ALSO BY BRAD LEITHAUSER

ESSAYS

Penchants and Places   1995

POEMS

The Mail from Anywhere   1990

Cats of the Temple   1986

Hundreds of Fireflies   1982

NOVELS

Seaward   1993

Hence   1989

Equal Distance   1985

THESE ARE BORZOI BOOKS PUBLISHED IN NEW YORK
BY ALFRED A. KNOPF

The Friends of Freeland

THE FRIENDS
OF FREELAND

Brad Leithauser

Alfred A. Knopf   New York   1997

THIS IS A BORZOI BOOK
PUBLISHED BY ALFRED A. KNOPF, INC.

http://www.randomhouse.com/

Library of Congress Cataloging-in-Publication Data
Leithauser, Brad.
The friends of Freeland: a novel / by Brad Leithauser. — 1st ed.
p.   cm.
ISBN 0-679-45083-1
I. Title.
PS3562.E4623F7   1997
813'.54—dc20   96-19618
CIP

Manufactured in the United States of America
First Edition

For my children
EMILY AND HILARY
with the hope
that theirs will be a world
where Freeland thrives

And where was it that he'd glimpsed or felt before (in a dream perhaps?) the place where he was meant to live? (Where else but in the free land of a dream had he beheld those white and gold and sea-blue streets, that low, not quite traceable skyline?)

Seaward

Was there ever a cause too lost,
Ever a cause that was lost too long,
Or that showed with the lapse of time too vain
For the generous tears of youth and song?

Robert Frost, "Hannibal"

Contents

I

II

III

IV

Author's Note

No island is an island is I suppose one of the lessons the writing of this book taught me. Regardless of how remote he chooses to make it, the novelist who creates an island is likely to find himself compelled to revisit, and disturb, that other, everyday world he thought his project would allow him to abandon. In my case, the depositing of a modest archipelago into the North Atlantic has forced me to alter ocean currents, modify the location of the Atlantic Fault, bend a few details of the history of Viking exploration, and even take in hand the world's largest island—Greenland—and nudge it a little to the left.

Although I've spent a couple of years in Iceland, I've tried hard here to do something more than merely portray that magnificent, puzzling nation under a funny name. For further inspiration, in addition to Inspiration, I've looked to my travels in the Hebrides, the Faeroe Islands, Newfoundland, Nova Scotia, and (giving fancy a free hand) the Oki Islands in the Sea of Japan.

1

1

A Dead Gull

Snow on this fourth of July is descending in loose, lacy flakes onto Independence Square, contributing epaulets to the uniformed shoulders of the four-man band, fuzzing the gray-gloved hand of its gray-bearded piccolist, pirouetting daintily into the open brass throat of the tuba—from which erupt thumpings that vibrate the windows in the ramshackle houses on all sides—and settling as well on the ragtag crowd of thirty or forty onlookers, some of them singing and some merely attending with dumbstruck expressions, some wearing caps or hoods and some by their bareheadedness marking themselves as penitents of exceptional heartfulness. We have suffered a loss and it is *our fault* and even now the littered Square speaks of sinful excess and of the potential for further, for irrevocable ruin. We've let our wealth, our leisure get the best of us. Like bodies of the slain after some unspeakable campaign, after a night of combat waged without quarter asked or given, they're scattered everywhere: beside one of the park benches a toppled bottle of gin; in the hotel's struggling flower bed a prone, dark-mouthed bottle of wine, bandaged to the neck in brown paper; pint bottles, quart bottles, liters and half-gallons, broken glass in front of the closed bakery, broken glass in front of the closed tanning studio. And even at the base of the statue of the armored Father of Our Country we find four gutted beer cans, twisted grotesquely into simulations of the maimed.

Truly, we have suffered a loss. This very morning, one of our bright lights, one of our investments in the future, one of our tender shoots—one of our children—was found lifeless on a wharf down at the harbor. What would a laboratory test reveal about the level of alcohol in the motionless bloodstream of the diminutive, jacketless corpse of Simon Olsson? How much did the boy drink last night, who was last glimpsed alive at an impromptu party in a parking lot behind one of our discotheques, and who—or so our possibly sentimental thinking now runs—was drawn seaward in sympathy with the spirit of his poor father, drowned ten years ago? In any case, whatever his motivations, little Simon—at sixteen still more boy than man—made his way down to the wharf, curled up beside a wooden crate, and entered a sleep as sound as a stone's.

In times of sorrow or danger, the bells in nearby Mariners' Church are rung for ten minutes on the hour every hour. Their just-finished tolling resounds in our ears, asking, What in the world is to be done with us? Are we truly hopeless? We've gone soft, haven't we? In bygone days, our children didn't hold parties behind discotheques. In bygone days, we *had* no discotheques. . . . At this early hour, horror often has a special harshness—the too-bright light of day falls like an accusation—and our tragedy this morning hints at another, vaster tragedy: our nation itself may have lost its way.

Meanwhile, they are a link to a solider past, the four-man band, these members of the forthrightly named Society for the Redemption of the Damned, who every Sunday morning in the summer offer us a concert in Independence Square. High summer, when our town spills over with more light than we possibly know what to do with, is for us an interval of giddiness, of dizziness, of outlandish and outsize desires. . . . We indulge ourselves, and, repenting of our indulgence, we come, we congregate, we listen, and—most of us—we sing, kiting our voices aloft into the brisk, sea-salted, ever-shifting skies.

If occasionally the quartet has looked a little quaint; if we've now and then questioned whether, given the pressing realities of modern life, we still need the Society for the Redemption of the Damned . . . well, such doubts vanish on a morning when the pale corpse of one of our boys brings coldly home the realization that we're flirting with our own extinction. This unreined energy of ours, this coarse gluttonous yearning for something more in addition to something more—what in Heaven's name can be done with us?

When in the name of God will we learn to pace ourselves, stumble out of our discotheques and tanning studios and settle on some sober long-sighted goals? And when will we finally understand that abundance fosters only an urge for greater abundance? Hasn't this undreamed-of affluence of ours—for we've recently stepped into a world where mere fishermen and farmhands own televisions and digital watches!—actually impoverished us?

Such questions, it turns out, are to be voiced by the big, disheveled mendicant of a man who shambles limpingly from the crowd and with an unexpectedly imperious wave of his hand silences the Society for the Redemption of the Damned. Wincing, he mounts a park bench to stand upon its flat cement seat. He sways there—he seems precariously perched. His eyes are bloodshot. He is one of those in the crowd who, drawn outdoors by the alarming bells in Mariners' Church, have stepped out bareheaded on this snowy July morning, and his thinning red hair is dulled with age and plastered flat on one side with a brown substance that doesn't invite close inspection. His mottled face is simultaneously pale and flushed. He seems, like the dead boy, to have mislaid whatever jacket he might have begun the night with. He is wearing a green sweater-vest that has mounted the hemisphere of his belly, exposing a white shirt tucked half in and half out of his trousers. His limp may be accentuated by alcohol, for there's little question he has been overindulging in the very vice whose ravages we have congregated to censure.

"My fellow countrymen," he begins. His voice is scratchy and thin. He clears his throat thoroughly, with ample patience, and from his full-lipped mouth he squirts a loosely bound eggy mass onto the pavement. He follows this with a belch and then, having bunched one of his big hands into a fist, with three hard, calming thumps on the chest. "We have suffered a loss," he begins again. "One of our bright lights, one of our investments in the future, one of our tender shoots—one of our children—has been taken from us and who among us by means of mere words can lighten even by the weight of a single snowflake the burden of our woe? Let us ponder that."

Ponder it? The crowd doesn't seem to ponder so much as simply to shuffle back and forth forbearingly in the cold. With a tinny clatter the piccolo tumbles to the cobblestones and when its owner stoops in retrieval his hands are so unsteady you have to wonder whether he too this morning might be feeling crapulous and unfocused. Was *anyone* sober last night?

"Who with mere words can add to this tragedy anything of more value than a pickled herring?" The beggarly speaker spits again, dribblingly this time, and does not quite manage to clear his scuffed black shoe from its descent. After this second ransacking of the throat his voice assumes a husky resonance. To anyone who did not know him—although, in fact, he is well known to everyone in the Square—it would already be evident that this ne'er-do-well has, improbably enough, a flair for public speaking. He is at once orotund and folksy, harsh and sentimental: "At such times, when a hammer falls out of the sky, flattening one of us, what must we ask ourselves? We must ask, *Where does our strength lie?* And to ask such a question is naturally to ask, *Where has our strength always resided?* I say, Let us ponder this question. I say, Let us look into our hearts. Where is it we've found the ability to guide our nation through the trials and travails of its history? And is it not true that if one ventures back to the very beginning, back to the Father of Our Country"—and here a pause, and, with deferentially lowered gaze, a nod at the statue of our armored Founding Father at the far end of Independence Square, none other than Erik the Other himself—"is it not true that our strength has always resided in a singleness of purpose? Steadily, clear-sightedly, we have coveted freedom. Freedom. I'd ask you to pronounce that word now, each and every one of you, in the privacy of your own skulls. *Freedom!* Our country endured long centuries of domination, when we were nothing but thralls to distant powers lying far beyond the cold gray reaches of the sea. And what did our masters think of us? When they condescended to think of us at all, didn't they consider us nothing but a supplier of wool and dried fish and nothing but a market for goods too shoddy to be sold at home?" And into the beggar-man's voice something like rage has arrived, warming it, weighting it: "During those dark centuries, I ask you, when we were nothing but a *colony,* where was it lay any real hope of salvation? Was it not in our determination to be a people of a particular ilk, people of a particular distinctive stamp?

"And what sort of people had we resolved to be? What is the one word encapsulating our aspiration? Haven't we always striven after one characteristic?" The bareheaded speaker halts, and amid this crowd, all of whom know the big, prepossessing word to come, one or two scattered dismissive groans arise, but these are themselves dismissed with indignant calls for a respectful silence.

And in the next moment there is no sound in this little square in this little capital city on this little island in this little cluster of islands perched in an unremarked corner of the globe except that of the snow falling—which makes no more sound than does Erik the Other at the Square's opposite end. The snow falls, Erik rusts, and the crowd waits upon a word.

Yes, the speaker has them: the crowd's in his hands, as he understands full well. His broad shoulders have straightened, his face has clarified. Oh, indeed, they are hanging on his speech—waiting, once more, to hear themselves defined in the terms so familiar to them. "Our goal? Hasn't our goal been to be *self-standing?* We would stand on our own, we ask for no crutches," cries this man who, though he walks with a limp, carries no crutch. "Does the word not ring like a bell in your skulls? Would anyone deny that we have always sought to be *self-standing* folk? Throughout the long years I have served you, the two decades I've devoted to the greater good of our commonwealth—" And perhaps here I must belatedly impart that this unseemly spectacle of a man, whose hair is plastered flat on one side with—yes—vomit, for the past twenty years has been the leader of our people. He is the President of our country. "—I have been guided primarily by a single principle: we Freelanders are self-standing folk. When we fail, as we have failed one of our children today, we must look to ourselves for the fault. The true friend of Freeland is the man or woman who believes in our ability ever to lift ourselves higher. The struggle is un-ending. Pain, such as we are all feeling so intensely this morning, is our benefactor and protector. It toughens the will. It improves us. In the pain we are feeling today lies the hope of a better morrow."

Yes, well and good, indeed, sure thing, okay, that's so, that's true, that's apt—and yet, notwithstanding all the wisdom in his words, we yearn for something more. Yes—something more. Even the skeptics in the audi-ence, of whom there are many, have somehow been beguiled across a mys-terious elocutionary threshold into a zone where they find themselves catching eagerly at his words. A transformation has been effected. This beggar-man has become a kind of vacant-lot fire—a ragged blaze made up of cardboard boxes, newspapers, paper bags, scrapwood—beside which we, turned mendicants ourselves, would now warm our raw, chapped hands. Our wish is an old wish. We say to him now, as innumerable times in decades past, *Define us, Mister President.* We say, *We'd forgotten . . . We'd some-how forgotten our mission and now you must remind us, Hannibal Hannibalsson, that we might go forward.*

More—truly the spirit is the thing inside a person that insists on something *more.* Our hearts are hungry, as Hannibal sure-heartedly senses. It's a question of pacing—he has broached too soon the notion of some reconciliation with our grief. We require additional thunder and brim-stone: Hannibal, we need more pain. And so our President, gazing out beyond his own discomfort on this wretched frigid summer morning, be-yond his own fatigue and the falling snow and his pounding head, digs deep into his kit bag of rhetorical devices.

"I stared this morning at the body of a dead boy and what did I be-hold? What did I see before me? I saw something of no more worth to me than a dead seagull lying smashed by the side of the road." Again Hannibal halts. He throws open his big empty hands, as though to declare himself dead flat broke; he has nothing more to give. Ah, but it's an old ruse. A sly one is what he is. We wait patiently, as the snow, capriciously turning antic in a gust of sea breeze, romps in the air between us.

Abruptly, Hannibal launches anew. "What did I see before me? I saw something of no more value to anyone than an old sprat, lying in an inch of rainwater in the bottom of a creel." Another pause, another shrug, and this time he actually begins to dismount from the park bench. He lowers himself—has one foot settled on the pavement, one foot still on the bench. Isn't it clear? The man simply has nothing more to say.

And yet—hmm, well, hmm, yes, it seems he might have a few more words after all. . . . Wincing on his bad knees, he hoists himself back onto his makeshift pedestal and re-clears his throat. His voice is little more than a whisper: "For that is all any of us is worth. You and I, my friends? We are dead sprats—if we lose sight of the true source of our strength. You and I, my friends? We are so many dead gulls, we are so many cracked eggs, our nation is but a few contemptible windswept skerries, all about to tumble into the sea.

"I looked this morning at the body of a dead boy and what did I see? What under Heaven did I see?" He peers hard into the thronging snow. Another change has come over him. Hannibal's chin has lifted, and now his voice dilates as he projects his words well beyond us, to Erik the Other himself, who founded our nation more than a millennium ago, and even beyond Erik to distant Great Blue Mountain. And in Hannibal's voice the fire has grown up once more, bigger than ever, and within it there is blaze enough to make the snowflakes wink out like stars at dawn, to loosen the immemorial grip of Great Blue Glacier itself: "I saw our fairest flower clipped before its bloom, I saw the light of the world snuffed out, for please each of you must understand that I believe now as I have always be-lieved that Freeland is the true world-light and if we remain faithful to ourselves we're the one true good hope of this troubled planet—*the one true good hope!* Life changes in Freeland, of course, and sometimes by acci-dent or oversight young boys die, but meanwhile, far away, out where the madness reigns, ever more brutal wars are waged, and ever more destruc-tive forms of leisure are conceived, so that war and peace are more and more interchangeable, the two streams uniting in a single rich river of blood, and to those misguided peoples we present a sanity—and ultimately the world must come questing after a sanity such as ours. I believed this when I began to serve as your leader, some two decades ago, just as I believe it now, in the dusk of my career: friends, fellow Freelanders, we are the light of the world."

The dusk of his career? Yes, unthinkable though it is on a day such as this in high summer, when night's a wolflike creature chased to lower latitudes, when there are no proper dusks and our nation has become in a literal sense the light of the world, Hannibal Hannibalsson has again made clear that his long tenure as our President is approaching an end. When the polls open on October fourth, he will not be standing for reelection. In exactly three months he will step down from office, and all of us are left to wonder: Who in the world could possibly fill a park bench as he does? How are we ever to carry on without him? Who but this splendid ruin of a man with spit on his shoe and vomit in his hair is fit to guide us?

2

A Liquid Sheet

The Lord God comes down one evening at suppertime and says to you, *Your behavior has pleased me. I would grant you a request.*

And you? Gaping, dumbstruck, you don't begin to know how to answer, and so the Lord God offers a helpful prompting hint: *There must be some interest or passion you would care to pursue. . . .*

And you reply humbly, "Well, beyond everything else in this world, I have always loved Mozart. Would it be possible—I don't want to trouble You—but would it be possible to hear tonight some of the music Mozart has written in Heaven?"

A smile plays upon the visage of the Lord, and poof!—a cloud of smoke—and Mozart himself stands before you.

"Maestro!" you simultaneously cry and whisper, and you pump his hand—yes, the hand of the man who wrote *The Magic Flute*—and you inquire, with a slight stammer, whether he has written any music in the last two hundred years.

Any music? The composer throws back his head and laughs so heartily white powder dances up from his wig. As of this morning, he has completed 27,272 symphonies, each more moving than its predecessor! The work he did upon earth? The *Jupiter* Symphony? The astonishing aerial architecture of the Twenty-fifth Piano Concerto? Mere dross . . . They possess, compared to the music he creates now, all the artistry of a child's drawing scratched in the mud with a stick.

Let there be a concert! the Lord God declares and—poof once more!— an amphitheater surrounds you, its walls a braver red than any tropical sunset's, its ceiling the vault of the firmament itself. *We have need of musicians!* the Lord God announces, and in the orchestral pit, row upon row, the players materialize, each shouldering a snowy pair of wings. Angels—angels in the pit! And Mozart, Mozart himself at the podium! But when you swing round once more, to offer your astounded thanks, the Lord God, already turning diaphanous, appends a final remark that, on its face, makes no sense at all. In a reverberating voice that sounds almost wistful—or is it amused?—the Lord God says to you, *They will play just as long as you wish. And when you have had enough, when you decide to bring the concert to a close, feel free to adjourn to the auditorium lobby, where you'll find a modest little snack of ham sandwiches and potato chips awaiting you.*

They will play for you as long as you *wish. . . .* By heaven, truly it shall be just as the French poet once declared: *Car c'est toujours Mozart / Que reprennent sans fin / les anges musiciens.* The concert begins, Mozart's Symphony no. 77 in A Minor, "The More than Everlasting," K. 1027. *When you have had enough,* the Lord God had declared, and was this a sample of Divine Humor? Had enough? For you will never have *enough!* So ravishing is this music, your body itself becomes an instrument, infinitely subtler in its vibrating niceties than any Steinway or Stradivarius. This is music whose every demi-semi-quaver is both indispensable and independently fulfilling; music that reconfigures the topography of your brain, opening sectors wherein thoughts have never penetrated and into which they now go surging with all the breathtaking agility of a flock of helical-horned gazelles bounding down a green savannah; this is music that evokes the word *ineffable* and dismantles it—*in a fable*—and eventually explodes it, sending sky-high, in a glittering alphabetic strew, *a*'s and *i*'s and *f*'s and *b*'s, for language is no longer of any use to us here.

The first symphony concludes.

The second symphony, Mozart's Symphony no. 727 in G Sharp Major, "Ascending Orders of the Infinite," K. 2500, commences. And it is far more beautiful still, you perch in your chair like a fern beside the perpetually sliding crest of Victoria Falls, absorbing the rainbow-filtered solar harmonies through your every cell. These melodies are aliment, they are Life Itself; indeed, they are more than Life, having as they do their origin in a zone beyond all questions of mutability, mortality.

The second symphony concludes.

Commences now the third performance, Mozart's Symphony no. 1779 in A Flat Minor and D Sharp Major, "The Borderless Beyond," K. 5339. And it is—how is this possible?—truly it is more miraculous still, minute by minute the potentialities of Art itself are being reconstituted . . . but wouldn't you have supposed that, unspeakably gorgeous as this amphitheater is, the seats might have been a little comfier? You shift, you wiggle, and blissfully settle in once more.

The third symphony concludes.

The fourth symphony, Mozart's Symphony no. 1997 in Q, "The Tetrahedron," K. 6996, commences.

He is a sort of god himself, isn't he, this Mozart who so tirelessly elicits the music of the angels. And how beautifully the angels play!—and why in the world would the Lord God have provided *ham sandwiches?* Jesus, wouldn't you suppose the food might be fancier at a "do" of this sort? Shrimp salad, maybe? Or some raw-milk Camembert? And isn't this music *astonishing?* Isn't this the greatest privilege ever granted a mere mortal?

The fourth symphony concludes.

The fifth, Mozart's Symphony no. 2525 in C, "The Circle Squared," K. 7777, commences, and isn't there something almost a little *eerie* in the way Mozart throws himself into his task? Good heavens, doesn't the man's attention ever wander? Or his stomach rumble? Presumably, the elevated dead never feel a moment of fatigue, which itself ought to be a very tiring experience, and surely this is the most beautiful music yet and why in the world *potato chips?* Admittedly, there can be about them something quite lovely—about potato chips, that is—a beautiful modest music of their own as one of their graceful arcs shatters with a rending little cry of fulfillment under the roof of the mouth. . . .

The fifth symphony concludes.

The sixth, Mozart's Symphony no. 3333 in *, "The Ideal &," K. 8989, commences, and isn't it just possible that you're not doing yourself any service—that in fact you're doing yourself, and Mozart, a *dis*service by remaining in the concert hall beyond the point where you can absorb the compounding dazzlements of this divine man's accomplishment? Hell, don't you perhaps owe it to Mozart to get up from your seat and get out of here before everything dissolves into some ravishing but dreamlike blur. . . .

So: How many symphonies do you listen to? How long is it before you find yourself standing out in the lobby, sheepishly and yet avidly tucking into a ham sandwich and a handful of chips?

And is the moral of my fable clear? Art is willing, but the flesh is weak. . . . Poor Mozart: he conducts so raptly he fails to notice how the amphitheater behind him empties. . . .

Even so, even so, what else is another composer—a thoroughly earthbound composer—to do but compose? What else but fill the trellis of his clef with grapelike clusters of notes—hoping that, years hence, the vintage will prove noble?

What is the struggling painter to do but clean his brushes and attempt another waterfall, another impossible sunset? And the writer? Fill the page, and hope some reader turns the page.

A train is carrying me forward in the richest of my memories. Rain's falling. The window beside me streams with water. Floating, warm and dry, above the sodden metal clatter, blissfully idle, I know I can't possibly be in Freeland, since my country has never in its history possessed a single mile of rail track. But there's a second reason for knowing I'm far from home. Although no objects are identifiable through the flooded glass, a color powerfully penetrates: green. It's a generous, deep, voluptuous shade, mounting nearly to the top of the window, and while I can no longer summon up my destination on that rain-washed day so many years ago, I do know it led me through a teeming terrain. Where *was* I? What lay on the other side? Was I maybe in Kyushu, traveling in my laughable disguise as a diplomat, Freeland's plenipotentiary to the Japanese nation? Or could this have been 1961, in which case the green behind the glass is the jungles of the Yucatán? Or could it stem from my one trip to an island then called Ceylon, the train lumbering away from Kandy, perhaps, and could those have been bamboo forests on the other side? And were there any people in the train car around me?

If there were any other passengers, in every aspect—voice and face and scent—they've disappeared. What I recollect is only the age of the train, brown seats seamed with dusty cracks, and a sensation of passing through something my rock-rich, tree-poor native land could never have vouchsafed me: fecundity, bounty, a vegetation with cosmic aspirations, loftily lifting itself some sizable distance toward the heavens. Between me—dark little me—and a densely enveloping mesh of brilliant foliage lay a sheet of glass, and on that glass a sheet of water: paired transparencies which, together, blinded me. Only a color managed to slip through the glass, and maybe a smell of damp growth. . . . In the richest memory I possess I am traveling through a country whose map and name, no less than my fellow passengers, have dissolved and flowed away. For this is nothing less than the Landscape of Elsewhere I pass through. I am dry and warm and blessedly far from home.

Kyushu, the Yucatán, Kandy . . . So lustrous in themselves, the names as I now inscribe them on the page carry for me an enhanced luster, born in a suspicion that they're unlikely to surface here again. Already, at my story's cleansed, rain-misted point of embarkation, I sense that the bulk of my narrative lies far from Kyushu, from the Yucatán, from Kandy. You see, I'm enough of an old hand at this game—I have forty-nine books behind me—to recognize right away how much of what most matters to me will not appear here. Once again the straitened, distorting business of narrative selection supervenes. Once again all the necessary lies begin to multiply, and in the pursuit of coherence and pace and proportion even the richest of my memories will be thrust aside. Again I will not do myself— I will not do Life—justice. The train will continue to roll, and the green to glow, but only in another, an as-yet-unwritten story. *This* tale's to be situated at the border between the Old World and the New. It's set in Freeland, which sometimes you'll find on maps of Europe, and sometimes on maps of North America, and sometimes—all too often—you won't find at all; we don't count for much. Not surprisingly, my story will occasionally touch down in Denmark—the horizontal, overfertile countryside of our historic oppressors. But mostly we will look in the other direction. In my lifetime, anyway, it has been the habit of my country to face westward. These days, Denmark lies over our shoulders and is to be accorded no more than a dismissive backward glance. We set our gazes instead on an America perceived as the fountainhead of all openness and opulence, and I'd like to think mine an American tale, suitably sweet and preposterous, the chronicle of a broken love affair between a giant and a gnat. . . .

My memory of the train is suitably counterpoised, then, by recollections of another journey. This time I can speak with specificity. The date is the thirtieth of June 1959, and I am heading off to my death. This is to be both my first departure from Freeland and my life's terminal pilgrimage. I have posted myself at the rail of a ship, a small Dutch steamer called, with poignant inappropriateness, *The Return*. It's bound for the New World. On the dock before me stands Hannibal Hannibalsson. Of all my acquaintances, he alone has come down to see me off. He is a young man, just twenty-two, a year older than I, and what an unforgettable figure he makes, stationed there on the dock! *He* rather than I ought to be the one voyaging out across the seas, for in his straight-shouldered, red-gold-haired, strong-jawed splendidness he is as perfect a Viking as ever navigated by instinct up a rocky, fog-clamped fjord. At the moment, the sun is blazing.

It's the thirtieth of June 1959, and I stand at the taffrail gazing out, for the final time, at my one true friend, my soul's genuine brother. Death isn't something pursuing me from without; I harbor it in the cellar of my lungs. I am tubercular, as was my mother, who died when I was two, when she was only twenty. My father deserted my mother less than a week after my birth; it seems he didn't like my looks. As it happens, they hadn't yet married—my mother's only child was a bastard son—and after my mother's death I was reared by her aunt, a stern woman who has refused, on this blazing thirtieth of June, to come down to see me off, lest she be viewed as sanctioning my departure. Had I shown the good sense to remain in my homeland, I might soon have looked forward to being buried right beside my mother, within the lych-gate of Starri's Church, and what more could a young man reasonably demand of life than to be spared a watery grave? What is this *utter foolishness*—my aunt being a woman whose reproachful philosophy of life coheres around the phrase *utter foolishness*—that would drive a dying young man away from the one hard comfort his existence offers him: the promise that, measly and cold and thin as is the soil of his native land, in the end it's hospitable enough to bury him forever.

In search of an unknown and probably unmarked grave, I stand at the rail and nod for the final time at my one true friend in the world. Does this sound unbearably melodramatic?

If so, perhaps justifiably so—for I was entitled to melodrama, having just now hacked up into my wadded handkerchief a fresh gummy plug of blood. Like me, Hannibal believed this was the last moment we would set eyes on each other. We'd come to a mortal juncture. Was he exhibiting grief, then? Had he given way to sorrow?

Nothing like, nothing like—for our Hannibal was showing fidelity to something more elevated and fine than grief and sorrow. Shoulders thrown back, chin aloft, he was seeking to invest the moment with epic grandeur. Nothing less could possibly do justice to its terrible gravity. Good son of the medieval Norse Sagas that he was, he must attempt an exhibition of quiet heroism. He was striving after magnitude.

Dimly, Hannibal sensed, on this thirtieth of June 1959, that our country's anguished past—two hundred, four hundred, six hundred, eight hundred, a thousand years of brutal subsistence living—now pressed upon two of its fair sons a legacy of strength and solemnity and stoicism. And with this image of him on the dock, it's possible today to see, more than a third of a century later, that Hannibal had already arrived at the shaping impulse of his life. For it governs him still, as dimly and as surely as ever— this sensation of being descended from titans, so that to declare *I am a Free-lander* is to ally yourself with the very noblest of the dead. Our roles are prescribed for us, and it matters very little on this June morning that his partner in this pathetic ceremony is a small, pallid, stoop-shouldered young man with the coarse, spiky hair of a rat and the quick, avid features of a ferret.

Of all the spots on the globe, the sun this morning has selected our own White Seal Bay for the display of its very brightest scintillations. The dirty steamer, hooting forlornly, pulls away. Hannibal Hannibalsson, dwindling from sight, lifts a long arm in farewell. It is to say, *The gods be with you, Eggert Oddason* and *You have acquitted yourself becomingly, my friend.*

And in truth I *have* done my best to lend these closing moments something like a regal equanimity. After I've disappeared in a blaze of lights, I want Hannibal to say of me, *Well done.* And yet . . . in the back of my sly ferret's head flares the nagging suspicion that this tragedy should never have taken place. I'm a victim of some little error in the bookkeeping of the gods. Yes: I'm dying as a result of some trifling celestial oversight.

You see, I can't quell my sense of being fated for something else entirely. It wasn't to enact the poignant tragedy of a flower clipped before its bloom that I was placed upon this earth. No, I was deposited here to embody fullness and fruition: who can doubt that my manifest purpose in life is to bring the world of modern letters to my backwater nation? Rat that I am, I'm also an arctic fox—wasn't I intended to create, from worthless scraps of fustian, the modern Freelandic novel, the modern Freelandic play, the modern Freelandic poem?

"Consumption," one of the sailors declares, summing me up. It's the second day out. He speaks in Danish. He has heard me coughing, evidently. He taps significantly at his chest.

We're belowdecks, in the shadows of a rusty corridor. He addresses me from ten or so feet away—maintaining a wary distance.

"A bad cold. That's all it is."

"Consumption," he repeats, and this time he grins merrily—horribly.

"It's influenza, actually."

"Consumption. I had it too, once." Dead square in the center of his forehead reposes an extraordinary growth—wart or mole or polyp, I don't know. It's the size of an ape's eye.

In time, even our most providential benefactors fade from our memories. . . . I've effaced the man utterly, except for that growth of his. The words and gestures I'm now ascribing to him are a fiction, and would he be realer for you if I fleshed him out, lent him in addition a stutter, a limp, a withered hand? I'd be happy to oblige, but in truth for me he couldn't be realer than he already is. The whole of the man has, as it were, been sucked into a funnel, leaving that single ineradicable bulge that was too large to fit through the funnel's neck—that eye of an ape, which even today levelly, magisterially contemplates me.

"Want to know how I shook it, lad? I was on a ship too, a passenger back then, just like you, and you know what I did? For four days I lived up there on the open deck. Four days, standing at the railing, hour after hour. Just stood there, breathing in, out, in, out, just as hard and as steady as you please. Hour after hour that's what I did, I took the air straight off the sea."

"The doctor recommends the opposite. To keep myself sheltered. And plenty of rest."

"Four days. And on my feet almost the whole time. Taking it all in deep. Think about your breathing, understand? About nothing but your breathing . . ."

Squeamishly, needfully, I peer into the man's third eye. Try as I might, it's hard to escape the sense of being addressed by an oracle.

"Rest is what the doctor recommends. And shelter," I repeat.

"Rest? No. Shelter? No. No no no *no*." The eye eyes me, and I? I'm spellbound. . . . "Four days in the sea-wind, standing till you're ready to drop. Right off the sea. *That's* how you've got to take it."

In truth, it was long enough ago—that shadowy belowdecks encounter—and the blood in the handkerchief is now so distant from my blood that I come naturally to speak in the third person, asking, What would have happened to young Eggert Oddason had he not followed this unlikely advice? Would he have recovered just the same?

In any event, let's leave him up there on the deck, young Eggert, the sea outspread panoramically before him. One might say of him he's on top of the world. On the deck of a ship called *The Return* he stands, breathing. And that is all in the world he does: he breathes and he contemplates his breathing. The light is unfading, perpetual—this is the season of white nights and the sky's a blue without flaw or stain. The steamer, too, is on top of the world, or nearly so: it's gliding across indigo Arctic seas. Its keel flips back the water with a practiced hand, like a maid turning down a bed, revealing a strip of white sheets under the dark comforter. Sleep is the comfort Eggert covets but he does not sleep. He stands and stands. He breathes instead.

3

A Word About My Country

At 67 degrees north latitude, just below the Arctic Circle, lies Thorskrist, our **capital city**. Its sloping streets and inventively patched-together houses face toward the sea. We turn our backs on the hills surrounding us on three sides, preferring to look instead upon White Seal Bay. But the hills are not to be slighted, and across the bay, its classic cone a reproach to the make-do qualities of our architecture, stands our Kilimanjaro, our Mount Fuji: Storblafell, otherwise known as Great Blue Mountain. Thorskrist is the northernmost capital in the world, and may well be the smallest—not so surprising when you consider that the aggregate population of the Freeland archipelago consists of some sixty thousand souls.

Our **nearest neighbors** on the right—I speak cartographically—are the Icelanders, whom we dismiss as a group of diluted, unhealthily modernized, cosseted grumblers who cannot hold their liquor and who have had, all in all, an easy time of it over the centuries. Did the Black Death epidemic of 1402–4 fell a third of the Icelandic population? *Our* epidemic wiped out nearly one half of ours. Did Iceland's great Skafta eruption of 1783 kill off half the country's cattle and four-fifths of its sheep? *Our* great eruption—of Storblafell, in 1810—destroyed nearly two-thirds of the cattle and ninety percent of the sheep. And so it goes, through smallpox, famines, shipwrecks, incursions of Algerian pirates, ice storms. It is something of a national pastime for us to illustrate, rigorously and dispassionately, that however horrific has been the rate at which Icelanders have fallen dead of one calamity after another, we have succumbed at a rate so much more precipitous that the Icelanders truly ought to be ashamed of themselves.

Our neighbors on the other side, to the west, are the Greenlanders, whom we dismiss as a bunch of insufficiently modernized, hardbitten, drunken wastrels who are racially dubious besides. The racial issue is especially delicate for us. When not an out-and-out Eskimo, or a half-Eskimo, or a quarter-Eskimo, your typical Greenlander still shows subtle tincturing hints of an Eskimo undercurrent in the blood. Doubtless this would not be so unsettling were it not the case that many a Freelander, although we're a fair people, shows a broad Asian cast to the bones of the face—as does my own daughter, Lilja, who looks something like a blue-eyed, blond-haired Mongol. Preferring not to be viewed as some sort of albino Eskimo, the typical Freelander holds firm to an ancient nugget of native lore which asserts that our pilgrim forebears, two or so millennia ago, started out near Russia's Lake Baikal. Over the centuries, resolutely bypassing one inviting, arable, promising valley after another, these people drove themselves toward their home of choice: a wind-rasped cluster of four arctic islands in the North Atlantic. I should add that there isn't one jot of hard historical evidence to support so ludicrous a notion. . . .

We live on **fish,** by **fish**—some might well say for **fish.** During most of our history there were two principal livelihoods, as reflected in an old Freelandic proverb, *A man ought to be free to choose whether he'll stink of fish guts or sheep shit,* which perhaps loses something of its wit or subtlety in the translation. . . . But in recent years the market for our wool and mutton has largely collapsed, and today the modern tourist in Thorskrist who, desperate for *some* keepsake, purchases a traditional Freelandic sweater may eventually discover, tucked away on a tag inside, that it was knit in Iceland.

Our **architecture?** Call it "antic bunker." Although a few older residences are modeled, freely, on traditional Danish designs, with gables and crennels, bell roofs and crest tiles, the standard Freelandic home is a squat gray bunkerlike cement structure whose effect is "lightened" by lace curtains and zanily painted rooftops. In recent years, however, a taste for modern, or possibly postmodern, effects has led to such extravagances as triangular stained-glass windows, bubble-shaped skylights, porches inlaid with particolored ceramic tiles.

We employ **patronymics,** identifying ourselves chiefly by first names—by given names. Last names, which merely denote paternity, therefore change from generation to generation. Thus, if a man named Benedikt Hauksson has a child he christens Ragnar, the boy will be Ragnar Benediktsson, and that boy's daughter Helga will be Helga Ragnarsdottir, and so forth.

Our **language** is Freelandic. It is a point of great pride with us that, among all the Nordic tongues, ours comes nearest to the Old Norse of the Viking settlers. While those other nations have deviated from that glorious heyday when Vikings were busy, from Byzantium to Lapland, from Russia to Vinland, splitting open with maces and pikestaffs the skulls of farmers and farmers' wives and farmers' children, we alone have maintained the faith. I should add that most of the linguistic evidence suggests that modern Icelandic, rather than its close cousin Freelandic, comes nearest in both pronunciation and vocabulary to the language of our bloody forebears.

Am I sounding a little cynical? I hope so, having accepted it as my duty, over a literary career spanning three decades and forty-nine books, to rail against my country and my countrymen, believing as I do that the true friend of Freeland must occasionally don the armor and bear the standard of its enemy. As the English poet once said, He loveth best who dispraiseth best . . . and if I take some textual liberties, surely I'm entitled to them, since "The Ancient Mariner" was the first gift I ever bestowed on my countrymen—the first of my many translations into Freelandic. It was a seemingly irresistible choice for a seafaring people. How could my countrymen fail to embrace it—and fail to embrace me, its importer? Yet the response was oddly quizzical. You're saying the man shot an *albatross,* Eggert? With a *crossbow?* Wouldn't surprise me a bit to learn this old Sam Coldridge never put in one good day's sail on the open sea. . . .

And **the land**? I suppose you might express it this way: what green is to Ireland, gray is to Freeland. Our slopes and fields are overlaid with lava so recent, geologically speaking, that its flow seems even now a liquid thing. It takes the form of rivers and riverbeds, sheets and cascades, tubes and dribbling strings. Add generous amounts of ice to the lava—an arrested flow atop an arrested flow—and you've hit upon a quintessentially Freelandic sight. Our winters are hard and tenacious. We are subject to storms of killing ferocity.

We come by our grayness naturally. Some eighty-five percent of all igneous rocks in the country are basaltic, one of the greatest such concentrations in the world. Here and there, our hills are lightened by flow-banded rhyolite and granophyric batholiths and laccoliths, darkened by patches of obsidian and pitchstone.

And yet, if our terrain's spectrum is narrow, its shapes are overtakingly varied: the volatile marriage of volcano and glacier has produced something of a paradise for the geologist. Our language is rich in everyday terms which, when translated, take on a specialist's air: scoria, tephra, brec-cia, tuff, talus, and so forth. It's said that the Greenlandic Inuit have some thirty different words for "snow"—although this statistic could well be based upon misinformation; subsequent linguistic analysis may reveal that a good many of these words are, simply, expletives. As they stare up at the sky, what those Greenlanders are saying, I suspect, is *Oh no, here comes some more of that shit. . . .* In any event, it can be reported reliably that in Free-landic there are some forty-plus terms for "lava." Any schoolchild knows the distinct words for pillow lava and ropey lava and block lava and lava bed and lava dome and lava field and lava fountain.

The degree to which the naming of our **four main islands** reflects drollery—as opposed to dishonesty or drunkenness—remains a matter of debate. They are: Braudeyjar, Blaeyjar, Demantseyjar, and Risaeyjar, or Bread Island, Blue Island, Diamond Island, and Giant Island. Giant Island is, perhaps not surprisingly, the smallest of the four. There's some specula-tion that it takes its name from a rock formation—said to resemble a troll's head—on its northern shore. Diamond Island is not diamond-shaped and, needless to say, has never yielded up a single gemstone, precious or semi-precious. It's sometimes claimed, by way of explanation, that Blue Island takes its name from Great Blue Mountain, which is no explanation at all, since there's nothing the least bit blue or bluish about Great Blue. And there is nothing loaflike in the shape of Bread Island, where—although it has always been the most desirable of the islands, or at least the most pop-ulous—our people no doubt starved over the centuries in proportions as great as anywhere else in Freeland.

In addition to the four main islands, there are an untold number of rackety, contentious, bird-overrun, otherwise uninhabited outcroppings and skerries.

Our country lies just barely within the reach of that great marine broom known as the Gulf Stream. When it comes sweeping our way, we can enjoy **seasons** of something approaching mildness. There are days in midsummer when the keen angling northern sun discovers on our hillsides not merely the green but the luminous gold glow of the low-growing lichens. On such a day, a person can forget absolutely that the weather, in another season, will come hurtling down from those round-the-clock factories of the North—from that industrial zone where the miles and miles of pack ice and shelf ice and the icebergs taller than our tallest houses are constructed and warehoused.

4

A Vision

These days, my dreams explore unpeopled terrain. It's quite a peculiar sensation. Although insomnia is my only steady nighttime companion—I sleep alone—I usually manage, once I've finally drifted off, to sleep "like a stone." And yet lately, as though an empty metaphor should suddenly assume an uncanny reality, I find I've begun to have the unblinking, unvarying dreams a stone might be expected to entertain. What sort of living man has lifeless dreams? Who am I? I awake to an awareness of a steadily contemplated landscape: a parade of smooth, balloonlike, lavender-brown hills, veined with long snow-rivulets; or a rusty-brown barnacled outcropping, glimpsed as though from a shore-cliff above, which the slate-gray, inrushing tide indefatigably conceals and discloses, conceals and discloses; or a lost green landscape immanently aglow through a downstreaming pane of glass.

In this particular dream, the one that held me when my telephone rang, the landscape contained two living creatures, myself and a horse. My dream counterpart, unlike my waking self, clearly had a feel and an affection for horses. I spoke to my mount through my hips and knees; my legs were the most alive part of me. We—the horse and I—might have been in Ireland or France. Though treeless, the land was too rich and plush to be Freelandic. We were coming down off a low, slow-sloping hill and in all its easy, open gradients the terrain outlying below me breathed an air of welcome.

In the distance, on a rise that twinned the one my horse and I descended, stood my destination, the limestone-gray rectilinear blocks of an ancient turreted castle. As my horse approached, I detected behind one of the merlons of one of the tall parapets a movement—the shifting of what

I took to be the head of a sentry, helmeted in black armor. Who was he? Had he spotted me yet?

But the next moment something horrible happened. The sentry's head cannonballed high into the air and, unfolding a set of wings, soared in an ever-widening spiral, and a cry went off like a pistol-shot. The head was a crow. The phone trilled again and this time it shook me loose. My horse's legs, draining downward, turned to mud; the living creature ebbed into the earth beneath me.

"I was visited by a vision," declared the voice at the other end. Hannibal, naturally. Oh, I didn't need to be fully awake to shiver at this particular cantabile tone. This was Hannibal at his most dangerous: sounding greatly pleased with himself.

"Mm?" I said.

"It was early this afternoon. I was riding Blesi, out in the Black River Valley—"

Even now I was drugged with sleep and his words perplexed me. This horse he spoke of seemed *my* horse, the creature of my exploded dream, and how in the world had he managed to steal my mount? Granted, Hannibal's talent for invading a person's life was without any serious peer in my experience—but what was this disturbing new potency of his that allowed him to make off with one of my dream-horses?

"I was thundering, really *thundering*, Eggi. I felt like—now damn it what's the word I'm looking for? You're the word-wizard. Both joyful and large—come on: *you* know how I felt."

"And you know how I feel about horses. . . ."

"Exultant? I suppose that's close enough. . . ."

Riding is a passion that yearly deepens as Hannibal's shattered athlete's knees crumple. He went on: "The sun broke through the clouds, casting my shadow forward, and there in front of me stood a kind of gateway. It was a rainbow, you see, and can you guess what? Now what was it lay on the other side of that gateway?"

"A wood nymph? A wee little fairy's child?"

"Great Blue Mountain, my friend. Good old Great Blue. Its tip was just tucked inside it, you see. The mountain's cone was perfectly enclosed by the top of the arch of the rainbow, and that's when the message came to me. Now can you guess what the words were?"

"*Take your daily dose of cod-liver oil*, perhaps? Or, *Never trust a Freelander who bears a Danish name?*"

"Not quite." Hannibal sounded miffed, he sounded offended. This *vision* he was describing was evidently not to be minimized or trifled with. "The words were these," he said, and offered them in English—the tongue the two of us resorted to when aspiring, self-consciously, for an affectionate solemnity: "*Hannibal, you will run again.*"

There was no mistaking what he meant—yet I mistook it. At some level, I suppose I'd seen this "vision" coming for months, but I was still so sleepy, or so resistant to his message, that I momentarily misconstrued him. I was thinking of his knees, I suppose. In any event, what came to mind was the act of running in the physical sense. He had been, once, a demon in a footrace—the hero of the First Freelandic Olympics, held on June 21, 1958. And between the two of us—as you'll soon see—footraces held a special significance.

"Run?" I said.

"Run," Hannibal repeated.

"For political office?"

"For President, of course. My country needs me."

Thump. Just like that, *thump*, an avalanche dumped down within me and I was fully awake. My heart was packed in ice.

"Good Christ, run for *President*, your country will *reject* you, toss you out like a week-old fish. At this point you haven't a hope in hell, Hanni. Not one hope. In hell."

"Do you know what I *actually* was looking at when that rainbow stretched before me like the gateway to some glorious castle?"

And now?—and now that bastard Hannibal was *stealing my castle, too!* Honestly, there was no end to him—he would rob us all blind! He would steal our very dreams from us! "You were looking at water vapor. . . ."

"And you a poet . . . ," he noted. I saw him, in my weary, jaded mind's eye, lugubriously shaking his head at me. "In truth, I was looking at the spirit of Freeland. *That's* what I saw. And it was beckoning to me."

"This time I'm not joking, Hanni. I really, truly am begging you. Let it go. Twenty years is plenty. Let it go, mm?" It wasn't as though I didn't have troubles enough already, but now a disturbing new thought hit me: "You haven't spoken to anybody else? About this vision of yours?"

Hannibal paused histrionically. "You're the first, Eggi. . . ."

He intended me to be flattered—and the awful, the mortifying truth is that I suppose I was, for a moment. But hard on that moment's heels came anger. Good strong anger. This was one lunatic's venture he wouldn't entice me into.

"Then let me be the last. Don't mention a word of your 'vision' to anybody. They're going to think you've gone soft in the *head*. I suppose we better have a talk."

"Give me five minutes. I'm on my way."

"You're doing this one alone," I said.

Alone? That's what *I* was. He'd already hung up. "This time you're dancing off the end of the dock," I continued, just the same, before hanging up my end of the phone.

I rose from my bed and peered thoughtfully over White Seal Bay. Today was the first of August. The wind was up, the water whitecapped. The sun was struggling to tear itself free of a patch of clouds—a local battle of fleeting consequence, for over Great Blue Mountain another mountain, of dark gray clouds, was assembling itself. Within moments, it would surely blot out the sun altogether.

Today was the first of August and summer was slipping by and when was I going to get around to starting my next book?

When I'm not staying out at the primitive little summerhouse in Birkidalur—Birch Valley—where I do much of my writing, I live in an apartment in the tallest building in Thorskrist. It's called Skyscraper Tower, a name most Freelanders employ without irony. I live at the apex, the penthouse, the ninth floor of the building.

I walked out into the living room and found both my daughter, Lilja, and her boyfriend, Helmut, listening to music. They were supine. Music tends to flatten them.

I don't allow rock music in the house, but they sneak it in anyway, by means of headphones. Each of their wired skulls was propped upon a pillow. Their hands were locked, their eyes closed. Were they asleep? I don't allow Helmut to spend the night here either—a rule he symbolically flouts by regularly dozing off on my living room floor. Lilja was wearing olive-green dungarees and a black sweatshirt that had, in her free abandonment to her music, crept some ways up her belly, revealing two or three inches of glowing white skin.

I nudged her calf with my foot. Her eyes, languid not with any landscaped castled dream, hell no, but with the raptures of her infernal music, opened slowly. She withdrew one rather than both of the headphone cups from her ears.

"Hannibal's coming," I announced.

"Lovely."

"Soon."

"Marvelous."

In my immediate annoyance with her, I wasn't about to render explicit the inference she should have reached on her own: that she might perhaps rise from the floor, as a very modest gesture of preparation for the arrival of our country's President. She didn't rise. Instead, she resettled the headphones over her ears and half-shut her eyes. But that wasn't all: from the depths of her Valley of Din she lifted an open palm to her mouth and blew me a kiss.

This last was a gesture that galled me the more for being, in its way, rather winsome. It was a stroke at once affectionate and dismissive—a beguiling bit of impudence.

I carried my disgruntlements out into what I naturally supposed would be an empty kitchen. But no. Here was my son, Sindri, fixing himself a cup of coffee. At the sight of him I guess I recoiled slightly, in surprise. I said, "You're back again."

His dark eyes looked apologetic. No, more than that: crestfallen. Oh, how in the *world* am I going to do justice to Sindri's eyes—those big green beseeching born-ladykiller's eyes—and if I can't adequately do them justice, how are you to arrive at any fair full picture of the boy, my son, whose soul always seems atremble right there on the surface of his face? Oh, that face!—which habitually wears a hurt, hopeful expression, as if to suggest that while you have, in truth, regularly and systematically disappointed him in the past, he is, nonetheless, choosing now to deposit his utmost trust in you once more.

"I was just having a cup of coffee."

"Do," I said. "Hey, help yourself."

"Is this a bad time? You seemed to start."

"I was merely surprised to see you again so soon."

"Soon?"

"Well, you were here just a couple of days ago."

"It's been a couple of weeks."

The clemency of the boy's correction, in alliance with his wounded and knowing gaze—his way of seeming at once sage and childish—outmaneuvered me, virtually compelling my hospitable reply: "Why don'tcha fix yourself something to eat?" I added, "I'm leaving anyway."

Taking all with all, Sindri's a good boy, really. He's at least quiet and neat—partnered virtues you'd never ascribe to his sister, three years his elder. And, at twenty-two, he seems, unlike his sister, to have found a steady job. She works for a cosmetics importer, for the radio station, for a restaurant—from one week to the next I can hardly keep track of her. Sindri, on the other hand, works, week in, week out, for Freefiskur, Freeland's largest fish exporter. He does something or other involving computers. I picture him doggedly logging each newly caught mackerel into a memory bank—what do I know? For a time he talked in a pitiably mooning way of becoming a writer and I naturally did all I could to discourage him. His was a poignant fantasy. Sindri lacks, among other things, the proper spirit—and I told him so. I spoke with firm certitude, knowing I represented not only his own best interests but those of that great cause which is *my* life's great cause: Freelandic literature.

As I say, Sindri's a good boy in the main, and we get along handsomely so long as I don't have him constantly underfoot like this. He grew up in Copenhagen, in the care of his mother—his late mother, Sigrun— and on the couple of occasions, long ago, when I visited him there, truthfully I can say I enjoyed my glimpses of the boy, who back then bore a Danish name, Svenning. I was introduced as his mother's "friend." The boy already had a "father," for Sigrun had married a Dutch engineer. But this father, or "father," eventually ran out on them—all the way to Jakarta—and when Sigrun ultimately came down with what proved to be Hodgkin's disease, she told the boy the truth.

But was it—was it the truth? Sigrun was always an impossible one to decipher, and the fact is, we were intimates only in the nakedest sense. Svenning/Sindri was the accidental by-product of a short, spirited, often pugnacious affair carried out in Odense, on the island of Fyn—the birthplace, as it happens, of Hans Christian Andersen. Sigrun was a woman who always harbored ill-defined grievances against me, and I've often suspected that, finding herself alone on a premature deathbed, she steered the boy my way in order to get back at me. What I mean to say is: within my heart of hearts, I can't quite believe Sindri is my son. But what was I to do? One day my bell rings, I rise from my study chair to answer it, and there in my doorway I encounter a pimply fifteen-year-old boy, who hails me with a loud, lachrymose cry of "Father!" and webs his arms around me. Ever since, in one way or another, our dealings have been mortifying.

I do constantly point out, for the boy's own benefit, that he might do better elsewhere. Any impartial observer eventually would have to ask: what sort of young man of twenty-two would remain so rooted in Freeland? Wouldn't any right-spirited lad of his age have moved off by now? At twenty-two, I'd already headed toward America on a steamer called *The Return*, my tubercular lungs thrown open to a westward seascape. Meanwhile, he's logging fish into a computer!

"How are the catches?" I ask him.

"The catches?"

Though I don't mean to bellyache about the boy, I *do* wish he would discard this particular charade. He always feigns a moment's confusion when I ask after his job—just as though he weren't spending some forty hours a week separating, electronically, the cod from the haddock.

"Hannibal's coming," I say—and, thank the Lord, the doorbell at just that instant sounds.

Hannibal in the doorway *fills* the doorway. There's an expansiveness to him, whose features bear a ruddy, portentous glow. I'd intended to invite him in, and his craning glance, which takes in the pair of supine young people on the living room floor, shows a piqued curiosity. Lilja's midriff is still bare. "We're off," I declare, and step out into the corridor.

In silence we ride the elevator down to the lobby. Hannibal shakes his head in a mulling, marveling sort of way clearly meant to elicit a friendly query; I ignore him. All business, I say "Where's your car?" when we step outside, under a sky whose sun is buried, just as those clouds from my study had predicted. Hannibal drives a big gray Land Rover. Needless to say, Freelanders often joke about Hannibal's "elephant." I'm in no mood for jokes now.

"First, I want you to understand it was an authentic vision, Eggi," he says, once he has the car started and has turned onto Skeggjagata, the main street of Thorskrist.

"It's authentic suicide," I reply. "It's the sirens calling you to the rocks."

"I don't want you to think I'm fabricating anything—pulling some sort of trick on you."

"And I don't want you to think you have a chance in hell, my friend. Have you thought about it? Really *thought*? At this point, everyone's lined up against you."

All at once, it began to rain. Hannibal adjusted the wipers, meanwhile nodding gravely as if to show me how attentively he was heeding my words—the old trickster! I might as well have been addressing myself to a stuffed puffin.

I said: "The fishermen are against you because catches are down, and have been down for the last three years. And more and more of what they *are* catching is trash fish. It may not be fair to blame you, but they do."

"It's the others. The big foreign powers. Polluting the seas. Overfishing. Dynamiting the coral reefs, it's enough to make a grown man weep. And they're dumping radioactive—"

"All beside the point. The *point* is, the fishermen blame you. And the farmers are against you, because the wool market has collapsed."

"It's those damned New Zealanders. It's the Chinese. And it's those foppish Italian fashion designers and this rage for dressing people in table-cloths. Curtain materials. Linen and all the rest of it."

"Maybe it's the Martians, Hanni. We're doomed all the same. Economically, Freeland has gone down the drain."

Hannibal stopped the car to let Linh Ng cross the street. She carried a delicate and quite pretty—i.e., imported—umbrella in one hand, a bag of groceries in the other. In the seventies, back when the sad saga of Vietnam was winding down, and the sad saga of the "boat people" was winding up, Hannibal arranged for Freeland to take in a dozen refugee families. As a proportion of our population, this represented a greater commitment than that undertaken by either France or the United States —those global powers responsible for the mess in the first place. By absorbing so many refugees, Hannibal had intended to "shame America back to a sense of her moral commitments." Some doubt in my mind remains as to whether we succeeded in doing so. As already should be clear, Hannibal has an appetite—unmatched in any public figure I've ever met —for grand symbolic gestures.

Unfortunately, the great majority of the refugees eventually found a way out of Freeland, most of them to America and Canada. I say unfortunately because in what Hannibal used to call our "Little Saigon"—a cluster of corrugated aluminum shacks at the east end of the harbor—his political support was unwavering. From Freeland's point of view, the fall of—Little—Saigon followed a sort of reverse Darwinism. The fittest— those marshaling the greatest talent, intelligence, material wealth, enterprise—all disappeared. Linh Ng is typical of the few hangers-on: after nearly twenty years in Thorskrist, she has yet to master more than two dozen phrases in Freelandic. Not even the Freelandic name we gave her— Linda—has stuck.

"And the so-called industrial base has been against you ever since the oil exploration collapsed."

"Now I have it on absolute *authority*, from a top geologist in *Oslo*, that there's oil in abundance down there. It's just a way of attempting to drive us down. To say nothing of secret payoffs from the Arabs. Tightening the screws, you see. Trying to make us desperate."

"We *are* desperate. Don't you understand? Damn it to hell, man, we have no electoral base. And the young people, they're against you because they think we're conspiring to keep their 'culture' from them, which admittedly is just exactly what we *are* doing, since in our secret hearts you and I both agree that the phrase 'youth culture' is an oxymoron. They want commercial radio. They want a lifting of the equal-time music requirements. They want to be free to blast themselves deaf, the little bastards."

In Freeland we have a good many regulations intended to deflect or disarm pernicious musical influences. Most are extremely complicated, and most—over the years I've served as the President's closest adviser—are of my own devising. We tax recordings by living "composers," and the radio, which is state-run, places various limitations on the number of hours devoted to "youth music." I've occasionally been called a fascist—not a name I shrink from.

Again Hannibal nodded with a look of devoted, *grateful* attention. He can be, without question, the most inspiring sham I've ever met.

"And I'll tell you who else will be against you. Rut will be against you."

Oh, but this time I'd actually managed to hit him squarely: Hannibal winced. "She'll come round," he answered, but in a voice stripped of that expansive insouciance he'd shown just moments before.

"Are you saying she'll actually support you?"

"In the end. Not at first perhaps."

"You're crazy, Hanni. Absolutely raving mad."

"You wait and see. She'll come round in the end."

But while advancing this claim, Hannibal swiveled my way a set of worried eyes. Beseeching eyes—for just a moment I might almost have been dealing with my boy Sindri.

"Stop a minute. Please. Now are we talking about the same Rut?"

And I myself had better stop to ask: How is a writer to do justice to Rut? I suppose I must begin with her name, Freelandic for Ruth, but so much more evocative in its three-letter form, with its hintings at *root* and *rut*. She embodies both connotations, and more, for our Hannibal Hannibalsson. Spoken, the name comes closer to *root* than *rut*—but with a rolling *r*, sliding upward from the rrroots of the throat to the rrroof of the mouth. She and Hannibal have been together, off and on, for something like thirty years. They have no children. In fact, they aren't married. But she is universally perceived as his *kona*, his woman—I suppose you could call her his common-law wife. Blond-haired, blue-eyed, square-jawed, broad of hips and shoulders, she is a big *root*: a very deep *root*. As Hannibal's wife, she has been Freeland's "first lady" for twenty years—surely the only first lady on the planet who works as a barkeep. . . . Oh my native land!

"She won't come round," I tell him. "Rut doesn't 'come round' any more than a mountain does. Great Blue Glacier will melt before she does. She's unbudging. She's an immovable object, Hanni, like something you'd encounter in a physics problem. She extracted a vow from you. You pledged not to run again. She'll hold you to it."

"She'll come round. In the end." But his gaze was positively beggarly.

"She *won't*. Christ, don't you see she's got just what she wants. She's behind Nonni Karlsson and she'll stay behind him."

And what to say of Nonni Karlsson? Of him little need be said, which I suppose is his great asset and virtue. In his blandness, his sweetness, his malleability, he has been accepted by almost all parties as a suitable replacement for Hannibal Hannibalsson. Nonni is comfortingly life-sized. He's thirty-nine and handsome and impeccably earnest, and his father was an honest-to-God hero who once dove into icy, raging water to rescue a fellow sailor. He's also Rut's cousin. And she dotes on him.

"Where are we going?" I say to Hannibal. The rain has halted as abruptly as it began.

"To see Thorgunnur."

"Well, I suppose you do have at least one vote. Provided she lives to Election Day."

"Oh she's got many years left. She'll outlive us both, Eggi."

"I fear you're right. Poor thing, she may be an immortal."

If, at this stage in my life, anyone on the planet might be said to serve as a mother-figure to me, I suppose it would be our old schoolteacher— yes, that ancient dog-faced bitch Thorgunnur Sigurdardottir, who instructed us in Freelandic and Danish and English and three or four other subjects. From among all the women in the world, I've selected a mother-figure who's a holy terror, who looks on my every accomplishment with disdain, who if she were a mother bird and I a fledgling would long ago have pitched me from the nest—what does this say about me? Hannibal and I were students together in the old Superior School, a building located beside the sailors' graveyard. Many of those graves are empty—memorials to bodies lost at sea—as likewise were empty the heads of many of her students, according to old Thorgunnur, sternest of taskmasters. My own mother died when I was two, as I've told you; the aunt who raised me, old

Dögg Danielsdottir, died when I was in my twenties; but Thorgunnur, born well before either, perdures. She lives in Thorskrist's Eldershelter. Her room looks out on Great Blue Mountain.

The Eldershelter was Hannibal's doing—a monumental construction project into which was plunged so much public funding that, for three years running, the Superior School had to struggle along without the text-books placed on order. By Freelandic standards, the Eldershelter is a veri-table palace. It's no accident that Thorgunnur's room looks out over the mountain. *Every* room has its view of Great Blue Mountain, which has served as the inspiration and the subject of half the oil paintings ever at-tempted in our land.

All of these paintings, by the by, have been atrocious productions—the Freelandic gene pool is wholly lacking in any flair for visual artistry—but if the soul of Freeland resides anywhere, it inhabits the cone of Great Blue. I suppose Hannibal's vision—another vision!—was that the elderly would pass their waning years meaningfully in its shadow. During the days when the hospital/nursing home's construction was capsizing our national economy, he made so much of those scenic views that a sprightly coinage sprang up in our language. "Going mountain-viewing" became impudent slang for "dying." Improbably—and truly, I think, rather beautifully—the phrase eventually shed its arch overtones. Nowadays you will occasionally hear a Freelander say, "Grampa went mountain-viewing," or, "When it's my time to go mountain-viewing," and no one seems to recall the phrase's birth in indignation and contumely. My own suspicion is that the entire magnificent structure went up purely to charm Thorgunnur—there's sim-ply no overstating Hannibal's devotion—and that the country was driven into temporary bankruptcy lest his old Superior School teacher lack a suitably elevated outlook in keeping with her elevated years. Her room lies on the seventh, the top, floor of the most expensive edifice erected in our nation's history. Unfortunately, she cannot have drawn much solace from the view. She was already all but blind when she arrived at the Eldershel-ter five years ago, at the age of eighty-eight.

In an only slightly altered world, this woman who in all her long life has never once departed from Freeland, devoting the whole of her profes-sional career to a little jerrybuilt school overlooking White Seal Bay, in-stead might have wound up holding a professorship in Copenhagen or in Oxford or in ivied New Haven. The intellect was more than up to the task. When it comes to sheer spread and tenacity of memory, I think I've seen its like only once, in the person of an American academic, a philologist at Johns Hopkins, who likewise was all but blind, and whose ugly tale of multiple betrayals I hope in time to unfold here—all sorts of ugliness will unfold here. But the Norse Sagas? Thorgunnur had them down cold; so far as I know there wasn't to be found in their pages an ancillary character—or even a stream or deserted homestead—whose name she couldn't provide on the instant. She had Hans Christian Andersen inside and out, but more impressive still, she could call up—in her burry Freelandic accent—page after page after page of Shakespeare, Milton, Wordsworth, Keats. She never married. She lived to read, and whatever she read she kept.

Hannibal had been her pet, her prize, her plum, the apple of her eye. That these words—pet, prize, plum—pierce me as I write them says perhaps more about me than I would immediately reveal to you. But hell, there it is, and let it stand: after all these years, even now, her rejection rankles! The *unfairness* is what's so embittering, for if anyone—*anyone*—was meant to be sensible to the peculiar charms of young Eggert Oddason, surely that person was Thorgunnur Sigurdardottir. For I was the bright boy of the class, of the school, of—perhaps—the nation. Hadn't I, with a pertinacity akin to her own, mastered my Danish and my English until I, too, could call up pages of it in my head? Didn't I, too, live to read? Hadn't I annotated—night after night, goddamnit—an entire *Webster's Seventh Collegiate*? And having finished that, hadn't I plowed straight through Mencken's *The American Language* and a dictionary of American slang? Were we not soulmates, then, she and I? And yet it was to Hannibal Hannibalsson, who scanted his books and confused his Sagas and stumbled over his English lessons, that the woman's heart went out. Shouldn't *she*, at least, have been able to look beyond our physical charms? Why did she distrust me? How had I acquired my ugly knack for stirring an instant, instinctive distaste in the people I met, particularly those whose approval I most coveted?

We took the elevator up. Hannibal knocked at her door, which was open, craned his head inside and said, "Hello, *oldrudkona*, it's Hannibal."

Oldrudkona—literally, "old woman"—has no exact English counterpart. A term of endearment, it's sometimes translated as *granny* or *auntie*.

"They say a storm is coming," she offered in reply. Old Thorgunnur was lying on her bed, facing away from the door, in the pose of someone scrutinizing the weather brewing around Great Blue Mountain.

"You're looking well, auntie."

Looking well, was she? Looking like *hell* . . . Hers was a face like something you might find out in the lava fields: gray and pitted, weather-scarred and -scored.

"And you are too, Hannibal."

"I have a friend with me."

At these words Thorgunnur swung round her white-haired head and, as God is my witness, she tested the air with her long nose. "It's Eggert Oddason, isn't it," she posited, with the uplifted chin of someone proud to have faced an unpleasant truth straight on. I swear it: she'd sniffed me out.

"Hello, auntie," I said.

"They say a storm is coming," she noted, and added, in heavily accented English:

> Late, late yestreen
> I saw the new moon with the old moon in her arms . . .

" 'And I fear, I fear,' " I said, picking up the ballad, " 'my master dear, there is going to be a storm.' "

"*Yes . . .*" She cleared her throat, threw in my direction a glance of impatient loathing, and returned to her contemplation of Blue Mountain. I vowed to keep mum.

"Auntie," Hannibal said. "I think I have arrived at an important decision. But I wanted to consult with you first. I need your advice."

"I'm listening, Hannibal."

The absurdity of this sentimental little tableau—the notion that a statesman might plausibly turn for useful political counsel to a blind nonagenarian ex-schoolmarm—was evidently lost on the two of them. A respectful, even reverential silence ensued, eventually broken by Hannibal: "The election is only two months off."

"Two months and three days," she corrected him, and this display of calendrical mastery brought a wrinkling smirk to her already fissured face. I suppose I haven't yet mentioned that she's a tall, large-boned woman, Thorgunnur—*still* is, even as she passes through decades that have stunted her contemporaries. That imposing pleated face of hers is a *big* face.

"Nine weeks," he echoed. "It isn't much time. The future must be planned for. I think perhaps I am going to run once more for President, auntie."

"It's a large decision, Hannibal."

"There will be difficulties, no doubt. I'm on the record vowing not to run again. The people have it in their heads that the next President will be Nonni Karlsson, who is—"

"Nonni Karlsson!" Thorgunnur huffed.

"Why, do you remember him, auntie?"

"Of *course* I remember him, and more's the pity. Am I going to forget that in my classroom he once misspelled 'Storblafell'?"—Great Blue Mountain.

"Well, in our youth each of us makes—"

"Now this was no *youth*, Hannibal. I remember it well. Here the boy was nine years old and he didn't know how to spell 'Storblafell,' and are we as a nation going to entrust our future to somebody who could not spell 'Storblafell'?"

We cast—all three of us—a respectful eye in the direction of Great Blue.

"Well, perhaps in the meantime he has—"

"Nothing went into his *head*, Hannibal. It went into his *face,* but not into his head."

Even now the old crone has a wonderful gift for invective.

Then she stared so long and hard at Storblafell—with such a look of discernment on her ruined face—I would have sworn she could make out the very runnels and outcroppings of its lower slopes, and finally she declared, with a schoolmarm's impregnable authority: "It's a question of national honor, Hannibal. You must run."

"People are saying I've been President too long. It's been—"

"Twenty years. On December first, it will be twenty years Hannibal Hannibalsson has served as our President. Some people said I taught school too long. Needless to say, I paid them absolutely no mind. Being a politician is like being a teacher, Hannibal. You must learn how not to listen."

There's no doubt the old bird has lost half her wits over the years—and no doubt that, even so, she's still wilier than the rest of us.

"You must *run*," she declared, and, with a flourish of dignity surprisingly grand in so simple a motion, she held out her hands to him.

And with a commensurate dignity—for there's no passion more potent for Hannibal than a love of the ceremonial—he took her ancient hands in his and declared, "Indeed I will run, auntie."

It was so abruptly intimate a moment that, truly, I felt like a trespasser. They might almost have been lovers. It's a quirk of Hannibal's dealings with the opposite sex that this sort of breathless intimacy is rarely displayed toward anyone he might actually be intimate with. But put him in the presence of a ninety-three-year-old woman, or a three-year-old girl, and his face goes moony-eyed, his voice croons. That's how he used to be with my Lilja, when she as a schoolgirl would perch upon his knee. And Lilja!—how in return she'd doted on her Uncle Hannibal! I shifted in the doorway, cleared my throat.

Thorgunnur withdrew her hands. "I read something in the paper today that concerns you, Hannibal. It concerns the two of you, actually." She reached over to her bedside table and fumblingly brought forth a copy of *The Torch*, the country's leading newspaper. She'd *read* something in the paper today? But surely her eyes no longer make out newsprint. . . .

She brandished the paper in our faces. "Do you know what this concerns? It concerns *The Freeland Saga*."

Oh, dear Lord, spare us—save us, save us, *save* us from any further dither about *The Freeland Saga*. It was the great cause, the idée fixe, of the old crone's existence. For how many decades had she been battling for the "return" of *The Freeland Saga*? Never mind that it couldn't *be* returned, since in the seven or so hundred years of its existence it had never once been to Freeland . . . Never mind that its contents—a rambling, almost incoherent tale of sheep-theft and blood-feud, only partly devoted to the discovery and initial settling of the Freeland archipelago—are of nugatory artistic or historical value, even to someone like me who has a passion for the Sagas. And never mind that it was almost surely written by an Icelander, almost surely in Iceland, about an Icelandic expedition! For in her mind it was our own testament, our Pentateuch, our Magna Carta and Domesday Book, our Landnamabok—and it must be returned. . . .

"Do you know what it says here?" Thorgunnur asked us.

"I think so," Hannibal said. "Perhaps a rough idea."

Of course he knew its contents back and forth. It had been a small story on the television news last night—which is probably how Thorgunnur had been alerted to its presence in this morning's *Torch*.

Still, bending her head over the paper, she did a credible imitation of someone actually poring over a newspaper column. "As you know, *The Freeland Saga* was written on sheepskin, which itself ought to give everyone pause, since most of the other Sagas were written on calfskin. Now, it says here that the sheep from whose skins the parchment was made must have weighed some forty or even forty-five kilograms. Now what does that suggest to you?"

"That's a mighty big sheep," Hannibal said.

"But what does it *suggest*, my boy?"

"Well," Hannibal said, obligingly acting the role of someone being led along an intellectual path of discovery, "Freeland has long been known for the generous size of its sheep. . . ."

"Precisely—or has been so known ever since the Reverend Gudmundur brought his breed here from Norway in—now what year was it?"

"Eleven fifty-six," Hannibal said.

"Eleven sixty-six," I corrected.

"In either case, a full century before *The Freeland Saga* was written. Now, what does this suggest to you, boy?"

"That those first chapters could well have been written on the skin of a Reverendgudmundur sheep?"

"*Could* have? *Must* have! Don't you see? It's as plain as the nose on your face. They stole our manuscript!"

"Or they stole our sheep," I pointed out.

Thorgunnur flashed at me a look of bristling annoyance—which suddenly softened in the recognition of my suggestion's usefulness: "Exactly. Precisely. Why, it comes to the same thing!"

"Well, this does appear to put the matter in a new light . . . ," Hannibal began.

"This time, *this* time around, you have to employ the full powers of your Presidency to ensure the return of *The Freeland Saga*. It's your duty, Hannibal."

"I'll do everything I can. As you know, they're very reluctant. The Icelanders . . ."

"They're thieves," Thorgunnur announced happily, and resumed a meditation on her mountain.

We said good-bye, rode down the elevator and slipped into the street. A dull pickax of sun was hacking through a hill of clouds. As we marched toward Hannibal's "elephant," I did not point out to him that a rainbow had opened on his right. Lord knows what gateway *this* one might have pointed him toward.

"Now if I were to run . . . ," he began, after he'd pulled out into Sudurgata.

"You've already *pledged* to run. And pledged not to," I added.

As though it were the smallest of quibbles, he waved my paradox away. "Eggi, I want you right behind me."

"*Behind* is impossible when you stand on two sides of an issue. . . ."

"I see us in this together."

"Do you? I see myself far from here. I'm off to Birch Valley and the summerhouse. I have a book to write—my fiftieth book. And maybe then, when it's done, overseas again. To Sicily perhaps. It's time I was leaving Freeland."

"Wait until after the election. I'll appoint you somewhere."

A diplomatic post? In theory, it was an enticing prospect. The trouble is, ours isn't a country that has the resources for any sort of credible overseas presence. I suppose that if reelected, Hannibal could again appoint me Ambassador to Denmark—we have a little outpost in Copenhagen, over on the south, the "wrong," side of the train station. Or he might cajole our good friends the Danes, or our good Nordic brothers the Swedes or the Norwegians, to clear for me a little broom-closet office in London or Paris or New York or even Tokyo. I've served, under various august titles—Ambassador, Economic Secretary, Consul General—in each of those places. Incidentally, it sometimes does strike me that I've lived an odd life. . . .

"And think of the Language Committee. What's going to happen if you're no longer at the helm?"

The helm? Hannibal seemed always to be visualizing our nation as some sort of Viking ship he was piloting into the fog-topped seas of the future.

Still, with this objection he'd prodded closer to my heart. I'm the head of something called the Freelandic Language Committee, a public organization which provides my only steady source of income. But Hannibal wasn't appealing chiefly to my pocketbook. No, here was to be found, in a folly-overrun planet operated by bastards and thieves, a cause to believe in.

The task of my Committee is to ensure that the language absorbs as few loan-words as possible. Ideally, all neologisms ought to come from Freelandic and its old Norse roots. What is to be our word for *microprocessor*, for *stagflation*, for *telegenic* and *gene-splicing* and *hydroponics*? Constantly struggling to absorb and contain the outside world, we on the Committee find ourselves asking: where in the Sagas, in the Poetic and Prose Edda, in the proverbs and folktales of our ancestors, is to be found the obscure, superannuated term that, through the revivifications of metaphor, might now be used to signify *sunroof* or *carjacking* or *freebasing* or *gentrification* or *yuppie*? It's a job that calls for a true poet's mixture of fancy and precision—which means, I'm afraid, that I'm the only one in Freeland perfectly equal to it. And if the job consumed far too much of my time—if it meant I was forever having to shuttle from one "expert" to another, one small subcommittee to another—oh, the satisfactions it provided me! Suddenly to grasp that there's an outmoded term for plague, current back when the Black Death ravaged our valleys, that might now be applied to AIDS; to realize there's an old word for a hand-held children's toy, fabricated out of pins and twine, that might now serve for *video game*. . . . *Who am I?* is what I sometimes ask myself, waking in the middle of the night from dreams of landscapes that hold no people in them. But there are times, working for my Committee, when I know that I am the head of my nation's language, which is to say I'm the head of my nation's culture, which is to say—truly, and God help us—*I'm the real brains of the body politic.* No, the Committee is essential, and if Hannibal's defeat were to mean some great curtailment in its functions, or—unthinkable—its dissolution, the loss would be grievous.

We were driving along Hafnargata, Harbor Road, not far from where the body of little Simon Olsson had been discovered. Mist rode in over the water, carrying sea-drizzle; we'd left the rainbows behind us.

"Good Lord, now look at *that*," Hannibal exclaimed, and veered off the road. We both got out. I lifted my collar against the rain.

We made our way to a pair of outsize garbage containers composed of a frog-green plastic that gave off an unearthly shimmer in the mist and drizzle. "The things some people will throw away . . . ," Hannibal mused, shaking his head in mixed censure and jubilation. For in between the trash containers someone had slipped two sizable sheets of plywood, each maybe four feet by six.

"I'll take one, you take the other," Hannibal said, instinctively assuming command of our two-man raiding expedition.

I watched him lift out one of the wet sheets and haul it to a big rock by the side of the road. He propped the board upon the rock and, wincing in anticipation at the shock to his knees, brought his booted foot down upon it. The board yielded with a soundless, fatigued crack.

I duplicated his gestures. I found my own good-sized rock—Freeland is rich, incidentally, not only in rocks but in boulders, pebbles, stones—and propped my board upon it. But when I brought my foot down, the board did *not* collapse. Instead, my sole skidded and slid, and I, losing my balance, dropped to one knee. The rain had turned everything slick. . . . And of course I wasn't to be given a second chance. Hannibal's big boot came down on my board, and this time, showing him spineless deference, it gave in utterly. "You take that piece, I'll take this one." And he stooped and gathered the larger of the two remnants into his arms.

Nothing about this task struck me as out of the ordinary. Hannibal's always on the lookout for fuel for his fireplace—broken fishing crates, housing construction castoffs, driftwood. He has an insatiable appetite for something his treeless native land is utterly unsuited to provide: big crackling blazes in the hearth in the study in his house out on Founders' Point.

Is the picture coming clear? This is a country where the President is a trash-picker, the First Lady is a barkeep, and the leading Man of Letters is an errand boy. . . .

"Time for a soak," Hannibal announced, once we'd stowed our cargo in the back of the Land Rover.

"I'm already soaked."

"Time for a hot soak. That's a different matter."

Freeland sits atop vast tectonic fissures. Everywhere you walk on our four islands—through cottonweed bogs, in rhyolite canyons, beside hillside clefts, along streambeds and lavafields and mossy heaths—the land is steaming. At times it's hard to escape an impression that we live on a terrestrial wound that will not heal, an endlessly running sore. Whereas other countries might offer glades, forests, copses, we abound in calderas, fumaroles, smoking tuff. In terms of geothermal resources, anyway, we are per capita the richest people in the world; you might say we have heat to burn. An old Freelandic joke . . . *Son to mother: I'm going to take a bath. Mother to son: Don't use up all the cold water.* We have dotted our countryside with open-air swimming pools, blithely casting our one great natural bounty up toward the snow-heavy skies.

We drove to the pool in silence. Anyone could see that Hannibal had lost that sweet glow of purpose which had draped upon his shoulders like a mantle when, only an hour before, he had come banging on my door. Perhaps he was fretting over Rut. She was going to be a problem—more than a problem, for she would never come round. Or perhaps it had struck home, with the fading of his vision, that his electoral defeat was all but certain. It wasn't a matter of whether or not, looking deep into his soul, he would "choose to serve." He was a fifty-six-year-old man with bad knees and thinning hair and a spreading gut whose country had had enough of him.

In the men's locker room I had a chance to survey that gut. Hannibal was cargoing some twenty-five or thirty surplus pounds. Our bodies in the mirrors across from the rust-stained urinals were a study in contrasts. I don't pack an excess ounce. I suppose it should be said that with age I seem at last to have become more inoffensive-looking; these days, I don't so often seem to stir that intuitive distaste which characterized my youth. I've learned to clip close to my skull my still abundant hair, which takes on a clumped and mangy look when I let it grow. Less feral too with time is my face: the sharpness of the nose and the quick jumpiness of the small-eyed gaze have gentled with age. I may be flattering myself, but I think that someone meeting me today would be less likely to think of a brown rat than of an albino chinchilla. There are mornings when I would swear my expression looks positively benign.

Even so, despite his spreading torso, around Hannibal's limbs there floated, as never would float around mine, a consummate athlete's grace. Is it possible to look at once adroit and presidential while rubbing cobalt-blue liquid soap into one's underarms and along one's dick? If this is possible, Hannibal managed it.

The soap? It was something called "Danish Blue," a term conceivably confusable with that lovely marbled cheese, produced from cows fattened on the Jutland plains, which is one of the Danes' few culinary triumphs; in fact, there's little such confusion in Freeland, since my countrymen, although usually susceptible to every Danish wile, are not about to have foisted upon them a comestible riddled with mold. We won't go near the stuff. When *we* speak of Danish Blue we mean a bright, gummy liquid cleansing agent dispensed in swimming pools and bathrooms around the country. We import it by the freighter-load, as we have been doing for decades. We ascribe near-mystical powers to it.

The dick? It was broad and long and—stately. Often you see fat men whose penises seem to have almost disappeared, turtle-fashion, into the hemispheric shell of their belly. This wasn't the case with Hannibal, though, who beneath the impressive overhang of his gut carried an impressive, balancing overhang.

We put on our bathing suits and, barefoot, headed outdoors. The sun was again splitting through the clouds. If you've never been to Freeland, you probably cannot imagine how rapidly our weather shifts. A twenty-minute drive may well take you through rain and sun, hail and sun, snow and sun. Just as we lead the world in geothermal heat, we probably excel it in rainbow production—and perhaps in displays of the northern lights as well.

Alongside the pool lay two hot pots. The one kept at 38–40 degrees

Centigrade contained some half a dozen people. The other, which is kept at 40–45 and isn't for the thin-skinned, was empty. It was our destination. I followed Hannibal down the stairs of the tub. A submerged bench runs along its rim. Hannibal sat down and tossed his head back. He was immersed to the neck in very hot water.

I sat down as well, but kept my head erect. I was studying him.

"She's going to be furious," I said. "Rut."

"Going to be furious," an abject Hannibal agreed.

"Can you imagine just how mortifying this might be? I wouldn't be surprised, I wouldn't be at all surprised, if she refused to support you."

"No, not surprised. Ohh, she's capable of it." And *he*, in his despondency, seemed capable, suddenly, of hearing my every word. I sensed his abrupt, acute vulnerability.

So I pounced on him; this was for his own good, after all. "Can you imagine? When in the entire history of the planet was there an election when a candidate's wife didn't support him?"

"This may well be a first, Eggi. I can see that. *You've* got to run with me, anyway."

"*I've* got to talk you out of this, my friend. You're contemplating a degree of mortification which, even by your own gargantuan standards, is altogether unparalleled."

"Such eloquence. It's marvelous. You do speak beautifully, Eggi. I've never seen such a gift for language. That's why I need you to help with my speeches."

"Spare me. And won't the Danes love this? After all your baiting remarks?"

"The poor Danes," he said. "They're being swallowed up by the Germans."

"And the Germans?"

"Actually, they're in a bad way, Eggi." He still had his head thrown back. He was contemplating the heavens. "They're being overrun by the East Europeans, the former Communists. Their economy is being undermined."

"You know what you're like, Hanni? Christ, do you know what your worldview is like?" Why had I not thought of this before? "Think of Annasigga, Hanni. Annasigga and the trolls."

We have in Freeland a favorite folktale, one with many international counterparts, which concerns a little shepherd girl, Annasigga, who one day stumbles upon a cavern stacked with treasure. She has never glimpsed anything like such riches before—gemstones and silks and heaping vats of gold coins—and for a long while she wanders, dazed and wide-eyed, among them. Indeed, she tarries too long, for after a while she hears behind her a thump-thump-thump and her exit is blocked by a stupendous troll. She goes into hiding. She sits shivering with horror behind a vat of gold coins, as one troll after another, each more fearsome and ferocious than the next, lumbers through the cavern's mouth.

Little terrified Annasigga huddles for hours and hours, as the trolls begin swilling their hogsheads of spirits and banqueting on the bones of men. Finally, they start to bicker over who among them is the strongest. They come to blows, axes and maces are drawn, and when the long, reverberating mayhem concludes, a miracle is revealed to the child. Somehow they have managed to kill each other off; death has come to each and every one. The little girl fills her arms with sparkling booty and runs home to her parents. . . .

"Annasigga?"

"That's what Freeland is for you, isn't it, Hanni? You seriously believe the other nations are trolls that will do themselves in, and we shall survive them all."

I had meant the words in ridicule, but—why hadn't I foreseen this?—instead they *heartened* him. He lifted his great shaggy head and gazed at me earnestly, admiringly. "It's true, you're right, you've got it exactly, Eggi. They're doing themselves in. Anyone can see it. They're forgetting how to live. Look at the Americans. Here is a culture that once brought us Fred Astaire in *Top Hat* and now they're exporting Arnold Schwarzenegger in *The Terminator*. They have ferocity without honor. Look at the Japanese . . ."

He left unspoken—apparently because it was so obvious—what was demolishing the Japanese. Caving in, perhaps, under their own material excess? Their islands—four of them, just like ours—beginning to sink under the weight of innumerable silicon chips, each as light as a feather of pumice ash, such as once began to snow upon the streets of Pompeii? The poor British, meanwhile, were victims of runaway anemia, the poor French of acute aestheticism. The Russians were going to back-stab the Chinese, who were going to back-stab the Russians.

"We have a mission, you and I," he declared, and I don't think the words would have worked so potently upon my spirits had the skies not chosen just that moment to unleash a stinging round of hail. Hannibal looked so fatuous right then, his heat-ruddied, trash-picker's face oblivious of the mean little pellets pounding down upon it, that my heart went out to him.

I nodded.

"You're in?" he asked in English—our language of private ceremony, and of raillery.

It was a pleasure, while embarking on something so potentially cata-strophic, to be able to wrap it in a joke.

"We're both in—in hot water up to the neck."

"You'll run with me?" Still in English.

"Don't say I failed to warn you."

"You'll run with me?"

"This shows a lack of respect not only for yourself but for everyone around you."

"But you mean to say you'll run with me, my friend?"

"If you were really my friend, you wouldn't put me on so disastrous a course. . . ."

"You'll run?"

"I'll run."

5

A Run Across Time

Why embark on anything so dim, so doomed, so open to ridicule? If an answer's to be found, I suppose it lies in the past; we've run together, Hannibal and I, for a long time.

The sun works its way free of the clouds at last, as is only fitting, for we return to its heyday, its highwater mark: June 21. The decades drop away, it's Midsummer's Eve, 1958, and today we celebrate the anniversary of our independence with the first annual Freelandic Olympic Games.

I'm recalling another, simpler era. . . . In the interim, our Olympic Games have been transformed. These days, they're held at the new track beside the new Superior School and imported technology reigns. The pole vaulters soar, birdlike, on fiberglass poles and drop into birdlike nests of honeycomb foam. The discus is a pliable, high-optic pink object that whizzes through the sky like a UFO. The shot-putters cradle indoor-outdoor spheres of duraline vinyl. The runners sport polychromatic, sweat-wicking uniforms and inflatable shoes. To evoke our First Olympics is to summon up an extinct world. Our shot put was a sea-rounded stone, dragged from the beach at Founders' Point. Instead of a track we ran in a meadow scored by sheep paths. Our hurdles were fishing crates. The javelin was a planed and sanded two-by-four.

Back then, there were only six events: the sprint, the javelin, the long jump, the shot put, the hurdles, and the long run. They were varied enough, nonetheless, to lead one to suppose that the victors would display a range of ages and heights and body types. The sprint might go to some lightfoot student, an ectomorph, quick with schoolyard games; the shot put clearly belonged to a fisherman, a mesomorph, shoulders burly with the daily hauling of the nets; and so on down the list.

But things failed to fall out as foreseen. One body type was winning all the events. One *body* was winning all the events, and in fact doing more than merely *winning*. In the sprint, across the lava-ash yard that served as our soccer field, Hannibal came in four or five paces before the silver medalist. His javelin soared another ten, twelve, fifteen feet beyond the little hen-scratches in the dirt that marked his fellows' aspirations. His long jump outdistanced by nearly the length of his feet his nearest competitor.

The gods had sent us, in endorsement of our ceremony, a day of crystalline beauty. The sky would have been the deepest blue imaginable had the waters of White Seal Bay not been bluer still. . . . It was a day for competition: blue contended with blue, depth with depth, under a sun that sparked the least vein of the least pebble on the rubbled outskirts of the soccer field. The air was warm; this was sweater and windbreaker weather, not coat and hat weather, and every eye followed Hannibal Hannibalsson, whose square shoulders, bare save for a woolen jersey, were broadening before our eyes. In our newly independent and rashly hopeful land—only recently rescued from the thieving Danes—we had discovered a true hero, someone reminiscent of the great Saga figures of old.

The gray stone of the shot sank deep into Hannibal's shoulder as he spun himself round and when it emerged it took to the air like any bird. His ankles, too, took to the air, on wings, as he sailed over the fish-crate hurdles. Only the long run, the two-mile, remained. If the wings on his feet held up, if his big heart was equal to it, he would accomplish a clean sweep of the events.

The two-mile distance was approximate. In the old meadow a rough rectangle, its corners marked by piles of stones, had been set out. It was estimated to be half a mile in all. The remaining gold medal would belong to whoever most quickly got around it four times.

The starter's gun was an ancient German pistol wielded by ancient Lars Larsson. Jostling at the starter's line, there must have been sixty of us assembled—yes, "us," for among the ranks of fair-haired, strapping competitors had slipped swarthy, scrawny Eggert Oddason.

The ancient pistol explodes with a thunderclap and the bullet, like a circus lion leaping through a hoop of flame, cuts cleanly through a cloud of acrid blue smoke. And as it sails onward, making its long arced flight over the sea, a host of runners spills forward at a sprint, determined to streak toward glory on this, the culminating event of the afternoon.

Eggert Oddason—I—wasn't among the sprinters. Eggert restrained himself, as did Hannibal Hannibalsson, who by chance had settled beside him. We were in the middle of the pack as we swung round the cairn that marked the first lap.

On the second lap, one by one, the rabbiting sprinters began falling by the wayside. By doing nothing more than what we'd done from the outset—settling stride after stride steadily across the grassy, knobby ground—we overtook them, until there couldn't have been more than four or five still ahead of us. The air, like the sun on the face of the water, was cool and warm at once. Down, down into the sea's darkening folds the bullet from the starter's pistol tumbled; up, up toward the blue of the heavens the cries of the crowd mounted; and on the third lap Eggert made his move.

Who would have supposed that bespectacled, smudgy-faced, sharp-nosed, book-mad Eggert Oddason ever had in him the makings of a runner? No one would have believed it of me, but I'd long suspected that in my driven darting nervousness I had the temper and the constitution of a long-distance runner. And now the moment was come when cloudy suspicions would cohere into glittering facts, when my countrymen would behold the vivid secret lodged within me from my earliest days: the knowledge that in the long sweep of time I was destined to surpass them all.

When I made my move it was as though the earth's gravity gave me a partial reprieve; I half-ran half-flew. One moment, Hannibal was beside me, his feet thudding, for they were growing heavy, his breath rasping, for he had reached the sill of utter depletion—and in the next moment all his noisy strainings were behind me.

And now it's fair to say the eyes of my country center on me. This is new. This has never happened before. In the panorama of my run their gazes blur, the multitudes melt into a single mass—with the exception of one gaze. One set of blue eyes remains apart, distinct and infusible. My talent as a runner is only the first of my well-buried secrets. Here's another: over these past few months I've fallen—breathtakingly—in love. Near the cairn that is both starting point and finish line stands my own start and finish, my alpha and omega, Gudrun Haraldsdottir, and surely her blue mild kindly eyes are dilated in amazement, for she would never ever have guessed that that peculiar bookish classmate of hers—the runty one, the intense one, whom she has allowed to walk her home from school on four or five occasions, from whom she has heard such queer and arresting talk—was destined to wear around his skimpy neck a gold medal. Now, for the first time, she is seeing him whole. . . .

On the wings of my inspiration I sailed past the other runners, one by one, to open a commanding lead.

Truly, ours being the sort of planet which regularly makes way for astoundingnesses, incredibilitudes, unbelievabilities, for things so striking they beggar the capacities of conventional language—a planet in which slinking hirsute one-centimeter-long creatures with far too many legs metamorphose over time into expansive butterflies—truly, might it not be possible that Gudrun, for all her sweetness, goodness, and circumspection, felt attracted to this other's bitterness, vindictiveness, recklessness? I mean, didn't she perhaps sense in him, all along, the possibility of some stunning redemption? Sense that under her beneficent influence he might cast off his many legs, unfold a pair of wings?

On their little walks he has explained to her about the world. The world—*that* is his subject. No matter that he, no more than she, has never once escaped this little necessitous cluster of islands in the icy North Atlantic. He has been reading about all the foreign lands; he is an insomniac who sometimes reads all night, who pores over the maps and the photographs, and in time he will, if only she permits him, escort her into the splendors of Copenhagen, Paris, New York, and Hollywood. On their walks he explains and gesticulates, amplifies and embellishes, and she, her eyes fixed on him, replies with sighs and little deep-throated grunts of something like wonderment. Just as you might feed a hungry pigeon crusts of bread from the palm of your hand, so he has been feeding her the world itself. There is a rapt appetitive keenness in her mild eyes, and he alone has put it there.

Yes, she has guessed, perhaps, a good deal about me—but not this! Who would have supposed I house within me the spirit of an athletic champion? My feet scarcely need touch the ground. I feel rather than see my lead expand behind me. And I feel, too, her eyes upon me and I know, with the certitude of virginal love, that under her approving gaze I am invincible—

Oh, that gaze of hers even today, a third of a century later, works its effects upon me. I saw Gudrun just a week ago. We might safely leave the race for a moment, while Eggert is inexorably broadening his lead, and now the sky again throngs with clouds. It's a drizzly gray Monday in downtown Thorskrist, and there stands Gudrun on the sidewalk, outside

Thorbald's Fishbooth. We are in our fifties now, both of us, and our paths have been crossing for nearly half a century. But for how much longer? She is dying of a rare form of cancer. It is called "Glowinski's sarcoma," and I suppose I might in time, as the head of the Freelandic Language Committee, fashion a native name for it, although the only thing I can think to call it is Gudrun's disease.

Often in the past couple of years she has been away, pursuing expensive treatments in Copenhagen and Stockholm. Now she has returned to us. Resignedly? Hopefully? There's no way to read the difference on Gudrun's face. Age and disease have dug away at the flesh around her eyes, and furrowed her forehead and neck, but the cheeks and mouth retain their look of ample contentment.

Memories of Gudrun run together, and now I backtrack once more, recalling a different glimpse of her, in winter, a year before this most recent sighting. She was walking beside her husband, Baldur Hermannsson, the two of them backlit by a street lamp as they trudged together through falling snow up the walkway to the medical center on Fellsgata. Baldur, whose father once owned the Hotel Snorri and who must have left his son a sizable legacy, has failed at everything he ever attempted. I once heard him describe himself as an "importer of entertainment," and over the years, with one harebrained scheme after another, he has brought to our shores a four-lane bowling alley, an indoor miniature golf course, and a restaurant specializing in ballroom dancing. Tall at the outset of his marriage, with a thick head of curly auburn hair, he has developed a middle-aged stoop and a monkish tonsure.

And yet to behold the look of grateful satisfaction on Gudrun's street-lamp-lit face, as she leans into him on the snowy walkway of that clinic whose tests can only confirm the inevitability of her demise, is to detect no recognition of his failure. The woman has not demanded enough from life, clearly. I watch the two of them marching side by side through the snow and a wild gloating frightened laugh rings inside my skull at the knowledge that the flesh around her eyes has been eaten, that Gudrun Haraldsdottir is dying.

A year later—a week ago—I run into her in front of Thorbald's Fishbooth in a fine drizzle, she's just back from Stockholm, both of us are alone, and she does not seem to resent my cold and appraising survey of her face. She talks cheerfully about her children: a trio of sons who show no more aptitude for success than their hapless father.

For Gudrun alone, my earliest, wholehearted, hackneyed verses were written. I suppose I feel toward her what other men feel toward the first girl they ever bedded. But more so. I feel nothing at all toward the girl who languorously took my virginity—a cousin of mine who was already, at the age of nineteen, a souse. No, if I feel any such inextinguishable tenderness it is toward Gudrun, who was not my first lover—not my lover at all, ever—but something far more meaningful: my first muse. For her, I paced the dark sleeted streets of Thorskrist, hour after hour, warming myself with visions of the two of us together, strolling different and needless to say more clement streets, for somehow or other I would guide her to Copenhagen, to Rome, to Washington.

And even now I can't fully shake a suspicion that if Gudrun had only taken me as her partner . . . if she had not, without consulting a soul, one day allowed herself to be carried off by Baldur Hermannsson . . . then she might . . . might have amended me? Freed me from most of my rancors, my envies, from all the bitter relish I take in the world's iniquities? She talks to me gently for a few minutes, in front of Thorbald's Fishbooth, and as, in farewell, she turns her still proudly erect body, I experience a sympathy and a sorrow that is a needle to the heart. At the sight of her, drifting down the street in a drizzle, I draw in my breath sharply—

The breath goes deep, deep into my boyish not yet tubercular lungs as I round the cairn that marks the halfway point on the final lap. All's become a pounding, revolving blur. My chest is burning, burning with crackling sheets of flame, and there's no longer time enough to expel an old breath before a new breath's needed. Still I hammer on. I am nearly there.

I've rounded the final cairn and I'm in the last eighth of a mile and there's not a single bend or twist standing between me and glory. It seems I've entered a voluminous tunnel like a cathedral, whose walls and vaulted ceiling are the clamor of the crowd, and at whose altar-end lies a blaze of downflooding sun—when I become aware behind me, seemingly less by hearing than by sensing, of a thump and a scrape, a thump and a scrape, a thump and a scrape. Hannibal—he's closing in.

I run on, I show him my heels, I borrow strength from my true love and muse, from Gudrun Haraldsdottir, who stands out there by the finish line urging me on, and whose urgings, heeded, are indomitable. I'm pursued by a thump and a scrape—by a man whose lungs sound like a car in need of a brake job—but I run on, I show it my heels, I carry the burning torch of my chest toward the finish line, which cannot be more than a hundred yards off. *There* abides my victory, my princely vindication. Defeat? Defeat lies as far away as Gudrun's cancer. . . .

How many hours, since, have I devoted to pondering why I lost the race? Perhaps there's nothing to ponder. Perhaps it's simply a case of the triumph of the faster and stronger; perhaps the better runner won. But I cannot, even now, altogether believe that. Better for me if I could, I suppose, but still I remain convinced, more than a third of a century later, that I might indeed on that golden afternoon have won and worn the gold.

Did I throw the race? If so, which of my inner demons should be held accountable? Suspects abound . . . Was it the one called You Loathsome Thing—was it self-hatred? Or the one called Kick Me—was it the desire, never to be fully expunged in my life, to be bested and dominated? Was it Pity the Poor Orphan Boy? Or Yellow-belly the Coward?

But when I think of that body surging past me in the final ten yards—its big legs thumping, its heart raging like a furnace under the sweat-matted jersey, and the blood-and-gold hair flashing in the midsummer sun—I'd like to think I was yielding to the incomparable notion that sometimes life, too, no less than literature, is larger than life.

6

And What Is Life Like?

The light lingers. On this Olympic Day, summer's solstice, night is as remote as a half-garbled rumor concerning some family long since packed up and moved from town. It is something native only to those southern latitudes of hopeless compromise, zones where you meet no true sun, no true dark, but only a fleeting faulty series of blinkings, a flutter like that of a night-moth drifting hungrily in and out of the glow of a windowpane.

When had we last laid eyes on such a hero? It seems Hannibal is the sort of young man after whom hilltops, or great geological fissures, are naturally named, and there's no physical contest of human devising at which he wouldn't prove the victor—just as there's no woman on these islands who could possibly deny him. How is it, then, that the light on the evening of his great glory reveals him walking under Great Blue Mountain with a girl of indifferent looks and an indifferent manner?

Perhaps it's ten at night, perhaps eleven, maybe a few minutes short of midnight, but the sun lingers even yet on his triumphs. It fingers, dotingly, the six gold medals around his neck. He tastes the air in great gliding swings of breath—never, never has he known breezes of such vivifying properties. Truly life could now be accepted as a process of attainable perfections if only he understood what ought to be done about the girl walking beside him.

How has it happened that, on this evening of evenings, she's the companion at his side? This was none of *her* doing, surely; one of this girl's puzzling allurements is the flat final uninterest he holds for her. And for his part, while admittedly piqued by the challenge she presents,

the truth is he'd had other, brighter prizes in mind. Thorskrist is so generously outfitted—it's not to be believed, really, just how *many* lovely
girls and women there are! So how has he wound up here, on Blue Island, with Rut?

And why should she alone, of all his countrymen, appear unswayed
by his accomplishments? She claims to have left the Games early, returning
home to Blue for lunch, but is this true? She'd certainly *looked* guileless
when inquiring after the outcome of the final race. . . . Had she somehow
failed to absorb the significance of the half-dozen medals around his neck?

She's a tall, broad-shouldered, high-breasted girl whose blond pigtail
braids beat upon the back of her fuzzy brown wool sweater. She walks a
few steps ahead of him on the narrow path. Her dress beneath her sweater
is brown as well. She has a cast in one eye, her gaze never meeting yours
straight on, which makes interpretation all the more difficult when she
volunteers some preposterous fact or judgment. She is speaking of her father, Bjartur Jonsson, a figure of near-legendary pith and stubbornness.
He's a fool of a stripe particularly dear to the Freelandic imagination: a
man who can be depended on, when encountering a closed door, to bang
his head against it rather than turn the knob.

As they wind their way round the base of Great Blue, Hannibal
begins to sense—what will come clearer to him in the decades to come—
that she is in truth something of a Daddy's girl, this tall tough broad-
shouldered creature whose plaits trail down her back.

"Rut," he says, and the shape of her name—perhaps the first time he
has spoken it alone in her presence—reverberates inside him. It goes surprisingly deep, this *root*—seems to touch down at some hardpan within
him. She swings around and a braid swings with her, pertly slapping up
against her face. "I don't want to be a farmer," he tells her.

"No, no, not *you*," she says, with a toss of her head. She might almost
be mocking him.

"Rut," he plunges on, "I don't want to be a fisherman either."

"No? Not a fisherman either? And what do you see for yourself?
Maybe you're meant to be an office boy for the Danes? Father always
says there isn't one of them isn't a bigger thief than the other. They stole
his sheep from him once. And everything else . . ."

"I'm not a thief, Rut . . . ," Hannibal tells her, in an aggrieved tone,
and this denial proves unexpectedly gratifying. He senses, with a pre-
science rare to him, that he could never be a thief. This is a day when the

future presses upon him as never before, when the multiplying choices a man faces in his life have a close-meshed, ramifying reality like nothing he knows. What does it remind him of? There are times when, everything on God's earth pressing upon him, he yearns to formulate a profound question, one which emerges—perversely, absurdly—as *What is life like?*

All the same, wherever his faults lie, whatever fatal compromises await him, he suddenly knows he is no more capable of picking a pocket than of assaulting a grandmother, slitting a baby's throat. "I'm not a thief," he reaffirms, his delivery having grown slow and expansive in its journey from indignation to self-congratulation.

"What then?" she challenges him. "What will you do? Where is the place for you?"

"Who can say?" he counters. "The world is large. I may go out in it."

He has never quite dared to credit the existence of those countries said to lie beyond the seas—not dared, that is, to suppose that their stones have the same heft as ours and their rain the same yearning penetration, to believe that their hillsides show the same palpable gratitude as ours do for a touch of sun on their flanks. But what is to stop him, he who wears six gold medals upon his chest, from journeying off to see for himself? Why should he take anyone else's word on this critical question of the reality of foreign lands?

"Father always says it's only a fool who can't find in Freeland whatever he's looking for. He said the world out there is no place for a decent man—that the bloodthirsty bastards would just as soon pry your eyeballs out of your skull in order to butter their bread with them."

Hannibal is just a little dumbstruck at how assuredly the profanity and the horrific image issue from the girl's lips. Her face shows the unblinking contentment of someone who has uttered a choice and impregnable judgment, and in this moment, challenged by this paternal certainty of hers, all his ambiguous feelings toward the girl suddenly clarify: he understands that he desires her. His body on this Olympic Day has accomplished extraordinary feats—he has prised from his limbs prowess as never before in his life—but only now does it grow apparent that each of the day's trials was a mere steppingstone toward the action he contemplates. His body does not covet medals or ribbons, beer or brandy, hot water or cold water; it wants this girl's body.

She swings her head around and again her robust back is to him. He watches her blond braids dance on her brown sweater. She is two, three paces ahead. Other girls, the path being so narrow, would have naturally let him lead. But she doesn't question his willingness to follow.

On his left, across the narrow strait, lies Bread Island and the city of Thorskrist, our ever-expanding capital. He can make out clearly the school and beside it the fields where the day's triumphs were enacted. It was repeatedly declared this afternoon that on only two or three occasions in the history of our country had so large a crowd assembled. Yes, Rut may choose to turn her back, but the nation's eyes had been riveted to him, the only man entitled to wear the nation's gold.

"Next year, I intend to do everything better," he tells her. "I will throw the javelin five feet farther than I threw it today."

This time she does not turn round. "Father always says we've grown soft," she replies. "He said that in the old times, in the days of the Settlement, this land was peopled by giants."

Grown soft, old times, the Settlement, giants . . . The words lash at him, prod him, galvanize him. Desire, positively identified only moments ago, catapults up from his belly and into his chest, his arms, his throat. This sensation—his body's yearning—is larger than he is. He can feel it spilling out from his fingertips, and with a clear victor's good decisiveness, a giant's own certitude about his limbs' every placement, Hannibal seizes the girl by the upper arm and spins her around. A braid whips by his cheek, and down below, in the borders of his vision, the cotton grass glows like so many thousands of candles. He might be standing in a great mead hall. The sea shines like armor-plate. He jams his face down into hers, twisting and locking his lips upon her waiting lips.

—And when he paused, a few seconds later, withdrawing his face far enough from hers that he might appreciate the shocked, pleased expression on her features, he felt a rustle against his chest. But it was all very quick. Her large right hand, balled into a fist, drove itself upward, *hard*, into the center of his face. There was a crunching, a gruesome shattering at the fundament of things, as the stays and props beneath his brain gave way. It was all so amazingly quick. She'd broken his nose.

Hannibal swung around and, crouching, dropped his head between his legs, his medals bumping up against his upside-down face. From this queer and humble position, looking out at the world from under the seat of his pants, he considered his existence. *What is life like?* When he lifted his head again, his features were bloodied, his nose was streaming.

Hannibal turned and looked at her, *hard*, and what he beheld in her face was a touch of fear perhaps, and maybe a dash of remorse, but not so much of either one really. He read in her features self-righteousness. He read anger.

"You've broken my nose," he announced quietly.

"You shouldn't have done that," she told him. And if her voice was quavering, still her gaze was firm.

Each held their position; neither was about to approach the other. They might have been two old farmers, calling contrary opinions on the weather across a river which, though narrow, is too deep and cold and rapid for fording.

"I was only kissing you—that was all."

"You said you were no thief."

"Thief?" What in the world did she mean? Why, when he stood before her with his face broken, was she still talking in riddles? He had always been good at overriding pain, but the fact was, he was hurting. And dripping blood, everywhere he turned.

Rut said, "Yes, a thief. You took the kiss from me. I didn't give it to you."

"It was just a kiss," he replied, and flinched to hear something almost plaintive in his voice.

"You had to ask first," Rut repeated. "Don't you see?"

He licked his upper lip and the soupy taste—just like the leavings in the pan where a leg of lamb has been roasted—was reassuring. It was only blood after all. "You've made yourself clear," he told her, and this time his tone was exactly what it ought to be, under the circumstances: wry, and witty, and utterly autonomous.

The girl, though, made a declaration that undid him a second time. She said, "You can kiss me now, Hannibal," and he stared at her without the least flutter of desire, needless to say, and yet with an attraction more crushing than any lust he'd ever known: oh, the self-possession of it! The unrattled, gorgeous, *gorgeous* audacity! Who in the world *was* this girl? What supernatural agent had laid a spell of enchantment upon her— where on earth had she come by her cross-eyed unflappability?

Hannibal merely stood there, dazed, puzzled, fazed, bedazzled, and *she* approached *him*, as if wading straight across that unfordable river between them, and deposited her hands flat upon his powerful shoulders. Again his lips met hers. And when this time their faces separated, she wore all over her mouth his living stamp: brain-blood, the fluid of his inner skull. He had dripped on her chin, on the collar of her dress, on the front of her sweater. They had, like any proper bride and bridegroom, come together in an initial rip and surge of blood, but in this case it was the man and not the woman who had supplied it. Her crossed eyes—the good one and the other—burned equally at him.

The girl took his hand and eased him to the ground and set herself down beside him. She asked him to tilt his head back, into her lap, to arrest the river of blood. His skull lay between her breasts. She drew from her dress a handkerchief and dabbed a few times lightly at his face. Then she placed one end of the handkerchief in her mouth, to wet it. He closed his eyes and it might have been her tongue going over his face, so lightly did she caress him with the dampness.

After a time she went away, to a stream whose gurglings lulled him, and when she came back the cloth, which she placed upon his nose, was thrillingly cold. She began to stroke his hair. He kept his eyes screwed shut. In a gruff, exasperated voice that wasn't quite her own she chanted, over and over, "Whatcha done this time, Rut-girl? Whatcha done this time, Rut-girl? Whatcha done this time, Rut-girl?," until eventually, in the hazy precincts of a dream, Hannibal ascertained that this was her father's voice, Old Bjartur Jonsson's. She was evoking the manner in which, when she was a mere girl, he used to reprimand her—sternly, for he was an exacting taskmaster, but also admiringly, for clearly he, too, had marveled at the ungovernable *force* of this creature.

Hannibal's head lay in Rut's lap, her breasts against his face. But he kept his eyes shut—so intimate and delicate was the message he had to impart: "You would actually be doing me a great favor if you did not inform the others just how it was my nose came to be broken."

She spoke in a new, simple tone belonging neither to the girl who had mocked him on the path nor to the ghost of her father: a voice as simple and solid and dependable as any rock rooted on a hillside. "I shall never tell anyone. Ever."

"And neither will I. I'll say I was thrown from a horse."

"Then that's what happened, Hannibal: you were thrown from a horse."

"So we've made a compact, have we, you and I?"

"We have," Rut declared. "Neither of us will ever tell anyone."

And neither of them ever did.

(And at this point my high and heartfelt hope is that I have a troubled reader. I'm hoping someone somewhere's just a little vexed, someone somewhere's wanting to know precisely *how* it is—assuming the two bloodstained lovers kept their vow—that I've arrived at my story. Indeed, is wanting now to know—the issue having been raised—how I came by each conversational turn, each nuance, each facial expression in an exchange that took place, outside my presence, nearly a third of a century ago. And to this very reader, to you, I would make some pledges of my own. . . . For you alone, viewpoints, verb tenses, chronologies will all be bent, modified, clarified—purely for the purpose of serving you. I will break every grammatical rule I know, snapping them like so many pieces of kindling, in order to lay a blaze at your feet. I will set down for you banquets I never ate, will lay before you long sweeps of beach; will wake you with bells and birdcalls. I shall crown your head with rainbows by day, with the aurora borealis by night, for my relationship with you—and mine is surely an ugly, challenging enough tale that I can say this without fear of looking either sentimental or presumptuous—is my life's mainstay. Oh, my Ideal Reader, if you knew, if you *knew* the hours I've devoted to your contemplation! I've pictured you in so many guises, so many sites. . . . You are a sixty-seven-year-old retired American schoolteacher, a widow, vacationing alone in the Yucatán. You have chanced upon this book in that rococo eyesore of a bookcase, two of its six panes shattered, located in your little hotel's lobby. It was abandoned by someone who lightened his backpack of the weight of me. The book was not for him, and that's all right. It's for you. And now you're reading it under the awning on the hotel's unscreened interior terrace, in the shelter of a sort of modest peristyle, as a warm rain, just a few feet away, collects in the cups of the tropical blossoms. Or you're a young man, who maybe still thinks of himself as more lad than man, recently come to Brooklyn from County Cork. You've been staying on Ocean Parkway, sleeping on the floor of the apartment of a friend who works during the day in a "tapas bar," whatever in God's name *that* is, and while he's off at work you've taken this opportunity to borrow his bed, luxuriantly curled up in which you've now begun to read about the friends of Freeland. Or you're a sailor. Or you're a pregnant young mother whose children—thirteen-month-old twins—have miraculously fallen asleep simultaneously, leaving you a few minutes now, the breakfast coffee having been reheated, to sample a few pages. . . . Or you're a shipping clerk in Rotterdam, overseeing bills of lading, whose hatred for your job and quiet wish to be fired encourage you to read fiction in the office, indiscriminately and desperately. Or you have plucked this novel from a shelf of your local library, as a means of avoiding the books about alcoholism that drew you here, for you've come to this sleepy building in response to a nightmarish suspicion that your spouse is—irrecoverably—a drunkard. You are reading this on a slow rocking plane, on a bullet train, in an old stone house in the Pyrenees, in an old wood house, mice-infested, on an old street of the old capital city of Kyoto, or on some tireless shore where a sluggish sea now and then, with a seething curl and crash, turns another page. . . . You have picked this book up out of curiosity, because you've never been quite sure where Freeland is located, or out of dire boredom, because the only other volume on the shelf is entitled *The Further Pleasures of a Pipe-Smoker,* or out of a murkily hopeful notion that anyone whose last name begins with the letters *o-d-d* must be employing a pseudonym and therefore his book stands a fair chance of being pornographic. . . . Well, even though this rucksack of a parenthesis is already packed to bursting, I would tuck a final sentiment into it. For I must add that the heart of my story lies here, in this moment when—in what I solemnly pledge shall be the book's first and final parenthesis—I reveal that the whole of *The Friends of Freeland* is for you, and other readers are nothing but a cheery inconsequence. My book is meant to meditate widely on the nature of friendship, but let there be no doubt—please, *hear me*—that in the ultimate footrace you alone are my true friend, we are running side by side, stride for stride.)

"Did you hear that?" she said.

"Hear what?" Hannibal opened his eyes once more. His aching head still slumped in the girl's lap. The smell of the sun was on her. Her breasts, though they had never seen the sun, smelled of sun; he knew this even though at the moment he could smell nothing.

"It sounded like a cry. Way far off. Could a voice carry all the way over the water?" She was staring off at Thorskrist.

"Maybe. Though it would take some very good lungs," Hannibal Hannibalsson said, and added, dismissively, "It was probably a bird."

7

Another Brief Word . . .

. . . about my country.

Early history: Discovered by an off-course Icelandic/Norwegian Viking navigator, Erik the Other, in A.D. 980. According to Viking chronicles, the four islands were already inhabited, thinly, by Skurlings—Eskimos or Inuits—although the exiguous anthropological and archaeological evidence suggests that these were people who may have had more in common with Labradorean Indians. In any case, their presence is something of a mystery, since at that time neither the Inuit nor the Indian was to be found even in neighboring southern Greenland, and both lacked long-range navigational craft. In recent decades, their presence has fostered, particularly in the United States, various speculations about their having been either guided or ancestrally derived from Stonehengers, Atlanteans, or extraterrestrials.

Questions of origin aside, this great appointment between the Skurlings and the Vikings represents a copestone in world history. For the first time, two human populations expanding across the globe in opposite directions encountered each other—a rendezvous that was at least twelve thousand years and five hundred generations in the making. Right here, on these small, easily overlooked islands, was enacted the moment when eastward-trending Asian peoples, having migrated over the frozen Bering Strait about the year 15,000 B.C. and having steadily made their way across Canada to Greenland and, finally, to Freeland, and westward-probing Europeans, having mastered the art of open-water navigation, at last looked each other in the eye.

This unparalleled event was celebrated, needless to say, by ferocious plundering and slaughtering on both sides, with the eventual result that the Skurlings were either exterminated or fully subjugated and absorbed.

Economy: Our lives rise and fall with the weight of our fishing nets as they rise and fall in the seas around Freeland. We export the cod and eat the haddock. It's a matter of superior merriment among us that the rest of the world perceives no large distinction between the two.

Currency: the kronur. Rates vary, but tend to hover around 50FKr = US $1.

Flora and fauna: No snakes. Only one native land mammal, the arctic fox, which provides farmers with an opportunity to vary their complaints about those other sheep-marauders, lungworm and tapeworm. Occasionally a polar bear will float our way on a Greenlandic ice-floe. Any such visitor to our shores is greeted with a bullet. Land mammals introduced by human settlers, and since become naturalized, include the brown rat, the black rat, the house mouse, the wood mouse, and the mink. We boast some two hundred species of birds.

Few trees grow on our hilly, sheep-overgrazed terrain, and those that do—commonly rowans and emaciated, dark-skinned birches—are low, shrubby affairs. Our forests are such that nine-year-olds can, like the illustrations of giants and giantesses in children's fairy books, peer over the tops of them. We specialize in mosses and lichens—some three hundred species of each—cotton grass, lady's bedstraw, low-lying gentians, angelica, campions, and, in the bogs, ling, saxifrage, squill.

Later history: Remained a Norwegian colony from the Settlement until 1387, when, as a result of the Kalman "Act of Union," reconstituted as a Danish colony. Change in colonial status brought few concrete alterations in daily life, which for centuries continued to blend subsistence farming and subsistence fishing.

Nineteenth century introduced increased contact with non-Scandinavian world, including American missionaries and whalers of various nationalities. Notable American painter Frederic Church sojourned here for two weeks in the summer of 1859. It was on our shores that, according to the travel journal of his companion, the Reverend Louis L. Noble, Church declared that he had "mastered the bewitching effects of Northern light at long last." Unfortunately, the three canvases deriving from this period were destroyed in 1903, three years after the artist's death, when a fire gutted a small outbuilding of the Oriental castle, Olana, he had erected for himself on the Hudson. Notable American novelist Herman Melville, on his sole North Atlantic whaling voyage, stopped here in 1850, quite briefly, but long enough to conclude that Freeland was a rival to the "emphatic uninhabitableness" of the Encantadas: he found here a "humble acme in the planet's perennial pursuit of utter desolation."

Famine of 1857, and subsequent famines over next four decades, resulted in mass migrations to Canada and the United States.

With the fall of Denmark to Nazi Germany in 1939, country effectively became British and American protectorate. Official independence from Denmark granted in 1947, an event perhaps somewhat overshadowed on the world stage by the independence of India in the same year. Unofficial "independence" from United States effected, against the will of many Freelanders, by unilateral American decision to close military base in 1967.

Religion: Ninety-eight percent Lutheran. The country officially converted from paganism to Christianity in the year 1066, but did so in a characteristically hedging way. The old Norse pantheon—Odin, Thor, Loki, Frida, Baldur, et al.—lingers on in our "Christian names," in our place names, in our oaths and proverbs. It is surely significant that when the name of the largest town—Thorshovn, or Thor's Harbor—was altered in the Year of the Conversion, it became not Kristshovn but Thorskristshovn: the modern-day Thorskrist.

National character: Proudly, surpassingly taciturn. Brooding; ironic; "weighty." A nation of chess players. It is sometimes claimed that we were put upon the planet in order to reveal that at bottom the Danes, the Norwegians, even the Finns, are insouciant, lighthearted, giggly, bubbly, warm, happy-go-lucky peoples.

Ways in which visitors to our country can immediately be spotted as such: (1) by refusing a drink; (2) by appearing on our streets garbed in some article of "traditional" Freelandic clothing, particularly a sweater; (3) by whistling. No Freelander would ever be caught dead whistling in public except angrily, at a dog.

Public physical contact: In the last few decades, Freelandic women have acquired the habit of kissing each other on meeting. This practice, regarded as ostentatious by the oldest generation of Freelanders, has recently burgeoned into the full-blown excesses of the two-cheek "Continental kiss."

Men and women will sometimes kiss each other by way of greeting, provided they are not especially fond of each other or are not romantically linked.

Men display little public physical contact with each other. They shake hands warily, as if reluctant to have temporarily immobilized their weapon-wielding arm, or, on occasion—throwing personal safety to the winds—will hurl themselves into great, back-clapping embraces. Intermediate contact of any sort is viewed with suspicion.

Private physical contact: The highest illegitimacy rate in Europe.

Zoological milestone: The world's last confirmed great auk died on Giant Island in 1847. Little is known about this occasion other than that the bird was eaten by a man named Isleifur.

National quirk: Only nation in Europe—and perhaps in world—to offer public subsidies to Psychics Guild.

National pastime, youths: Milling around on weekend nights, for hours at a stretch, in Independence Square.

National pastime, adults: Hole-digging. We are forever planning some commanding structure or edifice—a fifty-meter swimming pool, a sculpture gallery, a parking garage, an "interactive" aquarium—and getting only so far as an initial, asymmetrical hole in the ground. These holes are, psychologically and physically, the complement to the piles of stones—the cairns—that dot our rural landscape. The cairns serve as landmarks of where we are: they lead us through fog, mist, snow. The holes serve as landmarks of where we would be: they stand for the thriving, resplendent country we would become if we only had the money, the resources, the energy, the brute manpower to make it so.

8

The Escalator to Heaven

I first entered the New World by way of Vinland—or so even today it might be called had my Nordic forebears not mislaid their way and, with time, allowed chronicles and travelogues to mist into legend and hearsay. Embarking from the Eastern Settlement of Greenland in a single narrow ship, its keel a single oak timber whose caulking was a gum of tarred animal hair, they headed north, although their hopes lay southward; having no instrument for determining longitude, the Vikings habitually hugged coastlines. Eventually they took a left turn, into uncut seas, and soon came upon three lands fit for the finest fairy tale.

The first was barren and forbidding. They called it *Helluland*—Stone Land—and turned from it and headed south. The second was forested and flat, with white sand beaches, and they called it *Markland*—Wood Land—and again they turned southward. And this time they came to a fair-weathered terrain where they disembarked and found dew on the grass, "and the first thing they did was to get some of it on their hands, and put it to their lips, and to them it seemed the sweetest thing they had ever tasted." This intoxicating place they called *Vinland*—Wine Land.

It was an auspicious beginning. Like a dragon dozing upon a treasure heap, they were perched atop a continent of illimitable riches. Steeled as they were to hardship, steeped in bloody combat, they were raiders of a daring and, in their shallow-drawing, rapid, flexible-framed ships, of a technological seamanship elsewhere unmatched in the Mediterranean or the Atlantic, and one can envision an alternative history of North America in which the Norsemen plunged upon the continent with a full-throated cry of giddy, irresistible ferocity. The future might have been ours. Instead it fell to the Spanish, some half a millennium later, to take up the job of looting and rapine, of slaughter and hostage-taking, of sacking and desecration. The Vikings contented themselves with a few heaps of animal skins and some paltry loads of timber, and they seem, in their dealings with the small dark indigenes of those big bright forests, to have taken as many hard blows as they gave. It was, therefore, with a notion of ancestral opportunities lost, or of spoils too long deferred, that I entered the city of Halifax, Nova Scotia, on a patchy cloud-scrambled morning in July of 1959. My lungs, amazingly, had cleared. I would never die.

In the nineteenth century, recurring famines periodically stripped the human flesh from the rocky ribs of my country. Which is to say, we abandoned our broken-down farms, our tubercular fishing villages and exhausted parish councils, and we headed west, across the seas, this time less as conquerors than as mendicants. It's a haunting picture. . . . A steamship pulls out of Thorskrist Harbor into White Seal Bay. On one side, lined up along the taffrail, the emaciated, hapless bodies of the emigrants. On the other, on the pier, the emaciated, hapless figures destined to remain behind, gazing at the ship with an implacable rancor, a biting sense of betrayal—an animosity smoldering even now, more than a century later, in the collective psyche of my nation.

Canada was the destination of choice, particularly Manitoba and Saskatchewan. Today, it is estimated that something like forty thousand Canadians—more than half the population of my country—are by blood at least one-eighth Freelandic. But our language and culture only rarely survived transplantation, even to a land whose climate was likewise brumal and whose soil barren. You might say we throve and died out simultaneously. Freelandic enclaves also sprang up in Seattle and, nearer at hand, Chicago—which I, stepping ashore in Halifax, had fixed as my eventual goal. Manitoba? Saskatchewan? Not for me . . . I must of course go to the United States. After all, I had mastered the language: I spoke slang. I must visit the country where a man might at last say attaboy, bamboozle, chippie, dibs, eagerbeaver, feedbag, gams, hotsie-totsie, ixnay, jerkwater, knucklehead, as well as my favorite cluster of syllables assembled in any tongue since Babel tumbled: lollapalooza.

But there was no hurry. I had crossed the seas and reached Vinland. I would stay for a time in Canada, gather my strength.

Some fifty miles from Halifax, on a farm on the island of Cape Breton, lived a family of Freelandic emigrants who were dimly related to my aunt. Will and Heidi Anson was what they called themselves—they'd an-glicized their names. I immediately headed their way. I'd written a letter to them. They were, I suppose, expecting me.

The anonymous Saga writers of old wasted no time in dispatching any character no longer of use to them. Whoever it was, major or minor figure, out he or she would go in a single phrase—"So Thorolf leaves our story," or "and now Gunhildur departs our tale." It's an example I probably ought to follow with the Ansons, who in the end mean nothing to me or my narrative. I might pretend otherwise, but the truth is I can no longer summon up either of their faces. It's not a loss I much regret. I couldn't have understood this at the time, but my stay with them—and it was siz-able, the better part of a year—was destined to serve in my life as an inter-lude, a way station. It's one of the great peculiarities of human existence, I've often thought, that those periods fated eventually to slide almost wholly out of memory are not identifiable as such. They feel as real, as firm, as durable, as any other period. It has been impossible in my life to determine when I was actually living and when, in effect, preparing to live. Only in retrospect do patterns emerge, as various gaps in my life appear—whole months, years slither away into darkness.

Behind the Anson farmhouse stood a little "guest house" that was also a tool shed. That's where I slept. I had no electricity and carried out my nightly reading and writing by kerosene lamp. I suppose the Ansons must have been in their sixties, and both of them were, happily, well down the path to deafness; I was left alone. I was writing all the time—feverishly, hungrily, hopefully. A surviving journal-fragment informs me that in my first three months I commenced three novels, completed two plays, and composed forty-two free-verse poems, having first jettisoned all the Free-landic poetry previously written, not excepting my own. I'd concluded that, in a thousand years of hammering together quatrains, my country-men's only notable achievement was a matter of prosody: their cultivation of pararhyme. I'm speaking of rhymes like "bread" and "broad," "light" and "late"—pairings that, as I've perhaps already made evident in these pages, have lost no luster for me. All the other poetic conventions were to be scuttled. . . .

I was also translating. Into Freelandic I rendered—maybe "stuffed" is a fitter term for those fledgling efforts—Coleridge's Ancient Mariner and Keats's Autumn ode and Tennyson's Lotos-Eaters.

And yet I felt, for all this activity, oddly rooted and reposed. I had come to a gentler land than anything I'd ever known. To anyone raised in

Thorskrist, the hills of Cape Breton must seem humorously clement. I performed various undemanding odd jobs by way of earning my keep. Autumn and, before long, winter set in. The days stretched before me. I had no plans to return to Freeland. I wrote now and then to my aunt, who fulfilled all my expectations by never replying, and a couple of times to Hannibal, who I hoped might actually answer. He didn't. In fact, during the whole of my first visit to North America—an expanse which, when all was said and done, stretched out more than three years, and which would take me to Denver, and Seattle, and the Yucatán—I never once received a letter.

On leaving Freeland I had truly thought—justifiably or not—that I wasn't long for this world. My return to health made a new man of me. Wanderlust had been supplanted by daily-awakening wonder. Living in a little shack behind the Ansons' farm, what did I do with myself for days at a stretch, as summer gave way to fall, fall to winter, winter to the first numb proddings of spring? I marveled. That's what I did. Strangely, beautifully, my environs grew more rather than less fantastic with time. I gaped at the trees. Although it may not sound fully believable to you—these days, I hardly believe it myself—I'd never actually glimpsed real trees before, never before laid eyes on any variety of vegetation that dwarfed me; you might say these were the first specimens of the vegetable kingdom I didn't feel I could thrash in hand-to-hand combat. One after another after another, in the woods around me on all sides, burly barked boles soared toward heaven, unfurling themselves overhead in great fountaining crowns of sibilant verdancy—what a land this was! And I marveled at the queer, delicious food that sometimes came my way—cans of spaghetti, spicy "Polish sausages," even oranges in the dead of winter! And marveled at the animals—deer, raccoons, squirrels, skunks, otters. At dawn one morning, on a stroll through the woods, I came upon a moose, and if tomorrow on the streets of Thorskrist I were to encounter an extraterrestrial disembarking from his spacecraft, green skin aglow and antennae hyperintelligently aquiver, he surely wouldn't leave me any more thunderstruck than did that mobile alp of a creature. The largest wild mammal on Freeland is the arctic fox.

But if all sense of hurry left me from the moment when I settled in at the Ansons, when it did at last return, during an unseasonable stretch of February sun, it set my blood to boiling. A new decade had dawned, the year was 1960, and I needed to be off, nothing less than my destiny was awaiting me. Farewell, farewell, with a wave of the hand I left my half-deaf host and my half-deaf hostess—left them to totter ever farther into that increasingly muted countryside where all birds are songless and thunder does not follow lightning. My savings were low, my hopes were high. I took a bus and then a train—my first train—through Montreal, Ottawa, and Toronto, on down to Windsor, riding upright the whole time, across a timeless, ever-dissolving landscape: it rained continually, in blinding sheets, hour after hour after hour. Over a thousand miles in all.

The skies didn't clear until the trip was nearly done. Then they opened to reveal, across the river from Windsor, an upright realm whose tallest spires trafficked with the clouds. It was a *metropolis*. The syllables had long carried deep, cavernous associations. I knew the word but not yet the reality, and in many ways that's what my first trip across North America turned out to be: an ongoing process of affixing word to object, of mapping the coordinates of the two-dimensional page onto a three-dimensional nation. Oh, so *this* is an elevator. *This* is a supermarket. *This* is a synagogue. *This* is an expressway. All such sights were new; and yet all had been prepared for—my books truly hadn't misled me. Everything I'd ever read about could be found, provided I only knew where to look.

Yes, *this* is a metropolis. Across the river, in a single city, unbroken by scarps and glaciers, resided something like two million souls—a population ten, twenty times larger than that of the whole Freelandic nation! Washed to a pristine newness by the rain, the buildings ascended as though in dizzy, light-headed competition, adding a row of windows to another row of windows, and in each window one might well imagine a pair of eyes, glance intersecting glance intersecting glance in aerial interweavings so intricate it set the head to reeling; this was America. I crossed the Ambassador Bridge into Detroit on a bus. I was heading, vaguely, to Chicago, where my dead mother, that mythical creature of whom I hadn't a single memory, had left some likewise mythical cousins, and in another day or two I would surely have reached that still larger metropolis had I not crossed the Detroit River on a morning when the sun was blazing.

Footstep-size glints danced—soft-shoed—on the wide slow-flowing expanse dividing one immense country from another; the air was chockablock with invisible spirits. I was, in the deep meaning of the word, enchanted—as chronicled in the folktales of my childhood, where trolls and witches and elves and *huldufolk* robbed a person of wits and will alike. Once, years ago, while typing in my summerhouse, I produced "hope" when aiming for "home," and in a lifetime of misspellings and misreadings, of fingertip-stumbles and slips of the tongue, no other little linguistic

blunder has ever seemed quite so felicitous. That first day in Detroit, hope
sang in my blood—which is to say that in this city of two million strangers
I'd found a home.

. . . But not yet a place to sleep. I was a man without an address or an
explicable purpose and I kept waiting to be forcibly halted; it scarcely
seemed that in such a miraculous place someone like me—a Freelander, a
dark slight figure with a bulging rucksack and near-empty pockets—could
be at liberty to wander at will. Why were the people pretending not to
stare at me? What lay behind their cunning attempt to convince me I
passed unremarked among them? I found my way to J. L. Hudson's, the
central department store, and having watched a number of others negotiate it, and having assured myself that no fare or ticket was required, I
climbed aboard my first escalator; I was being drawn, almost despite myself, toward Heaven.

I wandered each of its twelve floors. Here was a precinct devoted,
surreally, to "garden furniture," one to men's suits, whole aisles to women's
undergarments, and a little room stocked with coins and stamps, which I
mistook for a post office. At the top of the building I, for whom this entire city seemed a sort of playground, found a floor given over to children's
toys.

I wandered back outside, drifted down Woodward Avenue toward the
river, peered furtively at the black-and-white stills of a burlesque house,
ate seven slices of bread and drank a Vernors Ginger Ale on a bench in
Grand Circus Plaza. I wandered at random, at will. I gawked at the buses;
at the women in their finery; at the abundance of Negroes; at a hurtling
fire truck whose siren as it receded recalled a squalling infant; at a squalling
infant by a bus stop, whose mother quieted it by placing in its mouth a
bottle filled with an electric-blue liquid. I wandered into another surreal
store, this one devoted to grotesquerie—to plastic ice cubes with flies
frozen inside them, and rubbery turds and pools of vomit, and masks of
Dracula, of Frankenstein, and of an otherwise comely man the left side
of whose face was melting in big, pendulous drops.

Have I ever felt more disoriented? As I wandered the streets, a sense
of being *lost* would suddenly overcome me—illogically, since there's no
getting lost where everything's equally foreign. Then I'd round a corner
and spot a familiar entryway or shop awning and an almost ecstatic sense
of being *found* would wash over me. And so it went, for circling hours on
end, foraying and backtracking, getting lost and finding myself once more.

I'd never seen such crowds. These Americans were dazzling, particularly of course the women, magnificently got up in nylons and girdles and beehive hairdos, with wonderfully lavish flourishes of lipstick and rouge. I started up an old game of my own devising called "Twenty Down," which is played like this: out of the next twenty women who cross your path, you must select your bride for life. And you must remain faithful to her, and she to you. You will live together for the remainder of your days.

In the game's purest, harshest, most daredevil form, called "Twenty Down and a Desert Isle," the two of you will pass the rest of your natural lives in solitude. Henceforth, hers shall be the only face you lay eyes upon, from the moment the dawn sun pinkens the fronds of the island's tallest palm until the moment the moon climbs over the shark-infested bay.

In either variant, all decisions must be instantaneous; and they are irreversible.

The game perhaps begins like this. The first woman who crosses your path is a moderately good-looking auburn-haired woman in her early thirties—she is maybe a dozen years older than you—and will you choose to spend the rest of your life with her? If you reject her, you may have to settle for somebody a good deal less appealing. So: reject her, and you'll naturally be hoping that among the next nineteen women you will find one who is yet more charming; accept her, and pray that no heartbreaking beauty subsequently materializes. In any event, one of these twenty shall be your bride: it is the cornerstone of Twenty Down that bachelorhood is not an option.

It was late in the afternoon when, having wandered some ways down Jefferson Avenue, I found a side street called Lyon Road with a house with a sign saying ROOM TO LET. I hesitated not one instant. Fate was guiding me and a moment later I was standing on the porch. What now strikes me as so remarkable was how smoothly everything went—how unerringly serendipity guided me. At the time, I don't suppose it *did* seem remarkable. I was in a land of miracles; I had slipped into a fairy tale; no wonder things must fall into place.

The middle-aged woman who answered the door was no one with whom you would have chosen to live out your days on a desert island. Her face was dominated by a large "strawberry" birthmark. I was reminded of the mask I'd seen earlier that afternoon, the man whose face was melting in great free-flowing droplets, and perhaps I winced at her? I tried not to, tried to hold my voice steady. "You have a room to let," I announced.

"That's right." And not another word. Just a skeptical once-over.

Well, it may have been my first day in America, and I may have been upended and bedazzled more than ever in my life, but if there was one ploy that I, as a good son of Freeland, knew how to negotiate, it was taciturnity. I glared right back at her.

"It's eight dollars a week," she said. "That all right with you?"

"Could be." I had stepped into an American movie. She might at any moment explode a bubble-gum bubble in my face. Was this what was called "moxie"?

"And I need four weeks' rent up front. That all right?"

For all my love of American slang, the phrase *up front* tripped me up, but just for a second. Her drift was clear. "Might be."

"You got that kind of money?" Her eyes tightened. I had a sense, standing out there on her front porch, that others—neighbors—were also squinting at me.

I lied: "That's right."

"No exceptions to the rule. The four weeks up front. You follow me?"

"I'll follow," I said, edging toward her. I wanted a look at the room.

"You a Polack?" she went on.

"No." Although I hadn't an inkling what she meant, I did feel fairly certain what she wanted to hear.

"You talk funny," she said.

"Thank you."

"You a Jew?"

"Unfortunately not," I replied, and these words brought an unexpected response. Her look of suspicion deepened—darkened—before abruptly giving way to a loose, abdominal grunt of laughter. She'd found me amusing.

"I'm a Freelander," I said to her. And of course she looked at me blankly.

"It's not the same thing as a freeloader," I went on, and needless to say I took great pride in punning so idiomatically in a foreign language. What a prodigy—no, call me a *whiz kid*—I must be! But the little joke only brought suspicion back to her face. Was this too glib? Too much like a salesman's patter?

"Freeland's a small island nation in the North Atlantic."

Information that did nothing to further my cause.

"In a sense, we're Scandinavian."

No help there either.

"Like Norway or Sweden."

Her face, which had become a sort of fist, loosened its grip on itself, as it were. "Uncle of mine," she said, "he was Norwegian. Uncle Torvald, but always we called him Terry. Everybody loved him."

"My name is Eggert," I said. "But you call me Ed or Edgar."

"Uncle Terry drowned," she added, with brutal satisfaction.

"I didn't," I said. "Not yet."

"Well, aren't you the funny one." And once again we wordlessly contemplated each other.

She was wearing a brown kerchief over her head, into which she tucked a straying clump of brown hair. Between the mud-colored hair and the strawberry mark her eyes had brightened and I thought perhaps I read there, in a language free of the imprecisions of words, what might be called a very welcome welcome. Could it be that this new specimen who stood before me, an *American housewife*, actually belonged to that rare species—akin in its rarity to the panda, the snow leopard, the black rhinoceros—which is, to my thinking, the most splendid of all God's creations? I mean, of course, was this a woman susceptible to Eggert Oddason's quick sharp ratlike good looks?

"And may I see the room?" I asked her.

She supposed I might. . . .

I followed her broad-boned, shrugging, agreeable bottom up a flight of stairs. She was wearing—though I didn't at the time have the word for them—Bermuda shorts. You can imagine how often we wear shorts in Freeland. These were a faded pink, and not absolutely clean. The house had a smell I couldn't place.

She led me to a room whose wallpaper consisted of neat, interlocking rows of green and blue and red dinosaurs. Some things you never forget. What sort of country was this, where dinosaurs roamed the walls? And where airplanes floated on strings from the ceiling?

I pointed questioningly at one of the planes and she said to me, "This was Stevie's room. Our boy." She had turned away. She was looking out the window. And two words: "He's dead."

"I'm sorry."

"He's gone to God."

"I'm sorry," I repeated, and she veered round to deliver an impassioned correction: "That's nothing to be sorry about."

"No," I said, and added what, to judge from the softening of her features, was exactly the right rejoinder: "I've had my share of deaths. I'm an orphan."

And again we examined each other. I liked this about her instantly: her willingness to show me a cold, hostile face. She was approximately my height. She wore a cross around her neck. She was busty. She picked up from the bookcase beside her a children's toy—a green model car. "My husband will be home soon. *He's* the one wants to rent the room. I don't."

"It's a fine room," I tell her.

"But he says if we rent it we must clear everything out."

"But you wouldn't have to clear it out for me," I reassure her. "I already feel quite at home here."

"I like to leave things *alone*," she says, and again she has turned toward the window. From the way her eyes seek refuge there, that son of hers, Stevie, might almost be buried in the backyard. "But that's not his way, my husband. Michael. He says the living have to move on."

"I can see wisdom in both approaches," I say.

"He's twice the size of you," she adds, with scornful relish.

"I'm actually quite big for my size."

It was as though, in this willingness of hers to repeat her gestures, we were together enacting some ritual or pantomime: again she gave me a dark and puzzled look, which again was succeeded by an abrupt grateful grunt of laughter. And she said once more, "Aren't you the funny one . . ."

"I've just begun . . ."

"And no meals thrown in. You'd have to feed yourself."

"That's no problem. I eat very little, as you can see. I live mostly on sardines."

"You'd need that thirty-two dollars," she said. "Do you have it or not?"

"In a manner of speaking. Most of it."

"There are no exceptions. It's his rule. Michael's."

"And he's bigger than we are. He's bigger than both of us put together. . . ."

"It's his rule." She shrugged.

"Let's say I gave you eight dollars now. That's payment for a week. With the remainder to come soon."

"He'd expect the whole thirty-two. Michael. He'd want me to *show* it to him. All the whole thirty-two. It's as simple as that." Another broad-shouldered shrug.

For all my dizzy foreigner's bewilderment in finding myself standing alone with her in a bedroom—a dead child's bedroom whose walls were festooned with dinosaurs—and all my uncertainty about how best to negotiate with this formidable broad-kneed figure in the smudged pink Bermuda shorts, I'd experienced from the moment I glimpsed the room-to-let sign a feeling of rightness and good fortune. How had it happened, then, that I'd come out in a cul-de-sac?

Evidently, it was time to leave. It might be possible, perhaps, to return later, when this twice-my-size Michael had returned from work. Perhaps he might make an exception for me. But I sensed, even then, that *he* was nobody I wanted to negotiate with. I identified him, already, as the enemy.

"You have a job?" she asked me.

"Looks like it," I said.

"What sort?"

"Any sort," I said. "I'm versatile."

"You're a regular comedian. . . ." But this time the scornful note in her laughter turned mild and wistful: "Oh I do like to laugh. I don't see any other way of getting through this life, do you?" And her eyes swung round at me—and held me, in their fervency, just as solidly as though she'd seized me by both arms.

"Beg your pardon?"

"But a rule's a rule, isn't it?"

Where was this conversation going? It suddenly occurred to me that, broken by grief at the loss of her child, this woman might not be altogether right in the head. . . .

Why, then, did I feel so determined to find a home beneath her roof? I don't know—but I wanted to stay. I plucked from the desktop a toy soldier. It was a knight, a gray plastic man in armor who bore a shield in one hand and a bent sword in the other. "This is my first day in America," I confessed. "I came over from Canada. This is the very first room I've looked at, and you know what? I already feel right at home in it."

And was this woman, Megan McKaig, whose name I didn't yet know, truly going to expel the orphan in her late son's bedroom? Was she going to refuse the knight in armor that the orphan brandished, crooked sword and all?

Again the woman stared out the window, down at that grave I'd mentally dug there. "I have a little money. A little money hid away from him, Michael, he doesn't know anything about." And having ventured into this new territory, the privileged musky realm of her domestic deceptions, she lifted her gaze toward the sky. Heaven help us. "I suppose if you gave me the eight dollars, I could add to it twenty-four of my own, you see. We could show him that. We could show him that, don't you see? *You see?*" Was it desperation she was leveling at me? Why did her eyes pop in her head and her voice sharpen so? "And when you paid me the rest, I could replace what I'd taken out, you see? I suppose we could do that like that. Do you suppose we could do that like that?"

It was as though she were pleading with me. . . .

"We could do that," I reassured her.

Our gazes met again, in the visual equivalent of a sweaty handshake. Yes, she made me wary, and uneasy. But even so, I felt encouraged too. And though I couldn't yet, of course, predict the future extent of our abrupt collusion, I felt keenly how auspicious a business this was—that we were already, some ten minutes after meeting each other, conspiring about how best to deceive her husband.

9

The Birth of Culture

It might be told this way:

Once upon a time, when our land lay under a curse, when we were overrun by invaders and devoid of all Culture, two fearless youths slipped out of their dwellings one moonlit evening and mounted the hills behind the capital city. The night was frightfully cold. Up and down over icy rocks they clambered, for six miles, all the way to the enemy camp, where, after consultation with the sentries, they were granted admission. Now, as it happens, a festive ceremony had been scheduled for that very evening, and the two youths were conducted into a spacious hall, from which the feasting tables had been removed, and they were accorded seats in among the enemy warriors. The lights were extinguished. After a few moments, a great gray flickering sprung up before them, like the dancing of ten thousand tapers. . . .

But perhaps I'd better begin my tale again:

One hellishly cold night in December 1958, a couple of kids, Hannibal Hannibalsson and Eggert Oddason, skipped out of Thorskrist and scrabbled over the hills behind the town, up and down for six miles, to the NATO base at Jardvik. Although this was a site strictly off-limits to Freelanders, somehow Hannibal managed to talk their way inside the barbed-wire compound.

Yes: success: we were in: we'd done it. This was forbidden ground. To the rest of the world, this was the only piece of Freelandic real estate of any consequence whatsoever. For this was the armamentarium, where were located the deadly tools that safeguarded and jeopardized the planet itself: these were the military forces that inserted submarines under the

Arctic icecap and jet planes into the stratosphere, these the people who hoarded megaton bombs as a miser might hoard silver coins—not to spend, perhaps, but for the glittering furtive frisson of possession. And we were inside it—inside the barbed wire! It was like one of those folktales in which a farmer is guided into the bowels of the mountain to where the trolls have their smithy and given a glimpse of that white-hot forge where diamonds and rubies and sapphires are sparked into existence. . . . And we were in, Hannibal had talked our way in, just as he'd said he would, and I was stumbling over my feet as we took up seats in the back, behind scores of crew-cut American soldiers. The white screen that confronted us was the tabula rasa of our cultural sensibilities. The lights dimmed.

Oh of course we'd seen movies before. . . . Every young Freelander of our generation had now and then warmed a seat at Biohofnin—literally, the Cinemaharbor—just off of Independence Square. But this evening the air bobbed with heightened promises, enchanted expectations. . . . This was not going to be just another movie. . . . We were about to watch diamonds and sapphires pulled from the forge, we were about to watch a film in the company of a troop of young soldiers born and raised in the United States of Hollywood.

The film was an old film, released a few years before that benign, generous war—the Second World War—which had loosened Freeland from the mortmain of the Danes. Even the least independent-minded among us, content to cling limpetlike to the Danish crown forever, had found it no easy task to remain a Danish colony while the Nazis sat in Copenhagen. Independence had been thrust upon us: there was no more Denmark! Yes, truly a benign and generous conflict: one which had, in addition, vindicated a long-cherished vision of which the rest of the world had heretofore been blind. The war pointed up, for anyone taking a truly global perspective, the pivotal, epicentral location of our archipelago. Suddenly we possessed something called "strategic significance." We were a key outpost in the North Atlantic—potentially, a surveillance center, a refueling station, a defensible harbor. The war brought the soldiers, who had come to stay.

The film was *Top Hat,* starring Fred Astaire and Ginger Rogers. Neither Hannibal nor I had ever seen them before and we were utterly unready for their effect on us. We were a couple of Thorskrist boys who'd just come in out of the cold, no doubt smelling of fish and mud and sheep dung. Our clothes didn't fit. Our lips were chapped and cracked, and our haircuts might have been executed with sheep shears. The ancient projector behind us whirred and clattered. Its interconnected circles, quaint as those of some Enlightenment orrery, began to spin. Before us, the screen came to life in dazzling black-and-white. The music—Irving Berlin's—was polychromatic.

The story opens with a sort of wave on a sort of sea—but not a wave on any sea ever glimpsed on our shores. This is a wave compounded of the black crowns of gentlemen's top hats, eddying into an establishment called the Thackeray Club. We are in London.

Fred plays an American dancer, Jerry Travers, come over the Atlantic to star in a show produced by his friend Horace Hardwick, played by Edward Everett Horton. And the others? What type of man belongs to a London "gentleman's club"? With my outsider's keen appetite for American slang, I knew immediately how to categorize them: stuffed shirts. And what is it like in a gentleman's club in London? It's quiet as a tomb— or it is until Fred, employing nothing but his explosive feet, detonates a sort of bomb. . . .

The two friends then enter Horace's hotel room, although I must confess that during our first viewing of the film it wasn't at all obvious that these palatial, gleaming, white-on-white quarters, outfitted with statuary and a sunburst mirror and glass tables and a parquet floor, represented hotel lodgings. I knew, after all, what luxury hotels in big cities were like: I'd been many times inside the Hotel Snorri in downtown Thorskrist. And yet the room through which Astaire and Horton disported with such proprietary ease had nothing to do with the Snorri. It was equipped with seltzer dispensers and cherry blossoms and a white telephone and a Classical statue. It was an Art Deco/Greco/Nippo triumph.

Horace advises Jerry, which is to say Fred, that it's time he settled down. Fred demurs. He is feeling restless. He's on the loose, with no yens, no yearnings, no strings, no connections, no ties to his affections—he has begun to sing—and he's fancy-free and free for anything fancy. And the better to illustrate his zippy anticipation, he begins to dance as well.

Ah, but to say Fred *dances*? That's to speak so matter-of-factly as to wind up telling a lie. . . . The man floats, he flits, he flutters; he has the balance of a cat, the spring of a frog, the bones of a hummingbird. I'd never seen anything like it—we'd never seen anything like it. We sat stupefied, with our bad haircuts and our dirty hands, in our heavy mud-and-sheep-shit-encrusted boots, sat in a drafty prefab hall that smelt of onions and cigarettes on an icebound island in the Arctic Circle, while less than fifty feet away a gentleman in a tuxedo swept and swooped around a hotel room large enough to hold the whole ground floor of Thorskrist's Hotel Snorri.

And now the camera does a magical and naughty and enviable thing: it drifts right through the floor, to enter, without knocking, the chambers of the woman lodged directly below. But to call her a *woman* may again be an understatement: for this is the slumbering form of a golden angel.

She will not sleep long, though, our fair-haired Aphrodite, in her bed with its quilted satin headboard. The crisp clatter of Fred's dancing breaks into her repose like rifle fire; unwittingly, he has loosed the first salvo in this latest chapter in the millennial war between the sexes.

So—Ginger wakes up in a snit. She emerges from her blankets to reveal a miraculous peignoir of white satin, with a lace collar and kimono sleeves and a train that trails behind her on the gleaming floor. She marches upstairs, a creature of steel in her ethereal gown, and gives Fred a piece of her mind. Fred is apologetic, and humble, and self-deprecating; he's smitten. And can it be that Ginger is smitten too, already?—and merely playing hard to get as she parries his compliments with wisecracks and stomps back to bed?

Love leads Fred to a brilliant stratagem. Having woken her up, he will put her to sleep. He will be, literally, her sandman. Ashtrays in this hotel consist not—as they would if this were the Snorri—of glass rectangles on whose bottom have been glued blurry color photographs of Copenhagen's Tivoli Gardens. No, they are cuspidors brimming with a white powder, pure as any pillow, upon which cigarettes are not so much put out as put to bed. Here is the "sand" Fred needs. And thus it comes to pass that he, like a man sowing grain, empties the cuspidor in great graceful handfuls on the very floor where his feet, just minutes ago, set up their staccato clatter. This time, the sound will be different.

Fred recommences. He dances on sand—smoothly, soothingly, strokingly. He is singing for Ginger a lullaby with his feet. Again the camera slips right through the floor. Ginger has returned to bed and Fred's plan is working brilliantly: her eyelids are flagging. Fred's dream-of-a-woman is about to enter the land of dreams. . . .

But the next morning she is crisp and authoritative once more as she strides into the hotel lobby wearing riding apparel. Evidently she has slept well. She is in the pink of health. She has arranged for a horse-drawn coach to take her to the park, where her own horse awaits her. If indeed her heart has already gone out to Fred, she isn't about to sit mooning over him.

But Fred has anticipated her. Disguised in livery, he has somehow arranged to make himself her coachman—to be, once more, her invisible custodian. Just as he guided her last night into sleep, this morning he will lead her to the park.

Ginger's *not* amused when she discovers Fred's newest trick, and as soon as they reach the park she gallops off in a defiant huff. A tough nut to crack, this girl. But now the heavens conspire to bring the two of them together. The sky begins to rumble, rain starts to fall. Ginger dismounts and scurries to shelter in a bandstand, where Fred soon joins her. They talk to each other—he eagerly, she warily. Another rumble overhead. Is she scared of thunder? he asks. Oh no, she answers, "just the noise." Another, an even louder thunderclap, and this one sends a flustered Ginger rushing into Fred's arms. And he begins to sing:

> The weather is frightening,
> The thunder and lightning
> Seem to be having their way,
> But as far as I'm concerned
> It's a lovely day.

And Fred begins to dance. He has a captive audience of one, and he can't help showing off a bit. Ginger isn't yet aware she's dealing with Jerry Travers, the internationally acclaimed entertainer, but Fred needn't boast to her directly; he can demonstrate for her, musically, that he's a man of superior attainments.

> Let the rain pitter-patter
> But it really doesn't matter
> If the skies are gray,
> Long as I can be with you
> It's a lovely day.

And you might say that here the flag is planted on the mountain's summit. Or that here the apex of the art is reached. For now arrives what for me will always stand as the most enthralling stretch of seconds ever unfolded on a movie screen. Unbeknownst to Fred, who is performing with his back to her, Ginger has risen from her seat. Fred is executing a little dance, which Ginger is matching sway for sway and step for step, with such loving exactitude that she captures even the easy masculine bravado of his stride. Fred turns, seeking to gauge the full extent of the impression he has made upon her, and here it is, the magic instant: the littlest and yet the richest of double takes, an incredulity that swivels his head but does not break the intricate sequence of his steps, as the realization dawns upon him that *he does not have an audience but a partner.*

We have in Freeland an expression, concerning a fish that has wholeheartedly swallowed a hook, which might be rendered as, *taking it in so deep it can only go out the other end.* Actually, the expression's more vulgar than that and might better be translated, *To get rid of that one, you'd first have to shit your guts out.* But however you care to translate it, we were just such a pair of fish, Hannibal and I: we'd taken it all the way, plumb in the entrails. I suppose we'd fallen in love at first sight, both of us, not merely with Ginger, or even with Fred, but with a vision of a refinement more comely and complicated than any we'd ever conceived of. In an evening, in an instant, in a repeatable cinematic expanse where time has no meaning, our notions of what dexterity and suavity and manhood itself consisted of had been upended. Our heroes had always been the weighty colossi of the Sagas, with their halberds and pikestaffs and their crashing fatalistic melancholy. But here we'd found a man who successfully wooed and won his princess by means of a glib line of jokes and a nimble run of steps. Here we'd found someone whose contrary ambition was not weightiness but legerity: the goal being, in one's inspired moments, to touch the earth as lightly and rarely as possible. Soon, perhaps in his very next movie, Fred might well escape the earth altogether and dance upon a cloud.

We watched a contretemps evolve as Ginger, in a silly bewilderment over names, confused Fred/Jerry with his companion and concluded that she had been, caddishly, wooed by a married man. We followed Fred and Ginger and Horace and Horace's wife, Madge, down to Venice—a city simulated with the most endearing, stylized, and preposterous of Hollywood sets. I'm not sure either one of us knew, right away, that this was no more Venice than Thorskrist was. For us, the gray screen was a Mediterranean eruption of gold and crimson, yellow and blue and pink. Fred rode a gondola in southern California, and Hannibal and I felt the hearts go out of our chests in Jardvik, Freeland. That's what Culture does to a person.

We watched a distraught Ginger marry another man, a vain Italian peacock named Beddini, although it would turn out that—unbeknownst to Beddini and Ginger—this was no marriage at all, since the minister was an impostor: he was none other than Horace's butler. No irrecoverable harm had been done, then, and Fred might still take Ginger as his virtuous bride, provided that nothing went forward—no bedding with Beddini—in the bridal chamber. But how was Fred going to halt them?

How else but secure the room above the newlyweds and begin to dance more cacophonously than ever before—a sound in which Beddini might hear a call to battle and Ginger the tattoo of a love-struck man. Fred, it turns out, has more brains in his feet than Beddini has in his head. . . . And the true lovers are united at last.

We clambered home in darkness, across Freeland's moony ridges and craters. In fact a full moon was overhead, so we walked upon the moon and underneath the moon. Had this extremely cold night grown still colder? Would we have noticed if it had? All the warmth of Venice rinsed our veins and to have complained about anything so paltry and local as mere weather would have been a betrayal of our vision. Hannibal and I had glimpsed some new configuration of our place in the solar system— and you might say that on this night was born a pattern of humor we've been evolving for a third of a century. If the specific jokes didn't take shape until later, it all started here: Hannibal would turn into Hanni, and Eggert Eggi, and the whole of our dealings become a sort of Hollywood send-up; we might have been Astaire and Horton in Venice, or Bob Hope and Bing Crosby on the road to Mandalay. We had ventured into the enemy camp and stolen away with a prize we might never have concocted on our own, in our own territory: an appetite for spoof, for lunatic patter, for self-parody.

10

A Lost Snapshot

In the grand scheme of things—that panoramic zone where he is most himself—he hasn't a doubt in the world about his mission: he must venture forth and seize his fate. Oh, he wouldn't have things otherwise. It's a duty he embraces, and he means to pursue it with strength, valor, and forbearance. But even so, he does wish his fate weren't so vague in its particulars. . . . What *is* required of him?

He feels himself floundering, though he has neither the willingness nor the vocabulary of self-doubt to confess to any such thing. He feels confused—even if unable to admit, quite, to anything so small and belittling as confusion.

Consider a snapshot of Hannibal Hannibalsson in the year 1960. He has wound up where good young ambitious Freelandic men generally do: Copenhagen. Freeland may no longer be a Danish colony, but it's still to the Danes we turn for trade and education, for polish and guidance.

In our snapshot, Hannibal is wandering morosely through the Tivoli Gardens. It's a lackluster hour, maybe six in the evening, an interval when most of the children have been bundled up and sent home for supper and the neon revelry of the evening hasn't yet shimmered into life. It's a lackluster day as well: a gray leaf-stripped November afternoon.

Hannibal's face shines pale on this pale day, although there is in truth no snapshot, or you might say the snapshot was lost, since nobody was on hand that afternoon to capture him on film. And—besides—the Tivoli Gardens are closed in November. I envision him no less distinctly for that. I see the sere branches, the brown flower beds, and a drizzle that catches no light in its descent, so that the sky might just as well be spilling not raindrops but spatters of flat-gray paint.

Hannibal refuses to acknowledge the rain by turning up the collar of his greatcoat. He ambles slowly through the gardens. Incisiveness of thought has never been and never will be his métier, particularly self-analysis. The whole process of close internal scrutiny is one he regards as unbecomingly small. In the voyage of his own life he pilots himself by instinct, which on this dark November afternoon informs him that something somewhere in his existence is out of kilter.

He has taken a job with Det Store Danske Dampskibselskab—The Great Danish Steamship Company—whose ships have always been, ever since he was a boy, the pride and envy of Thorskrist Harbor. For a young Freelander of Hannibal's generation there is no position more promising than that of a DSDD executive. These days he regularly has money wadded in his pockets, and he sports fine clothes and carries the key to his own apartment.

Before him a plausible and profitable future outstretches. What is life like? Well, he might remain permanently in Copenhagen, henceforth apportioning to Freeland only occasional, perhaps biannual vacations. And he might marry a Dane—one of those beguilingly cosmopolitan, fashionable, fast-talking women he sometimes sees at night near the Royal Theater or on weekends in Orsteds Park. Or he could marry a French girl, or a German or an Italian, a Venetian count's daughter whom he might, one impossibly warm star-overrun evening, deflower in the curved prow of a gondola. . . . In settling himself in Copenhagen he has experienced a sensation new to his islander's heart: an indeterminate haziness at the horizon, an awareness of arbitrary borders drawn by committee rather than Nature's hand, nations slipping seamlessly into other nations, a whole continent packed like an overstuffed footlocker below him. Why stop at Copenhagen? Why not make his way to Berlin, to Paris, to Rome, to Constantinople? Where is the fitting end to all his fiery ambitions?

He carries in one fist a dense hemispherical half-loaf of rye bread, from which he every now and then, with idle savagery, rips off a mouthful. He likes the way the rain penetrates the dense grain of the bread, turns its heaviness heavier.

He wanders past a carousel that is shut down or broken. It offers a wide variety of mounts. Not just horses, variously festooned—caparisoned, plumed, side-saddled—but a veritable quadrupedal menagerie: here children can ride like sultans on the bumpy backs of camels, like mahouts on the domed backs of elephants, like Sioux chieftains on the shaggy backs of bison. In the islands of his homeland, from one end of Freeland to another, there's never been, needless to say, anything like this carousel. When he was a boy, what would he have felt merely to clap eyes on such an apparition? *What would he have felt?* More amazed, surely, than if he'd glimpsed a troll, skin the color of cigarette tobacco, humping over a kame. More amazed than if he'd seen a circle of *huldufolk* prancing round a moonlit campfire. The troll, the *huldufolk,* these things were imaginable—but the carousel belonged to a world beyond all conceiving. . . . There's a puzzle here. Within the gulf between the dumbstruck rapture the carousel once would have brought him, in boyhood, and the drizzly melancholy he feels this afternoon, in the height of his young manhood, lie a number of pieces he cannot quite assemble.

Hannibal continues to tear and chew his bread. The rain thickens. A fog seems to be rolling in, which cheers him a little; he likes fog. He had especially liked to wake in Thorskrist on sightlessly white mornings, lounging in bed a moment while listening to the foghorns in White Seal Bay. There is one sort of blindness where everything goes dark, and there's another odder, dizzier, even better blindness where everything goes white and the sound of a foghorn is the needy call of a lost father, a brother, maybe even a lover. . . . And he misses the storms, particularly the big screaming northwesters during which the heavens seemed to vow, *This time, we are going to level this town*, and merely to be sitting inside, sipping a cup of coffee and gnawing a buttered rope of dried fish, was, triumphantly, to issue a wordless denial: *Not yet, uh-uh, not this time.* . . .

A continent lies outspread before him, like a stage whose painted backdrop has, by sheer magic, extended itself, unrolling outward into a third dimension, and why exactly do none of the performances he visualizes for himself feel absolutely vital? He has made some forays into that backdrop, he has glimpsed the Alps while winding along on a powerfully coiled train south of Zurich—those Alps over which his namesake, two thousand years ago, traveling on foot, guided not only his troops but a team of elephants—but what was the landscape's missing ingredient? Where had the world's magic gone? What made these peaks so much less moving than Freeland's own much smaller Great Blue Mountain? And why, finally, were the women he saw in Orsteds Park, or imagined for himself in Berlin and Paris and Venice, so much less warmly tactile than that girl who once shattered his nose during a midsummer night's walk on the eastern slopes of Blue Island? The world was calling upon him to perform sizable feats and yet—simultaneously, perversely—was conniving to lend anything he might accomplish an air of unreality. He was like a man bewitched by a phantom lover, destined to have the body he would clasp to his chest dissolve away to nothing in his arms—but who has laid the spell upon him? And where was he to turn for help? There was, as yet, some crucial linkage missing between him and this new continent he inhabited. It wasn't a case—about this he felt confident—of any shortage of imagination. No, there was no fatal provincialism in his character which might render him forever unable to cast his lot with foreign lands. Could anyone feel closer than he did to the Greenlander Leif Eriksson, who founded a new community in the New World? Or to Magellan, or Drake, or Caesar, or Alexander? Or William Smith, whom the world has forgotten, who died a pauper back in England—even though he was the last man in history to discover a continent? Smith found the seventh of the continents, the one tucked away at the bottom of the planet, and what sort of world was this that would provide no more than seven continents?

He ripped another mouthful from his rain-impregnated loaf. A woman carrying a pink umbrella, a fair-haired woman in a gray coat with fur-collar trim, clatters by on red high heels, and if Eggert were here he would surely not let such a woman pass without throwing her a glance of transparent longing. Forget any sense of dignity—Eggert's availability must at all times be made obvious. Oh life is no doubt easier for Eggert, off in America—if that's where he is now—industriously compiling his unpublished and unperformed plays, chasing indiscriminately after any woman who does not spit in his eye. For someone like Eggert, the world's a relatively simple place—isn't it?—merely a matter of assembling the books he wishes to write, bedding the women who allow him into their beds. Poor Eggert would not understand this—this what? This huge wet mulling vacancy at the core of everything. Eggert has taken shelter, for life, in the sublime simplifications of Art. . . .

Better the higher, the harder road, which, on this afternoon in the Tivoli Gardens, Hannibal is searching for, but what in the name of heaven does that road have to do with the papers on his desk, these customs forms and fees, FOB and CIF, these towage liens and contracts of affreightment, and these bills, bills, bills—of lading, of entry, of adventure, of health, of sight? What does it have to do with these clean bills and negotiable bills and ocean bills and on-board bills? If the Tivoli Gardens or the Alps or even the sheep meadows on Jutland all lack some final, firm actuality, what could possibly be said about the offices of The Great Danish Steamship

Company? Sometimes it seemed they had no reality at all—as if with a simple spirited sneeze he might topple the very walls. . . .

Since his arrival in Denmark some link has been severed and the worst of it is he cannot say with certainty whether it would be restored even if he *were* to return to Thorskrist. Assuming he *did* go back, what in the world would he do with himself? Carry on working for Danish Steamship in a diminished, an outpost office? Become a teacher, like old Thorgunnur, sacrificing himself for Freelandic youth, for whom he could not answer the fundamental philosophical questions that now bedevil him? Turn to sheep farming? Oh, there are days, in the office, gazing in the distance at the spire of Nikolaj Church, when he dreams of just that. He will do what Freelanders have done from the beginning: he will lead his sheep out from the cotes in spring, herd them into the cotes in the fall, henceforth he will center his conversations on talk of grass and ringworm and weather, will become one of those down-to-earth folk for whom the only hypothetical questions worth speculating over involve the price of wool and mutton in the fall. Yet even as he transports himself to Freeland, attempts to see himself bounding across little streams and fissures, this vision, too, has an air of unreality.

He is waiting for a celestial bulletin: a list of lucid ultimata. But it is as though the actors, having long stood ready in the wings, only now discover that the wrong sets have been erected. *What is the name of the play? And what is its plot?*

How is it, given the amplitude of his dreams, he has come to this pass? Hannibal Hannibalsson walks through the Tivoli Gardens in the rain, on a gray afternoon in November 1960, and knows what? Knows nothing, but suspects that something's gravely amiss, that his life, like a pail set under a leak in the roof, sings out the need for repairs. . . . Even the bread, as he rips into it with his teeth, isn't quite real. Worse, even the slight discomfort the bread gives him, the scraping in his throat as he forces down one uncompromisingly large, ill-chewed hunk after another, isn't quite real. Worse, even the liquid in which the bread has been steeped—rainfall, that most pure and truthful of all natural phenomena—isn't real, and when even the rain has stopped being real for a man, where under heaven is he supposed to go next?

11

The Vow: There Will Be Laughter Either Way

A corner seat, the wall at his back, Hannibal Hannibalsson is camped out in the Cod's Head. He watches his adversary warily. She's on a reconnaissance mission, patrolling from table to table. No shots have been fired yet.

Hannibal has brought with him his most trusted deputy, Eggert Oddason, and the two old soldiers sit forward in their seats, conducting a desultory conversation while tracking events from the corners of their eyes, as out from the kitchen Rut occasionally brings a plate of fried haddock, a hamburger steak embogged in a pool of gray gravy, hills of boiled potatoes with squibs of mutton-fat wedged into their valleys. But what she mostly transports are steaming mugs of Freeland's "strong coffee."

And now, momentarily shifting roles, I find that the happy task falls upon me of detailing the supreme, surreal folly of my country's drinking laws. . . . It is forbidden in Freeland to sell alcohol except by the bottle, in state-run shops whose task it is to depress consumption both by punitive taxes and by a rationing system based upon nontransferable coupons, around whose transfer a lively black market has sprung up. Meanwhile, another sort of black market has evolved around *brugga*—home brew— usually derived from raisins. Meanwhile—this is a subject which gives birth to many "whiles"—venerable Freelandic tradition deems it immoral to deny a fisherman a drink.

Which explains the Cod's Head, situated at the harbor's edge. It caters mostly to fishermen. On its premises alcohol is never glimpsed by the patrons. The Cod's Head sells both coffee and "strong coffee." The latter includes, depending on the whim of the proprietress, two or three ounces of vodka or gin or indeterminate *brugga*. The proprietress is the nation's First Lady, Rut Bjartardottir.

She runs the place with a firm and cunning hand. Her wile is law. Men who aren't real workers—aren't fishermen or farmers—are quietly discouraged from the premises, mostly by way of weak drinks served up at "strong coffee" prices. Many are the stories of young kids swaggering in to order "strong coffee"—only to wind up meekly emptying their wallets for spirits left undecanted in the kitchen.

Rut has run this place for more than twenty years. The sailors love her, perhaps; they are afraid of her, certainly. They abide strictly by her rules, which include No Singing, No Fighting, and No Open Lewdness. The beauty of Rut's system of governance is that she can curtail whom she wants when she wants, all without a word. It doesn't do to cross her. She has a long memory.

And yet, crossing her is precisely what Hannibal this evening plans to do. He, too, loves her perhaps and is afraid of her certainly. He has brought Eggert along to bolster him. The two of them drink strong coffee at a back table. Each sips from his cup nervously, gaugingly—hoping to determine from its precise alcoholic potency just where he stands with Rut this evening. Hannibal is waiting for the Cod's Head to close. He has his announcement to make.

Each time Eggert hints at a departure, Hannibal forestalls him with a heave of his shoulders and a sweep of his arms. Those arms and shoulders are prepossessing. Their placement on the table likewise makes clear to all patrons that he is not to be disturbed tonight. He is to be nodded at, merely.

Eggert feels sweaty and shaky. The coffee and the alcohol and the general state of his nerves have converted his stomach into a precarious layering of uncertainties—like one of those shoddy hotels you sometimes read about, erected for a song in some "developing country," one of whose floors gives way, collapsing the one beneath it, the two of them collapsing the one beneath, and so forth, a masonry avalanche that ends in piles of moaning rubble. He watches Rut patrol the room. She knows something's up. She is ignoring the two of them.

Striding from the kitchen with a steaming plate of haddock in one hand, a mug of coffee in the other, she's an imposing presence. Her beauty, even as a young girl, always had tendons of toughness underneath. When most of her beauty left her, the toughness persisted, flourished. Her bones have broadened with the years, the cast in her eye grown more pronounced. And just this past year she has lost an upper canine. Evidently, she doesn't plan to replace it.

Each time a customer enters or exits, the tail ends of fierce winds whip through the Cod's Head, carrying the smell of rain. A storm has sprung up.

Hannibal and Eggert have been sitting for a moody hour or so, their conversation repeatedly gusting and fading, like the room's storm-sweepings, when a new wind washes in two young men wearing dripping yellow rain gear. After they remove their jackets the shorter of the two stands revealed as Eggert's son, Sindri. It's an unexpected arrival and, though Eggert has a genuine soft spot for the boy, gives him something of a start.

To his relief, followed immediately by a sense of some slight pique, his son does not come over to greet him. Perhaps Sindri, too, has read the heavy defensive thrust of Hannibal's shoulders? And Sindri's companion, with the wistful yellow mustache, who is he? There's something foreign about him. Is it the neat part of his hair? An Englishman, maybe, or a Frenchman. Eggert has lost track of his son's friends.

Sindri's hand leaps here and there, in uncharacteristically broad movements; he is evidently giving his friend a descriptive tour. It's almost as though the boy, rather than broadening his life by travel to foreign places, has chosen instead to bring his country alive to foreigners. A couple of months ago Eggert happened to run into Sindri as he was guiding a pair of very young Japanese women around the harbor. How it had come to pass that these two girls had wound up, unchaperoned, in Thorskrist, Freeland, and how, having done so, they'd linked up with Sindri, was an unplumbed mystery. Unmistakable, though, was the bright glow of the boy's face, his pleasure in playing cicerone.

When, after some twenty minutes, Sindri and his companion don their rain gear and, with a wave of farewell, shuffle out, this seems a signal; Eggert waits a couple more minutes and then says, in English—the language of their most jocular camaraderie—"I'm feeling fagged, Hanni," and rises from the table.

This time Hannibal does not protest. He glances up unhappily, squints at Eggert as though to make out who is addressing him, and nods in pensive agreement. His face is red, with drink, with nerves, with the cruel wear of time. Now and then it comes sharply back to Eggert just how long ago it was that Hannibal took home all the Olympic gold. Years, decades. There have been other Olympics since, of course, but never again did Hannibal—or anyone else, needless to say—come close to sweeping all the events. After the first Games, the country's athletes variously devoted themselves to practicing this event or that one; the age of specialization had come to Freeland too. Hannibal at that first Games had been a boy—younger, even, than tour-guide Sindri.

Hannibal, peering over the top of his coffee cup, watches his old friend make his way out of the Cod's Head—watches that slight, grizzle-headed figure who, though he threads his way with exaggerated care, nonetheless manages to jar a hip against a table. Poor Eggert always has lacked for physical grace.

So the President sits alone. There was a moment—it now seems weeks ago, although it was indeed earlier this very day—when a vision had descended from the sky and had, like some angel in an antique painting, sung in his ear. He'd felt an old expansiveness, something like what Leif Eriksson must have felt when, from the open prow of his ship, he'd watched mist give way to a high-timbered shoreline. But the lands had drifted back into mist, and the mist given way to pelting rain.

He sips from his coffee. How much alcohol does it contain? Of course it was unfair that Rut should be allowed to determine just how much Dutch courage would be allotted him—but battles with Rut were rarely fair.

The other customers have departed. Rut has locked the front door and, sponge in hand, goes briskly after the tabletops. A sharp stink of disinfectant cuts the air. She is waging a battle here, too, broad forearm locked in combat with whole armies of bacteria. They don't stand a chance, those forces of squalor. . . . Has she guessed the message he brings? She knows something's brewing. Meanwhile, he cannot clear his head. . . .

He waits until she is across the room, head bowed as she goes after some sort of congealed spill, before he declares, "Rut-my-dear, I've decided to run again. For President."

She needn't say a thing. The wind, coming in across the harbor, and falling at last, with a happy shriek, on solid objects that can be pulled and pelted, speaks for her. Its cries pierce the walls.

Rut continues to scrub, then snaps her head upright, sends arrowing his way one poisoned glance, and lowers her face once more. Her hand has never stopped scrubbing.

"I didn't know until today," he tells her. "You mustn't think I've been keeping it from you."

The wind hurls a handful of cold rain at him. It smacks against the glass.

"I was riding out in Black River Valley. It was the way the light fell on the hills, I suppose, and then there was—well there was a rainbow, and maybe I was reminded of that moment in *Njal's Saga* when the horse stumbles and Gunnar happens to look up at the hills and only then realizes he isn't about to flee Iceland as planned, that he will stay and face his Fate dead on, and if this means his enemies will strike him down, so be it. He declares, 'How lovely the slopes are, golden cornfields and new-mown hay.' You could say I had a sort of vision. I knew in that moment I must stay at my work. One more time. One more term. Complete the twenty-five years. I will give a quarter century to Freeland."

What is she going to fire at him? Hannibal had expected an immediate explosion. He hadn't expected to be allowed to justify himself in this leisurely fashion, and consequently hadn't prepared any detailed explanation. But the words are arriving. He feels, despite himself, a frail but uplifting hopefulness, like a banner held aloft against the wind. She will come round.

The words trip lightly from his throat. "I am a man of abiding loyalties. I have given myself to you, Rut-my-dear, and I have remained true to that vow."

At this juncture, certainly, she might find cause to object, since it isn't quite the case that his attentions have been constant. Mostly—mostly constant. But she says nothing. Is he softening her? Is she accepting his comments in the spirit he offers them? He cannot see her face. She has moved to another tabletop and is attacking this one, too, with abstracted fervor. He pushes his luck: "When you have called upon me, I have been there. For all my shortcomings, you've known you could depend on me through thick and thin."

Will she let this one stand? She raises no protest, and to have been permitted such a pronouncement seems such an unexpected bounty that he plunges right on: "And I have given myself to Freeland. When she has called upon me, I've been there. This is who I am. You see before you," he concludes with a flourish, "a man of few but enduring loyalties."

"I don't allow singing in my place," Rut says.

"Mm? Singing?" What is she on about?

"Nor lewdness. The first man pats me on the rump, I toss him out on his ear."

"Yes. Of course you do, darling. If you weren't so capable of it yourself, I'd toss him out for you. No one pats my Rut on the rump. . . ." But where is this going? Hannibal feels himself drifting through fog. . . .

"And fighting. There is no fighting in here."

"Quite right. And everyone knows that. You have them all cowed, lovey."

"But there's another thing, there is something else I won't have in my place," Rut says. Her head is again lowered.

"Oh? And what's that?"

"I won't sit in my own place and listen to a man go back on his word."

Across the room, at last, Rut lifts her face and her sockets are hot and bright as candle flames; they could singe the hair right off your wrist. And they are cold as ice; they could needle your feet with frostbite. What in the world had he been thinking? She'll *come round*?

"Gone back on my word, love?"

"*One more*, you said. Five years ago that's what you pledged. You said, *One more*. You said, I will serve Freeland for twenty years, I will give my country a fifth of a century, you said. And you pledged your word. Just as surely as snow sits atop Great Blue Glacier, you promised me, and you promised your country, that we'd have an end to it."

"But Rut-my-dear, it came in a vision today. Surely you're not about to hold a man responsible for what arrives in the form of a vision!"

"And how did it arrive last time, Hannibal? Huh? Was *that* the time when you were hiking through Widows' Valley and the spirits of the dead warriors urged you to seek reelection? Forgive me if my memory's no longer clear on this point. Or was it the time you were standing out at Founders' Point and the sea itself spoke to you, whispering, *Twenty years, twenty years*? It's hard to keep track in the end, isn't it?"

His head has begun to spin. Last time around? Speaking of fading memories—what *happened* last time around? His head feels too jumbled, too jumbled and sorrowful and hampered and muddled, to sort this out right now. . . .

"You're a man of too many visions, Hannibal. Too many visions and too little sight: that's you."

He winces—this one bites. Yet even while he's conceding that she has drawn blood, he must pause in admiration: *too many visions and too little sight*. He has never known a sharper-tongued woman. What a splendid, challenging adversary she makes! "My country needs me," Hannibal offers, and these words are so beautiful, in their compelling simplicity, surely even Rut must defer to them.

Yet she doesn't. She says, "The economy's a shambles. Catches are down."

"It's the Brits and the damn Japs—they're overfishing. Truly, it is a tragedy beyond anything the world—"

"Bankruptcies are up."

"It's the Danes. Squeezing us dry, the bastards. What else have they been doing for—"

"The young have turned to drugs."

"Now *that's* the Yanks. Have you actually seen one of their movies lately? They've become a malignant culture. I pity them. Truly I—"

"And crime—we're in the middle of a crime wave. We had a woman's purse snatched just last week on Skeggjagata. A month ago Olafur Agnarsson had his entire pipe and snuff-box collection stolen from his house while he was *sitting down to Sunday dinner.*"

"Now that's the Yanks *all over.* Surely you can see it as clearly as I. They are marketers of barbarism. They're becoming the cleverest, most comprehensive thieves the world has ever seen. They're a culture selling lawlessness and mayhem—and they sell it to you by means of sixty-page legal contracts! The fiendish *ingenuity* is absolutely boggling. Think about it. . . . These people are muggers who crack open your skull not with a brick but a law dictionary. That's why we have to protect ourselves. That's why Freeland needs me. We've got to keep the TV out anyway. That's what my opponents are promising, you know? To expand the TV. Bring us those American programs. That's why my country needs me. Because we've come to a point so debased that as a campaign promise we would offer our people American television."

"Anything needs to be done in the way of protecting ourselves, Nonni will see to it."

"Nonni Karlsson! But darling, he's an empty suit! A coat wrapped around some moss and a cobweb."

"He will make a fine President. You mark my words. . . ."

"Goodness, well, yes, I know the lad's your cousin, and I know you've a soft spot for him, Rut-my-dear. We all do. And he's comely—oh, he's a very comely boy. And I don't doubt he might make a good President—in time. *Seasoning* is what the boy needs. Now you just let me season him for five years, you let me take the lad under my wing—" Again Hannibal feels a sort of spacious hopefulness open up within his chest. How could she possibly refuse a proposal at once so judicious and so generous? "—and

I will *personally* mold him. My love, I'll make a leader of that boy. Trust me. You simply need to trust me."

"You say 'Trust me' on the day you've proved yourself the nation's biggest liar? *Trust* you? Trust *you?*"

"This is larger than I am, Rut. Larger than all of us."

"My father used to say, There's nothing larger than a man's word. And I've remembered that. . . ."

"Oh, your father. Your *father* . . ."

Old Bjartur Jonsson wasn't someone of whom Rut often spoke these days; she was too wary about being teased as a daddy's girl. But in moments of dudgeon, when vitriol got shaken up with elevated principles, out from the grave would crawl that unkillable old bastard Bjartur Jonsson, as fierce and purblind as ever. Old Bjartur, who at the age of seventy-eight had no more sense than to go out in search of a lost lamb in a murderous blizzard and wind up drowning in the Two Day River . . .

"Bjartur Jonsson was a fool," Hannibal declares.

"A *fool?*" Rut meets him with shrill incredulity. She is herself a murderous blizzard.

But then a change comes over her features and she says softly, chantingly, "A fool? A fool? Oh a fool indeed, yes, a fool to the last of his sore old bones, a true fool and nothing ever nothing bless him but a fool. But I would ask you now, Hannibal"—and her voice is a sort of purr—"when was the last time Freeland saw a fool on a scale like his? And how many generations will it be, I'd ask you now, before Freeland again sees a fool of his dimensions? Now *there* was a man who in the last year of his life went dead flat bankrupt trying once again to build himself a proper home, he who never had two sticks to rub together, and what does he do when the bank forecloses? He says, I'm going to start over. He says, I'll move to another island and build my palace yet. And *you* presume to talk about foolishness, Hannibal. Well you mustn't. No. It's unseemly. It's undeserved. You don't know enough about it yet. You poor thing, you don't yet know enough about the big true wholehearted foolishness of the old, true sort. . . ."

Her voice had gone mild, turning melancholy, perhaps even tender, and could it be she was coming round? He senses opportunity here, the possibility—unexpected and devilishly subtle—of righting everything at a single stroke. It is merely a matter of locating the proper words. He needs to explain to her, perhaps, that he is as much a fool as anyone—as anyone, at least, in this wan and diminished day and age—could ever hope to be. . . . And if she wanted to talk about scale—well, who in the world saw a larger world than he did? He glimpsed it huge and whole at times and this, *this* is the vision he must convey to her: that he saw the world huge and whole and he recognized, as others did not, that the whole damn thing was collapsing. *The world is going to hell*, people say. You hear it all the time: *the world's going to hell*. It's a mere expression, though, a remark tossed off when the cigarette lighter in your car goes dead, or when a printers' strike silences the town newspapers for a day, or when you pop open a can of beer and find the contents have gone flat, but to use it like this, as an idle lament, is gradually to bleed its true significance: the *world* is going to *hell*. In his office across from Mariners' Church, in the two-room, sixty-five-square-meter Presidential Suite, nervously, gingerly he thumbs through the magazines on his desk, *The Economist, Time, US News & World Report, Politiken*, and contemplates the map of the world on the wall opposite.

Hannibal sits in the Presidential Suite of the northernmost capital of the world, and considers the world that lies—speaking latitudinally—below him. In the 67 degrees down to the equator, and perhaps more tellingly still in the 90 further degrees to the south pole, the writing on the wall map is unmistakable: the world is going firmly, resolutely, unswervingly to hell. They are poisoning the air and they are ripping down the forests as if these were a stage set, needing to be struck overnight; they are eliminating species not yet named and at the same time they themselves are pullulating like jackrabbits, copulating blindly and indiscriminately, in valleys on whose hillsides heroin poppies and coca leaves unfurl in the sun. Worse yet, they are killing that holy womb wherein all life began. Yes, they are turning the sea into a desert, into an acid-bath. They are fishing it dry and they are—an image that pinches the heart in his chest—dynamiting the coral reefs in order to bring blast-victims floating to the surface. . . . Eggert in his witty and often incisive way had been quite right to invoke the tale of Little Annasigga in the Cavern of the Trolls. Eggert had said that in Hannibal's mind little Annasigga was Freeland and the vast, lumbering, murderous trolls were the superpowers of the world—all of which was apt enough. Witty Eggert! But Eggert hadn't been quite fair—or simply hadn't perceived that in Hannibal's mind it wasn't at all apparent that things will turn out for Freeland as they did for Annasigga. In the girl's case, the trolls fell so ferociously upon each other that, miraculously, not a single one was left, after which she could slip out of the cavern with a sackful of troll-pelf slung over her shoulder. But would that other Little Annasigga, the one called Freeland, likewise escape un-scathed? She might instead be struck dead by the stray missile of a stone, aimed elsewhere; she might be roasted alive by an errant firebrand. The nations of the world were out to destroy themselves and they might just, inadvertently, take Freeland down with them. . . . And the reason he must run for reelection is because at bottom his opponent, Nonni Karlsson, does not grasp the meaning of the fable of Little Annasigga in the Cavern of the Trolls. Nonni believes they perhaps can be negotiated with, those trolls, may even be finessed or manipulated into sharing the glitter of their bounty. He does not understand that they would eat Little Annasigga without a compunction, their only regret, as the girl's dis-jointed bones crunched under their molars, that she did not have more flesh on her limbs.

Hannibal senses, yes, a fleeting opportunity to right everything with Rut, but where to begin?

He says, "I am not doing this for me. I am doing this for the world at large."

It's the wrong thing to say—she hoots at him. For how many years now has she been hooting at him? *I don't want to be a farmer*, he'd confessed the very first night they walked together, on Olympic Day, at the base of Great Blue, and she had hooted at him—before breaking his nose.

She says: "The world replies, *No thank you to you, Mr. Hannibal Han-nibalsson. The world answers, We don't need you to save us.*"

"You know what our country is like? It's like Little Annasigga in the fable. . . ."

Rut shakes her head astoundedly. "You? You've had too much coffee. There are things I will not listen to in my own place. Singing. Lewdness. And the ditherings of a lunatic."

"After I am reelected, you will see—"

"That day will arrive only when Annasigga's trolls all become vege-tarians. That day will arrive when Freeland opens its first beach resort. Don't you see? You will *never* be reelected, Hannibal. You are doomed, doomed, doomed, and you would doom anybody who would go down with you."

"Up or down, Rut-my-dear, sink or swim, you must be beside me. I count on you."

"You count on me? You *dare* to count on me? You go back on your word like this, and still you dare to count on me? Only an utter fool would go along with you now," Rut says—and yet, wasn't full-blown foolishness just what, mere moments ago, she'd been extolling? His head's aswim. . . .

"Well this time I will not stand beside you," she goes on. "You will never have my vote."

"Well the vote's a private matter," Hannibal begins. "Many an unexpected and unreported thing has gone on in the secrecy of the voting booth. . . ."

"Private matter? You understand *nothing*, do you? You don't grasp it at all, you great muddleheaded walrus. I shall not remain *private*. I shall proclaim it to the world. I shall tell all and sundry that I no longer stand beside you."

"Rut-my-dear," he begins, but he knows this is sheer futility. She is a boat slipped over the horizon—she has gone out well beyond the reach of his words.

"You don't understand," she says. "This time they will turn you into a figure of *ridicule*. How many swan songs can one swan sing? They will show you no mercy. And when they go at you with stones and clubs and arrows, when they decide that this is a swan to roast and baste and spread on a platter on their dining room table, how will I respond? Hear me, Hannibal Hannibalsson, because now I make you a vow: I make a vow that I will lift not one finger to protect you."

Her words are thrilling. All right: well and good: even conceding that he has lost her, still the very sound of *I make you a vow* sets his blood to spinning. Let there be war between them, then—only let it be a war of solemnity and grandeur. Fatigue, confusion, hopelessness all slip like a heavy rucksack from his shoulders. Hannibal sits up straighter, lighter, younger: he is being summoned to battle.

"And when you're defeated," she goes on, "they are all going to laugh at you. And do you know what I'll do then? I will laugh at you along with them. . . ."

"And now, Rut-my-dear," Hannibal replies, "I shall make you a vow in return." His voice is venturesome—it goes out to an entire electorate and beyond; it reaches out toward the great ranks of warrior dead in Valhalla: "There will be laughter either way. For when I have proved you wrong, when I have won this damn election, do you know how I shall proceed? I would ask you to hold one image in your head. Keep this one in mind. For on that day I shall head over to Blue Island and I shall take a walk at the base of Great Blue Mountain and there I will stand upon a rock and send my laughter echoing over the sea."

He rises from the table and his left knee—as sometimes happens when he has been sitting for a long stretch—shoots out a pain so vivid he almost collapses. But he remains on his feet. He throws his jacket over his big shoulders, downs the last of his spiked coffee, and steps out into the howling censorious night.

12

A Job with Opportunities

I acquired a nifty new phrase: cash under the table. A job went with it. I was washing dishes and bussing tables at a place called Buck's Eat Shop off of Detroit's Jefferson Avenue. I'd established a life—an American life. It was 1960 and the sun shone every day of the year, without fail.

There wasn't now and never had been any Buck, a discrepancy that nagged at my Freelandic sensibility; perhaps we take names more seriously than Americans do. In any case, the owner was a seamed bald little man— three or four inches shorter than I—with gray and yellow pouches under his eyes, and his name was Aaron Shlomowitz. Such was my worldliness at the time, I was some weeks in identifying him as a Jew.

And I was years away from understanding that in America a tacit compact of cohabitation had been arrived at by which the prominent names of the Old Testament belonged to the Jews and those of the New to the Gentiles. In Freeland, where something like ninety-eight percent of the population is Lutheran and there are doubtless more out-and-out Odin-worshipping pagans than Jews, Old Testament names abound. I grew up around Isaks and Josuas and Eliases and Solomons and Jakobs. A name like Moses Hreggvidursson does not look peculiar to my eye— certainly less so than, say, Scott Drill or Peggy O'Shea.

In addition to Buck's, Shlomowitz owned Charley's Floor Covering across the street, where tile and carpet and linoleum were sold, and Uncle Orwell's Antiques around the corner. He was a genial, jittery man who would sometimes press fruit on me as I was leaving work: an apple, a banana, an orange, even a cantaloupe. He was hoping to sell his worldly empire—Buck's, Charley's, Uncle Orwell's—and move to Florida for his wife's health, about which he fretted himself to the point of torment. He was himself such a frail, wispy man—the "ash of a feather" as we Free-landers say—that to hear him describe a creature frailer by far than he, that "poor thing" his long-suffering wife, was to evoke someone scarcely able to cast a shadow under a street lamp. I certainly wasn't prepared to be introduced to a stout-boned woman of robust, ruddy complexion.

So new, back then, was everything around me that I had no means of recognizing Shlomowitz for the rare and appealing species he was: a hypochondriac-by-proxy. If anyone ever wore a look of imminent mortal-ity it was Aaron Shlomowitz, who daily waned into a grayer and smaller and frailer being, as he agonized over Mrs. Shlomowitz, who daily waxed fuller of figure and rosier of hue. When she came by the restaurant, as she sometimes did in the late afternoon, she could usually be prevailed upon to "sample" a little something. Mr. Shlomowitz would watch with an ex-pression of avid concentration on his gray face as she consumed a plate of short-ribs and gravy, but a moment later would be speculating that her stomach must be troubling her when she refused a scoop of vanilla ice cream on her second piece of apple pie.

In time I came to think of the man who sometimes waited tables and always served behind the cash register as Buck—his name was Mack, which was close enough. He was large and plump and freckled, with tight-set eyes of a washed-out blue. He secreted a gun, a pistol, underneath the cash register.

He was passionately devoted—if passion may be attributed to anyone of such waddling deliberation—to television westerns. Photos of some of the leading actors were taped to the cash register. They were realer to Mack than any blood-family. Maverick. Cheyenne. Bat Masterson. He seemed to feel I was pulling his leg when I asked him to identify one of them, and I can hardly blame him. Truly I was a singular creature: some-one who had never seen "Gunsmoke" and yet who could identify Mack as a "hashslinger." If I hadn't happened to have been me, I never would have believed myself.

I'd been working at Buck's for a couple of weeks when Mack intro-duced me to what he called "the drill." His willingness to take me on as a partner was, I suppose, a sign of the trust he'd grown to repose in me. We were to assume that a robber had come. Mack would be stationed behind the cash register, which the robber had ordered him to empty. I would be at the end of the counter, my hands thrust high in the air.

Well, at the end of this counter sat a stack of four plates that never moved from the moment we opened the doors for breakfast at seven until we closed at four in the afternoon. On the day the robber came, and ordered me to "reach for the sky," I was to await an opportune moment and then send the plates clattering to the floor, simultaneously diving behind the counter. At the sound of the crash, the robber would turn, allowing Mack just enough time to seize the gun beneath the register and "pop him one in the chest."

I took the drill seriously; I did as I was told. After closing hours, the shades drawn, we would practice it over and over, having first replaced the stack of four breakable plates with a pile of plastic dishes. I'd reach for the sky. I'd wait for the imaginary intruder to let his guard down. Then I'd send the dishes clattering and I'd frog-flop behind the counter. And Mack would draw the gun and sink a couple of slugs into the malefactor's chest. What could be simpler?

And was Mack a lunatic? I didn't think so at the time. To be sure, what he was contemplating was all but unimaginable to me. Some years, Freeland has no killings at all. The year we had four, not long ago, the newspapers took to thundering about our "murder wave." But what was so oddly appealing about Mack was his managing the whole business with such quiet, unruffled certainty. "He's coming," he would say—uttering the phrase with some of that unbudgeable assurance with which I've heard it delivered, though in a wildly different context, by religious fanatics. "One day he's going to walk right through that door, and we're going to be ready for him, little fella."

I'm afraid, yes, you will have to put up with this, since I did too: he called me "little fella." Perhaps he *was* a lunatic. But I watched, I listened, I nodded. He was remarkably well informed about crime in the neighborhood. Lucky's Party Store, over on Gratiot, had been hit by a pair of thugs last Wednesday. Lacy of Lacy's Soup and Sandwich had been mugged right out in front of her store, at six in the evening. The Sunoco on Gumble? Burgled in the night. And so the chronicles accumulated, the inevitable neared. *He* was coming.

I've thought about Mack surprisingly often over the years. What in the world ever happened to freckly tiny-eyed broad-bottomed Mack Ketchum, who rolled through life with such waddling certainty, who watched his Westerns every night and waited all day long for the arrival of his "bad guy," his masked bandit, his desperado villain? And the odd truth is, given the mounting ferocity of America's inner cities, Mack more and more looks like a realist.

For as the years went along, if he remained posted behind the cash register at Buck's, who can doubt that eventually, yes, the day arrived and *he* showed up

—but with what result? What occurred when the long-awaited day materialized? I see one of three things happening: all the practicing paid off and Mack drummed his adversary full of lead; Mack himself met a bullet; or paralysis set in, and in that frozen moment all the comfy futility of his existence—his hidden pistol, his drills, his nights before the television—was exposed for what it was, hollow as any spent bullet casing. I suppose I must have liked Mack, since I'm unwilling to wish any of his three probable fates upon him.

Sometimes in a magazine or a newspaper one comes across a glowing collection of little testimonials addressing the issue What America Means to Me. One of the things it means to Eggert Oddason, who thinks of it fondly, is a succession of afternoons in that last year of Eisenhower's reign when he found himself reaching for the sky, motionlessly breathing in and out the warring aromas of onions and hamburger patties and mustard and vinegar and cinnamon-dusted doughnuts, while waiting for an invisible intruder fractionally to relax his guard. . . .

Its smells used to all but overpower me. I hardly knew how I felt about the place—I knew merely that the atmosphere was almost too rich for breathing. Only in retrospect am I able to recognize it as one of my life's holy sites: I loved Buck's Eat Shop. It was homely, and it was heavenly. I was a magician when I held the whipped cream dispenser: sweet clouds emerged with the merest nudge of the nozzle. And there was magic and romance too when eggs, having first been beaten in a bowl, met the vast skillet in a searing, cohering kiss.

We opened up at seven to serve breakfast. Later there would be a lull, and then a lunch crowd, and then a straggling afternoon assortment of pie-eaters and coffee-drinkers. We closed before dinner. I'd clean up a bit and, walking observantly along Jefferson Avenue, be back at Lyon Road by five, a good hour before the true man and master of the house returned. I would go home ostensibly to read and to write, but it usually wasn't more than a few minutes before Meg—who in my mind soon became Meggy, and in time became Meggy to her face—would find me out, with a tap at my door. She'd bring tea, coffee, cookies, a ten-cent two-part Mounds Bar of which I was free to accept a nickel's worth. Or she might bring me, although she'd warned me I would have to fend for myself at dinnertime, a sandwich of tuna fish mashed up with mayonnaise and sweet pickle. She soon came to understand that, although I'd rebelliously thrown off my background, I was still enough of a Freelander to feel a near-compulsive daily need for fish. Even now, it's hard for me wholly to regret any day in which I've consumed a codfish cake. . . .

She called me Eddie. I called myself, in secret, Eggi; by nicknaming her Meggy I'd made her, so to speak, my mate in rhyme. She would appear shyly, the faint blush on her cheeks gracefully easing the hurtful contrast between her face's natural pallor and the blood-flooded strawberry mark on her throat and jaw. It was striking how thoroughly had vanished that toughness with which she'd initially greeted me. Even in her own house she now moved hesitantly, gingerly. The Bermuda shorts of our first encounter had given way to a shapeless and faded blue housedress. She usually wore a cross around her neck.

It would have been difficult, I suppose, for her to maintain any semblance of authority once I'd met Michael, who ruled the house with a presence so amplitudinous as to leave other inhabitants pressed tight against its walls. There's a sizable portion of Celtic blood in the Freelandic gene pool, and on first glance I experienced a vivid recognition of his type: big-boned and fair-skinned, flashing blue eyes and thinning red hair. You might see his Freelandic cousin prowling down Skeggjagata, fresh off a fishing boat, hunting for comfort or excitement, for an embrace or a brawl—whatever, it doesn't much matter which. But even so, while I'd seen more than my share of drunkenness in Freeland—including the coarse, drowning drunkenness of sailors on a spree, complete with ragged sea chanteys and spewings in the street—Michael's steady, purposeful, indrawn, bitter pursuit of oblivion was something new. Virtually every night he'd pass out downstairs on the sofa, in a fetid cloud of Lucky Strikes, with the television running and scraps of popcorn or Ritz crackers or potato chips—Michael *crunched* on things—scattered everywhere. That sofa was Meggy's pride and joy, the one piece of "first-class furniture in the house."

It had come to Michael's attention that I was a poet. Meggy had let this information drop—a revelation that cost me dearly. Much about America still needed to be clarified, but already I understood that verse-writing was a practice a man acknowledges shamefacedly, like admitting to a fear of fast cars or to a fondness for warm milk—a pair of weaknesses I might, in utter honesty, also have confessed to. So it was hardly surprising when Michael began addressing me as "Little Poet," or when, home from work, he would greet me by asking, in a wee, piping voice, "Write any *verses* today, Eddie?" What *was* surprising was that Michael, on a couple of occasions, when deep into the bottle, would begin to expatiate upon the "living poetry" in the blood of the Irish. Your true Irishman, it turned out, was a *born* poet, songs in verse were as natural to him as rain or whiskey or boiled potatoes, and so Michael might rise from the couch, glass in hand, and—as God is my witness—recite Longfellow's "Excelsior," or Joyce Kilmer's "Trees," or Kipling's "If," or Edgar Guest's "Equipment." And it was my peculiar good fortune to be living cheek by jowl with what surely must have been one of America's leading proponents of Berton Braley. I heard "Success":

> If neither cold poverty, famished and gaunt,
> Nor sickness nor pain
> Of body or brain
> Can turn you away from the thing that you want,
> If dogged and grim you besiege and beset it,
> *You'll get it!*

And "That's Success!":

> It's sharing sorrow and work and mirth
> And making better this good old earth;
> It's serving, striving through strain and stress;
> It's doing your noblest—that's Success!

And "Start Where You Stand":

> What has been, has been; yesterday is dead
> And by it you are neither blessed nor banned;
> Take courage, man, be brave and drive ahead;
> Start where you stand.

The source of such poems was no mystery: they must have been drummed into him as a schoolboy. But that he'd retained them *was* a surprise. Michael McKaig may well have been pernicious—among the ever-swelling ranks of men I've disliked in my life, he stands near the forefront—but he was a more intricate character than I'd first taken him for. He had dozens and dozens of verses inside his brain. He was no mere drunken Irish layabout. The poor man fancied himself a poet.

As with Mack at work, so with Michael at home, a routine developed, though this time I was a thoroughly unwilling partner. Michael would first draw thoughtfully upon his bottle. After a while, he would begin to muse upon what a "tough town" Detroit had become. I would agree, or I would disagree, or I would say nothing, it was all one: "Eddie, you gotta be taught to protect yourself," he would announce, dutifully hauling himself to his feet. There was nothing for it; I must wrestle with him.

No demurring, no expostulating, no dissuading or postponing availed me. And whether I succumbed easily, or hit the floor in a great grunting maelstrom of thrashes and kicks, my feet digging into his shins and my elbows into his ribs, in the end it always came down to the same thing: he liked to bury my face in the crotch of his elbow, locking it blindly into place, while with his free hand, back and forth with a scouring motion, he'd rub his knuckles—hard, very very *hard*—across the crown of my head. I'd been in Detroit a couple of weeks, I guess, before I discovered one day at Buck's, idly running a hand across my scalp, that he'd abraded the hair there: he was literally rubbing me bald.

—A discovery that all but overwhelmed me. A discovery so humiliating it called for some severe escalation of the covert war I'd been scheming against him. But how could I raise the stakes any further? I'd already vowed, in repayment for his jokes about my verses, to seduce his wife. Oh, I was bitterly resolute: another sort of wrestling would go on in that house. Yes, dear God yes: Michael would in time put himself to bed between sheets damp with the amorous sweat of my narrow-shouldered torso. . . .

Coming home from Buck's at the end of a workday, I would slip quickly up to my room and shut the door behind me. I was erecting obstacles for Meg. If she wanted to talk to me—and each passing day made more apparent how desperate she was for someone to talk to—she must seek me out. I would wait. The knock would come. Our conversation had two main subjects. Mine was Freeland. The place had piqued her curiosity; she wanted to know how we "did things there." Poor Meggy, she didn't perhaps understand just why she hungered so for reports from elsewhere—the farther away the better. Kicked and tethered, she led a dog's life.

When *she* talked, the subject was likely to be her son, her late son, her heart's own Stevie, the mere recitation of whose name set her face aglow and her voice atremble. She had suffered a loss so monumental—I see now—she couldn't bear to talk about it and yet couldn't bear not to talk around it. Although she hadn't expressly asked me to, I'd kept the shrine to her son intact: to judge from how little my belongings had impinged upon the place, you might have supposed it was still a boy of eleven, and not a young man of twice that age, who inhabited it. I'd left the model cars on the bookcase top, the planes dangling from the ceiling. They served as decoys, lures.

For didn't they help to explain why, on my return at the end of a day, she could bear to wait so few minutes before summoning me with her timorous tap-tap—and why she hesitated so soulfully on the threshold of my doorway? She could hardly endure it, the place called her so.

My talk turned endlessly to the flexible, haphazard social arrangements of my native land. I told her—which happened to be true—that we have the highest illegitimacy rate in Europe. I told her—which, so far as I know, happened not to be—that my own father had sired eight bastards. "A woman back there who has a child out of wedlock is applauded for her independence," I told her, and Meg's eyes grew wide, the years slipped from her appealingly careworn face. "As for sexual intercourse"—I began, and the launching of this phrase, the utterance of it so dryly and authoritatively, launched me elsewhere: I felt a deep combative prodding against the confinement of my underwear—"sexual intercourse is something we Freelanders treat as completely natural." Oh, Margaret Mead among the Samoans had nothing on me! I drew for Meg a picture so captivating in its clement, insouciant, casual carnality that I myself succumbed to its spell. Freeland's ice-hammered, rock-ribbed coastlines were replaced by evenly banked saffron sands, its scree moraines by mossy beds, its lurching drunken midnight grapplings by heady palm wine–enhanced daylight comminglings, its pasty sunless malnourished bodies by bronzed torsos plumped up on mangoes, papaya, breadfruit, coconut oil.

Meg said to me one day, "I could never have slept with Michael before I married him." She added, appealingly lifting her chin with pride, "He knew better than to try." Oh, he didn't leave you much room, did he, Meggy, for anything like a healthy defiance. Only here, in the land of imagined slights and oversights, could you stand up to him and say, *You're out of line now, Michael McKaig, and you better watch your step*, for in the other world, the one of everyday degradations, you took with nothing but a whimper whatever kicks and curses he administered. And another time, after I'd waxed brilliant about the adulterous intertwinings of my countrymen, you said, "I could never sleep with someone I wasn't married to, it's sinful," and touched the talisman of the crucifix at your neck. Did such proclamations reassure you? Render gorgeously unreal my talk of orgiastic foreign lands? What was the harm—you might have supposed—in listening to what so patently had nothing to do with your life?

And so my Meg attended me steadily, mouth set in a tight scowl but eyes aglitter, as I unfolded the story of how I'd lost my virginity to a fair-haired farmer's daughter on the night of the day I won the Long Run at the Freeland Olympics—an exquisite fabrication, my tale, from start to finish. Actually, it wasn't as though I had no sexual escapades to offer her—but was I going to serve up the truth? That I'd lost my virginity to an acne-scarred cousin who, drunk and weeping when I met her on the street—she'd been ditched by a sailor who'd taken up with one of her friends—was drunker still when I had my rendezvous with Eros? Was I going to confess I'd stolen my aunt's "sleep medicine" in order to bed my cousin in a deserted warehouse that reeked of fish and urine? If over the previous few years, despite my obvious shortcomings, I'd had a few women, weren't these successes wholly the result of a dogged persistence, and a thick-skinned willingness to endure humiliation and rejection? *Endure* it? Perhaps I might better say, *Enjoy* it, for sometimes it seemed my appetite for humiliation and rejection was as great as for sexual gratification. Hence, when I propositioned a woman, I could hardly lose. . . .

And what did she have to lose, Meg McKaig, attending to tales about a place so remote it might as well have been imaginary? It was a harmless means of whiling away an hour—that deadly, dusky, nerve-rattled hour before her husband came home and the night commenced in all its surly, slumping devolutions. How bad would it be? Would Michael manage to pass from rancor into incoherence without breaking anything, or hitting anyone? And *if* nothing was broken and nobody had been struck, couldn't the evening be judged a success of sorts? Given the shape of Meg's days, what harm was there in listening to this young foreigner who was—who was almost young enough to be her son?

It was her son, not surprisingly, who prompted our first bodily contact. Without knowing when it might come, or what it might look like, I'd been awaiting a signal, and one afternoon, as a gentle rain was laving the windowpanes, I gave her an account—the purest, gentlest of fictions —of the uncle of mine who'd lived with three women, each of whom had borne him twin sons.

"All twin boys?" she said.

"That's right."

Meg moved from this detail to that other which was for her the more incredible still: "He lived with three different women?"

"Three." I nodded solemnly.

"At the same time? Lived with them at the same time?"

"All in the same house. It was a farmhouse. On Diamond Island."

"And at night?"

"At night?"

"They—they would—how would they—"

"How would they—" I echoed, prettily feigning confusion at her confusion. . . .

"They slept—I suppose he moved from one—"

Inspiration came to me all at once, in a warm heap: "They all slept in the same bed."

"Dear sweet Lord," Meg murmured and, drawing back from me, actually placed a hand behind her to steady herself. In doing so, she dislodged one of the little model cars on the bookcase, sending it plunging earthward. There was the most delicate of rending sounds—what you might hear if you snapped a grasshopper's leg in two—followed by a heart-ruptured moan: "Oh *no!*" She dropped to the floor.

I dropped to the floor beside her and withdrew from her clutching fingers the model car. It was a lime-green convertible. The bar at the top of the windshield had shattered.

"I can fix it," I told her grandly.

"You can fix it?"

"Certainly I can fix it."

Both of us were still squatting. This was the moment, unmistakably it was, and I placed my hands upon her shoulders and, in a rush born partly by an off-balance forward toppling of my weight, set my lips firmly upon hers and held them there, one, two, three.

I was more moved by what I'd done than I had reason to be, perhaps—my blood was racketing in my veins—and yet I had sufficient wits about me that when, with one hand clutching the cross between her breasts and the other rubbing at her lips, as though the effects of me might yet be effaced, Meg sighed, "Dear Jesus Christ," I replied, "No, no. Just Edgar, my dear."

I dropped from my squat to my knees, steadying myself, and, again planting my hands on her ample shoulders, worked her to her knees as well. We might have been preparing for prayer. This time when I kissed her I took the weight of her breasts in my hands. In the strained, squeezed-out cry that escaped her there was no telling whether the dominant emotion was shock or agony or relief or fear.

13

Rut Loses Something

In almost every situation there's at least one way out, an escape from the forces hemming you in on every side, only it must be seized at quickly—quickly and deftly and audaciously—as was true for Jason in the old Greek myth, who, Scylla menacing him on one side and Charybdis on the other, divined that the way past them was in fact the way through them, and therefore plunged his ship the *Argo* straight in, taking so clean and daring a course that he won his way through to the sun and safety on the other side. . . . If in Copenhagen he wasn't as easy in his mind as he knew he ought to be and often pretended to be, yet on his return to Freeland—a month's vacation—a sense of rightness followed him everywhere. Just like that: doubt left him. And if perhaps he wasn't finally destined to be a clerk for The Great Danish Steamship Company in Copenhagen, he was absolutely meant to return to Thorskrist as a person of obvious eminence and visible promise. Money jingled in his pockets as never before. He had new, dazzling clothes on his back. He had become a personage to consult. The old and the young looked to him for reports. Whither the price of salt cod? Would the market for wool hold up? Was it true that a touch of lunacy ran through the Danish royal family? Who drank more—the Germans or the French?

He would arrive at Gisli's Cakehouse early in the morning and casually select a table. There he would sit, in his beautiful new rust-brown three-piece suit, a gold pocket-watch dangling from a belt loop. He would bring with him a magazine, a Danish newsweekly, but often wouldn't be allowed to make his way uninterrupted through a single page. Bashfully, eagerly, others would approach his table. Young boys, net-faced ancient fishermen, whispering housewives . . . Did he require any more coffee? Or a sweet-roll, temptingly smothered in a white-sugar glaze, into which lovely crunchy black raisins had been strategically placed?

The invitations came like freshets at thaw-time. Did he want to go riding? How about fishing? What about a small party, featuring an endless reservoir of the finest *brugga* and a beautiful leg of lamb, smoked to perfection? A dance? How about a dance?

All the women were pursuing him. . . . The teenagers came at him shyly and hopelessly, with hand-muffled giggles and pretty tosses of the head. Those his own age were more forthcoming. But still more forthcoming were the old crones, who saw in him just the match for their niece, their neighbor's daughter, their accomplished granddaughter. Had he ever met, did he perhaps recall, vivacious Aslaug, who has filled out so beautifully? Magnificent Eyglo? Incomparable Drofn, the pride of Sand-gilsheath? Lovely Una, whose father'd recently erected a handsome new barn? Charming Bjork, who sings like a lark?

He carried a little alligator-skin-bound book reserved—oh, the wonder it incited!—for his personal appointments. Would it be possible for him to come around to meet old Yrr Magnusdottir's niece Swana on Thursday at four, when there might be a cake waiting for him? *Thursday at four . . . Let me just consult my book.* . . . This Saturday afternoon, Sveirir Brynjolfs-son, whose daughter by the way . . . *Saturday afternoon, let me see . . .*

And yet it wasn't as though he lost sight of where his true obligations lay; he was no mere vain peacock slighting all thought of duty. Didn't he make his way over to the Superior School to visit old Thorgunnur, appearing one afternoon in his magnificent rust-brown three-piece suit just as the children were fleeing the place? He strode against the tide of them—a giant among them—and arrived just as she was gathering up the books on her desk. It was pleasing to behold, in this city in which so many landmarks had dwindled, that Thorgunnur was as prepossessing as ever—she was, herself, a giantess. "Teacher," he called from the doorway, "I haven't done my homework," and out came the scowl he'd hoped for.

The scowl lingered, however, which disconcerted him until he remembered her failing eyesight. "I have returned from Copenhagen," he said.

"Hannibal!" she cried. "I've long expected you."

He bounded toward her, meaning to bestow upon her a kiss of greeting—he was bringing to Freeland a Continental lavishness with kisses—

but her eyesight was not so dim that, catching sight of his intentions, she didn't wave him peremptorily toward the rows of desks. He took a seat. Instantly, he might have been her pupil once more.

"And how are you, my boy?" she asked him. In Danish.

"I am fine, I am fine," he answered. In booming Freelandic.

"Tell me, tell me of your life," she said. Again in Danish.

Well, of course: another oral examination. And so he spoke to her in Danish, recounting for her a little about his travels, his arrival in Thorskrist, the weather—

She cut him off in mid-sentence, with a contented shake of her head. "You've mastered the language," she said. "Finally."

"I didn't always complete my homework."

"You got it done in the end."

He sat at a schooldesk and, good pupil that he was, informed her about his promotion, his apartment, his visit to Switzerland. "I'm going to stay a while longer in Copenhagen," he concluded.

"That's as it should be. You were meant to go away."

"I'm not sure I'll ever come back, back for good," he said—words that left odd, unsettling echoes in the air. The classroom had a partial view of Great Blue Mountain: its rising northern slope. All his years in this room, how many times had he looked across White Seal Bay and found the crest of Great Blue hidden? To see it in entirety—he remembered now—you had to lean right up against the window and place your nose against the glass.

"Oh you'll come back," old Thorgunnur declared—words still more odd and unsettling. The truth was that in his heart Hannibal husbanded all sorts of venerable Freelandic superstitions about prophetic women— seeresses. You came to a woman like Thorgunnur not for chat but for consultations.

"I don't see what opportunities I would have here."

Her reply rebounded back: "Of course you don't. For that is your quest, isn't it?"

Was there another word in the language that thrilled him so wholly as *quest*? Not *riches* or *honor* or *cunt* or *immortality* . . . Thorgunnur in her surefooted way had hit on the word precisely. She spoke so confidently about his forward fumblings—surely she might, if she wished, elucidate his life for him.

"I had a letter from that friend of yours," she said.

"Friend?"

"The little one. The dark one."

"Oh, Eggert. Yes. Come to think of it, I think I owe him a letter. Or a couple letters . . ."

"He reports that he is writing *poetry*," old Thorgunnur huffed, with a scorn perhaps unexpected in someone who had given her life to cultivating literature in the minds of the young.

"Oh, Eggi, yes," Hannibal countered cheerfully. "He's wildly ambitious: plays, novels, poems. He says he's going to bring modern literature to Freeland."

"I should think we have plenty of literature already."

"You mean the Sagas?"

"The Sagas of course. We're a small country, Hannibal. The Sagas are far, far larger than we are."

An old mischief stirs in Hannibal's breast. It is a mark of his privileged status that he's permitted to goad her, gently. He says, "But the Sagas belong to the Icelanders, teacher."

Old Thorgunnur upthrusts the prow of her nose: "They were written by Norsemen, by peripatetic Vikings who happened to jot down their thoughts while sojourning on Icelandic soil. The language they wrote in, Old Norse, is of course far closer to Freelandic than to Icelandic—or for that matter to Danish or Norwegian or Swedish. No, the Sagas, including our very own *Freeland Saga*, 'belong' to the Icelanders only in the legal sense; they have them in hand and won't relinquish them. But they *belong* to us. Never forget it, Hannibal: we are as close to the anonymous writers who told of Burnt Njal and Egil and Grettir the Strong as it is possible to be after seven hundred years."

"I won't forget." He adds, impulsively, "That's part of my quest."

What does he mean by this, exactly? He hasn't a clue and yet to judge from her hearty confirming nod he has voiced a far-reaching and subtle truth.

And then this woman who just moments before had spoken dismissively of poetry utters a line that is as gnomic, as nornlike, as intricate an interlacing of meaning and mystery as is achieved by only the highest verse. She declares: "When you come back to close the circle, Hannibal, you will discover it will not close. But in the gap there, where the circle almost closes, that's the place where the truth will emerge. . . ."

These are words to ponder—even as he must also ponder, fleetingly, whether there might be some basis to those occasional unkind rumors about the old girl's having gone off her nut at last. . . . He was attempting to close a circle, anyway, when, two days before departure, he found himself walking with Rut Bjartardottir at the base of Great Blue. It was here he'd brought her on Olympic Night, six medals of gold dangling on his chest. He was similarly resplendent this time around, in his princely rustbrown suit. He told himself that this visit to Rut was an afterthought—hadn't he waited until the penultimate day before departure to look her up? Yet even so, the girl was an afterthought he'd given much forethought to; she'd been constantly on his mind. He'd repeatedly seen himself doing just what he was doing now, and looking as he was looking now: seen himself, that is, altogether splendid in his handsome three-piece rustbrown suit, walking with Rut Bjartardottir along the base of Great Blue. Well, he'd kept up his end perfectly . . . but Rut was another matter.

Could it be that, for this young woman, the bloom was already ever so slightly off the rose? Or—more likely—was it a matter of Copenhagen's having schooled him to view her as a more discriminating world would view her: an impoverished, uncultured farm girl raised at the chilly, winddenuded ends of the earth. Her breasts were still high and broad, but it seemed her skin had lost some freshness—become more like dough than milk—and the cast in her eye grown more pronounced. Her reticence had enchanted him once, but now her limited range of conversation, her faint sullenness, her shocking lack of curiosity—these seemed less the expression of a charming self-possession than the product of a pinched provincialism. He explained to her about Copenhagen, about Danish Steamship's plans for expansion, his trip to Switzerland—was she listening at all?

"Now tell me," he said, after he had rattled on for a while, each of the avenues of conversation having concluded, inexplicably, in a cul-de-sac, "about your life."

"Mine?" She laughed at him.

"What has been happening with you?"

"With me? Nothing—nothing," she cried.

"But there must be new things. Nothing ever stays exactly the same on a farm."

"My father bought a new cow," she said.

"A new cow. Well that's splendid. And what's her name?"

"Titla."

"A splendid name. Is she a good milker?"

"Milk? I hardly know. She is the most intelligent cow in the world, though."

"Well that is splendid, that is marvelous!" Was she having him on?

"Last Christmas, I decided to prepare her. So, a week before Christmas Day, when I go to her in the morning, I hold up seven fingers. 'Seven,' I say to her. 'Seven, seven, seven.' "

Rut's face had brightened. Yes, she was as pretty and vivacious as ever. The sun—it was a patchy, cloud-scattered day—approved of her, emerging to light her hands as she held up for Hannibal's inspection seven white, long, plump fingers.

"And the next day, when I go out to her in the morning I chant, 'Six, six, six,' and I hold them up." Rut lifted six fingers.

"And the next day I hold up five and chant, 'Five, five, five.' And four the next day—'Four, four, four.' And three the next—'Three, three, three.' And the next day two and I say, 'Two, two, two, two.' And the next day I hold out one finger and I say, 'Titla, old girl, tomorrow is Christmas, and I shall tie a bell to your tail now and tomorrow I want you to ring the bell to show me you understand it's Christmas morning.' And you know what? The next day I hardly step into the barn when I hear *ring, ring, ring, ring, ring!* She knew, the old girl knew. . . ."

Surely Rut was having him on? He bantered back at her: "I'll bet the smartest cow in the world would make good eating."

As it happened, it was the wrong thing to say. Rut's face went dark, her eyes crossed hopelessly. And the sun itself registered disapproval of dapper Hannibal by ducking its head behind a cloud.

"I'd like to meet your cow," he offered by way of reparation.

"You can't," Rut said.

"And why can't I?"

"Because—" She paused reflectively. "Because she's dead."

"Dead? When did she die?"

"Last week," Rut said. "Worms crawled out of her nose."

"I'm sorry," he said.

"Animals die," Rut noted cruelly, and, more cruelly still, she added, parroting him, "Nothing ever stays exactly the same on a farm."

"And how is your father?" Hannibal asked.

"Father is well." She pondered a moment, dipped her head from one side to the other, as if to gauge him from each of her imbalanced eyes, and said, "He is going to build us a proper home."

"A proper home?"

"A proper home with two stories and doors on brass hinges and windows in every room."

"A proper home?" Had she not mocked him a moment ago, Hannibal might not have pointed out the harsh but obvious truth: "But he'll never do it."

Old Bjartur Jonsson was as tough and hard-working and self-sacrificing as any Freelander alive, but he was one of those luckless old muckshovelers who, battling for independence his whole life, had nothing more to show for it than a couple dozen sheep and a listing turf-roofed hovel that looked ready to collapse in the first good storm of winter.

Rut's eyes blazed up: "*Never do it!* If Father says he will do something, then of course he will do it! And that's that. He has promised to build me a proper home."

"But how will he pay for a two-story house with brass hinges and windows in every room, I ask you?"

"It might just interest you to know"—oh, she was furious with him!—"that in Thorskrist there are powerful men who have more faith in Father than you do. They are businessmen like you, even if they don't put on a fancy manure-colored suit before taking a walk through the mud, and they have offered him credit."

"Credit? Many's the farmer who wound up on the parish after he accepted that."

"If you think Father's going to wind up a pauper, I have nothing more to say to you. . . ."

And Rut was ready to walk off, to leave him—just like that. Hannibal was either going to speak conciliatory words, or none at all; she would be gone. So he said, "There's no tougher man alive than your father. I've worked beside him. Sixteen-hour days out there with a scythe, one after another, trying to get the hay in before the rains."

And Rut was apparently mollified. She said, which was quite a concession, after all, "Father says you're one of the few young ones who actually knows how to fit a day's work into a day. . . ."

Hannibal tried to exploit this shift in her tone: "I've thought of you often," he said.

"Of me?" And she shifted her tone once more: she snorted with laughter.

"Have you thought of me?"

"Not often. Life is very busy on the farm."

"And when I've thought of you do you know what I've thought?" Hannibal halted. She was intended to halt with him, to gaze up into his eyes. But she kept right on walking down the path. He watched the blond braid tap-tapping on her back and cried after her, after it, "I've thought that you are very beautiful."

"Beautiful?" She snorted again without bothering to turn round.

"And on those occasions when you *have* thought of me," he continued, striding forward with long steps to lay a hand upon her shoulder, "what have you thought?"

He knew enough, this time, not to attempt to swing her around. She must come around of her own accord. Rut looked up into his eyes, her own eyes dancing, and she said, "I've thought you're amazingly arrogant."

"Arrogant?"

How in the world, just how in the *world* could she ever have concluded such a thing? Did she truly fail to understand that he knew his place precisely? He was descended from men who, without motors or radios, had explored unmapped northern seas whose waters are so cold the drowned never rise to the surface: the buoyant gases of decomposition fail to form. He was descended from Erik the Red and Leif Eriksson, as well as Njal Thorgeirsson, who would sooner be burned alive than surrender, and Grettir the Strong, who survived nineteen years of outlawry. Oh, he knew his limitations: he felt—daily—the full heartbreaking extent of his falling short. . . . Arrogant!

She said: "I remember that day, the Olympic Day, when you won the last race, the Long Race, and there it was all over your face: you were the most arrogant boy I'd ever laid eyes upon."

"But the last race—the last—but you didn't—you—you didn't even *see* the last race." It was as though a sandstorm had blow up in his brain, hurling grit everywhere; he couldn't, for the moment, find his way clear of her words. "You'd gone home."

Rut hesitated. "I did go home. But I happened to come back. I'd lost something. I came back to look for it."

"Lost something?"

"A glove."

"Oh but that was a very warm day," Hannibal pointed out. And a calm settled upon him, the sun broke through. What a shameless little fox she was. . . . "No one was wearing gloves."

"Maybe it was my lunch sack—that's what I'd forgotten."

"But you'd gone home for lunch. . . ."

"I can't remember," Rut cried.

"No?"

"It was a long time ago. . . ."

The words pricked and tore inside him, like a needle snagged in the muscle of his heart. Olympic Day wasn't such a *long time ago*—just a few years!—and yet for him, too, the day of his purest triumphs felt remote. In a changed, throatier voice he told her, "I meant what I said. I think you're beautiful."

Her eyes held his eyes. Her crossed gaze was naturally difficult to construe, but he sensed within it a wavering, as if she were weighing divergent responses. What she said was, "And I think you're arrogant."

He went on, unperturbed, "I've seen the finest women in Copenhagen. I went to the opera in the Royal Theater. I went to a reception at the French embassy and drank nine glasses of champagne. So I know what I'm talking about. I have a basis for judgment when I tell you you're lovely."

Her eyes held his. "And I have a basis for judgment, too. I have lived around men all my life. I think you're pompous and conceited."

"What would you have me say?" he went on earnestly. He had taken her hands. Surprisingly, she had not withdrawn them. "Should I lie to you? Tell you you remind me of a muddy sow? That you remind me of some old, flea-bitten, milkless cow?"

Her eyes brightened. She squeezed his hands. "You're a strutting rooster whose neck's about to be wrung by the old grandmother of the farm. You're the fish that ate the plastic worm!"

"And you? You're a freshly sheared sheep rolling in the muck to restore its sense of cover," Hannibal said. "You're a beached, putrid whale that must be burned to chase its stink away."

The lights of the entire landscape had entered into the lusters of her face: the bent, hooked glints upon the stones and upon the sea, the bright candlelike tufts of the cotton grass and the blazing crystal mass of Great Blue Glacier. Her hands squeezed his. He had reached her: at last he had reached her.

"You in your fine suit, you're a baby seal that one of our children will club and skin. You're a skinned rabbit. . . ."

And now arrived the moment when, having reached her, having clasped her hands in his hands, General Hannibal showed his flash of tactical genius. He redeployed his troops and switched directions: "And you, my darling? You're an angel. You are a vision to make Ivory Frida redden in jealousy. You are a portrait painted on ivory that a knight carries in a locket. . . ."

The switch totally upended the girl. Her hands jerked in his, but he held them tight. "You're a pail of rotting fish," she declared, hoping to lure him back onto familiar ground.

But she was not going to lead him—he was not going to be led. At last he knew where he was going: "You are the girl in the locket that the knight carries as he battles dragons and trolls and witches for her sweet sake. You are the princess for whom he ventures into Devil's Wood. You are Guinevere, you are the Lady of the Lake."

"You're the dead rat at the bottom of the wharf," Rut called—hopefully, desperately.

Hannibal swung his forces around and hit her again smartly on the other flank: "You're the blood sausage that has burst its casing. You're the roach floating in the soup."

He had let go of her hands to seize her upper arms, which were young and full and beautifully strong enough to break a man's nose. He eased his hands across her shoulders to her breasts—young and strong and full as well. Her eyes were afire.

"Drowned dog," she faltered. "You—you're nothing but a dumb drowned *dog*."

And he shifts on her once more. He need no longer pay the slightest attention to what issues from his throat, since the tongue of the poet speaks within him now: "And you are a creature of roses and cotton grass and rainbows. You are the milk in the green hay. You are the girl who stepped from behind the waterfall to enthrall a pilgrim's heart."

"Butchered pig," she mutters feebly. She is in full retreat—falling into disarray, repetition. "Rotten fish."

As lightly as his words trip off his tongue his fingers slip up the back of her dress. The buttons come undone at a touch. He need do no more than graze them with his fingertips—they unbutton themselves. Her clothes, one by one, fall away with a will of their own and Rut Bjartardottir, in all her blue-veined flesh–packed whiteness, as bare as at God's creation, stands shivering in his arms.

"Stinking bear," she pleads. "Stinking, stinking, *stinking* bear."

And now he summons as witnesses to the act they are contemplating animals these islands have never seen, near-imaginary creatures of mythical squalor: "My mud-wallowing hippopotamus," he chants. "My farting camel." And holding the girl in his arms, he lets go of reality entirely: "My slippery swamp-serpent. My monkey-skinned weasel."

He pulls off his jersey to make for her a bed of sorts and he lies beside her, just off the path. The smell of mud is overtakingly sweet; it is as though someone has lifted away the whole front of his face, and for the first time in his life his brain takes in the smells directly, rawly, unfiltered by his nose. Her body is ready for him and yet she shudders, clenching deeply, folding in on herself when he enters her. After a moment he halts, props himself on his elbows, looks down and realizes their genitals are aswim in blood. "It's your first time," he whispers.

"Mm?" Rut is far away.

"Your first time—" The words fill his mouth, his head—they fill him as much as, more than, he could ever possibly fill her. . . .

Her eyes drift open, toward the light. Her voice struggles to find its familiar farm-girl fierceness. "Isn't," she protests. "This—this," she says. "Done this—this lots of times . . ."

Oh, it's apparent she'd rather he took her for a harbor whore, some old hand who led the drunkest of sailors to a filthy cot, than for what indeed she is: a newcomer to this prickling form of exchange, this misted meeting of limb with limb. "Oh my angel," he cries, descending once more upon her, breathing his wonder into her hair, into the mud at the base of Blue Mountain. "Oh fairest *fair* creature. Vision of visions. Vision of vision of visions," Hannibal sings.

14

The Dump of the Kingdom

"Once more. Huh? It's a question of deepening our acquaintance," Hannibal began.

"This one runs deep enough as it is."

"But it has to be freshened," he insisted. "Come on. One more time."

"And why should I? What's in it for me?"

"In it? We're in it together. Our fates are meshed."

"God help me," I said.

"Today's the day, Eggi. We're going to rediscover Freeland."

"Today's the day, Hanni. I'm going to stay home and nurse a bottle of vodka. You look horrible, by the way."

"I feel marvelous."

Did Hannibal feel marvelous? His voice was big and bright. He was wearing a freshly laundered white shirt. He smelled powerfully of cheap aftershave.

And he looked horrible. Last night he'd broken the news to Rut about his plans to run for reelection, and although I'd been treated this morning only to an abbreviated, close-mouthed account, it was apparent she hadn't "come round." But was he intending to brood over it? Was he about to unveil doubts, reservations, second thoughts? Perhaps even entertain the notion of relinquishing this doomed new political ambition? No, he had identified this morning—a perversely bright and cheerful Sunday morning—as a perfect opportunity to "rub shoulders with our voters." We were going to get the "feel of the country." We were going to take a walk through the Silfurnama.

In the mid-eighties, the country's first underground municipal parking garage was constructed, near City Hall, in downtown Thorskrist. On weekdays it tended to fill up aggressively—surely the last two survivors on the planet will, in the year A.D. 3066, battle to the death over a parking place—but on weekends it stood empty. One day, an enterprising young man, Albert Salvarsson—"Albert the disco millionaire" as the newspapers called him, an epithet offered, I'm afraid, not in ridicule but in admiration—presented our municipal authorities with a peculiar proposal: he wanted to rent the garage on Sunday mornings.

The "disco millionaire," who owned a string of places with names like The Hole and The Dead Parrot and False Friends, wanted to rent the garage on Sunday mornings? What was he going to do, open up a Sunday morning disco, ha ha ha? Obviously he'd gone soft in the head, all that racketing music had pounded his brains to mush, and from the city's standpoint, this was a boon and a windfall, this was found money—seize it, before the blockhead sobers up. And so, much to the subsequent mortification of certain politicians—most notably, Hannibal Hannibalsson—it came to pass that the city had for ten years leased away, for a pittance, the rights to a gold mine. Or silver mine, for that's what Albert called it: Silfurnama.

What did Albert do with his deserted underground parking lot? He set up a flea market. Here, sheltered from the slamming give-and-take of Freelandic weather, anyone and everyone wanting to rent a table from Albert could do so. They lined up in droves outside his office door. They'd waited for years, it seemed—hoarding until now their hobo bundles of curios and gewgaws.

You might suppose that Hannibal, having been finessed so disastrously, would have been too abashed to show his face at the Silfurnama. Nothing like it. The place held for him a perverse attraction: he felt there the "pulse of the country." He found it as energizing as I did deadening, for in truth the place disheartened me, pointing up as it did just what dupes and gulls my countrymen had always been. But grumbling, remonstrating, on this bright Sunday morning I went along.

I would like to think there was a time in my nation's history when we were still largely free of all the clutter of the world's castoffs, its knick-knacks, its bric-a-brac. But if ever there was such a time, those days are long gone. Though in the world's eyes we lie at the ends of the earth, we are spared nothing. In recent decades the globe has become so manically fertile in this area—in junk production—that no country on earth can remain untouched. Some days, I feel sure it's the defining trait of our era: ours has become a world of such powerful manufacturing capabilities that the streets of even its remotest outposts are lined with imported garbage. Ambling through the Silfurnama, you'd swear that Freeland has become a sort of dump-of-last-resort, the site where the very shoddiest and stupidest products come finally to stay, there being no remote people still more be-nighted upon whom these things can be foisted. Hence, we're reduced in the end to shuffling them among ourselves—these Korean-made Martian dolls whose antennae rise at the touch of a remote-control device; these Mexican car-fresheners available in male and female scents, the former providing a "rugged whiff of spice and pine," the latter an "ultra feminine exhale of lilac"; these balky ballpoint pens advertising a Miami-based company called Day-to-Data; these fluorescent kazoos; these jars of Colonel Khyber's rainbow tropical fruit relish. No doubt each of these objects has its own distinctive and far-flung story, and I suppose that's the Silfurnama's appeal for Hannibal: strolling in this menagerie of a flea mar-ket, he feels himself wired to crisscrossing networks of multinational com-merce. Look at this, Eggi—this electric corkscrew was manufactured in *Singapore!*

He exults and expands, visibly, just when you might expect him to doubt and to dwindle. A decade or so ago he and I traveled to Copen-hagen for a Nordic Cultural Summit—or some such preposterous enter-prise—and the Danes put on a show of lavish pomp and sumptuosity. I remember champagne and caviar and a limousine tour over to Roskil-deand and a multilevel department store with chandeliers and a tour of the royal castle with an appearance by King Frederik himself. As we flew back toward Freeland, the clouds thickened, night fell, lightning snapped and angled, and by the time we arrived, in the middle of the night, the wind was howling and spiteful hail was clattering against the windshield of my little Fiat, whose heater was broken. But as we crossed Spine Ridge and the scattered lights of Thorskrist came into view, Hannibal crowed: "Look at it, Eggi. Just *look* at it."

Yes, there it was, our weather-eaten capital, its shedlike houses of cor-rugated aluminum and cracked concrete twinkling feebly against the pounding hail. But in a voice whose concluding giggle could not wholly hide its megalomaniacal outreach, Hannibal went on: "Eggi, look how vast, how *vast* is our kingdom."

In the vast capital of our vast kingdom, the underground parking lot fills with people. The emporium of the imperium—the very treasure of the realm—is on display. Buy, buy—what would you buy? A seashell-encrusted candlesnuffer? A pair of brown wool blankets which, if perhaps not certifiable antiques, unquestionably date back a couple of decades? A water buffalo horn, carved by a guaranteed Thai artist into the likeness of an owl? An almost-matching pair of souvenir ashtrays from friendly Bulgaria? A bottle of guava concentrate? A bag of homegrown potatoes the size of brussels sprouts? Or a bag of brussels sprouts not much larger than good-sized peas?

Hannibal moved and mused, shook hands and called greetings. With each passing minute, he was looking less and less like death warmed over. The crowd had begun to work its old magic upon him: he'd begun to fluoresce. Nothing about this place depressed him, not even the elderly woman with the ear trumpet, Hallbera Valtysdottir, whose earthly wares consisted of a tin of Tetley Tea, twenty-something jars of Malaysian mixed citrus and fruit marmalade, seven cans of a Scottish antiperspirant called Mist o' the Morning, a gray cactus, three not-for-resale mini-packs of American cigarettes, a pair of what were in all likelihood her late husband's bifocals, some polycolored refrigerator magnets that spelled RANCE—only the initial F was missing—and a shrink-wrapped copy of Norman Mailer's *Harlot's Ghost*.

Limping along on his shattered knees Hannibal works the crowd—steps up to sample some pickled shark, stoops to examine a baby in a pram, pets a dog, pats the shoulder of a dotty old woman who confides that today is but six days from the twenty-ninth anniversary of the night when her Bjarni was drowned off Founders' Point, punches a high school swimming champion in the biceps, pinches admiringly a cellophane-wrapped wedge of salmon, swaps a couple of salty jokes with a pipe-smoking jack-tar, sweeps a six-year-old off her feet, the better to examine her new hair ribbon. He is followed, a few steps behind, by his truncated shadow, short dark Eggert, who cannot help marveling that his sunny friend is a sort of miracle worker. Can it truly be that the electorate will reject this man?

By the time the two of them step out into the street, they're both feeling a good deal better. "Fish, fish, fish," Hannibal chants. As it so often does, politicking has made him hungry.

They amble over to Valhalla and take a table by the window. While they're waiting for their plates of haddock to arrive, the most outlandish car in Freeland passes by—Vikram Jakobsson's custom-painted egg-yolk-yellow Mustang convertible. It was a sight that, by all rights, ought to have been hugely depressing: this young, aimless, brainless kid circling round and round the streets of Thorskrist with his top down, his radio blasting. And yet it wasn't. The world is full of things, Eggert has often remarked to himself, that have no business being depressing and yet are deeply so: children's choirs, gymnasts of either sex and any age, Christmas, sun-bathing, the coming of spring. All too rare, though, and the more valuable for their rarity, are experiences, like the sight of Vikram behind the wheel of his yellow Mustang, which hearten us unpredictably, illogically. In the end, Vikram was so *beautifully* brainless that one had to applaud his free-wheeling narcissism, his larky callowness. It's a joy to watch him navigate our streets, one moment slowing to a perambulator's pace and the next moment jamming his accelerator, suddenly hell-bent on escaping—like a miner in a cave-in, scrambling toward a patch of azure—a distant traffic light. In his car's movements we detect a tale of our country's boundless opportunity and beneficence. Dark-skinned Vikram, our adopted son, was brought as a child thousands and thousands of miles, from near-mythical Calcutta, in order to be clothed and sheltered here, to be reared and edu-cated here . . . all so that he might in the end cruise our streets in a blazing yellow Mustang convertible!

Hannibal and I were feeling cheered, something close to jubilant, and the white-on-white fare at Valhalla—boiled haddock in a cream sauce, boiled potatoes, a dab of snow-white cabbage in mayonnaise—further el-evated us. Voyaging to the other end of the spectrum, we ordered coffee.

As it happened, Vikram's disappearance was soon followed by the emergence of another odd and distinctively Freelandic sight: Odin Pals-son. He's the head of the Psychics Guild, a civic organization that—like the boys' swim club, the Women's Temperance Society, the International Freeland String Quartet, the International Youth of Tomorrow—receives a modest public subsidy. Ten years ago, which is to say two campaigns ago, Hannibal's hapless opponent, the late Thorthur Engilbertsson, had tried to make hay of the fact that public money was being squandered on "foolish-ness and superstition." But Hannibal had sensed then, as I hadn't, that the subsidy to the Psychics Guild wasn't any potential liability. It was an asset. It comforted the public to know that we were, apparently, the only nation in the world willing to fund a paranormal organization—a gesture con-necting us, somehow, to our glorious Viking heyday.

We watched Odin walk by. He's a staunch political ally—as he ought to be, given our financial support. Unfortunately, he's also a lunatic, who, although he can sometimes be cajoled to read tea leaves or a person's palm, prefers to work his divinations by way of objects "close to the body"—old shoes, undergarments, a soiled handkerchief. The very least he could do, it seems to me, is to look like a prophet. He could carry a staff or grow a towering beard—repay our generosity by becoming something of a tourist attraction. Instead, he wanders around in high-top tennis shoes and American athletic gear, which he never washes—the better, perhaps, to read his own future. All the same, he peers into Valhalla and grins at us. It's a gesture which might be taken—so, at least, we choose to take it—as an auspicious comment on the upcoming, still unannounced, candidacy.

"It was good to see your boy last night," Hannibal said.

"My boy?"

"Sindri."

"Not his sort of place, generally. The Cod's Head. I think he was giving his friend a tour. He's a great tour guide."

"And Lilja?"

"Lilja?"

"She's well?"

Hannibal always takes, it seems to me, a somewhat too healthy interest in my daughter. "She's very well. We're a thriving family."

And then my old muse, whom I hadn't glimpsed in weeks, enters Valhalla and nods fondly at me. Yes, it's sweet-faced Gudrun, for whom, like some lovestruck windup automaton, I paced the streets of Thorskrist night after night after night some four decades ago. How does she look today? Feebler, perhaps? How must it feel to be dying of a cancer so rare there's no word for it in your native language? She's accompanied by her husband, round-shouldered balding Baldur—a sweet fellow, too, in his way.

I watch her out of the corner of my eye. I'm hardly listening to Hannibal, who is now rattling on about *energy*—not, it turns out, petroleum, or kerosene, or our geothermal reserves, but the *personal* energy at the Silfurnama.

Hannibal goes on talking but my attention has been claimed by a table across the room. Food is eventually brought to it, and I realize that only Baldur's eating. Gudrun has ordered nothing but a cup of coffee. Has she no appetite? Is this another sign of illness?

I interrupt Hannibal. "Baldur and Gudrun have just come in."

"Oh?"

"She was my first muse," I tell him. He nods attentively, politely. He has heard all this before. "I asked her to marry me, you know. In so many words. And there she is instead with the man she chose in my place, who has failed at his every business venture, and now she's dying. It's odd to be sitting in a restaurant and to know that across the room sits your muse, who is quietly dying."

Hannibal deliberates, nods, drains his coffee cup in one long swallow. "Well I am no poet, Eggi. But you could say I had a muse, too."

"Mm?" What is he talking about?

"Mine is Rut Bjartardottir. And let me tell you, it's also queer to have your muse accept you, to live your life beside her, and then to find she ultimately abandons you. Your muse rejected you at the outset, mine accepted me. And I'm not at all sure, my friend, which is the odder arrangement in the end."

I thought for a moment. "When you spoke of your muse, you know who I thought you were going to say?"

"Mm?"

"Old Thorgunnur. And *she* hasn't abandoned you."

"No, worse yet. I've failed her."

"Failed her? Good heavens, you've become the country's *President*. What more could she possibly ask of her old student?"

"But she has charged me with a task."

"Oh, Christ," I said. "Not *The Freeland Saga*."

Hannibal nodded unhappily. "She wants me to get it back. From the Icelanders. It's not as though I haven't been trying."

"Get it back?"

"Didn't I lie on my belly on some frozen lake all one endless afternoon, ice fishing with their Minister of Culture?"

"Did you say, 'get it back'?"

"And when he got cold, I actually gave him my last flask of vodka. Wouldn't you think he'd feel beholden to me?"

"Get it back? It was never *ours*, Hanni."

"Whatever. Questions of right and wrong aside, the Icelanders don't want to relinquish it. It's worth too much. It's our bad luck that it happens to be a one-of-a-kind: the best-preserved, and far, far and away best-illustrated Saga manuscript in the world."

"Maybe they won't relinquish it for other reasons as well? Because it was written by one of their own? In their own country? About their own expedition?"

"Does that matter? In the end? Thorgunnur has charged me with a task. And she feels I've failed her. . . ."

We'd been feeling cheered? All that was gone. Cheer, jubilation, anticipation, elevation—these things had climbed into the backseat of a yellow Mustang convertible and roared out of town.

15

The Worst Thing Anyone
Ever Did to Anyone

Three snapshots:
    • Summer, 1986. Here's a glimpse of a middle-aged Eggert, rak-ishly leaning over the front desk of a posh hotel, chatting up the pretty receptionist. She presents him with his bill. He reaches into the inner pocket of his sports coat and, with a happy flourish, slaps down upon the counter a fat cellophane-wrapped stack of lunchmeat.
    • Fall, 1980. Eggert again, standing in a stranger's kitchen. He's emptying pricy cognac into his personal flask when a plump middle-aged Asian woman enters. Her eyes dilate in surprise, in shock, in mortifi-cation, and she retreats, buttocks first, back through the swinging door, bowing at him frantically.
    • Summer, 1960. Eggert as a boy-man, hurrying up the steps of a modest American home. As he nears the front door he throws a rattled hare-eyed glance up and down, up and down the street.
    What's the shared thread, what do the pictures have in common? All offer variations on the theme of Eggert the Thief, a role he plays with slinking but clumsy gusto.
    The hotel was one of Copenhagen's finest, and the pretty reception-ist was not a Dane but a Swede, just returned from a year in the States, where she'd been studying "international relations." Our conversation it-self might plausibly be described as something of a high-level international encounter; I was traveling in my role as Freeland's Ambassador to Den-mark. The hotel offered, included in the price of a room, a bountiful breakfast buffet, and earlier that morning, falling on the ham and the

salami, I'd surreptitiously assembled the innards of a lunchtime sandwich. The stack was so thick my fingers mistook it for my wallet.

The second snapshot? Taken in Tokyo. I'd come to Japan as a guest of the Institute for Better Whale Research. The name was something of a brazen misnomer, since the only research the Institute seemed to undertake involved feasibility studies to determine precisely how many yen a Japanese business executive dining on an expense account might feasibly pay for whale sushi. The ever-growing international furor against whaling—the imposition of various moratoria, the threat of rock-band-led boycotts—had inspired the Japanese to embrace, indiscriminately, global allies wherever they could be found. Suddenly, Icelanders, and even God-help-us Freelanders—whose whaling days peaked a hundred years ago—were being extended invitations to visit Japan for "fact-finding" visits.

Earlier that day, in my role as a fact finder, I'd been invited to some lectures on the "psychology of the whale"—an animal, it turned out, whose keenest ambition was to grace a sushi counter in the Ginza; these are creatures wholly dedicated to the principle of serving others by being served. Fearing that this educational event might unfold in a painfully dry state, I'd filled a flask with vodka, into which I'd made a few inroads in a men's room just before the lectures began. But the lectures had been brief, and the ensuing celebration, which boasted beer and sake and champagne and Scotch, had been lengthy, and the party had evolved into another party at a steak restaurant, and finally into an invitation—extended to a small group of hangers-on—to Mr. Naohiko Takagaki's house. Mr. Takagaki was the president of the Institute.

I had enough familiarity with Japan to know that home invitations of this sort are few and far between. Perhaps Mr. Takagaki was rebelliously drunk. Perhaps he was bowing to Western ways. Perhaps he'd wanted merely to show off his apartment—a "spread" by anyone's standards, and a palace to the Japanese. In any case, I'd wandered off in search of a toilet and somehow found my way into a kitchen, where I'd spotted an open bottle of VSOP Napoleon Cognac. It had been the work of a moment to empty my flask into the sink, rinse it out, and begin decanting the cognac into it. Of course it was just at that moment the woman entered—presumably Mrs. Takagaki—whose horror was perfectly understandable. She felt unspeakably ashamed at having done anything so heinous as to catch one of her guests pilfering her husband's liquor.

The third snapshot? I'm returning from my job at Buck's Eat Shop, glancing up and down the street for a glimpse of Michael. I should have a good forty-five minutes before his return, which means—unless I tarry too conscientiously over niceties—I can safely bed his wife twice by the time he mounts the porch with his heavy tread.

Oh, the jittery exhilaration of those days! I'd committed all sorts of acts in my life that might plausibly wind up with my getting my front teeth dislodged or a rib cracked or an eye blackened, but this was the first time I'd engaged in any pursuit that could well have concluded with my taking an andiron through the skullbone or a knife in the abdomen. I'd grown up! I liked Meg's nervousness, her religiosity, and all those scruples which, in being gradually overcome, proved to be so ticklishly piquant. She refused for a while to go near her marriage bed with me. In this, as in much else, I wore her down with a steady underhanded patience, and it's a pleasure even now to recall our first time in Michael's bed, and how, in those moments when my exultation was at its highest, I acknowledged my gratitude—though I was usually a nonverbal partner, communicating chiefly by grunts and sighs—with a hot string of obscenities in her licked-wet ear. We'd shattered some barrier together. Call it the bonds of decency. . . . Whatever, it was thrilling.

But in the end, surprisingly, the forbidden fruits were greater, their flavors richer and tarter and sweeter, within my own room, which of course was not my room and never would be my room it was the dead boy's it was Stevie's, and to strip naked there and to place body-things on and into body-things—a rushed and indiscriminate laying on and in of hands mouths ears buttocks nipples testes vulva—was to call up a treasured audience. We were exhibitionists, I suppose, choosing to perform serio-comic exercises in front of a ghost.

In truth, it mystifies me now, so many years later, how little I was able to stand back and survey the clear, cold dynamics of that affair. Where was my *brain*? Given how deep my obsession ran, and how strikingly unsentimental I was for a young man, how willing, even at that age, to acknowledge the ruthless self-interest behind most of my pursuits—wouldn't you think I'd have done a better job of identifying the game we played at? A woman bereft of a son symbolically takes on a new one, and as if to ensure that *this* one never abandons her, she clasps him to her bed; a young man whose entire life's been colored by a sense of parental abandonment locates a new family where the father can be hoodwinked and the mother outmaneuvered. Why couldn't I see even this much? My understanding, back then, extended little ways beyond an awareness of an underlying rage. . . .

But what a rage! It was the worst anger I'd ever known, my blood scorching my veins each time our little male ritual was enacted: *it's a dangerous town*, Michael would point out, and I needed to learn to protect myself, and then the sweaty grappling would begin. . . . And as he stooped apelike before me, arms asway, crazed eyes burning below his brow-ridges, I'd silently howl at him the most punishing declarations I could conceive of: *I was in your wife twice today, you drunken sloppy-stupid bastard*, and *Those are my privates you taste in your wife's kiss*. But I didn't even then recognize the obvious—that Michael no less than his wife had a kind of hunger for me. For him, too, I was a revenant. Repeatedly, regularly, he needed, in his cigarette-puffing, brain-pickling, doggerel-chanting way, literally to lay the ghost that stood before him, to wrestle his son once more to the ground and, in the guise of parental solicitude, of teaching self-sufficiency, to grind the doomed kid's head raw with his knuckles.

What ought I to say now except that I've learned to see my blindness more clearly? I remember one afternoon in my room when, arms laced round the back of Meg's plump thighs, I thrust her feet high into the air. Eggert the Marauder, eyes screwed tight, was having his way. Yet catching the feel of an abstraction below, he fluttered open his eyes and met in the woman's gaze a faraway look—which he, surreptitiously pivoting his head, followed up her legs to reveal, dangling between her low-arched, homely, yellow-callused feet, a model airplane. Hung from the ceiling. Stevie's. Wasn't Meg simultaneously giving herself to me and—her feet doing a little toe-pointed ballet in the air—sheltering from harm her son's model of Lindbergh's plane? I remember thinking—a joke so propulsively funny it hurtled me on toward climax—that it must be every woman's fantasy to have the *Spirit of St. Louis* between her legs. But still the import of it escaped me.

She was willing to take me on, or take me in, but what she seemed most to covet was the chance to stroke me. She might almost have been blind, the way she hungered for constant contact at the fingertips. She'd run her hands over and over over my pinched chest, my knotty legs, my bony hips, my feet, as though, weeks after our first illicit contact, still she couldn't believe in my presence. And in order to be obliging—though I've never been able, quite, to see the point of physical contact that is not orgasm bound—I would stroke her body: her heavy breasts, her lax wan belly, her plump upper arms and thighs.

How many hours did we spend in all, running hands over limbs? Enough, anyway, that the question's inescapable: what did it all add up to?

The lover naturally assumes they're imprinted on the brain, indelibly—these caresses. You will never lose them: and never lose that little unlatched cry of hers, in the back of the throat, when you first enter her; the particular responsive feel of this particular buttock in your hand, of this particular nipple against your tongue; the constellated cluster of reflections—three in one, two in the other—crystallizing in her eyes; the warm rising blood-sausage smell of your mingled bodies after withdrawal; that hesitancy in her speech which habitually beguiles the tongue-tip forward; the flutter of the eyelids, the shiver, the sigh that shifts deliciously into a yawn, the laughter at the end of the corridor. . . . And how much is actually retained? What do they achieve in terms of permanency, all of these touchings, all of these minimal, precious, unhygienic transfers of fluid? If today, miraculously, Meg were returned to me as she was, led into a bedroom where I awaited her blindfolded, would I in my sightlessness recognize her by her feel in my hands, by her smell, by the plunge of her breathing? Or would I—like the knight of a thousand folktales, or, for that matter, the traveling salesman of a thousand jokes—accept the familiar as the novel and exult in my newest conquest?

Not long ago, I was sitting at my study desk one wind-whipped day, morosely contemplating Blue Mountain, when it struck me: the woman was dead. Meg was dead. Although I sometimes joke with my daughter about my "poet's intuition," actually I'm a rarity among my superstitious countrymen in seldom making any claims of clairvoyance. But this time I knew it, *knew* it to a certitude: at some point in the past Meg's body had been boarded up, like a room behind shutters—she'd been boxed up and stored underground. The light of day had closed on the woman forever, and grief—pure grief, the sort that makes the very bones of your face hurt—overwhelmed me. I would have wished, even after all these years, to bid her farewell. Or would have wished her a different life. I would have wished her a different world—one where all our back-breaking, dangerous couplings provided her with some final refuge. In my dealings with women—as with the writing of books, the study of a language, the grasping of a landscape—I tend to place my faith in numbers. Too much faith, perhaps: I plot my literary output against the years, five books, ten, twenty, forty-nine; I annotate my daily block of Webster's *Seventh*; I set out systematically to master not only the specialized terms that describe my native land—sinters, erratics, steepdowns, pahoehoe lava, welded tuff, solifluction—but also the heights of its five tallest peaks, the approximate size of its glaciers, the fish catches in tons, and so forth. And yet, as regards women, whatever numbers I reach, I'm left finally to wonder—to wonder whether, blindfolded, I could identify the body that once was sun and moon to me.

Of course we're each in the end a body of numbers. Not long ago I read an article about the health care systems of the future. Each of us will effectively become an Everest of digits in the memory bank of a master computer. Our every internal organ will be surveyed by noninvasive probes, its location and precise millimetric size documented: our hearts, our livers, our prostates, our ovaries will be meticulously recorded, so that even the most minute alterations in shape or dimension can be promptly detected and investigated. Medical scientists will approach that tabulated Ideal in which, as in the biblical vision, the very hairs of our heads are numbered.

But what of someone for whom there is no more flux, no further additions or subtractions? Who was Meg McKaig? Oh she was an appealing, homely woman who, married to a vicious boozing lout, had lost the son who was sun and moon to her, and who, while passion stormed the room, used to lie on her back with her feet in the air, the *Spirit of St. Louis* cruising safely between her legs.

And who was Eggert Oddason, the dark body sprawled upon the fair, where was he in this? What was he up to?

—What he's always up to at such times: frantically, as his bony hips rutted, or rooted, he was ransacking his mind, chasing after the phrase that would lend some overarching coherence to it all. For that's what coitus has usually been for him—an internal, solitary groping after an elusive phrase. In all the accounts of sex he has pored over over the years, the ever more graphic novels arriving even from countries reputedly puritanical and straitlaced, he has repeatedly met up with the phenomenon of the "simultaneous climax"—man and woman exploding together like cannons, like fireworks, like rockets, like supernova. And oh, how he has wished those explosions would stop—enough, enough, *enough* he cries! It's a literary occurrence that, in its ubiquity, strikes him as both statistically implausible and—far the graver sin—psychologically dishonest. All these cannons and rockets and fireworks and supernova—what connection do they have with the act as he knows it? How's he supposed to match them up with what has always been for him a private scrambling search, his mind digging around like a hand rummaging through an overstuffed overcoat pocket for a slender, single key—only, in this case, it isn't even possible to say what the key consists of. . . .

Will it be a color? A landscape? A down-spiraling smell? More likely a phrase ... I remember once, at the conclusion of an extremely brief affair, being locked in one of those acts of love which, once launched, promise no exit. We were in my little hotel room—this was in Amsterdam—a dormer with a sloping roof, and my partner, like Meg, had her legs up, she had placed them on the tilted ceiling, and turning my head and seeing them rooted there, the looked-for phrase arrived, *Look where she's planted herself,* and with this vegetal metaphor my partner ramified, became something richer and larger than I could ever wholly embrace. . . . A savannah, a grove, a rain forest oozily at home with resinous beings like myself.

Sometimes I've gone off in quest of a color and probably, if I were a painter, the exploration would be a hunt after some rare tint, some happy juxtaposition of light and shade. I can imagine how the composer clambers up and down his black and white scales, seeking his missing tone—how the mapmaker's forever gauging the variable contours beneath him. For me, it's been a coupling of word with word, a search whose origins are pleasurably languid but whose finale is a thing of overrunning desperation—the mind like a trodden-on anthill, like a beehive riven by a logger's ax. The realization dawns: time is running out, physical release is imminent, yet the looked-for phrase still is nowhere to be found—and as far as I'm concerned the only vital meaning of "simultaneous orgasm" describes that moment when, as the lemminglike armies are tumbling through the vertiginous pass of the urethra into the abyss of another body, the mind seizes hard upon its phrase. Mind and body momentarily united—now *that* is togetherness.

Sometimes I jot the phrases down. Word-spills is what I've come to calling them in the shorthand of my journals, and stripped of their context they have a wan and meager look—much as our bodies do, or I suppose most of us feel our bodies do, who can only hope our purest acts of love will be accepted like valuable gifts indifferently wrapped. Some of my word-spills are tender near-nonsense phrases: *You're the world's warmest mitten* or *This beats all beauty.* And of course there are a good many self-disparagings: *I'll fill you with folly* and *You're home to the homely.* And little silly plays on words: *Yours is the jelly role* and *Into the shoot chute.* Actually, the sillier ones are for me the most heartening—testifying as they do to the somersaults in logic and taste I once, for an instant, experienced. I'm fondest of those in which I detect no sense at all—*numb as the gum-time, humbler*—or those absurd little puns which, in their single vital moment, seemed prodigies of felicitous compression, as when, one afternoon on Lyon Road, the word *fleshlight* went on in my head. It lights my way even now, I sense a way back, and once again a kind woman lets a homely, angry young man into her body, and he reaches out and discovers *To probe your caverns with a fleshlight.* . . . Oh, poor Meg—who once brought me to climax with the help of a grotesque rhyme: *Eat your Eggi, Meggy.* She touched me. I remember once touching *her*, on her large strawberry mark, which must have covered something like a hundred square centimeters on her right lower jaw and neck. "Does it hurt?" I asked her. "It looks as though it ought to hurt."

And speaking of compression? I glimpsed a human soul there, distilled, in the wincing squint of her eyes. "Well," she said. "Not to the touch."

Perhaps it says more about me than her, that I think of her as "poor Meg"—since I can scarcely think of anyone I've ever taken to bed as anything other than "poor so-and-so." What a pitiable business it is, being a lover to Eggert-the-Self-Despising. All the same, in Meg's case the "poor" is justly applied. It used to break my heart—even then, in my youth, when her situation's true heartbreak wasn't evident to me—to hear her endless fretting about her living room sofa. It was the *one good piece of furniture we have.* It was—more sweeping still—the *one good thing I have.* They'd bought it less than a year before, not long after Stevie died. It was the house's one furnishing of any value, and Michael was going to destroy it. Oh, she was sure he would!

Most nights, in a reek of cigarette smoke and whiskey, Michael fell asleep—passed out—upon it. Given all the cigarettes smoked in a boozy haze, it was a miracle, she said, it was one of the Lord's miracles—and at this point her fingers would stroke the crucifix round her neck—that he hadn't yet burned a big hole in the only decent thing she had. Night after night she would sit up with him downstairs, simply to ensure the couch's preservation.

Oh, it pulled my heart. . . . Here was a woman whose marriage was an unspeakable calamity; whose few good looks were going; who had lost her son; and the source of everything decent and presentable in her existence had come to be symbolized by a tawdry sofa. Oh, it pulled at me, to see her turn her face away whenever I'd hint at leaving Detroit. I must soon be moving on. . . . Once, one unseasonably chilly, autumnal afternoon when rain was overspilling the leaf-choked gutters, she said to me, "If you went away, would you take me with you, Eddie?"

The words simply hung there in the air. They didn't move—they had nowhere else to go.

What could I reply? For I saw in that moment just how pitiful it all was, just how cruel the world could be: that any woman would plausibly look on *me* as her lifeboat. In the pause that ensued, I'd like to think I read correctly the acknowledgment in her eyes of the impossibility of everything she asked. Otherwise, she might have called her Eddie a liar for saying, "Sure, Meggie, sure I would."

But there came a day when she went far beyond "poor Meg"—she became the victim of the Worst Thing Anyone Ever Did to Anybody. That's how I came to think of it. There was something else Michael had inflicted on her—something intimate and very deep—and at this point in my narrative I hesitate. I balk, wince, squirm. The whole business sounds so farcical—and yet why doesn't my heart respond as though to farce? Given my willingness to confess here to such a broad range of nastinesses, to all my selfishness and cruelty, why do I feel so much shame about something I'd played no part in? For this particular cruelty was Michael's doing. . . . We were in bed, Meg and I, I was stroking her naked back, and she made some reference to her private parts, calling them by a term—her spuggly—unfamiliar to me.

"Your what?" I said.

She blushed deeply, my Meg, who was in many ways such a prude, and yet blushed proudly as well. For it was something of a feat for her, my proud prude, to have spoken the word aloud.

Well, my own pride was likewise at stake: she had challenged my command of off-color American slang. The word shimmered provocatively.

I came alive with questions. Where had she heard the term? Was it common? Did she know anything about its origins?

Oh, she'd heard it from Michael, of course, and all she knew was that it belonged to the double-swears.

The double-swears?

Yes, the you know, the ones that are *doubly* bad, you mustn't say them ever, except perhaps maybe once in a while in bed with your husband.

The double-swears?

Yes, the double-swears. Maybe they don't have them in Freeland, in Freelandic? But they have them in English, the worse-than-swears.

There are others—other worse-than-swears? Can you tell me others?

Well, she blanched at this—blanched and reddened. But in the end, while my heart thumped loudly behind my ear, she gave them to me: the double-swears for sexual intercourse and anus and penis and cunnilingus and fellatio, the words that are far, far worse than those other words for such things. . . .

And of course it wasn't immediately clear to me, it took me a long while to divine the obvious truth: as God is my witness, he'd made them all up. Yes, mad Michael had invented his own intimate language, and pressed its vileness so convincingly upon his wife that she'd never breathed a word of it to any outsider until I came along.

Is the awfulness of what he'd done quite clear? Is it obvious why, even now, I wouldn't dream—couldn't bear—to inventory one further example of Michael McKaig's inventions? Has that "ugly" lurking in "spuggly" poked its sorry head yet in your face? The man who, deep in his cups, had recited for me Edgar Guest—"With your equipment they all began. / Get hold of yourself, and say: *I can*"—this man who fancied himself a poet, had converted his marital bedroom into a sort of unspeakably filthy limerick. . . . And I begin to rage. . . . But let us return to that couch that was the house's "one decent thing." For eventually there came a time when I was sitting regularly on it with the two of them. Most nights, I stayed in my room—reading, writing, scheming. But now an epochal event arrived: the first televised presidential debates. John Fitzgerald Kennedy, Senator from Massachusetts, and Richard M. Nixon, the Vice-President. This was history unfolding in a million different homes simultaneously, bathed within the spectral blue televisual glow of modern geopolitics, and I was urged to observe it.

And they were fascinating—those gruesome evenings. . . . For Kennedy's mere appearance, even diluted to a small and monochromatic screen, did something dangerous to Michael—charged him, heated him up. An *Irishman*, a Boston Irishman and a Catholic to boot, was running for the presidency of the United States, and *this was history, huh!* This was something monu-expletive-mental! Michael would take his whiskey in great gulps, eyes wide like a child's, hooting with laughter at a Kennedy witticism, sneering and pouting at a Nixon retort. He applauded and booed, clapped and cursed, pitching back and forth in his seat like a man rowing a boat. He was so keyed up, every debate must close with the observation that Detroit was a *rough town, Eddie,* and the apelike arms hanging down. . . . The foreigner's bony boyish head must again be knuckled raw.

Eggert, needless to say, distrusted Kennedy, and was hardly surprised, years later, when the Camelot erected by this bootlegger's son was exposed in all its gaudiness and treachery. Secretly, in his tight avid heart, Eggi liked Nixon—felt an immediate kinship with the man's solemn humbug and jumpy-eyed uneasiness.

On these evenings Michael would plunge even deeper than usual into the whiskey, eventually snoring away on the sofa with a mottled glow on his besotted features. I watched Meg once, looking older than her years, pluck a still-burning Lucky Strike from her dozing husband's hand. "He's going to," she said, shaking her head grimly. "I know he will. Going to burn a big black hole in the one thing of value in this house." I nodded grimly back. I felt even more certain of this than she. For I'd recently come up with a plan to ensure that he did.

16

Collared

I jumped when a key began its quiet icy probing at the lock. And instinctively dropped a concealing hand over my work.

My motions surprised me: something inside me was feeling far guiltier about what I was doing than I'd previously admitted to myself.

Only two people had keys to my apartment and my visitor must be either my son or my daughter. I called a hello but remained seated, waiting at my study desk.

The lightness of the footstep led me to picture Lilja in the doorway. When, instead, Sindri's narrow head slid into view, my morale sagged slightly. He's a good boy, and I'm fond of him, but I would have preferred Lilja at that moment.

"You're working," he said. He was dressed in black.

"Not really. Well maybe. I'm writing a speech for Hannibal."

"A farewell speech?"

The lie sprang from my lips so automatically I can't say I played any substantial role in its utterance: "Yes—something like that."

"He wasn't looking so well the other night. At Rut's."

"The other night, yes, I did see you there, Sindri. You should have come over and said hello. I don't bite."

"Hannibal looked ready to."

"He's a burdened man. But you had a friend with you. Looked foreign."

"Dag—he's Norwegian. He's a linguist."

I do have to say, to Sindri's credit, that his friends are almost invariably bright and bookish. In the last few years I've grown somewhat embittered about Sindri's generation. It's a feeling dating back at least to the moment when Hannibal, capitulating to widespread demands, accepted the idea of a "Youth Hour" three nights a week on Freeland's one, public television station—a disastrous decision, as he would now be the first to admit. If "Youth Hour" is ultimately nothing more than a thorn in our side, it has pricked us far more fiendishly and frequently than even I foresaw. To be fair to Sindri, the sort of young people I associate with "Youth Hour"— boys with bleached punk haircuts and particolored shirts, girls with glasses and cigarettes and military jackets—are not his typical companions. In his own way, he seems as estranged from all of that nonsense as I am.

I was willing, then, to give him credit where credit was due, but did he have to loiter in the doorway with quite that mixture of puppyish hopefulness and hangdog despair? For years now he'd been subjecting me to this—eyeing me with a yearning expectancy. He seemed always to be seeking assistance of some sort, but what more could I do for him? All along, dating back to his arrival in Freeland as a teenager, I'd provided whatever help I could. And hadn't I helped him as an adult, too, on the afternoon when, a grown man, he'd showed up in my study doorway bubbling over with childish, doomed talk about becoming a writer? Though it hurt me to do it, I'd let him know, forcibly, that he wasn't cut out for the writer's life. Had it not been for my advice, he might even now be floundering here and there, notebook in hand, a habitué of coffee shops, never having found the line of work he seems best suited for: he "does computers" for Freefiskur. He can hold his head up high. Now, if somebody were to say to him, Your forefathers for generations pulled fish from the cold and challenging sea, whereas you sit in an office and store fish catches in a computer, I would advise him to answer, *It is not everyone who finds, as I have, work matched to his temperament.*

On the other hand, I never admit to him that his work—his entire life—weighs upon my spirits. I am protecting him even now, you see. Still, a basic respect for candor requires me to confess that I would've preferred another career for the boy—and would have preferred a son who, having entered into his twenties, did not still loiter in my study doorway with eyes that murmur *Help me.*

"He really wasn't looking well," Sindri said.

"Who?"

"Hannibal."

"Wasn't looking well? What do you mean? What are you talking about?"

"The other night. At Rut's place."

"Oh *that* night. Well, he has a lot on his mind."

"*I'll* say."

"What do you mean by that?" I ask, perhaps a little astringently.

Sindri shrugs. "Well, everything. The economy. Unemployment. Drugs. People are talking about Freeland's first 'crime wave.' "

"Well, if that's what we're in the midst of, it's the work of you young people," I say, again perhaps a little pettishly. "We never should have given you 'Youth Hour.' "

In fact, we were outmaneuvered. When the opposition, whining about political bias at the television station, demanded "equal time" and "alternative programming," we stood firm. The station was independent and impartial, we declared, and there was an end to it. But they got round us by stirring up the kids, mounting petitions in the coffee shops and the discotheques, and this time, when they came back looking for "youth involvement," we caved in. We gave them an hour a night, three nights a week—Tuesdays, Thursdays, and Saturdays. Actually, that's even more time than it might first appear, it's effectively every other night, since Freeland has no television whatsoever on Mondays. That's our "family day."

And we wound up giving them carte blanche. What real harm could a couple of kids do, anyway? It turned out, though, that one of them, a mere boy in his early twenties, had spent a couple of years studying film at a California university and—to give the Devil his due—he was funny and mordant in ways that the old governmental television crew had never been. The attacks were flagrant but implicit: a cut from a shot of Hannibal's face, looking perhaps slightly booze-bloated at the end of a state dinner, to the glazed snout of a haddock on a block of ice; a cut from Rut emerging from the Cod's Head to a scavenging polar bear; my face juxtaposed with a spider's. There were free-for-all talk shows, where more than once I was called a fascist—which is accurate, anyway, to the extent that I don't think people who call me a fascist ought to be privileged with access to the airways.

But much the worst of the show is Ulvar's Puppettheater. It seems that my ever-indulgent native land, in one more of its misguided coddlings of the young, had awarded an educational grant to one Ulvar Ormsson—whose name, translated literally, means Wolf the son of Worm. He was allowed, for two years, to squander scarce taxpayer funds in the study of puppet theater in Strasbourg.

Now, having effectively robbed his countrymen for twenty-four months running, you might suppose Ulvar afterward wouldn't have dared show his face in his homeland. But he not only returned, he originated his five-minute puppet skits for "Youth Hour." I was sitting with Hannibal in my apartment on that first occasion when we both appeared in Puppettheater. Hannibal watched open-mouthed, more flabbergasted than angry when a wild-haired Viking, sporting an ahistorical bullhorn helmet, came limping into view. King Carthage. The skits are set in the Viking Age. I felt no amusement—none, only a frigid and murderous rage—when King Carthage's assistant sprang forward: a small, swart lickspittle of a man, who sports a spider in his hair and is occasionally given to a storm trooper's goose-stepping.

There are times when—unfairly, as I would be the first to acknowledge—I hold such affronts against Sindri. If only the boy were not so soft! If only those black clothes sought to look imposing rather than to make him invisible! He fails to understand—and in this regard, anyway, he is typical of his generation, he is marching shoulder to shoulder with Ulvar and all the bespectacled, ferocious women of "Youth Hour"—that Freeland will not be preserved unless it's fought for. They don't sense their own imperilment. The true friend of Freeland will undergo calumny and ridicule—will be depicted as a goose-stepping sycophant—in its defense.

I look down upon my notebook page and ponder the words most recently written there: "All the world may not be mindful of us. But all the world has need of us." Had I spoken the truth? Are these sentiments authentic? It seems they are. They would certainly be authentic when Hannibal declaimed them. Has anyone, ever, in the ten centuries of my country's history, believed so convincingly in its sacred mission? I had already planned the setting and the weather. The words would be spoken on Giant Island, where, according to legend, the founder of our country, Erik the Other, established his first homestead, in the year 990. A light breeze would be ruffling Hannibal's hair. In the background, limned by sunlight, Great Blue would weigh in with its mute but unshakable support.

I underwent a sudden shift of heart and inched toward a disclosure: "What would you say, Sindri-my-boy, if I told you the speech I'm working on isn't a farewell speech but an announcement that Hannibal will seek a fifth term?"

What sort of response was I looking for? Clearly I hadn't expected Sindri's gape of incredulity: "But he can't. . . ."

"Can't? And why not? The Constitution sets no limit on the number of terms the President may serve."

"But he *can't*. . . ."

I didn't fully fight down my annoyance. "And why in hell not? Speak up, son."

"Well, all the—just think . . . Think what they'll do to him. Think how they'll go after him. And you, too, Father."

Was this genuine—his concern for my well-being? In any case, it mollified me somewhat. "We've taken our share of fire in the past," I reminded him.

"He's going to look ridiculous. Last time around, he must have said it a hundred times: *I will never ask for your vote again*. You remember . . ."

Oh, I did. I'd written a good many of the lines myself. *4 × 5 = Prosperity* and *The last five is the best five* and *This time I'm fishing for votes; next election I'll be fishing for trout*. "Politics," I declared, "is an inherently volatile profession. Surely you understand that."

Sindri nodded. "Yes, but I'm not sure you understand"—and with this hint of a rebuke, temperate as it was, his eyes dropped unsurely to the floor—"something has changed in these last few years. Freeland has changed. When I was a kid, Hannibal really was a sort of God to us—to the kids. But in the last few years, I don't know if it's the effect of 'Youth Hour' or what, maybe just time passing and his getting older and a bit more, more—" Sindri faltered and began again: "Among the young he's seen as—well, as something of a national embarrassment. He has these sterling principles, yes, nobody denies that, but the grandiosity is, well, it's—how do *you* feel, Father, when he threatens to cut off trade with the U.S. over its foreign policy? Or when he threatens to embargo Japan?"

"Surely you see, Sindri, that principles are not a matter of wealth or might."

"Oh I do. I do see it. But surely you see"—and he was looking me square in the face now, the green ladykiller's eyes ablaze in the comely mortician's face—"that there's something *ludicrous* in our threatening to embargo French goods because of their nuclear testing in the Pacific. Our letter reaches Paris, and some *fonctionnaire* is momentarily left wondering if Freeland is maybe a new African nation, one of their former colonies? Or is Freeland one of the actual atolls threatened by the tests? It's mortifying."

"Freeland is a cause I believe in," I said.

"It's a cause I believe in too," Sindri countered.

"So let me ask you again: what would you think if I told you I wasn't writing a farewell speech but an announcement that Hannibal's seeking a fifth term?"

During the messy pause that succeeded my question I felt, for maybe the first time in my life, a fear of my son's sliding out of the reach of my control. It shook me—chilled me. Hence, when he offered words that were not a full endorsement of my position, perhaps, but were a statement of some deference, nonetheless, when he said, "I would answer, *I wish you both well*," I responded warmly. I said, "I'm grateful to you."

We eyed each other. "And work is proceeding all right?" I ask the boy.

"I have no major complaints."

"That's good. I'm proud of you."

"On the other hand, there are times—well, let's put it this way: I am determined it won't consume my real life."

"But you do want to keep your eye on the job. That's a good boy."

"In fact, I've begun to feel I might have a wholly different life. . . ."

"A different life?"

"Well, I feel as though—" Sindri hesitates, regards me with those ever-pleading eyes. When in the world will he learn to conclude a sentence? "In fact, the truth, the nub of it is, you see—"

I sense in the boy's fumblings the imminent arrival of some unwise and utterly disheartening disclosure—some impossibly far-flung aspiration, some poignantly unrealistic self-appraisal—and to spare him, as well as myself, I interrupt: "No doubt any job takes some getting used to." I add, "So what brings you here tonight? Just come round to see what it is your old dad's working on?"

"It was Lilja actually. I'm looking for her," Sindri says, and at that very moment—as if clairvoyantly, as if to demonstrate the almost unnerving affinity the two of them share—a key turns in the lock. "We're going out to a party."

"The party's in here," I call to the girl.

Lilja appears and she's wearing, I'm afraid, soiled blue jeans and a military jacket. What would a pop sociologist make of youthful fashion in Freeland, in which the boys are the peacocks, in their floral prints, their pastels, their fancy Italian shoes, and the girls favor a pared, paramilitary look? And what would a psychologist make of Sindri's contrary habit of donning undertaker's black? Lilja nods at me, says, "You're working," and kisses her brother on the cheek.

"I'm writing a speech for our friend Hannibal."

"Good Christ, you can do better than that," she says. But these words, happily, are directed not at me but at her brother. "I told you something *bright*. Why *must* you always look like a mortician?"

Sindri's laughter, anyway, is bright—bright and childlike, a boyish string of airy chuckles that Lilja's presence alone seems able to elicit. His pleasure in her company is patent: his cheeks blaze, his eyes glow. It has sometimes struck me that my two children, half-brother and half-sister, are closer than perhaps they ought to be—it seems but one more sign of Sindri's housebound sensibility that, at his age, he should draw so much sustenance from the girl. What in the world has happened to good old sibling rivalry?

Or am I merely showing envy? Women—of any age—seem to find irresistibly appealing the boy's wistful, wishy-washy melancholy.

"So I brought you something," she says, and he says, "Brought me something?" and his face has the avid, tremulous expectancy of a child presented with a gift he fears may be a practical joke.

She draws from a pocket of her military jacket a square of color: a paisley silk scarf. "I told you I wasn't going to a party with a mortician."

"Really?" Sindri eyes the scarf fixedly, uneasily—like a dog presented with a new collar.

"Really. Now hold still."

Lilja circles round behind him and gives the back of his head a little shove. His chin drops to his chest. She ties the scarf with a tiny flourish— she's deft with her hands in a way I've never been—and tucks and pats. The effect of the scarf, much of it buried within the neck of Sindri's black shirt, is not so garish as I'd feared.

"Perfect," she says.

"Really?" Sindri grins nervously at her.

"You're working," she says to me.

I repeat myself word for word, since it doesn't appear she'd bothered to listen the first time: "I'm writing a speech for our friend Hannibal."

"A swan song, eh?"

I exchange a glance with Sindri, who surely gathers from it my wish that he hold his tongue. "Something like that. . . ." In truth, I'm not fully confident I can bend the girl, even to the extent I've just now bent her brother.

"We'd better go," Lilja says to him.

"You're off to a party," I say to her.

"It isn't easy convincing this one to come along," Lilja says, and pulls playfully, flirtatiously on the collar of Sindri's black shirt. He beams at her. "He'd rather stay home and sit at his nasty desk all night."

"That's exactly what I plan to do," I say. "Me and my nasty desk. I'm looking forward to it."

But the fact is, once the two of them are out of the apartment and I contemplate the spotlit sheet of blank paper below me, I look forward to nothing. Under my tired eyes, its desolate whiteness carries all the dolor of a snowy field on a day when more snow's expected—a blankness destined to yield to a deeper, deader blankness.

On the far left corner of my desk, from which I avert my eyes, is a list of English words for which, as part of my too-long-neglected duties as head of the Freelandic Language Committee, native substitutes must be found. *Carjacking, copycat killing, co-dependent, ecocide.* It's endless. They're always coming in, day after day, word after word, wave after wave, hitting our shores like so many soldiers clambering out of amphibious landing craft. And the attack never stops. In the World Language War, every day—day after day—is D-day.

I knuckle my eyes, to rouse myself, before settling my gaze on the last sentences I'd written: "All the world may not be mindful of us. But all the world has need of us." I attach a postscript: "There may even be those in our own homes who begin to doubt us. To them I say, *We will surmount you.*"

17

A Weight, a Flame

When for a long time you've been carrying a heavy bag with a string handle and you halt for a rest and painfully prise open a hand all but locked into a claw, you discover that your future's been erased: the trackings of your palm, your lifeline and loveline and all the rest, have dissolved into the virulent red grooves cut by the cord. You have become your burden; your load has obliterated the rest of your life.

Weight sometimes has a way of doing just that to you, and a feeling of weight on different levels, physical and psychological, was what Meg increasingly deposited upon me—the physical being the more obvious of course. Had you placed us in chairs strapped to opposite ends of an enormous swing-balance, hers would have plunged earthward, mine soared skyward; she must have had forty pounds on me. But I wasn't soaring skyward—quite the contrary. More and more, I felt pinned to the ground, squatted upon.

Not that we didn't continue to share powerful satisfactions, some of them indeed attributable to that discrepancy in our weights. To the vanished son's bed I brought bone and tendon and muscle, Meggy brought flesh and flesh and flesh. I supplied urgency; she, ease. Her breasts were broad and lax, her belly broader and laxer. It was not I but she who sweated profusely and I'd come away bathed in her saltwater. Like the son who'd disappeared but had once swum in her amnion, I was immersed in her; body to body she would make me clean.

And what would I do for her? I'd like to think I was likewise useful—I want to think we helped each other. *She* helped *me*. A mirror hung over the dead boy's desk, and one day, catching sight both of ample Meg, crossing the room with her undergarments clutched to her chest like a tattered packet of billet-doux, and of narrow-chested naked young Eggert, sitting cross-legged on the bed, I realized one of the great intimate verities of life: the female body, as it deviates from the ideal, becomes humorous; the male, grotesque. Within the fairest alabaster Aphrodite on her pedestal at the Uffizi there's a plump, off-balance, waddling creature waiting to emerge; in the comeliest Adonis lurks a goat-footed, limb-twisted deformity. Oh, I did love that mimed, unconscious comedy which Meg in her nakedness presented to me—the spill and bounce of her shuffle, the dimpled jollity, the sliding clump of rump all but broadsiding me as she'd stoop to retrieve some panties from the floor. And she—bless her—valued the ugliness of me: savoring this chance, in the long late-afternoon minutes, to stroke my chest, my arms, my thighs. When, she seemed to be wondering, was she ever going to assimilate her life's stark actuality? When would this affair with a boy some twenty years her junior begin to seem fully real?

It's hardly surprising, I suppose, if she couldn't even yet, for all our doings, accept what we'd embarked upon. She was sleeping with a Freelander? Doing *it*, doing that thing which the young man himself was always insisting, in his bookish way, on calling *sexual intercourse*—or calling it that when he wasn't, in the act itself, calling it something else again, alternately filling her ears with filth and licking them clean? Doing *it* with someone from an Arctic island nation she'd never once in her life heard of before he, guided by a troubling Providence, showed up on her doorstep? And what would be next for her, the man in the moon? This Eddie who was no Eddie and no Edgar but an Eggert Oddason was an apparition, a ghost, a creature of the air.

And she, for me, was increasingly the very embodiment of the burying earth. Weighty, weighty those plump, chthonic upper arms of hers, resting upon my chest. Weighty her marriage, to a man with a mind like a sinkhole. Weighty the dead boy, weighty the unflushable blood in her birthmarked face, the disfigurement which, even in the prime of youth— itself a dimming memory—would have kept her from prettiness, and weighty her endless sad fretting over that garish new couch, on which the gut-swollen weighty drunkard sprawled. Weightier, by the day, the stubby hands of the clock, weighty the pages of the calendar and the tomorrows surely grimmer even than her grim todays.

The last time, ever, I went to bed with Meg, I knew it was the last time. She didn't. It was all as grotesque as it could be, the glutting organ waving a sort of good-bye—a last spill of another couple hundred million stunted prototypes of myself. Forgive me.

Should I have let you know I was leaving, Meg? From the moment when I sensed—some months ago, morosely staring off at Great Blue from my study desk—from the moment, I say, when I sensed you were dead, I shuddered to think how unbalanced our accounts remained. I'd like to assume you guessed the gist, that by the end you accepted the logic of everything I did. . . .

Thump, thump, on his big heavy-booted feet the Lord of the Manor came home that night in an especially foul mood. Upstairs in my room, sitting beside my packed rucksack, listening hard, I heard him grunting and pacing, heard the chink of bottle on glass, the click of the television. I might well have been little Jack and he the giant—I might have climbed to this place on a beanstalk, to steal the pale white-gold of his wife's, the giantess's, flesh, thump, thump. I heard underneath the television's rattle another clicking of bottle on glass. I gave him an hour or so, came down-stairs to find him sprawled on the couch, face promisingly flushed. He was smoking a Lucky Strike. The television was running. Meg was clean-ing up in the kitchen.

"I had some good news today," I announced, standing at the foot of the sofa, over whose edge his stocking-shod feet were hanging. There was a hole in one of his socks, through which protruded a toe whose nail cried out to be clipped.

"Good news?" Michael's gaze paddled toward me. For a moment I would have sworn he failed to recognize me.

"Mr. Shlomowitz said I'd been doing such fine work he wanted to give me a raise."

"A raise?" Confusion became vexation. "Without your asking?"

To my regret Meg stepped out of the kitchen. I would have preferred to brazen this out without her.

"Completely without my asking," I went on. "And so, to celebrate, I bought us all a surprise." I drew from behind my back a fifth of Bushmill's finest Irish whiskey. It gleamed like an apparition. This was costly drink, of a quality such that—so I'd learned from Meg—Michael permitted him-self a bottle maybe once a year, as a Christmas present to himself.

I rotated the bottle, letting it catch and throw off the lamplight. The expressions that contended in Michael's face were varied. I read there, at the very least, incredulity, greed, and jubilation. "Let me pour you a glass," I said. "Let me pour you both a glass."

"Some glasses, some more glasses," Michael cried, not taking his eyes off me, or off my bottle. I'm embarrassed even now at the unoriginality of my ploy—defensible only because it succeeded. Mine was the old-est trick in the book—but then I don't suppose Michael had ever read a book.

Meg trundled off to the kitchen. Michael heaved himself up into a sitting position. I took a chummy seat beside him on the couch. When Meg returned with two more glasses, she lowered herself into my usual chair, across from the two of us. I cracked open the bottle.

I poured three generous glasses. Meg wasn't much for drink. Neither, back then, was I. But she took, as ever, what I offered her. . . . "To the three of us," I declared by way of toast. We drank.

The television droned on. We watched a sheriff rescue a cow from a pack of coyotes. "Would you like another?" I asked Michael, as his glass came down empty on the coffee table. He would. I poured.

After a while I said, "I think I might go out and take a walk."

"A walk?" Meg said.

"Walk where?" Michael said thickly.

"Just a little stroll. Here and there. You know," I went on, "Michael's always saying this is such a tough town, but I've never had any trouble."

"Tough town, tough town," the Lord of the Manor repeated darkly.

"I'm starting to wonder if it *is* such a tough town."

"Tough, tough," Michael chanted, nodding his head in solemn agree-ment with himself. "Very tough." He sipped again from his whiskey. Somehow he wasn't getting my hint. . . .

"Well, I feel ready for it." I stood up and lunged my arms forward, wrestler-style. "I'm prepared, if they want to get tough with me."

He shook his head in weary dismay. It pained him—clearly it pained him that the world had ever spawned a male specimen so stupid and puny and hapless as I. "The Little Poet's ready?"

"Sure," I answered. "Absolutely ready."

"Ready—there's a laugh." But still he did not rise.

"Some stumbling Mick comes along? Wants to start something? I lay him flat." I threw an imaginary Irishman hard to the pavement. Of course, like the stammering Oxford don who compiles a lexicon of London wharf-rat slang, I loved this sort of talk; I had a bottomless appetite for a breezy, stylized, Hollywood-tongued vernacular.

"*You?* Ready?" Michael laughs. His voice is thickly fogged in; it comes from a place no one can see. "A little kike like you."

It seems he has never fully abandoned the suspicion that he might be housing a Jew.

"Come on, Michael, I'll show you how it's done." I stood before him, arms outstretched.

Seated on the couch, Michael peers up at me uncomprehendingly. He has always been the one to initiate our wrestling matches. Laboriously now, he draws himself to his feet and I realize just how thoroughly intoxicated—every vein bathed in its own sweet liquor—the man is. Drink has not only reddened his face; it has discomposed and rearranged his features, robbing them of all symmetry, so that one eye seems to float a good inch above the other. Meg has risen to her feet and is standing by the television—hoping, I suppose, to prevent either of us from putting a foot through the screen. "Tough, tough, tough," he chants, and there's a sort of savor, almost a tenderness, in his delivery. "Tough town. A tough town. A real *tough* town."

I go at him quickly, darting low, catching one of his legs in my arms, and I yank hard. Somewhat to my surprise, with breathtaking speed, he goes down. There's a crisp thump, which I register in the back of my mind, and the heavier groan of the floor crying out against our foolery. I'm moving fast. In just a moment I have one of my sharp knees pinned against Michael's chest.

I poise there confusedly. I've momentarily triumphed, which isn't at all what I'd been seeking.

Then a hand reaches up and seizes me by the ear. My head goes down, *whack*, face squashed into the carpet. A knee or an elbow catches me sharp in the ribs and all the breath's punched out of me. My hair is yanked and my slack-jawed head flies up and is inserted, with driving, nose-smashing fury, into the crotch of Michael's elbow. Oh yes. *This* is what I want, *this* is what I've come for. The ritual must be played out. This is but a step along the way.

Powerfully, over and over and over again, the knuckles rake the back of my skull. And I suppose I'm exulting as much as it's possible to exult in so pained and humiliating a position. "Tough . . . tough . . . tough," Michael chants, as though accompanying himself as he plays his primitive instrument—the back of my head—and his faraway song is at once spiteful and blissful. "Tough, tough, tough, tough, tough . . ."

Again he yanks back my head. His disassembled features are less than a foot from mine. His breath is hot on my cheeks. Something splatters on my nose. Blood. It's streaming from his temple. When I took him down, he'd cracked his head against the table.

"You think you're ready?" he asks.

"Maybe not," the Little Poet stammers.

"You'll never be ready. Never, never, never."

He takes a knuckle and roots it deep into, scarily deep into, one of my eye-sockets. A crowning, crackling shower of sparks explodes inside my head. . . .

Michael rose unsteadily to his feet. I sat on the floor. With a cry of alarm, Meg ran to her husband, handkerchief in hand. My head cleared and I understood her distress. She feared blood on her sofa.

Michael poured himself another whiskey, sat down, and began watching television as though nothing had happened. He was panting, though. Meg bustled back and forth, bringing him a washcloth wrapped around ice cubes. He shrugged it off, but she held it to his head as a compress. His breathing slowed. I took a seat on the sofa. We watched a sheriff rescue a town from a pack of wild Mexicans.

I sat down and poured a few more drops of whiskey into my glass. I was motivated not by thirst but by a desire to reestablish proprietary rights over the bottle. My plans necessitated that I be in charge of timing.

Meggy was flagging—I could see it in her face—but she was reluctant to leave us alone. She was worried about her sofa. She was unnerved by the hint of something more-than-usually malign in the air.

She urged us both, a number of times, to make our way up to bed. Michael dismissed her, first with a grunt and then, more dismissive still, with a wave of the hand. He wasn't going anywhere while so much of the bottle remained.

"You go ahead," I told her after a time, and added quietly, "I'll see to everything."

And though it may have been fully justified, though her suspicions were in truth well founded, still the look of distrust she shot at me hurt me. What had we achieved in all our intimate afternoons if she would now doubt me like this? "Go on," I told her, and this time—still uneasy, with a docility born not of trust but of sheer fatigue—she nodded agreement.

She turned away and I heard her mount the stairs. "Good night, Michael," she called. She added, "Good night, Eddie," and I swung around for one last look at her.

But already I was too late—or mostly too late. From where I sat, the ceiling bisected her body. Her head was gone. What was left—my last glance at the woman—were those broad haunches of hers, that ample bottom which, packed that initial afternoon into a pair of pink Bermuda shorts, I had followed up those very stairs on my first day in America, half a year before.

I turned to the business at hand. "Michael, might I offer you a little more whiskey?"

"You speak welcome words."

Michael nodded contentedly at himself; his features had that dangerous glazed look they'd assumed the night he'd first recited Edgar Guest's "Equipment."

I poured him a tall glass. We sat, we drank, we talked—though what was spoken has vanished utterly from my mind—and Michael smoked another Lucky Strike, and another. I returned to the bathroom, where I washed my face, and when I came back he was snoring on the couch, his blotchy, nasty features blindly upswung toward the lamplight. There was dried blood in his hair. On the floor beside him lay his Lucky Strikes, and a pack of matches.

On mouselike feet I made my way upstairs. I drew my rucksack from my room and set it out in the hall. Then, on tiptoe, I walked to their bedroom door and heard—faint, more sigh than snore—a sound tinged with disappointment. Somehow, even when unconscious Meg conveyed a sense of having been dealt a raw deal in life. . . .

I carried my rucksack downstairs. I took a seat in the chair beside the sofa. For ten minutes, maybe twenty, I watched Michael snore. He was deep into it now.

I retrieved from the floor his matches and cigarettes. I lit up a Lucky Strike. I was sweating, but my hands showed admirable steadiness when I brought the lit end of the cigarette to the sleeve of his shirt, just above the cuff. The smoke was instantly, powerfully acrid.

Michael continued to snore.

Were he to awaken, I was ready to bolt out the door with nothing but my journal under my arm. Surely the man who had taken second place in the Long Run in the First Freelandic Olympics was not about to be pursued and captured by a dead-drunk middle-aged Irishman.

When the smoking hole was about the size of a dime, I licked my thumb and forefinger and pressed them to its smoldering edge. The flame bit into my flesh but I held on tight, until I knew it was extinguished.

Then, with my lit little wand, my artist's paintbrush, I drew a pretty new opening in Michael's pants, where the material bunched at his crotch.

I was doing him a favor; he'd be able to pee without taking down his zipper.

Michael continued his snoring. I was sweating heavily, which I rarely do, but I managed to keep my motions slow and circumspect. I had visions in my head of Meg behind me, at the foot of the stairs, having somehow made her way down without my hearing. She would cry out—a sharp wounded yelp of astonishment and betrayal. But no cry came. The house had gone to bed.

Only one task remained to me, but it was the important one—the one for which I needed to steel myself. I'd resolved to burn a good-sized hole in the sofa itself. Not on one of the cushions, where the damage might be concealed simply by flipping it over. No. On the top. Where it must show.

This I would do for Meg's own good. I had all the unyielding certainty of youth behind me. I knew she needed a sharp, stiff blow, needed to be shown, in some painful and irreversible stroke, that she had wed herself to disaster. I would open her eyes.

I stood there, twenty-two years old, with the burning cigarette in my hand.

I was sweating, and out of breath.

Below me, sprawled in all his distant hateful ugliness, lay the lord of the domain: the woman's oppressor, her soul-killer. She needed my guidance. She needed to be roused, however painful her awakening might be.

And yet, as I pictured her up there, snoring disappointedly, I hesitated; my too-soft heart once more got the better of me. I waited, cigarette in hand. . . .

What I had envisioned was a great gaping scar—a disfigurement no more to be hidden than that strawberry mark she'd carried on her face every day for forty-four years. But I couldn't bring myself to do it. No. The most I could bring myself to do was a tiny singe on the sofa arm, more a pockmark than a great soul-arresting cicatrice. I held the cigarette in place for a second or two and heard the world's tiniest hiss, like the first sound ever to issue from the throat of a new-hatched snake. Then I laid a licked finger upon it, gentle as any kiss.

I gathered up my bag and my papers. I walked briskly down Lyon Road. The night was cold, the constellations bright. I might almost have been in Freeland, but I was not about to go back there—yet. I was accumulating experiences. I owed it to myself to continue my travels. My debts to myself were deep, and still mostly unpaid.

18

A Mountain of Zeroes

And here's another photograph of Hannibal Hannibalsson, one which, unlike the snapshot of him as a young man strolling moodily in the Tivoli Gardens, recalls a genuine event. You could dig it up in the archives of *The Torch*. The caption below reads, "His Finest Hour." But first some background . . .

It's September 27, 1982, and Hannibal is seated in the Presidential Suite, entertaining important visitors—a pair of fat cats. They're Danes, come to discuss the possibility of setting up a pumice-grinding factory. The commercial prospects are favorable, but they're unhappy about our "unpredictability," our "unreliability." With ill-disguised condescension, they are letting Hannibal know that he, no less than his countrymen, embodies a collection of antiquated, unprofessional attitudes. For it seems that we Freelanders fail to understand that a modern legal document is not meant as a record of goodwill, or as window dressing, or as a loose, advisory body of aspirations. It is a binding document.

Hannibal is bored not only with them but with life itself. These days, he is largely incapacitated. Some weeks ago, the old athlete's knees having gradually given out, he'd finally consented to arthroscopic knee surgery— a delicate operation which was in fact carried out in the city from which these two tedious visitors have come. Let's give credit where credit is due: those hospitals in Copenhagen are a wonder.

Hannibal's on crutches. He must stay off his right knee. This he has been told, and told, and told. He must give it a chance to heal.

Hannibal is chafing under the regime, of course, but doing his best to conform to it.

Meanwhile, the Danes are droning, and he is nodding. His life is a much-diminished thing. The salt had lost its savor, but when the salt is nothing less than your very lifeblood, what's a man to— And then he hears a thrilling, a gorgeous sound: the grim tolling bell in Mariners' Church, announcing peril or tragedy. And even as he is reaching for the phone, an exultant inner voice inside his head is crying: *my country needs me.*

Why is the bell ringing in Mariners' Church? The answer turns out to be the most horrifying, the most exhilarating news he has heard in all his life: the peril announced by the bell applies to that selfsame bell. Enough riddles. Lord in heaven: Mariners' Church has caught fire.

Mariners' Church—the chief architectural jewel in our capital city!—has *caught fire!* And Hannibal is on his feet, he has no more use for either the Danes or his crutches, he is out the door.

And here is our unforgettable snapshot, taken a few minutes later: Hannibal's face is aglow in the flame that waves like an incarcerated lunatic from one of the broken stained-glass windows. He has taken charge of the rescue mission. He is, on that broken knee of his, swinging an ax, and wielding big strapping hoses, and bearing on his back—as a lifeguard might salvage from the sea an unconscious swimmer—the pulpit itself. And the poisonous, acrid air is beautiful, the victory the townsfolk are achieving is beautiful, his heart is thumping like a dog's tail in his chest. He is saving Mariners' Church and has he ever in his life been a happier man? The blood in his veins is singing, *Some men live their whole lives without ever once having the chance to rescue Mariners' Church.*

And some men live whole lives without ever serving for twenty years as Freeland's President. Could he make it twenty-five? I scheduled the announcement of Hannibal's candidacy for three o'clock the following Saturday afternoon. I figured this would be late enough in the day to throw the bastards at "Youth Hour" into temporary confusion; clever as they might be, they were unlikely to concoct anything fiendishly pernicious in time for their eight o'clock broadcast. And they wouldn't get another shot at him until Tuesday night, by which time, the story become stale news, their outrage ought to be blunted.

The announcement would take place on Giant Island, alongside the site where, according to legend, our founder, Erik the Other, established his first homestead. He is reputed to have come ashore initially on Bread Island—at Founders' Point, where Hannibal's home is located—but to have traveled thence to Giant Island and a hot spring known as the Waters of Truth. It says something significant about our founder, doubtless, that he chose to live on the island least favored by modern-day Freelanders—

the most storm-ravaged, the least arable—and perhaps some additional words should now be said about dear Erik and all our fanciful attempts to dignify a man who, though a thousand years in the grave, gamely resists all the trappings of dignity.

Erik's original epithet, as set down in old Thorgunnur's hobbyhorse and idée fixe—the medieval Icelandic manuscript known as *The Freeland Saga*—was *skitugi*, which might be translated as The Squalid or The Unwashed or even, literally, The Shitty. The Saga also occasionally referred to Erik as The Hairless One, and it was as Erik the Bald that he was known to generations of my countrymen. But over the centuries, as Freeland belatedly inched into the modern era, this description, too, was perceived as a trifle unrefined. Unfortunately, he could not be known as Erik plain and simple. Some sort of tag was essential to distinguish him from his—in the eyes of the world, anyway—more accomplished namesake, Erik the Red, who founded the Viking settlements in Greenland and who fathered Leif Eriksson, discoverer of Vinland. It seemed that *our* Erik, Freeland's, was the *other* Erik, and thereby in time a new epithet was born: Erik the Other . . . Which is to say, Erik the Minor, the Second-rate, the Also-ran. I've reserved this choice little anecdote until now, hoping that my reader will have come to grasp that the Freelandic sensibility accepts as only natural a dash of clownery in its leaders. Hence, Hannibal in this regard, too—no less than in his physical prowess and straightforward good looks—was made for us.

What better place than Giant Island, and the Waters of Truth, for Hannibal Hannibalsson to accept, with understandable weariness but an unquenchable desire to serve others, the burden of another term?

Freeland's a place where it's risky to schedule any event outdoors. But we seemed to be in the midst of a mild spell, and, anyway, we had a substitute plan. We had reserved a municipal auditorium in Nordvik, the largest village on Giant, which would serve us if the weather turned. I prayed it wouldn't. I had the event clear in my mind, where it played beautifully: Hannibal Hannibalsson standing beside the Waters of Truth, with the sun on his face. In the background would loom Blue Island's Great Blue Mountain. He would deliver stirring words, ringing words—those I had composed for him.

Our entourage included two television cameras and two cameramen. It seemed a little risky to bring out so large a technical crew—one camera was deemed sufficient for most presidential events—and I worried about raising suspicions in the "Youth Hour" crew. But it was essential to capture the speech adequately on film. With luck, it would all be over before the "Youth Hour" bunch knew what hit them; they would meet a fait accompli.

We took the ferry out to Nordvik and disembarked at one o'clock. I immediately began dropping artful hints about the imminent arrival of a momentous occasion. I visited the post office, the seamen's home, the little grocery store, and of course the old folks' home. Mysteriously—who can say where such things originate?—home brew materialized and began to flow. People were curious, interested. . . . Would they perhaps like to follow us out to the Waters of Truth? Something historic was about to unfold. I wanted a large gathering. It would be lovely if the cameras had something like a crowd to pan across, and Hannibal would profit by having the feel of a genuine audience.

As best I can reconstruct it, everything went beautifully until two-fifty, ten minutes before the speech was scheduled to commence. We arrived at the site of Erik the Other's old homestead to discover that some witty prankster had dumped a whole box of laundry detergent into the Waters of Truth, converting the hot spring into an outdoor bubble bath. A broom was dragged from the back of somebody's truck and frantic restoration work was begun. Needless to say, the sight was piquant: clouds of pinkish bubbles being swept over the moss. Clouds—real ones—were simultaneously thickening and blackening overhead.

Then the far more reliable of the two cameramen managed to tumble into a narrow fissure, badly wrenching his back and lacerating his thigh. Few sights are more cheering to the Freelandic soul than a mishap involving a generous outpouring of blood, and a jolly, helpful hue and cry went up, resulting in the injured party's being energetically bundled into a pickup truck—to the great detriment of his wrenched back, doubtless—and hauled off toward Nordvik.

Somewhere in the heavens a celestial knob was turned clockwise and the sky began to drizzle. By my count we had forty-two people assembled as audience, but most were looking skeptical. We decided to go ahead with one cameraman, and here I suppose I must dutifully introduce hapless Trausti Hauksson—untrustworthy Trausti—who I'm afraid will reappear now and then in my story. Others might see him as a pitiable spectacle, but I feel less pity than distaste when I fix him in my mind's eye: bean-pole thin but potbellied, lank unwashed hair trailing over his nose, mouth collapsing around a couple of missing teeth. It's often impossible to make out what Trausti says, and there's no telling whether the mumbling's a result of a shortage of teeth or an excess of alcohol; I don't think I've ever seen him completely sober. Why had we brought him? What did he have to offer us? The most feebleminded of virtues, I'm afraid: loyalty. He's utterly, unimpeachably devoted to Hannibal Hannibalsson. And Trausti's close affiliation with us, his status as semi-official presidential photographer, is but further evidence of Hannibal's unhealthy willingness to sacrifice competence for devotion.

As soon as we had the soapsuds under control—they floated off quite prettily across the lava fields, like a new, ultra-hygienic form of tumble-weed—Hannibal began to read his speech, which I had typed out for him. I was worried that its ink might run in the rain. Drunken Trausti stood at his post; the camera rolled.

Hannibal appeared to be coming down with a cold. His nose was red and his voice was hoarse. "At this point I am not thinking purely of Free-land," he declared. "I am thinking of that greater world out there and Freeland's mission in it. I am speaking of history."

Before him stood, in their dark, ill-fitting coats and patient, forbear-ing expressions, some thirty-three wet Freelanders—nine had wandered off. The camera continued to roll.

"Do some of you question me? Do I see some of you look at me sharply when I speak of our mission?" These were Hannibal's extrapola-tions, for of course no one in this glazed-eyed group had looked at him *sharply*. Still, after all these years, I knew enough not to second-guess him as he advanced one of his rhetorical challenges. When he wasn't blunder-ing badly—dropping what I'd dubbed a Hannibalistic missile—he was apt to be stirring hearts and swaying minds. At the right moment, he can be a peerless political genius.

This was not the right moment.

The drizzle thickened. And turned colder. A few members of our bedraggled audience laughed, for behind Hannibal a querulous-looking sheep, its coat mud-matted, had stumbled onto the scene. "The large na-tions get larger. You might suppose things would even out, the small and the large would more and more resemble each other, but it is a defining peculiarity of modern life"—and let me interrupt my President to say I'm hoping my reader has already guessed that Hannibal had returned to text of my own devising—"that the huge become huger. Their unimaginably vast weaponry becomes unimaginably vaster. Millions become billions— billions of dollars, billions of people, billions of throwaway cans and bot-tles. Their talk slides into the trillions—trillions of dollars of debt. What does another set of zeroes matter when they are already sitting on a mountain of zeroes? This is what their system of governance boils down to: adding zeroes. Multiply everything by ten and the books will balance, surely everything will come right. Do you understand? They have lost all sense of scale." The sheep, I was relieved to see, had wandered off. The rain was not letting up.

"We in Freeland have scale. We know that these islands of ours, which people Down Below think of as mere dots in the sea, are expansive. They are large enough to sustain a people, a heritage, an outlook, a language. We know that Great Blue—" And here Hannibal turned, as I had instructed him to do, and nodded at the mountain. Unfortunately, mist had settled in, and Blue was lost in gray. "—is as large as Mount Everest."

A wet bottle slipped out of somebody's fingers and smashed upon the rocks. A collective mourning grunt went up from the crowd, and so intimately did I know my people that the subtle characteristics of their grunt, its particular down-sliding pitch and duration, told me that the bottle had not been empty.

"Let me ask you a question. When Erik the Other came to this very island, to our own sacred Giant, did he come looking merely for ease, for a place in the sun, or did he come—as I know that *you* know he did— with a sense of mission? Surely the man had a *vision*. What would he make in Freeland?" The text was back in Hannibal's uncertain hands. "He had resolved that in Freeland he would make—Freeland. *That* was his vision, making Freeland in Freeland, a vision carried down to us lo these thousand years."

Gamely, Hannibal dragged on. The weather drizzled on. Did the audience understand which harbor he was sailing toward? And when he arrived, how would they greet sight of his sail? With ringing bells, or with a fountaining of arrows? The same sheep, or another sheep with an equally sour expression—they're a grumpy lot, your typical Freelandic sheep—had wandered in behind Hannibal. The country is overrun by the damned things.

"I have served as your President for twenty years. Five years ago, it was my intention—no, more than that, my *hope*, my dearest personal wish—to finish what I set out to do in twenty years. But in these last few weeks I see now that for you"—and Hannibal outflung his hands to encompass a *you* far, far larger than the assembled crowd—"my task remains unfinished. I have listened to your wishes. I am no less your servant now than five years ago, or ten, fifteen, or twenty, and that's the reason why, accepting your mandate, with solemnity in my heart but also the joy that comes of imminent triumph, I bring you an announcement: I have decided, once again, to run for the presidency of Freeland."

What were we expecting? Triumphal rainbows blazing and breaking in halos behind his head? The sun streaming forth in corroboration/coronation? In any event, we were expecting more, I suppose, than the tolerant hush which ensued—understandably inducing Hannibal, as though the crowd simply hadn't heard him, to deliver another arms-outflung declaration: "I accept—I accept your wishes."

This time we had some scrappy applause, a few scrannel cries of support—encouragement sufficient, anyway, to launch Hannibal into the next installment of his speech.

"I have spoken of the broad and the general, but now I would speak of the narrow and specific. I have spoken of visions but now I speak of practicalities. I see four main issues I plan to address in my next administration."

This portion of the speech was designed to counter charges of woolly-headedness. It was a harmless, unexceptionable list of objectives; a candidate running five years hence, or fifty, could probably recite them just as they were, nothing changed. But Hannibal enumerated them vigorously and, I thought, well.

One, he was going to see to the diversification of the economy. After an unbroken millennium of subsisting on fish, we would now branch out and tap the full range of our human talents and resources.

Two, he was going to see to an improvement in public works and services—better roads and bridges, better ferries, better telephone and mail services, better health care, better schools, all to be achieved not through a levying of additional taxes but through greater efficiency and streamlining.

Was this streamlining—someone in the audience called out—to be achieved through loss of jobs? No, he cheerfully explained, such streamlining was to be achieved through greater efficiency, just as the efficiency was to be achieved through streamlining. Hand in hand, you see.

Three, he was going to increase tourism by means of a heightened awareness of the natural bounties and unmatched warmth and openhandedness of the Freelandic nation. A new slogan had already been conceived by the Office of Tourism and Convention Management: *Freeland—Experience it!* "Can anyone question that ours is a country of almost unnatural natural"—he paused to peel apart one rain-sodden page from another—

"beauty?" When the world fully, belatedly learns of us, it will arrive at our shores in packs, droves, multitudes.

Four, he would further improve the lot of the elderly. It had been—he wanted to remind us—a matter of great pride, perhaps the proudest moment of any of his four terms in office, when he had overseen the ground-breaking ceremony of Thorskrist's Eldershelter. It was a moment matched only by the day of its completion, when he had escorted through its hallways his Superior School instructor, the legendary Thorgunnur Sigurdardottir—who had taken it as her holy task to teach our youth the responsibilities and the God-given privilege of being a Freelander. He was able to inform his old teacher that here was a building with ninety-two rooms for the elderly, each with its own unobstructed view of Great Blue Mountain!

In addition to being a cause Hannibal cherished, the tending to the needs of the elderly made hardheaded political sense. Election after election, they were his faithfulest constituency. If he could but keep them alive forever, in their rooms overlooking Great Blue, he had a perpetual electoral base. They remembered harder times, so that when things went well—when fish catches were up and the country riding high on one of its delirious short-lived boom-cycles—they thanked Hannibal for their prosperity. And when the cycle went bust, they shook their heads with nonjudgmental resignation. No one was to be blamed for such things, for hadn't life always been miserable in Freeland? Wasn't misery, they insisted proudly, what being a Freelander was all about?

No, it was the young people, with all their fickle and inordinate appetites, their unquestioning trust in their own outsize prerogatives, who caused us most of our trouble. They wanted *things*, and they vociferated when they couldn't have them. Why couldn't they have what the Danes had, and the Brits and the Swedes, and the Americans, whose opulent, malignant movies they queued to see every weekend, in rain and wind and sleet and snow? And what about the Japanese, those diminutive and humorously impeccable business-suited fish merchants who now and then descended on Thorskrist looking for halibut or lobster, and who had been known to spend more than a hundred and fifty thousand kronur in one of our souvenir shops? One hundred and fifty thousand kronur for authentic—albeit occasionally Icelandic—Freelandic woolen goods: blankets, sweaters, hats, gloves, scarves. Such money was out there! Beyond our own cold niggardly seas there were other, warmer seas—seas of cash—upon which the rest of the world was floating. Why should we not, too, own microwave ovens and DAT stereo systems, possess wine cellars and leather couches, pamper ourselves with Italian shoes and French perfumes, call greetings to each other across bowling alleys and indoor tennis courts, lament the weather on telephones installed in our imported automobiles?

"I come to you with dreams. I come to you with practical plans. I come to you with respect for our past. I come to you with hopes for our future." Things were winding down, which was all to the good since the rain was picking up. His final words were a conceit of mine, done up with Hannibalistic embellishments: "I have served four terms, which I now regard as the four fingers of a hand. The fifth shall be the thumb. It is the fifth which shall give me the adaptive power to shear a sheep, wield a net, sign a document, make a fist. It is the fifth that shall lend completion to the whole. This time, as your President, I will be more useful and I will be stronger than ever before."

He brought the whole business to a reasonably fervent close, and for a moment, despite the ominous weather, I allowed myself some optimism. But it wasn't more than a minute later that Trausti, our hopeless cameraman, came forward to shatter my well-being.

How to begin to describe his excruciating eccentricities of speech? For there's not *only* the toothless lisping and the slur of drink, but also the endless weaving of proudly, maddeningly roundabout locutions, so convoluted I sometimes suspect him of being genuinely demented. Does he think he's being witty? Doesn't he realize I'm yearning to strangle him?

"Everything go all right?" I ask him.

"By and large. By and large, Eggert. When things go smoothly a large share of the time, and not so smoothly only a small share, how are we to justify complaining? Every sea has its rough patches." He pokes his chin at me. His eyes shine merrily. Rain is falling onto his misshapen face. He has all the time in the world, clearly. "It's true we had a little what you might call mishap at what you might call the hind end of the speech, but why count your troubles when you could just as soon count your blessings, eh, Eggert? Is the glass half full or is it half empty? My theory is, if you own a glass at all, you're sitting pretty. . . ."

"I beg your pardon."

"Right there at what you might identify as the climax of the old boy's speech, that stirring passage about answering the call it was, well that was the moment of true delivery. One of those sheep happened to wander into the picture with a call of its own, if you see what I'm getting at."

"I'm not sure I do. You've got a sheep in the background?"

"Part of a sheep, anyway. More like the background quarters of a sheep in the background. Which wouldn't be a subject worth troubling you about, Eggert, sheep being sheep, if he hadn't chosen just that moment to express himself, and they say we all wind up as grass, but isn't that just begging the question? What I'd liked to know is, what does grass wind up as? If you follow the question through, you see it's not just a case of us eating the sheep, but vice versa. When you and I are grass, it isn't *lions* we're going to be worrying about, if you see how it is: the lamb may lie down with the lion, but who's to say which one will get up the next morning?"

"What in the world are you on about? Good Christ, spill it out. You don't mean—"

"You have it precisely. 'Spill it out''s the very phrase. Or gave way to what he'd been keeping pent up inside him is perhaps more like it?"

"—and it's on film?"

"Well I suppose you might say the old boy, I'm speaking now of the sheep and not our President, shat like an elephant. If you don't mind my speaking pungently. Dropped a precious heavy wet load, I suppose you might say."

"On film?"

"On the ground, but even so, that's bad enough. Right at the actual moment he's announcing his candidacy is the truth of it. 'He' here being our President again. Sort of a simultaneous announcement is how you—"

"Oh good Christ—so what are we going to do?" I was shouting, I realized. But the rain was coming down, and I was talking to a lunatic. . . .

"Maybe he could deliver it again. . . ."

Exasperation was undoing my wits and with that word *deliver* I truly thought Trausti meant the sheep. "Again?" I shouted.

"Just the actual announcement. With no sheep this time?"

But could Hannibal be convinced to announce again? When we'd at last isolated him from his audience, each of whose stories he needed to hear, each of whose right hands he needed to shake, and when our difficulties were explained—which had to be done a couple of times, a politician's "high" having settled over him—he burst into whooping, deep-chested laughter. "Won't be the first time, I suppose, these people watch a sheep mint some pocket change!"

Pause for a hypothetical question: Would I actually *want* to know how many creative hours in Freeland, accumulated over the centuries, have gone into the creation of new ways to describe a sheep's defecating? Probably not . . . In any case, I understood in my heart how hopeless the whole business was. The rain was pelting now. All speechifying was over for the day. . . .

A sweeping melancholy settled over me on the return ferry. I managed to find a remote corner in the lounge, and leaned my head against the vibrating window. Rain had turned to rattling hail. I thought of my neglected summerhouse, which of course was where I should have spent the afternoon, with the kerosene lamp glowing and my sock-shod feet propped up before the little gas heater, a notebook open in my lap. My clothes were dripping. News of Hannibal's announcement would travel fast. Our enemies would soon be upon us, and I didn't have the strength to deal with them. I resolved to drive straight home, to lock the door, to take the phone off the hook, to lie down and rest.

But when I reached the apartment, cacophonous music was spilling from the open doorway of Lilja's room.

Even before stepping through that door, I knew she knew the news.

I impose few restrictions on the girl. She can live with me rent-free, and though she usually stays with her boyfriend, there are enough nights when she arrives here abruptly, in a tight jangling fluster, to suggest that she and Helmut have an on-off relationship. She can eat for free and borrow the car when I don't need it. Virtually the only limitation I impose is that in my apartment she listen to her baleful music through headphones.

The music was a protest.

I stepped through the doorway into a thicket of sound. Lilja held a book in her lap. As a child, she was something of a bookworm—a practice which, I suspect, she renounced purely to annoy me. "Hello," I shouted. "I didn't realize anyone was home."

"What?" she shouted back.

I couldn't tell whether this was her way of defusing my little joke or whether—not unlikely—she simply hadn't heard it.

"Would you turn that down a bit?" I yelled again.

Lilja turned it down. A bit.

"More?"

She brought it down to something like a human level.

"You were reading a book," I said.

This was an accusation she was quick to counter: "It's about palmistry."

"Oh I see. Well that's all right then. So tell me," I said, holding up my palm, "what's in my future."

She had dropped her eyes to her book once more. Without looking up she said, "You will become a national laughingstock."

"Would you turn that racket down still further."

She did. Another bit.

"I've been out on Giant Island," I said.

"Oh?" she said.

"Hannibal delivered an announcement. He's going to run again."

"And did you write the speech?" Her head remained buried in her book.

"I did. Or most of it anyway."

"And did your speech make reference to 'the spirit of Freeland'? And did the phrase 'the friends of Freeland' come up?"

"It may have. . . ."

"This Freeland you believe in, y'ever notice it's an anachronism? Actually, that's overly polite. You might just call it stinking dead."

I answered her with a show of great, considered sincerity: "Indeed, I have noticed it is an anachronism. Like most of the things I believe in. The printed word, say. Or hummable songs. Or the recuperative qualities of labor."

Lilja has, even in combat, a sense of fair play—it's one of the traits I love best about the girl—and justice now dictated that she acknowledge the neat eloquence of my response. She glanced up from her book. Her brow was gently furrowed, with lines that even a non-palmist could read. She was incensed. And she was, despite herself, faintly amused.

"Now let me guess," she went on. "Did it conclude with some practical proposals?"

"You know, I believe it *did*. I think there were four. It's the part of the speech I'm least likely to write of course."

"And let me guess . . . Is he going to restore the economy? What did he promise to do this time, the big bloody stupid Viking—swim out into the sea and pull in the haddock by their tails?"

"Actually, he's hoping to diversify the economy."

"Oh *is* he? Isn't that sweet? And what will we invest in? Our emerald mines? Our tobacco fields?"

The girl truly has a delicious talent for invective. Perhaps I bestowed on her a half-smile; she certainly deserved it.

"And he pledged a more streamlined government," I added.

"Streamlined? Him? The man's developing a gut the size of a walrus's. . . ."

"And he's going to strengthen the tourist industry."

"Will they come for our snorkeling, do you fancy? Or primarily for our glittering opera?"

"And there's to be better care of the elderly."

"Oh? And what about the young?"

"The young? They weren't specifically addressed I suppose."

"No, I suppose they weren't. Not *specifically*."

And then I did a surprising thing, one that, so precipitatedly did it come on, took me aback no less than Lilja: I laughed. No chuckle, no snicker—uh uh, and there was nothing wry or rueful or ironic about it. The whole full-blown absurdity of the day—the rain, the lackluster crowd, the cameraman's fall into the fissure, Trausti's drunkenness, the "expressive" sheep—suddenly goosed me in the rib cage and I let go with a belly laugh: what a country my country was!

Needless to say, mirth was fleeting. A moment later, all sobriety, I continued, "No, it's true he didn't address the *youth issue*."

The *youth issue* . . . And merely to utter the phrase was to introduce, so soon after my attack of laughter, another powerful feeling—this one far from merry. Someone or something pressed a switch inside me, and I saw that I was wrong and Lilja was right: it was that simple. The youth issue *was* the central issue, and not just for Freeland. Oh, to be sure, Lilja's views about it were cockeyed, and whatever solutions she espoused would be disastrous, but ultimately the real issue had nothing to do with whether the elderly had handsome views of Great Blue Mountain. The question was: What about our young people? To ask this was to ask nothing less than, What is the future of Freeland?

Just think of them assembled there, out in Independence Square every Friday and Saturday night. Out in rain, wind, hail—any weather that isn't positively murderous. Some nights, you'd swear every young person in Freeland is loitering in Independence Square, hundreds and hundreds of them in the darkness, at two in the morning, at three, at four, long after the discotheques close, huddling by their little newspaper fires, stumbling about, slipping on each other's vomit. Just because they're unworthy of it doesn't mean the future doesn't lie with *them*. In that moment I saw my whole country sliding into an abyss and my head spun. I took a seat on the edge of Lilja's desk.

There was a good case to be made—and I was in just the state of mind to make it—that the whole history of Freeland was written in those crowds of drunken teenagers and post-teenagers in Independence Square. For something like a thousand years, thirty-plus generations, we'd struggled to free ourselves from the torturing rack of nature. We drowned when the seas were rough, starved when disease carried off our sheep, froze to death when the polar cold came down. We gnawed on moldy stockfish and subsisted on a prayer. Just a couple of generations ago, many of us were still living in turf houses that Erik the Other, aka Erik the Fetid and Erik the Bald, would have immediately recognized as home. And nowadays, if not a rich nation by the standards of the tourists who visit us, we have nonetheless become a land whose fishermen do not drown, whose farmers do not starve, whose every home has heat and a real floor. We have accomplished the impossible goal, we have liberated ourselves from the icy multiarmed grip of cruel Mother Nature, but in all our thirty-plus generations it turns out we never had time to determine what we might do if we actually won our liberty. What have we been fighting *for*? That's the question our young people confront. That's the Youth Issue. They're no longer needed on the farms, more and more of which are abandoned each year. A single ship—provided it's a two-hundred-ton floating factory manufactured in Norway—can haul in enough fish to feed not only everyone in the village but foreign multitudes as well. The young have leisure, freedom to do what they want when they will—but the only place they can think to go is Independence Square, and the only thing they can think to do is to stand around, in the drizzle, swigging vodka.

I sat on Lilja's desk, my head spinning as though *I'd* been drinking, and the problems of the world came clear. Oh, there are still places on the globe where the fishermen drown and the farmers starve, but for those other countries, the ones that call themselves developed, surely the "Youth Problem" is *the* problem: think of the punks, earrings in their noses, lurching through London's Piccadilly Circus, think of the timorous crowds of middle-aged people making way for the skinheads marching down Berlin's Kurfürstendamm, think of the illiterate, armed youngsters patrolling the rubbled streets of Detroit. And think of them, packed shoulder to shoulder, bobbing to their poisonous music; think of them with hallucinogens joyriding down their neural systems like a vehicle packed with explosives; think of them off to the cinema, queuing up to behold, as realistic as our hypersophisticated technology can make it, eviscerations, decapitations, throat-slittings, eyeball-gougings. . . . What in the world has happened to the young foreigners who find their way to Freeland? It used to be I understood them. They came with topographical maps and coils of rope—they were looking for unspoiled hills to climb. They came with field guides and notebooks—they were here to observe the birds. They came with journals or easels—they were artists chasing after unspoiled Nature. And now they come to stand, to stand for hours on end, in Independence Square. They come bringing puzzling, unplaceable skills: they come to juggle, to sing folk songs, to give mime performances. They come to play some sort of South American panpipe; they come to do card tricks; they come, in pink leotards, to do shivering pliés and arabesques and pas de deux. They come—in the end—to panhandle. They, too, are part of the "Youth Problem." The Swedes and the Brits and the Germans and the French send their problem children to us, as we send ours to them, and why don't you all go home, I want to say to the crowds, massed like a demobilized army in Independence Square. . . . Oh, Lilja, my eyes itched and burned to see you sitting there, your own eyes regarding me suspiciously. You with that peculiar priceless face of yours—my dear blue-eyed fair-skinned broad-faced Aryan/Asian princess—don't you understand that all my anachronistic and fascistic efforts are meant to provide you with a world closer to the one you deserve?

I must have been looking rather strained, to judge from the change in Lilja's tone. If she still sought to instruct me, her voice held far less reprimand than solicitude: "Let me explain the Youth Problem. Do you know what we're listening to right now?"

"I've got the essence of it down. It's satanic in both origin and intent."

"Now I'm going to explain something. I'm going to clarify just why it is that Hannibal doesn't stand a ghost of a chance in this election. What we're listening to is Ingolfur Snorrisson singing 'I Can't Get No Satisfaction.' Ingolfur Snorrisson is Freeland's Mick Jagger."

"I'm not sure I follow you down every last byway here."

"No, I suppose you don't. But let me nonetheless point out that before this we heard Adalheidur Grimsdottir singing 'Papa Don't Preach.' Adalheidur is Freeland's Madonna. She has even dropped all trace of a last name in order to make the kinship all the more striking, although some might plausibly argue that, as names go, 'Adalheidur' doesn't have quite the international cachet that 'Madonna' does. Are you following me down the last byway here?"

"Well, dear, perhaps not the very *very* last one, no."

"I figured as much, but I'll go on anyway. Before that we heard Bubbi Skarphedinnsson's 'Just the Way You Are.' Bubbi is Freeland's Billy Joel."

"I'd have to confess even now, despite your plethora of examples, to some minimal degree of haziness."

"Yes, but as you *do* understand, since you were instrumental in writing the law, our country has various regulations about how much radio time can be devoted to non-Freelandic artists."

"A good law," I said. "Promotes local industry. You notice I don't call them artists."

"A good law with one problem. It turns out that no Freelander has ever written a single song, not one, that any other Freelandic young person, however drunk he or she may be, has ever wanted to dance to—let alone listen to while sober, without dancing. If there's a gene for rock composers, it's not in our collective gene pool."

"Further proof that we are indeed God's chosen people."

Although she wasn't about to grant me a full smile, fairness demanded that her lip at least lift slightly. The fact is she's never been able to resist my joking.

"The result of this law is that we play music written by others but recorded, incompetently, by us. Thus are born Freeland's Madonna, Freeland's Mick Jagger, Freeland's Billy Joel."

"Told you—promotes local industry."

"The problem is that no one particularly *wants* to listen to Freeland's Mick Jagger—not even his girlfriend, who happens to be a friend of mine. When she goes home does she put Ingolfur on the boom box?"

"I recently came up with a lovely Freelandic term for 'boom box,' by the way."

"Does she put on Ingolfur? No, she puts on Mick Jagger."

"These things take time, Lilja-mine. Give Ingolfur two or three more years, I'm sure he can learn to sing every bit as badly as Mr. Jagger."

Again that upper lip curled.

"Now you'll notice they're playing many Freelandic artists right now. An attempt to promote local industry?"

"I'd certainly think so."

"This is a phenomenon known as checklisting, Eggert."

Whenever my daughter is feeling my obtuseness especially keenly, she's apt to address me, schoolmarm fashion, by my first name.

She went on: "Notice that this is an hour of the day when they might figure not so many young people are listening. So they're building up a bank of credits, allowing them to play tonight what people actually want to hear. There was talk for a while of broadcasting Freelandic artists non-stop from four to six in the morning. You'd have two hours of credit before the day actually began."

"I *like* that—that's clever. Although we will have to close that loop-hole, won't we?"

"Eggert, let me put this as simply as possible: *we want our music.* And we want it in the form we want. We want Madonna. You could say *she's* the one who's going to cost you the election, Eggert."

"Then we'll go down in a noble cause, won't we? Denying you Madonna?"

"Eggert, I don't read books. Maybe I should, but I don't. I don't even always read *your* books."

I flinched, needless to say, but tried to keep a steady face.

"I know you think I ought to be spending the afternoon with *Erbyggja Saga*, some medieval manuscript about how two men fought over who had first pissing rights to a particular boulder, but I don't actually feel the slightest inclination to do so. You'd be surprised, really, to learn just how *little* interest your daughter has in the bladders of medieval men. The truth is I would trade away all the Sagas ever written for a two-CD collection of Sting's greatest hits."

I stared into my daughter's inscrutable moon-Mongol face. Were ever blue eyes more impenetrable? Then I made an announcement: "Well, my darling, it's with this last remark you've managed to cut me to the quick. Many women have tried to break your father's heart but few have suc-ceeded. You've managed it—like your mother before you. I'm going to bed."

I'd not yet eaten dinner, but I went straight to my room, closed the door, slipped off my shoes, and dropped headlong, in my clothes, onto my bed. Quickly, mercifully, sleep came down over my head.

19

Concerto for Hovel and Winds

"You've been a busy young man."

True enough, but why did this sound like a reproach?

"Absolutely."

"And so young—you're not yet twenty-five."

"Not yet, no."

"And two books. Not just a single novel but a *pair* of them. It takes an exceptional level of confidence for a young man not yet twenty-five to submit for publication *two* books. You've been quite prolific."

"Oh I wouldn't want you to think I've written only two," I told him. "I've finished five novels in all. The other three weren't worthy of me."

"Worthy of you?" And he laughed at this. Could it be he found me a little pompous? He was an obscure figure in all sorts of ways—not least in the immediate, material, visible sense: his big-bellied, blond-wooded pipe had erected a soft gray wall between us. The air in this airless office was suffocating.

"Not worthy of my reader," I corrected.

"Your *reader*, yes." And behind his wall of smoke he seemed to find *this* amusing too. The room was dark, the shade was pulled. Why didn't he turn on a lamp? The brightest light in the room was that of his match, and the second brightest was the glowing bed of shredded nerves in the belly of his pipe.

I didn't know what to say.

"And you wrote them in America?" he went on.

"Yes—in America."

"You were gone—what? Two years?"

"More than three."

"That's a very peculiar place, America. Where did you spend your time?"

"Detroit. Chicago. Denver. Seattle. And Canada too. And nearly two months in Mexico, most of it in the Yucatán. I suppose I liked Seattle best. Have you been to Seattle?"

"Seattle? Seattle, no."

"Although there was a substantial, if rather naïve, charm to Denver." Yes, I'm afraid that's the sort of tone that I, in my youth and nervousness, was taking with the great man; I, too, was producing a smoke screen. "To the Freelandic imagination, there's something irresistibly alluring in any city so far from the sea. Have you been to Denver?"

"Denver, no."

"What is your favorite American city?" I was of course eager, after that embarrassing exchange about the *worthiness* of my books, to establish an affinity. We would be voyagers together.

"My favorite American city? Well my boy, I think I prefer Copenhagen to them all," he declared, and in a flash I understood, with a potent, contrary mixture of relief and unease, that he'd never been to America. He was of that generation for whom a trip to Denmark was a voyage to the center of the map.

"You were working?" he went on. "At jobs, I mean."

"Always. I always found some sort of job."

"And writing always?"

"Always writing."

"Where did you find the time?"

"I very rarely sleep."

His slow rumble of laughter—a bump-bump-bump like a pram going down a flight of stairs—suggested that I'd been joking. So I repeated it, only more emphatically: "I very rarely sleep. I'm an insomniac."

This time he launched at me, over a fresh cloud of pipe smoke, a penetrating glance that said, *Who are you really?* He'd probably never heard of me until two days ago, when I scuttled into his office toting a ratty paper bag that, it transpired, contained a pair of novels. Total duration of my first visit to his office: less than sixty seconds.

I'd known about *him* almost since the beginning of time. He was Saint Peter, keeper of the keys to Heaven—which is to say, he was Magnus Ingisson, publisher of Great Blue Press. He had figured in my daydreams for years. He was going to establish my name. Together we would awaken and reconfigure Freelandic literature.

He said, "I understand you've become a homeowner."

News travels fast in Thorskrist. "A landowner, anyway. I don't know how much longer that home of mine is going to stand."

He laughed at this, too, before—evidently thinking better of it—puffing furiously, one might better say spitefully, at his pipe. *Who are you?*

I'd returned to Freeland eight days before to discover that my aunt Dögg—the woman who'd raised me—had died only a month before. She'd left me "everything," which was in truth only a little more than nothing. I'd been all the family remaining to her, but even so she surprised me by leaving me her small all. She'd never much cared for me, frankly. Still, she'd fed me and sheltered me and darned my socks and shirts; I had, you might say, no bone to pick with her skeleton. She'd been an accountable creature who, having accepted me as a charge, never publicly rued the decision. She saw it as her obligation, I suppose, to leave whatever legacy she had to her nearest kin. Nonetheless, and grateful as I was to discover, on my return to Freeland, that I not only still had a roof over my head but now *owned* that very roof, I think I would have been even more heartened had that dogtrot old woman, scoffing at duty, instead bequeathed her house to some scabrous, unwashed rogue of a sailor, or to the Catholic Church, or to a spiritual medium. If it's true—as my calling as a novelist encourages me to suppose—that every life encloses at least one marvelous story, it's likewise true that most people take their sole story with them to the grave. Into the ground they and their story disappear, without leaving behind even the perennial flower of one memorable anecdote. . . .

"Will you be staying here awhile, Eggert?" Magnus Ingisson asked me.

"That's hard to say. That depends on a good many things."

"How does your homeland look to you after three years away from it?"

"Interesting—very interesting. We come from a very interesting country, don't we, you and I?"

Oh, I hardly knew what I was saying! No wonder he, puffing prodigiously, scrutinized me as though I were some lunatic. But in truth these inquiries of his meant nothing to me. One question, and one alone, was at issue here—though I didn't quite dare to ask it, and he at every turn seemed to sidestep it.

"You must have been at the Superior School with Hannibal Hannibalsson."

Oh, Hannibal—everyone knew *him*.

"Indeed I was, he's my closest friend."

"Your closest friend?" If I hadn't felt so nervous, I might have felt insulted. The man's incredulity was patent. His look said: Hannibal Hannibalsson found a close friend in the likes of *you*? "I understand he's working on a farm out on Giant," he went on.

"For the moment. He's had enough of the Danes, I gather."

If there is anything my countrymen relish more than stories about a Freelander's runaway success in Denmark it is a tale of a Freelander's thumbing his nose at such success. Hannibal had managed both, evidently.

"A most extraordinary young man," Magnus said.

"I've always thought so."

"You have seen him since your return?"

"No. Not yet. I will."

Magnus's next unasked question—*Why have you been back for a week and not yet bothered to look up your closest friend?*—hung loose as smoke in the air. I could not tell him that my answer depended on that other question, the vital question, beside which no other talk counted for anything: *Mr. Ingisson, is Great Blue Press going to publish either of the books I submitted?* A portion of my mind believed utterly in those books, and in the illustrious fate they presaged, but I would be rewriting my personal history if I didn't also confess my nervousness. Wasn't it possible that the manuscripts were barren, and Magnus Ingisson was about to reveal that all my months of work—my entire journey to America, even the deep recuperative breaths I'd taken into my infected lungs three years before as *The Return* pulled out of Thorskrist Harbor—came to naught? Before I went off in search of Hannibal, I needed to know where I stood.

"You write in Freelandic," Magnus said—with a hint of reproach?

"I do—at least I have."

"It is customary for Freelandic writers to write in Danish. That has always been our literary language."

Like Moses, I spoke confidently into the burning cloud: "Oh, I could write them in Danish. Or in English, too—I speak English better than the Americans do, not just literary English but the American vernacular. I like slang." I used the English word and it rang—*slang*—hanging in the air around us. "I've studied it as hard as I've ever studied anything. No, I could have gone all sorts of ways. I've chosen Freelandic on principle."

"Danish has always been our literary language."

"Seven hundred years ago, when the Sagas were being penned, those anonymous writers did not compose in Danish—there was no Danish.

They chose to write in Old Norse, which is to say in Freelandic. I always thought *that* was our literary language."

The cloud cogitated. It had met something unexpected in me: a fine stony defiance.

"There are moments in your books more—more believable to me than other moments. Now in the one called *The Annals of Nils*, where our hero arrives in Canada, in Nova Scotia, and befriends that colored man, the African whaler, Ishmael—well now, all that has the flavor of real authenticity to it, doesn't it? But that first woman he meets, Peggy, the one with—with the scar on her face, there's something highly improbable, isn't there, in a woman of her age, in all their amorous—their amorous—" Doubt, disapprobation momentarily stilled him.

"Even so, even so," Magnus went on, fuming once more, "*The Annals of Nils* has about it a—well, it has a youthful—a certain youthfulness, doesn't it?"

Youthfulness? Me? But I nodded in agreement.

"A youthfulness that would make it . . . It speaks to the Condition of the Young, doesn't it? Which is why I'm proposing we do that one first, and *Vinland Voyages* perhaps six months later."

The import of these words was unmistakable, and yet I needed to have them outright: I needed to have them denuded of every last vestige of smoke and shadow. "Does this mean," I said to him, "that you're consenting to publish my books?"

I was met by another descending rumble of laughter, another penetrating look, fresh clouds of smoke—as well as, eventually, by a "Yes, my lad, yes, Great Blue is going to do them—do them both. These two little books of yours."

What abruptly followed was a lengthy and again almost hostile disquisition—this one about the parlous state of Freeland's economy, the especial tenuousness of the publishing world, the slovenly reading habits of Freelanders generally, and the long decline of literacy since the great Middle Ages, when every shepherd's boy could, on demand, forge a serviceable quatrain. The elaborately-arrived-at conclusion was that I could of course expect no publisher's advances and should, naturally, expect neither of these books to butter my bread, still less to buy me a new pair of shoes. I scarcely heard him. Although *he* was the creature of fire and smoke, when we parted some twenty minutes later, with a wispy handshake, it was I who walked with steps that didn't touch the ground.

I stepped out into a capital city that was *mine*: I held Freeland in freehold. Although there was some question whether I still belonged to this country, there was no doubting that *it* belonged to *me*. My first thought, standing there on Skeggjagata on a blue, breezy day in August 1962, combing the street from one end to the other, was, Where's Hannibal? I wanted *him* to see me at this moment, when Thorskrist itself lay in my hands. It seemed we were still running our footrace on the playing fields by the Superior School. I wanted him there, but where was he? Racing sheep up and down the slopes of Giant Island!

I stepped forth into the streets of a city I owned, but even in those instants of my apotheosis, wasn't I feeling intimations that the city was no longer everything it once had been—that my triumph was hollow? For eight days now, ever since the corrugated aluminum houses of Thorskrist first glittered into view, I'd been fending off a sense of the scantiness of my native domain. To step into Halldor's Booth, which had lately come to calling itself a supermarket, was to invite despair. To eat in Valhalla or even the dining room of the Hotel Snorri was to invite despair. To climb into one of our five city buses—each representing one-fifth of the country's mass transit system—and find that the windshield was cracked in half a dozen places, the driver making his rounds through a fractured city, was to invite despair. To inspect our clothes and our haircuts, to buy one of our newspapers, to meet a flyer for "An Evening in Old Vienna" as rendered by the International Freeland String Quartet—all of these were to invite despair.

I sauntered down to the waterfront, where I met an old tar, Torfi Torfason, who had known my aunt. He walked with a cane—he'd had an accident many years back. He was seated on the dock, eating a piece of buttered dried fish and drinking a Coca-Cola.

"Fish, Eggert?" he said by way of greeting, and held it out. It was just the greeting you might expect. I hadn't laid eyes on him in more than three years.

I ripped off a companionable shred of fish and chewed for a minute. "Do you think the butter's gone bad?" Torfi asked me.

"Maybe a little."

"I don't have any taste buds left."

"It doesn't matter. The butter's mostly for lubrication." If you decided to eat your hiking boot, you'd probably be grateful for a little butter, rancid or no. It's much the same with our dried fish.

"I hear the old girl's dead."

"A few weeks before I arrived. So I never saw her again. I'd gone to America."

"You were away," Torfi said. "And the house?"

"The house is mine."

"Well then."

Torfi held out the fish and I tore free another shred.

"Storm's coming," he said, staring out to sea.

"When do you estimate?"

"Soon now. Two hours, three."

"I think I'll head home then."

The word rang oddly in my ear: *home. My home.* It followed me crookedly down the street like the tolling of a cracked bell: *home, home, home.* Is this where I *lived,* this tumbledown shack of rust-riddled corrugated siding and splintered cement?

Home—and if not here, where? This is where the old woman had lived her Dögg's life. She'd left the place neat—stripped, indeed, of most of its narrative interest, though I did find in her chest of drawers my letters, a tidy packet tied with a green ribbon. Eleven in all. She'd been true to the vow she'd made on my departure, answering nary a one, but she'd kept them all—whether out of duty, again, or perhaps, I'd like to think, out of Romance in the broadest sense: these were messages from another, an unimaginable world. . . . I'd set them beside her obituary in *The Torch.* Dögg Danielsdottir. Deceased.

So: one more infinitesimal shifting in the great human balance: a single unit subtracted from the unreckonably vast multidigit number of the living and added to the unreckonably vast multidigit number of the dead. . . . Yes, there in black and white was the face of the deceased, and there as well were the life-statistics which said, finally, little about that life, and it occurred to me that a whole novel might be devoted to the rewriting of a single obituary. Think of them, the daily departees, all those faces lined up in their black and white galleries, all of them mutely clamoring for a truthful voice: so many books to write!

But not today. I needed to settle in first, and it was comforting when, just as if Torfi had the heavens at his beck and call, the wind began to blow as he'd scheduled. The old house creaked, protesting in its resigned, long-term way. It's a prehistoric, a primordial marriage—that between wind and shelter—and one in which, like the oldest of human marriages, the gender of the partners ultimately blurs, until you can no longer say whether it's a mad old man raging, out there on the heath, or an embittered harridan. Whose are they?—whose are the sighs of the roof and the walls and the floor?

Celebration is something I never seem to have any flair for. . . . How was I to meet this news from Magnus Ingisson? How acknowledge the realization that Freeland belonged to me? I began rereading *A Midsummer Night's Dream*, which hadn't yet been translated into anything resembling true Freelandic. I owed it to my country, and to Shakespeare, and to myself: surely I was meant to live in a land whose language contained a competent version of *A Midsummer Night's Dream*. . . .

I would contact Hannibal on the morrow. If the race we were running belonged finally to me, I would rise above all gloating. Was he chasing sheep out on Giant while I was being crowned as the father-to-be of modern Freelandic literature? I would not gloat. For hadn't he climbed with me over the hills behind Thorskrist on a gelid pitch-black night, and hadn't he somehow talked the two of us onto the NATO base, and hadn't we sat there transfixed in the flickering half-dawn of the movie projector, watching wide-eyed and slack-jawed as Fred sang to Ginger, "as long as I can be with you it's a sunny day"? We were blood brothers.

Somewhere, far from Freeland, Oberon had deposited, diaphanous as a fairy's wing, a gauze of sorcery on Titania's eyelids, and somewhere far from Freeland Fred pursued Ginger through a mazed Venice erected of plywood and Bakelite by unionized carpenters in southern California, and who is to say where the boundaries of enchantment cease? There have certainly been occasions when it has reached across the years and miles to tap with its potent improbable wand Eggert Oddason as he hunches over his writing desk in Thorskrist's Skyscraper Tower, momentarily allowing him to slough off his orphaned upbringing, his pinched rodential features, his raging petty grievances and animosities.

By the time I went upstairs to bed the wind was really up and the whole house was shaking, as if in a fever—a cold fever. I fell asleep under the sloping roof in the bed where, over the years, I'd grown inch by inch from boyhood into manhood, ossifying through time into the grasping, ambitious, spiteful, and yet on occasion nearly admirable grown-up I'd become.

And I woke in the middle of the night to a familiar darkness: *my* darkness, defined by an angle of the roof that was *my* angle, by a collection of smells that were *my* smells. In the swampy inner purlieus of the brain, where, improbably, sights and scents are alike transformed into the numbers of an ideal geometry, a statistically implausible harmony had been achieved. The old woman—bless her—was truly dead. And yet her house perdured, creaking and sighing and remonstrating in all its aged, deathless ways. Oh, these were *my* sounds, these were the finest fiercest music I knew: that of the old house in a storm, granted at last its chance for commentary, and responding with creaks, rattles, bangings, whistles, sighs, all of which I knew intimately, and yet all of which were freshly conceived: music timeless and new.

Wind and shelter, the oldest marriage that ever was, and in my state of half-sleep I, the product of their union, experienced an acute moment of distress: Wasn't it almost over? Would this concert soon stop? Better than Mozart it was, even his Symphony no. 5252, "The Circle Squared," and how could such a meager, destitute land as my Freeland sustain so opulent a music?

But the next moment, as my mind drifted elsewhere—closer to sleep? closer to wakefulness?—I understood, exquisitely, the groundlessness of all such fears. In this particular resource, the rising of the wind in the middle of the night, no country on earth was so well endowed. Hours, days, rolling treeless eternities—the wind might go on and on and on. My land was inexhaustible.

20

The Gray Closes In

Afternoon after afternoon, looking up from my desk in my study, I relish the arrival of a storm. Even now, with all my years here, the changes in our weather are something to marvel at. A flawless blue day will unwrap itself, ninety-three million miles of uninterrupted clarity between the sun and Thorskrist, and now appears on the horizon a single gray cloud, no more weighty than a child's balloon, and of no more moment than a mumbled profanity . . . and yet here's another and another and another, a long string of dark invective, assembling themselves into a tumbling tirade, a local rage that feeds upon itself, and abruptly in the whole of the heavens there are no more than two or three tightening pockets of blue, and in these urgent instants they become the human spirit itself, don't they?—struggling to hold intact some sense of perspicuity, music, freedom.

Something like that feeling, a sense of being squeezed in a cloudy vise, followed me relentlessly throughout the weekend of Hannibal's announcement. The process was entirely soft and insidious. But all the exits were narrowing. The gray was closing in. . . . On television, his speech looked even more absurd—more sodden and chaotic and woebegone—than it had in life. And despite the shortage of time I'd imposed on them, the "Youth Hour" bastards came at us that evening with drawn swords. Worse was still to come, of course, but they did manage to put together a particularly vile Puppettheater, in which King Carthage's court fool revealed himself in a new role, as a puppetmaster: the royal monarch wiggled and danced in his hands. I was struck not so much by the rancor as by the injustice of this portrayal, for, whatever my wrongdoings, in this particular campaign I'd been—as the record clearly shows—far more the manipulated than the manipulator. We were—all of us who worked on Hannibal's behalf—alike subordinate to that "vision" of his. We were slaves to that perfect rainbow which had called upon him to seek a fifth term.

Freeland has three daily newspapers. Hannibal and I have traditionally enjoyed with the *Torch*, largest of the three, a close and amicable relationship, and in their editorial pages they came forth in immediate support of us. And yet there was, wasn't there—and I don't think I'm being overly thin-skinned—something maybe a little grudging in their endorsement? Wasn't it an avowal phrased without passion? *Dagbladid Stormur*—*The Daily Storm*—typically forwent any immediate judgment, but in the guise of an impartial recounting of events they were unmistakably hostile. And *The Daily Ledger*—to be known here henceforth as *The Daily Liar*—exceeded even the outraged howls we'd expected. Truly, their spluttering bile was a shock. One sensed something new to modern Freelandic politics, or new at least in the domain of broad public utterance: a rage approaching hatred. If nothing else, my country's native pessimism—fostering a sense that life would never go *very* well, irrespective of who was in office—had always encouraged a healthy resignation.

Meanwhile, Rut had carted off her few belongings from Hannibal's house on Founders' Point—the two of them have maintained separate residences during the length of their "marriage"—and on the couple of occasions when he telephoned, she refused to speak to him. And my children ostracized me. But more distressing yet was the chill I met from strangers—at the supermarket, at the bookstore, at the fishbooth. *Everyone* seemed to be feeling betrayed, and, ironically, I did, too—betrayed by their very sense of betrayal. How could they be so stony-hearted? Weren't the most revered of our nation's heroes those old Viking warriors who, bleeding from multiple wounds, nonetheless fought on? And if the odds were insurmountable—so much the better! Had my countrymen forgotten Gisli, who survived fourteen years of outlawry in the West Fjords, and when he went down, on the slope of Einhamar, it was a battle of a dozen men against one? Or Njal, who consented to be burned alive rather than surrender to his enemies? I wanted to denounce my countrymen as hypocrites, to harangue them, to shake sense into their heads. How could anybody calling himself a true Freelander turn his back on the one modern leader imbued with the great adversarial spirit of old? Who has betrayed whom here?

Dispiriting, too, was the speed and efficiency with which our opposition marshaled against us. Forces were rallying behind Rut's cousin with an intensity I wouldn't have thought possible: How could anyone rally enthusiastically behind a nonentity like Nonni Karlsson? All weekend, ominous rumors circulated. A consortium of Danish businessmen, out of sorts with Hannibal's erratic uppityness, was going to donate a million kronur to Nonni's campaign. The Japanese, impatient with our waffling on the whaling issue, were going to supply Nonni with a panoply of the latest electronic equipment—microphones, television cameras, video cameras. The fishermen's collective, weary of declining catches and sinking prices, and superstitiously convinced that, even if Hannibal *was* doing everything he could, he'd nonetheless become irretrievably unlucky, was cuddling up to Nonni. So were the teachers, and the police, and so, believe it or not, was the Psychics Guild, who had divined a rosier future under a new administration. The opposition of the young took an eye-catching turn in the person of our beautiful, feckless Vikram Jakobsson, he of the solar-yellow Mustang, who festooned his vehicle with banners and graffiti proclaiming *Nonni Yes* and *No more than Four* and *Nonni Karlsson = Freeland's Future* and, despite the raw weather, drove it with the top down around and around the streets of Thorskrist, beeping his horn and blaring his stereo.

I wanted to throttle the boy by his comely throat, while saying to him, *The reason you are here at all, and not lying dead in Calcutta of those many maladies you carried with you to this country, is precisely because of the policies of that "old fart" you ridicule, who in his doubtless too generous and grandiose way has dreamed always of making Freeland a haven for the hurting.* I wanted to slap Vikram's silly face while saying, *It was Hannibal who dreamed of establishing Thorskrist's Chinatown, its Little Saigon, its Little Rio and Little Lagos, and it was his efforts to modify the laws of a country that had never made any allowance for foreign adoption that led to your salvation.* But what, finally, can a middle-aged man say to someone who on a frosty day cruises the town in a yellow Mustang convertible decked with banners proclaiming *Out with the Old*?

We waited, all weekend long, with dread in our hearts, for Monday and Tuesday, when the workaday world would reawaken and "Youth Hour" detonate the bomb it had no doubt spent the weekend fiendishly devising. Oh why wasn't I elsewhere? Drinking a cup of Darjeeling tea in Amsterdam's Hotel de l'Europe; strolling through the Tivoli Gardens or the Jardin des Plantes; sitting on a boulder, shirtless, shoeless, in southern California, while watching—oh, how briskly in the end our wildest youthful fantasies come to life!—women in bikinis batting a volleyball. . . .

Hannibal and I arranged to watch "Youth Hour" together at his place on Tuesday night. I arrived twenty minutes early and, to prepare myself, began sipping vodka, neat. He was drinking Brown Death, our traditional schnapps. It's a beverage which, for all my Freelandic chauvinism, I've never been able to stomach. Since there's nothing brown about either the bottle, the label, or the contents, the sobriquet remains something of a mystery. One story has it that the original glass bottles, long ago, were brown. Others insist that it refers to the running havoc it wreaks in your digestive tract.

"Youth Hour" . . . Of course we fully expected to be the lead-off story. Instead, we were treated to an account, upbeat and innocuous, about the performance of Freeland's handball team in a competition in Oslo. This was followed by news of an art show of paintings by a young woman who, despite having painstakingly converted her hair into a palisade of purple spikes, devoted her artistic talents to largely recognizable Freelandic landscapes, painted by means of a brush, on canvas, with oils. What in the world was going on?

A woman in an army jacket—dressed alarmingly like my own Lilja—announced that a special feature about the election was forthcoming. There was mischief—more than mischief—in her gaze, and I waited for something cataclysmic. . . . But the camera shifted not to the United Nations Building in New York and an announcement that by special dispensation of the Secretary General a multinational expeditionary force had been authorized to invade Freeland if that unregenerate ass Hannibal Hannibalsson were reelected; no, the camera opened on some young newlyweds whose passports and money had been stolen in London's Victoria Station. Huh?

Next appeared a young man in a purple shirt and a green blazer—one of the "Youth Hour" stalwarts—who was standing out by Thorskrist Harbor. The wind ruffled his hair. He was holding an unlit cigarette. On top of all his other offenses, he was outstandingly good-looking. These days, he might be expected to turn young female hearts much as, in another era, the six-gold-medal winner of the First Freelandic Olympics used to do.

His tone was cheerful but somber—which is to say bright and duplicitous.

"It won't be long before all of us, young and old, go forth to elect a new President. It's a grave responsibility. This may well be the most important collective decision we've ever made."

He paused to sweep his gaze over White Seal Bay and it pleased me to feel, within my heart, dislike solidifying into detestation.

"Now it's our conviction, here at 'Youth Hour,' that *both* sides in what will surely be a very heated election have their virtues." What in the world was the bastard getting at? Where was this going? I poured myself another vodka. Hannibal dipped again into his Brown Death.

"We thought, for tonight's 'Youth Hour,' we'd look into the virtues of Hannibal Hannibalsson. Now it's the feeling among the staff here that the best way to discover a candidate's virtues is to go to that one special person who knows the candidate most intimately. So we've done just that. The results"—and the camera tracked toward his face, revealing the ghost of a smile on his handsome lips—"were a great surprise."

Even at this point, I must confess, I had no inkling what they were up to. I don't think Hannibal did either, but that's less surprising, since he seems constitutionally convinced that there's something unmanly in detecting an ambush before it has been sprung. He was probably as surprised as I when the camera, sliding down the quay, halted before the Cod's Head. The young man, speaking in voice-over, went on: "And so we went to Rut Bjartardottir, beloved proprietor of the Cod's Head, who has been intimate friend and close adviser to our President for more than three decades. If anyone has a clear vision of who he is and why we should vote for him, surely that person is Rut Bjartardottir."

Forgive my stupidity, but even at this point I wasn't fully prepared for what followed. I guess I was denying the obvious. In any event, the very next shot brought us an undeniable presence. There was our Rut, looking ill at ease and impatient, but also imposingly resolute as she stood beside the young man in the purple shirt and green blazer.

"*She isn't going to do this . . . ,*" Hannibal whispered.

"Do you think . . . ," I whispered back.

"Lately I've often found myself wondering," the young man said to Rut, "whether you, with your wide experience in our politics, have given any thought to the upcoming election."

"Plenty—plenty of thought . . . ," Rut mumbled.

"Now you have known our current President for—well, for, perhaps, let's see, some—"

"For a hell of a long time."

She had no patience, clearly, with the young man's coy circumlocutions—as he evidently sensed. He must curtail the irony, or he would lose her. He ran a hand through his blond hair and, thoughtfully pursing his lips, nodded sympathetically. He said: "Hey, let's get to the point. Given your long acquaintance with our President, surely I'd be right in assuming you plan to cast your vote for Hannibal Hannibalsson?"

"You would be . . . dead . . . wrong."

"I beg your pardon?" And the young man popped his eyes in a fine simulation of flabbergasted confusion.

Rut glared at him. There was no doubting that the boy had heard her and had been, in addition, fully prepared for her answer. Well, this sort of histrionic nonsense wasn't the least to her liking. But after a moment's deliberation—weighing annoyance with annoyance, grievance with grievance—she chose to save her ammunition for the greater target, for the chief and original cause of all her discontent. Looking away from the young man, she stared fixedly at the camera—or as fixedly as anyone with a cast in one eye was capable of—and declared, "Dead . . . wrong. I will *not* be voting for Hannibal Hannibalsson. I will be voting for Nonni Karlsson. Five years ago Hannibal pledged, time and again, that he would not come up for reelection. He made a pact with us. That was part of the bargain when we voted for him, and now he is going back on his side of the bargain. He is proving that he cannot be trusted."

The room was going dark. The only light in the world was the unhealthy glow of Hannibal's television. The only nourishment in the world was Hannibal's Brown Death, which he splashed deep into his churning, battered vitals. "*She is not doing this . . . ,*" he insisted.

Oh, but she was. With her one good eye, she was peering hard into the cyclopean eye of the camera and she was saying, "Before Hannibal's announcement, I declared that I was supporting Nonni Karlsson in the upcoming election, and I, anyway, am going to stick to my word. This should come as a surprise to nobody, least of all to Hannibal himself. . . ." She was now addressing him alone, the rest of the nation was as nothing to her, the feud lay between her and Hannibal only, to whom she was saying, "When you told me you planned to run again, I made a vow. I said, When others ridicule you, I will not defend you. I said, When others attack you, I will not lift a finger to protect you." She halted. "I will stick to that vow. . . ."

"Well this is startling, *amazing* news—amazing, *startling* news. Could you please tell us, tell the nation if you will, whether this untrustworthiness you speak of is part of a more general psychological pathology, something that perhaps goes to the very *character* of the man you have known for—"

But with a testy brush of a hefty arm, Rut waved him off. "I've got coffee to serve," she said, and swung round squarely. She looked even bigger on the screen than in life—as sizable as any troll as she clambered down into her cavern.

The room went absolutely dark. I suppose the television was still running, the lamps still burning, but when Hannibal said, a moment later, "That's really it, isn't it?" he was speaking into a dwelling gone black as pitch.

It was unnecessary to add a thing. Yet merely to show him I, too, was present in the darkness—seated beside him on the floor of Hell's basement—I said, "That's it, all right." After an unilluminated pause I added, "We're finished, my friend."

II

21

The Heavy Hand of Fate

Eggert the Needle-nosed threads the streets of Copenhagen, Eggert the Sharp-eyed is playing Twenty Down. *You will spend the remainder of your natural life on a tropical island deserted of everyone but your wife, whom you will select from among the next twenty women who cross your path.* The sky is blue—buoyant, even bouncy—on this brisk summer day in June 1967. *The instant a woman crosses your path, you must arrive at your decision whether to marry her or let her go. All decisions are irreversible.* Outdoors, people are drinking coffee from toy-sized cups. Metropolitan life—continental life!—and a child walks by, hilarity spilling from his fine features, who trails kitelike in the breeze behind him a grapey cluster of five purple balloons. Lord, the opulence of this place! *You cannot remain single. The game ends when you have selected a wife, or when, reaching twenty, the twentieth is selected for you. . . .* Eggert likes to imagine that somewhere in the streets of Copenhagen a beautiful female creature—he sees her as tall and young, a green-eyed redhead whose creamy freckle-dotted skin evokes the cup of warm milk dusted with nutmeg he likes to nurse before bed—is simultaneously playing Twenty Down. Complementary games are being enacted as the two of them, unwittingly, wind their way toward a rendezvous near Rosenberg Castle. On her circuitous journey, the beautiful female creature happens upon a number of plausible mates—blond young men all, with strong jaws and square shoulders—and yet she, trusting to some darting inkling of an intuition, chooses to pass them by. Twelve, thirteen, fourteen . . . Her husband must come soon!

And our Eggert, too, passes up all sorts of enticements, for he likewise heeds his intuitions. A sky so blue, a heaven so fair, must surely in the end, at a bare minimum, dish up one angel. Fourteen, fifteen, sixteen . . . Soon now, his wife must come soon!

The numbers mount, the pressure builds, and imagine the two of them poised at the very brink: both have rejected nineteen candidates, both are pricklingly aware, as a corner nears, that the very next person who swings into sight will be their mate into eternity. Now, yes, the moment ripens, this is it, the corner is turned and—and, right before your eyes, stands your future! And imagine the rapturous joy rippling through Eggert's little body! Inside his chest, it's as if popcorn were exploding, for there she is, his sweet promised partner! And imagine, equally, the girl's horror, her desolation! Think of her sense of cold betrayal within—it's like having a shovelful of wet clay dumped over her intestines—on discovering that before her stands, in place of the prince she was clearly meant for, Eggert the Hamster-faced . . . and already, already the handsome, seductive streets of Copenhagen are dissolving into a mist, she is being transported, as a sweeping, sour wind screams through the entrails of a dripping cavern, to that imprisoning isle where the runty, swarthy, hirsute body before her is to be her one-and-only, is to be her all-in-all. . . . What a vision it is! So delectable is this combination—her beauty yoked to her pitiful despair—that it makes Eggert's head spin, for however bitterly she may bewail her fate, however fiercely the very winds of the earth may rage at the rank monstrousness of this coupling, the Rules of the Game must be honored, and Beast shall have his Beauty. And—who knows?—Beauty may learn in time to cherish her Beast. . . .

It's one of the best games Eggert knows, fusing as it does romance with frustration, disappointment, even heartbreak, and all of them delivered in the name of Cosmic Justice. The Rules must be obeyed *scrupulously*. There's no speeding up one's pace, or slowing it down, or changing one's course for the purpose of in any way altering the progression of women who pass you on the street. Your romantic life is securely in the hands of the gods, and the lesson they would teach you is, Your lot is meant to be grim. Passion stumbles, love withers.

But not today! The streets are singing in Eggert's ears, *Another game! Another game!* So far, his luck this morning has been spectacular and what else would you expect in a city of such spectacular women? The first time around, he'd pledged himself to a young tall bosomy creature with appealingly protruding ears who arrived—bless her!—at the nick of time; she was number nineteen. On the next pass-through he'd taken as his bride an engagingly gentle-faced woman, maybe fifteen years his senior, who had the air—or if she didn't have it, he was happy to lend it to her—of being handsomely widowed and what does it say about his knotted psyche that he can think of no more erotically charged word-coupling than *handsomely widowed*? In the next round, he committed himself early, marrying a young woman who looked Indonesian; there was pleasure to be taken in the notion that the island of their banishment might recall to her the tradewind-fanned site of her birth.

On the next round, though, his luck appeared to sour. Very early into the game he passed up a pigeon-toed girl walking a bicycle, sufficiently attractive but with acne peppering her cheeks and something lackluster to her gaze. And now he was paying for his choosiness. Fourteen, fifteen, sixteen, he was offered a trio of women, all older than his aunt Dögg would be if his aunt were not now bedded in a cemetery under Great Blue Mountain. Freeland's climate treats its dead with a clemency it rarely shows the living; those bodies under Great Blue Glacier decompose far more slowly than in a temperate land. But for the living, it's another matter, and a voice in Eggert's head today announces, You are alive, Eggi, you are alive! Seventeen, eighteen, nineteen . . . I had nowhere else to go, I was at the end of my rope, and now from round the corner stepped my wife-to-be.

She cuts off the sun, she blocks most of the light on the street, for this woman is more enormous than *enormous*, this is perhaps the vastest woman—the vastest human being—Eggert has ever laid eyes upon. Eggert adores large women but this one is so colossal her arms cannot hang down on anything like a vertical line. The girth of her hips lifts them out, at an angle, lending her arms a flipperlike look, and here comes my wife-to-be, outweighing me by what cannot be less than two hundred and fifty pounds, and unless the heavens intervene, we will be wed within moments, in the instant we pass one another. I myself am, according to the Rules of Twenty Down, powerless to obstruct or hinder our encounter. I cannot even slow my pace, let alone cross the street; my only hope is she'll suddenly turn in her tracks, push her way into a store, drop dead of a heart attack, simultaneously combust. I step toward my wife, and she marches down upon me. . . .

And the heavens intervene. A bus swirls by on my right, and a boulder flies into my right eye—an object so large and razor-sharp I cry out in pain. I cradle my head in my hands, tears stream down my face, and then the boulder tumbles loose. Gone—quickly as it came. I wipe my eye on the sleeve of my jacket, stand erect, peer in front of me, peer behind me, and discover that the woman has indeed spontaneously combusted. Not even a trace of smoke.

And at that very moment, bursting out of a shop on my left, steps my new wife-to-be. She is quite a large woman—though she seems, after her predecessor, a mere slip of a girl—and she is handsome, with masses of unkempt blond hair and a blouse of which one tail has worked its way loose of her slacks. I do love female dishevelment. She holds in her hands her purchase. She tears it open hungrily and, letting the cellophane flutter to the ground, plugs a cigarette into her mouth. Her littering, too, appeals to me. She starts walking in my direction. A breeze brings the cellophane along with her, and I step decisively upon it, in a ceremonial way, just as she—making our marriage official—passes me by.

This time, the heavens had truly intervened. This was no mere mutual, lifelong banishment to a deserted island. No mere marriage until eternity. We shared a far deeper bond than that. The heavens had intervened, calling upon me to do what I would otherwise never have done: I turned and followed her. Two blocks later she entered a cafe, auspiciously called The Meeting Place. I followed my wife inside, taking a table two tables from hers.

My wife almost immediately drew from her sacklike purse a book, which faintly disconcerted me—life was going to be far more difficult for us if she admired the wrong writers—and then almost as quickly, with a forehead-creasing look of impatience, she set it down. Which likewise disconcerted me. Life would be hard going if she had no respect for books. She ordered a coffee and a pastry. I ordered coffee, too, though money at the moment was a bit tight and the Meeting Place was scandalously overpriced.

When the coffee and pastry emerged, she left her cigarette burning, and variously drifted, in sips and bites and puffs, from one refreshment to the other to the other—which, too, was a little unnerving, but which did not stop me from shortly appearing at her side. I asked her, in Danish, whether I might borrow a cigarette.

"Afraid I don't speak Danish," she replied, in what sounded like good Danish. Was I being dismissed? She hadn't glanced in my direction long enough to dismiss me.

"I don't either, when I can avoid it," I said in English. "Where are you from?"

She didn't answer this one. Had she even understood? I had at my disposal a couple of other languages I might try before abandoning this first foray.

"I'm from a place perhaps you've never heard of," I said. "I'm from Freeland."

My wife gave me a piercing look and said in an odd-edged English I could not place, "My father went there."

"Your father did? What was he doing? We don't get many visitors."

"Buying it, I suppose. He's a merchant."

"And not a very successful one if he went and bought Freeland." And I gave my little wisecrack an extra, extended laugh to compensate for the woman's stoniness.

"And where is he based," I asked, "this merchant father of yours?" Again she didn't answer me. "I was hoping to borrow a cigarette. You know what it's like when you're out . . ."

This plea softened her enough, anyway, that she shot me a fleeting glance and nodded at the pack on the table. Of course I was now obliged to smoke one of the hateful things.

"Do you have a light?" I asked her.

You might suppose, to judge from her air of weariness, that I'd been troubling her for two hours rather than two minutes. She nodded, my wife, at the lighter on the table, which flared like a blowtorch when I spun it with my thumb; some like it hot.

I did a good job, I thought, of dissembling urgent need as I pulled upon the cigarette, but I'd no sooner released an impressively bountiful bouquet of smoke than she said, "You're no smoker, are you?"

"Not when I can help it," I replied. "It's something generally to be avoided, like speaking Danish." This seemed to amuse her, slightly, and I went on, "By the way, I don't want you to think I actually look like this. I'm actually tall and fairhaired and dressed in a camel's hair sportscoat. I'm in disguise, you see." This one brought the ghost of a smile to her lips, which were ghosted as well with powdered sugar, and I risked a "May I sit down?"

"I can't stop you," she said. "It's not my restaurant."

I seated myself and I said, "But you owe me an answer. I asked where this merchant father of yours is based."

"I owe you nothing."

"I owe you a cigarette. But since I didn't want it, I suppose we're even."

She exhaled a field of smoke that seemed to reach out, horizontally, a full two meters before her. "Amsterdam," she said. "He's Dutch. I'm Dutch."

"And what goods is he a merchant of?"

"Shipping," she said.

"And what does he ship?"

"Diamonds, rubies, peacocks, dynamite—who knows? He's filthy rich, the thieving bastard."

This was profoundly cheering news. I'd recently arrived at a high-principled resolution: I would marry for money. My new ambition was to enter into wedlock with the first reasonably well-off woman who would have me, irrespective of her appearance or personality.

So why do I call this a high-principled decision?

Because by nature I was of course an incurable romantic, someone who'd always supposed that, if he married at all, it would be in furtherance of some overwhelming passion. My new resolve went against all my deepest instincts. But I was tired of having no money; I was tired, most, of the *distraction* of having no money—of the endless serial run of dead-end jobs I'd taken to keep some sort of roof over my head and some sort of meal on some sort of table before me. It was more than a lifetime ago that I'd spilled out of Magnus Ingisson's office, afloat on the news that he was planning to publish my first two novels. Freeland on that day belonged to me; I was the spiritual heir to the whole place. But it subsequently turned out that my inheritance would hardly book me one-way passage on a boat to Iceland, would hardly bring me a plate of boiled haddock or a Coca-Cola. In addition to that initial pair of novels, I had published three others, as well as two collections of short stories, a play, two books of verse, an assortment of essays, a travelogue about America, and another about Denmark, and the royalty checks were still scarcely large enough to buy me a bed for the night in a flea-bag rooming house behind the train station in Copenhagen. I'd come to Denmark looking for a new book to write. I'd been here for two weeks and already I was nearly broke. Next door to my rooming house was a sex shop whose window boasted a matching set of battery-operated his-'n'-hers genitalia—whoever or whatever you were, you didn't need to add a thing—and I suppose this equipment would have struck me as funny if its price tag hadn't exceeded the advance I'd received for my last book of poetry. . . . Could there be in this world a more forlorn moment for a poet than the realization that even the pimping purveyors of *artificial* sex make more money than he does? I was still reduced at times to washing dishes, busing tables, raking leaves, distributing leaflets. The press of mere externalities was impinging on my art and therefore I'd resolved to sacrifice mere personal feelings on the altar of a Higher Good: I would marry myself to money. My art—Art itself—demanded nothing less.

And yet, having framed this self-sacrificing resolution, having agreed out of principle to forgo so much of what I cherished in life, I now found myself seated before a woman who apparently could offer me both beauty *and* money. For I liked my wife's looks—and this is perhaps the moment to reveal that, yes, this woman, Kornelia Alslost, in time did indeed become my lawful wife—yes, liked the tangled thriving hopeless chaos of her hair, the broad full-cheeked forcefulness of her face, the small cloudy untrustworthy blue eyes, and liked best, naturally, the big-boned bigness, for I'd always harbored what I suppose is a small man's appetite for the outsize and the outflung, the hint of spiritual boldness and entitlement emanating from an overspilling female form. No other preference has ever made much *sense* to me, frankly. If in the end, carnivores all, we're destined to feast off the bodies of our lovers, who in the world would favor a scrawny, tendon-riddled haunch over a dimpled, fat-marbled one? It's especially true of marriage, a state whose progress might reasonably be likened to a waterless trek through scrubland, where what nourishment you can depend upon will be only that which you had the foresight to transport yourself. Big, well-fleshed bones. I'd always aimed to marry "above me" in the literal, the physical sense.

And having been threatened, on the street just moments earlier, with a woman the size of a house, there was something all the more gratifying in finding myself seated before a woman who was no larger than a single bedroom.

"Thieving bastards have a hard time of it in Freeland," I said. "There isn't much to steal."

She seemed amused by this one, too. A twitching smile played upon her lips and I was getting a hopeful, beautifully amplitudinous feeling that I just might have located here, after weeks and weeks of futile searching, one of those priceless women who are susceptible to Eggert the Rodent-face's guileful good looks. Back then, it seems I used to give off, in my hunched and fast-featured way, an exciting zigzag quickness, a crackly skittering of static electricity.

"So what took him to Freeland?" I said.

"The devil knows. I really did think he'd gone there to buy it. He went with some Danes. He's very *thick* with all of these Danes."

"And you," I said, "you're not thick with any Dane?"

"Not me," she said.

"Well then," I said, and glanced her hard in the eye—the first inkling she'd had, perhaps, of that rooting forcefulness which complements my low, darting elusiveness. "Who is it you are thick with?"

"Thick with? Me, myself, and I," Kornelia said—a remark far more perceptive than either of us supposed at the time.

She stood up. "I've got to buy some soup bones."

"Soup bones! I don't mean to boast, forgive my arrogance, but I know the best soup-bone store in all of Copenhagen, perhaps in all of Denmark!"

Again that smile perked her lips, which still bore a trace of powdered sugar. She drew hard on her cigarette, exhaled a voluminous cloud, and said, with something of the clipped unquestioning briskness with which a mistress might summon a tarrying terrier, "All right. Come on along."

Did I enjoy being addressed in this fashion? I suppose. But I'd like to think I also felt clear forebodings when the used-up smoke of her cigarette slapped me in the face.

Even so, what was I to do but go along? She was my mate, after all.

22

With Pieter de Hooch
One Sunday Morning

I dreamed recently I was walking down Oudezijds Achterburgwal, the handsomer and more sumptuous of the two lovely canaled streets that are the parallel arteries of Amsterdam's red-light district. It was early in the morning—perhaps a Sunday morning, to judge from the clear, clement, sleepy, scrappy, sun-scattered feel of things. It was one of those enchanted interludes when the city, shucking its brazen tawdriness, seems bent on demonstrating that in spirit it still belongs to Jan Vermeer and Pieter de Hooch and Jacob van Ruisdael, artists who would have awakened on such a morning and cried, "My God, I must be up and out before the light changes!" But Vermeer and de Hooch and Ruisdael would not have known *what* to make of the queer, castoff, childish emblems that were bobbing in the canal: balloons, toy boats and toy airplanes, stuffed animals and huge lace-festooned chocolate Easter eggs. The water flowed briskly.

I'd come to the end of the street when an Asian woman in a canary-yellow bikini leaned out of her doorway. Her bosom was ample, her smile prodigious. "Stop for a visit, darling?" she said. Her voice—and even amid the dislocations of my dream I detected something incongruous in this—had a cockney overlay. It didn't belong to her; she might have been an actress in a hastily dubbed film.

And yet she seemed to think she knew me. Her chatty companionability drew from me a complementary, distancing formality: "Pardon me, but my destination is the train station." In truth I was heading south, away from the station.

"But darling, the trains aren't running today. You have time for *un petit rendezvous. . . .*" And now my cockney Asian was seducing me in French.

Taking refuge in my best university diction, "I have but ten kronur," I said, confessing to my poverty in the currency not of Holland but of Freeland.

At this reply, she ran her hands ruminatively across her only-half-clad buttocks, and after a moment, in a dry voice utterly at odds with her clothing and her motions, she said, "This morning, this morning only, love, I'll let you come *coucher* with me for ten kronur."

Pushed to it, ransacking my brain, I answered, "I cannot visit this morning, my dear, for I must be hurrying off to the hospital, where my wife is having a baby. Lilja—she is just now giving birth to blue-eyed Lilja. . . ."

I waved good-bye and, loping purposefully into Damstraat, heard a soul-wrenching squeal. I swung around: coming at me, slowly but nonetheless unstoppably, with all the hulking mass of Newton's clean-angled, unambiguous physics behind it, was Vikram's canary-yellow convertible. It was bearing down on my knees, which would in just one moment bend in a direction they had never bent—no, they were incapable of it, and everything I stood upon must, into a thousand pieces, shatter. . . .

I woke with an upward lurch and I was at home—I was in my bed, I was in Freeland. And I knew as I hadn't known before just how deep ran my feelings of betrayal over that car of Vikram's, with its flags and banners in support of Nonni Karlsson.

Perhaps life's cruelest everyday irony lies in its many ingenious ways of squeezing from us an expected, a stereotypical response. We cry out, passionately, heartbrokenly, the very words anyone might have predicted we would cry out—with the result, naturally, that no one heeds us. . . . These days, in my hunched middle age, I find myself eyeing the elderly with a sort of fastidious removal—like that of a religious fundamentalist who, having always regarded the theory of evolution as the devil's own handiwork, meets uneasily the look of recognition in the eyes of a chimp in a monkey house. Yet, for all my sense of removal from them, I'm constantly having to squelch within me the elderly man's hidebound lament: *You don't appreciate what I've done for you.* For this is *exactly* what I feel. . . . Vikram cruises around Thorskrist in a ludicrous fantasy of a vehicle, proclaiming loudly and extravagantly his support of Nonni Karlsson, and does he for a moment pause to ponder that he may owe his very existence to the forces he's opposing? I can't help it, I begin to take up the anthem of the aged: *You don't appreciate what we've done for you.* And this time I long— by means of a megaphone, having installed myself in the belfry of Mariners' Church—to proclaim the words to Freeland herself.

It was to me that Vikram's parents came, nearly twenty years ago, when they resolved to venture out in search of a child. This was 1973 and Hannibal had just been elected for the first time. I had been appointed something whose title escapes me. Secretary of State? Presidential Chief Adviser? Panjandrum of Geopolitical Planning? I've held a great many posts over the years. It was generally understood that while I was not an elected official I had my hands in things—foreign affairs especially.

And it was out into the wide world of foreign nations, what we in Freeland tend to think of as the world Down Below, Jakob and Perla had decided to go. Neither had ever once traveled beyond our shores, and they might well have lived out their entire lives within our little brace of polar islands had they not together given birth to the seed of a dream. They would adopt a child. Yes, they would pluck some homeless, hapless orphan from out of the reckless chaos of Down Below and transport it up to the high sane sanctuary of Freeland.

God, what a pair they were! And in their benighted, hopeless hope-fulness, how persuasive, how powerful! To begin with—and I speak as someone with his own unignorable claims in the field—they were almost comically ugly: I don't know if I've ever seen a homelier couple. First thing in the morning, while my stomach was still empty, I would find them hunkered outside my office door. . . . Jakob a broad, big-bellied man who suffered from a skin disorder I thought of as carbuncles. Maybe they were boils or shingles or pimples—those red, often runny sores, on hands and face, finally so eye-catching the eye must flee from them. So one glances over at Perla, who has no chin. Where a jawbone should assert itself her face subsides loosely—grotesquely—into the flesh-folds of her neck.

The two had recently learned they couldn't engender a child. A cruel joke had sprung up—most Freelandic jokes are cruel—that their marriage was barren because neither could bear to couple with anyone so unsightly. But, undeterred by any thought of their own homeliness, they had re-solved to adopt an infant from abroad.

Our laws back then made no provision for such things. The notion that a couple might choose to import a foreign child to Freeland—a country that, over many destitute decades, had come to specialize in the export of its people—seemed cockeyed. Through the centuries we had arrived at an ideal solution for childless couples. Our families are large and flexible, and childless couples traditionally perfect the roles of aunts and uncles, perhaps in time inviting a niece or nephew into the home permanently—an arrangement which, especially when times were hard and there were many mouths to feed, suited everybody. Or almost everybody. Jakob and Perla did not want to be uncle and aunt, or godfather and godmother; they wanted to be parents.

I remember them sitting in my office—absolutely resolute, absolutely ignorant of the world Down Below from which they were determined to snatch their prize. They came to me with questions. Contacts would have to be made—could I make them? Some sort of law or dispensation would have to be enacted, that the child might be granted citizenship—and how best ought this be done? The first time they showed up in my office I gently, painstakingly illustrated for them the implausibility of their scheme. They nodded in agreement, thanked me, and filed out. They were back two days later. . . . *We dream of a child, you see.* I reexplained, they were reconvinced, and I kindly sent them packing. They were back two days later.

A firm chin and a strong jaw are universal emblems of obstinacy, but in my mind it's chinlessness—Perla had all the boneless tenacity of an octopus—that stands for a persistence that cannot be evaded. It's Perla Juliusdottir materializing yet again. It's that quiet voice of hers emerging from a voice-box buried within a quivering, tormentingly vulnerable throat. *We dream of a child, you see.*

What they could not perceive was the far-fetched implausibility of the task. The complications were unending. Someone would have to go forth and communicate to some distant officials a notion like this: *There's a couple who dream of bringing a child across the seas to the edge of the North Pole, to a faraway little country you have never heard of.* And how was this official going to feel when the prospective parents shuffled out and they looked like stand-ins for a horror film?

Someone was needed forthrightly to explain it to Jakob and Perla: The two of you are simply too repulsive to play the roles you covet. But no one came forward to explain it. And they persisted. And precisely in this blindness of theirs, this inability to see the unseemliness of their scheme, resided their enduring strength. No one could bear to deny them outright. And so the impossible ultimately began to look possible.

In the end, with a great deal of indispensable if reluctant help from me, a little girl was located, an abandoned, six-month-old Guatemalan, but how in the world clumsy carbuncled Jakob and chinless Perla, who had between them almost no English and not a word of Spanish, managed to make their way to Reykjavik, thence to New York, thence to Miami, thence to Guatemala, there successfully to negotiate with various no doubt corrupt officials, then managed to reverse the process, arriving in Thorskrist with a dark-skinned black-haired child in tow—is almost too dizzying to contemplate.

Well, an unforeseen thing happened when they returned with their little girl, who was nicknamed Sola—Sunny. This man and woman who had formerly been derided and dismissed, this couple once lampooned for both the impracticality of their scheme and the horrific expenditures lavished in its pursuit, were now recognized as heroes. Jakob and Perla . . . Thorskrist's own dear Jakob and Perla had voyaged all the way to Guatemala on a benevolent raiding mission, in order to bring to our shores a beautiful girl, named for the sun. What a bold feat! And how typically Freelandic in its boldness!

And the girl—the girl! With her limpid brown-black eyes, her abundant black hair bunched in a ponytail atop her head, Sunny was a beauty of a sort these islands had never known. What a tale this was, for the newspapers and our budding television station! Hadn't we always been a nation of clever, enterprising voyagers, of dreamers, of unquenchable visionaries? Here was this lovely gem, her pigmented bronze skin adapted to a sun whose true force and bounty we under our dilute northern skies would never know, and she had been *given* to us! There was, Down Below, a world so profligate and foolish that this matchless creature had actually been *abandoned!* Fortunately, thank the Lord, she had found shelter in a nation of sane, solid, businesslike, and yet courageous people who would nourish and cherish her. . . .

When, a couple of months later, Perla peered into the child's crib one morning and discovered that the sun had gone out, the bronze girl was cold as metal, the nation did more than merely mourn. For days on end, a soiling shame colored our every motion. We'd been hoodwinked, or had allowed ourselves to be hoodwinked; somehow we'd accepted a scheme whose impossibility we had identified from the outset. Deep in our leery hearts, we knew the little girl's death was a judgment. Good God, *what had we been thinking?* It was time to bury the little alien bundle under Great Blue and never again speak of her. One more of our imprudent dreams had come crashing to the ground—and now deep into the frosty ground it must go.

But it turned out that Jakob and Perla did not have the common sense, the simple human decency, to relinquish their dream. Eight months later they were back in my office. *We dream of a child, another child. . . .* To most people's eyes—mine included—there was something faintly obscene about this. Though Freelanders have always prized pursuers of hopeless causes, we have nothing but disdain for the fools who refuse to heed the signs and reprimands of the lowering heavens. Only a numbskull ignores a portent. Clearly, this dream of theirs wasn't meant to be. . . .

And yet clearly, in their obtuse tirelessness, the two of them thought it was. *We dream of another child. . . .* I delayed, I obfuscated, I temporized, but there was in the end no putting them off.

This time, when the child was brought to Thorskrist, we accorded it no fanfare. Unmistakably, the scrawny, cough-racked, ill-colored little creature was doomed. They had heartlessly dragged the boy forth from a Calcutta slum where he might soon have been buried among his fellow slum-dwellers; he might have had, at least, a warm and companionable grave. We were not going to be made fools of again. We weren't about to become complicit, through our big-hearted welcomes, in this imminent, tasteless tragedy. We would let him vanish quietly into the lap of Great Blue.

It is a well-established law in Freeland, one which over the years I've done everything in my power to enforce and to tighten, that all citizens must bear traditional Freelandic names and surnames. The Ministry of Deeds simply will not register a citizen otherwise. Thus it was for my own Sindri, who was originally christened Svenning. The statute was established around the turn of the century to thwart those who would attenuate our heritage by aspiring to the trappings of Denmark, that wellspring of all culture, power, urbanity. It later served—particularly with the advent of Hollywood movies and the NATO base at Jardvik—to preserve us from the Americans. Ours was not going to be a culture overrun with little boys named Errol or Humphrey or Montgomery, girls named Ginger or Myrna or Claudette.

But you see, the boy's name is Vikram, Perla explained to me. But you see, he cannot be officially registered under that name, I explained to the two of them in return. Until you abandon this outlandish and inappropriate moniker and give him an everyday, practical name, something like Yngvinn or Thjodbergur or Hjalmtyr, he cannot be said fully to exist. *But it is not a case of our trying to give him a foreign name. He already has one.* And what about Thorvaldur? There's a good Freelandic name for you, and one that simultaneously carries exotic overtones. You will recall of course that in Saga days Thorvaldur Vidforli ventured as far as Constantinople.

They sought a dispensation; again they were asking that an exception be made. There they sat in my office—no longer two ugly creatures but three: carbuncled Jakob and chinless Perla and that nameless malodorous drooling doomed bundle. The creature, lacking the strength to cry, whimpered endlessly, and, unable to keep any food down, threw up everything, converting it first into a green gummy swampy substance that belonged properly to the alien viscera of a bullfrog or a salamander—but not to the belly of anything resembling a human being.

I hoped, naturally, that the infant might die before the legal issue could proceed. If it was going to perish anyway, the child might do us the small favor of protecting our legal system from a dangerous precedent. . . . Yet the boy held on, and chinless Perla held on—*but he already has a name, just as much as you do, Eggert*—and in the end, soft heart that I am, I concluded that the creature's tombstone might just as well carry the name originally given it. The stony syllables would stand as a cautionary tale. So, various initiatives were initiated, various resolutions resolved, all culminating in the poor, puking child's being registered as Vikram.

Miraculously, perversely, the child held on, not growing or filling out, but not positively dwindling any further either. Still it could not manage to hold down anything of substance, though all the foods you might naturally give an ailing infant were attempted: codfish cakes and cinnamon rolls, ground mutton and gull's eggs and lamb's liver and Coca-Cola. Still the doomed boy persisted, and to come upon Perla in the streets of Thorskrist wheeling around her death-infant in its elaborate, wastefully extravagant new pram was, of course, one more morbid mortification for us all.

And still the whining, wheezing, sickly, gaunt, death-stamped child held on, afloat in its ever-renewed bacterial seas of vomit and diarrhea, until its parents, throwing good money after bad, decided the boy should be taken to medical specialists in Copenhagen, in defiance of nature and common sense and national pride, all of which dictated that it be allowed to die without further obstruction. The Copenhagen doctors, after lengthy examination, concluded that the situation was grave—something a veterinarian might have told them—and recommended a series of intricate and no doubt bootless procedures, all of which, at enormous expense, were undertaken, and still the child held on.

Somehow, into the hands of the two stubbornest parents in the world had fallen the world's stubbornest child, who went on living, sickly and sallow, underweight and undersized, as the years passed, five, ten, and then one day, in spring perhaps, a miracle unfolded. . . . Some good fairy we Freelanders had never conceived of, perhaps some multiarmed creature like Shiva, waved a wand over the boy's head and the stunted limbs elongated, the yellow whites of his eyes whitened, his skin assumed a ruddy glow. Not for him the acne lesions and the scratchy froggy voices and the gangling motions of his classmates, on whom adolescence had fallen like some sort of tragicomic plague. Overnight, Vikram metamorphosed into the most beautiful child in Freeland.

Or was this too narrow a judgment? Wasn't it only fair and just to call him the most beautiful boy in the world?

And all at once there were no bounds to our adulation and goodwill. Having ignored and scorned him, having consigned him to the grave, we rallied to his daring good looks with a giddy blend of guilt and jubilation. Oh how we wished, belatedly but wholeheartedly, to embrace him! There wasn't a soul in Thorskrist immune to his charms. *Vikram*, Ursula the baker would call, *try one of these cinnamon rolls, fresh from the oven*. And *Vikram*, old Solveig in her fishbooth would cry, *I have some big shrimps you must take home to your mother*. It was *In truth I'd been planning to put this item on sale*; it was *There's a little nick here, in the back, I can't charge you full price for this one*; it was *I need the shelf-space actually*. And Vikram moved in this new element gracefully and hauntingly and without the faintest edge of reproof.

I say he "moved," but better say *glided*, or *skated*, or *flowed*, for he was one of those people—rare anywhere, but almost nonpareil in Freeland—who are born with a dancer's fluxing grace: a cushioned fluidity belongs to them, a soft-cadenced footfall, a hint of meaning to the most trifling of their motions, as if each workaday errand were but one more unraveling anecdote in some rich, ongoing mime-narrative. Dear Lord, he was beautiful! And if he was spoiled, wasn't this nothing less than what his magnificence demanded? He who had battled so manfully, long before the onset of manhood, merely to stay alive, was evidently finished with battles of any sort. Henceforth, his was meant to be a cosseted life. It was our common accomplishment: he would be collectively pampered.

Even now, for all the years he'd been with us, he remained a not quite believable sight. Who among us could quite compass the image of Vikram Jakobsson at age fifteen strolling down Skeggjagata in a preposterous and gorgeous double-breasted shark-gray silk suit and an apricot-colored Italian silk necktie? And who could resist the image of Vikram Jakobsson at age nineteen, circling round and round Thorskrist in that canary-yellow Mustang convertible his parents had doubtless mortgaged their lives to purchase for him?

And yet in the lucid land of dreams, this was the vehicle, and this the driver, that bore down grimly upon my legs, my knees, my life on an innocent Sunday morning in Pieter de Hooch's Amsterdam, while I, fleeing the red-light district, hastened virtuously forth to view my newborn daughter.

23

The File Called Kornelia

S ighing resignedly, muttering apologies under my breath, I pull out
that file in my head called "Kornelia," knowing in advance that its
haphazard contents won't begin to explain the tumble of events we
lived through. Details haze over. Crucial pieces are missing. And little of
what I did makes any sense to me. Why did I put up with things as long as
I did? Was I, as I think I was, a better, more patient person back then—or
merely a larger fool? It sometimes seems that each of my voyages Down
Below has worked both to enrich my books and to darken my soul—
although I'd append, paradoxically, my belief that in darkness alone lies
my particular redemption. . . .

I thumb through the file's contents, I arrange them chronologically, I
dust off the mental snapshots. What was the power she held over me? To
the reflexive cynic, the answer comes easily: there was her father's money.
To which I answer, Yes, there was her father's money and it was both a
boon and a lure and I regret only never getting my hands firmly on a
larger portion of it, though as for that I have no real complaints: from the
day I moved in with her until the day I moved out, I never held a job and
oh, what a blessing that was! But I'd add, Surely there are easier ways to
make a living than to be married to Kornelia Alslost.

How did she hold me? In addition to her money, I liked her slovenly
good looks. I saw in her dishevelment a titillating hint of the uncontain-
able; I roused at the way her body was continually coming loose of whatever bindings or coverings she imposed upon it. Her hair was always
springing loose of its pins or ribbons or barrettes. Her shirttails wouldn't
stay in her skirts, her tights wouldn't stay up on her legs, and I even liked
the way her toes poked through her tattered gym shoes, as if they, too,

were saying, *Don't ever seek to confine me.* When she wore lipstick, it smeared; when she cooked, warring aromas drifted off her hands and face; and even when she yawned, she did so ravenously, biting off a big piece of the room's air with her strong jaw.

When we became lovers, I liked, I suppose, how this sense of the not-to-be-contained extended even to the act itself—I mean, I suppose I liked the rodeo aspect to it, how she in her tumultuous heavings was forever expelling me at crucial instants. Afterward, one didn't ask so much whether things had gone well or badly but only whether they'd gone approximately as aimed. Fun? Clearly sex wasn't meant to be fun—it was meant to leave you, at its best, with the winded feeling of accomplishment savored by a man who has just squeezed himself and his baggage onto a crowded subway train.

Oh and I suppose I liked about Kornelia the conflicted sense she gave me, so much like my own, of simultaneously seeing deep into my rattiness and seeing beyond it. Hers was a tinderbox temper, and early in our affair I remember her, fire blazing in her eyes, calling me a "twisted little man." Well, there was a profound satisfaction—in addition to something too molten to be labeled *satisfaction*—in having outspread beneath me, *just twenty minutes later*, a Kornelia who was calling into my ear *More, more . . .* More, Kornelia? More of your *twisted little man?*

And what else—as I seek now to perceive myself through your eyes, Kornelia—did you like about me? You enjoyed, hugely, having to explain to everybody where exactly Freeland was. To have on hand a boyfriend who "grew up with the Eskimos" was a thrill, wasn't it?

But thumbing through it all again, it's clear that the very things Kornelia initially admired about me often contributed to our undoing. She joyed, at first, in the fierceness of my industry. Job or no job, I never stopped piling one scrawled paper atop another. In my sleepless way, I would be scratching and scribbling as she padded off to bed, I would be rising in the middle of the night to subjoin a sleepy thought to a sleepy thought, I would be up at dawn to scratch out the inky missteps of the day before. I was assembling poems and a novel, I was sending off pieces to the *Torch* and the *Daily Storm,* I was translating into Freelandic *The Winter's Tale* and Hamsun's *Hunger* and Jacobsen's *Niels Lyhne.*

She liked my misanthropy, I suppose, for despite all her rhetorical flummery about peace and love and universal brotherhood—she was deeply infected by the prevailing winds out of California—at bottom she remained a woman of titanic resentments. She liked the fact, perhaps, that on that eventual day when cold and hostile disillusion hit her, I would be there to reassure her that nothing could have been done to avoid it. I was there to say, *The game is fixed* or *I knew they weren't to be trusted* or *They're all bastards anyhow*. I was there to say, *You're too sweet and trusting, darling. You mustn't put your faith in people.*

She, too, had no job. In effect she was living—and, as soon as I'd moved in with her, *we* were living—on a parental allowance. Her father wired her money, sporadically. The old man moved with maddening capriciousness. I thought of our funds as coming in *shrugs*: I saw him, every now and then, aimlessly shedding a windfall with the rise and dip of a shoulder.

In the end, though, he could be counted upon to deliver the goods if Kornelia seriously threatened to move back to Amsterdam. They didn't get along, needless to say. She had left Holland and come to Denmark to learn to paint, or so her story went. And far be it from me to explain why anyone wishing to study art would migrate from a country whose artists at least *used* to know how to paint, magnificently, to one where they'd never, in their long history, confidently mastered the business.

Over the first months we lived together, in that summer and fall of 1967, there was usually some newfound and absolutely unforeseeable reason why Kornelia was not, at this particular moment, actually painting. The light was bad. The canvas was wrong. She was distracted. She was too happy to work. She was too sad. Increasingly, it was the state of the world itself that obstructed her.

You might say the world spoke more urgently to Kornelia than to me. For she carried with her a conviction, absolutely alien to my upbringing, that the planet was amenable to wide-scale improvement. She believed in the feasibility of "revolution," a word that tripped off her tongue as smoothly as "pickled herring" might spring from my own. A new social order would usher in a broadened justice, a cleansing altruism, a renewed spirituality. She was, in addition, smoking prodigious quantities of marijuana—one of those aesthetic pursuits, like listening to atonal music or eating seaweed or contemplating ceramics, whose "pleasures" I've always found not merely elusive but rebarbative. Still, she kept urging the stuff on me. She saw it as a failure of mine, increasingly irksome as the months passed, that I refused to "give in" or "submit" to the marijuana experience—curious phrasing, actually, given how little her own behavior under the drug resembled anything I recognized as giving in or submitting. Kornelia on a marijuana high was, unbelievably, a heightened and a yet-more-imposing Kornelia, coming at you in enhanced form through every avenue of the senses: louder, brighter, warmer, more pungent, and, when kissed, more acrid-sweet. She was, when launched on the drug, subject to quick and peremptory impulses—turning up the music and plunging herself into a floor-shaking dance, or emptying the shelves of their every eatable. Truly, her appetite at such times wasn't to be believed: she might consume six jelly doughnuts in an afternoon, or a one-pound box of mocha-cream chocolates. Meanwhile, the music hammered on—the Beatles, the Doors, the Rolling Stones—and she'd sometimes ask me to dance. Of course I disliked this music, hated the dancing. *She* never seemed to need to pause and sit and digest her food. She was drugged and poisoned and, withal, lovely.

A new and tenderer era was upon us, or about to break upon us: an Aquarian Age. She was, for all her physical stolidity and self-absorption, remarkably attuned to delicate oscillations in what I may as well call the zeitgeist. That wayward, wind-turned mass of hair on her outsize skull might have been an antenna. She had a gift, notable if unenviable, for sensing where a society's youthful energies were trending. She'd come early to marijuana—early, anyway, for a woman of her background—just as she'd come early to sitar music and black lights and unisex clothing and bralessness, and opposition to the Americans in Vietnam.

Oh, those damn Americans! What *was* to be done about them? Just as the planet was ascending to new levels of brotherhood and enlightenment, here come the bastard Yanks, seeking to embroil the family of nations in a racist and colonialist war. How she raged at them! They were undermining the new karmic investigations that young men and women like Kornelia—brave young navigators willing to ride their drug-tides into new and unnamed territories—were working so hard to achieve.

Forgive the bitter sound of this. But predictions about a better world have always sounded like gibberish to my Freelandic ear. We take it as a given that the people Down Below move in inexplicable cycles, driven by greed and ferocity, and all a person can do is to shake his head and hope for the best. Unexpected boons or bounties, goods or goodies, now and then may come our way. The First World War was one such blessing—a span of years destined to be recalled warmly by every true friend of Freeland. Somewhere, far far away, a madman had shot a fool, a single stray bullet, and as a result indiscriminate, interminable slaughter had unfolded, as the Lunatics battled valiantly to quell the Crazies, and the Crazies fought with equal valor to free the world from the yoke of the Lunatics, and prices for Freelandic wool and fish skyrocketed as never before, fostering in my country the impossible but irrepressible hope that, if only the slaughter continued for another decade or so, we might raise ourselves out of our turf and tarpaper hovels and build stately homes of brick and wood. . . . What was to stop us from having radios and paved roads and streetlights? . . . It was a Golden Age, one whose glories were equaled only, perhaps, by the Second World War, which ushered in not only premium prices for our goods and the lovely sight of the proud Danes humbled but also the arrival of the freewheeling, candy-carrying Americans, who out of the overbrimming kindness of their hearts wanted to construct for us a modern airport, on which perhaps their own planes, too, military planes, might land. . . .

Have I made myself clear? To trust, as Kornelia did, in the notion that that pair of enormous troll-dens lying at Freeland's feet, the one called Europe and the other America, might nurture a new dawn of the spirit—well, this ran counter to everything I'd ever learned. A man might well fall in love with the jewel-work of these clever trolls—with their architecture, with their dolled-up women, with their *Midsummer Night's Dream* and their Fred Astaire films—but you would never trust them to behave civilizedly. They were trolls, after all. When I learned that one of the politicians I'd watched so closely during my days in Detroit, the fair Irish boy who had defeated Dick the Self-Implicating, had had his head blown into various-sized pieces by a rifleman in Dallas, I felt no surprise, none. Such things happen Down Below. Ages ago Freeland, too, had been a place where a chieftain might well expect to have his skull stove in—though by a broadax or halberd rather than a rifle. But it seems that the mayhem of even the darkest stretches of our Dark Ages had been lightened by ideals of valor, pride, probity. The crack of the rifle in Dallas, the echoing snapfire in the paddies of Indochina, the ongoing crescendo of armaments in the ever-more-bloody movies Hollywood exports to the world—was it unfair to hear in these sounds the ascendancy of an age that had perfected our old barbarousness while shedding our old trappings of honor?

We, too, liked to fight—Kornelia and I. We sniped at each other through vaporous clouds of marijuana smoke, and sometimes—particularly when I ridiculed her nebulous talk about peace and love—she'd push and shove at me, and I at her; nothing made her more bellicose than to see her pacifism attacked. She was the larger, I the quicker. We were a good match, and in time we would be married. . . .

I last saw Kornelia half a dozen years ago, in Amsterdam. She'd been through all sorts of things, including a couple of massive spectacular break-downs, in whose wake a weird and slow-speaking and seemingly amnesiac calm had descended upon her. She had a new husband, her third, this one a beautiful miniature Spaniard. My immediate successor, her second hus-band, had been a Frenchman, an art dealer, who was also smaller than I. Kornelia meanwhile had steadily expanded, and when I saw her that day in Amsterdam I knew on first glance that she'd forever outstripped even my taste in ample-bodied women. Perhaps I'm all too eager—as some-thing of a connoisseur of melancholy—to label this or that discovery the world's most forlorn experience, but what *can* be more depressing than to encounter a woman whom you once craved the way a timberwolf craves the moon, and who now awakens in your sleepy veins not even a single blood cell? In our kiss of greeting, there in the flower-overrun foyer of her beautiful old canal house on Herrengracht, something in me declared, for the last time, *Farewell, Kornelia.*

Eggert was small and the Frenchman smaller and the Spaniard smaller still, while Kornelia was steadily becoming a sort of Mardi Gras float—a sort of Kornelia-balloon—and isn't it a shame that our fleeting stay on Planet Earth doesn't allow us time to pursue our deepest impulses to their indicated conclusions? Give her not decades to work with but centuries, and surely Kornelia must wind up with a husband who stands to her as Arrow-odd did to the giantess Hildigunn in the old Saga: Arrow-odd became her dolly, her plaything, her "tiny little pip."

And thus does it turn out—why didn't I see this coming?—that the Rules of the Game, the game of Twenty Down, prove inescapable. The first time I glimpsed Kornelia, that sunny day in Copenhagen in 1967, I'd thought her an emissary from heaven, sent to save me from the woman I'd glimpsed just moments before: the largest woman in the world. But it turned out Kornelia *was* that woman. She was the largest woman in the world reduced, temporarily, to a human size.

In 1980, years after we'd parted, Kornelia's father finally passed away, and his house on Herrengracht became hers. It's a shame the tireless old crook didn't drop earlier; I would have liked living there. The canals of Amsterdam have always struck my Freelandic soul as more than pic-turesque; they inspirit me. Any true city will possess some potent re-minder or presagement of the sea. He—my father-in-law—was toxic, a man of viciousness without wit or irony. He managed to be both exces-sively fastidious and physically odious. After shaking hands with me, he would regularly wipe away my touch on a white handkerchief—and yet he had the most disgusting mouth I've ever seen, and as a Freelander I'm used to looking into unappetizing mouths, ours being a country where sugar's consumed by the sackful and dentists are thin on the ground. But old Ruud's mouth was something out of the ordinary: fleshy lips, buck teeth that were not merely brown but—so one sensed, not daring to look too closely—gray and green as well. I used to see him at times strolling round Amsterdam's red-light district—and the thought of him applying his mouth to any portion of a woman, even her elbows or feet, was harrowing.

And perhaps it's here I should confess to being endlessly, irresistibly drawn to the district myself, though not—as should by now be clear—as patron. What kept me chaste wasn't moral scruple, obviously, but a sense of there being nothing but hurt for me there. Self-protection. With a small dash of voyeurism. Looking back on an utterly disarrayed romantic life, I suppose I've always taken a somewhat adversarial approach toward love, viewing myself—with pride, with loathing—as a being at once more elevated and coarser than those men I scrutinized so sharply as they went shopping for a lover. Because for me a seduction that didn't involve overcoming the love-object's reservations and distrust, as well as her possible distaste, offered little to celebrate. My greatest romantic ambition? To be told—laughingly, fondly—*You're not really as awful as you seem.* Kornelia and I presented dear Ruud with a fait accompli. By the time we arrived in Amsterdam, in the fall of 1967, I was not a suitor but a son-in-law. I had bristled at the prospect of coming as a supplicant; I wasn't going to ask any man for his daughter's hand. Ruud might welcome me or he might bar me from his door, but he would not be able finally to reject me: I would already have gained admittance to his family.

To marry after only a few months' acquaintance was perhaps a crazy idea, but we had embraced what was, in retrospect, a plan crazier still: we would pack our bags and move to Freeland. Yes, the newlyweds meant to pursue a purer existence. Free of the distractions of the city and the dissipations of her drugs, Kornelia would begin to paint in earnest: those bright, puissant, audacious canvases she clearly had it in her to do. And Eggert? Well, he would write books of course, but he would do that anywhere. The vision his daydreams kept gravitating toward was that of appearing on Skeggjagata, Thorskrist's main street, with a large, strangely dressed, unmistakably foreign creature on his arm.

Kornelia would be the materialized proof of just how capacious was my muse. Once, years ago, I'd taken as muse a Freelandic girl, who had upped and married hopeless Baldur Hermannsson, but Kornelia Alslost was to be proof positive of how much larger my imaginative powers had grown in the interim. My oeuvre was expanding and my muse along with it.

Given her penchant for outflung gestures, Kornelia would have much preferred to present her father with both thunderbolts simultaneously: she was a married woman and she was moving to Freeland. Strategically, this seemed unwise to me, and the encouraging truth was that Kornelia was learning to acknowledge my cold cunning.

So we informed him instead that we were moving to Amsterdam. He would be seeing a great deal of us, wasn't that wonderful? There would be many opportunities to introduce his clever if swarthy son-in-law-the-poet and his pretty if increasingly blowsy daughter-the-painter to his business associates. On the other hand, there was some slight chance that this happy prospect might have to be postponed . . . for there were some pressing, quite favorable business considerations that might hurry the newlyweds out to faraway Freeland for quite a lengthy stint, although, as for that, the expenses of transplanting ourselves to such a remote country might of course render this venture impracticable, etcetera, which would be a lamentable shame, given its great promise. And so forth. I played the old man beautifully and in the end our tale extracted from him a wedding gift of forty thousand guilders, or about eleven thousand dollars—which made this fiction of mine far and away the most profitable creation so far of my young but prolific writer's life. We sailed for Thorskrist, and arrived in late November.

Arrived, that is, at that exquisite time of year when the full Arctic dark is coming down and the sun, so low to the horizon, becomes just another scrawny hovel-dweller, shivering in its bed of ragged red clouds. Was it the frailty and the brevity of the light that so quickly undermined Kornelia? Or was it, as she insisted, my country's remoteness and architectural ugliness and culinary repulsiveness and ignorance and cultural benightedness and close-lipped reserve and complacency and resignation and deadness of spirit and a hundred other things? Perhaps it was the absence of drugs, for in those days—so backward were we Freelanders!—alcohol was virtually our only narcotic. In any case, within a few days something novel and ominous—a grimness that wasn't contentious so much as supine and nagging and bitter—had overcome her. We settled into what had been my aunt's house, and *how could anyone ever have endured living year after year in such a dump?* We slept upstairs—*had the Lord ever seen such a bed, it leaves your every bone aching!* We ate downstairs in the kitchen among *horrible ghastly knickknacks.* In truth, *the tackiness of this country is not to be believed!*

We had come for purity, and just outside our door the purest wind in the world, brought to us straight from the North Pole, was there for the breathing, and right over our rooftop the purest darkness on earth arched overhead, but Kornelia didn't care to venture out into the pure wind and the pure darkness. She hunkered down, in our overheated new home, keeping the windows shuttered. Meanwhile her new paints and canvases, which we'd purchased in The Hague at such great, worrying expense, at a fancy shop around the corner from the Maritshuis, sat untouched in a corner. They wore the air of funerary accessories.

We were fighting again, constantly, but on Kornelia's part there was more retreat than shove, more resignation than pugnacity. Gone was that sort of pushing, frontal drive that had a hungry neediness in it—and gone, for the most part, were those sweaty acts of union that so often culminated our contendings.

How in the world did you manage to eat this slop for all those years? No wonder you're such a runt. . . . It was an accusation that, to my ears, spoke not of my own but of *her* aesthetic poverty—since, as every Freelander knows, it's only a superficial soul that cannot be sated, perpetually, on a diet built around the four basic food groups of fried haddock, boiled potatoes, cinnamon rolls, and Coca-Cola. The only element of Freelandic cuisine that seemed to hold any appeal for Kornelia was what we call cream ships, our sole native delicacy. One begins with a sweet dry yellow pastry, of a texture—depending on freshness—lying somewhere between a cake and a biscuit. It is cut in half and piled high, sandwich style, with whipped cream, onto which chocolate, or some chocolatey substitute, is drizzled, and it can be topped off, as you wish, with either a green or a red maraschino cherry. Kornelia was polishing them off at a prodigious rate— six, eight, ten a day. Fleets, veritable armadas of cream ships sank into the sunless depths of her belly.

I came home one afternoon in December, on a day when the minuscule shreds of sunlight we might have experienced had been concealed by cavernous clouds, and found Kornelia at the kitchen table with two cream ships before her. To judge from the empty box on the table, she'd brought home six and already eaten four.

Now the truth is I didn't actually want one. But I wasn't about to let her go marching through the entire box unchallenged. "How very appeal-ing that looks!" I announced, and took a seat across from her. "Many thanks, my dear."

"I brought these home myself. I went out into the goddamn sleet and muck to get them."

"Now wasn't that *kind* of you . . . ," I answered, and reached tenta-tively across the table.

"They're mine," Kornelia declared. She circled her hands around the plate, embaying the two remaining ships in the haven of her arms.

"What's mine is yours and yours is mine," I responded gaily, and again reached toward the cream ships.

"Get your damn dirty hands away from me, Eggert."

I corrected her: "It isn't *you* I'm reaching toward, my dear one. . . ."

Now, my hands may well have been dirty but at least they were not deadly. Hers were: she had wrapped her fingers around the handle of an old knife.

Whether the knife happened to be on hand for the cutting of the biscuit, or had been there all along as a proprietary weapon, I couldn't say. But there it was, and the blade glinted in the lamplight. It had an ivory handle, yellowed with age, and I knew its edge was keen; my aunt used to clean fish with it. Was Kornelia willing to open up her husband's belly, just like gutting a trout, for the sake of a Freelandic cream ship? In my mem-ory, the blade goes on shining and wavering, and nowadays I find some-thing faintly splendid in the scene: from the point of view of Kornelia Alslost, marooned in a dark, sleet-pelted, indigestible land, the light of all the world had been spun, miraculously, into a nourishing froth.

There it was on the plate before her: and aren't we all searching for the light of the world? The woman's husband, wily and malign Eggert, was trying to steal from her the planet's last remaining scraps of sun; wasn't there something handsome and even noble in her standing up for princi-ple like this?

The knife goes on glinting and I used to entertain fantasies of being eviscerated in my sleep. When apprehended by the law, she would plead cabin fever, or light deprivation, or malnutrition, and the Freelandic au-thorities, boggling at the burden this big bohemian foreign lady would place upon their undersized jails, would see fit to release her.

What's the matter with you, how can you possibly bear to live in a country so far away from everything? To be fair, Kornelia was even more isolated than I. While in Copenhagen, we'd somehow never stopped to consider that in

Freeland she wouldn't be able to read the papers and wouldn't be able to understand what little radio and television there was, even assuming we'd owned a radio or television. Dutch magazines were of course nonexistent in Thorskrist; now and then an American or Danish one would float ashore, but it was apt to be many weeks old. How could I endure to live so far from everything?

The answer seemed obvious: when everything was collapsing, as it surely was, where else but Freeland would you want to be? This was the winter of '67–'68, and the crisis gripping our little nation was something on a human scale. It involved the Christmas raffle at the Superior School. Could it be mere chance that the Minister of Education had won both a radio and a toaster oven—or was it possible we were all victims of a fraud? It was the winter of '67–'68—elsewhere a season of such pervasive planetary madness that nothing but cosmic ray bombardments could account for it. At Kornelia's insistence, we used to go sometimes to a neighbor's and watch the news on television. Blue-faced in its glow, Kornelia would stare with a raptness all the sadder for her incomprehension of what was being said. The images alone aroused her: thousands of Ibo dead in the Nigerian jungles; Che Guevara shot dead in a Bolivian jungle; American and Vietnamese dead lying side by side in the jungles of Southeast Asia; and meanwhile roses falling from a blue sky, dropping onto a desert land— 17,532 roses, one for every day of the Shah of Iran's life at the time of his coronation. I'd hear a voice inside me say, *Eggert, it's a lunatic world*, and a second voice add, *And you've married a lunatic, Eggert.*

Those were hard times for most everyone, I suppose. Hard times for Hannibal, anyway, who'd once again left Freeland. A few years before, with both farming and the Great Danish Steamship Company behind him, he'd gotten involved with a Thorskrist fishing concern that had refused to float—or you might say it floated all too rapidly, belly up—and now he was traveling in faraway lands. Hannibal was in Italy. He was in Moscow. He was in Malaysia. No one seemed to know where he was, other than far away.

Far away is precisely where Kornelia wanted to be. She started going out at night without me. How pitiful, in retrospect, the picture is—this impulse to paint the town red when the town happens to be Thorskrist, Freeland, and the year is 1968. Where could she possibly go? There were no nightclubs, nothing resembling a civilized bar. . . . On weekends there were establishments where a young person might thrash around to primitive pounding music—I think we'd belatedly begun to call them discotheques—but weekdays were another matter. We simply didn't have the wherewithal—to say nothing of the liquor allowances—to pursue dissolution on a daily basis. We didn't have the money to go to the dogs in any brute animal way. Her hope, I suppose, was that she might encounter people from Elsewhere—some errant hippies, maybe, who would understand her clothes and who would bring with them talk of a wider world and who might even have on hand a communal contraband cigarette. Or a stray Continental businessman, perhaps, his suitcase full of current magazines and German cold cuts. Or even some sailors, frantically fun-loving, with rucksacks stuffed with bourbon and pistachios. Perhaps on occasion she found what she was seeking, for there were a couple of nights when she stumbled in at dawn—or at what would have been dawn had we not been living in an Arctic nation whose winter daybreaks arrive at the lunch hour—and toppled down beside me with a heavy groan of weariness and satiation. In truth I hoped she would find what she sought—hoped, indeed, *she* might find a new partner and *I*, one sweet morning, find her gone.

Our marriage had come undone, seemingly before it began. It was an undeniable disaster—so how did I respond? How did I proceed when my wife threatened to filet me like a sheep in a smokehouse, or came stumbling home at six in the morning? I did what anyone would have done: I began the task—"The raven himself is hoarse / That croaks the fatal entrance"—of translating *Macbeth* into Freelandic. I put my head down and wrote more poems, plays, essays, chapters of a new novel.

I had vowed to do the sensible, hardheaded thing—to stay with Kornelia at least until we'd spent her father's wedding gift. Prudence and common sense—to say nothing of simple respect for my own work—mandated this line of behavior. Yes, I knew that's what I *ought* to do, I knew where my responsibilities lay. . . .

But—my great handicap—I've always been an incurable romantic, and I now resolved, in typically softheaded fashion, to dump my wife while there were still thousands of guilders to spend. I knew it was callow and ill-judged not to make good use of the money—hadn't I won it by cleverness alone? But my foolish heart directed otherwise, and it has been my lifelong weakness to heed my heart. All right. I would propose that she sail home, for Amsterdam. To make things easier on both of us, I would feign an intention to join her in the spring, when I'd finished my newest novel.

I mulled the matter over, letting a few days pass. I was looking for the right moment. In the meantime, against the grim weeks when I'd be cut off from our financial reserves, I laid in a bank of provisions: baked beans, flour, sugar, sardines, pickled herring, Spam, deviled ham, spaghetti, sugar cookies, Coca-Cola, coffee, dried fish. I was waiting for a propitious moment.

It came in an afternoon of howling winds and thick, blind hurlings of snow. I'd spent the afternoon in the little town library, noting with pleasure, whenever I'd glance up from my work, the accelerating ferocity of the storm. By the time I headed home the wind was so high I could hardly keep my trudging, small-stepping feet planted on the ground. It was a day when *anyone* might long to leave Freeland.

Kornelia was not where I thought she'd be. I'd expected to find her in the kitchen, huddled over a cup of coffee and perhaps a cream ship, but she was upstairs, in the bedroom, lying down. I thought she might be in her bathrobe. Some days she didn't bother to change out of pajamas, but today she was dressed—a peasant skirt and a bulky sweater. She was flat on her back, hands folded across her stomach. Oddly, disconcertingly, a smile was playing upon Kornelia's face. I never felt quite comfortable when my wife was smiling.

"Hello, my dear," I said.

"Mm?" She could hardly be expected to hear my mumbled greeting. The wind was *loud* up here. I remember worrying that it might lift off the roof.

I'd planned to broach the subject gradually, but the primitive wind seemed to dictate a primitive dialogue. Standing over her, looking down at her from the foot of the bed, I said, "Kornelia dear, we can't go on like this."

Her face lit still brighter. Had she—had she somehow got hold of some drugs? She said: "You *know* . . ."

And today I'm prepared to swear that, right then, at these peculiar words, the wind suddenly died. Something momentous was about to be sprung. And it was *eerie*—the implication that I had some clairvoyant affinity with this lounging, glowing-faced lunatic.

"Know?"

"Then you *don't* know?" A teasing coyness was in her tone and in her face. She'd unearthed, from our buried past, a manner I'm tempted to call flirtatious.

"I do know it hasn't worked out. Freeland. Your living here."

"Ah, but then you *do* know," she cried ecstatically.

"I'm afraid, Kornelia dear, I don't see what it is you're talking about."

"Ah, but then you *don't* see, you don't see at all." And she giggled at me.

Mad . . . I remember thinking it wasn't drugs at all—no, her sugar-overloaded brain had snapped, relinquishing whatever ties she'd once had to the sane and the rational.

"Perhaps you'd better explain, Kornelia dear."

"Well, I have two announcements for you, Eggert . . ." If her eyes, inflated like balloons, were to grow any larger, they would float right out of her skull. "We're moving to America!"

"I think perhaps you'd better proceed directly to announcement number two. . . ."

"Certainly," my wife answered, and giggled again. "That's where we're going to have our baby."

24

Baby's First Puff

Our baby sits across the table from me, puffing a cigarette. I wish she wouldn't smoke, as she understands full well, since I remind her constantly. I've known some real smokers in my time, Michael McKaig being one, and Lilja's own mother being another, who used to take the smoke in avidly, *greedily*, just as she took in everything else: cream ships, beer, cheesepuffs, stuffed mushrooms, stuffed grape leaves, stuffed chicken breasts, stuffed zucchini, stuffed clams, scalding handfuls of French fries. But anyone can see from the idle, unmindful way Lilja pulls upon the hateful little cylinders that her heart isn't in it, and I can't believe smoking offers her any substantial pleasure other than the dubious satisfaction of flouting me. The world is full of young women of Lilja's age who, fearful of bringing paternal wrath down upon their heads, smoke in the presence of everyone except their father. It would make sense, given my willful daughter and my own life's perversities, that I'd be the only dad on the planet whose daughter smokes exclusively in his presence.

Our baby sits across from me and if my memory were better I could perhaps recollect the very night of her conception. The range of possibilities would have been narrow. In time, the tasks of love became bigger, or my ambition smaller, and I shrank, physically, from the job of maneuvering my wife out of her voluminous peasant skirt.

And yet, for some inexplicable reason—the devil alone knows why—one more tentative, fumble-fingered attempt at bliss is tried. Two bodies unite and for some impenetrable reason—the Lord alone knows why—one of the flagellating, almond-headed cells puts its heart-to-be into its struggle. The waters it navigates have been poisoned—laced with a chemical designed for its extermination. But the cell keeps swimming. It's looking for something. . . .

I'm a creature whose occasional clairvoyant feelings usually turn out to be misguided; you might say I have nearsighted second sight. From the outset, I was convinced Kornelia was carrying a boy. Inside her ample belly, a young Eggert had taken root: a dark homuncular hirsute explosive bundle of a boy. And later, when the long nine-month wait was over, the living creature deposited into my arms seemed a hoax, a trick. . . . To be presented with this wide-eyed, fine-featured, fair-skinned tranquil beauty of a girl was, among other feelings, dumbfounding.

How in the world could *Eggert Oddason* have produced a beautiful baby? Eggert can remember holding his child when she was just a few months old, and staring down into her pale Oriental face, and quietly chanting to himself an antiquated Asian litany, *Tartary, Cathay, Formosa, Siam*, and these superseded place names held for him, so long as he himself held his child in his arms, more richness than "season of mellow fruitfulness" or "the dearest freshness deep down things" or "yellow the wet wild strawberry leaves." Where had she come from? It was as though his daughter had been smuggled out from the other side of the planet, from the other side of the moon. I'd envisioned another Eggert—dark, squat, hairy, irredeemably male—and instead met a new species entirely, a Lilja: a creature of turquoise and of ivory and of gold "to an airy thinness beat." Here she is—beautiful still, at the age of twenty-five, her eyes as broadset as they ever were, skin as fair as it was back when the bathing fluids of her mother's body were freshly rinsed from her newly aired skin.

Eggert Oddason's beautiful child nonchalantly exhales a cloud of cigarette smoke into her father's face. Like mother, like daughter. He doesn't mind. He is a sexist, or reverse-sexist, at least to the extent that he feels twinges of sympathy for any man who has no daughters—feels, in truth, that the father who has only sons is a short-changed figure. She is the apple of his eye, this vexing young woman who lounges at his dining room table in combat gear, dispensing smoke. She is angry with him, which pains and disturbs him. It turns out—as she has forthrightly let him know—that he's a reactionary and a would-be dictator. A fascist. A liar. A manipulator. A party-pooper.

How do I defend myself, Lilja? With the argument that I'm defending *you*, who have so far yet to travel. Unmistakably you are a voyager— and one who doesn't quite know what sort of landfall to hope for. Your father, too, has had far to travel, years on the tramp, but he has had the advantage of knowing from the outset the crystallizing form his journeys must eventually take. On the shelf before him, as he writes these words, he has his forty-nine books as testament to the relentlessness of his pursuit.

Lilja was given to me as a Christmas present—Christmas 1971. The girl was three. Her mother, passing hurriedly through Freeland in the dead of winter, dropped her off for "a while." It was almost as though, for once, Kornelia had shown the good sense to prepare for the future—for it wasn't more than a few weeks later that she suffered some sort of breakdown and wound up in a little rest home outside Rotterdam, not far from the world's largest tulip fields. The details are unclear—I made a point of making no pointed inquiries—but I gather she underwent hydrotherapy, and electroshocks, and the Lord knows what all. What *is* clear is that when Kornelia subsequently reassembled her life she did so, in part, by effacing her past with me, including our child. It turned out that when she'd dropped off Lilja for "a while," she meant a lifetime, which was of course fine with me.

So, both of my children have come to me as strays. In Lilja's case, the transition went far more smoothly than anyone might have supposed. It was as if, though she hadn't yet learned a word of Freelandic, the girl immediately knew she'd come home. Lilja was, from the first, a Freelander, just as her half-brother Sindri, however long he chooses to remain here, somehow will never be.

I remember when Lilja first discovered Culture. She must have been about fourteen. She came home one day with a glossy Italian fashion magazine and I scolded her for wasting my money on something she couldn't read, written in a language she had no intention of learning. The very next day, she found her first job, clerking after school in a woolen-goods store. I kept my mouth shut. And what did she do a few weeks later, on her first payday? She arrived home with what must have been ten foreign fashion magazines: French, English, Danish, Italian, American. It was, I fancy, one of her life's most enchanting experiences. What she felt, struggling home with her heavy cargo under her arms, was surely akin to what I had felt as Hannibal and I scrambled back from the NATO base, that freezing night when Fred pursued Ginger to Venice: truly, that world Down Below could be more ingeniously beautiful than anybody would have dreamed. . . .

What keeps the girl here? Wouldn't it have made more sense for my Asian princess to be Asia-based? Pounding a mallet into a sun-baked cliff-side in the Indus Valley, painstakingly exhuming some four-thousand-year-old Harappan potsherds? Or learning ceramic glazes in Hokkaido? Or drifting on ponyback through a bamboo forest, a rifle outfitted with a hypodermic needle under one arm, searching for a panda that she means to anesthetize and outfit with a radio transmitter? Instead, she sits on the top, the ninth floor of Thorskrist's Skyscraper Tower, wearily enumerating for her fascistic father the errors of his ways.

"The campaign doesn't seem to be going very well," she says.

"I'm hoping, my dear, that's no gloating light in your eyes."

"It isn't as if I didn't warn you."

"And it isn't as if I haven't ignored warnings all my life. I'm much too old to start listening now. . . ."

"Oh, you're not as old as you want to be. Poor man, you want to be older than ancient Thorgunnur, sitting in her room in the Eldershelter, too blind even to do any mountain-viewing. The sad fact is, you've got a number of laps yet to swim, Pappalingur."

The term is Lilja's own invention—a variation on the informal Free-landic *pabbi*, or dad, by way of *pappi*, or cardboard, with a diminutive suffix attached. Literally, she calls her author-father "little heavy paper"—while suggesting "father-tongue" or "father-language." She's her daddy's girl: a clever girl.

"Not so old? Me, not so old? How dare you suggest such a thing. Listen, I've written forty-nine books. If the writing of a book ages a man two years—surely a conservative judgment—I'm ninety-eight."

"And no doubt you have another forty-nine books inside you. I'm eventually going to have a father who is a hundred and—and ninety-eight."

Clever though she may be, I'm afraid her mathematical training has been shockingly deficient.

"Ninety-eight multiplied by two makes a hundred and ninety-six," I point out.

"I never claimed a mind for figures. That's Sindri's domain."

"He's very precise."

"He's not only precise. He's brilliant."

"Why is it that everyone seems to have a taste for bright-eyed, breathless superlatives except my reviewers? But as for Sindri, it probably *is* a good thing that he, and not you, tallies the fish-catches at Freefiskur, or whatever it is he does."

"A good thing for Freefiskur, maybe. Not such a good thing for Sindri."

I feel something bristle within me. "That's an excellent job," I remind her. "Freefiskur's as secure as things come in Freeland."

And Lilja bristles, too, her eyes flash fire at me. "He's better than that job."

I feel an impassioned, wide-ranging tirade coalescing within me—something about maturity lying in the realization that people are large and jobs are small, and about the lamentable state, generally, of European youth, and about how much I dislike, particularly, boyfriends of hers who doze off on my living room floor—but I swallow it all down. "In my own case," I say, "I'd like to think the reverse is true. My job—writing books—is better than I am."

"That's what makes you lucky."

"And old," I reply.

"Old? You're not any older than poor Hannibal, who was born in the Middle Ages. At least. He may date all the way back to the Settlement. But still that doesn't stop him from chasing after a kid my age."

Her words transfigured the air in the room. Or the light in the room. Everything changed.

My hands on the tabletop, which I'd been idly staring at, now, as if with the adjustment of a microscope's focusing screw, shifted into almost preternaturally sharp clarity: I became aware of every thready hair on the backs of my palms, both the black and the white, and of the tortuous twisting of my prominent veins, laid athwart the hungry-looking tendons, and of the crusty wart in the lax scoop of flesh between thumb and fore-finger, and of my nails, snugly packed with sediment. "A kid your age?" I said. "What are you talking about?"

"You don't know?"

It elated her—merely to utter this question. Unmistakably, Lilja had been hoping to draw the befuddled look I gave her.

"I'm not sure I do. . . ."

"About Hannibal and Elva?"

"Elva? Elva who?"

"You really *do* don't know. . . ." Triumphant—my girl was triumph-ant. "Elva Gizursdottir."

"Gizur Steingrimsson's daughter?"

"Exactly."

"But I don't think I know her. I can't picture her, anyway. . . ."

Could it be, was it truly possible that Hannibal had taken up with Gizur Steingrimsson's daughter? It seemed unlikely—and yet possible.

Generally, Hannibal wasn't one to go chasing after women, particularly young women. Although he'd never married Rut, he was in various recondite ways of the spirit the most married man I knew. He always returned to Rut. However far from Freeland he'd gone, however long he'd stayed away, always he'd returned to her. There was no fathoming such devotion. Why has he stayed so inextricably bound, when other, brighter opportunities beckon at every side? His wastefulness in this regard—the worst sort of wastefulness, from my point of view, that of romantic opportunities unexplored—seems to haunt me far more than him. How did Rut hold on to him? Who knows, but hold him she did. . . . Even so, there have been occasions, especially when he and Rut have had a public falling out, when Hannibal has ostentatiously sallied forth, like a man with something to prove, and affiliated himself with some other woman. These affairs have never lasted, though.

"I'm surprised you can't," Lilja said.

"Can't?"

"Can't picture her."

"What do you mean?"

"Well she's so amazingly pretty."

If you looked closely enough, that wart between my thumb and forefinger formed a little face. By wiggling my thumb, I made it grin lopsidedly at me.

"But surely she must be—why she's just a kid," I protested.

"She's my age. Come on, Pabbi. What difference does that make?"

"I don't know what you mean."

"Come on. You may be the oldest living Freelander, but let's face it. It isn't as though you've lost your eye for pretty young girls, now have you?" And young Lilja laughed, prettily.

25

On the Shelf

It was that year in America when everybody seemed to be shoving—when not shooting—each other, and I bitterly regretted having settled ourselves at the very hub of the turmoil. But I suppose it was the nature of the times to foster everywhere a sense of being plumb at the center of the storm and no doubt I would have felt much the same had we, in that spring of 1968, wound up in New York or New Haven, in Chicago or Ann Arbor, in Berkeley or San Francisco, instead of in Boston. In any case, I take it as proof of my ability to transcend the merely topical that most of my memories of that year are of steady industry. Those were productive months for me.

Actually, we wound up not in Boston but in one of its suburbs, Arlington, selected because it was home to Kornelia's American cousin, who worked for a chemical company. Our destination might just as well have been, as one of those post office displays would have it, Anywhere, USA; Kornelia was determined to get out of Thorskrist at any cost.

The cousin turned out to be nothing but a lighthouse; he brought us safely to harbor and, once we were there, immediately became an irrelevance. We had one meal with him—this a candlelit affair at an Italian restaurant near the Public Gardens. He was a fair-haired, clean-shaven, handsome man with strikingly mobile features and the horror he felt on first perceiving us—an oversized woman in a red-checked flannel shirt and a trailing peasant skirt, and her dark-skinned husband with the veering narrow eyes of a petty thief—was broadcast on his face with admirable openness: he literally gaped and shuddered. Perhaps he'd been hoping, bless his heart, for a dash of European elegance. . . .

In truth, Kornelia had no need of any cousin—of any blood-connections whatsoever. I was beginning to perceive that she, in her grasping way, had an incomparable talent for imposing herself on others. Indeed, she was so gifted as to make me almost regret my decision to leave her just as soon as the baby was born. But there it was: my secret, my reserve of strength. I would soon be free. I would soon be far from America, and what in the world did it matter if military induction centers were being firebombed or people were dodging yellow clouds of tear gas in the streets?

Kornelia was already free. She was in her element at last. The play she was daily enacting—the Kornelia Alslost Story—now had a swollen, rapidly rotating cast; I could never keep everyone straight. She had a new life. No longer vaguely political, she'd become an *activist*. Eggert, the times are so exciting!

She found us an apartment, or part of an apartment, and managed, in her irresistible vigor, to get the rent reduced. For our room—a big second-story paint-peeling room overlooking a maple tree—we paid $90 a month. We shared a bathroom and living room and kitchen with a former law student who slept all day and played cards all night, and a farmer's son from Michigan who'd dropped out of Harvard to peddle drugs. Kornelia was smoking pot ceaselessly, exhaling clouds of smoke that—so my memory has it—were the size of armchairs, of sofas, of refrigerators.

The times were stressful, as I've said, for it used to gnaw at me: the image of that little fetal Eggert ingesting illicit drugs through what I suppose one might call the water pipe of his placenta. Couldn't she show a little *pity* for the lad? Utterly in the dark he was, and upside down to boot—did he need any *further* disorientations? I was sentimentally drawn to the boy and felt I owed it to him, before leaving his life, to see him safely out of his mother's body. Out of the dangerous womb and into the comparative safety of the dog-eat-dog world-at-large.

Of course I'm being much too flippant. For it troubled me, it *did*, it stirred me up: the thought of another Eggert unloaded on the planet, destined like his father to make his way on quickness and slyness, and perhaps, too, destined to court and curse a world that recoiled from him, when it noticed him at all. Wouldn't that endless greedy string of wizened cigarettes blunt the boy's wits?—an especially disturbing thought because an Eggert stripped of his guilt-guile was no Eggert at all, was nothing but a three-legged fox, a cracked gull's egg, an ebony duck afloat in an oil-slick.

Kornelia was not altogether neglecting the child's health. Nutritionally, the boy lacked for *nothing*. After the unspeakable deprivations of a winter in Freeland, she obviously deserved to indulge herself: fried chicken, chicken-fried steak, cheese steak subs, Italian sausage subs, lasagna and moussaka and spaghetti carbonara, sesame noodles in peanut sauce, peanut butter cake and brownies and fudgies and ice cream cake à la mode. . . . There was, I'm tempted now to say if I wouldn't have said so then, something noble about her resolve. The problem of the Self and the Other having stymied Western philosophy for millennia, wasn't Kornelia's solution as good as any? She would break down the boundary. She herself was expanding, day by day, magnifying Self while diminishing Other. Given enough time, the earth-mother would eat the earth and all would be One.

In the meanwhile, our bed was no longer large enough for the two of us. That was fine with Eggert, who slept on the floor. Most things were fine with him, for this young married couple had worked out a tacit arrangement for the weeks until the baby's arrival. Kornelia could spend her days as she wished—going to meetings, smoking contraband, dancing to music, raising or otherwise fine-tuning her consciousness. And Eggert would spend the days as he wished: in solitude. He had finagled a pass that would get him into the stacks of Harvard's Widener Library.

Edward Gibbon, when contemplating the "incredible multitude" of volumes lost in antiquity's most painful fire, was ultimately less moved and impressed by the Library of Alexandria than Eggert Oddason by the Widener, who marveled and went on marveling at the third-largest library in the world. Here were the true King Solomon's mines, the cavernous repository of what was always Solomon's greatest treasure: wisdom. Here were, among other things, reams of Saga materials not to be found in either Reykjavik or Copenhagen. Here were as well Danish books and Icelandic books and even, astoundingly, a section of Freelandica. In my quiet bibliomaniacally driven way, I was undergoing raptures. Were the times explosive? Was society—out there on the other side of the library's little windows—coming apart? That's not how it felt. In my mind, those days are lambent with a slanting late-afternoon sun; they are mild and contemplative and as inebriatingly pretty as the purple lilac blooming everywhere in robust grapelike clusters. Such was the light, anyhow, on that first day when I explored the shelf of Freelandica, and discovered tucked within it—one of the great beatitudes of my life—a book entitled *Nilssannals*. The Annals of Nils. My first novel. Right here. Eggert, meet Eggert. It—I—had been here, on the shelf, all along. Awaiting me.

It was understood I should no more be expected to follow Kornelia to her meetings and parties than she to follow me to Widener. We had our days worked out. If she had the friends and I the solitude, that was beautifully all right with me.

Nights, however, posed something of a problem. Unfortunately, there were evenings when Kornelia stayed home. In the later stages of pregnancy her body was finally growing so mammoth that, for all her titanic energy, she was slowing down, and more and more often there were evenings when she and Warren Bradburn—the Michigan boy, the Harvard dropout—would sit on the floor and dig into his cache of pot and a slow-speaking languor would permeate the place. As far as I was concerned, Warren was a mystery, though not a terribly engaging one. He remains of interest solely because of the appeal he held for Kornelia, and she for him; they were oddly devoted to each other.

When I first met him, I felt we might have something in common— I was thinking of my long sojourn in Detroit eight years before. But his Michigan wasn't mine. He'd attended a small high school in the northern, rural part of the state. The Bradburns grew cherries. He himself was—a condition clearly of fateful moment to him—the first graduate of his high school ever to attend Harvard. In high school he'd been a high jumper— another fact often alluded to, since it naturally fed into the joke he prized above all others in the world: "Even then, I loved getting high." Much of the time he was a hopeless mumbler, but when he was far gone in his pot a voice of precisely calibrated enunciations—pitched higher than his usual voice—would emerge. There was something uneasily feminine about him. He was small, though I suppose I'm in no position to touch on anyone's smallness, with little flourishing turns to his movements. He would become positively flouncy when approaching the metal weights and scale of his dope trade. Yet in some unplaceable way he seemed to be half in love with my Kornelia.

One night I came home from the library to aggressively witless music and the two of them puffing on a water pipe. How long had they been sitting right here, absorbing this racket? By now, poor little fetal Eggert surely had a splitting headache. . . .

"Eggsy!" Kornelia called. "Come sit with us."

To judge from her startled and jubilant tone, I was the last person on earth she'd expected to see. What in the world was I doing arriving in my own apartment at the end of a day, just when I usually did?

"Long live the republic of Freeland," Warren proclaimed. "May its sovereignty long endure." His voice again had climbed—its pitch lifting

with the smoke—and I heard a note of self-congratulation in having produced with such distinctness a word so prepossessing as sov-er-eign-ty.

I lowered myself to the floor, across from the two of them. They were
seated almost shoulder to shoulder. And speaking of sovereignty, I needed
no drugs to see that the water stain on the wall opposite created a map of
a low alluvial territory. I'd come to think of it as Potland. It was a muggy
and pestilential place, but careful scrutiny revealed a few outlying, doubtless uninhabited islands where a man might live a pure, drug-free life. In
place of the one I currently inhabited, I was ready to settle for *any* other
land—real or imaginary—although like any true artist I preferred the
latter. Away—I would get *away*. . . .

Kornelia began, in time to the music, to tap her foot against my knee,
to clap her hands against her hipbones. "You hate this music, don't you
Eggert?" she said.

"I don't much like this music," I said.

"You never want to dance," she said, and she pouted, first at me and
then at Warren. "He never wants to dance," she explained to him.

"Not to this music, no," I said.

"Little Baby wants to dance." She drummed her hands upon the
mushrooming dome where "Little Baby" was warehoused. Did it ever
occur to her that the kid might need some sleep? "Little Baby wants to
dance with its Daddy."

"Daddy doesn't wish to dance," I said.

"But Little Baby wants to dance—to dance with its Daddy."

"As it happens, Daddy, however, who has put in a very long day in
the library stacks, doesn't wish to dance."

"But Little Baby wants to *dance* with its Daddy," she repeated. Only
this time she'd swung around; she was addressing the boy, Warren.
"Daddy," she said to him, "will you dance with Little Baby?" Warren
giggled.

Was I supposed to find touching, or threatening, the melting fondness
of their long, lingering glance? In truth it did leave me wondering when
the last time was that Kornelia had bestowed such a look upon her husband. Had she *ever* regarded him with just this sort of dewy affection?

"And Daddy will dance," Warren declared.

Well, recall that this pregnancy of hers began in Freeland, months before our arrival in Boston. Kornelia was already big with child by the time
we'd crossed Warren's path. But if the boy now wanted to claim paternity—that was all right with me.

Slowly, unsteadily, Kornelia and Warren climbed to their feet. Their new altitude—heads at a radically different elevation in the room—momentarily befuddled the two of them, but soon they began to writhe around. They were not touching each other, quite, but their bodies shrugged in unison. Shoulder moved with shoulder, hip with hip. Kornelia at this point was so large that Warren might just as well have been an inebriated camper dancing with his pup tent. But the absurdity didn't seem to reach either of them.

They gazed at each other adoringly. Limb mirrored limb. And then Warren with a clench and thrust of his groin sent a symbolic shower of semen her way.

He turned to see just what I'd make of this. Kornelia, too, looked at me—gloatingly. I stared back at them, hoping my own triumph was emblazoned in my gaze.

What use, what possible purpose was there in Warren's sending a deposit, mimed or authentic, her way? The woman's womb was already full to bursting. From a biological standpoint, from the point of view of that battle, all the more ruthless for being invisible, between competing clusters of genes, Warren was an irrelevance. Hence, he was shamming. She was shamming. He had fallen half in love with her because at some level he'd ascertained that she wouldn't or couldn't have him, and she solicited his advances precisely because she recognized their innate limitations.

And as for me? Mine was the exaltation of the man who has out-brained his would-be persecutors.

26

Doomed?

Eggert's baby is back at the kitchen table, lounging and—I'm afraid—smoking another cigarette. It's one of life's piquant ironies that this creature who in youth discovered Culture in the form of an Italian fashion magazine now in adulthood goes around mainly in combat gear. Still, it's a hopeful sign that she would visit again so soon. There was a period, right after Eggert announced his intention of working toward Hannibal's fifth term, when the girl was hardly speaking to her father.

"You're not doing enough for Sindri," she announces.

"For Sindri?" But the boy is now a grown man. What in the world ought Eggert to be doing for him?

"He doesn't feel he has your full support."

"My support . . ." It's the most absurd accusation that grizzled old Eggert has ever heard. In large matters and small, when had I failed to support him? Hadn't I just a few months ago lent him my car when he'd arrived with some vague lament about a burst water pipe in his apartment? And when he'd come to me with sugary talk about "wanting to write," hadn't I taken the boy in hand and, though it hurt me to do it, made vigorously clear that he must abandon all such feckless dreams? Wasn't I directly responsible for the boy's finding solid work at the nation's largest fish processor?

"He feels that you favor me."

Naturally, what I want to reply is, *Of course I do.* I want to say, *After all, you are my daughter and he is merely my son.* Why do social conventions so regularly coerce dishonesty from us? But in deference to the girl's quaint, youthful notions of an evenhanded fairness that runs counter to everything in human nature I answer, "It's not a matter of 'favoring' one over the other. I treat him as a son, I treat you as a daughter."

"I just think you might be closer to him. After all, you're so similar."

"Similar? Sindri and I?" What is the girl thinking?

"Your brightness, for one thing."

"Sindri's brightness? Well, of course he's extremely bright, no question about it. In his methodical way. I don't doubt for a minute that when it comes to logging fish catches into a computer, or whatever it is precisely that—"

"Pabbi, look at the facts. The boy comes to Freeland at the age of fifteen, knowing hardly a word of the language, and three years later he's at the very top of his class. That's not where *I* finished up, you'll recall."

"Indeed, all too well I recall it. You didn't study. I'm still chagrined about that, by the way. Don't think for a minute I'm about to excuse indolence when it cleverly conceals itself behind a lack of cleverness."

"What you have to remember about Sindri is: still waters run deep."

"Indeed, indeed they do. But they also run slowly. The fact is I've never quite seen the point of that particular aphorism. If I said, Still waters go stagnant, would you feel I'd been—"

Again my daughter interrupts me: "What's your plan for today?"

"I thought I might do some work. You'd be well advised to follow my example, incidentally."

"How about giving me some time?"

"Time? I thought I was giving you some of that right now."

"May I take you on a tour?"

"A tour?"

"Of the electorate. You ought to know who it is you're leveling your speeches at."

"Another tour guide, are you? Hannibal's always giving me a tour. We usually wind up at the Silfurnama, where somebody's selling a food-stained wall-hanging from his auntie's trip to Dublin."

"We won't go to the Silfurnama," Lilja assures me. Her wide eyes are fast upon me. It isn't as though I don't acknowledge that my daughter has much to teach me. It's merely a matter of our somehow not being able to align our thinking. . . .

"Now let's suppose I were to agree. Just where on earth might we be off to?"

Of course Lilja interprets this as a full assent. "I haven't yet decided where we're going," she replies.

I let her drive my old Volvo. The day has turned quick and breezy—energetically pretty—with now and then whipping little flashes of rain. Lilja finds a parking spot on Skeggjagata, just beside, as chance would have it, Vikram's yellow Mustang—the vehicle that has cruised its way into my sleep. Somehow, until this moment, I'd all but forgotten this particular Amsterdam-based nightmare—the one in which, after shrugging off a prostitute's wiles, virtuously bound to glimpse my newborn daughter, I'd turned and seen Vikram's car come barreling down on me.

On the driver's side, in paint that has run in the rain, somebody has written VOTE FOR THE FUTURE.

Surprisingly, the coffee shop we enter feels far from hostile. I'd always avoided it because of its name, The Alternative. The walls are kelly green. Over the stereo someone is singing, with unnecessary embellishments, "The Way You Look Tonight." Nonetheless, it's a hard tune to kill absolutely. It's the one an imploring Fred sings to a resentful Ginger in *Swing Time,* enticing her from behind her barricades. I thought Vikram might be found in the Alternative, smiling beautifully, but the faces within—nobody aged more than thirty—happily belong to nobody I recognize.

"Not such a bad place," I tell Lilja, once we're seated.

"This is one of the spots kids'll go who're trying to score some dope," Lilja ripostes.

"I'm well acquainted with the phenomenon," I counter. "Your mother and I used to live with a dope-seller. In Massachusetts."

"So you've often told me."

"Before you were born, your mother was smoking so much of the damn stuff, I used to think you were one-third sperm cell, one-third egg, and one-third tetrahydrocannabinol."

"So you've said before. You put it in a poem."

"Did I?" I never seem to know quite when I can presume that those around me have actually read my books. . . . Mine is no commonplace role, being the leading man of letters in a country that most people could not find on a world map, and a country that is, as rapidly as it can, trading in its literary heritage for a handful of pirated videocassettes and a closetful of boom boxes.

The music, though still reasonably quiet, has shifted into another mode entirely: we've drifted into a song about the razing of a concrete wall with a pickax and a jackhammer.

A menu in a clear plastic frame stands upright on the table. Brownies, mousse chocolat, cappuccino, nonalcoholic wine spritzer. Given that these are things I enjoy, by and large, why does it depress me to see them available in a coffee shop in Thorskrist? While there's *some* consolation in the notion that very likely this wouldn't be a very *good* brownie or mousse chocolat, there's not as much comfort in it as you might suppose. "We were discussing how much you and Sindri have in common."

"*We* weren't discussing. *You* were expounding."

"You know, Pappalingur, he has very fine literary taste."

"Taste is nothing," I tell her. "Scores of people have it. In the end it's a matter of imagination."

This is valuable enough wisdom that I expect from her something like a grateful acknowledging nod, but she's too enmeshed in her own argument to hear me.

"I used to envy the two of you that," she says. "The two of you always feeling you might find exactly what you were looking for in a book. But I long ago gave up the illusion that any really serious answers to *my* life would be found there. And you know what? That's an advantage in some ways. I think it makes it easier for me to understand most of the people who come in here—easier to grasp just why it is your friend Hannibal's going to get something like two percent of the youth vote. Do you know where the senior class at the Superior School went for their senior trip this year?"

"Their senior what?"

"Now come along, it doesn't help matters if you're *willfully* ignorant. If you truly understood how ignorant you are, you wouldn't feel any need to put on a show of feigning it."

"Touché."

"Their *senior trip*. Each year, as you well know, the seniors take a trip together. Do you know where they went this year?"

"To Great Blue Glacier? A little climbing expedition?"

"They went to Rome. And do you know where they went last year?"

"To the old whaling station at Sudurvik?"

"They went to Berlin. And next year they hope to go to Hong Kong. Do you grasp what I'm saying? These kids go to Rome or Berlin or Paris, they see the clubs and hear the music, they see the movie theaters and the restaurants, they see the street life and the clothes, and they discover that drinks are cheap and—wonder of wonders—there are no alcohol-rationing coupons, and drugs are plentiful too if you want them, and the television miraculously goes to bed after you do and gets up before you do and more miraculous still it's not devoted to some Eggert-

Oddason-inspired investigation into obscure Norse etymologies. Do you see what I'm saying? How are they supposed to feel when they return to Freeland?"

"Glad to be home, I suppose."

"Well that's *not* how they feel. They feel shortchanged. Don't you see? It's not your fault—not your government's. Though you don't want to admit it, I can feel you're blaming yourself. Don't. It's not a case of a failure to teach us properly. And it's not *our* fault either—not a case of a failure to listen. We've listened, we've heard, and we've discovered there's a whole rich fun exciting world out there, and however much Thorskrist is never going to be Paris—more's the pity—we know it doesn't have to be quite so pure and godforsaken as the image you would impose on us."

"I'm rather fond of the old place."

"Your Thorskrist is a necropolis."

"I can think of worse destinies for a city. Who wouldn't prefer to live in Pompeii, even after the eruption, than in modern-day Naples?"

"It's doomed, Pabbi."

"Doomed? Perhaps, but you'd have to admit we Freelanders have always had an especial softness in our hearts for doomed settlements. Why else would we settle these islands in the first place?"

"It's sinking, it's fading, it's falling, it's collapsing right before your eyes! The question is, What will arise in its place? Maybe the outside world has never heard of Freeland, but it's invading us all the same. Mindlessly. It can't help it. That's what that world Down Below was born to do: mindlessly invade."

Oh, with this last remark of hers, my heart sang! If indeed we're sinking, fading, falling, collapsing, let us by all means do so with just this sort of trenchancy! I needed to save these words, to deposit them into one of my books: *That's what that world Down Below was born to do: mindlessly invade.* She can be such an appealingly bright creature, my Lilja. If she could only somehow get her thinking turned round 180 degrees, what a force of positive good she might be!

"Don't you see that the Great Ship Freeland is sinking?" she added.

"Maybe it is," I told her. "And I don't want to sound mawkish, Lilja-my-dear, but I suppose I've always hoped that *if* we're all going under, into the great cold dark airless depths, you might just choose to go down with me. . . . I'll have the mousse chocolat and a cappuccino. How about you?"

27

The Whole Package

More than once I've had a dream in which I'm clutching under one arm a bloody package—a freshly dressed chicken? a plump dripping leg of lamb?—and trying with frantic wavings of the other to lure a taxi from out of the tight, hurtling, blind rush of traffic before me, and can you blame me?

As her time drew near, Kornelia resolved to give birth at home. She would have nothing to do with those forces of soullessness, repression, sterility, and greed embodied in a modern hospital facility. She had a friend, her dear and wonderful friend Wanda, who was a midwife, or who was studying to be a midwife, or who was seriously interested in midwifery, and everything would be *fine*. We had a van—Warren's van—to get us to the hospital in an emergency.

Kornelia had grown still larger. She'd become a kind of astrophysical force field, pressing even upon the clock on the living room mantel; in our apartment, as at the unimaginable racing verge of Einstein's universe, time had stopped. She would never have the baby.

And yet the clock went on ticking. Meals continued to be served. I carried bags of groceries upstairs and bags of garbage downstairs. The sun entered timidly, with a benign lack of intrusiveness, through the ivied little windows of the Widener stacks. I worked all day. I would come home at night to a figure grown not only too big for its bed but too big for the room, too big for the apartment, and what else must be the rational culmination of this process but my winding up squeezed motionless against the wall, asphyxiated?

Or, alternatively, what else was its logical culmination but to come home late one afternoon and find the entire apartment being squeezed, like an accordion, by colossal groans and grunts and cries? That's what happened, anyway. My own wife was giving birth, or trying to give birth, on the big waterbed in Warren's room. She was outspread in all her pale naked enormousness, a sort of snowy subcontinent of hills and slopes and valleys, and she was sweating and grunting, she was looking creased and worn, and Wanda, too, was creased and worn, and a sort of wide-eyed blindness settled immediately over Eggert, a sort of open-eared deafness, so that everything was being taken in but nothing indeed was being taken in, and of course he didn't straightaway perceive that something was amiss, Wanda was disturbed and frightened. It was all unfolding in a blur.

This was a blur destined to turn still blurrier with succeeding years, so that nothing clear and tangible of that unprecedented afternoon remains but a tight tugged knot in the viscera, low in the belly. It will never be loosened. Merely to write the words *that unprecedented afternoon* is to experience it again. I don't think I've ever felt so pressed, so frantic, so terrified. Everything slid—and the jaws of Hell opened. . . . For things weren't going quite right, Wanda confided in me, something might be a little wrong, or something was frightfully wrong, and I must go fetch Warren's van, it's around the corner, here are the keys, we're going to take her to the hospital. And I can hardly see, there's so little air anywhere, and breathlessly I tumble down the stairs, keys in my fist, and of course when I find the van and turn the ignition the result's a sluggish low reluctant moaning, a drugged effort at arousal, and then a heavy spiteful terminal thud. And then silence. A cold, gummy sweat oozes from the palms of my hands. Somewhere above me, in a second-floor room, a mountain's writhing, the earth mother herself is agonizingly struggling, and Warren's goddamned pothead's junk heap of a van will not start. I turn the key—I curse. I turn it—I curse. Nothing! A tomb, the engine is nothing but a tomb, and the proper response is to race upstairs and summon an ambulance, but I'm off my head and the only thing I can think to do is to go lunging into Massachusetts Avenue swinging my arms wildly, signaling a taxi, a truck, an angel of the Lord. In that moment my recurring nightmare is born: the one where I'm signaling a taxi with one arm and carrying under the other a bloody, leaking sack of meat, and over the years the nightmare has interwoven itself with my memories: the dream becomes realer than the reality, and now when I think back upon it I see myself clutching what I suppose is my butchered son under one arm.

My son! . . . and at some point I must have rushed back upstairs, although that ascent has vanished from my mind, and an ambulance must have been telephoned, though that call has vanished from my mind, but I do remember two men—brawny men, built on a scale fitting for the magnitude of their errand—who appeared in response. One was black and one was white and I remember them hoisting her up to her feet, and lifting, and grunting in answer to her grunts, and I remember, suddenly clear as day, a hospital waiting room where was hung a painting of two country boys lounging on a riverbank, long fishing poles dangling before them. Great leafy trees arched over their heads and the boys were alike dressed in raggedy little shorts and T-shirts and straw hats, and needless to say they lived far, far from Freeland. Sentimental? It has always been my credo that any form of art that implicitly denies the existence of Freeland is sentimental, and it was in this waiting room that blind panic gave way to a clear-eyed fury, and I can remember internally raging at Kornelia for having drugged and abused our little Eggert, and reassuring myself that the long ordeal was nearly over: I would leave her soon. I would set far behind me all the drugs, including the drugs of political activism and domestic compromise and fisher-boys in straw hats. She would have to make her way on her own. The boy, too, would have to make his way on his own, but hadn't I gotten along without a parent at all? He would at least have Kornelia. . . .

Why was I not in the delivery room with my wife? After a quarter of a century many details haze over, but it seems that in the hospital I'd blacked out, or nearly blacked out, and I'd been babbling, or raging, and could it be the doctors and nurses simply grew tired of me? Who led me to the waiting room? I can't remember. Nor can I summon up the moment when the news finally penetrated my skull that Kornelia had birthed not a son but a daughter. The nurse's face is gone, the one who informed me I was the father of a bonny blond blue-eyed girl. But I remember thinking this must be some sort of ruse or mistake. If I just sat tight, the whole situation would be rectified.

I'm tempted to declare that the nurse's announcement was the great overtaking surprise of my life, this the moment when I felt as though the planet itself had abruptly halted on its axis, for a second or two, and then begun, widdershins, to rotate. But that wouldn't be quite accurate. No. For the great surprise was sprung a few minutes later. It arose when I was given an all-but-weightless living bundle to cradle in my arms: my very daughter, a being so naked it wore no name.

Man is the creature that names the other creatures. . . . And yet humanity's far-flung web of words—in whose extensive mesh lay predinosaurian theodonts that died out more than two hundred million years ago, and millimetric acanthocephalans, the spiny-headed worms that invade the viscera of antarctic icefish—had still to affix a syllable to this particular anima; so new as that she was. A pure packet of warmth she was, a flushed fleshed pulse, a pair of remote, wide-set eyes. And looking down—tumbling down—into that gaze of hers, I experienced a thump inside my chest that resounded in all two hundred and six bones in my body, and at that moment arrived my life's one great surprise: love

—love at first sight, the only time anything of the sort has ever happened to me.

Leave America? I was not about to leave. . . . I was not going anywhere. I would work things out with Kornelia. We would find a new apartment, with a crib and an assortment of Freelandic baby blankets—the finest wool in the world—and an igloo-sized pile of snowy diapers. Money? Once I'd completed Adam's task of naming all the animals, including this helpless one in my arms, I would take up Adam's curse; I would come down out of my Garden of Books and enter the Fields of Toil. I would find a job. God help me, I would become a family man.

28

The Kick

I suppose one reason I have so little patience with Hannibal's "visions"—which seem to come on him about once a week, catalyzed by a salted herring, or a photograph of a jeep in a barber's window, or a sock with a hole in the toe—is that I've waited my whole life for something of that sort to descend on me. Truly it would seem, having worked so purposefully, having spent so many solitary and often spooky night-hours chained to my writing desk, hoping something odd and noteworthy would occur—truly it would seem I *deserve* no less: to step into my kitchen and meet there not Sindri but John Keats making himself a cup of coffee, or to have the telephone ring and hear the voice not of my daughter's boyfriend Helmut Knudsen but, yelling over his deafness, Knut Hamsun.

I suppose the closest I've come to a vision arose on the night of October 30, 1979. I was away from the city, out in Birch Valley, at my summerhouse. It was the middle of the night and I'd been working hard beside the hum of my gas heater. I stepped out my front door to see whether the northern lights, which had been blazing a few hours earlier, were still putting on a show.

Well, there was indeed a show out there, one that practically everyone else in the country was already watching. . . .

Great Blue had begun to erupt.

I'm a Freelander born and bred in this regard, anyway: volcanoes reign over the home fields of my imagination. But more than most of my countrymen, I knew a little about them. Over the years, in my dogged way, I'd sifted through a compact shelf of geological textbooks. I'd done this, admittedly, with less passion than duty: if I was going to be the Voice of Freeland, I needed to master what was distinctive about the place. So I'd done my homework on plate tectology, volcanology, glaciology, and had gotten myself invited on many useful hikes with geologists. Eskers, kames, erratics, firn, grabens, horsts, glacial till, kettle holes—I'd learned to bandy terms with the best of them.

There hadn't been, as I say, much passion in my scholarship, but to step out of a summerhouse in Birch Valley on an October night and to behold, in the distance, a crown of sparks cresting high above Great Blue Mountain, its slopes rolling with seams of flame, was like nothing I'd ever seen under heaven.

And standing there that night, a little figure in a big black valley, breathless and alone, I recalled a hypothetical illustration from one of my geology textbooks.

If you were to take a lemon from your refrigerator and breathe upon it, the film of moisture condensing upon its cold skin would be deeper—relatively speaking—than the oceans. By which I mean, if the earth itself were shrunk to the size of a lemon, the black hadal depths of even the Marianas Trench would be shallower than that moist breath of yours gathered on the lemon's skin.

The seas run less than seven miles deep in the Marianas Trench, while the radius of the earth measures some 3950 miles. The oceans penetrate no farther, then, than some two-tenths of one percent of the way to the earth's core. The remaining distance is metal and stone, solid and molten.

The tides? The great Gulf Stream? The ships sailing upon them? They are a cobweb perched atop a pediment on the Parthenon—no more substantial than that. And the poet on the shoreline, contemplating the "eternal sea"? Hah!—he or she is an artist fallen under the diverting spell of a scrim, a film, a vapor.

For the real sea—as I came to ascertain on that October night in 1979, while standing alone in Birch Valley—is the sea of stone. Under the scrim, the film, the vapor, lay the true ocean—circulating to tides that, over time, rearranged the continents as a child might shift a set of blocks.

Strictly speaking, mine wasn't a "vision," I suppose, and yet as the sparks flew and the red runnels went arrowing down the flanks of Blue, I was an inhabitant of a planet far vaster than any I'd known before.

And if the seas are nothing but a membrane of breath-vapor, think how sere to the point of infinitesimality are the forests, the cultivated valleys. The poet of the jungle? He is—like the poet of the desert, or the poet of the pond's edge, or the poet of the savannah or the taiga—beguiled by superficialities. He has no depth. What we must strive to be, clearly, is the Poet of the Stone.

And where better to accomplish this goal than in Freeland, where a helpful, instructive Mother Nature has stripped away for her privileged children the distortions of trees, bushes, and most forms of animal life? Visitors to our country often lament the lack of sun, which even during the white nights of summer tends to be tepid and mist-hung. But here, too, aren't we liberated from a distraction? Aren't we reminded that the sun is but one middling star among illimitable myriads of stars, and *can* a man, given the innate curbs on his body and intellect, ever arrive nearer the truth than when he stands, on a dark October night in Bread Island's Birch Valley, watching as Great Blue struggles to give birth to the sea of stone below? Forgive me for saying so, but it sometimes seems the earth is more *truthful* here than anywhere else on the planet.

Of course there are other sorts of birth which the Voice of Freeland must do justice to. . . . We step out of the Valley and into a Volvo; Eggert's fair-haired daughter continues to lead him on a tour of the capital, circling round Hafnargata, the street that lines the harbor, and coming out on Kelduhvammur, which something like half a century ago, when Eggert was a little boy, used to mark the boulder-strewn fringes of town. But these days, on what used to be open hillsides, home after home after home has been assembled, new aluminum roofs gleaming. The ancient battle between sheep and fish, between farmer and fisherman, has seemingly been resolved at last. In recent years our agriculture has mostly collapsed, the farmers abandoning the old crofts for work in the fish-processing plants, and we outgrow the harbor that has contained our town for a millennium. Birth? We're giving birth to a metropolis! That's what Thorskrist is becoming! Nearly nineteen thousand inhabitants at the last census, and heaven only knows how many now.

Lilja pulls into the empty driveway of a home Eggert does not recognize. "This is a friend of yours?" he says.

"You could say that. It's where Sindri lives. . . ."

"Where Sindri lives?" What new absurdity is this? Sindri lives on Bragastraeti. When he isn't to be found in Eggert's own apartment.

"He moved out of his place a couple of weeks ago. Some pipes burst. Don't you remember him telling you about burst pipes?"

She has caught me off guard. "You must understand, it's been a time of great distractions. . . ." Then I realize there's nothing to apologize for. I have the perfect rejoinder: "Actually, I remember it very well. I lent him my car, after all. I gather he wanted to move some things."

"Anyway, he's been staying here the past couple of weeks. With Dag."

"Dag?"

"A friend of his. Norwegian—a Norwegian linguist. Sindri will be here a couple days more. Till the repairs are done."

"He isn't here at the moment?" It isn't that I don't want to see the boy. It's just that I don't feel ready to face both of my children simultaneously. Lilja's a handful on her own.

"He's at work."

"And Dag?"

"He's out on Diamond for a couple days. Looking into dialects."

"Then what brings the two of us here?"

"Some things of mine. I want to pick them up."

The door is locked; Lilja has a key. I follow her into a surprisingly tidy kitchen and with a proprietary ease she motions me toward a chair. She disappears into the flat's interior. I look around, idly, for some trace of my son. Dag, the Norwegian, has a taste for flowers—all sorts of rooted lives are blooming on the window ledge.

Lilja returns with a sweater under her arm. "You left it here?" I say.

"I lent it to Sindri. You know how he is." She shrugs. "Always going round in some little jacket whose sleeves are too short."

I've never been able to determine just how consciously the boy cultivates his waiflike air. There's no question, though, of its effectiveness: women with even the most vestigial of maternal instincts find something irresistible in his false frailty. Meanwhile, my daughter in her military jacket appears prepared to carry a forty-pound pack across a mountain range. She looks at times absurdly, laughably healthy.

I have risen to my feet, ready for departure, but Lilja signals me to the table once more. "I'll make us coffee," she tells me. And I feel it suddenly: she's up to something.

Or is she? There would seem to be nothing but daughterly solicitude on her face when she places on the table two cups of coffee and some slices of buttered mountain bread.

Lilja sits down, squeezes into her mouth half a slice of bread, and mumbles, "I've been hungry all day."

"Nothing new in that," I tell her, which is true. Neither of his children share Eggert's peculiar indifference toward food, his absentminded ability to subsist all day on a couple of crackers and a tin of sardines.

"You're working hard on the campaign," Lilja says, broaching again the sensitive topic.

"Not that it's doing us any good. But I take my pride in it all the same."

"You *should* be proud," the girl says, and adds, in a far less grudging way than I would have expected, "Hannibal's speeches have been wonderful."

My eyes catch hers over our upraised coffee cups. "Does this mean you're eventually going to forgive me, in the unlikely event he wins this election?"

"Oh I don't have as much invested in it as you suppose. Actually, Helmut and I are thinking about going to Berlin for a while."

"Helmut?"

"Helmut Knudsen. You know him. Your son-in-law."

"Son-in-law?"

"Son-in-law."

I try again: "Son-in-law?"

"We're married. Legally. Man and wife. Which unquestionably makes him your son-in-law."

Dear Lord, those eyes of hers! They burned me once—turned my soul upside down—in an American hospital one afternoon a quarter of a century ago. I haven't, even yet, recovered my equilibrium in the face of them.

The dryness I bring to my voice is, under the circumstances, a formidable accomplishment: "No doubt you've been extremely busy lately too. What with one thing and another. But apparently you somehow neglected to inform your father that you had entered into the state of matrimony."

"I was angry with you, Pabbi."

"When was the ceremony? Did you have a large church wedding perhaps? Was there dancing? Were there multitudes of guests?"

This elicits a grin. "A civil ceremony, needless to say. A week ago. Two weeks ago, I guess."

"Are you to be congratulated, Lilja? Or is this the moment when by rights I ought to come forward with some sort of precious paternal advice? It's odd, it's very odd," I confess, "but it seems I never know quite who I am when I first meet one of the milestones of fatherhood. . . ."

"I'd settle for a blessing."

"Easy enough, then. God bless you, girl." I stare into my coffee cup. In that moment, for a moment, I cannot meet her eyes.

"He's a good man, Pabbi."

And would any of the women I've known intimately ever have thought to begin a description of me in such terms? Would the girl's mother? Probably not. Would Sindri's mother? Certainly not. Is it envy burning at my throat? For my throat is—you might say—crying. It's overflowing with a hot, salty liquid I cannot swallow down. Still peering into my coffee cup, I say to her, "I suppose he is. I guess I've never really talked to him. It seems every time I see him he's got those damn headphones clamped on his ears."

"They're to please *you*. You're the one who won't allow music in the house."

"Berlin," I say. "Did I hear you say you were thinking of moving to Berlin?"

"Maybe. None of our plans are quite fixed."

I shift my gaze to the plants on the windowsill. I wind up staring at a cactus, a stout specimen of such plentiful but slender needles its branches look not so much armed as furred, and it's just as though this radically transplanted creature, conveyed to Freeland from God knows what warm and faraway land, provides me with some welcome mental distance. I pull back and observe. I see that Lilja brought me here in order to announce her marriage. And see that all day long she'd had something to say, which she hadn't wished to impart in the green-walled Alternative, over brownies and cappuccino, still less in the fortress of her father's apartment. She had taken shelter behind Sindri. It was at *his* lodgings—temporary though they were—that she'd chosen to make her confession. Although the boy initially appeared quite late in our household—out of the blue, with that cry of "Father!"—brother and sister have become such inextricable intimates that these days my memory counterfeits vivid pictures of the two of them consorting as little children: playing on the rug, walking hand-in-hand down Skeggjagata. This cramped, dispiriting apartment of Dag's may only be Sindri's temporary quarters, but there's enough of him in the air that she'd sought it out for spiritual reinforcement.

"Does Sindri know about your marriage?"

"Of course he knows. . . ."

"That's an *of course* I would have thought also pertained to me."

"I told you—I've been angry with you."

"No longer?"

"Let's say less so."

"Hell, let's say no longer and leave it at that, Lilja. I have enough enemies at the moment. If nothing else, I need your pity." The words cheer her, charm her: they pump radiance into her face.

"*Pity*'s one thing you'll never get from me. You slippery old trickster, you're the most manipulative man I know."

These words cheer and charm *me*. We laugh together.

"I suppose the question is, Can I manipulate a whole nation? This campaign is looking doomed. We're lucky to get two dozen people for one of Hannibal's speeches, eloquently crafted though they may be. His own common-law *wife* has gone over to the opposition."

"If you fail, it won't be for lack of conniving."

"Or for lack of conviction. Don't forget the other half of the equation. Has any politician ever believed in himself more than Hannibal does?"

"Oh, *Hannibal*." And the dismissive way she utters his name, as if nothing more need be said, gnaws at my heart.

"He's worth ten of your Nonni Karlssons," I tell her. "As he himself well knows. What he can't quite believe is that all the rest of you don't know it."

"The election isn't about *worth*, Pappalingur."

"If Nonni wins, you might say it's about worthlessness."

"It's the trouble with both of you, you take everything so personally."

"How do you expect Hannibal not to take an election personally? Good Christ, girl, he thinks he *is* Freeland."

"And what about you?"

"Tell you the truth, I think he may be right. Is he beautiful and foolish? It took a sort of beautiful foolishness to settle here in the first place."

Lilja laughs again. "You *are* a slippery one. What I meant by my question was, What do you think *you* are?"

"I'm a man with a willful daughter. Next time you get married, promise you'll inform me first."

"Actually," Lilja says, "I have two—two announcements."

Mm?

The phrase volleys, it reverberates, it tolls back and forth across the decades. *Two announcements* and it might just as well be her own mother speaking, for these are the words, the precise words, Kornelia offered me on that raw day a quarter century ago, in the sloping-roofed bedroom of my late aunt's house, as the storm howled so loudly I worried the roof might be lifted off. And you might say the roof *was* lifted off, for that was the afternoon when I came home to tell her we must go our separate ways and she preempted me with her *two announcements*, the first being that we were moving to America. . . . With those *two announcements* the woman reconfigured my life, and of course it's possible Lilja is echoing her mother's words subconsciously, having previously heard the story from Kornelia.

Yet it feels as though Kornelia herself is speaking, ventriloquially—feels as if mystical affinities are arcing through the air. In any event, intuitions are flying with such speed and certitude that I could plant in Lilja's mouth the words issuing there: "I'm going to have a child."

A child—Lilja's child—and Eggert can envision the newborn perfectly: a little blond girl with a splayed stare. A more delicate Lilja. His own Asian-eyed fair-skinned granddaughter. Well, he'd been willing, grudgingly, to make room in his life for a son-in-law, but now he recognizes that his mind already, some time ago, set aside space for a granddaughter. There was a vacancy all along. The cold truth is, a son-in-law isn't necessarily a permanent fixture in your life. With any luck, Lilja will eventually send Helmut packing. She'll write him a note—GO AWAY—and pass it to him while he's sprawled on my living room floor with headphones clamped over his ears. But a granddaughter represents a permanent enhancement. This little girl will help me see out my time. Oh, she will *love* her queer, crusty, frustration-ridden Freelandic grandfather! As he will love her. . . .

"When?"

"Not till spring . . . I'm just two months along."

My brain is reeling. I try to sort it all out. . . . "So you decided to get married because you were pregnant," I tell her.

"No, I didn't *know* I was pregnant, not until two days ago. I thought I *might* be, but it was important to get married *before* we knew. You understand."

I don't, fully, but I do understand that the distinction matters enormously to my girl.

"Now *this* is news," I say. "This is lovely, lovely news. I'll have to take you out, out to celebrate. We'll have a dinner next week at the Hotel Snorri."

"Take the two of us?"

And does Lilja honestly think her father is *quite* so prickly? Does she truly think I'd seek to celebrate my daughter's marriage and pregnancy by leaving my son-in-law at home? In any event, I have the perfect—the absolutely gracious—rejoinder. "No," I say, and savor a dramatic pause before dropping a surprise of my own: "The three of you."

I follow up this surprise with another. Although Eggert rarely touches his children—the laying on of hands is an aspect of parenting which has always felt alien to him—he reaches across the table and sets his hairy bony-knuckled hand flat upon the girl's belly. And what happened next is physiologically implausible, as he'd be the first to admit. Nonetheless, he would swear—a final surprise!—he felt the baby give an ardent, molten kick in answer.

29

Jason, Mason

I had pledged myself to an altered existence, that of the paterfamilias, and there were moments when I would have sworn a metamorphosis was possible for me. Though she tipped the scale at only eight pounds—and, holding her in your arms, you might have supposed she weighed half that—our sweet-tempered new charge emanated subtle powers of enchantment. Under her influence, what previously had been one of the world's oddest and most incongruous couples was transformed into a mystical triangular union called a *family*. Potentially, there was something beautifully elemental about it all. Our little quirks and queernesses would be smoothed away as we undertook, each of us, our ambitious new roles: we would become the *father*, the *mother*, the *baby*. Only, something in my life—in the patterns of our combined life—obstinately arranged it so that between me and Kornelia nothing could ever change substantially. I continued to sleep on the floor, because the extent to which Kornelia was smaller than at the full noon of her pregnancy was precisely compensated for by the baby. Moving into the newly vacated niche, Lilja slept beside Kornelia. I protested endlessly but in vain over this—fretting that Kornelia, always a loglike sleeper, might roll over upon the baby, who would be suffocated by one of the breasts intended to sustain her—but Kornelia brushed all my fears aside. Her friends continued to visit in dizzying, kaleidoscopically shifting profusion, and it seemed I had no meaningful role among them. We lacked a common language. I was, after all, the man who had "grown up with the Eskimos," and conversationally I had no place among either the vivid blacks and whites of their fervent political debates or the pretty pastels of their mellower drug-musings: *everything* in the apartment smelled of pot. No, my colors, my personal spectrum, have always reflected the igneous grays and mossy green-browns of my native land. Warren continued to mumble and grumble in the mornings and to volunteer fussily finicky enunciations in the evenings. He continued to peddle pot and to remind everyone that he was the first student from his high school to attend Harvard.

I was prepared to amend my life, but could anyone tell me precisely what my new role consisted of? Even had I been willing, Kornelia made it clear she didn't *want* me attending political rallies or joining the little circle gathered around the home-fire of the water pipe. Likewise, she made it clear that my paternal attentions were superfluous. She'd acquired a blue denim contraption of snaps and buckles which allowed her to carry the child—I'm tempted to say, to *wear* it—on her hip, and any attempt to remove the baby seemed tantamount to picking her pocket. Before too long I fell, willy-nilly, into my old routine, spending most of every day at the library. After all, I was doing what the Lord meant me to do: I was piling up pages.

From the first, Lilja was an amazingly sweet and placid creature. Almost too much so: as if contentedly drugged. Weeks passed. The plump little thing became plumper. Pages accumulated. We were running out of money, which agitated me far more than Kornelia, who greeted my queries with an impatient shake of her fuzzy head. She had evidently transcended material considerations.

And yet in her own way she, too, was fretting over things. I gathered as much the afternoon when I came home from the library and she greeted me with the words, "Eggert, I'm leaving you."

There was no one else in the apartment—nobody but Lilja, who was napping on the bed, face tranquilly upturned toward the desk's blazing fluorescent lamp. The afternoon was heavy with a black promise of rain, and Kornelia had responded by switching on every light. An uneasiness with darkness was one of the lingering effects of her stint in Freeland. She habitually fought the night with costly explosions of electricity.

I'm leaving you. . . . It was the world's most familiar line, a staple of hundreds of novels and films. And yet somehow, though abandoned by some highly determined women over the years, I'd never encountered it directly before.

"But you need me, Kornelia." I would find my true voice in a minute; meanwhile, this solemn counterfeit would have to do.

We sat across from each other at the kitchen table.

"We have nothing in common." This was accompanied by a resigned and *knowing* shake of her head. "Not a single thing."

"Very little," I agreed.

"You don't like movies."

"Not when I feel I'm *in* one, as I do at this moment. But I do like movies. I like Fred Astaire. I like *The Shop Around the Corner* and half of *Double Indemnity*."

"*New* movies."

"New movies? No, I don't like new movies."

"You don't like parties."

"Parties? No."

"Or picnics."

"Picnics? Good heavens, no."

"Or sunshine."

"Sunshine? I don't like sunshine? Now that's not true—whatever gave you such an idea? It's the sun *overhead* I don't much care for. I like it just fine when it knows its place. The sun in Freeland never climbs more than, say, forty degrees above the horizon."

Actually, this line of conversation was encouraging me. I felt we were getting somewhere. . . . I was doing my best to match her splendid dispassion, her lovely lucid objectivity. I like lists of any sort—including lists of things I don't like.

Kornelia's thinking was often as fuzzy as her hair, and I'd forgotten just how capable she could be of a pared, analytical approach to things. How admirable, truly, was this woman who was saying she was about to leave me!

"Listen, it isn't your neglect I mind," she said.

"I'm as attentive as you make it possible for me to be, Kornelia. If I'm neglectful, it's not out of neglect. So to speak."

"You know what I think the biggest problem is? There are lots of big problems, but you know what I think's the biggest problem? Your personality."

"My personality?" This seemed something of a low blow. "Look, I'm aware that I have an unappealing personality. For heaven's sake, I know I'm unlikable. But let's be fair, darling. You knew that about me when you married me." I added, rather sweetly it seemed to me: "Marriage is surely a matter of overlooking such things."

"You know what's the biggest problem? You don't really like *people,* do you? I'm someone who likes people and you don't really like people, do you?"

"I don't know if I've ever stopped to think about it in just those terms."

So I stopped and gave the matter a couple of seconds' thought. "I suppose in the main you're right," I concluded fair-mindedly. "People by and large aren't perhaps at the very head of my list of favorite things. But then, let's be fair. How many people are there out there in the world who are apt to say, *Gee, that Eggert Oddason is a real peach,* or, *Eggert's the cream in my coffee,* or, *That guy's a balm to my heart.* I do believe I'm a good deal fonder of the world than the world is of—"

"You turn everything into a grievance."

"But I don't see why my fondness for people, or lack of it, has to be such an obstacle between us."

"You *don't see why*?" She was meaning to convey incredulity, I think.

"No, I don't," I told her candidly. "You don't like winter, which strikes me as an enormous aesthetic oversight—think how much longer winter has been on the planet than people have!—but I'm willing to overlook it. A good marriage demands no less."

"That's why you have no politics," she said. "You don't really care what happens to *people.*"

Did I have no politics? What I said to Kornelia on that dark afternoon was: "When my cause arrives, I'll dedicate myself to it." And it heartens me now, having given so much of my subsequent life to politics—to that great cause so majestically and buffoonishly embodied by Hannibal Hannibalsson—that I intuited even then my capacity for a commitment eclipsing her own.

"I won't be around to see it, Eggert. To see your cause arrive."

"But Kornelia, my dear, you mustn't say such a thing. You're in the pink of health. . . ."

"I mean I won't be around because I'm leaving you."

"Oh of course," I answered. "But the truth is, you need me, Kornelia."

"That's just it—I don't. If you stop and think about it, that's a very insulting thing to say—that I need someone like you."

It was hard to argue with this particular aperçu. So I said: "But the baby does. Lilja does. I'm her father, after all."

"That's just it—you're not."

All of the banter went out of our little talk. All right: the woman was out for blood. All right: let's get vicious. She was lunging at me with a blade as cold as ice—a blade that burned like ice. I said: "Goddamn you, of course I am."

"Eggert, it's not as though I was sleeping around all the time back there. . . ." *Back there*, Kornelia would always say. It was as if, even now, so many months later, she could hardly bear to utter its name: oh, Freeland! "I don't think I could've if I'd wanted to, I swear to God half those men couldn't find the crotch of their trousers with both hands. . . . But there were a couple of occasions, and given how you were forcing me to live, and what you were *forcing me to eat*—I'm not exactly excusing myself for what I did to you, Eggert, but I can't imagine there are many women in the world who would blame me if they knew about the so-called meals you subjected me to."

"And yet you survived it. Even if you sometimes had to protect your cream ships at knife-point."

"Goddamnit, don't get me started, Eggert."

At knife-point? This was perhaps the only time in my life when I would have picked up a knife if one were handy, and brandished it at her. Surely the woman read murder in my eyes. I had a sense of rolling my words out one by one, just as a man in heavy fog takes each step singly: I was *blind* with rage. "Listen, I suppose I'm willing to concede you were unfaithful, Kornelia. What I'm not willing to concede is that Lilja's not my own."

"*Look* at her. Just *look* at her. Does she look like you?"

"She looks," I went on, "like a strikingly faithful replication of the child I would wish to create for myself. I mean to say, She is absolutely and *conclusively* true to the image in my mind's eye." And I felt a good deal better, suddenly.

"Look at the facts, Eggert. Take your nose out of your books and look at the simple numbers. How *could* she be yours?"

"Of course she could be." Even more than the issue of paternity was at stake. Kornelia seemed to be denying the very substance of my past. It was my life being repudiated here. "There was never a month," I reported to her, "when we did not reconsummate our wedding vows." And I smiled benignly at her—at Kornelia, my wife.

"But would you call it likely?"

"I suppose I would call it very unlikely. But in just the same way

I would call the existence of each and every person on the planet very unlikely. Did you know there are something like two hundred to three hundred million sperm cells in the average male discharge? To call each of us a million-to-one shot is a huge statistical understatement. Let's face it—we're miracles, each and every one on the planet. Four billion miracles. And the only thing that makes any of us believable is that we happen to be here. What makes Lilja's being my daughter believable is that she is my daughter."

"But she *isn't* yours, Eggert," Kornelia protested, and, though I hadn't seen them form, a couple of tears balanced on her plump cheeks. Meanwhile, black raindrops began rattling the windows.

And another wave of fury went through me. What right did *she* have to cry at a time like this? Tears seemed in all fairness my prerogative—though one I wasn't about to indulge. Kornelia was staring down at her lap. "I'm sorry."

"Look me dead in the eyes, Kornelia." I challenged her: "Look me dead in the eyes and repeat these words: *Lilja is not your daughter, Eggert.*"

Well, Kornelia did—she did look me dead in the eyes. And "Lilja is—" she began forthrightly. But her glance wobbled, and a shadow went over her face—that face so much bigger than mine. Her words thinned into wisps of sound.

Within me, I clung of course to another gaze, one against which to weigh Kornelia's. A few months before, I'd caught the wide-eyed scrutiny of that creature whose existence was then still measured in minutes, whose scant hair was flattened with the waters of the primordial mother-swamp, who had peered into my eyes with eyes that cried *Father.* . . . Let the scientists draw their own conclusions about a neonate's vision, let them explain how the photomechanics of retina and rods and cones takes a few hours to begin to process the incoming bombardment of light. The scientists have nothing but science on their side. What do they know of an encounter like this one? It was pure stuff: soul to soul. I needed no other corroboration. . . .

"—she may not be yours," Kornelia finished lamely. "Look, shit, it doesn't matter. That's just it—I'm leaving you. I'm going to move in with Mason. He loves me, by the way."

"With Mason?" Truly I *had* been trying my best to invest the conversation with its full due of solemnity, to lift it free of its hackneyed conventions—but why in God's name couldn't my wife do the same? "Who the hell is Mason?"

"That's just it—you wouldn't even know, would you? Mason O'Grady. He's been here three or four times, you've *talked* to him, he was here just last Sunday night, and yet here you are just a few days later and you don't even know who he is."

Sunday night? I cast my mind backward. Mason—yes, good Lord, I did remember him. There'd been a number of visitors, sitting on the floor, passing around a water pipe. Mason! The truth was he'd been unexpectedly appealing. A graduate student in mathematics. I'd admired his quietness, which had verged on unsociability. He'd sat in a corner with a book. Tall, thin, with a likably angular, acne-pitted face, and a faint stutter.

"I remember him well."

"I'm taking the baby and moving in with him. He loves me," Kornelia repeated, unnecessarily.

What was I feeling at that moment? All sorts of things, all sorts of things, but perhaps relief primarily. I would be free of Kornelia. *I would be free of Kornelia!* We had met as the result of a game of Twenty Down—*you must select your life-mate from among the next twenty women who cross your path*—a pastime that makes no allowances for misgivings or second thoughts. For the game to make any emotional sense, the relinquishments it contemplates must be perpetual—*all decisions are to be instantaneous and irreversible*—and yet I was, in effect, being airlifted right off of the island I'd been sharing with my Kornelia. I was being returned to the world. It's true I would be losing my daughter, but hadn't I already somehow lost her? I was exhausted, and, under the circumstances, I wasn't going to battle Kornelia for long. Someday I would get my daughter back. I think I sensed this even then. But right now? Now was the time to yield. . . .

Nonetheless, I yearned to manufacture some words or gesture equal to the moment's amplitude. My marriage was dissolving, after all. I had no money, and soon, again, I would have no family. An inspiring icy barrenness—as inspiring and cold as Great Blue Glacier—outspread itself, and in order to do justice to *it*, anyway, I told her, "He isn't what I would have expected for you. That's not a criticism. Quite the reverse. Somehow I would never have pictured you with a mathematician."

"A mathematician?" So wide apart did Kornelia open her eyes that for a moment I thought, for the thousandth time, she must truly be demented. She had smoked her brains too much, just the way you'd smoke a trout too long in the smokehouse, and now she was mad, utterly mad mad mad mad mad, and the mad woman had fabricated utterly her mad tale of mad extramarital liaisons and madmen who loved her and her preposterous, mad plans for leaving me. "A mathematician? Jesus, what in the world are you talking about, Eggert?"

I had been seeking after dignity, but the moment was to possess none. . . . None! She laughed—a huge whoop of laughter. Having only moments ago announced she was leaving me, my wife was laughing right in my face!

"You're thinking of *Jason*," she said. "He's the mathematician. I'm leaving you for *Mason*. Mason O'Grady. That's just it," she said, "you talk to these people four or five times and they mean so little to you you can't bother even to remember the name of your own wife's fiancé."

My own wife's fiancé?

What to reply? What a phrase—what a phrase this was! Now, if it were true, as seemed apparent, that even the most cataclysmic events in Orphan-Eggert-the-Oft-Abandoned's life must have their farcical elements, what else was I to do but play the farce as best I could? As circumstances required, I laughed in return and said, "Well then, dear, do tell me, pray. Who the hell is *Mason*, darling?"

30

A State of Mind

On the evening when the political event is to take place which, according to every prediction, will reach a larger television audience than any in our history, President Hannibal Hannibalsson arrives at the studio with his full panoply of media consultants, pollsters, spin doctors, speechwriters, executive gag-suppliers, public relations specialists, domestic advisers, foreign policy experts, press secretaries, handlers, bodyguards—which is to say, he arrives with me—some twenty minutes before the debate's scheduled to begin. In fact, although I am his sole assistant tonight, he has been well guided. At dinner, knowing him likely at times like this to look for broad-based support in a bottle of Brown Death, I'd restricted him to three smallish glasses. His face when he arrives at the studio is only mildly flushed and my plausible hope is that the television camera will translate this into an athletic glow. In addition, I've made on his behalf some clandestine inquiries, through an old friend at the station who owes me a favor or two, into the possibility of suddenly pulling the program off the air due to "transmission difficulties" in the event Hannibal seriously missteps.

Was I being too cautious? Probably. I eventually decided we didn't need "transmission difficulties." Hannibal could take care of himself. If he will occasionally wedge his foot in his mouth—and, having done so, will stubbornly deny, in a voice muffled by shoe leather, that he's experiencing the slightest difficulty in expressing himself—he's a remarkably effective speaker as a rule. You do have to grant him that. Although an accident of birth fated him to enact his political drama on a diminished scale, out along the drafty wings of the global stage, he has an innate genius for that oddest of social art forms—the one devoted to convincing total strangers you hold their interests foremost in your heart. His was a persuasiveness born of fidelity. For he *did*—he *did* hold their interests foremost. He believed in what he was doing. Others around him might be different, as he himself understood. I don't think he would have been flabbergasted, though maybe indignant, to learn that I'd explored the possibility of "transmission difficulties." But he himself was above such manipulations, perhaps less as a matter of principle than of personal dignity: as a competitor, Hannibal could be ruthless, but never small. Me, I'm willing to be small, if the cause is large enough.

I'm quite jittery as we enter the studio, and yet a mere glimpse of our opponent restores me. There sits Nonni Karlsson on a sofa, surrounded by advisers—*young* advisers, wearing unappealingly bright and stylish clothes. But what team of henchmen, however dapper and cosmopolitan, could surmount the unalterable fact that if you bored into the head of Nonni Karlsson, venturing behind his handsome features and bright smile, you would discover no light and no heat? His brain simply doesn't have enough logs on the fire to keep a blaze going. He may be—he *is*—our opponent, our sworn political enemy, but it's even harder to take him seriously than to dislike him. For we are dealing with a man who, as the ancient schoolmistress Thorgunnur would eagerly point out, reached the age of nine without knowing how to spell Great Blue Mountain. Pull the debate off the air? Whatever for? Hannibal will carve him up, leaving him as limp and harmless as a gutted trout.

The moment he sees us, Nonni springs from the couch and bounds forward with round face alit and hand extended. If Hannibal can hardly dislike Nonni, still less can Nonni dislike Hannibal, who has been President throughout Nonni's adult life. This man whose hand Nonni eagerly pumps is the most successful leader our nation has known since the days before we became thralls to the Danes, in 1387; Hannibal's natural rivals wore mail shirts and carried pikestaffs.

The boy—and for all his thirty-nine years Nonni seems a boy to me—looks desperate for Hannibal's approval. They linger over their handshake. Raptly I study Nonni's features, determining that his good looks derive from his high and smooth cheekbones, without which his would be a face nobody could take seriously. This is handsomeness of a seamless boyishness: cheeks plump as if with unshucked baby fat, little bridgeless nose, neatly parted hair piled in an insouciant wave upon his rounded brow. . . . No edge: the boy nowhere has any edge. We have nothing to fear from Nonni.

The one whom we did have cause to fear, and who had *not* come over to greet us from the dark corner where he was lankily standing, was Ulvar Ormsson, Wolf the son of Worm, among whose collection of marionette creations was an SS officer bearing a striking resemblance to Eggert Oddason. Through a series of what I suppose must be called missteps on my part, it had been arranged that Ulvar would make up one-third of the panel of interviewers. Televised debates are relatively new in our politics and their protocol is uncertain. It was eventually decided that one of the three interviewers ought to be neutral, one in Hannibal's camp, and one in Nonni's. I'd ingeniously worked it out that the neutral party would be Matthias Jonasson, a mild-seeming old friend of ours at the Ministry of Fisheries who presumably could be counted on to kick Nonni once he was down. But in securing Matthias I traded away any sort of veto on the third panelist. The result was Wolf the Puppetmaster.

Safely, beautifully on our side was old Tryggvi Gunnarsson, Deputy Editor of *The Torch*, who sported the bushiest, most striking eyebrows I've ever encountered. Either one of these, if surgically transplanted to his chin, might have served as a respectable goatee. To him had fallen the honor of posing the first question.

Clearly, Tryggvi's a man unused to being interrupted. Even his most routine remark—a request for more coffee, a comment on the weather—can come off as momentous, and he was more than usually so tonight. Ruminating deeply, huffing and halting in his gravelly voice, he delivered up a powder puff, a cream ship: Candidates, how does your foreign policy experience match up against your opponent's?

The question went first to Nonni, who initially seemed prepared to argue that his extended stay in Fairbanks, Iowa, as a high school exchange student, equipped him with a strong background in— But he thought better of this tack, wishing instead to go on record as declaring that our country's foreign policy has been riddled with the most— But he thought better of this line, too, and allowed that in the particular area of foreign policy his esteemed opponent, the President, might conceivably— By the time his three minutes were up, he'd all but endorsed Hannibal.

I was sitting on a folding chair in a shadowy corner of the studio, having detached myself from the crowd for Hannibal's benefit. My plan was to begin signaling if and when he went grievously astray.

But he handled Tryggvi's question with all the platitudinizing aplomb it merited. He was manifestly a leader, as Nonni just as manifestly wasn't. Midway through his answer, actually slapping his knee self-reproachedly—

as though scolding himself for getting carried away with the sheer pleasure the question brought him—Hannibal said sternly, "But specifics: let us turn to specifics." Was he not, he reminded us, on long and intimate terms with the highest of the higher-ups in the government of our friends in Denmark? And had he not succeeded in luring to Freeland a Vice-President of the United States—the number-two man at the world's number-one superpower? And was it not true that by luring Mr. Quayle out onto the world's northernmost golf course he had single-handedly created a news story that had appeared in magazines and on televisions across the globe, with the direct result that we'd seen a ninefold increase in tourists coming to Freeland expressly for its golf, some of them from as far away as Johannesburg, South Africa, and Nagoya, Japan?

The second question came from Matthias and was directed first to Hannibal. It involved the price of cod. Given current market conditions, which involved diminished catches and diminished world prices, what steps did Hannibal envision taking for the betterment of Freeland's cod industry?

Well. He, Hannibal, wanted to express first how gratified he was to be asked this very question. He was reminded, coincidentally, of a passage from the earliest written account of our ancestors, for does it not say in *The Freeland Saga*—and here he must be excused if he hasn't the wording exactly right—doesn't it say that "after many years of plenty, in that spring the nets came up empty and bellies were lean"? In truth, he *did* have the wording exactly right . . . finally. After years and years of delivering this answer—which I had incorporated into his very first campaign speech—he'd finally gotten it down verbatim.

Hannibal went on to point out that although this hungry lament was written seven hundred years ago, the story remained unchanged. Freeland was a fishing nation and although many initiatives were currently being undertaken to diversify the economy—diversification itself being a subject he looked forward to addressing later in the evening—Freeland would always be a fishing nation, which was indeed a defining aspect of the grand privilege and adventure of being a Freelander, which is to say the salt in our blood, our fates rising and falling like the tides, although the upward motion, the sense of incremental progress, was of course inescapably clear to anyone taking an extended reckoning of the history of our beloved country.

It was Nonni's turn. With much backtracking and throat-clearing—he was even less an orator than I'd supposed—he criticized Hannibal for a lack of specific solutions. He, Nonni Karlsson, was indeed prepared, first taking proper counsel, strong measures clearly being imperative, at least for the moment, fishing being a chancy business after all, had, that is, already resolved to submit to the United Nations, in New York City, a strongly worded document protesting the problem of overfishing, said document to be delivered, directly, to the proper authorities in Japan, the United States, England, and any other government suspected of depleting the stocks around Freeland. There. And this was only a start. Other measures would be formulated and postulated in due time.

Meanwhile, Wolf the Puppetmaster surveys these proceedings with a look of icy amusement. A sneer flutters over his features. It is to his credit, I suppose, that although devoted to a cause I regard as quasi-insurrectional—the removal from office of King Hannibal—he apparently disdains Hannibal's would-be successor. To judge from Wolf's nasty face, he finds equally distasteful Hannibal's fluent grandiosities and Nonni's flaccid denunciations.

Now it's the Wolf's turn for a question. He regards the ceiling with an expression of willed tranquillity—something like a Hindu holy man striving, effortlessly, toward some final tableland of spiritual enlightenment. But when his eyes return to us, they are lit not with some becalmed otherworldliness but with a feral gleam. "Nonni Karlsson," he says, "I would like to read some statements made by your opponent five years ago, when he was last running for office. On June the tenth, he remarked, and I quote, 'I shall never again come looking for your votes.' A week later, June seventeenth, he said, quote, 'Believe in me this last time, and I'll never ask you to support me again.' On August first he said, 'I am not a man with an infinite appetite for power. Five years from now I shall happily devote myself to fishing and riding.' August third: 'You can trust me when I tell you this is my final campaign.' August sixth: 'You have my word that this is Hannibal Hannibalsson's last fling.' Now, you have often gone on record citing your esteem for your opponent. You've done so with such frequency that no one would question your goodwill. But how would you answer those many people who, unlike you, might simply say, *Hannibal Hannibalsson is a damned liar.*"

I watch Nonni's face as he follows the question's turnings. You might have expected its cruel, twisting ironies to puzzle him momentarily. But no. And just as soon as the Puppetmaster, with a nod, concludes, Nonni is absolutely at the ready. He smiles generously at Wolf, and says, or recites, "I am, frankly, as puzzled by these inconsistencies as you are, and in order to give my opponent proper time to address them I will forgo my three minutes and grant them to Hannibal." And I sit there flabbergasted.

Well, the exchange of grins and nods was transparently, shamelessly collusive. There was no doubting that Nonni had known what was coming and been advised how to meet it. Black, bitter gall welled up within me. Had our nation sunk as low as this?

Obviously, it wasn't the willingness to cheat that incensed me. I suppose an outside observer might even see some sort of rough ethical parity in *my* willingness to take shelter in "transmission difficulties" and *their* decision to crib and conspire. But of course *my* scheme boasted all sorts of virtues that any true friend of Freeland would instantly recognize: boldness, novelty, and a willingness to risk becoming a laughingstock. Whereas *their* scheme was something a couple of schoolboys might hatch. There was no *scale* to it. . . .

Wolf nods gratefully at Nonni's response and then—the clever bastard—begins reciting the question again in entirety, quotations and all. Hannibal fidgets. He has gone quite red in the face and one can only hope our viewers will attribute this to drink, not shame. He's clearly nonplussed, else he wouldn't let Wolf run on so long, repeating all those damaging declarations. Too late, Hannibal snaps to attention and says, "If it's all right with you, I've already heard the question."

"Oh I'm happy to cut it short." Wolf's grin really *is* a wolf's grin: it has a steamy, pink-tongued, panting quality. "That will give you more time to respond. I'm very *eager* to hear how you would answer those blunt people I'm talking about. . . ."

To his credit, Hannibal now shoveled up a reasonably credible mix of fluster, bluster, and poetry: oh yes, indeed, those quotations did bring him embarrassment, but far more they brought him *sorrow*, since truly it was his dearest dream to abandon public life for the pleasures of the natural man— fishing and camping and riding in what surely is, and was there anyone present who would disagree?, the world's most beautiful country. I worried that he might at this point broach the subject of his vision—of that horsebacked moment when a glimpse of Great Blue through a rainbow prompted him to seek office again—but he held the reins adroitly: nonetheless, there are times, he pointed out, when even one's dearest dreams must be postponed in deference to the needs of the commonweal, and this was such a time, and so forth, the threats to our way of life never having been and so forth.

End of Round One, and if our side was a little bloodied, surely we hadn't taken a knockout blow; Nonni, too, had felt the thump and sting of a couple of sharp jabs to the face.

Round Two opened with our friend Tryggvi, eyebrows toiling up and down, asking how each would appraise his own efforts thus far on behalf of the elderly. Nonni tripped over this one, too, being reduced in the end to pointing out that both his maternal grandfather *and* his great-uncle were old people. Hannibal, meanwhile, no doubt directing his comments at half-blind Thorgunnur, sent his words soaring: the elderly are the living threads that link us to the great tapestry of our past. They bind us to the incomparable heroes of the Sagas, to Grettir the Strong and Njal and Gisli, and to the heroes of the Settlement and of course to Erik the Other, and so on.

Over to Matthias, who, sailing from the subject of fresh cod to that of frozen cod, asked each candidate to comment on the commercial future of the new fish-processing plant on Giant Island, whose prospects, both candidates agreed, were excellent.

And now the Puppetmaster was back.

A few years ago, our nation issued a communiqué threatening to cut off commercial and diplomatic ties with France in response to her policy of nuclear testing in the Pacific. Now, indubitably noble as this policy was in terms of global disarmament; and commendable in its expression of solidarity with tiny island nations everywhere; and affecting though it may have been as a piece of eloquent rhetoric; nonetheless, how *would* we counter those spoilsports and malcontents who might claim that our foreign policy is in something of a shambles, in the light of indisputable evidence that when, twelve days after our communiqué was issued, the French consul/chargé for Freeland—who prefers to base himself in Copenhagen rather than Thorskrist—was contacted about the official French response to said communiqué, he replied that he "wasn't sure it had been noticed yet." What would we say to those people of narrow, literal-minded vision who might claim that a foreign policy that went absolutely unnoticed by the foreign powers it censured and threatened was something of a disaster? Nonni was, it turned out, so disturbed about so disturbing an implication that he was again willing to grant his time to his opponent. Hannibal gulped once, then leapt into the center of the ring. He danced around—sidestepped, soft-shoed, put his foot down, backpedaled—and we were, if bloodied a little more, through Round Two.

Peering hard into his soul, old Tryggvi—bless him!—was still curious about the elderly and wanted to know how each candidate felt about the country's most costly edifice, Thorskrist's Eldershelter.

Who, at this point, was going to criticize the Eldershelter? True, its erection had nearly broken the bank—it had been constructed with shocking if not criminal inefficiency—but these days, perforce, we'd all come round to viewing its monumental extravagances as a virtue. Didn't even its cost overruns attest to our humane, no-cost-spared solicitude for our forebears? Nonni, in a state of high agitation, wound up praising Hannibal, who in turn sang a song of praise to himself.

Matthias, veering markedly from the subject of cod, wanted to know what each candidate thought about the decline of the smoked salmon market in the face of Norwegian overproduction. . . . Needless to say, the Norwegians themselves, as well as their flabby-fleshed and disappointingly bland product, were roundly deplored. The superiority of our native waters was reaffirmed.

This time, the Puppetmaster wanted to shift his focus to the young. In particular, he wanted to know how each of the candidates felt about the Give Us Our Music movement that was sweeping the country.

The Give Us Our Music movement? Sweeping the country? The question's phrasing was spitefully clever. It left Hannibal boxed in, since to confess utter ignorance of this movement that was "sweeping the country" would be to declare himself hopelessly out of touch with the young. I could see he was even more in the dark than I would have been, for I anyway had had Lilja's hectoring guidance to make clear that any such "movement" must be aimed against those of our radio laws which sensibly limit the broadcasting of foreign pop music.

After huffing and puffing for a moment, Hannibal displayed a side-stepping dexterity I'm not sure I would have expected from him: since this was a question devoted to the young, he thought he might best pass it back to his very young opponent. For his part, Nonni made a beautiful botch of things, lunging forward with the bright-eyed, gliding gawkiness of a man who has a pat answer at the ready. He first pointed out that music is the soul of food—then corrected himself to say that food is the music of the soul. By the time he got around to laying it out correctly—music *is* the food of the soul—he was ready to quit. In closing he observed that a tradition of censorship belongs more properly to Communist China than to Freeland, but surely this was no very telling condemnation in the eyes of those young people to whom it was addressed; they, in their military jackets, were surely not displeased to have their country compared with exotic and glamorous totalitarian China. We'd finished Round Three. I checked my watch. Things were going roughly according to schedule. It looked as though we had time for two more rounds.

Old Tryggvi, after foraging deep in his soul, found himself curious as to the place that traditional Freelandic culture held in our future. This was clover for a horse as far as Hannibal was concerned, who traipsed while Nonni tripped. Then Matthias, navigating into new seas, expressed himself curious to know how each candidate felt about the export future of so-called novelty herring—glass jars of herring in mustard sauce, herring in sweet tomato sauce, herring in a green-orange curry sauce, herring in a pumpkin-colored cheese sauce, herring in a pink tropical-fruit sauce. Hannibal pointed out that these products were bound for huge commercial success in the long run, since the world was—whether it fully appreciated this fact yet or not—famished for the pollution-free purity of Freelandic fish products. Nonni corrected Hannibal by pointing out that their inevitable success was chiefly to be imputed to the ingenious blending of pure fish products with flavors the wider world was already hankering after. Hannibal corrected *him* by pointing out that this explanation failed to do justice to the culinary experts in our own Department of Foreign Trade, who had devised these confections only after the most extensive gastronomical research ever conducted in the history of Freeland.

It was time again for the Puppetmaster.

Would either of the two candidates care to comment on various curious anomalies involving alcohol consumption in a country that maintained the strictest liquor laws in Europe and among the strictest, surely, anywhere in the non-Islamic world? If one closely analyzed recent statistics, released by the government itself, they quite unmistakably revealed that high-level public officials, who were exempted from the alcohol quota system by virtue of the ostensible social demands of their diplomatic positions, were purchasing spirits at a rate some eight times higher than that allowed the average citizen. . . .

Yes, indeed, Nonni would like to comment on this. Speaking as someone who was mostly a teetotaler—his abstemiousness was a matter of public knowledge—he sympathized with and supported those who called for stricter regulations on alcohol, particularly when applied to those currently exempted from them. On the other hand, as someone who liked as much as the next man a drink at a party or a dance or during the holiday season or after a day's fishing or on weekends, he sympathized with and supported those who called for a liberalization of Freeland's archaic drinking laws.

Hannibal had thrust himself forward in his seat. Unmistakably, his big body longed to be let loose. It is generally agreed that in modern-day Freeland we've never had an act of political terrorism—though there are those who contend that the hurling of a five-kilogram crate of frozen baby shrimp through the kitchen window of the Minister of Fisheries was not the act of a drunken vandal but the first in a fortunately abandoned series of accelerating steps of public terror. Hannibal looked ready to shatter our pacific tradition. He was set to throw Wolf the Puppetmaster headlong into the dark abyss at the edge of the stage.

But Hannibal held off. Again, to his credit, he offered up a high-minded blend of evasion and doubletalk. He asked whether anyone had stopped to consider just what a large portion of the state budget was generated through our tax on spirits—money that had gone into building the road from Bitsnes to Ritsnes, the tunnel through Asgardfell, the new swimming and fitness complex on Giant, and the aforementioned Elder-shelter, whose each and every room provided a view of Great Blue Mountain, which he need hardly remind us was the very first geological feature of our country glimpsed by Erik the Other, who in the year of our Lord 990, while drifting bravely through unknown seas, had descried the cone of Great Blue in the distance above its lap of clouds. End of Round Four.

Tryggvi Gunnarsson wished to point out in the time left him, the shortage of which was so acutely vexing, since he still had so many tormenting questions in his mind, but having time for one only, he wished now to discover what each candidate thought about the notion that our trading partners might prefer to continue dealing with someone they knew and trusted rather than someone who was to them a dangerous unknown? And wasn't it possible, too, that the dramatic increase in tourism over the last six months, which had included visitors from every continent, except South America, as well as an international conference of volcanologists, might not be a reflection of our growing reputation on the international scene—a growth accomplished through steadiness and continuity of leadership?

The length and dual-pronged nature of the question seemingly lost Nonni, who in the end was reduced to pointing out that, as regarded tourism, he himself had been responsible for bringing five visitors to our country in just this last year—his cousin Floyd Hamm from Manitoba, and Floyd's wife, Marie-Therese, and their three children—all of whom reported that Freelandic weather seemed mild and the landscape excitingly varied in comparison with the high plains of Saskatchewan. Hannibal countered with the proposition that while it was well and good to bring five visitors here on a onetime basis, he himself had constructed a slogan and a theme meant to draw visitors to our shores not only next year but for years to come. The modern world is becoming a streamlined place, you see, where one has to speak with brevity and bite if you're going to capture the attention of societies aswarm with video cameras and mobile telephones and these so-called fax machines, and how were we in Freeland going to compete in it? Well, he was tonight proposing that henceforward our slogan was to be The New World Begins Here. Yes—and how was *that* for forward-thinking? How was *that* for a slogan that might encapsulate, too, the aspirations of a forward-looking administration?

Hannibal went on: When people talked of the New World, they generally meant America, they meant the Caribbean, they meant Mexico and the riches of Montezuma, meant the Incas of Macchu Picchu, Brazil and Virginia and Massachusetts, but didn't the New World actually begin here, in Freeland? Didn't it start at that point when Erik the Other left Iceland, the westernmost satellite of Europe, and made his way still farther west, in the hope of a new frontier? In this sense, wasn't it only reasonable to view places like Canada and the United States and Argentina as our spiritual descendants? And when the people of Canada and the United States and Argentina came properly to grasp that their national experience was in effect an imitation, a mere replaying, of our own, wouldn't they inevitably seek out the fountainhead? Hannibal handled the whole business handsomely, with the enthusiasm of someone who had actually devised the slogan; it was mine, of course.

Matthias wished with his final question to broach a new topic entirely. Shifting, then, from fish to fish eggs, he wanted to know whether either candidate had anything to say about the possibility of somehow educating a pitifully misguided world Down Below where individuals were reputed to pay ten or twenty dollars an ounce—he'd once read forty dollars, but that was evidently a misprint—for fish eggs drawn from the befouled waters of Russia, from the so-called beluga sturgeon, whereas we in Freeland could not get $1 an ounce, on the wholesale market, for our lumpfish caviar, harvested from our own pristine waters and dyed, to suit consumer tastes, either ebony or scarlet? To which Hannibal pointed out that in a world that was daily coming to realize the extent of its own besmirchment, it was inevitable, with time and patience, that our fish, as well as our fish products, must achieve the premium in the market they deserved. Nonni, who was beginning to look done-in by the hot lights, chose to agree, though adding that our cheeses, too, derived from a nation that, unlike France, held not a single plastics factory or nuclear power plant, were destined for the world's esteem.

The Puppetmaster had come to his final question. We were almost home.

And how would you, Nonni Karlsson, respond if pressed by one of those niggling critics who insist on jamming statistics into our faces—who, specifically, wanted to point out that five years ago unemployment stood at 4.2 percent and now stands at 7.9 percent. Or that five years ago inflation stood at 8.7 percent and now stands at 15.3 percent? Or that five years ago cod catches were 80 tons and this year 74 tons? Or that five years ago we had a total of 231 crimes against property and last year 301? Or that five years ago the country had one reported murder and last year—a 100 percent increase!—we had two? To repeat the question, how would you, Nonni Karlsson, respond to that carping critic who, citing such statistics, concluded that the country was *going to the dogs?*

Rousing himself at the eleventh hour, pounding his fist and projecting his round jaw at the nation, Nonni declared himself as declaring that he wanted to go on record declaring that this was clear evidence of the need for new leadership. The country had stagnated, it had lost its spunk and direction, it was floundering, it was drowning. It was—to put things bluntly—going straight to the dogs, make no mistake and irreversibly, though with the right sort of leadership the nation could flourish and prosper as never before.

And how, the Puppetmaster began once more, would you, Hannibal Hannibalsson, if confronted with one of those critics with a niggling taste for statistics, who presented you with the following facts, who pointed out that five years ago—

"I heard the question the first time," Hannibal broke in.

"Five years ago," the Puppetmaster went on, "unemployment stood at four—"

"I would tell that critic his numbers were nonsense."

"Nonsense? Nonsense . . ." Wolf managed to look thoroughly nonplussed. In truth, he should have been; it was Hannibal who was beginning to talk nonsense. . . . "Aren't these the figures compiled by your very own agencies? Aren't these the official—"

"I would tell him his numbers meant nothing to me."

"Nothing? Nothing . . . I see. Are you saying, then, it doesn't concern you that unemployment has risen from 4.2 to 7.9 percent in a matter of—"

"I would tell him his numbers are unreal."

"Unreal? Unreal . . . I see. I don't see. Forgive me if I'm a little confused. Are you saying, then, that the people those numbers represent, the ninety percent increase in unemployment, are—"

"I would tell him that Freeland is not numbers. . . ."

"Not numbers. I see. Are you saying, perhaps, that in Freeland we cannot count?"

"I'm saying we're above counting."

"Above counting. I see. Are you saying, then, that the people these numbers represent are not Freelanders? Are you saying—"

Both men had turned red in the face. I was of course signaling frantically at Hannibal. I recognized all the symptoms. The most dangerous thing in the world was happening to him: he was submitting to the urge to philosophize. It's an activity his head simply wasn't cut out for. Nonetheless, in his wonderfully visceral brain, he was now struggling for some sort of cerebral pronouncement. I signaled still more frantically. When Hannibal wrestles with the angel of an abstraction, there's no telling what might ensue.

In hushed, self-congratulatory tones, warmed with a conviction of his own sagacity, Hannibal declared, "I am saying that Freeland is a state of mind."

"A state of mind? Freeland is a state of mind? I see. I see. So are you saying, then, that those people represented by the unemployment figures are not real?"

Hannibal took a deep breath. "That's correct. And not just them. You see, the numbers are not real. The jobs are not real." I wasn't only signaling with both arms at this point—I was coughing and spluttering to boot.

"Freeland itself is not real," Hannibal went on. "No, we are a state of mind. A conception. We are a dream, a creation in the head of—"

But he didn't quite get the name of Freeland's creator out: "Do you think your—your conception of us as a *conception* ought to be reassuring to the person who has just lost his job?"

Never, ever retreat—right, Hannibal? When your horse buckles beneath you, an arrow in its windpipe, proceed on foot! And when your sword breaks, throw yourself into the fray armed with a hilt only, you brawny brainless damn doomed rube. Oh, my pulse was racing—my heart was breaking! Shut *up*, Hannibal. Shut *up*!

But he went on: "I should think it's the greatest reassurance he or she could possibly have."

"I should think most people would rather have the job."

"Then they're dead." And the word *dead* recoiled. It was a gunshot that backfired, and the speaker on the stage, our President, was a victim of self-assassination.

—A victim who went on talking, unfortunately. Oh, the foot was so deep in his mouth I hoped he would choke on it, falling to the floor in a seizure of airless writhings, but still he managed to get the words out clearly: "They don't have the vision to look beyond their mere unemployment."

"Their *mere* unemployment?"

"Many's the Freelander who—"

"Dead?" the Puppetmaster repeated.

"Dead. Dead. Dead. They have no vision—"

My own vision was unmercifully lucid. Oh, I sensed just how devastating this was going to be, just how ludicrous Hannibal would be made to look. And if I didn't immediately recognize all the extravagant shapes the ridicule would take—*The Daily Liar* headlines reading "President Tells Nation: You Don't Exist," and the placards declaring "Another Dead Person Against Hannibal," and Vikram Jakobsson's yellow Mustang festooned with a banner proclaiming "The Dead Need Jobs Too"—still I knew we were in for it. Some weeks ago, when Rut had appeared on the television screen to denounce him, I'd heard Hannibal, in a voice like torn metal—the sound a ripsaw makes on encountering a nail concealed in a pineboard—cry out, "We're done for." The words had been vibrating ever since. Now his lament found its complement, as a second soul went howling down to hell. In sudden darkness, my head buried in my hands, I called out, over and over, "It's over, over, over."

III

31

Whistler

Right down Skeggjagata at high noon somebody goes whistling. Were he to amble along the street clad in a silk kimono and a pair of wooden geta, or stand bare-chested in Independence Square wearing fringed buckskin pants and a crown of eagle feathers, he could not announce any more unmistakably *I am a foreigner here*. For, as I've pointed out before, we don't whistle—except perhaps when summoning a sheepdog across a valley. To do so in public, for one's simple entertainment, is a sure sign of feeblemindedness.

Well, it was a slow day—it had been a slow year, I suppose—and I followed our whistler. He was a short, plump, bespectacled figure with what I think of as a flat-top haircut, though it seems that's a term, like "muttonchop whiskers" or "mustachioed," expressive of a bygone age. He turned into a tobacconist's and I followed him inside. Then something unexpected happened: he addressed the shop-boy in fluent Freelandic.

The cadences were stiff—he was indeed a foreigner—but I was manifestly in the presence of one of those rare individuals for whom Freelandic was a comfortable second language. Not many outsiders have gone to the trouble of mastering a tongue spoken by well under a hundred thousand souls in all. To us, foreign accents sound *foreign*.

One surprise followed another. He asked the shop-boy whether there were any Danish newspapers or magazines. But surely he wasn't a Dane. . . . I'd already classified him—correctly, it would transpire—as a Yank; he could only be an American academic. The music he'd been whistling? What tune was in his head as he strode down Skeggjagata on a summer day in June 1973—rendering its huge orchestral dynamics with a cheery, can-do dexterity? It was the "Ode to Joy" of Beethoven's Ninth. Hot diggety dog: an American.

I followed him round the corner to what was then a relatively new establishment, the Cod's Head. My friend Hannibal's woman, whom he'd still not married—and never would marry—had found her calling in life. She'd entered into a career as maître d' and bouncer, cook and barkeep— yes, barkeep, too, for here, so the rumor went, a man might get hold of some "strong coffee." This all depended on the formidable caprice of the proprietress, who tended to look favorably only upon men in work clothes, fishermen and farmers. The alcohol was reputed to be *brugga*— moonshine.

Back then, even less than now, the Cod's Head was hardly the sort of place where a pudgy, cheery, flat-topped, bespectacled whistler sporting a bright yellow anorak and carrying a thick notebook might expect a robust welcome. So: as he seats himself, on this June afternoon, he's eyed with a sort of reserved belligerence. He doesn't notice. He throws a sprightly glance around the room and I realize he's one of the few adults I've ever met who might fairly be described as pink-cheeked. I take a seat at a table nearby. He orders coffee. I order coffee.

With the quick gauging glances of a carrion bird, Eggert studies this plump new creature through the steam of his upraised coffee mug. The Yank has drawn out a fountain pen and begun recording brisk notations in his journal. Eggert senses opportunity. What it might consist of is impossi- ble to say, but how often is Skeggjagata going to throw your way a flat- topped trilingual in a yellow anorak who is whistling Beethoven as he bounces along with a thick journal under his arm? The novelist in me springs alive. I'm searching, as ever, for a narrative so universally captivat- ing it will liberate me from a cruel cycle of publish-and-paucity—of mi- nuscule advances converted into niggardly stores of rice and coffee and sugar and beans, all of them consumed before pen first meets paper— and a spectacle so outlandish on the main street of Thorskrist is simply irresistible. Here is a gleam, a burnish, a promise of good things.

I'm thirty-five, that summer of 1973, and already graying at the tem- ples. As for my literary reputation, I'm already too old to be an enfant terrible, while too young to have my snappishness affectionately termed *curmudgeonly* or *crusty*. I'm still living in my deceased aunt's house near the harbor—my move to Skyscraper Tower remains a few years off. Half a dozen pails and cans are scattered on the floor, to catch rainwater; it seems I can't manage to keep a real roof over my head. These are hard days, and

I take some comfort, I suppose, in the notion that my fellow long-runner is floundering a bit: Hannibal is just back from a year in Norway, where he'd gotten himself involved with an ill-founded lumber concern.

As should by now be clear, I'm not the sort who easily strikes up a conversation with a strange man in a restaurant, and in the end I was reduced to asking the Yank, in Freelandic, if he knew the time.

His wristwatch was massive—in deference, I was later to learn, to his myopia. Even so, he was a moment in getting his glasses and the glassed face of the watch into a workable alignment. "It is precisely a quarter past the hour of noon." He beamed at me.

I flattered him: "Are you Freelandic?"

"No, I am an American."

I nodded sympathetically, and said in English: "And what brings you to Thorskrist at precisely a quarter past the hour of noon on a Monday in June?"

"Why just *this*—" he said, and took in all of the Cod's Head with an inclusive sweep of his hand.

"Our coffee? I take it you're keen on Freelandic coffee?"

He laughed with just the sort of abandon you might expect from somebody who'd been whistling "Ode to Joy" on Skeggjagata just minutes ago. And when his laughter trailed away I sensed in his gaze—behind the thick wall of his glasses—a kind of reciprocal avidity. He looked both gratified and greedy. It seemed he was on a quest himself, looking perhaps for brightness, for raillery, for something that might approximate Freelandic mother-wit.

"It's talk I was seeking, if you want to know the truth. I'm a student of the language, you see."

"That's all to the good. Talk is cheap in Freeland," I said. "Coffee isn't."

Again laughter—generous, pink-cheeked laughter—and a look of piqued satisfaction. Let's face it: someone looking to study Freelandic could do no better than to run into Eggert Oddason in a coffee shop on the edge of the harbor. "You're of Freelandic descent?" I said.

"Actually, it's the one gene pool I *can't* seem to lay any claim to. My name is Geoffrey Simple but the name's frightfully misleading. In truth, there's nothing simple about it. Despite the name, I'm only a quarter English. I'm also a quarter Lithuanian, and a quarter Swiss, and a quarter Andorran, which you perhaps may not—"

"A principality located in the Pyrenees between France and Spain."

"You've been there?"

"Never. But we Freelanders take an interest in any commonwealth that might be perceived as feebler and obscurer than our own."

The smile on his face was transparent: he was beginning to consider me a real find.

"Yours is a very interesting country—Freeland."

"There are those who might say that yours is more interesting still—America."

I delivered this in my best Freelandic blend of gravity and humorlessness. For a moment he peered at me quizzically: then Geoffrey Simple's features lit, he smiled, he quipped, "Now who in the world would say that?"

The mixture of nationalities in his veins had not blended harmoniously: he was a queer-looking man. Perhaps I am, too, but in looks we shared almost nothing except height—or the lack of it. Indeed, Geoffrey was a sort of mirror complement of me: fair as I was dark; glabrous as I was hirsute; round as I was angular; his complexion freckled as mine was pocked. His laughter was always lifting toward a bubbly giggle, mine toward a husky cough; and he was myopic, whereas I, despite tireless years of reading, was sharpsighted as a hawk. There was, withal, something childish about him—or I should say something about him children might adore: he looked like a Christmas elf.

"You are an academic," I said.

"To judge from your tone, a profession you disapprove of," he replied. This was astute. I'd learned, in all my threadbare years, to resent these American academics, with their lavish sabbaticals and fellowships, their assistants and assistance; Freeland extends to its scholars nothing of the sort. "I myself," he went on, "would like to think it's more or less an ethically neutral profession. Like being a chef, or a hotelier." When he delivered a remark which satisfied him, his head would give a little upward off-balance jerk, just as though he were—perhaps Ulvar and Ulvar's Puppettheater have come to haunt my thinking—a marionette whose head was attached to its handler by a single, off-center string.

"Neutral professions? The former encourages gluttony. The latter, lust and sloth."

I thought he might lean across the table and kiss me, so pleased did he appear with my witticism. He darted a longing glance at his notebook. Did he wish to preserve my words there? Instead he said, "May I buy you dinner tonight?"

"If you do, you'll have me wishing we were in America. Freelanders are irredeemably proud of the inedibility of their native cuisine."

"You are not an academic," he said.

"Something less neutral still. I'm a writer."

"A writer? In Freelandic?"

"I can hardly deny it. After all, the shabbiness of my coat attests to it."

The inevitable question followed, and of all the inquiries regularly made of me it's the one that most consistently anguishes me: *What is your name?*

The truth is, it's an excruciating process: first I mention my profession to a foreigner, then I'm asked my name. . . .

I had at that time written some two dozen books. I have at present written forty-nine. I'm the most prolific and prominent author this country has ever seen. And yet what predictably ensues when, either loudly or softly, defiantly or embarrassedly, I supply my name? Blankness. A blank nod.

This time, though, something else—something vertiginous—occurred. "My name's Eggert Oddason," I said, and this fleshy elf uttered words of spellbinding enchantment: "Eggert Oddason! Good heavens, I've been reading your books! How fortunate! What a—what a marvelous coincidence."

A coincidence? More than that, a godsend! *Good heavens*, he'd declared, *I've been reading your books!* and at this point I was prepared to scale Great Blue Glacier barefoot behind Geoffrey Simple, to swim to Greenland in his wake. . . . I loved him!

He had been *reading my books*? No, he'd been doing more than that: for it soon became apparent he'd been etching them into his memory. . . . He appeared to know them better than I did. I had been, unwittingly, one of his instructors; he had been teaching himself the nuances of the language through me.

He had been *reading my books*? Yes, yes, he cried—and in the process had amassed so many questions he hardly knew where to start, but why had I taken up unconventional spellings in *The Bitter Heathen*? And why was the dream sequence in *The Annals of Nils* in the future tense? And speaking of tenses, was my perpetual wavering between past and present tenses, sometimes within a single paragraph, a nod at the Sagas? And why had I so often shifted viewpoints, veering from first person to second to third, in *Under the Yucatán*? And was I aware that Burl and Winfield, two characters in *Rats' Kingdom*, were, etymologically speaking, siblings?

And were the archaisms in *Guests of the Glacier* a deliberate echo of *Egil's Saga*?

As I would come in time to see, in his domain, which was philology, Geoffrey Simple was an absolute monster of erudition: a phenomenon of not always human limitations. He was breathtaking. His abilities were big big BIG, and, attempting to set Geoffrey down here, I feel him spilling over my paper, so colossally BIG he was. I'd always thought old Thorgunnur, with her ability to call up lengthy swatches of Danish and Freelandic and English verse, possessed the most commanding memory imaginable, but in his penetrating way, in his urge to track a word from language to language and variant to variant, Geoffrey was something I'd never conceived of. In the universe *he* inhabited, the man who would utter a word whose etymology was unknown to him was irresponsible, unseemly. To do so was a kind of cheat, like hanging on your wall the reproduction of a painting you couldn't identify. A spot of ignorance *goaded* him, and he held to his findings with a barnacular tenacity. If he could no more write a poem or short story than levitate, and indeed rarely had anything very trenchant to say about the contents of the literature he so avidly ingested, nonetheless when he was in his element—turning over linguistic niceties of phrasing and structure—he was invincible.

We talked in the Cod's Head for three hours. I adored him. Geoffrey would throw out a question and I would answer, he'd throw out a question and I'd answer. Sometimes he recorded what I said in his notebook, and is any sensation in the world more flattering than to know that one's utterances are being, so to speak, doggedly tracked by the bloodhound's nose of a fountain pen?

He taught in Baltimore, Maryland, at Johns Hopkins University. He was forty-seven. He spoke French and Spanish and German, had studied Latin and Greek and Sanskrit in school, had worked on his own to master Danish, Icelandic, Freelandic, Old Norse. His specialty—a process as delicate as any paleontologist's erection of some fabled, never-glimpsed creature—was the reconstruction of Proto-German, in whose pursuit he had delved into Old Frisian, Old High German, Old Saxon, and Gothic. He was too good to be true.

Too good to be true, too—this time, they were his words—was his wife, Constance, who at that moment was resting up at the Hotel Snorri with their daughter, Bella, but who all but certainly would be joining us for dinner. "She came into my life relatively late, which is to say relatively recently. I was forty-one, and I thought myself ensconced in a confirmed bachelorhood. Connie thought otherwise." *Isn't it amusing?* his grin seemed to say. *I was utterly mistaken!* It was a look I would see now and again in the weeks to come: a happy incredulity on discovering himself fallen into an error, although in truth he fell into them all the time. If he was almost infallible within his linguistic domain—when he supplied you with a cognate or an etymology, it did not need to be double-checked— in his social dealings he stumbled as often as he strode; he had no mind for appointments, maps, names, family relations. "She was twenty-seven at the time. We were affianced five days after we met and married a fortnight later. She has given me a whole new life."

"And a new life's a better life almost by definition, isn't it?"

"I'm trying to determine whether it's idiosyncratic to you or whether it's a Freelandic trait: you rarely smile when you crack a joke, do you?"

"Freelandic humor is a grim business," I told him. "You must understand, we pride ourselves on its being not the least bit funny."

32

A Fetching Corpse

"Dad," Sindri began and while I don't mean to sound needlessly pettish or peevish or prickly is it unreasonable to hear something faintly bullying in the sheer frequency with which he finds occasion thus to refer to me? Why couldn't he find a less inflammatory term? Isn't he staking a claim once again in the disputed territory of his paternity?

"Yes, son." And does he detect the blade of irony in this? He can be an unsettlingly earnest boy. . . .

"There are some things I was wanting to talk to you about. Do you have a minute?"

"More than one. I have eight or nine. Then I'm off to Hannibal's."

"It's not much of a night for driving out to Founders' Point."

"Oh I've gone out in worse."

A storm had blown in. Rain had hardened into sleet and even in my weathertight quarters in Freeland's sole skyscraper you could hear the wind screaming; I might just as well have been living once more in my aunt's shack-of-a-house on Hafnargata.

I was seated at my desk in my study. Sindri was where he always seemed to be—loitering in an entryway. I said, "You managed to get yourself here."

"It was rough. The pavement's like glass."

What in the world, then, had impelled him over here? What had he come to talk about? My heart, my spirits plummeted.

"I've seen my share of storms," I reminded him.

"Dad, I've been worrying that you're angry with me."

"Angry with you? Whatever on earth for?"

"Well—about Hannibal, for one thing. I wasn't exactly supportive, was I, when you first told me he meant to run again?"

"It's a personal matter, politics. I impose no demands on you."

"But I think it's important for family members to stick together in a crisis. . . ."

"It's all a matter of individual judgment. Stick together? A real family respects their differences."

"But you must be candid. . . . Weren't you perhaps a little disappointed at my response?"

"Candid? When was I ever less than candid? I should have thought my problem was, if anything, a superabundance of candor."

The hurt, importunate look he sends my way leaves me mistrusting myself—leaves me feeling I indeed must be hoodwinking him. I have to stop and remind myself: what I'm saying is true. Whatever my shortcomings as a father, I've generally dealt forthrightly with the boy. Still, it's not easy holding your own against that gaze which is his defining, his paramount feature: those large eyes saying, *I implore you.*

Freeland was still an uninhabited place, century after century its fiercest storms broke on unpeopled slopes, back in those days when some anonymous Mediterranean scribe pointed out that the eyes are the window of the soul, and I'd like to think the gazes of each of the principals in my story speak volumes. You could tell more about Eggert than perhaps you'd want to know from that avid bolting analytical glance of his. And Lilja, too: to stare into her broad Asian eyes is to sense both stupendous distances—windpicked steppes—and a hazy centerless lack of focus; it's to contemplate a soul at once larger and obscurer than, perhaps, your own. And Sindri? The boy was born to beg. It's a look constantly suggesting that you happen to be in possession of something which, once again, he's in need of—oh, and wouldn't life be *perfect* if he might only be granted this one unspoken thing he needs. . . . And Rut and that cross-eyed elusive gaze of hers? Only eventually do you recognize that the left eye is, even now, a girl's. It's the eye that will never stop trafficking in heroes, in all the great Freelandic forebears whose last legitimate heir was her father, Bjartur Jonsson, who, as an old man, having reached an age when he might rightfully have put away his boots and gloves, marched out into a storm to search for a missing sheep and wound up drowning in the Two Day River. And Rut's other eye? The one with the cast in it? It's the coldest eye cold

Eggert has ever seen. It knows with certainty to anticipate, from a world whose every kindness is a self-serving sham, nothing but cruelty and heartlessness.

And Hannibal? Yes and what's to be said about *his* gaze in its various phases—as he stands on the Thorskrist docks, for instance, twenty-two years old, somberly watching his closest friend, who is surely dying of tuberculosis, sail off toward America? Or, thirty-four years later, as he returns from the bathroom on his hurting knees in the middle of the night and halts to bask his eyes upon a naked body, the most beautiful female form he has ever beheld—but I get ahead of my story. . . . Let me say only that if this book did not already have so inviting, so fine and musical a title, I would call it Hannibal's Vision. I'm fond of titles—I sometimes joke that I've written so many books in order to attend so many christenings.

But I was talking about Sindri's gaze as he stood in my study doorway one evening while the wind howled, having fixed on me that beseeching look which women, in particular, have never been able to resist. His sister inevitably bends to it. But so do girl shop assistants, elderly lady customs agents, middle-aged divorcee bank clerks, and I suppose jealousy may lie at the root of my impatience. . . . Oh, in one's dealings with women to be free of language! For once in my life, free of the endless patter-prattle of the ingratiator! Merely to peer into a woman's eyes and to say, mutely, *I implore you* and to meet in reciprocation a gaze saying *But don't you understand? You needn't utter a word.* . . . It is one of the great spiteful mockeries of Eggert's life that he continues to feel, at fifty-plus, that if he would only attempt it once more, throw his full-blooded soul into the task, his face might speak of tenderness, spaciousness, enlightenment, clemency.

Now and then I need to be photographed. Perhaps for a new dust jacket. Or for an article in *The Torch*. In any case, the humiliation is inescapable. Each time, in my romantic, naïve, hopeful, dear, childish way, I plunge my gaze fervently into the camera's eye, funneling into it an outlook so generous and susceptible and soulful that this time I must, surely, be apotheosized. . . . And each time what leers back at me from the photographer's contact sheets is a sharp-nosed, sharp-eared, cruel-eyed stoat.

"Well," Sindri goes on, "let's just say you can be hard to read."

"Cruel words to an author of forty-nine books. . . ."

In response to a joke, Sindri has a way—this is a difficult thing to describe precisely—of curling up his lip and giving a little self-dismissive shrug, as if modestly shaking off acclaim or credit for the humor. It's an act of gentle appropriation. If the boy often seems mildly pathetic, there is also about him a sliding slyness. He wants watching. "Let me change the metaphor," he says. "How about hard to fathom?"

"In all the Sagas, I suppose my favorite epithet is Unnur's. Hers is even better than the Freehanded but Food-Stingy—you remember Half-dan the Freehanded but Food-Stingy from *Hrafnkel the Priest of Frey*? No, I prefer Unnur the Deep-minded. Literally, the Deep-minded Wave. It makes Alexander's 'the Great' look cheap or superficial, doesn't it?"

I suppose I was stalling for time. I certainly wasn't about to plumb the question of why he did or didn't find me decipherable.

"You've heard the news about Lilja's baby?" he begins again.

"She was kind enough to let me know. . . ."

"I've been *urging* her to tell you. I said you had a right to know."

Perhaps it was mostly the storm outdoors, howling so menacingly. Anyway, I felt out of sorts with the boy. An explosion of rage, a lashing stormy howl, was brewing in my chest. I swallowed it down. But his little remark rankled in all sorts of ways. . . . Didn't it imply that I might still be ignorant of her pregnancy, if not for his ministering hand? And what business of *his* was it how I chose to handle my daughter?

"Everything in its own sweet time," I said.

"You're going to be a grandfather—"

"Does the picture seem incongruous? Eggert dandling a little Lilja on his knee?"

"You're assuming it's a girl," Sindri observes, and again his eyes flash with cunning. Is there any sensation in the world more jarring for a man than a look from his son which says *I have your number . . .* ?

"A poet's intuition . . ."

"Well for those of us of more prosaic intuitions, it can be hard to read what's in another person's mind."

But what in truth could be harder to read than the mind behind the boy's mirthful, mocking eyes? How much of it was mischief? And how much sweetness? He went on: "Lilja says it too. She calls you the King of the Brooders."

"I'd like to think I write such an abundance of lines that there's no reason ever to read between them. . . ."

"I guess what I'm saying is, I would like to have a closer relationship with my father."

Well, these words struck me a hearty, concussive blow. When I was a schoolboy, a hundred years ago, I once got into a tussle that concluded with my taking the round wooden end of a shovel so deep into my belly that I would've sworn it bumped up against my spine. It laid me flat upon the ground for hours, for timeless ages, while milky-gray galactic swirlings rose and dissipated, and still that blow remains for me the symbol of an overwhelming assault. The reflex to protect myself from a similar attack persists; seated at my desk, I fanned a protective hand across my belly. . . .

How in the world had I failed the boy, how in the world had *life* so failed him, that he would come into man's estate—would have entered his third decade—and still be looking for a *closer relationship with his father?* Did he honestly fail to see how damning and grotesque this was? I never knew my father, who abandoned me at birth, and if I cursed him—as any son will—I've never once longed for his return, and still less for some sort of "close relationship." *Get yourself a daughter, Sindri,* is what I yearned to say, *if it's closeness between parent and child you seek.* But how in the world can I utter these words when he contemplates me with those needy bread-crumb eyes of his? My softness of heart again gets the better of me, and it is perhaps to this weakness of mine that I must look when accounting for the boy's painful unseemliness; no doubt I've spoiled him, should have been tougher with him all along. Instead, despairingly, I offer up a pretty pleasantry: "Oh I suppose we're closer than you realize. Perhaps we need fewer words between us than you think."

Of course it breaks my heart: to see just how cheered he looks. I turn off my desk lamp and rise to my feet. "I'd better be going," I say. "Driving's going to be slow."

"You be careful," he advises, and isn't there in this solicitude one more confusion of roles—isn't this the tone of a parent addressing a child?

I hurry into coat, gloves, hat, and with a heavy heart step out into the storm. The sidewalks are sheeted glass and the wind's so violent it almost blows me off my feet. Even in my gumboots I proceed to my car in baby steps; it simply isn't possible to go any faster.

It takes a while before the engine turns over. The wind seems to be blowing in four directions at once, hurling with equal ferocity at every window of my Volvo. I back into Vatnastraeti and begin to crawl— I've gone from baby steps to a baby's crawl—toward Hafnargata and the harbor.

This is drowning weather. In the old days, on nights like this, the fishermen's wives would sit at home and knit and pray for all those who hadn't yet found a harbor. And one hardly dares to think what it was like a few hundred years before that—to be pitching on such seas in a Viking ship. My Volvo has four-wheel drive but tonight it slips and slides on the ice. On the afternoon of the First Freelandic Olympics I surely ran faster than I'm driving now. "Jesus," I say.

Something dark and wet—maybe a newspaper, maybe one of the souls of the dead—flaps its arms against my windshield, lifts away and sails on. I'm the only one left alive and I'm returned once more to that image, so key to my imagination, of an unpeopled Freeland, storms brewing and breaking over a blind, deaf, unfeeling land.

My car creeps under a streetlight that must have been rammed by a truck: it careens dangerously, ready to topple onto the roof of my car. A big ghostly vehicle looms out of the mist. A bus. Sliding, I pull to the side of the road, and wait for it, too, to topple upon me.

I reach the Customs House and in the corner of my vision I spot something untoward: something unnerving. It's—good Christ yes it's a body. It's a corpse, a drowned sailor, it's a drowned sailor's corpse, washed up from the sea, but this corpse is still moving. Crawling. On the ice in the Customs House parking lot.

I inch the car in that direction, my foot riding the brake, my head full of visions in which my Volvo's blown right on top of the body and of course the world will say it was murder. The *Daily Liar* will announce that I set out and killed a man. . . .

I turn the steering wheel until the headlights catch the figure front on, and the body's head lifts, and I see it's a woman. Her legs, her white knees, are bare. It's a young woman and I halt the car and the woman lifts herself, attempting to stand. She slides a few feet and drops back down on all fours.

The shoes she's wearing have no traction, and there's simply no way she can proceed upright in wind like this on ice like this. I watch her crawl to the front of the car and she disappears—presumably she has found something on the grille on which to secure herself. Seconds pass. What next? Am I to be visited by a sorceress, a witch, a norn? The passenger side door clicks open and out of the howling darkness she crawls forth, wet as a dog. She's beside me. The door shuts.

"Good evening," I call over the wind.

She nods at me.

"Can I take you somewhere?"

More nodding. She's young. She lowers the hood of her coat and a sort of cataract—composed of fair hair—tumbles onto her shoulders.

"I'm going to Founders' Point," she declares.

This time it's my turn to pause. "Me too," I call.

Neither of us says anything more. I let her catch her breath.

We turn onto Saebraut and the cliff-face cuts some of the wind. We don't have to shout so much.

"I recognize you," she says to me. "You're Eggert Oddason."

"Perhaps you know me from Ulvar's Theater. I'm the puppet with the spider in his hair. And you're—"

"Elva Gizursdottir." Yes: Hannibal's new girl.

"You must have been glad to see me," I say.

"It was just that damned parking lot. That's where the bus let me out. I knew once I rounded the hill I'd be fine."

She isn't about to admit any gratitude, evidently. In truth she seems very little discomposed by her ordeal.

"Bit of a storm," I say.

"I've been out in worse," she says.

"I hope those other times you were better dressed for it. . . ."

" 'Scuse me," she says and withdraws something from a pocket of her coat. "I took them off because I didn't want to tear them."

"Mm?" I can't see what she's talking about.

But her wiggling and bending and squirming soon say everything. Right here in the front seat of my Volvo, in this cramped and makeshift harbor from the storm, Elva draws a pair of black nylons up her long white legs.

"There we are," she says contentedly.

"Here we are," I answer.

33

Whistler's Wife

Spare a moment for your conception.

A minute's thought to its lengthy sightless slide in the dark, its whipped-up jab and jostle: the limbless groping, the quest as blindly outflung as a hurled handful of confetti. And ask yourself, How much better do we do in the daylit world of courtship? Isn't it blind either way? —or how else explain what brought Geoffrey Simple and Constance Quimby together? Who would have predicted it? What matchmaker, heady with drink or drowsiness, would have said to one or the other of them, *I have just the mate for you . . .* ? And what novelist, seeking to weave under his readers' feet a coherent rug of relationships, would have knotted these two in holy matrimony? And yet here they most unmistakably were: shoulder to shoulder, patently devoted to each other.

She was immensely, irresistibly tall, towering half a head above her husband, who couldn't have been more than five foot seven. The crown of Connie's head must have topped six feet. She had unending legs—narrow and straight like her feet, her hands, her arms—and straight blond hair usually worn pulled back in a way calculated to throw her proud nose into relief. She had a fair, freckled complexion—if she had been a book, my fair Connie, she would have been papered not with vellum but with onion-skin—which, for all its look of sere perishability, had withstood the years beautifully. She had the seamless face of a girl closer to twenty than thirty; and she was thirty-two.

Such were my first impressions, anyway, as the three of us sat in the dining room of the Hotel Snorri pursuing the pretense of gourmet dining in Freeland. That's a pursuit grown slightly less outlandishly amusing in recent years, but which even these days is ripe for humor. Remember that, as a concession to the temperance movement, alcohol is not legally served in Freelandic restaurants, and the importing of most cheese and meat is, as a concession to the farmers, forbidden. Back then, in 1973, the business was quainter yet. Dear Freeland was still a place with one "good" hotel, one "good" restaurant; competition hadn't yet clarified some of our most glaring shortcomings.

Still, the three of us were doing our utmost to impersonate gourmandizers. Didn't our cold cabbage salad, supplemented by crunchy peanuts and crunchy raisins, show exemplary vitality? Had anyone ever tasted *fresher* fish than our halibut slabs in mushroom gravy? On my part, as the guest of the Simples, such effusions came spontaneously and heartfully, for this was indeed a splendid and a promising outing. It thrilled me to be so unmistakably a *prize*. It's a sensation which orphaned Eggert has savored too rarely in his life: this feeling of being taken up by an approving couple. Truly, they felt *lucky*. They had not only located a genuine Freelander; more, they had chanced upon the very essence of the nation, the man who had written the books, who had spent his life seeking to bind up and paginate the Freelandic experience. Dessert? Surely we must all experience dessert! Chocolate cake? Yes, for all, and what big-hearted wedges these are! How sumptuous the whipped cream!

"Now isn't this marvelous," Geoffrey cries. "I don't often eat cake."

"Why Geoffrey, that's an out-and-out lie. You stuff it into your mouth every chance you get, like a schoolboy at a birthday party."

And he beams at her, grateful to have been corrected; and she beams at him, beautifully grateful for the task of keeping Geoffrey Simple's observations in line.

And coffee?—certainly coffee! And isn't it splendidly thoughtful and pragmatic, the way Freelanders will set on the table before you, even in a fancy place like this, not a pot of coffee but an immense fire-engine-red plastic thermos, which so hospitably suggests that you may wish to linger awhile? And what is this placed beside the coffee cups? Sticks of chewing gum? *Wonderful!*

I see I've neglected—significantly—to mention the fourth party at our table. The Simples had a child, a daughter of six named Bella. I was soon to learn that she'd been diagnosed as "mildly retarded." One expects, somehow, that the offspring of a genius—and Geoffrey came as near to that exalted condition as anyone I've ever encountered—may suffer from violent mental disorders: madness, schizophrenia, manic depression, and the like. But there was nothing at all violent about Bella, the most pacific child I've ever known. For long sessile minutes, with a vacant half-smile poised on her lips, she would sit passively, a sweet-faced round-faced sandy-haired girl who clasped in her arms a sweet-faced round-faced sandy-haired dolly. Now and then she would lift her dolly to whisper something in its ear. Minutes later, she would hold the dolly to *her* ear, to catch a dilatory reply. Something like catatonia or autism would then come down and she would sit motionless and dreamily half-smiling once more. She was herself a doll—a clockwork doll in need of a brisk winding. That night, I scarcely noticed her.

The one I noticed, minutely, was Constance, who returned my looks of frank appraisal. She was dressed demurely, in a powder-blue sweater. Her fair hair was pulled back, under a pink floral headband, revealing square silver earrings in her large, shiny-pink ears. Her small gray-blue eyes, so securely rooted on either side of that aristocratic wedge of a nose, spoke of restraint, reservation, unflappability. They spoke of a *dryness*—as did her lower lip, chapped at its corners, and her negligible bosom, and her slightly rasped voice—which tugged on me beguilingly. In her presence I felt winningly vigorous—bustling, resinous, headlong. Yes, and they were *lucky* to have met me.

"Connie didn't like coffee before she took up with me. I'm afraid I've *corrupted* her." Geoffrey's face reddens and he laughs proudly.

"Now Geoffrey, you do know, don't you, that that's abso*lute* nonsense. What I didn't like before I met you was this sweet silly drink I've subsequently become addicted to—in which one takes a perfectly serviceable cup of coffee and adulterates it with cream and two packets of sugar."

That night, Constance wasn't eager to talk about herself. In time things would become clearer; I drew out her story in pieces. She was a New Englander, whose family lines for generations had been strung across Connecticut and western Massachusetts. There had been some money in the family but the primary legacy, as attested to in her upright carriage, her deft table manners, her unhurried speech, was a social assurance: a self-possession in sharp contrast, needless to say, to Eggert's rodential view of the external world as a place to be explored in a series of hustling, hunting forays. For a time she'd been a graduate student in French literature at Johns Hopkins, where she met Geoffrey. "I was told that this man called Simple was the most brilliant member of any of the language departments." She smiled affectionately at her redoubtable husband—who was reaching over to filch a spoonful of leftover whipped cream from her dessert plate. "My source was reliable." And was it here one ought to look for an answer to what united them? At bottom, was young Constance Quimby prodded to pursue the abstracted, pudgy, confirmed bachelor Geoffrey Simple by a desire to draw into the long line of Quimbys the brainiest man available—a pursuit that had eventuated in the round-faced, languidly retarded girl who waited so patiently for some further communication from her squalid dolly? Or had Connie seen in Geoffrey a comforting, matching dryness? Had his discarnated air appealed to her?

On the other hand, from the start I felt I understood Geoffrey, as well as one can ever understand a nonpareil. He was a benign freak of nature, a genetic caprice, to be accepted as one accepts—as outside all categories—the duckbilled platypus; if Nature can produce an egg-laying mammal, she can give us a Geoffrey Simple. Blessed at birth with myopia and an irretrievably unathletic constitution, he had—much as a baby otter naturally perfects its swimming, or a falcon masters flight—thrown his considerable energies into the business of learning. As a child, he would ultimately have been too genial, too remote with a sort of abstracted goodwill, to have suffered much from schoolyard bullying. He would have been the sort whom other children taunt for a while with cries of "Four Eyes" and "Butterball," until their leader mutters, "Oh leave him alone," and they troop off in search of some quick, slinking little boy into whose belly the wood end of a shovel might be delightfully shoved.

Leave him alone . . . Geoffrey would have been left alone, too, by both the grandmother and the housekeeper who, after his mother's death in a traffic accident on the boy's third birthday, reared him, while his widowed father—a grieving, shell-shocked accountant for Du Pont—slipped off to work and home from work. Idly, almost as a courtesy to his arthritic grandmother and his dropsical housekeeper, he learned to speak to them in, respectively, French and German. They, in return, left him alone with his library and notebooks, his files and word lists. Indeed, these might have been a fitting and not unhappy epitaph to his life, *I was left alone*, had the long, book-lined tunnel of his life not been forcibly broken into by a bright, demanding, solicitous, self-assured New England giantess who stepped forward on feet larger than his own to claim him.

"The first night I met Geoffrey, he demonstrated a little parlor trick. Perhaps we might prevail upon you, darling? Would you like our new friend to choose a number between one and a hundred and fifty-four?"

Her tone was that of a mother proposing to her toddler, "Would you like to sing your 'Twinkle, Twinkle' to our guests?" And Geoffrey? The blazing eyes and down-tucked chin were just exactly those of a little boy about to break into song.

"I'm to choose a number between one and a hundred fifty-four?" I said to her.

"That's right."

"One hundred twenty-three."

"And now," Constance went on, "you're to choose a number between one and fourteen."

"Seven."

"And now a number between one and ten."

"Nine."

"Geoffrey?" she said and regarded her husband expectantly.

Geoffrey's eyes returned a look of triumph. "The answer is duh," he told me.

"I beg your pardon."

"*Duh*," he repeated, with incandescent satisfaction, and of course the idea occurred to me that both husband and wife might be touched in the head. A pause opened.

Then Geoffrey said: "The ninth syllable in the seventh line of the hundred and twenty-third of Shakespeare's sonnets is *duh*. The word is *desire*. The line is *And rather make them borne to our desire*."

The silence resumed. Was I ever going to find my voice again?

And what good was my voice?—what could anyone offer in reply?

"*Duh*," Bella said, or something similar to it, and Geoffrey said, "Connie dear, you must learn Freelandic, in order to read our friend's books."

"Freelandic? Geoffrey, what *are* you thinking? I can hardly remember my French."

And another silence. I was still too thunderstruck for words. . . .

Meanwhile, the two of them went on undermining me in yet another way, bantering with each other in a manner that could only inspire envy and jealousy. There was something so—so *connubial* about it? What better word for the way she was forever correcting him, he forever chuckling gleefully in having been corrected? *Honestly, you don't remember a thing!* she was forever protesting, and this man with the memory of an elephant-sized computer would squirm in merriment. What she meant by her protest was that the world of everyday social discourse was, unlike the world of print, forever slipping from his grasp; she would serve as his lifeline to a peopled environment of names, faces, appointments, parties, purchases. In return, he reflected back at her a charmingly inaccurate portrait of herself as a woman who could do virtually *anything* in that concrete world wherein he, in his myopic way, was forever stubbing his toe or barking his shin. When, that evening, I happened to mention a newspaper article about a man who'd sailed solo across the Pacific, Geoffrey actually suggested to Connie, who had done a little sailing in college, that she might someday wish to do the same. In his mind, his able wife stood prepared to climb Mont Blanc, to salvage Spanish moidores from the sunless Caribbean depths, to bicycle across America, and, by the by, to speak any language that he did.

"Oh your French is all there, Connie dear. You're just a little out of practice. Actually, Freelandic might help you there, since the two languages share a surprising number of cognates, though nothing like German and Freelandic, of course."

"Geoffrey, you're forgetting that my German is abysmal."

Ah, but the reading of Freelandic, I pointed out, wouldn't be absolutely necessary, since I was an international author, in a way, a couple of my books having appeared in Danish editions, in authoritative translations—my own. And there were a few English translations which, though not yet successfully allied with a publisher, might be obtained in manuscript form.

"You're an extraordinary man, Eggert. Connie, we've had the good fortune to stumble upon one extraordinary Freelander."

But she wasn't ready, quite yet, to grant me this: "Well, it's quite an interesting *country*, isn't it, Geoffrey dear?"

"Indeed, oh indeed, and *luck* was with us this time. Oh"—spooning up another scoop of his wife's whipped cream—"luck was with *us*."

"You want the little girls' room, don't you, Bella dear?" Connie said.

Bella did not answer—she did not seem to hear. How had the child, absorbedly pondering the dolly in her arms, communicated any such need?

"Bella dear," Connie called again, "the little girls' room?"

The child nodded, sweetly, and Connie rose, just as Simple was repeating, "Lady Luck was with us this time."

Connie in rising to her feet had placed me eye to eye, so to speak, with where her navel must be. From beneath her narrow rib cage, her hips bloomed unexpectedly. She was skinny above the waist, and skinny in the legs. In her hips alone her body took some comfort in the cushion of the flesh, and a stirring, a surging of freshened desire climbed through me. But what were my chances of, as line seven of Sonnet 123 would have it, ever seeing this particular object "borne to my desire"?

I speak of seeing, but of course what I wanted was *not* to be seeing. If only Lady Luck were with *me*, I knew where I'd be off to: the long sightless slide in the dark, the whipped-up jab and jostle, the quest as blindly outflung as a hurled handful of confetti.

34

Figments, Shadows, Ghosts, and Daydreams

Discretion admittedly was called for. There was Rut to consider, and beyond her, if one could look beyond so bulking a presence, there was an electorate not likely to welcome the news that their President had formed an attachment with a girl easily young enough to be his daughter. Still, you might have expected—*I* did—that Hannibal would choose to open his heart to his closest friend and adviser.

He was staying mum. I had to read between the lines so far as Elva was concerned. I never saw them touch. Nor did I ever see pass between them anything resembling a yearning or adoring glance. She was simply *there*—repeatedly *there*, someone to draw aside for whispered consultations, to dispatch on a little errand, to drive home with after a night of speeches, questions, handshakes, grins.

The girl was, if anything, harder still to draw out. I did my level best to make something significant out of the circumstances of our meeting. Hadn't I come along like a knight in white armor—or in a white-armored Volvo—to save her from the deadly elements? But she would have none of it. The killing storm had forged no bond between its survivors.

What was I to make of her stubborn distance? Perhaps it was nothing more than an all-too-familiar form of revulsion. What was said of Mr. Hyde—that he "gave an impression of deformity without any nameable malformation"—might fairly be said of me. And yet in this particular case, I had the distinct feeling that her coolness wasn't a matter of instinct but of principle; she disliked my politics. As my daughter is forever reminding me, I am *known* among the young. I am the joy-squelching bastard chiefly responsible for the laws limiting the radio time given over to rock music; I am the wet blanket conspiring to ensure that Freelandic television is backward, boring, and scanty. I am, in concentrated form, the *they* inveighed against in laments like *They want to keep us down* or *They're trying to silence us* or *They think because life here was miserable when they were growing up we have to be miserable too.*

To be held in such disfavor by the young logically ought to ensure, in compensation, some measure of loyalty among those who are getting-on-in-years. But I'm afraid that among them, too, I'm regarded coolly. They see me, I suppose, as a schemer, a wily fanatic.

Well, if what estranged the girl from me was a matter of mere politics or principles, I wanted to tell her, *My beliefs are malleable*, to tell her, *My convictions can be suspended*. For the truth is she fired my spirits as nobody had in ages. She was no creature of the hour, but a figure of durable fascination. Her beauty was as clear as glass and it cut like glass. Once, many lifetimes ago, back when I was still writing books that might conceivably be labeled romantic, I spoke of a woman so lovely she set the nerves in your teeth to singing and I observed that it was no wonder you stood open-mouthed before her, since it's in the nature of any singing thing to crave the open air . . . and I don't think I've ever done a better job of conveying the numb jittery desperation which beauty of a certain rare sort instills in me. Yes, in Elva's presence the nerves in my teeth began singing and I'd sense that the branched pursuit I'd based my life around—the preservation of Freeland in both poem and ordinance, novel and statute—would all be gladly forfeited if I might pass a single night with her in the penthouse of Thorskrist's Skyscraper Tower. One night. Meanwhile, I longed to say to her something like this: I recognize that you yourself are claimed, linked up with the only man on the planet I don't think I could bear to betray, but don't you perhaps have an identical twin? Dear magical Elva, whose name evokes for me those elfin sororities that are so rich a source of mischief and mystery in our folklore, where am I to locate your double?

Elva was neither kind nor rude to me—merely curt to the point of utter dismissal. Did she know my daughter? Yes, but not very well—Lilja was more a friend of a friend, you see. Pause.

And did she know my boy, Sindri? Oh yes, yes, though not very well, but of course she admired him. Admired him? Yes, well he's very artistic, isn't he?

Artistic? Sindri the Fish-tallier?

Naturally I was left to ponder what Elva saw in my friend Hannibal. What was the nature of her feelings? How deep did they run?

Was she vicariously playing out the erotic daydreams of her mother, or maybe an aunt—the fantasies of some slumping middle-aged woman who had been struck, in best romantic fashion, by one of Cupid's darts thirty-plus years ago, on that golden day when golden Hannibal Hannibalsson won every medal at the First Freelandic Olympics? Or was it a case of a girl who, seeking a father, gravitated toward the man sometimes referred to as the father of our country? Or could it be—a prospect so torturously appealing I could scarcely endure its contemplation—that Elva was someone who appreciated my friend for all those traits that she as a military-jacketed member of the Army of the Young might be expected to ridicule: Hannibal's reverence for the antiquated virtues of valor and self-abnegation, his powerful sense of having undertaken an indefeasible compact with the mighty dead, his near-mystical conviction that Freeland held some sort of unique role in the global scheme of things?

What did she draw from him? And he from her? In my sidelong way, I scrutinized them painstakingly. To another observer, my questions might have looked absurd. What in the world was there to *explain*? Why should a young woman not be drawn to the still-vigorous President of her country? And where was the mystery if a middle-aged politician who had just suffered a falling-out with his common-law wife was lured toward a beautiful young woman? But I sensed in their dealings something odd, something askew or ajar. I go back to that lack of "meaningful looks" between them. From Hannibal, anyway, wouldn't you have expected a few swiveling, doubt-gnawed glances of passion and possession? Instead, he seemed to gaze upon her with a kindly but detached affection. It didn't make *sense*.

I drove out to Founders' Point one night in a drizzle, pulled the Volvo into the driveway, and saw, a moment after extinguishing the headlights, Elva enter the little kitchen. She was wearing a baggy white T-shirt and a pair of jeans. The curtains were not drawn. The two of them were hiding nothing.

Evidently Elva hadn't seen me. She reached up toward the cupboard and simultaneously her red-gold hair—the color of Hannibal's hair, once—tumbled backward and her breasts rose sympathetically with the motion. That such beauty was utterly unselfconscious—she had no inkling she was playing to an audience—painfully intensified her allure.

She poured something from a bottle into a glass and swung away, out of the room.

I seemed to have no choice; I stepped out of my car and tiptoed around the front of the house and peered into the study window. There sat my friend Hannibal, his back to me, slouched in his big brown broken-down leather armchair. He was staring into the fire. Was it a driftwood blaze? *The icy sea will warm you,* or so I'd written in a poem long ago. At the moment, I was shivering. Elva was standing beside his chair. I had thought she was bringing him a drink—the glass was a wineglass—but she lifted it to her own lips and drank with that special, undesperate ardor of youth. On the end table, at Hannibal's other side, stood a bottle. He was nursing Brown Death. The girl, too, stared long into the fire. Her feet were bare.

Who could have predicted what I would see in that window? Would I have hung there patiently, a meticulous observer, if the two of them had disrobed and begun making frenzied love on the carpet before the fire? I suppose so. But no passion whatsoever emanated from the room I peeped into. I've said I never saw the two of them touch, but I suppose I mean I never saw them touch publicly, for now Elva lifted her free hand and began idly, empathetically, to stroke the thinning graying gold crown of Hannibal's head. And I continued to stand there, a cold rain stroking my own head. . . .

The scene seemed packed with significance. To watch the girl's hand roaming on the tired crown of Hannibal's head was to feel myself near the nub of some crucial and useful epiphany.

And yet it simultaneously pained me—each repeated flowing of her hand—and while I suppose I could have watched with something like equanimity if I'd caught the two of them in the thrash and pitch of love's delivery, I could hardly bear to see her stroking his head in that lax fashion. This wasn't a picture of great happiness. To the contrary, a creeping sadness pervaded the room. Even so, the scene overwhelmed me with longing, and with envy. I felt—that white hand of hers! those bare feet!—as though my squeezed heart would rupture. I balled up my fist, envisioned myself thrusting it—explosively—through the window glass. Instead, I turned around and drove back home.

The following morning I studied his naked body closely. We met at the swimming pool at seven, and as he soaked in the shower stall weren't there hints of that glutted ease which follows a night of answered passions?

Wasn't there, in the way the heel of one hand struck so commandingly at the button of the soap dispenser, sending deep cascades of Danish Blue into the open palm of the other, the air of a man who feels himself beautifully partnered?

O Danish Blue, let us now sing a hymn to you—our soap, our deodorant, our fungicide, our shampoo, our cologne all rolled into one! A deep, unnatural, even ominous shade, it looked like something that might lubricate the underside of a car, and when first applied to Hannibal's limbs, in a thick film not yet broken into lather, he took on the sheen of something unpacked in a laboratory: *Today, students, we will dissect a very rare creature, one of the last of the true Freelanders.* We imported the stuff from Denmark by the tanker-load, since the average Freelander applied it as Hannibal did: with a devoted, almost superstitious liberality. No doubt, this very day, somewhere in our archipelago a stooped grandmother was informing her little granddaughter that Danish Blue is concocted in the finest medical laboratories of Copenhagen. Folk wisdom . . . For decades we had been greasing our limbs with an electric blue soaping agent and savoring in its slippery touch a moment's communion with that lustrous mainland where technology, sophistication, art, and fashion are hatched.

I watched Hannibal again, and again, strike the soap dispenser button with the heel of his hand, noted the gingerly way he lathered his shaky, collapsing knees, the conscientious probing approach he took toward his crotch, the slow, ruminative spread of Blue over his aggressively expansive belly, and asked myself, Are these the motions of a man whose body still hums in the aftermath of sensualities equal to the mind's outermost fantasies? In other words, had my friend found Heaven?

His face, to be sure, wore the care-worn gravity-drawn features of a thoroughly earthbound creature. But this was only to be expected; he had a great deal on his mind. Tonight was to be the second of the televised debates. We were still staggering away from the debacle of the first. Hannibal's assertion that Freeland was a "state of mind" continued to haunt and hurt us. The "Youth Hour" bastards wouldn't let up. In their most recent foray, they hypothesized an election night in which Hannibal lost by a landslide among the "human voters" but triumphed among "figments, shadows, ghosts, and daydreams." They unrolled banners declaring, "No sweat, Hannibal is only a state of mind" and "My late grandparents are supporting Hannibal Hannibalsson." *The Daily Liar* was no less nasty, just a good deal less clever.

We marched outside in our bathing trunks and strode slowly through an icy needly early morning rain to the hotter of the two hot tubs. There was no one else inside it. The heat was intense. Hannibal issued an elephantine grunt.

"We can't afford another disaster tonight," I told him.

Hannibal stared across the bubbling surface of the pool—the two of us might have been the key ingredients of a witch's vat—and nodded ponderously at me. An odd docility had lately settled over him. He felt—we *both* felt—that catastrophe was imminent, and for perhaps the first time in his life he was facing defeat not forcefully but passively. Defiance had at last leached from his bones. There was a new vacancy in his gaze, which required that he be, in effect, summoned across a considerable distance; these days, he often had to be called twice, or even three times, before his eyes lost their meditative spaciousness.

"World cod prices were up last month," I went on. "Not much—something like four percent over last year at this time, which admittedly was a disastrous season, but the point is that down is down and up is up and things are getting better. As every housewife knows, the cod are going to reinvigorate the entire economy. That's the point you've got to make tonight."

"I'll make it."

"Four percent. Drum that figure into your head. You've got to look specific tonight. On top of the facts. We've got to counter all that Freeland-is-a-state-of-mind business."

Again he nodded lugubriously. You might suppose, after contending with him for so long, that I would find it refreshing to deal with a docile Hannibal. It wasn't. A docile Hannibal, it turned out, was no Hannibal at all.

"Fortunately, Nonni's the world's least effective public speaker. I don't think they realized just how atrocious he would turn out to be. He's easily flustered, Hanni. Come across as a man in clear command of the facts, and he'll fall apart on you. Then you can go in for the kill."

"The kill?" Hannibal echoed. From some distance off.

"Exactly."

"Imagine going in for the kill against *Nonni Karlsson*." Hannibal released a single grunted laugh. Even as defeat stared him full in the face, he couldn't see his way to taking Nonni seriously.

With some asperity, therefore, I said, "Well the fact is *he's* killing *you*—he's killing *us*. Nonni Karlsson may be no more than Nonni Karlsson, but he's got the blade at our necks, my friend."

Hannibal traced a big, thoughtful hand across his own neck, which was bright red with the heat; his life's blood was pumping close to the surface.

"And another thing," I went on. "Whether we like it or not, we've got to do something about this so-called Youth Question. I'm afraid we must make some sort of treaty with the savages. Or trick them anyhow. They're bleeding us, Hannibal." Speaking in English, in the language of our youthful venturesome dreams, I added, "The damn kids are bleeding us," just as a kid—a quick vision of lean lissome legs, an artful curve of hip and waist and bust, and isn't it astounding how beauty, authentic beauty, can assert itself so rapidly?—slipped into the pool. "Hello," she said. Elva.

She was, as I've earlier noted, insistently *there*—at the end of a speech, *there*, at the winding up of a press conference, *there*. Why in the world should I feel surprised, then, that she should tiptoe, near-naked, into our pool?

"Good morning," I said. Hannibal nodded at her.

"Has anyone ever pointed out to either of you that this thing is hot as *hell*?"

"We're steaming our badness out," Hannibal told her.

"Going to be a long soak." And Elva laughed—or nearly did. She puckered her lips in a wry grin—the closest hint I'd ever seen in her of something playful.

Through hooded, half-shut eyes I studied her intently. She was sitting very erect, perhaps as a way of keeping some substantial part of herself removed from the heat. She wore a pink bathing cap and a sky-blue suit that was a cousin-color to her eyes. Her nose was clean-angled and firm, her cheekbones high, her chin strong. The mouth was small but plump. Swatches of red-gold hair peeked out from beneath the rim of her bathing cap. The heat brought an instantaneous flush to her cheeks.

On the surface of the water, stray reflections—stray parts of her—dance and shimmer. They are pieces to the puzzle called Assemble the World's Fairest Young Woman. . . .

"And you," I muttered, through my still-half-shut alligator eyes, "how long a soak will you need?"

"Till Hell freezes over." Again she twisted her little mouth. "The funny thing is, there was a time I didn't need this pool at all. . . ."

A pause followed and Hannibal said, "Eggert and I were discussing my Youth Problem. Do you think I have a Youth Problem?"

"What do *you* think?"

"I mean our so-called Youth Issue. Perhaps you've come to clarify it?"

"I'm not one of them," Elva muttered.

"Mm?" Hannibal said.

"Not one of those youth people."

"In that case," I said, "you carry your advanced years remarkably well."

Elva again twisted her mouth, although this time not with amusement but with disdain.

"Elva seems to feel a certain disaffection from her peers," Hannibal explained.

"They're not my peers."

"Eggert insists that I'm not going to get a single youth vote. Can you tell him otherwise? Do you plan to vote for me?"

"Nonni Karlsson is an ass."

"That's not the most ringing endorsement I've ever received. Still, I suppose I'll take it."

"You're going to have to. That's all you're going to get. Either of you." And with these words she rose to her feet, as fair a Venus as ever surfed ashore upon a clam shell. She eyed me frankly and I felt positive she sensed just how paralyzingly desirable I found her. And wasn't there perhaps something just faintly insolent or contemptuous in that glance of hers? Things could be worse, I suppose. Better to inspire insolence or contempt than indifference. Maybe. "I'm going in for a swim. And then I'm off to work."

I watched the girl pad unhurriedly through the cold, needle-sharp rain in her sky-blue bathing suit. We'd had a spell of gray weather these last few days and this suit of hers was the closest thing I'd seen recently to an open blue sky. At the pool's edge our Venus dove cleanly back into the depths that had birthed her.

"She mentioned some sort of work. What does she do?" Actually, I'd already been told. She worked for Goldkjor, the food importers.

But Hannibal's reply surprised me. "She works on a computer."

"A computer?"

"For Goldkjor. She's a sort of bookkeeper."

What had I expected? I suppose I'd pictured her stacking packages of English lemon-cream sandwich cookies, or unloading a precious load of greenish oranges from the Canary Islands. "Like Sindri," I said.

"Mm?"

"My son. She packs fruit into a computer, he loads fish in. You do realize, don't you, Hanni, that in the twenty-first century we will reach a point where every young person on the planet will have a job loading things into a computer."

"Zero unemployment. End of our Youth Problem."

"And just a few years later, someone will design a computer to load everything into the master computer, throwing everybody out of work."

"One hundred percent unemployment. They will look back at the present day as a golden age for the working man and woman. Speaking of a hundred years, we have an errand to run."

"A hundred years?"

"She's close to it, anyway. We've got to go see Thorgunnur."

"Hanni, it's not yet eight in the morning. She's probably asleep."

"Asleep?" He was indignant on her behalf. "Auntie keeps teacher's hours. First classes start in an hour."

"She hasn't been in a classroom in twenty years."

"You'll see."

But seeing was just precisely what I didn't want to do by the time we reached her wing of the Eldershelter—didn't want to see *anything*. The years advance on me, despite my near-perfect health, and the more outlandish forms of aging press on my psyche; I shiver at what once amused me.

We might consider, for example, senile dementia—isn't it amazing just *how* cruel Mother Nature can be? On the way to Thorgunnur's room we pass a withered old woman who, cradling in her arms a stuffed animal, a bright green frog, croons to its glossy plastic face, "It's cold now, *cold*, my little darling, you have to bundle up." Enough to make you glad you were an orphan . . . Then we pass—more horrific still—a white-whiskered man who, on spotting me, flings out his hand and, as God is my witness, cries, "Son!" My heart seizes up in my chest.

The worst of it—it takes me a moment to realize the worst of it—is that for all I know this man *is* my father. And wouldn't it be perfect if he was? Mightn't this be Fate's ingenious way of balancing that stupendous moment, seven years ago, when I opened my apartment door and a pimply teenager cried "Father!" and threw himself into my arms?

Lunatics, *lunatics*, and in the face of such unsightly collapses I suppose I expected to find that Thorgunnur had soiled her bedclothes or was chanting obscene lyrics about the bishop and the fisherman's wife, but in fact she was, as ever, maintaining an unimpeachable dignity. Her long legs were stretched out on her bed, which was impeccably made, her back was propped against the headboard.

Shrouded in rain clouds as it was, she couldn't have begun to descry Great Blue, but even so she stared off in its direction with a look of discernment.

"Auntie," Hannibal said.

The great head rotated slowly: it was as though she'd been expecting him. "Hannibal," she replied.

"I have company, auntie," he said, and again her nose uplifted—truly it was as though the detestable creature meant to smell me out.

"Eggert Oddason," she said.

"Good morning, auntie," I said. "You're up early."

"Early?" The purblind eyes focused on me scornfully before settling, for relief, on Hannibal once more. "Young man, I want to hear what you plan to do for this country in your next term of office. . . ."

"My plans? Have you been listening to my speeches?"

"Perhaps I hear a speech now and then. Unfortunately, I evidently missed the one where you discussed the matter of *The Freeland Saga*."

Ah yes, here it was, as here it always must be. . . . For there was one true political issue and one only: when would our national Saga, inscribed on sheepskin seven hundred years ago and now entombed in Reykjavik's Arnamagnaean Institute, be prised from the thieving hands of the thieving Icelanders and restored to its rightful home? Yes, she used the word *re-stored*—about a manuscript written by an Icelander in Iceland. Such is the destitute artistic fate of our country that *this* would become our national saga. Did Eggert Oddason have any choice but to become a writer? Would he have been compelled to amass forty-nine books if his country had any literary heritage to speak of?

"Well as you know, auntie, that's a slow and a tricky business—negotiating with the Icelanders."

This line, or something like it, was usually sufficient to summon from Thorgunnur an anathema or two against our treacherous neighbors to the east, succeeded by an impatient but forbearing sigh. Today, however, she took another tack: "I sometimes think I shall not live to see it restored to these shores."

The words unnerved me—I was still feeling uncentered, I suppose, by those back-to-back encounters in the corridor—and I leapt in: "Oh, you mustn't say that, auntie. You've still got many, many—"

She silenced me with a wave of her hand.

Outside, across White Seal Bay, icy rain fell on the ice of Great Blue Mountain.

Hannibal said, "Oh, I think we're all going to see a great many surprises yet. Let's not sell any of us short."

The words seemed to hearten Thorgunnur. Clasping the railing of her hospital bed with a hand that had no flesh on it—pure tendon, vein, and bone—she told him, "You're the *only* one who can do it, Hannibal."

Another painful pause.

Hannibal said, "I have a television debate tonight, auntie. Did you see the last one?"

"It's a shocking thing, isn't it?"

"Shocking?"

"Setting that poor Nonni Karlsson up there just as though he might ever actually lead Freeland." She snorted at the thought.

I cleared my own throat, preparing to point out that virtually *everyone* was predicting Nonni's victory in the upcoming election, now only six weeks off, but thought better of it.

"I remember the day he misspelled 'Storblafell.'" Another pause opened, as Great Blue Mountain, that impervious pincushion, absorbed some one million additional needles of rain.

"People are saying I didn't do so well in that last debate. There has been a great deal of ridicule. Perhaps you don't recall the end of the debate. . . ."

"Don't *recall* it?" Admittedly, she was a woman easily affronted. Yet in the great hierarchy of insults to her dignity, few stood nearer the apex than any challenge to the powers of her memory.

But then Thorgunnur offered another unexpected observation: "Well, they're absolutely right, Hannibal. You did *not* do well."

"No?" And he hung his head. Truly he might have been a schoolboy again.

Of course it gladdened my heart to see Hannibal downcast. Hope, blessed hope rose in my chest, for this was *precisely* what he needed: a stern rebuke from the one person in the world whose censure he might actually attend to.

But all such optimism was cruelly short-lived. For the blind woman's very next remark was, "That business about how people who lack vision are dead? Oh, you were *right,* of course. You were absolutely right."

"I was?" And the big head lifted from the ursine shoulders.

"You were right about Freeland. You understand the central issues, of course you do, and that's why you must *lead* them, my boy: you're almost the only one left who understands them."

I could hardly bear it—to hear these words, to see his face so fatuously aglow.

"But you didn't make it *clear*," she said.

Hannibal nodded vigorously. "Yes," he said. "*Yes.* I see now. I failed to make it clear."

"You were hazy."

"Precisely."

"You have to clarify it."

"Exactly so."

"You need to be *firm* with them."

"Of course." Another pause. Icy rain fell inside my chest. Hannibal turned upon me a look of dangerous resolution.

35

The Answer to Someone's Prayers

"**M**y husband extracted a solemn vow from me—"
"Yes—" I said.
"—which I do plan to keep."
"Sometimes there are ways—"
"He made me promise to pay for dinner. So you must consider yourself my guest."

This was twenty years ago—the early seventies—and in those days the news that a woman I scarcely knew planned to buy me dinner was likely to prod me into vaguely gallant protestations. But for once I kept these to a minimum. For one thing, money was tight. For another, instinct told me that the erection of a web of obligations—whether I to her, or she to me—would most quickly narrow the distance between us. Yes: let Constance buy me dinner.

"He's so sorry he can't be here. These things come on him—there isn't any telling why or when. But I am to act as though he's here—"
"Well we needn't—"
"—and make sure you have everything your heart desires."

As I'd already begun to see, Constance was partial to remarks which ought to have been double entendres but which, scrubbed clean by her cheery, plainspoken delivery, carried almost nothing of the racy or risqué.

"My heart's desire? I hardly know where to begin. But do tell Geoffrey I'm sorry. Have these things long been a problem for him?"

These things were migraine headaches, which afflicted Simple a couple of times a year. At the moment he was upstairs, in his hotel room. I pictured him supine on the bed, eyes shaded by a towel, while Bella, equally silent and not much more mobile, sat playing in a corner.

"Ever since I've known him. I think they have to do with his eyes."

"His eyes?" To ask this question was to conjure up Geoffrey's enormous spectacles, and to sit, uneasily, under that glassed-in gaze.

"Oh he's had all sorts of problems with his eyes. It's all the reading, presumably."

I took this, I suppose, as some sort of challenge. "But nobody reads more than I do and my eyes are perfect."

"Well, Geoffrey's blind as a mole without his glasses, and that's just the start. He has retinitis, which means a thinning around the retina, which can lead to hemorrhaging and all sorts of gruesome things, and he has cataracts. It's as though something's wrong with the whole wiring system in the front of his head, for in addition to his eye problems, Geoffrey has no sense of smell. I sometimes think it's the price Fate exacts for his brilliance. It's just as though, in payment for that, he was given faulty wiring in the front of his head."

I confess I've never been able to listen tranquilly as a woman—particularly an attractive woman—praises the mind of another man. But I held off on qualifying or questioning her. Constance was not only dressed in the same powder-blue sweater and navy-blue wool slacks she'd worn the night before, but had reconstructed her yesterday's self down to the narrow pink floral hair band and squarish silver earrings. What to make of this? That in her travels she was the world's most lightweight packer? That she was, true to her name, a demon of consistency? That she, in her easy prettiness, intended to transcend matters of fashion? Or was it a case, as I preferred to think, of working to dampen the little sparks that inevitably fly whenever a married woman has dinner alone with an interesting, intense single man? Wasn't there something flattering in her implicit assertion that this evening was nothing to dress for?

"And *your* wiring?" I said. We were seated again in the dining room of the Hotel Snorri. We'd returned because the fish had been so "marvelous"—a rationale that kindly sidestepped the fact that the streets of Thorskrist weren't exactly chockablock with inviting bistros, taverns, *ristorantes*.

"Mm?"

"Your health, your wiring," I went on. "And what is it that Fate exacts from you, in payment for all your bountiful gifts?"

"Me? Well, I'm strong as an ox."

In her place, another woman might well have said *strong as a horse*. Constance had a taste for self-portraiture sketched in the most disarmingly mundane or even homely terms. I once heard her describe herself as feeling "lazy as a grub worm." In such remarks there was a denial of her attractiveness which I could never corroborate and which, indeed, I chose to read as the reining in of a powerful sensuality. I chose to see her as a woman working hard to quell her passions. I took as my symbols the telltale plumpness of her lower lip and the sweet plush unexpected breadth of her hips, which flourished in such alluring contrast to her otherwise clean-angled, no-nonsense good looks.

"And you?" she said. "Your health?"

"I? I'm as hardy as the creature that thrives on the poison that was laid for it. I'm the rat that eats the tainted cheese and, feeling bully, comes back for more."

Was this a surprising thing for me to say? The words, which emerged at a stroke, surprised *me* a little. A *rat*? In searching for an animal-sibling, why not look to the hawk, the otter, the fox? But I suppose instinct was telling me that Constance had begun responding precisely to my less savory aspects. I was keenly attuned to the symptoms—the most interesting symptoms, from my point of view, another human being could possibly manifest. It's an impulse something like miscegenation—I'd hesitate to call it bestiality—in which the most wholesome-looking creature in the world reveals a temporary desire to wiggle into an intimate embrace with the weasel-man, the rat-man, the snake-man. What did Connie see in me? Didn't she sense an unappeasable scrambling vigor, an unpoisonable avid ruthlessness that was vitally at odds with her languid gentility?

And hadn't she already sensed, at our first dinner alone, how fervent was my conviction that she was meant to be my ladder to a higher evolutionary plane? My look said, Make a *man* of me, darling. In all the fairy tales ever collected, no story's more resonant for me than that of the frog waiting for the freeing imprint of the Princess's kiss. And how does a frog attract a Princess, save by singing? And who has sung with more wide-mouthed hopefulness, more commendable unquestionable steadiness, than Eggert Oddason of the forty-nine books?

"I can't tell you how pleased my husband is to have met you. Geoffrey's so *excited*. He says you're the genuine article."

"And what does he mean by that?"

"Why, a real Freelander."

"And what, pray tell, does he mean by *that*?"

When challenged, even in a gentle and bandying way, Connie had a habit of blinking sharply once, twice, perhaps three times: a righting gesture that restored her to all her well-bred composure. Usually she'd choose to meet her challenger head on. So if I was playfully calling for a detailed answer, she would gamely give me one: "You see, Geoffrey spends so much time in the past. He's positively brilliant with living languages but in his heart I think he prefers dead ones like Anglo-Saxon and Old Norse. The man has spent countless hours with the Icelandic Sagas, as you know, and learning Freelandic was simply one more way of getting close to them. I gather that Freelandic and Old Norse are very close."

"Quite. But there are traps. Pitfalls for the unwary."

"But you've said it all much better than I have, haven't you, Eggert?" Had Connie ever spoken my name before? It was like a first glimpse of a bra strap through the armhole of a blouse, the first chance brushing of fingertips on the street: a fleeting familiarity that spoke of the possibility, far down the line, of a thrilling intimacy. "He sees you as the man who can guide him around the pitfalls." And then she uttered one of the most stirring pronouncements I've ever heard: "He calls you the answer to his prayers."

I am not very good at holding gazes—constitutionally shifty-eyed, I suppose—but it was Constance, after an instant of firm reciprocal appraisal, who glanced away. She went on swiftly: "That's why we're both so much hoping you'll take us up on our offer and come stay a couple of weeks. You've never been to Washington, isn't that right?"

"Never."

"You could bring your daughter."

"She's quite happily settled. She's summering at a farm on Diamond Island."

City-dwelling Freelanders customarily ship their children off to a farm for the summer. I'd billeted Lilja with a distant cousin who had twin girls her own age.

Our main courses arrived. Constance had again ordered the halibut, and when tonight the weighty wedge, ringed by boiled potatoes, steaming away mightily beneath its gray mushroom gravy, was deposited before her, didn't I detect a slight shuddering of her bony shoulders? Was she wishing she might be served instead an endive salad, a slice of aged mimolette, a fruit plate? In any case, she pushed on: "Geoffrey says you could be an incalculable help. I think he sees the two of you retreating into his study after dinner, talking etymologies and connotations and denotations into all hours of the night."

To this extent, anyway, Simple had a remarkably accurate vision of

the future. . . . Our talk would indeed prove inexhaustible. Or I might better say that when, a few weeks after the Simples' departure from Freeland,
I followed them out to Washington, and settled myself into their narrow
guest room in the top floor of their narrow Georgetown town house, *he*
proved to be inexhaustible and I did my best to keep up. I used to read
aloud to him from the Edda or the Sagas—he was saving his afflicted
eyes—and we would go over them word by word. With its faded Persian
carpet and walnut paneling, that study of his was a comfortingly cavelike
refuge. Beyond its walls, the traffic was jostling through the streets of an
overheated city that was excitedly contemplating its own collapse, for the
year was 1973 and you might say dishonesty had reached the point of
hyperinflation. Already the Nixon administration was proving to be un-
equal to the task of minting lies fast enough to save itself. But from within
Geoffrey's study, Nixon's beleaguered world seemed farther away than
some squabbling over sheep and grazing rights among Icelandic settlers
in the year 1102. I was, in Geoffrey's failing eyes, the ideal guest.

Of course if there were aspects of my trip that Simple vividly foresaw,
others he glimpsed not at all. It was in regard to some of these that I said
to Constance, after our dinner in the Hotel Snorri, "But what about you?
Do you think it would be a great inconvenience to have me for a couple
of weeks?"

I'd led her out into the lobby. The two of us were standing before
the largest, and arguably the finest, nineteenth-century Freelandic oil
painting. It commemorates the birth, nearly a thousand years ago, of the
hotel's little namesake, Snorri Thorfinnursson, the Viking child, the first
European born in the New World.

Connie was reflexively gracious: "Why, no inconvenience at all! If
you don't mind staying in our tight little guest room."

I pushed the point: "Can you honestly say *you* look forward to having
me under your roof for a couple of weeks?" I sensed that at some level she
found beguiling these attempts to drive her out of the artifice of etiquette,
from the conventional to the visceral: "Are you being candid with me?"

Again that flurried righting blink, followed by a foursquare declaration: "I'd be delighted. We would—my husband and I."

And another pushing of the point. In all sorts of ways, she was a good
deal bigger than I. Physically, of course, and financially—no doubt she
could have bought up my hovel of a house with a stroke of her pen. And
she had at her disposal a security of upbringing, of education and breeding, utterly alien to my sensibility. Even so, she had trouble standing up to

my forcefulness. "Your husband sees me as the answer to his prayers. I'm worrying you might see me as the punishment for your sins. Honestly, how are you going to feel when I show up on your doorstep?"

"Delighted. . . ."

Around the infant Snorri's birchbark cradle were ranged a companionable assortment of people and animals. Notwithstanding the crowd's inclusive variety—Vikings, Indians, deer, wolves, sheep, two upright bears, and a splendidly antlered moose—each gaze manifested a kindred expression of tender pride. Why couldn't two different worlds, Old and New, or Man and Beast, flourish together?

"Truly? Well then I *will* come. If I can count on your delight . . ."

Why did I feel so sure that in this regard, too, two different worlds might come together? What encouragement had she given me? Only her gaze's promising faint fluster, only a few ambivalent gestures of hospitality and retreat . . . And yet, it was as though the whole business were clearly laid out before me—the giddy airless couplings in that steamy little upstairs guest room, the receding protestations, the occasional outright attack on my character, on my heart and compassion and decency, these to be succeeded by new breathless couplings, each of them psychologically presided over by the house's pair of complementary ghosts: the little retarded girl whose wide eyes saw so much and understood so little and the man with the ailing eyes who understood everything he saw but saw next to nothing.

"Geoffrey will be so pleased," Connie said.

"No more than I. I can't think when the last time was, if ever, I was the answer to someone's prayers."

36

A Morale Boost for the
Light-Deprived

I didn't like the look of the sky, the smell of the sea, the feel of the breeze. I was a man goaded by qualms, pricklings, obscure bodements, and although I'd agreed to meet Hannibal at the television station at seven-thirty—the second debate was to be held tonight—at six o'clock I drove out to Founders' Point. My thumpings on the door, which was uncharacteristically locked, raised no answer. But encouraged by the sight in the driveway of Hannibal's "elephant"—his gray Land Rover—I kept at it. Eventually he appeared, looking tired and flushed. He hadn't combed his hair. His shirttails were out. Was that the smell of gin on his breath?

"I thought we might go over things one more time," I said.

"I thought I might ponder it all on my own."

"Nothing I can help with?"

"You're a good friend, Eggi, but at this point it's a solitary business."

He seemed to be using his considerable bulk to—actually—bar me at the door.

"I'm feeling nervous." My words were offered purely to make myself sympathetic; but once they were uttered, I understood just how true they were. "Do you have anything resembling a drink?"

"A drink?"

"An alcoholic beverage?"

Over Hannibal's shoulder I caught a glimpse, fleetingly, of a fair-haired head—crossing from the study to the kitchen—and for one unscrewed moment I was reminded, though this head of hair was red-blond and half a foot longer than my daughter's, of Lilja.

Hannibal sighed. "I suppose I could find you a drink."

I followed him into the study. The leather sofa still bore the press of its slim-hipped previous occupant. I settled my buttocks as precisely as I could into those narrow contours and said, "I'd kill for a gin."

"I don't think there is any gin."

"I'll take Brown Death if that's what you have, but I'd love a vodka."

"There may be some vodka."

But Hannibal did nothing to fetch the drink. He reached under one of his shirttails to scratch ruminatively at his belly, then strode over to the bookshelf and uplifted a plastic glass. I thought this might be intended for me, but he downed its contents at one go. He then took a seat in his leather armchair.

"That brooding look of yours is making me nervous, Hanni."

"I'm thinking about Auntie Thorgunnur. And what she was saying this morning."

"Forget it. Forget all of it. In regard to the last debate, the one idea and the only idea you need to keep in mind is that it was a disaster. A catastrophe. Let's be clear that it's *not* a matter of not having made yourself clear. It's a matter of having made an absolute ass of yourself."

"But there are things I need to *say*."

"Things?"

"Things—" Hannibal pushed on vaguely, and motioned vaguely with his arms. "Certain things to say, regardless of how they're received. Regardless, even, of how much they're ridiculed . . ."

"Hannibal, honestly, what more can there possibly be to say? You've been talking at these people for twenty *years*. Now if you'd like to lay some ideas before them, I'd be happy to organize them for you in some suitable—"

"Did you enjoy your swim?"

She had materialized in the doorway. She was wearing tight blue jeans and an immense turquoise blouse—many sizes too large—of an indeterminate Asian style. It shone. Silk, I suppose. Despite the dim light, the blueness of her eyes vaulted across the room. Her bright, wavy hair haloed her limpid features and it alarmed me to see just how pretty she was—how much prettier with each viewing. At this rate, before long, her youthful shoulder blades must bud, they must sprout a pair of white wings.

"Swim? What swim? I enjoyed my soak."

"I brought you a drink," Elva replied, and indeed her hand held a heretofore unnoticed glass tumbler. Again she was barefoot—those same lean high-arched feet which she'd slipped this morning into the hot tub, and which I'd studied the other night when, a drizzled-on Peeping Tom, I'd watched her stroking my friend's head as he stared into the fireplace. The drink turned out to be another surprise: the gin whose existence had been denied, plus a little vermouth and a twist of lemon. She possessed wisdom far beyond her years. God bless her, she'd made me a dry martini.

"To your kindness," I toasted, and swallowed deeply.

Elva shrugged and walked over to the bookcases and, with a young person's limber swiftness, dropped to the floor, where she sat cross-legged. "Is this boy-talk?"

"I don't know how you'd classify it," I said. "It's political strategy."

"Sounds like boy-talk to me . . ."

"It doesn't need to be. We're thinking about how certain issues ought to be treated in the debate—we're thinking about the best way to show up Nonni Karlsson."

"Sounds like Settlers and Eskimos."

She was referring to a children's game. Little Freelandic boys play not at Cowboys and Indians but at Settlers and Eskimos. Hannibal broke his silence. "Sounds a lot like a sheep's fart to me." His face was deeply flushed. He rose from the armchair abruptly, wincing at his broken knees. We waited, Elva and I, she from her position on the floor, I from my seat on the couch. He was panting. Clearly some sort of outburst was upon us.

"The notion, the very *notion*, that after the twenty years I've served as President of the Republic of Freeland you're now expecting me to come up with *strategies* for defeating a little whelp like Nonni Karlsson! Is this what we're reduced to, Eggert? What in the world, what in the world would you reduce me to? Don't you see there are certain games you must never enter? And not because they can't be won? But because only a lost man would play them? I'm going for a walk."

"A walk?"

"Along the shore. Alone."

Bad knees and all, he flung himself from the house, crashing the door behind him. I was still sitting on the sofa, Elva still on the floor. We eyed each other. *You in the glowing blue blouse*, I wanted to say, *how would you like to be my muse? And I will bring you poems much as a cat brings limp mice and frogs and birds to his mistress: proudly.* "I'm worried about him," I began.

"He's all right. You caught him at a bad time."

I noticed then that her dazzling blouse was misbuttoned and was it purely fanciful of me to hypothesize that I might have materialized at the front door just minutes after some rushed and not altogether successful act of love?

"I'm worried about how he'll handle it if he's defeated."

"That's not the thing to worry about," Elva told me.

"No?" Needless to say, I was taken aback by her cool certitude. Who in the world was *she* to tell me anything about Hannibal's character?

She went on, "The major worry is how he'll handle it if he doesn't feel he went down fighting. On his own terms. You're not doing him any good, you know, if at the end of the day you leave him feeling he fought your war and not his."

The surprising vistas opened up by her remark were almost too rich for immediate contemplation. Could it be that this creature, this Elva, was not only achingly beautiful but psychologically astute? I replied, "I still say we have to think in terms of victory."

"I'll let you do that. I'm tired. I'm going to take a rest."

"I'm heading back to town. I could drop you."

Besides my own, there was only one car in the driveway, Hannibal's, and at the moment he clearly wasn't to be disturbed. If she was going home to rest, she'd need a ride from me.

But Elva offered a further surprise: "I think I'll just pop upstairs," she said, and with the ease of someone who'd lived there all her life she rose from the floor and disappeared through the study doorway.

I heard her bare feet on the bare wood. "See you at the studio," she called back at me.

I went into the kitchen, found the gin bottle, poured myself a couple of splashes, downed them, and, on a sudden impulse, decided to drive to the Cod's Head. I hadn't been there since the night when Hannibal and Rut had had their set-to and the heavens came unstrung.

As I stepped into its smoky interior I couldn't honestly say whether or not I hoped Rut would be there; I only knew my stomach felt shaky. But when, from across the room, I caught her eye—that cold, cross-eyed glance—I instantly regretted coming. I sank my head between my shoulders and took a seat by the door.

With images of Elva still fresh before me, scowling Rut was no pretty sight. Heat from the kitchen had mottled her features, and her bad eye caromed around in her skull. Had she put on weight in the last few weeks? Her big-boned frame seemed to be supporting an additional ten pounds.

I worried that she might let me sit there unattended—in her domain, Rut does precisely what she wishes—but after an interval she came over.

"Haddock," I said. "And a cup of strong coffee."

She merely nodded, walked off. When she returned, a few minutes later, with my order, I too for a moment said nothing. I sipped from the cup she'd placed before me and noted, with relief, that it was indeed "strong coffee." I'd passed another hurdle. I said, "Rough weather."

"I've seen worse."

"You getting along all right, Rut?"

"Getting along just fine, Eggert."

"I wish I could say the same . . ."

Rut has never liked me, I suppose, but over the years we've come to an understanding—or a series, a network, of respectful accommodations—deep and complicated enough to render mere liking or disliking almost irrelevant. We had long been collaborators, whose shared task was the management of Hannibal Hannibalsson, and while I'd inured myself to her dislike, it now rankled me that she might suppose I'd shirked this fundamental duty. She mustn't think I'd betrayed a trust. I said, "I hope you understand, Rut, that all of this—his running for office and the rest—was never my idea. I urged him against it."

"You didn't talk him out of it," she observed.

"Neither did you."

I had her there—she knew I had her there. She regarded me angrily, but expectantly. I said, "There was simply no arguing with him. The idea came to him in a vision."

"A vision," she said.

"I'm afraid so."

"Well you can tell your friend Hannibal that he is not the only one around here who entertains visions. You can tell him that cross-eyed Rut Bjartardottir has had a vision, too."

"Yes?"

"And in her vision, do you know what she saw? She saw him going down to utter defeat in the upcoming election. Tell him that. And that's not all. You know what else she saw? She saw him being subjected to more and more humiliation, she saw him being attacked on every side, and in his defense she lifted *not even one little finger*." But of course Rut had no "little" fingers; her hands were sizable as a gorilla's, or so they looked as she wrapped them into fists and set them down before me on the tabletop. "That is my vision, and that is my vow"—and Rut swung round and disappeared into the kitchen.

It was apparently my day to have people abruptly walk out on me. I downed the rest of my coffee in one long swallow and drove over to the station. Perversely, I took the same corner seat I'd occupied last time, when disaster unfolded, and was I, unconsciously, hungering for some follow-up catastrophe? Was I looking for some final all-hope-destroying collapse, one that would extricate me from any further efforts to sway a stubborn, ungrateful electorate?

In the event, the debate's early rounds did not go so badly, and the denouement was—well, it was a thing of beauty and a joy forever. At first Hannibal seemed overly subdued, almost lackluster, but Nonni was cheeringly inarticulate. Could he, even today, spell Great Blue Mountain? Through some rather devious maneuvering I'd managed to get rid of the interviewer most dangerous to us, Ulvar the Puppetmaster, and the woman replacing him on behalf of the opposition turned out to be, despite the prematurely rucked severity of her young face, a harmless enough interrogator. She kept harping on the "Youth Issue," but with little effect. So far as I understood Nonni's circuitous, backtracking, cryptic answers, he pledged that the national radio's two channels would play rock music twenty-four hours a day, breaking only to issue storm reports to fishermen, who had been of course the backbone of our society for a thousand years. He may also have promised daily sacks of french fries to all voters under the age of twenty-five, the conversion of City Hall into a wine bar, and mandatory drug use in the Superior School, I'm not sure. The surprising thing, though, was that Hannibal handled the questions with a combination of aplomb and grace. He came alive a bit. Was he addressing his words to Elva? Or had he actually been listening to some of my tirades? He was anecdotal yet demanding, generous yet focused: "When I was a young man, too many years ago I'm afraid, I was desperate to see the world. I left Freeland as soon as I could for Copenhagen, where I worked for the Great Danish Steamship Company. But later I quit the Company and traveled on fishing boats and buses and trains—anyway I could, for I had very little money—through America and Italy and Spain and Greece and Turkey. I worked here, I worked there, often unsuccessfully. At the time, I didn't know what I was seeking. But now I see I was looking to bring back to Freeland little pieces of these exotic places. I wanted to enrich my native land. So, to these young people who seek to bring from Down Below new music and new movies and new television programs, I can say, I understand the impulse. I'll say more: I sympathize with it, admire it. I would only ask them to consider, with each of these importations, *But is it good for Freeland?* We must begin with that simple question."

Old Matthias was back among the panel of interviewers—bless him—so there were inquiries about haddock, cod-liver pills, fishing treaties, and did the candidates think this was mostly a fad and a publicity stunt or was it true the Japanese people actually preferred to eat their fish raw? This was a riddle securely laid to rest by Hannibal, who pointed out that as it's a well-known fact that cooking brings out the full flavor in fish—just as it does with lamb or oats—the Japanese penchant for this so-called *sushi* was an obviously ingenious attempt to mask the taint of the soiled waters from which many of their catches are drawn. Things grew rather monotonous, the room's one pocket of excitement belonging to the third row of chairs, where the body of a beautiful woman was aswim in an aquamarine blouse: Elva was sprawled in her seat, her head thrown back, making not the slightest attempt to disguise her boredom.

I was beginning to wonder whether the governance of Freeland might not be such a small-scale operation that a single debate could suffice for airing all the significant issues, when the "something wonderful" that I'd been praying for occurred.

Nonni was asked a question about the balance-of-trade problem. The answer should have been obvious to him. It was obvious to everyone else in the room. He was being called upon to make a plea for diversified exports. The essential, unhappy truth is that we export two things to the world—fish products and sheep products—and we import everything: oil, steel, wood, plastic; tea, coffee, grain, fruit, vegetables; clothing, furniture; telephones, televisions, stereos, washers, dryers; cars, motorcycles, buses, bicycles; ice skates, swimming trunks; medicines, wheelchairs, condoms, diapers . . . We regularly vow to begin peddling a wider array of goods Down Below—but what else do we have to offer them? We regularly vow to purchase less from Down Below—but who among us is willing to forgo Down Below's comforts? The politician's obvious line, then, is to call vigorously and vaguely for an improved balance of trade. It's an insoluble problem.

And yet Nonni failed to do the expected thing. "Today I had an idea," he began, and his big round face bobbed like a runaway beachball, drifting in a choppy surf. "I'd gone for a swim, and as I was washing up, I looked at the soap dispenser and I said to myself, 'Now why is it we need to import our soap from Denmark?'"

I straightened in my chair, just as Hannibal did in his. Something flickered within me—something as lovely as a candle flame glimpsed in a snug little window on a drizzly late afternoon. Could this be? Was Nonni Karlsson really so witless as to suggest that the people of Freeland abandon Danish Blue?

"Why can't we make our soap right here?" he went on. "Isn't it time we rid ourselves of this last vestige of our colonial status? Isn't it time we—"

Hannibal interrupted him: "Do you by any chance know how many years it is we've been importing Danish Blue?"

Now this was, according to the protocol of the debate, strictly verboten. The contenders were enjoined from entering into anything resembling a tête-à-tête: all exchanges had to be mediated through the panel of interviewers. Some grumbled protests went up, which Hannibal fielded magnificently. Erect in his seat, he brandished his hands with imperial weightiness: "My opponent has touched on a matter that goes right to the heart of the health and hygiene of our commonwealth. As such, it's vital that we immediately investigate a matter of concern to virtually every man, woman, and child in this nation. I would like to know whether my opponent has any idea how many years we have been importing Danish Blue?"

The auditorium grew still. This was, I suppose, partly the silence of a crowd that, dutifully decorous but thoroughly bored, had hushed itself gratefully at the prospect of some spectacular bloodletting. But we were also cowed. Hannibal Hannibalsson had somehow managed, once again, to step forward as the mesmerizing guardian of our nation.

No, Nonni mumbled, no, no, maybe he wasn't exactly sure of the date?

And did he have any idea, before proposing so unprecedented and one might say radical a course of action, just how life-expectancy figures had trended during the years that we'd been using Danish Blue?

Well, yes, maybe, no one was disputing that our life-expectancy figures are the envy of the world. . . .

And did he fully understand that Danish Blue was a cleaning agent formulated by master scientists in Copenhagen expressly for inhabitants of a cold and tempestuous climate?

Well, he was in no way impugning the quality of Danish Blue, he was merely indicating his faith in our own—

Was he, then, challenging the claim that the distinctive, one might

fairly say *unique,* color of Danish Blue had been selected for its scientifically tested morale-boosting effects on the psyche of inhabitants of polar
regions subject to light deprivation in the long winter months?

Well, as for that, he was second to no one in his admiration of a
color—

And was it not the case that Danish Blue was a product for all intents
and purposes universally accepted by the people of Freeland, men and
women, elderly and children alike, and did Nonni perhaps mean to imply,
with his extraordinary proposal, that the collective wisdom of the Freelandic people was to be dismissed wholesale?

No, he meant merely, which was to say quite to the—

Truly, you almost had to feel sorry for Nonni. It was all too easy to
envision how he'd landed in this unhappy fix. Standing in the shower this
morning, he'd been visited by a small inspiration. Ideas didn't come to him
often, and this one was all the more welcome in the light of a gathering
uneasiness—which his handlers regularly sought to assuage—that the
public sometimes ridiculed him for letting his every move be orchestrated
by those selfsame handlers. Well, he would demonstrate independence of
thought! He would spring his idea on a dazzled nation!

Nonni's not a small man. He must be six feet tall, and probably a hundred and eighty pounds, but under Hannibal's probings he seemed to fold
in upon himself, like a collapsible suitcase, while Hannibal himself reveled
in what was perhaps his greatest gift: his ability, in moments of urgency, to
become larger than life. Somehow it wasn't until the second of these debates, in the twentieth year of his presidency, that I formulated this point in
its essential clarity. A voice in my head announced: *Hannibal is a very large
figure in a very small country.*

And the moment I'd articulated it, a host of insights opened up. It was
well and good for the Japanese, poised in the confidence that the twenty-
first century belongs to them, to elect time and again a Prime Minister
who's blandly interchangeable with the manager of shoe sales in a
Takashimaya department store, just as it was well and good for America to
be steered through the Great Depression and a world war by a man in a
wheelchair. For Japan and America are such monumental commonwealths
that they almost require, in order to render their scale livable, a homey,
undersized figure at the top. But Freeland needed—more than it needed
export diversity or modernized fish-canning factories or a foolproof
vaccine for sheep ringworm—a figure who, by being larger than life,
might convince a nation that was smaller than life that it had attained just

the proper size. In all his outflung rhetoric and bombast, Hannibal set our world to rights.

And with this realization, I had to believe all predictions were wrong and the election must ultimately go our way. Wasn't Nonni Karlsson revealed tonight as painfully—banefully—*small*? While Hannibal was grinding his hapless opponent into powder, I looked over at Elva, who had spoken of her lover so perceptively, and at last found on her face what I'd often expected to find but had so far sought in vain: a look of affection lapsing on adoration. Despite all this fretting over our Youth Problem, could anyone doubt that Elva was ready to go through fire and ice for Hannibal? In the end, didn't all of them—even the young—have to love us?

Our future widened and, simultaneously, my throat, overcome by emotion, narrowed. Addressing that incomparable figure seated in the center of the bath of television lights, my voice emerged as a triumphant croak: *"All of it, Hanni. It's all of it within our grasp."*

37

Heat

Heat collecting under the arms, heat against the back, heat adhering to the wizened elastic band of my undershorts, sticky insupportable heat in the crotch, and the soles of the feet burning. "You must be perishing in this *heat*," they would exclaim, "you're not used to it," and I, smiling damply, would grit my teeth and reply, "It's an interesting change." Heat's supposed to make you dopey, dozy, supposed to dull, dim, deaden you, but it had brought my every tendon to a teased fineness. My nerve endings had swollen until my fingertips felt ready to burst.

I was sleeping in the Simples' upstairs dormer guest room, which had no air-conditioning. I'd been given an electric fan, but before long its grating, erosive clatter took on malign undertones, and so I chose to pursue sleep in a breathless but at least quiet inferno. I'm not usually someone disturbed by noises in the night—I relish the howling of the wind, the soft slapping of rainfall, even the lacy scamper of mice—but the Simples' electric fan stroke by stroke fed a cosmic dissonance into my brain. It was the sound of the minutes and seconds of my life being run through a coffee grinder.

Downstairs, snugly enfolded in her mild but irremediable stupidity, the little blond girl, Bella, slumbered in her air-conditioned room. Downstairs as well, wrapped in a curious blending of brilliance and stupidity, slept my friend, Geoffrey, and slept as well my lover, Connie, in their enormous bed, in their air-conditioned room. Meanwhile, Eggert the Itchy rolled over, twisted and turned, twisted and turned, recalling more vividly than he had in years those clenched, terrified days when his lungs had suppurated and he'd begun coughing up blood.

Long ages ago, on a ship called *The Return*, I'd sailed for the New World and my lungs had cleared and I was given a New Life. Now I'd returned to the New World, this time by plane. In my native land, a revolution had intervened in the meanwhile—the Twentieth Century had rapped on Freeland's front door and the Middle Ages had scooted out the back window like an illicit lover—but my personal situation was unchanged: I couldn't seem to get my breath.

Surely, *surely* I must leave. That was the message the weather was giving me, my lungs were giving me, and my skin, too, was giving me—for I'd broken out with hives or heat rash or fungus. I had constellations of red bumps on my rib cage and hostile red patches on my inner thighs. My red fingers were dotted with little vesicles of golden oil, and the skin between my toes had turned a soft sodden vegetal color: a milky green. My skin prickled and chafed. I scratched here and there with my fingernails, the ends of pencils, drinking straws, my elbows, the down-at-heel soles of my shoe. "You must be *perishing* in this heat." "Oh it's an interesting change."

All this itching and chafing was indisputably the price I paid for having taken on Connie as a lover. Steered by the faintest of love's electromagnetic signals, I'd traveled thousands of miles, and in the end I'd been vindicated. If such things can truly be fated, if a mouse can be *meant* for a monarch, I'd say we were meant for each other.

I seem unable to accept love at face value and for a woman to offer herself to me is inevitably to raise the question, Why is she doing this? I wanted to conclude that I represented for Connie a physicality otherwise absent from her life: I liked to presume, that is, that in matters of the bedroom Geoffrey was uninterested or, better still, unable. I constructed a pretty scenario in which Bella's birth, and the gradual revelation of her deficiencies, had worked to create a chill between her parents. Connie, incidentally, gave me no encouragement. On the couple of occasions when I probed directly, she insisted, to the contrary, that their love life was "very satisfying," and the truth is, however misleading she could be, Connie rarely seemed a liar. And yet she would now and then, always unprompted, speak woefully of Geoffrey's "coldness." It was as though she wished to confess to something, but only on her own terms.

Why was Connie drawn to me? Didn't it have something to do with her particular uneasiness toward the past? Gradually, as I learned to make my way around the city, it began to make perfect sense that she'd settled in Georgetown: that she lived in a house of old family furniture and old family portraits. Those Quimbys who had come from Yorkshire to Rhode Island in 1656 had evolved into a distinguished American line, which included mayors and a couple of congressmen and also newspaper owners and missionaries and a wayward poet or two. And yet they were not senators and governors, were not press moguls and expedition leaders and literary luminaries. They were sufficiently distinguished to have published a family history—it sat, leather-bound, in a place of honor on the Simple family shelf—but not so august that such a book might have been commissioned without family financing. Needless to say, I pieced all this together slowly—I was utterly out of my element. But even to me, her burden became unmistakable. These were people long proudly conscious of their prominence—while simultaneously aware that, among the truly prominent, they failed to occupy the first rank and, moreover, theirs was a family whose size and fortunes were waning. There were few uncles, aunts, cousins in Connie's life. While she did have two brothers, neither had produced any children. The elder, a divorced lawyer, lived in Hartford, Connecticut. He had problems with drink. The younger, a bachelor, had been thrown out as headmaster of a boys' private school.

Thrown out? I asked.

For improprieties.

Improprieties?

Advances. On a student.

A student? But I thought you said it was a boys' school.

I did, Eggert.

Surely, under the circumstances, I had no cause to express either shock or disapproval. We were lying on the narrow bed in my dormer room, not a stitch of clothing to show between us. An hour before, Geoffrey had taken the girl, Bella, off to Johns Hopkins, in Baltimore. She was undergoing a new round of tests. The great driving hope of the Simple household—too fervently embraced to be expressed outright—was that the cause of the girl's "mild retardation" might be traced to a simple chemical deficiency. So far nothing had turned up. The parents' desperation was rendered all the more poignant by the girl's habitual vacant beatitude; she herself would ask for so little. . . .

But I wander from my subject. The issue is *Why was Connie initially drawn to me?* and am I being fanciful in supposing my orphaned state had something to do with it? Did she not see herself as perched on a sort of withered limb of her family tree? There she was alongside a brother who drank and another whose appetite for schoolboys had cost him job and home. Which left her alone to perpetuate the line, and what had she produced but an afflicted creature who, best projections suggested, might eventually inhabit a "halfway house" located between a Georgian town house and a padded sanatorium. Surely the family history in the library reproached her! Surely the past confined her, as did a cohering tightening sense of needing some line of work. But how in the world was she ever going to pursue her degree in comparative literature while mated to a language-eating colossus of erudition—that rarest of species, a linguivore—who casually, effortlessly comprehended her discipline better than she ever would? In the face of such constrictions, what better figure to represent liberation than a man like me who had no family, whose ancestral past was a muddy sloppy field of sheep farmers and fish smokers, and whose future lay in the creation of a modern national literature for a nation that had none? Perhaps I'm indulging the storyteller in myself—making mine, in the recounting, a tale richer than in life—but how else explain why this particular princess chose to stoop and kiss this particular frog?

How else explain, that is, why Connie Quimby showed up in my room one morning, after I'd been a guest for some two weeks, and closed the door behind her and wordlessly contemplated me for one extended moment and declared, "I have never been unfaithful to Geoffrey. Do you believe that?"

Oh for days I'd been flirting with her, making use of every opportunity to touch her, to nudge her, to brush her, throwing "meaningful glances" her way and piling up one double entendre after another—but still the fact is it was Connie, not me, who promoted us from the tacit to the tactile: *she* crossed the threshold first.

"If you tell me so. I'll believe what you tell me, Connie."

"No, Eggert. That's not good enough." The jabbing vigor of her delivery unnerved me. She seemed, for just a moment, leaning her six-foot frame against the door she'd closed behind her, a good deal more than a rattled, ratty, heat-rashed Eggert might handle: I felt just a little frightened. I want my women to be bigger than I, but I don't want to feel like a moth impaled on a pin.

"You have to believe it absolutely," Connie said.

"Then I believe it absolutely."

"No, Eggert. Not good enough. *Look* at me. *Tell* me. *Say* it. Say it now: I believe you've never been unfaithful to Geoffrey."

"I believe, I do believe," Eggert chanted. "I believe you have never been unfaithful to your husband."

Connie nodded—and then with a surprising, heaving swiftness

yanked her sweatshirt over her head and stood before me in her lacy small-cupped bra. What was so striking in all of this—so monumentally alluring—was her regal assumptiveness; she never questioned my own availability. She felt no need to consult me, and oh, I adored her for that. I stood there transfixed, and she came forward, on her lovely big-boned feet, and undid, from the top down, the buttons of my shirt, and slipped it off, and laid it—a quiet coupling of fibers—upon her own.

Did she begin our affair seeking just this feeling of mastery? Did she enter into it with a notion of holding on to absolute control? If so, she was eventually to be taken by surprise—taken any way I could—by my passion's countertuggings. I was out of my head—we were out of our heads. Oh I would have her, yes, again, and then again, and the chances we took were breathtaking. Had Geoffrey decided to walk down to the corner to post a letter? Well, that ought to give us six or seven minutes—enough time, surely, to apply something to something, insert something into something. We were desperate people.

And do I contradict myself if I say I thought of Constance—still do—as virginal? For there was something finally unreachable, unreached, about her. She had that gift of detachment—more common in women than men, surely—which radically disjoined upper from lower body. To my great surprise, it turned out she had a naughty schoolgirl's taste for profanity, but her *shit* had no stink or squish—it was nothing the heel of your shoe could mash with a sickening sliding lurch—and her *balls* had no hair. There was something wonderfully improbable to the twist of fate which had led this perpetual student to sign up for Depravity 101, which discipline was, in the absence of an accredited professor, to be led by a substitute student-teacher.

I'm simplifying of course—and also venting an anger I thought I'd scuttled long ago. I suppose a cumulative lesson of these rapidly multiplying pages is that I've abandoned no angers, no resentments, not one. This is Eggert the Grudge-holder, angry at Thorgunnur Sigurdardottir for not recognizing his genius—for failing even to thank him when he sent along complimentary copies of his books; angry at his first muse, Gudrun the Good, for marrying herself to mediocrity and later succumbing to cancer with an evenhanded sweetness of temper; angry with the parents who'd abandoned him; angry at Michael McKaig, for teaching his wife the "double-swears" of that realm of literally unspeakable obscenities which he alone inhabited; angry at the Freelandic notion that, having thrown off all oppressors and achieved liberty at last, one must immediately look for new feats of subservience. And angry at Connie Quimby Simple for—what? Her poise? The sense of something with-held—incorruptible—plumb in the plump center of those hips of hers? Or for having the boldness to initiate our affair? Or for punitively refus-ing to make love with me anywhere except in that cramped and steamy guest room? Or for her willingness to take into herself, and in the end remain undisturbed by, the full range of my passions? I'd spill them all into her—my rages, my bile, my desperate climbing ambitions—and she, like Mithridates of the poem, would absorb them equably. . . . God-*damn*it, she was going to outlive me. She was going to outlive us all. . . . Wasn't I angry, then, at her willingness to take upon her smooth fair skin this feverish furry creature whose own skin—whose pelt—was blistered with hives and heat rash and eczema, pustules and scrofula, "jock rot" and athlete's foot, and in the end show herself untarnished by the contact?

Daily she would inform me I must consult her dermatologist, daily I would promise to do so on the following day. But somehow the appoint-ment never was fixed and weren't we both somehow reassured by the eruptions of my body? Wasn't my own prickling hirsute skin meant to be the hair-shirt I must wear as penance for my fleshly vices?

I was not so enfevered that I didn't have time, in my sleepless nights, to ponder the connections between my current situation and the world I'd created for myself, years ago, when I first came to America. All of that early sojourn had grown quite distant: Buck's Eat Shop, with Mack standing beside a cash register to which photographs of cowboys had been taped, waiting to gun down his robber, and cadaverous Mr. Shlomowitz fretting over the health of his robust wife, and McKaig holding me down to rub my scalp raw with his bare knuckles, and his wife naked underneath her dead son's dangling model airplane . . . They were so far away as to hardly belong to me, they were characters in a book, which in itself wouldn't have been so dispiriting had it been *my* book. But no, they seemed too dis-tant to be mine, they inhabited another life, they were another man's story—and yet the story of a young man who'd placed himself in a situa-tion strikingly similar to my own. Part of me hungered for progress—yearned to feel that my life was going somewhere! But I was once again a boarder entered into an affair with his landlady and surely something in this domestic configuration attracted me fundamentally; for me, there was a rightness about its wrongness, there was something comforting in its manifest discomfort. They were my parents, perhaps, the Simples, just as the McKaigs once had been, and I was the child who slept in the child's bedroom. But if so, what a tangled Oedipal tale we now enacted, the Simples and I, for this time around I was older than my "mother." And it was not I, young Oedipus, but my cuckolded "father" who was going blind.

And here was something ghastly—something I hadn't foreseen. I happened to arrive in Washington at a time when Geoffrey's vision was undergoing an ominous downturn. His cataracts had degenerated and he was brought in for an operation that had not gone well. It turned out— wouldn't you know it?—that Geoffrey had a very strangely shaped eyeball, which the anesthesiologist had punctured at the outset of the operation. So now Geoffrey had to worry about not only retinitis and severe astigmatism and cataracts but also a punctured eyeball with the attendant risk of a detached retina. *I sometimes think*, Constance had said to me back in Freeland, with a sort of philosophical bravado, *that it's the price he pays for his brilliance. He has faulty wiring in the front of his head.* The words had lost whatever levity they once held. The father-figure was going blind.

Not that the full, opaque weight of this tragedy seemed to press upon Geoffrey himself. He remained cheerful with a sort of constantly fermenting mirth.

He was buoyant, yes, he was effervescent, and yet, and yet—with something perhaps just faintly desperate to his joggling energies. Certainly there was something unnerving, as well as enviable, in his pyrotechnical displays of erudition during our after-dinner retreats to his study. A typical evening might go something like this:

I would begin to read from "Völuspá," the great cosmogonic introduction to *The Poetic Edda*, but I would get no further than the first two lines:

> Hljods bidele allar
> helgar kindir . . .

"That's an autoantonym, isn't it?"

"Beg pardon, Geoffrey?"

"*Hljods.* Meaning either 'noise' or 'silence.' It's an autoantonymous entity. The coinage is hardly acceptable to the pedants, I suppose, but I'm the last one who is going to call it antiphrasis or, Heaven forbid, anantiosemy."

"I'm not sure I'm familiar with the term."

"Think fast."

"I don't think under the circumstances—"

"Think *fast*."

"That's not going to do any good when there is no initial—"

"Think f-a-s-t. Because that's one of them. An autoantonym. A word incorporating its own opposite. Meaning either moving rapidly or absolutely motionless. Like *cleave* in English."

"A word which—"

"—which can mean either 'to sever,' as in 'meat cleaver,' and 'to unite,' as in 'cleave to your spouse.' As a linguistic phenomenon, autoantonyms would seem to be inherently unstable, wouldn't you suppose, like some sort of radioactive isotope"—Simple paused to empty from the bubbling decanter of himself an overflowing spill of mirth—"but in fact both senses of cleave, with roots in Old English and old High German, and with variants too many and tangled to mention, go back a millennium. Shakespeare uses the I suppose you could call it disjunctive 'cleave' in *Macbeth* and the conjunctive 'cleave' in *Hamlet*, make of that what you will."

"I'm not sure much *need* to be made of—"

"And speaking of *Hamlet*, let us not forget *let*. So to speak. You remember Hamlet's cry: 'I'll make a ghost of him that lets me'—this in the sense of hinders rather than allows. The prohibitive rather than the enabling *let*, I suppose you could call it. And surely we mustn't forget *enjoin*, although I suppose the purist might protest our calling it an autoantonym."

"The purist? Who, if not you, would qualify as—"

"Autoantonomy is a testament to the innate flexibility of language, I suppose, or if you wanted to be cynical you might call it a sort of collective Anglophonic schizophrenia." Giggle. "I'm not aware that Freelandic has many autoantonyms."

"I suppose that *hljods* may be the only—"

"Of course there's that peculiar little *hinn*, isn't there? Meaning both the object directly under one's nose, *the* object, and also meaning the other—"

"Yes, of course there's *hinn*."

"One of the odd things about German, as you have probably noticed, is how comparatively free it is of autoantonyms. Makes you almost believe, doesn't it, in all those stereotypes about the orderly hierarchizing—I know you'll forgive the clumsy groping at a neologism—Teutonic mind. The Romans, on the other hand, while also commonly viewed as exemplars of order—for what is a paved road, after all, but a concretization, literally, of the notion that we can get to Point B from Point A with rugged directness? And yet their tolerance of autoantonyms is one of their most remarkable—or perhaps, given all the Germanic overtones in that word's etymology, I had better say *prominent*, traits. I'm not thinking merely of *altus*, meaning either high or deep, since my suspicion is that with that word the Romans were negotiating a concept whose subtlety we've lost. But consider *tollere*, to build up or to tear down, and it's almost enough to make you believe in some divine linguistic poltergeist that in English we would have, while springing from completely different roots, a near-autoantonym meaning exactly the same thing."

"You're thinking of—"

"Raise and raze. You might call them autoantonymous homonyms, I suppose, and that's a field you might want to investigate. Very little has been done, so far as I know. But I interrupted you, didn't I? You were explicating 'Völuspá' for me."

Sitting there before him, I didn't yet absolutely see just how insufferable all this was—how drastically my feelings toward Geoffrey had changed. No, that became evident only a few days later, in bed with Connie.

"Lord, I'm so tired," she sighed. "Geoffrey didn't let me *sleep*."

Jealousy itched at me, from within, where I couldn't begin to scratch at it, and in my impotence I ran my fingernails over a scruffy patch on my rib cage. "He didn't let you sleep?"

"He woke me up when the dictionary fell."

"The dictionary?"

"He was looking up a word. With a flashlight. I said to him, *Excuse me, but what are you doing, Geoffrey?* And his face goes all sheepish, and he said to me"—and here she parroted his voice to near-perfection, conveying all of the man's shiny-faced energy, his whiz-kid's praise-hungry maddening brilliance—"he said to me, *I was having a little trouble sleeping, my dear one.* And I said to him, *Why were you having trouble sleeping, Geoffrey?* And he said to me, *Well, it's the silliest thing, Constance, but I simply could* not *recall the etymology of 'alfalfa.'* "

And, as I say, the woman had her husband down: she captured him even to that marionette's off-center jerking flourish of the head. I said to her, "The etymology of 'alfalfa'?"

"It's a sort of grain," Connie noted, which of course wounded me deeply.

"I *know* that," I told her.

Constance resumed her Geoffrey impersonation: "It's Arabic, by way of Spain. *Al-faṣfaṣah*. So why in the world was I thinking it had some sort of Amerindian derivation, my dear?"

Can anyone fault me? Am I possibly to be criticized for the realization, which arrived in that precise instant, that I *loathed* him? Had lust energized him in the middle of the night, I suppose I would have been jealous, but I could have overcome it. But that my rival would wake up my lover because he found himself sleepless upon discovering he couldn't remember the etymology of *alfalfa*—how could I do otherwise than *loathe* him?

No, the mystery was that *Connie* didn't seem to loathe him. How was it possible to capture, down to the most minute gestures and intonations, all the naked vanity, all the childish boastfulness of the man—and yet continue to speak of him with affection?

Ought I to have blamed myself for hating him? I didn't—I couldn't fully blame myself. No, couldn't feel *anything* fully, in the heat, the heat, the heat, while a voice inside said, *Surely it's time to leave* and another said, *But to do what? To go where?* Where perhaps I *was* to be blamed—where I did, anyway, blame myself—was for the afternoon when, with Geoffrey off at the university and Bella taking a nap, I led Connie to my room. I'd never known the little girl to mount the stairs to my bedroom, so I am perhaps not wholly to be censured for leaving the door slightly open; if somehow Geoffrey were to return home early, I wanted to make sure I heard the rattling of the front door.

I can only conclude that the child must have been extremely quiet. Connie and I had just finished up with things and she, stretched out on the too-short bed, had pulled on a blouse. She was naked from the waist down. I was naked utterly.

I had stood up, to gather my clothes, when I heard a rustling behind me. I swung around. My penis should have dropped by now, but it was standing firmly at the horizontal.

I swung around, and there was a chilly, unblinking moment when, through the one-inch interval between door and frame, the child saw my organ point her out, accusatorially. I stared first into her eye—rounder than ever with wonder—then down at myself, no sight for a child: big and red and lachrymose, for I was trailing a long tear of semen. I walked across the room and closed the door in her face.

"Mm?" said Connie, drowsily. Her dear broad pale bottom was turned outward, toward the door. She hadn't noticed a thing.

When Connie opened the door some ten minutes later, the child was gone.

38

A Vote from the Fumaroles

Hannibal Hannibalsson rises to a sensation of need, low and deep in the belly. There is a good long distance to be crossed, but he's up to the task, shakes off one obstruction after another, rises, he rises, rises and in a state of fine defiance he wakes: yes, he is awake, and arrived to find a mission waiting for him: he must pee.

A light is on—the desktop lamp is burning. Good Lord, he hadn't even managed, in getting himself to bed, to extinguish all the lights.

From his too-warm bed he rises, grimacing at his knees, and hobbles down the hall, making for the comfort of darkness. His feet are bare. He's wearing nothing but an old T-shirt. He turns on no light in the bathroom and leaves the door open, letting himself be guided by whatever stray glimmers from the desk lamp have rounded the corner and draggled down the hall behind him. Right beside his face, the wind's howling, lashing against the little windowpane something heavy—rain? sleet? iron chains?

Hannibal takes his slippery organ in hand and in darkness commands a letting go. There follows that moment when no echoing splash arises and for a fraction of a second he's left flustered, almost panicky—is his aim off entirely? Then the hospitable sound of liquid joining liquid wells up in his ears and he can relax fully into the task at hand.

This emptying of himself goes on and on. There's been too much to drink. Oh, he'd been good most of the day. After a lunch of cheese-and-tuna casserole he'd delivered a speech to the temperance people, most of them elderly women: just his sort of audience. He'd railed against the effects of overindulgence, pledging no "radical changes" in the rationing system while slyly suggesting that Nonni Karlsson's "outside money"—

only the rankest fool doubts that the Karlsson campaign is being run and financed by powerful people from Down Below—derived from those Copenhagen brewmasters who have steadfastly envisioned the reconquest of Freeland through the stupefying, ambition-sapping effects of their sophisticated beers and liqueurs. History is quite clear on this point, isn't it—that the Danes have had but one overriding national obsession for the last millennium, the subjugation of Freeland?

Afterward, feeling parched of throat after so much talking, he'd fortunately run into Kristjan Logason, who'd wanted to discuss the wool business—the sad fact was that his souvenir shop on Skeggjagata might be going under—and who'd invited Hannibal up to his flat and produced some good strong coffee, liberally laced with fine imported brandy. Then over to the television studio, where he'd talked briefly about the Youth Problem, which he was determined to confound his critics by confronting face on. They hadn't known what to do about this, frankly; he could sense their confusion at his forthright, aggressive manner of taking up the topic. They are the heirs to the kingdom, these young men and women—oh, but what are they going to do, these boys, these girls, who do not grasp the plenitude of their task and the perilous delicacy of the bequest they shall inherit? He loves them, Hannibal loves them in his swollen heart, and he knows, as the wind howls and his distended bladder disgorges itself, that they lack discipline.

The wind in Freeland howls and it goes on howling. It is the sternest of schoolmistresses, hurling rebukes down on the people of this young nation, rapping their knuckles with hail and sleet and flying grit, seeking ever to impose upon them a little discipline. It is of course his duty to intercede on their behalf and he whispers a plea of extenuation: "Ah but we're still an inexperienced people. How many countries on this earth have been inhabited for merely a thousand years?" The wind, however, will have none of it. It shrieks derisively at his words. Says to the sleeping citizens in their stolid gray homes, *You will never grow up.* Says, *Year by year you become more childish.*

After the television studio he'd headed down to the old guild hall to make another speech, this one to a small group of businessmen, mostly importers and exporters, salt of the earth, to whom he'd pledged continuing efforts to foster trade, particularly with Denmark, where, as many in the audience will recall, he'd spent some of the happiest years of his young life, as an executive for Great Steamship. Someone had passed him a mug of very strong coffee, laced with vodka maybe, and then another. They'd all eaten boiled haddock and boiled potatoes and drunk more coffee. Afterward he'd removed an adhesive dab of boiled potato from the lapel of his suit jacket and surreptitiously popped it into his mouth—not realizing until it had been chewed and swallowed that there was something peculiar about its flavor. There was a crusty chewiness to it, a queer fishiness to it, and belatedly it dawned on him what this little morsel must be: a stray dab of cheese-and-tuna casserole, which evidently he'd been carrying around on his lapel since lunch. It was a disconcerting revelation, which he'd washed down with more strong coffee and a coffee nightcap.

The ferocity of the wind on the other side of the pane heartens him a little. It is on his side. If given the electoral franchise, surely the winds of Freeland would cast their votes unanimously for Hannibal Hannibalsson and it's a measure of how thoroughly this battle over the upcoming election has permeated his brain that he has begun dividing even the inanimate world into supporters and opposition. Clearly, the wind endorses him—as does the sea, as do the valleys and the sheep that dot them, the fumaroles and the calderas, as do the northern lights, notwithstanding all their evasions, and as does the Seamen's Home, and the statue of Erik the Other in Independence Square, and the Eldershelter, and as does, naturally, Great Blue Mountain. In the other camp are the tanning studios and the new Toyota dealership on Fallen Hill and the proliferating satellite dishes and the Go for Broke Music Store and the espresso machines and the new mosaic-inlaid bus stops which had provided "work" for local artists and the roaring hair dryers at the Central Swimming Pool, under which, stooping, bronzed young men with earrings can be found fashioning their hair. Against him are the Frozen-in-Time Experimental Theatergroup, and Pasta Paradise, and of course Vikram Jakobsson's sun-yellow Mustang convertible, and the polychromatic joggers—who, for all their effete peacock finery, no doubt could have left gasping in their wake the winner of the Long Run at the First Freelandic Olympics. Against him were the concertgoers, and the graffiti-scribblers and—quite painfully, for hadn't he as a young man traversed freezing hills in pitch blackness in order to catch a glimpse of Fred Astaire?—the movie theaters, which in their comedies no less than their tragedies notify him that, however lax and disorderly life's lately become in Freeland, barbarism is ascendant Down Below.

Meanwhile, down below in the other sense, his bladder seems, after a number of spurting farewells, to have achieved a depletion. But you never know and although he's wearing no underwear he practices a habitual feint. He pretends to tuck his penis away, as though wholly trusting in its signals.

Then a few seconds later he whips it up and out again, and a hot treacherous dollop of fluid is released. It's a simple but invaluable trick, this Fake Putaway of his, against a dumb but tricky organ that is of course always seeking to mortify a man.

He shuffles back down the dark hall. In the doorway of his bedroom he stops to contemplate his very own Youth Problem: the young woman he'd left a few moments ago in his too-warm bed. In rising he must have yanked the sheet and blanket off her shoulders. Her slumbering body is swung toward his and her torso is bare.

He studies her form, her tranquil face. For a long moment he lets his eyes play upon the dips and swells of her body, seeking to clear his mind of all worries, all memories and observations, and to absorb purely the overtaking beauty of the girl.

It's a shame, really, that she's *quite* so lovely. It will break his heart to leave her. Never in his life, perhaps, has he had available to his eyes and to his hands a creature of such surpassing fineness.

He peers at her breasts, which lift and fall on the gentle sea-swell of her breathing, and how many poets have scribbled verses extolling their lovers' breasts and how many have gotten the matter right? Melons, beds of roses, cushions, mossy riverbanks . . . Fancy steals over the poet and he begins to sing, but isn't the very first thing poets do, when a melody strikes them, is close their eyes on their inspiration? This is a point Hannibal has tried time and again to make, and has never yet succeeded quite in making, to his friend Eggert, who in calling Art the highest truth ignores the existence of a pure love for the blessed things of this life which might be called artistic and yet which, in its very purity, disdains all traffic in the false approximations of the "creative impulse." No, this is a love that high-mindedly refuses to dilute with pretty lies the sea and the lichen-rugg'd hills and the galloping of a horse and the sound of a fish briskly frying and the rib cage of a beautiful woman. The way, just now, the one breast, the right one, for all its hefting uprightness, has come to rest upon the mattress, and the other, the left, has come to nuzzle up against its twin, as if less in support than in a casual alliance of beauty with beauty—who would be fool enough to try to clothe this in words? Why clothe it at all? And oh, how hard to leave her!

To contemplate a life without Elva is to feel a burning like that of the coldest wind off the sea, stinging the cheeks and tearing the eyes. Whenever he goes to a movie house these days, which he rarely does, it seems the men on the screen are continually weeping. They are either shooting people in the head, with ferocious pistols designed to burst open skulls as effortlessly as a man's hiking boot might flatten a plover's egg, or they are weeping.

Tears are not the Freelandic man's way of handling grief, he supposes—or at least not *his* way. But the feeling overcoming him these past few weeks while making love to Elva has been close kin to weeping. It's as though his body rather than his head is shedding tears. It is as though what he time and again sends coursing into the flowing center of the girl's hips is not a stray assortment of his would-be heirs but a bitter distillate, released from whatever organ it is in the bowels of the body where griefs are banked. He is weeping into her loins.

No one but Rut knows—not even clever Eggert, although he may, just may, have guessed it—that the Father of the Country cannot be a father. Years ago, far from the gossipmongers, he'd had the tests done in Copenhagen. The clinic lay behind the botanical gardens—that haunting symbol, with its thousand shades of green, of all the upthrust fecundity and irrepressibility of life—and his count had turned out to be *extremely low*, and what back then had been *extremely low* must by now have receded to nearly nothing. He'd been given some numbers, which meant little to him. He needed instead an image, which arrived eventually: the seas inside him were all but fishless. However strong the tides might be, however tempestuous the whitecapped swells, the nets must come up empty.

He understands anew, as he loiters like a visitor on the threshold of his own bedroom, surveying the world's comeliest young woman, that something's out of kilter in this latest affair of his, and how much longer can he go on weeping into the space between her hipbones? Her body was not made for such things—and there is something wrong, a kind of defilement, really, in subjecting her to it. Not that she's unwilling, bless her. But what he is suffering isn't properly her concern. And it won't do—it isn't right—to make other people carry the burdens that don't belong to them.

His knees are hurting him and he must return to bed and it shall not be tonight, anyway, that they go their separate ways. No, not tonight, thank God, and he is grateful again for the wind and the snow, and the astoundingly generous outlays of that body of hers. He needs her again, now. She will not leave tonight—not tonight. Though just a moment ago, when he'd gone to piss, he'd found himself still slick with her inner fluids, still slippery with the flowing gift of her, it appears he needs her again. She would take his sorrows for her own. She would take within her a weight he can hardly support and a few minutes later she would rise on her long slim legs with an insouciant bounce to her step and isn't the only Youth Problem worth discussing the fact that some of us are no longer young?

39

The Second Worst Thing Anyone
Ever Did to Anyone

Connie Quimby once fell sound asleep while I was discussing my lifelong problems with insomnia. That's an image to keep in mind as the rest of her story unfolds. . . .

Something arrived that was only a little short of miraculous: a letter from Hannibal. It appeared at the Simples on the morning of a day whose mercury was again predicted to reach into the nineties. It was written in English—our old language of conspiracy and comedy and adventure, the one in which those two roving, laugh-a-minute Freelandic cut-ups, Hanni and Eggi, shared a black-and-white cinematic camaraderie.

The letter read:

Dear Eggi,

Come back, come back. I'm running for office★ and I need your help.

Hanni

P.S. Please prepare en route a Charter for the Newly Reborn Nation of Freeland.

★President

I read the letter over and over. It was—it was a thunderbolt. And it was no surprise. No surprise, and yet why had I never seen this coming? Hannibal was thirty-six. You must be thirty-five, according to our Constitution, to serve as President. He was running in the very first election in which he was eligible. How long had he had this goal in mind?

A long time? If so, why hadn't he entered politics before? Was that, too, part of his plan? Had he determined, with characteristic boldness, that the only place to begin was at the top?

Or was he, like me, stumbling around a bit? Had the idea come in a redeeming flash? Was he, too, looking for renewal and, more important still, had he conceivably found it? Was it possible, in other words, that in that Long Run he and I were running he had somehow—astoundingly—bounded into the lead? And was it possible—more astounding still—that in his redemption lay mine? The invitation called to my soul. *Eggi, come back, come back.* And while you're at it, please prepare en route a Charter for the Newly Reborn Nation of Freeland. . . . Could Freeland itself be my deliverance?

Heaven knows it was time to leave the Simples, and Hannibal's letter provided a necessary prod. Even so, it seemed some final extension or clarification was lacking, some decisive freeing stroke. . . . I was enough of a storyteller to yearn to see events tilted toward some resolution, however unseemly, to long for some fateful unraveling of our tale. The individual threads of our shared narrative must be respected, blood be spilled or curses delivered, omens solidify into fact.

The last few days, the heat had intensified, and my skin, like some sort of thick filmed stew left to simmer too long on the stove, heaved and broke in slow molten blisters, and we went on being lovers, Connie and I.

On the day the letter arrived, Geoffrey was over at the hospital, submitting to a battery of tests. I was alone in the house. Connie had gone to drop Bella at her "special school" and was to stop back at the house, briefly, before heading off once more to the hospital. I waited for her in the study. There was self-punishment in the choice, for the room's air conditioner had recently broken down and the day was already sweltering.

Geoffrey's inner sanctum, the site of our nightly seminars, wasn't a place I often entered on my own. Things had been different when I first came to the Simple household. Initially, with its floor-to-ceiling walls of books, this room had drawn me like a magnet. But I'd avoided it ever since Connie and I had begun our affair; it was too much Geoffrey's. The room even smelled of him, though heretofore I hadn't been aware, quite, that Geoffrey possessed a smell: a flowery scent something like talcum powder, and under it an unplaceable, unpleasant odor. . . .

"I'm in here," I called to her, when I heard the front door open.

Connie made no reply. I repeated my greeting. Again no answer. Then she stepped through the doorway and at the sight of me, seated on her husband's maroon couch, a quick anguished look pinched her features. What a burden I must have seemed! She wasn't to be blamed, surely, if she flashed a twinge of revulsion.

Still, that look on her face hurt me, disturbed me, challenged me— and thrilled me, yes, for wasn't there something splendid in the way we were striving, the two of us, toward some harsh, candid clarity? *She is no fool,* a voice in my head declared, and I liked her all the better for that. . . .

"Come sit," I said.

So: there she stands, Connie Simple, whose husband's in the hands of one sort of medical team and whose daughter's in the hands of another, stands in the doorway of her husband's study, contemplating her fierce little lover, on whose baking skin a plague of sores has descended. Is it any surprise she maintains her distance, taking a seat at the far end of the couch? I found this vexing, and alluring. The goal I'd set for myself this morning was clearly even more formidable than I'd supposed.

"Things are a little tough for me today," I began.

"For you? For us all."

"For us all," I agreed, nodding lugubriously. "I don't mean to burden you, burdened as you already are, and perhaps I shouldn't even mention it. But today is my anniversary."

"Your anniversary?"

I'd piqued Connie's curiosity. Wariness remained in her voice but didn't I detect, too, a grateful note? Surely she liked this about me—the fiendish invention that went into my manipulations? "What anniversary?"

I tried to look offended and probably managed it; I suppose I *was* offended. "My wedding anniversary. You're not the only one around here who once took wedding vows."

"It's just that you so rarely talk about it. . . . Is—is it very hurtful?"

Everything in her positioning was meant to affirm her distance from me—everything but her dilated eyes. The fish had taken a first nibble at the hook.

"Maybe that's why I don't often talk about it."

"And you want to talk now?"

Had I only imagined, moments before, that look of revulsion? Or had it been genuine, and was I now being hoodwinked by the open solicitude on her face? Probably, she'd counterfeited neither expression; her feelings toward me, like mine toward her, must have been a hopeless tangle.

Yes, this new look of concern, too, was genuine, and this was Connie at her most vividly appealing: she was easily touched. Her sympathy was one of those great vulnerable extravagances of Nature—like the bird of paradise's plumage or the angelfish's trailing veils—whose persistence over time, in a world so rife with razor-toothed predators, must be marveled at.

"Yes, it's painful," I confessed.

"Does it trouble you like this every year? Your anniversary?"

I suppose the short answer would have been *no.* The long answer would have been that today wasn't, completely, my anniversary. The date was correct, but the month—indeed the season—wasn't. I found a mid-length response: "I try not to let it. Terribly much."

"I guess the breakup of any marriage must be painful. Even an unhappy one, and from what you've said of yours, it must have been quite unhappy."

She was wearing on this hot summer morning a purple and yellow sleeveless floral blouse, a pair of baggy wrinkled linen shorts, and on her otherwise bare feet a minimal pair of sandals. I liked the way her thin legs had little more curve than a pair of stilts. They simply went about their business, which was the elevating of the crown of Connie's head to its towering six-foot height. "Indeed it was. But that isn't what's bothering me today. You know what's bothering me today?"

"Tell me."

"It's that I never had any proper ceremony to begin with. Not only did the marriage itself collapse, but I never had that full solemn moment of ceremony and finery. Have I ever told you that the bureaucrat who married us stank of liquor?"

"You never told me that. . . ." Wider still—her eyes. She was leaning toward me, a little, the better to siphon her outflowing sympathy my way.

"Absolutely reeked of it. Now can you imagine? What that's like? To know not only that your marriage was a disaster but everything was a fiasco from day one? You at least had the pleasure of a golden moment. I can see it in your face." And I nodded not at Connie herself but at the wedding photograph on Geoffrey's desk. Geoffrey had been a little thinner, Connie's prettiness perhaps slightly more angular, but really it was remarkable how little either had altered. He was wearing a blue double-breasted suit, she a long white dress with a veil.

"And you once had your child taken away from you. That must have been hard. . . ."

"I look at that picture and, I'm sorry to say it, self-pity comes washing over me."

"Did you miss her? I mean your daughter, not your wife. I know you didn't miss your wife, you poor creature. She sounds absolutely dreadful."

She had such lovely manners, Connie always did. By contrast, it seems fair to say of my wife Kornelia that she embraced boorishness as a moral imperative—believed she was doing the *right thing* when she hunkered on the floor rather than in the chair offered her, or lit up a cigarette in a movie theater, or arrived at one of her father's parties wearing a food-stained peasant skirt, for by such gestures wasn't she subverting all that was sterile and hypocritical in the established order? But for Connie the issue of etiquette went far beyond a respect for appearances. It was a spiritual preserve, and the more uncomfortable our affair made her, the more likely she was to show me, abruptly, a sweet and faintly absurd civility. I can hear her even now saying *you poor creature* and following the phrase with a bright unspontaneous laugh. But was I, this morning, being detoured deliberately? Did she already sense where I was guiding her?

"I did miss my Lilja. And I miss the sense that there wasn't a single thing about our life together, Kornelia's and mine, that wasn't tainted from the outset."

"Do you regret not having a boy? Ever miss not having a son?"

"A little. Yes—yes I suppose I do," I opined.

I'd never mentioned to Connie that I already had a son, or—given my doubts on the issue of paternity—perhaps had a son, who was living in Denmark with his mother, Sigrun. "It would have been lovely to raise a boy," I added—and, in later years, I've often superstitiously speculated that by tempting fate with this particular whopping lie I lit the long fuse that burned until that stupefying day when I cracked open my apartment door and a fifteen-year-old Sindri exploded into my arms with a cry of *Father!*

"Of course you still may," Connie said. "Have a son, I mean. You'll meet somebody else. Do you see what I'm saying? We can't keep this up, Eggert. You know that."

In truth I did know it and a sprawling silence slumped over the shuttered room. We sat, radiantly hot, on our opposite ends of the couch. Some five or six feet of depleted air sat between us. Above our heads, in serried rows, bookshelves overhung bookshelves, all waiting to give way in outrage at the affront being carried out against their gentle owner; those volumes desired nothing more than to crush and smother the two of us in a dusty avalanche of print and paper.

"What I do know," I said, wandering out of the Hills of Duplicity into the Plains of Candor, "is that I'm haunted by you, Connie. I know I will always be haunted by you."

Another pause. We scrutinized each other from our opposite ends of the couch and now arrived a third, a distinct new expression on my Connie's face. The plush-lipped mouth had drifted apart, the gaze had melted, and though I might conceivably have been mistaken in reading either distaste on those features when she'd entered the room or sympathy when I'd started chronicling my troubles, there was absolutely no doubting this one: she desired me. Yes, she did, despite the state I was in, despite who I was, despite my suppurating skin—truly, the workings of the Lord are a wonder to perceive! Meanwhile, elsewhere, surrounded by darkness, one of the oddest and ablest intellects I'd ever encountered was being prodded at by minuscule lights that, digging deep, were rooting around in the nerves behind his oddly shaped eyeballs; and meanwhile, also in a sort of darkness, a rescue search was being carried out, as a "special teacher" of a "special student" sought to locate and vitalize a dormant mind. Meanwhile, vast bacterial armies were no doubt darkly massing in preparation for a new assault on my skin, as I steered my schemes toward that white, sacrosanct object which must lie buried somewhere in this house. I would bring it to light again.

"And I by you. There is no getting around it, Eggert. I think you may be the strangest man I've ever met."

"Thank you."

"It's one sign of your strangeness that you would take that as a compliment."

"I was speaking facetiously. It's called 'irony.'"

And didn't the merest jab of mutual dislike—just a blink—kindle in our eyes? In any case, her tone shifted—turned theatrically reflective: "Who *ever* would have thought I'd take up with a Freelandic poet?"

"What is amazing about that photograph," I said, picking up my task anew, "is that you haven't changed at all."

"Balls. That's absolutely nonsense, Eggert." This was precisely the sort of reproach Connie was forever directing at Geoffrey, and why was it when she tossed such fierce words at him her mock-sternness was playful and flirtatious and intimate, and now it was nothing of the sort? "I'm developing lines around my eyes. And in my forehead. And my jaw is going soft."

"But you haven't gained a pound."

"Yes I have. I've probably gained six or seven. And all in my hips." More laughter. "I'm developing a fat ass."

"If so, those six or seven pounds have gone only to perfect you. As the poet said:

> "An hundred years should go to praise
> Thine eyes, and on thy forehead gaze.
> Two hundred to adore each breast:
> But thirty thousand to the rest.

"If I were a better poet, Connie, or at least a less feverish one, I could give those hips of yours its thirty thousand." Marvell is one of the poets I've translated into Freelandic.

"You're very sweet, Eggert."

The heat had frayed my nerves raw, I guess, and her words vexed me. "No I'm not. But I do make up for it, somewhat, by being very passionate."

Laughter, which she then brushed away with her hand, as though it were cigarette smoke. "You don't want to admit it, but you are *sweet*." And why was she making this word sound like an accusation? What was I actually being accused of?

"No I'm not."

"Well you've certainly become more so since the first day I met you."

"Don't flatter yourself. At this point in our lives we don't change in our fundamental natures—or I don't. Any more than you've changed from your wedding picture. Why, right now you could step in for that girl bride. The same face. And right now you could slip into that dress. . . ."

Did she see where this was moving? She did and yet she didn't, I think. Certainly she managed to look repulsed when I, a minute later, made my proposal explicit. And yet, on another level, I think we were marching together; I think she yearned, no less than I, to have what followed follow.

"I should be going," she said. "To the hospital."

"I suppose I *would* be a better person," I said, "if I didn't envy Geoffrey so much."

"Envy Geoffrey? With his head this morning getting poked at by all sorts of spooky instruments?"

"Envy you, then. I suppose that's what I mean."

"Envy me?"

"You have parents and I never really had parents. You have a family with a genuine family history. You had a genuine wedding ceremony and I was married by a sodden lout. I never even had *that* comfort, Connie. I had the pains of a divorce without the pleasures of a wedding. I have a special favor to ask of you."

"A favor?"

"Just one."

"Well?"

I looked at her. I didn't say a thing.

"*If you could see your eyes, Eggert Oddason,*" Connie said, marveling, shaking her head at me. "You look positively feverish."

And still I said nothing.

Her voice sharpened: "What in the world is it you want of me?"

"I want a favor. One. No more than that." I took a deep breath. "Won't you put on your wedding dress for me, Connie? I just want to *see* you in it. Once, just once." I had slid across the couch, in my quick fashion, and seized the hands in her lap.

And I'll never in my life forget the look she gave me. *If you could see your eyes* she'd said, moments before, but now *her* eyes flashed as I'd never seen eyes flash. No doubt about it: I'd horrified her. There was ice in her eyes, ground glass in her eyes, rage and recoil—there was far more than I could contend with, and I felt myself cowering before her, fully revealed as the cringing, thrashing miserable creature I am.

And yet, damnable soul that I also am, I pushed on: "I want to see perfection. I want—"

Connie interrupted me: "What you're proposing is the most—the most— You're—you're—" Truly I'd shocked her speechless. "You're not well."

And even in my sudden fear of her, and of myself, even in all my excruciating discomfort, still I saw and relished the humor in her euphemism: *You're not well.* It was amazing, truly: just how deep that woman's habits of good breeding ran.

And in perceiving this, in knowing myself in possession of an acuity equal to the matter at hand, I found the voice of my continuation: "Of course I'm not *well*, Connie. Christ, I'm ill, I'm sick, as you said yourself

I'm feverish. I'm ill and sick and feverish with love for you, darling. Love isn't *healthy*. Look at the flaming skin on my chest and neck—I'm burning up with love for you. Christ, what sort of man would I be, what sort of monster, if I could be *well* under these circumstances?"

"It's absolutely out of the question. You *do* know, Eggert, that that's *the* most appalling, *the* most tasteless suggestion I've ever heard? I'll forget you ever said it." Good Lord, she *did* look appalled—more than that, revolted—and yet her hands still lay in mine.

"Don't," I urged. "*Don't* forget it." I took another deep breath. And I dove in again: "As a favor to me, if I've ever meant anything to you, I'd ask you not to forget it. I'd ask you to pledge never to forget what I requested of you today." The words came all in a torrent, straight from the bloody roots of my lungs. I'd been aware, up until this point, of when I'd been posing and when I'd been candid, but now the words tumbled forth in a cascade whose vigor made any question of veracity look irrelevant: "Even if you choose not to satisfy me, Connie, in this the one most intimate request I'll ever make of anyone, I'd ask you to remember, always, that once you were loved so wildly that your lover risked appalling you, he risked perhaps even disgusting you, in order that he might, for a single moment, dream you were his bride. Will you promise me at least that much, Connie? Pledge it. Promise never in all your life to forget how one torrid summer morning in Georgetown your lunatic Freelandic poet asked you to put on your wedding gown for him."

Slowly, on the long stalk of her neck, Connie rotated her head back and forth. Had I confused her? Moved her? Probably both, for I'd confused and moved myself, and I was sweating, Geoffrey's study was an oven, and our hands in her lap were a damp, boneless, steaming mass. "That's the strangest promise I've ever been asked to make. . . ."

Another pause opened. I could feel her blood—the spirited expulsions of her heart—in her fingertips.

"I received a letter today," I said.

She leaped happily at what seemed a change of subject. "Of course you did. I was so rushed! I forgot to ask you who it was from. . . ." It was the first letter I'd received since my arrival.

"It was from my friend Hannibal."

"Yes, of course it was, you've told me so many interesting things about him." This was volunteered in her brightest social manner. But she was still panting, as I was still panting. I was absolutely out of my head: I could hardly *see*.

"He has momentous news. He's planning to run for President."

"President?"

"Of the nation. Of Freeland."

"Of the whole country? Can he *do* that?"

"Why in the world not?"

"Yes," she concurred. "Why ever in the world not? But it's an enormous job, isn't it?"

"Is it? The size of the job is one of the questions I keep struggling to determine. We're talking about a country made up of less than sixty thousand souls. You could say that what he's doing is on a scale with running for mayor of Roanoke, Virginia. On the other hand," I went on, "Freeland *is* a nation, one which, according to some fair portion of its citizenry, myself included, has some sort of holy mission, and there are days when I'm convinced that being its President is the largest job in the world."

Her eyes were pinned to my face. She was waiting—prey anticipating the next move of its predator. And I went on: "He's written to ask me to return home. He wants me to help him."

"Help him? How in the world help him?"

The truth is, I hadn't until this moment asked myself how indeed I was to "help," and it embarrassed me to discover I had no answer at the ready. "Why, to clarify his thinking," I replied. "To do—to do just what I do for Geoffrey. To help him see Freeland clear and whole." I'd simply taken it for granted that if Hannibal Hannibalsson was running for President, he needed my assistance. The undertaking spoke straight to my soul.

"To see it whole and clear?" Was this—her quizzical look asked me —what politics consisted of in Freeland? Was this what our campaigns were all about?

Inspiration came to me suddenly: "And of course I shall write speeches. Through Hannibal, I will speak to my nation."

"Of course you will."

"And yet—" I went on, finally feeling that my every spidery impulse was stitching its way toward a splendid webwork intricacy, "how am I possibly to leave? How can I go fulfill my duty, when to do so would mean leaving *you*, Connie?"

She tried to pull her hands free of mine; I held on tight. She tugged harder and, extricating one, ran a long-fingered hand over her damp forehead and offered a dignified resolution: "Well, you must go. Clearly you must."

Again we halted, like boxers gratefully savoring one of those little gasping intervals between rounds. Once again, once again in that shuttered room we regarded each other, faces no more than a foot apart: eyes bursting with anger, resentment, importunacy, disgust, lust, affection, complicity, gratitude—and all of it so intermingled there was no separating whose gaze expressed what. We were both breathing audibly, straight into the other's face. I turned away and took up my task again: "I suppose it would all be so much easier for me, if only I left with some image of you I could hold to clearly. I suppose I'm back to the subject of that wedding dress, Connie, and is it such a large thing? To ask you? Look at it this way, darling: Geoffrey not only got to see you in a wedding dress, he got to marry you for life. And what does Eggert get, who loves you as fully as anyone ever could and who pursued you from the Arctic to what feels like the heart of the tropics? If Geoffrey gets you as bride for life, is it so unreasonable that Eggert might take you as bride for an hour? Where is the *injustice* in that? Doesn't justice tell us, darling, that this is the smallest least littlest thing I deserve, and that to fail me in this would be an injustice?"

"And don't you see it's impossible? Absolutely fucking impossible? The thing is sitting in a box. Up in the attic. I'm sure it's all *wrinkled*. And dusty."

"Am I to worry myself with *wrinkles*? Am I to worry myself with *dust*? Look what I've endured to be with you, Connie. Christ, I'm not *used* to this heat. Look what it's done to my skin. Rashes and sores all over my body! I've become a leper for you, Connie, and do I mind becoming a leper for you? If the question were put to Eggert directly, if he were asked, Are you willing to be transformed into a leper in order to have your Connie Quimby briefly, what would he say except, Willingly, gladly, unquestionably, immediately. . . ? What would he say except, What a small price to pay! And what would he ask in return? So tiny a thing! So modest a thing! Only to be given, for a few entrancing moments, what you've given his rival for life. I'm a poet, Connie, a man devoting his life to the pursuit of imagery, and what image, ever, could be more beautiful than Connie Quimby in a wedding gown? Yes, I think I could honestly leave here, I think I could go fulfill my duty to my nation, if only I might carry the sense that you for one minute—one brief minute, Connie!—were as wholly mine as I have been wholly yours from that first spellbinding instant when a tall creature of enchantment, a figure of magic drawn from some bejeweled medieval poem, a Keatsian faery's child, strode toward him across the lobby of the Hotel Snorri."

Keeping her hands in hand, I stood and tugged reasonably upon them, and this was the pivotal moment, and when my eyes found hers they seemed to lock almost audibly into place, like the click a metal nut and bolt make when a socket wrench gives them a cinching turn. I said, "Dear *heart*, how can I be expected to go off and serve my country, knowing you and I will meet again only God knows where and when, unless I carry with me this fair symbol of what we've meant to each other?"

And my head began to spin. I was suddenly dizzy with the room's airless heat, everything occurring through a sort of gray-around-the-edges blur, and whether in retrospect it ought to be viewed as a fair quid pro quo or as shameless blackmail, I don't know. But I made my offer explicit at last: "If you'll do this for me, Connie, I swear I'd get the hell out of here. I'd be gone in a day or two."

"A day or two?" Again she swept a hand over her forehead.

"I swear."

"You'd be gone—"

"To faraway Freeland," I said. "Where I belong," and I tugged upon her hand and slowly she levitated from the couch. It was as though she were in some somnambulistic trance.

"This is lunacy, lunacy, lunacy," the woman chanted softly.

"Truly it is," the little man echoed, guiding her toward the stairs, "but it's inspired lunacy, isn't it, and how better are we who are under its dominion to describe the imperatives of love? It's the moon on the reedy estuaries, isn't it, and the moon splintered on the glaciers, and the moon stroking the leaves of the bamboo thicket," and as we began to mount the stairs I remember dazedly asking myself, Has any man ever wooed his lover more movingly than you do now, Eggert? The air was aflutter with great butterfly-packs of words and I had only to put out my arm to have them swarm into my net.

"If I did this for you, Eggert, it would be for a minute only."

"Agreed—agreed—agreed," I sang. "And yet this minute will be an hour, won't it? A day, a month, a lifetime, for I will latch it in my heart forever, untouchable and incorruptible. And my gratitude will stand like a monument to you, forever, Connie—" and meanwhile, as I sang of stability, of towering monuments immune to Time, my hands were in a hideous palsy on the balustrade. Connie was shaking and I was shaking and a good stiff breeze would have knocked the pair of us off our feet, but we kept ascending, united in our common undertaking. "Lunacy, sheer lunacy," she kept softly chanting, and I knew I had to be grasping her fingers or the spell of our mission would be broken. I must follow her, up, up, up into the attic—must be at her side as she searched out the trunk where the sacramental garments lay. . . .

"You might say I'm going off to fight in my country's wars," I told her and it's a measure of our heat-doped, done-in state that such melodrama struck neither of us as absurd.

Access to the attic lay in Bella's room. This was a staircase I'd never glimpsed before. Connie threw a light switch. The steps were narrow, too narrow for walking abreast, and I let Connie guide me, although I held tight to her hand as my head and her hips ascended together. The air was hotter yet, and extremely close; it was asphyxiating.

We reached the top, gasping for oxygen, and I found myself standing in what was, evidently, a sort of Quimby graveyard: painted portraits, old photographs, old books, old furniture, old rolled-up rugs, their ends frayed. The family heirlooms had come up here to die. Dry and discouraged, the light from the single, dangling bulb fell on a stuffed raven, who would croak his "Nevermore" never more. He looked moth-eaten and—a darker hole in his dark face—one of his red glass eyes was missing.

I was sweating from head to foot. I let go of Connie's hand. At the far wall stood a cobwebbed window. There must have been a fissure somewhere in the roof, for a number of black wasps crawled stickily on the inside of the pane.

Connie had said she would never be able to find the dress and yet amid all this high-piled and dusty clutter she continued moving with a sleepwalker's sureness of touch. She threw open a trunk and there, wrapped in clear plastic, it lay. She stooped over it, motionless a moment— evidently immersed in thought. I stood beside her, cupping her hipbone in my hand.

"It's *beautiful*," I said, which should have sounded absurdly hackneyed. But we had entered a domain so infernally hot that all words, the trite and the profound both, meant nothing.

"It all seems so far far away," Connie murmured, but in a voice so unlike her own, so thin and so queerly strained, as to leave me feeling it was she herself who was far far away: I was losing her.

My hand stroked the swell of her haunch and I said, "Come on, come on now, Connie darling, we've must hurry now, hurry, or truly we'll *suffocate* up here."

But she went on eyeing the dress, while my blood hammered in my ears, and I feared, right at the threshold of our little ceremony, she would balk. She would leave me—so to speak—alone at the church gate.

But I was wrong to doubt her. An efficiency of purpose seized Connie's limbs, a characteristic get-to-it resolution: if this was lunacy, she nonetheless went at it in a no-nonsense manner.

I'd expected the donning of a wedding gown to be an elaborate, time-consuming process; I suppose I'd seen too many movies. But Connie moved with haste. She pulled her blouse over her head and dropped it to the floor, unbuckled her shorts and let them fall, stepped out of her sandals. In nothing but underwear—white bra and pink polka-dot panties— she ripped the clear plastic and lifted the dress free.

It was a simple gown. I know nothing about fabric but I recall that this one rustled as she lifted it high and dropped it over her head. "Do the snaps," she commanded, and turned her back to me.

I was proudly equal to the task of readying my bride and I relished the feel of expensive fabric against my sweating fingers. The buttons themselves were covered with fabric. All of my eyesight, nearly all of my brain, went into the task; I focused fiercely, which was my way of countering an odd feeling that, somehow, I wasn't—that neither of us were—quite there. We were neither one of us there. Where were we? We weren't anywhere. Where were we? Nothing was anywhere, nothing was fixed—we'd moved into a universe without gravity, without moorings, without mortar or binding: everything floated.

Connie stooped again to the trunk and lifted from it something white and—weightless. Her veil. She turned her back to me. A moment, two moments, three moments of adjustment. I scratched at one of the rash-patches in one of my fiery armpits and watched, across the room, the wasps trudging vertically on the dusty panes. From its single red glass eye the raven scrutinized the room's two interlopers.

Slowly, my veiled, barefoot bride turned round, and something momentous happened inside me—I suppose you might say my heart leapt up

—or perhaps I'd better say my heart leapt sideways, halfway out of my chest, and I felt a hundred things at once. I was thrilled and proud and also unnerved, I was *spooked*, as Connie lifted her veil, over her head, and vacantly regarded me; her eyes too might have been glass. I'd told her she was unchanged from that girl in the photograph, but the woman looming before me in the cobwebbed light was faded and lined: she was the careworn ghost of the bride in the frame downstairs. A wasp, a little airborne sac of poison, buzzed around her waist and Connie brushed it away with her hand.

I came forward and took that hand—bigger than mine—and pulled upon it. "Come on. We're going to suffocate up here. Let's go downstairs."

"*No.*" She tugged back, hard. "I said *one minute*, Eggert. Now I'm going to change back."

"Come on, come on, come on," I chanted, continuing to yank at her. I had no other words left—the poet's tongue had departed altogether.

"Damn it, Eggert, I'm not going downstairs in this damn thing."

"Ah but you must," I said. "You must." Both of us were panting in the heat. "If you will, I'll go away."

"You're a fucking lunatic."

"Yes, no doubt, of course *yes*, but if you do it for me, this fucking lunatic really will go away," I sang, and wasn't I speaking with greater truthfulness than I'd ever shown her? Wasn't I in effect saying, *I know I'm stubborn and repellent and devious, but you can be rid of me, rid of me, rid of me, if only you'll indulge me in this*. . . . Where was my pride? Everything was dropping away. . . . We were suffocating, we were going to be found dead underneath a dusty stuffed raven, a pair of corpses to puzzle every newspaper in town, and in my desperation for a rescue I jettisoned all inessentials: I threw away self-esteem. "I'll go away," I went on, "and the heat will break, and everything will be in place again. . . ."

Connie came then, reluctantly, tugging back on my arm. I led her down the attic stairs. We said nothing. She was behind me, her hand in mine. I led her through Bella's room and to the head of the next staircase, where a window blazed: the city on the other side had turned blindingly bright. The dress of my bride rustled on the stairs behind me.

Did she sense where I was going? I'm not sure I did. We could have turned into her air-conditioned bedroom, but that wasn't what I was looking for, somehow; I led her into Geoffrey's study.

Tall and bright, a fair-fleshed lighthouse, Connie towered motionlessly in the middle of the room. Behind her, in the same dress but far far away, a copy of herself kissed a round-faced groom. It was a different groom—lean as Death—beside her now. . . .

Surely the day cannot have been as hot as my memory has it, but I see the two of us gasping, swooning, melting through roiling waves of heat. I expected her to protest when I collapsed at her feet and, beginning at her ankles, ran my knuckly hands up her bare pale freckled legs, but she said nothing.

I maneuvered her back to the couch, where she lay down, her up-lifted dress folded under her. As I stepped out of my clothes she made various adjustments with her dress, as if to ready herself, but when I slid in atop her—the bunched bridal fabric teasing the bare rashed skin of my chest—she whispered, "I'm unprotected."

"Mm?"

"Diaphragm."

"I'll pull out," I countered, for there was no more time; we would run out of air if we didn't hurry.

Somehow the veil had settled over her face, by chance perhaps, or perhaps because she preferred viewing our actions through a film or filter. Everything was unfolding in a blur and for a minute or two continued in a blur. I was all the way in her—she was my bride, I was her groom, I was breathing into a veil, she was breathing out through a veil, and my open mouth bit through a delicate lace, my teeth sinking through mesh into the pith of her lower lip. Her hand reached up, or mine did, and the veil was lifted between us and we fell into each other's eyes and the blur vanished and it was as though we'd pushed out of a swamp into a clearing. *You're sweet*, she'd said to me, not so many minutes ago and in this very room, but surely she saw now how simplistic this was. I'd like to think for an instant she saw me dead on. And that for an instant I saw her, too, clearly, for if I didn't do so then, I suppose I never did. I saw that she, too, for all her pretty civility, those manners I could never wield with such charm, wasn't *sweet*. We couldn't afford sweetness, either of us. For wasn't she spilling into me—as I into her—a cry of resentment, against a life that had placed her beside an idiot daughter and a disembodied mate, with ghosts in the attic and impenetrable books in the study, and wasn't she saying to the woman who year after year gracefully endured all such things, *Screw you . . . ?* Wasn't there a reasonable loathing at the base of it all?

I was clumsy in my exit and I'm afraid there was a smear of something—a yellow mud-mustard color—on the bridal fabric. We'd made a mess. I turned on my side, propped on my elbow, my back to her, and for a long moment contemplated my crotch—my scrotum, actually, which in the room's dim light looked gray and dry and wizened. What did it remind me of? Behind me, I heard a long tearing sound, and for a moment it was as though she were ripping fabric in her hands.

But the sound was coming from her throat—Connie'd begun to cry. I scarcely heard her. I knew I was close to locating my metaphor, which alone held out to me liberation. I needed a phrase, an image. . . . Gray, dry, wizened, what did it remind me of?

When it came to me—a *wasps' nest*—I recalled a scene from one of my travels. A hot day, a luxuriant green landscape, and a man—a farmer—all bundled up, despite the heat. Rags around his hands, rags around his face, he was a sort of mummy—an armed mummy, for he carried in his hands a tire iron, which, with a dry sinking thud, he drove into a wasps' nest lodged in the crook of a tree. Where had I seen this? Mexico? In Sri Lanka? No, on television—yes, wasn't that it, hadn't I seen it on television? Or had I made it up?

In the richest of my memories, I'm traveling by train, through a rainy unidentified landscape whose vegetation, filtered through a rain-flooded window, has become the vibrant green glow of life itself.

In the ugliest of my memories, somebody is crying, and a dress is stained and torn, and the living creatures in my privates are packed with poison. Even so, even so, I'd succeeded in reaching bottom—at a time when I wasn't sure there was any longer a bottom to reach—and I'd found a message there, a message and a cause. From Hannibal. *Come back, come back.* It was time to go home.

40

The Troll in the Bowels

I was awakened by the telephone. Two minutes after two said the bed-side clock. In the morning. "It's Helmut," the voice at the other end announced, which I heard as "Holm," and so I'm to be forgiven for replying, with some asperity, "*Who?*"

Admittedly, the boy had the perfect rejoinder: "Your son-in-law."

"Good evening," I said.

"I'm calling about Lilja. She's fine."

Lilja was fine? Well and good, but surely *she* wasn't the one we needed to worry about. Helmut, on the other hand—had he lost his mind? What was he calling for? Lately, more and more I'd been beset by a feeling that everybody I dealt with—the whole damn populace—had a screw loose. It was painful to wake up, and I was awakening only slowly, into such a world.

"That's the main thing," my son-in-law continued. Always deep and hollow-sounding—as though his chest were empty—his voice sounded particularly robotic tonight. "But she had a little fall."

"A fall?" Had Lilja broken something?

"A little one. But there was some bleeding." Bleeding? "Naturally we were very worried."

"A fall?"

"But they think the baby's going to be fine."

Somehow I hadn't immediately thought of the baby. . . . But this was *that* sort of bleeding: between the legs.

I woke up fully. "Where's my daughter?"

"She's at the hospital. Listen, they don't think there's anything to worry about."

"The fall—where was the fall?"

"At the Prison Cell."

"The—I beg your pardon?"

"It's a disco—a discotheque."

"Lilja was at a discotheque?"

"She fell on some stairs. They were dark."

It was remarkable, the velocity with which concern turned to indignation. But in a flash I saw the whole sordid business: Helmut suggests they go dancing; Lilja all too quickly accedes; drinks are ordered; and I'm going to lose my granddaughter because my daughter can't, even for a few months, resist pickling her brains inside the satanic cacophony of a discotheque. Why hadn't I seen this coming? Rock music was going to kill off my progeny.

And Helmut was drunk. *That's* what all the pauses and the enhanced mechanical hollowness indicated.

"Maybe I better come down."

"There's no need," the boy protested, which decided the issue; I must thwart him wherever I could. "I'll be there in ten minutes," I said, and hung up the phone.

My daughter was bleeding and I myself was riding on a wave of hot red rage—slamming the apartment door, punching the Volvo's accelerator. How could she *be* so stupid? Most of my fury dissolved, however, on the instant when I laid eyes upon my girl—in large part because a *girl* is what, in her blue hospital pajamas, she so pathetically seemed. This was a Lilja of an earlier vintage. Propped up by pillows, her body was positioned midway between sitting and reclining. She looked not only blanched but dwindled. She had a magazine upon her lap, but her gaze lay elsewhere. It was focused on the wall before her.

Warily, I looked around for Helmut. Scared off? Sleeping one off? The girl was alone. Cheerily I said, "Pardon me, miss, but I'm looking for Lilja Eggertsdottir."

"Pabbi," she cried. The magazine slipped from her fingers and slithered brightly to the floor.

"You and the magazine both," I said.

"Mm?"

"A little fall."

"In my case, more a scare than a fall."

"I'm almost tempted to say it serves you right," I said. "The Prison Cell . . ." I shook my head sternly at the girl.

"I'm almost tempted to say you're the most chilly-hearted man I know," she said. "Somebody whose idea of extending sympathy to a bedridden girl is to deliver a lecture."

It's one of the prime delights of my Lilja: her breezy skill in the art of the barbed exchange. She contends with me. Unlike Sindri, who merely looks wounded when given a little prod. There's no possibility of real raillery with the boy.

"It's going to do us in," I said. "Rock music."

"At least we'll go down dancing," Lilja countered.

"Where's Helmut? I thought you were a married lady."

"Funny thing, I did too. Have you checked the Billiard Palace?"

And so it proceeded, for ten or fifteen satisfying minutes. Then I went out into the corridor, in search of a rest room, and perhaps my nerves were still jangled: my eyes played me a trick.

At the far end of the corridor, laboriously shuffling in my direction, a familiar figure approached. It was my First Muse—it was Gudrun—but something radical, something horrendous, had befallen her. She was all hunched over, she was progressing with a cane, and inside my chest someone nudged an icy sliver of glass up against my heart, denting but not rupturing the thick, toiling membrane: all at once, I felt terrifyingly vulnerable.

I blinked my eyes, or the fluorescent lights flickered, and I saw that this wasn't Gudrun. No no. This particular somebody-who-was-dying was somebody else. It was an elderly stranger—the Muse, perhaps, of another someone, himself long dead. . . .

And I was left panting. I felt both reprieved and shaken, and when I returned to Lilja's room I took a new tone entirely.

"So my dear, you did a very foolish thing. But I talked to a nurse on the way in and she says you're out of danger."

Lilja instantly adapted: "I don't know . . . Am I ever out of danger? I sometimes feel I'm walking over land mines, Pappalingur. It was all very frightening."

"Speak truth now. You'd been drinking, hadn't you?"

"Not so much." Blood drained into the rims of the girl's eyes; she looked near tears.

"More than you should have, I'm sure. Even a little is probably more than is good for you. In your condition. Now have you learned your lesson?"

"*We've* learned our lesson," my daughter replied and indicated, by arranging her hands tenderly around her belly, just who this unified and chastened plural was: mother and child. It's a gesture perhaps no man can escape envying: that motion whereby, simply by embracing yourself, you embrace another.

"Technically, I'm not supposed to be here. These are hardly visiting hours."

"You got round them somehow."

"I got round them somehow."

"Always such a sly one." Her lips hinted at a grin.

"And you, always such a reckless one. You worry me, girl."

"You don't have to worry about me, Pabbi. *I'll* worry about me. If you want to worry about one of your children, worry about Sindri."

"Oh the boy's all right. Don't believe all that moaning you hear, profits falling at Freefiskur and all the rest. His job looks steady. They're lining their pockets as never before, the big shots, while—"

"That's not what I meant. He looks so pale. And he never wants to go out. I don't believe he *likes* that job. He's too big for that job."

"But that's precisely what a job is," I explained to her. "Almost by definition, it's smaller than we are. Otherwise it wouldn't be *work*, you see. That's what people are doing all over the world—*working* to cram themselves into a box smaller than they are."

There's something about being near the top of the world—I speak literally, latitudinally—that fosters in me an occasional urge to make global pronouncements. I suppose you might say I sometimes feel I'm looking down on everybody else. I once figured out on a pocket calculator that something like 99.999 percent of the world's population lives to the south of me. . . .

"Well I don't want to be fit into a box that's smaller than I am and I don't want it to happen to my little brother either. And I don't want it to happen to my child."

"Girls are luckier. They're supposed to be unhappy. In the modern world, to call yourself a contented woman is to declare yourself a"—and a lovely English word popped into my head—"a *nincompoop*."

"But surely Sindri is just as entitled as I am to be unhappy. . . ."

"In theory. None of us lives in the domain of theory, though. Maybe the world will be different by the time that girl inside you is carrying my great-grandchild."

"It's a boy, Pappalingur. Inside me. Call it feminine intuition."

"It's a girl, darling. Call it a poet's inkling."

"So how is your election fight coming along?"

"Still badly. But better. I sometimes think we may go down to an honorable defeat instead of a humiliating rout."

"That was something, wasn't it? Nonni and the Danish Blue. I suppose you've been responsible for all the absurd data?"

I laughed merrily. "Most of it."

I'd generated various statistics and managed to get them planted on the TV and in *The Torch*. How Freeland's increasing consumption of Danish Blue over the last seventy years corresponded with greater longevity for both men and women. With lower infant mortality. With the virtual extirpation of tuberculosis and cholera, and higher admission to foreign universities. Furthermore, not a single case of leprosy—a great scourge among us only a century ago—had been reported in that time.

"Poor Nonni." She shook her head. "To be *such* an ass."

"That's what I keep hearing from the young people—who nonetheless all plan to support him. I can't fathom it."

"You know, Pabbi," my daughter reflected, "it doesn't really matter who wins this election."

"Oh but that's where you're dead wrong, my young miss. You couldn't *be* more mistaken. Assuming Freeland matters, this matters enormously."

"Let's say, just for argument's sake, that Hannibal loses, and Nonni and his lot step in. We all live with the aftermath, don't we? The future goes on, doesn't it? Or Hannibal somehow wins, and he holds on for five more years, and then Nonni and his lot, or someone just like him with a similar lot, step in. It comes to the same thing, doesn't it? You're fighting a rearguard action, the two of you, but in this battle you're not fighting the Danes, or even the Eskimos. You're fighting the future, and that's a battle nobody has ever won. Not even someone as brutally clever as you, Pabbi, not even someone as magnificently mad as Hannibal Hannibalsson."

When I'd first stepped into this room and glimpsed my daughter in her blue-green pajamas, she'd looked less like someone about to have a child than like a child herself. And now she was dispensing wisdom at me—and the truth was, there was wisdom aplenty in what she had to say. Her new role distanced the girl from me. . . . My daughter was journeying off on her own, so that it made perfect sense, it seemed to follow naturally, when she said, "I'm going to miss this crazy country. . . ."

"You speak as though you were leaving it."

"For a while. After the baby's born. Helmut and I have decided to go to Germany."

"Germany?"

"He thinks there's more opportunity there."

"Doubtless that's right. But opportunity for what?"

"For something like a normal life?"

"Germany? *That's* normalcy? I'll miss you, Lilja," I added. "I sometimes feel as though I'm getting too old to be left alone."

"You won't be left alone. You'll have Sindri."

"I've been looking forward to playing with my granddaughter."

"Your grandson. Trust me. Trust my female intuition. And we'll be back, or you can come visit."

"I think I *like* the idea of a granddaughter."

"You'll have to be very patient then. After this boy's born, we're going to wait awhile."

"Maybe Sindri will supply me with one."

"Not very likely. Let's face . . . Pabbi, it's— Look: about Sindri. Look: Sindri's *gay*."

Gay: she too had had recourse to English.

Gay she'd said and my first coherent thought—amid all the detonations in my head—was that she might not understand the term's vulgar slang sense.

The light in the hospital room thickened. It was still bright in here, truly as white as ever, but a sort of fog had set in, and like a man in a fog I proceeded slowly, tentatively: "I don't think I see what you mean."

"Pappalingur, he's a homosexual."

"But that's impossible," I told her.

"Impossible?" Lilja laughed. "How in the world impossible?"

But I'd no sooner spoken the word than I'd begun to feel just how *possible* it was. In my mind's eye I beheld that face of his, lingering in the doorway, wordlessly saying to me, *I beseech you*, and there was to Lilja's announcement a narrow and fatal logic. Of course. Of course. Wasn't this only the final corroboration of all the inklings I'd had over the years that the boy wasn't in fact my flesh and blood?

"Are you absolutely sure?" I asked her.

"Sure I'm sure." And Lilja laughed once more—she seemed to find the whole subject greatly entertaining. "Don't tell me you're going to be a bigot about this *too*?"

In the face of the revised future so abruptly revealed to me, my heart sank like any stone. I'd been looking forward to seeing the boy pass on— or perhaps I had better say pass through. I'd looked forward, that is, to the day when he graduated from his state of perpetual need and the importunate look departed his eyes and he no longer came to me seeking a "better relationship." A better relationship? Why hadn't I seen this coming? And why couldn't the two of us have had, instead, a *normal* relationship—in which he eventually cursed and discarded his father just as, long years ago, I'd learned to curse and abandon the man who had abandoned me? Surely it's one of the cruelest, slyest tricks that fate ever deals out: to burden a truly sensitive man with a "sensitive" son. Good Christ, Sindri was *never* going to pass on, to pass through, to graduate to a less needful state. . . .

"But how long have you known, Lilja?"

"Oh in some ways I suppose since he first came to Freeland. Age fifteen. My unexpected brother. He didn't really turn candid about it, though, until a couple months ago. For a long time I don't think *he* knew what he was. This isn't the easiest place to be gay, Pabbi."

"A couple of months ago? The boy has said absolutely nothing to me. . . ."

"He's tried to. A number of times. He says you evade him. He wondered in fact whether you already knew, and for some reason didn't want to discuss it. . . ."

Knew? Evaded him? Where in the world had he come up with such notions—what was going on in his *head*?

"He thought maybe you'd guessed when he moved in with Dag."

"With whom?"

"His friend Dag. The Norwegian, the linguist."

I now remembered having seen him once—Dag, the Norwegian linguist. It was in the Cod's Head. It was that ominous night when Hannibal had been preparing to break the news of his plans to Rut, and Sindri had entered with a little bespectacled boy who wore a wispy mustache.

"Sindri moved in with his friend because of a burst water pipe in his own apartment," I explained to her.

"That's true. Or it was initially. But he stayed two months. . . ."

And I'd been in Dag's flat. Not with Sindri but with Lilja. She had led me there to retrieve a sweater. Or so she'd said. But she'd used the site to announce her pregnancy.

"And Dag?" I said.

"He's gone back to Norway."

"And Sindri? Is he going away too?"

"Oh I wish he *would!* He needs a change. But I'm afraid Sindri these days is more Sindri than ever. Doing his job, never wanting to go out. Wearing more and more black and getting paler and paler. As I told you at the start of this conversation, if you want to worry about one of your children, *he's* the one."

But wasn't Sindri, in effect, beyond the point of worry? It—worry— implies some small measure of hope. Worry cherishes the possibility that by dint of careful fretting the gods of catastrophe can be fended off and some unlikely happy ending can be arrived at. But what possible happy ending was to be written for Sindri? Here was a young man, implausibly claiming me as a father, who spent his days casting fish into a computer and his nights mooning over a dapper Norwegian with a scraggly mustache. Lilja talked on, we both talked on for some time, but my heart was, as we Freelanders say, valleyed elsewhere. I kissed her good-bye—my dear blue-pajamaed little girl, my sage instructress—and went out again into the corridor.

And down at the other end, costumed in his undertaker's vestments, stood—oh, good Lord, would this night never stop?—Sindri. What was he doing here, at this ungodly hour?

He was—well of course he'd come to visit his sister. And yet . . . and yet there was something sinister, all the same, about his appearance. He was chatting with a woman in white, a nurse, and I was sure he hadn't yet spotted me. The two of them, the man in widower's black and the woman in bridal white, were waiting for me at the end of the long corridor.

My immediate impulse was, naturally, to turn the other way—to swing around and beat a quick retreat down the back stairs. . . . But after one quick glance over my shoulder, which did in fact reveal a clear escape, I changed my mind. No, I would face the boy straight on. I started marching toward him.

And as I went forward, the strangest thing in the world began to unfold: he melted away, my son.

As I advanced, he became somebody else entirely, a young man who looked very little like Sindri. . . .

And was I, like ancient Thorgunnur in her room in the Eldershelter, going blind? Twice—twice tonight, and both times in this very spot, my eyes had played a trick upon me. . . .

The conversation at the end of the long corridor broke up. The nurse vanished behind a door. As the young man came toward me I saw that he wasn't even a young man. Middle-aged. He was carrying an open tool box, out of which projected the claw end of a hammer. A workman, come to make some sort of repair.

Oh, but no ordinary workman! My reading in my nation's folklore runs deep, its images are no less in my blood than my leukocytes and hemoglobin, and as he trudged in my direction, aging visibly with each step, I recognized this figure for what he was: some variety of troll. By the time he was half a dozen paces from me, he was my age, at least, and were we to converse for a few minutes it would become evident he was as old as the hills—that he, with his troll's bag of tools, had *built* the hills, in whose bowels he now resided.

"It's late to be making repairs," I noted, and nodded at his tool kit.

His reply was just as gnomic and portent-rich as I could have wished: "It's never late to be making repairs. Water pipes keep late hours."

Was he, too, relishing the exchange? Didn't I catch behind the gruffness of his words a supernatural glint in his eye?

"It's good to know you're keeping the roof over our heads."

"Oh, the roof's coming down. Make no mistake about that. It's all just a question of when."

IV

41

Two More Dead Gulls?

Snow on this fourth of September plummets out of a gray and wind-less sky, homing earthward with a weighted urgency, straight as rain, onto the bare heads of the expanding little crowd, some of them singing and some mute; onto the empty bottles and the shattered glass that confess to another night of excess; onto that oxidizing error-prone explorer Erik the Other; onto the gloved hand of the piccolist; onto the tight brassy intestines of the trumpet; into the open, receptive throat of the tuba, whose lugubrious thumpings once more set the windows resounding on the far side of Independence Square. The singing is heartbroken, for we have suffered one more loss, at least, and maybe two losses—the second of them far too big to shoulder. Our mourning is perplexed and fearful. We are puny souls huddling underneath a cruel, cavernous, capacious sky. We do not know yet the full extent of the blow, but if our worst suspicions are confirmed, how in the world will we bear up?

Snow has just begun to fall. The large, adhesive flakes settle in with certainty, with seeming finality—they will never melt. Grief's come plunging down and our spirits are shattered. The bells in Mariners' Church only make it official: the final Ice Age is upon us, when Freeland will lie soundless and still, as painstakingly encased in ice and snow as, once, Pompeii in stone and ash.

In our uneasiness, in our fresh pain, we crave the reassurance to be found only in solemnity of the old high style. . . . And so we wait, hope-fully, needfully, for the sole figure who can right us. No one in Indepen-dence Square doubts that the role of speaker belongs to Hannibal Hannibalsson. The man who has declared himself Hannibal's opponent is also to be found in the Square—yes, there's Nonni Karlsson, over there, hunching in a new knee-length burnt-sienna leather coat in front of Ursula's Bakery—but nobody thinks to look to him. Doubtless, he scarcely thinks to look to himself. No less than the others, he is feeling depleted and fazed and destitute. He, too, is instinctively hoping that Hannibal Hannibalsson will come forward to poultice our collective hurt.

Hannibal stands alone, at the periphery of the crowd, out on the wheel of concrete that encircles the statue of Erik the Other. He spits, frowns, scratches at his ear, grinds a shard of glass underfoot. Snow collects in his thinning red hair. Nobody approaches him. Everyone understands he is gathering his words together—he is preparing to assist us. Now the makeshift, ragtaggle members of the Society for the Redemption of the Damned break into our national anthem, and Hannibal lifts his head and joins in with the rest of us:

> These are our boulders
> These are our hills
> These are our home-fields
> These are our seas.
> Stormy and smooth
> Stormy and smooth
> These are the seas of Freeland.

Hannibal draws a handkerchief from the pocket of his greatcoat. A small object clatters to the sidewalk—evidently something he'd wrapped up inside it. What is it? He peers quizzically at his feet, identifies the gray object as a chicken drumstick, and, satisfied, wipes his mouth with the handkerchief and launches into the second verse:

> Here are our homesteads
> Here are our farms
> Here is our lych-gate,
> Home to the fallen.
> Standing and fallen
> Standing and fallen
> We are the friends of Freeland.

When Hannibal steps forward, hobbling a little on his early-morning knees, the music, instrument by instrument, ceases. He positions himself in front of the musicians, directly across from rust-eaten, snow-fringed Erik the Other. The crowd in response forms a horseshoe shape around him. Everybody is silent. Help us, Hannibal. These are our hard hours and you must reconcile us to our loss.

Hannibal's looking rumpled and disheveled, as if freshly roused from bed. His face is saggy and baggy and splotchy with—presumably—last night's overindulgence. His text this morning must be, in part, the sorrows and perils of alcohol, which he can be expected to address with the subdued authenticity of the man whose skull is pounding and whose belly seethes with those lively little snakes whose transparent, invisible eggs gestate in bottles of high-potency spirits.

"As most of you know by now," he begins, mildly, levelly, "a body was dragged this morning out of the Two Day River. This was one of us, this was one of our countrymen, and we are all diminished by the loss."

He pauses. Around the corner, the bells are ringing the alarm in Mariners' Church and people are stumbling out of their houses, not quite dressed, into Independence Square. A television crew has arrived.

"One of *us*, one of our *own*, was dragged this morning out of the Two Day River, and this is not the first time a brave Freelander has gone there to his death. When we mourn the dead today, we mourn as well all those who have ever fallen there. . . ."

Was he thinking of the man who might be referred to as his common-law father-in-law? Old Bjartur Jonsson, Rut's father, who one blizzarding night drowned in the Two Day while seeking a missing lamb? And would Rut hear these words? And accept them as a peace offering?

"But *this* time, the tragedy has a special power and a special poignancy. For this was one of our children. This was a sixteen-year-old boy."

So far as I knew, I'd never laid eyes on this boy, whose name was Thorsteinn Thorsteinnsson. Few seem to have known him and through the crowd the bare-bones summary of a life has been rapidly circulating: he was one of the many bastard children of Thorsteinn Loftsson, who fled our shores years ago for Norway. The boy was something of a trouble-maker and last year he'd had to pay a sizable fine for spray-painting a tobacconist's window. And he'd been homely, with his incorrigible father's pinched pig-eyes. An indifferent student. It was said he sold drugs.

The charges mounted. . . . We collected them eagerly, for it was with just such smug unkindnesses that we initially sought to mitigate our sense of loss and responsibility. And having successfully diminished the boy, we now look to Hannibal Hannibalsson to elevate him. These are the two sides of our reconciliation.

Twice, twice in these last few months we have suffered a blow like this—in fact, the last one occurred two months ago to the day. July fourth, and snow falling on that morning, too. In each case, it's a loss all the more grievous for being wholly unnecessary. For the truth about last night, as best as we've been able to reconstruct it, is that the boy was wandering along the banks of the Two Day in a state of deep inebriation. He'd slipped and fallen in.

"Yes, he had been *drinking*." Hannibal delivers the word unflinchingly—we take it square in the face, as a slaplike reprimand we fully deserve. "A sixteen-year-old drunk boy wandered toward the Two Day, slipped, and there is one life gone forever. Thus do we lose one of our children."

Another pause. Elbows into neighbors' sides and quick, relayed whispers. The grieving mother has arrived. She stands by the entrance to the Hotel Snorri, an ashen-faced woman in a threadbare ash-gray coat, half among us and half on the outside, meeting our furtive glances with a face of twitching abasement. Her look says, *I deserve your censure.*

It seems as though Hannibal, in his plainspoken condemnation, is now prepared to spell out what is apparent to most of the men, certainly, and perhaps to many of the women as well: what must have happened last night is that this boy Thorsteinn, while a passenger in a friend's car, had felt a sudden need to urinate. They'd been drinking heavily, the two boys, as the empty bottle of vodka found this morning in the front seat attested. They'd stopped just below the bridge over the Two Day, and Thorsteinn, heeding that universal male desire to conjoin his waters with greater waters, had wandered down toward the bank of the river, where he'd misstepped. End of story.

But Hannibal says nothing about what might have led the boy to the bank of the river. He takes another tack—a comfortingly familiar line: "What are we to think when we contemplate the corpse of a sixteen-year-old boy who drowned because he'd had too much to drink? What are we to feel as we stand before his not-yet-full-grown body? Does this corpse mean anything more to us than a dead salmon washed ashore? More than a smashed dead gull by the side of the road? I say to you surely *it does not*, the dead boy means not a jot more than a dead salmon, he means nothing more than a dead gull—"

Pause. We know this particular rhetorical caesura and we're grateful for it. As the snow continues to plummet and the bells to ring, our glances volley back and forth: to the stricken mother, to our neighbors, to the seasoned orator.

"—unless we make of our pain a better commonwealth. Ours has been from the outset a country of grinding hardships, and of uncertain futures. Ours is a land where Death, as the old proverb tells us, is always a near-neighbor. I repeat: this is not the first body our rivers have swallowed. The challenge we have always had to confront, and always shall confront, is this: how are we best to love a land that treats us so harshly? How love a land that now and then destroys our children? Until we've answered these questions, the dead boys are dead fish, they are dead gulls, and they have died for nothing.

"Now listen to me: this is the second such death in only a few months. We had another on July fourth. *One* dead boy, *two* dead boys, and perhaps I should not stop at two. For we face this morning the possibility of another death, don't we?"

And here a whisper, a whimper issues from the crowd. We cringe before him, for Hannibal has delicately prodded at our central, our insupportable grief. We can reconcile ourselves to the death of a useless pig-eyed vandal like this Thorsteinn Thorsteinnsson, whom most of us had never heard of before this morning anyway. But it appears that Thorsteinn was with another boy, who is still missing. We may be confronting this morning not one teenager's death but two.

"In the face of such a tragedy we must ask ourselves, Where are we to find the strength to preserve our nation's young? Where do our safeguards lie? Imagine, if you will, that a native islander from the Pacific South Seas were suddenly dropped in our midst. He would naturally suppose he understood island life. He would know all about winds and currents and small-scale farming, and he would say to us, Your climate is too severe for survival. He would say, Your stony soil is too meager for survival. He would say, Your seas are too rough for survival."

Even while Hannibal is delivering his oration, an extensive and frantic search is being conducted, up and down the raw terrain alongside the Two Day River. Though ours is a treeless land, there are surprisingly many places where the body of a boy—alive or dead—might conceal itself. Our lava fields are everywhere riven and cratered, there are boulders and depressions, cairns and crevices.

"And how would we answer him? We would answer him with the

best answer there is, for we would say, *But we have survived*. And how have we survived?"

Some hundred meters up from the spot where Thorsteinn Thorsteinnsson's body was discovered, an empty car was found. It was Vikram Jakobsson's solar-yellow Mustang convertible.

"We have survived through pride of place, have we not? Survived through a determination that our lives were to be built right *here*, and not in America, and not in any South Sea island."

Yes, the possibility we're confronting this morning—or would be confronting were it not so hurtful, so horrifying—is that the comeliest boy in all of Freeland has been taken from us. The enchanted prince, the one who was brought to these islands from an antipodal domain—the legendary hellhole called Calcutta—who was adopted not merely by carbuncled Jakob and chinless Perla but by the nation as a whole, may have perished last night, and how are we to survive a revelation of this sort?

"We have pledged ourselves to the ongoing business of creating the sovereign nation of Freeland, and this is the only resolution that can protect our children when the storms howl and the rivers are in spate."

Old Perla, Vikram's mother—the homeliest mother in all of Freeland—also hovers at the crowd's edge. *She* meets no one's eyes, not that anyone can bear to look at her. She has fixed her gaze in the sky above Hannibal's head. That queer, unsettling nest of flesh in her throat, that sickening sac of tissue floating where her chin would be if she had a chin, is all atremble. In truth, at this moment it's as though none of us has any bones, we are all of us quivering sacs of flesh, shivering in the falling snow. . . .

If Vikram Jakobsson didn't drown, where could he be? His car was abandoned in the middle of nowhere, a mile away from the nearest farmhouse, where nobody has seen hide or hair of him. He is not asleep in their barn. The most plausible explanation—or, at least, the best hope we have—is that the boy wandered off, as drunk as his companion, and came to rest on a bed of moss somewhere. The night not having been *terribly* cold, he might well have survived it. . . .

But already a dark shadow has affixed itself to his gliding form. Wasn't it *wrong* to bring the boy here from Calcutta? Isn't it *clear* he wasn't meant to live among us? Already our grief is vitiated by a bitter sense of betrayal: we feel tricked. After all, what was that surpassing physical beauty of his except a ruse? That loose-limbed loping walk, for instance, which marked him, even a hundred yards off, as an authentic exotic among us—what but a ploy designed to burst our hearts? She has done it to us twice, Perla Juliusdottir, that stubborn, chinless bitch of a woman: has twice smuggled into our midst an irresistible creature that wasn't *meant* for us. She deserves in this miserable hour of trial not our empathy but our execration.

Snow falls straight down, putting up no fight against the primal call of gravity, and the only thing upholding *us*, keeping the crowd, too, from falling prostrate to the ground, is the red-faced hungover man who hurls his willful futilities across the frozen Square.

"There is a proverb," Hannibal says, lifting his gaze to contemplate the Mountain in the distance, his voice at last beginning to vault over our heads, "an old saying among our farmers that Freeland will not truly be ours until there's been a death for each and every snowflake on Great Blue Glacier. The land will exact nothing less of the people who came here a millennium ago, who came here in Viking ships, to claim her. At times like this, I'm mindful of that proverb. Could it be that in Freeland, anyway, there are no deaths in vain? Each one, you see, each death, however heart-breaking, brings us ever so slightly closer to that day when we have paid for the land in full and made her ours."

And has Hannibal invented the proverb on the spot? It's something that I, a student of such things, have never heard before. . . . And what does its provenance matter, when he has truly for a moment steeled and ennobled us? His words have unlaced a knot within us, and now we can spare some minimal sympathy for Thorsteinn Thorsteinnsson's mother, however wayward and irresponsible her behavior, now we would pardon even chinless Perla, from whose misshapen head oily tears have begun to leak. . . .

"We are in the midst of an election," Hannibal Hannibalsson begins anew, and the crowd immediately shifts, it grows uneasy. Surely—surely he isn't about to use Vikram Jakobsson's death for his own political advantage? Thorsteinn Thorsteinnsson is one thing—the boy was a delinquent. A budding sociopath. A drug addict. But our Vikram, he who day after day cruised among us in a yellow Mustang brighter than our feeble northern sun, he who in his yellow Mustang *was* our sun and our son—no, no, he mustn't be appropriated in this way. . . .

"It is a time of bitterness. A time of divisions that have come to re-semble hatreds. But on a morning such as *this*, faced with losses like *these*, it's surely apparent to everyone that our communality runs far deeper than our differences. And that is why"—and Hannibal Hannibalsson begins, limping slightly, to stride across the Square. Where is he headed? He is

THE FRIENDS OF FREELAND / 378

headed toward Nonni Karlsson, who stands goggle-eyed before him—
"that is why I would ask each of you this morning to turn and approach
whoever it is from whom you have grown distanced or estranged, anyone
with whom you've let a barrier grow up. For these are the moments when
our nation must come together."

And the roused crowd swings this way and that way, hungrily seeking
out the very figures it heretofore sought to avoid—and in particular hungry to express, one after another, with tears and sighs, our affection for
dear Perla, our sympathy for poor dear Thorsteinn's mother.

Meanwhile, the old politician has extended his hand to the
younger

—and Nonni lunges forward, clasps the hand offered him, and with
his other hand seizes Hannibal by the arm. Nonni looks transfixed: he is
thrilled. Clearly, no less than anyone else in the snowy Square, he *loves* the
older man. Nonni does not long to defeat him so much as to feel himself—flesh to flesh—in possession of the President's incomparable respect
and approbation.

42

Banishment Management

Restive and irresolute. Gnawed at, needy. Morose, remorseful, needled by grief-pin-pricklings that seem the harbingers of a pervasive, paralyzing despair. Warily Eggert wanders the streets of Thorskrist, playing a weary middle-aged-man's version of Twenty Down. This one's called "Twenty Downed." Like Twenty Down, it makes use of an uninhabited island. In this version, you're a mainland emperor who, like Aegeus, is compelled to send away from your nation a set number of citizens each year. Twenty. But in your case no harm will come to them—no ravenous Minotaur waits at the other end. They will simply be sent Away, forever. Off they go, to an uncharted tropical isle, where the twenty of them will pass their natural lives together.

The possibilities are manifold and allow for plentiful mischief. In order to keep the islanders on their toes you might, just for fun, place in their midst one sociopathic criminal, or one seething schizophrenic. Or you may decree that the group of twenty shall be exclusively male, thereby eliminating any possibility of regeneration. Or you might restrict the group to twenty employees of *The Daily Liar*—sending them off to snoop and snitch on each other into perpetuity.

Grief swims across the skies. Every hour on the hour, for ten straight minutes, the bells in Mariners' Church resound, tolling our loss and the promise of further, catastrophic loss; neither Vikram nor Vikram's body has yet materialized. The yellow Mustang convertible has been returned to his parents' house. Teams of searchers—on foot, on horseback—continue to comb the countryside.

Eggert on this snowy and rainy Saturday morning wanders over to what he sometimes facetiously refers to as his "annex office"—the Hotel

Snorri, where a lifetime ago he first met Constance Q. Simple. He orders a thermos of coffee. It's not yet noon. The day is early yet. Should he be out ransacking the hills? Vikram's disappearance has left him feeling illogically guilty. Not long ago, in an Amsterdam located in the Land of Dreams, Vikram—or Vikram's car—came barreling down on Eggert. . . . Is Eggert now culpable, or can he plead self-defense, if Vikram last night drowned in the Two Day River?

Eggert is staring forlornly out the hotel window onto Independence Square, languidly playing Twenty Downed. He dispatches to the tropical island the Puppetmaster, that bastard Ulvar Ormsson, who in a hundred lifetimes will still not be forgiven for depicting Eggert as an SS officer. The image of Ulvar seeking to pursue his "craft" with native, island-grown materials—trying to construct puppets out of banana leaves, palm fiber, coconut shells, fish scales, volcanic mud—is utterly delicious and Eggert sips gratefully from his coffee.

He banishes next Nonni Karlsson, who is less to be disliked than pitied perhaps, a simpleminded sailor launched on trickier currents than he can negotiate. It's all a question of scale; Nonni is too small for the role he aspires to. In truth, he would make an *ideal* President for the tropical Isle of Twenty, and isn't it in fact less malice than a sort of sage kindness that prompts Eggert to ship Nonni to his new, unmapped home?

He bids adieu next to the Norwegian, Dag the linguist, who has guided Eggert's hapless son toward a path that can only be disastrous. It would be a real pity, of course, if the band of twenty included someone who subscribed to Dag's appetites—a pity, that is, if the Island became a place of diverse sexual gratifications. Far, far better if Dag could find no partners—or at least should find only those who yielded to him limply and shamefully.

Eggert also exiles a stranger, Pall Sigtrygsson, a name attached to a recent review in *The Daily Liar* which concluded, "The forty-odd books that Eggert Oddason has constructed are a wall that must be dismantled to let the sun in once more." There isn't a young writer in the country who would openly admit to admiring Eggert's books—but then there isn't, in the last analysis, a young writer in the country. And while Eggert is at it, he banishes the four top names on *The Daily Liar* masthead—Editor in Chief, Chief Editor, Deputy Editor, Senior Editor. This brings us to, let's see, a total of eight on the Isle of Twenty.

Across Independence Square meanders Mrs. Thieu, a blue plastic bag in one hand and a red plastic bag in the other. Why *is* the woman never glimpsed without a burden under her arms? She's looking not merely abstracted but utterly lost, although she has lived in Freeland for a couple of decades now. Most of them have departed—those Vietnamese refugees we harbored in the seventies, back when Hannibal grandly talked about Thorskrist's "Little Saigon."

The fall of—Little—Saigon was a piecemeal process, as one or another of our refugees found further refuge in Canada, the States, France. Most of those few who still remain manage, like Mrs. Thieu, to look congenitally disoriented. Has anyone told her that Vikram Jakobsson is missing and that another boy has been found dead? Does she understand why the bells are sounding? One might send *her* to the Isle of Twenty purely as a favor. Perhaps it might recall to her those comprehensible purlieus she mislaid twenty years ago and has been seeking ever since. . . .

Instead, I dispatch my downstairs neighbor, a determinedly dejected and homely woman whose breathtakingly jubilant coital cries, penetrating the carpeted floor of my bedroom, have sometimes kept me awake. To keep her company, I send also her sullen, sallow teenaged daughter, last seen cracking a smile a decade ago, on her sixth birthday. Perhaps the sun will do the girl some good. . . . We have reached ten. Our Isle of Exile is half full.

I send as number eleven Michael McKaig, who once rubbed bald a patch of my scalp. Strictly speaking, he doesn't belong on the Island; technically, the Rules of Banishment Management allow us to traffic only in those known to be still alive. I justify his inclusion on the basis of an intuition. Somehow, though I haven't seen him in a third of a century, I feel confident he's still among the living—just as I feel that his wife, dear starcrossed Meggy, is in her grave. Pickled—preserved—in alcohol, Michael continues to smoke and stink, to bully and swagger, and my wrath is such that even now I want to call out after him, as the ship carrying him toward the Isle that will be his grave pulls away from the wharf, *I burned those holes in your shirt.* . . . And, *I could have blinded you as you lay there in your drunken stupor.*

Eggert sends also to the Isle the electrician whose recent repairs to the apartment have resulted in one blown fuse after another—*May you devote the rest of your life to wiring the coconut trees*—and by way of providing him with companionship also sentences Hallbera of Hallbera's Laundry, who two years ago could not bring herself to apologize after losing his favorite necktie. Perhaps they might jointly open some sort of shop. . . . Twelve, thirteen.

The Island fills, but his heart is hardly in it. . . . Eggert's gaze sweeps out over empty Independence Square. Lost Mrs. Thieu and her plastic bags are gone; she has carted her confusion elsewhere. But there stands rusty Erik the Other, who was lost, too, when he chanced on Freeland. There are days, I'd swear, when it seems we are the original Island of Lost Souls. The skies have shifted and it's begun—halfheartedly—to rain. At this very moment, are icy drops plopping down on the bare, beautiful, unfeeling features of Vikram Jakobsson, lying with face upturned in some shallow ravine, whose choice of a resting place was the final decision of his life?

Eggert thinks about banishing Helmut, his son-in-law, but reluctantly decides against it. No use making a martyr of the boy; better to wait for Lilja to eject him on her own.

As a way of hurrying things along, he adds a foursome to his list: Oskar Magnusson, the present editor of Great Blue Press and the son of the late, perpetually pipe-puffing Magnus Ingisson, who has doubtless found even the environs of Hell not smoky enough for his liking. For good measure, Eggert dispatches Oskar's three sons, each less literary than his predecessor. Were they allowed to remain, Freelandic publishing would be assured, for another generation, of dim-wittedness at the top.

That brings him to seventeen. Three to go . . . Across Independence Square trudges Gudrun's husband Baldur, and the first word that rings in Eggert's head is *eighteen!* But with a closer look at Baldur something unusual occurs.

It's just like the core of a three-minute egg when you lift off its crisp white cap with a serrated knife and confront its tremulous goldness bare: that's what Eggert's heart is like. For years and years—indeed, ever since Twenty Downed was first invented—Baldur has unwittingly been a regular participant. Eggert has banished him repeatedly, sent him off by boat and plane and kayak and iceberg. Baldur's offenses are plain to see. He deserves banishment, first and foremost, for having stolen from Eggert the one woman who, in her limitless sweetness of temperament, might actually have made a better man of him. He deserves banishment for his hapless, recurrent business failures. For his ever-softening plumpness. For his careless baldness.

And yet, watching Baldur from behind as he trudges hatless across the Square, wet and stoop-shouldered with worries, Eggert for the first time in his life actually sympathizes with the man. Gudrun seems to be dying. Baldur is about to become a widower.

But sympathy is followed immediately by another irrepressible emotion, hard to name, an ambition which mixes triumph and self-pity. And what *is* the matter with Eggert's brain? Why does he now find himself enthusiastically scheming up ways that he might, side by side with Baldur, be appointed one of Gudrun's pallbearers?

43

Providential

At noon, haranguing bells wrangle with bells. The clocktower in Mariners' Church begins its ten-minute call of alarm, a hybrid cry of mourning and warning, which is temporarily challenged by the bells in Starri's Church, down by the pier. Vikram has not yet been found.

I'm awakened from the reverie induced by the sight of stoop-shouldered Baldur and suddenly cannot bear to sit any longer in the Hotel Snorri. I need to be off—but where? An overmastering sorrow threatens to engulf the whole country and perhaps at such times the only sensible policy is to carry on just as you'd intended. My original plan for the day had included a drive over to the airport, where, according to Nonni's staff, an election "surprise" is to be unveiled. So I step out into the cold rain and climb into my Volvo. What will happen—assuming the boy is dead—to Vikram's sunny Mustang? Will it be sold? Preposterous as the vehicle is, the thought of anyone else owning it and cruising our streets in it is more than preposterous: unimaginable.

To the rower's beat of my windshield wipers I steer my thoughts elsewhere. What might Nonni's "surprise" consist of? The flight's arriving from Denmark. Most likely, the news is commercial—Nonni has managed to cajole over to our shores some well-heeled Dane, to dangle before us a new soft-drink bottling plant or a new market for woolen blankets . . . provided, naturally, that the fine people of Freeland demonstrate the good sense to elect an administration more hospitable to foreign investment than its predecessors. Or has Nonni hooked up with some Japanese? A reciprocal trade agreement, wherein we're to be supplied with the latest in fish-processing plants and they—whose compact bodies conceal an ungodly, monstrous appetite for seafood—are guaranteed another ocean-depleting round of meals?

The "surprise," in any event, is destined to undergo an eclipse. Nonni and Co. had doubtless been hoping their coy announcement would draw a gaggle of curiosity-seekers. But the airport's all but empty. The crowds are dispersed, either combing the hills for a boy's body or, stationed in their homes, awaiting news on the radio. Nonni had probably been hoping for a television crew, but those cameras are elsewhere, in search of a story far larger than any election "surprise." The single cameraman at the airport is, oddly, one of ours, and he carries only a Nikon. It's the drunk, Trausti, Hannibal's friend and the closest thing our hopelessly bedraggled campaign has to an official photographer. What brings him out here? The moment I spot him, I swerve into a chair and bury myself behind a hastily erected wall of newspaper. A minute later my wall rustles. I lower the paper and find myself staring full into Trausti's pickled features.

"Eggert!" he calls jubilantly.

"Trausti," I say.

"What are you doing here?"

"Well, Trausti, I'm expecting a mail-order bride from Kathmandu. What are you doing?"

"I'll let you in on a little secret. . . ."

"Don't feel you have to."

"I'm keeping an eye on *him*."

"On whom?"

Trausti cups one hand and places it—a sort of umbrella—atop the other. Within its shelter, he extends from the lower hand a gingerly index finger. He's pointing, evidently, at Nonni, who stands across the waiting room, looking both mournful and petulant, like a child who has just learned his birthday party must be canceled because the family house burned down.

"I'm tailing him," Trausti whispers.

"Tailing him?"

"You just wait. He'll slip up somewhere. And when he does? Trausti will be there." And Trausti actually winks at me. There is something amusing and appealing, and also drainingly sad, in the relish he takes in his own ingenuity, and what am I to conclude about myself when I consider how virtually everybody else associated with Hannibal's campaign is naïve and arrogant and *stupid*?

I don't manage to get rid of Trausti until the aircraft, only twenty minutes late, alights. It's a DHC-7, a fifty-seat prop plane. In deference to the rain, the pilot taxis in as close as he can to the waiting room, through whose windows I watch the door of the plane swing open. Down the stairway they come, the international travelers.

Will the "surprise" be identifiable on its face? Freelanders one after another disembark. It's interesting what little things go into making up a nation, details often so minuscule they're daily overlooked. For I discover now—or recognize now, for I suppose I've known this all my life—that there's a characteristically Freelandic way of stepping into rain. Others, the world over, might huddle against it—particularly against a rain as cold as this one. We tend toward another approach. The chin comes up, the heavens are surveyed skeptically, as if to say, *You presume to call this rain?*, and we march forth with a proud obtuse obliviousness on our faces.

Nor would I have supposed, I suppose, that in motions so basic as the descent from an airplane one could reveal oneself instantly as an American. But here come three men, Americans all, though physically they could hardly be more unlike: the first tall and blond, broadly grinning; the second balding and pudgy, with an anxious, darting look on his face; the third short and bespectacled, his soft, round Asian features further softened and rounded by fatigue. I can identify the nationality of each merely by the way he disembarks from an airplane, just as I identify them, instantly, as the "surprise."

The first off the plane and the one I take to be the leader—the blond one, the tall one—reaches the ground and makes a quick reconnaissance. Our airport lies in the middle of a lava field and the terrain answering his glance is scarred, crannied, pitted, lunarly lifeless. Dismay clouds his features, but briefly. His smile snaps back into place. He gives the impression of having a more-than-human number of teeth—like a shark's dentition, teeth behind teeth in tidy, carnivorous rows.

Bypassing the customs-and-passport-inspection booth, which is unaccountably empty, our would-soon-be-king, Nonni Karlsson, and some half a dozen members of his would-be court make their way onto the tarmac to offer greetings and introductions. I watch through the waiting-room window. Out on the windswept rainswept asphalt, handshakes and greetings are exchanged.

When the little crowd shuffles into the waiting room, awkwardness and uncertainty devolve into paralysis. What's next? Then a second cameraman bumbles eagerly forward. I don't know him; clearly, he's "one of theirs." For the benefit of the camera, new handshakes are extended, frozen ones. Click. But there is no flash.

The cameraman wears a jolly, dopey expression and my happy thought is that he, too, may be drunk. With luck, the pictures will be as blurry as his features. He tinkers with his camera, while the Americans look on uneasily. The tall blond man holds a smile. The Asian yawns. The short, pudgy man pats one pocket after another of his coat, sportscoat, and pants, finally unearthing a pack of cigarettes. He repeats the entire process and comes up with a lighter. He sets a cigarette into his mouth and has just brought the flaming lighter to his lips when the cameraman calls out: new pictures. The cigarette is stamped out on the floor. New handshakes are extended. There's another click, this one illuminated. Relieved laughter.

Nonni draws from his pocket a folded sheet of paper. He is pretending not to see me, but my hope is that my baleful stare will rattle him. "Dear People of Freeland," he begins.

If you subtract his half-dozen retainers, this is the meagerest of crowds. It consists of an aged stewardess who is wearing a pink ankle bandage, a seamed old man in a fisherman's sweater who is smoking a pipe and his seamed wife who is smoking a "lady's cigar," a skinny bespectacled black man who gives every impression of having landed in the wrong airport, and a young mother whose two little boys are dueling with swords made from the cardboard tubes of toilet paper rolls.

"Today I welcome to our country three specialists from the United States."

But isn't this a virtual redundancy? Is there anyone in America who is not a specialist?

"These three distinguished gentlemen, Mr. Kevin Wilhelm"—he nods at the blond one, with all the teeth—"Mr. Anthony Paradiso"—who has finally got his cigarette lighted, and as greeting to our nation blows a puff of smoke our way—"and Mr. Ken Kanekyu"—the sleepy-looking Asian. "They are electoral consultants."

Electoral consultants?

"This is probably the first time any electoral consultants have visited our land. It is certainly the first time any have come in a professional capacity. I consider this a great national honor.

"In keeping with the modern, innovative, reform-minded campaign I have waged from the outset," Nonni goes on, "I have brought these three gentlemen here: Mr. Wilhelm, Mr. Paradiso, and Mr. Kanekyu. My hope is that they will help me, in the exactly one month remaining before Election Day, to run the sort of modern, forward-looking campaign that all of you expect from me. Their job will be to help me to recognize and address your needs. I hope you will regard them, as I do, as servants of you the people. I would ask all of you now to join me in giving—"

Nonni halts, flustered. Doesn't his text call for a ringing round of applause? If so, as he only now discerns, he isn't likely to get it from a "crowd" of this variety. . . . After some throat-clearing, he recommences: "I'd ask you all to join me in welcoming these distinguished American gentlemen to our shores."

The two photographers, ours and theirs, each snap another picture. Theirs then dips into a black bag and withdraws a tape recorder. Evidently, he's meant to serve as interviewer too.

I'm beginning to like him. It's hard not to be charmed by the uncomprehending way he peers at the machine in his hands. He pokes at it with a wary index finger. A red light blinks, at which he nods emphatically, grins, and hoists the machine under one arm. He marches over to the visitors and stabs the attached microphone brusquely into Wilhelm's face: "What're you doing here?" he demands.

I suppose you'd have to say that, by and large, the interview is one of those modern art-forms we in Freeland have yet to master. On radio, on television, the artificiality of the whole business seems to balk us. We're just no good at it—the cheery dissembling stream of chatter during which you pose at a one-on-one conversation while steadily aiming your words elsewhere. So this thrusting of microphone into face is due less to the bumptiousness of drink, perhaps, than to a rational conviction that the fatuous burden of such an exchange ought fairly to fall on the party who is selling something—whatever that might be.

Wilhelm, after the most minute of pauses, screws his smile into place and says, "I'm very glad you asked me that. Our goals, it turns out, are quite specific. We see ourselves as detectives, actually. Modern-day Sherlock Holmeses. And what are we seeking? As detectives, what is our mission? You well might ask. Yep, you've asked a very good question. Our job is to locate the *hidden issues* in this campaign. Our job is to find the problems not being addressed, to find the discontentments not being dealt with. We're here to ensure that the beautiful democratic system you have here functions as it ought to. We're here to see that all of *you* have the system you deserve."

One of the two dueling children jabs his toilet-paper-roll-sword into his brother's eye, who wraps his hands around his skull and starts to keen. The scrupulously evenhanded mother thrashes each son twice on the side of the head, hard, and leads the two boys—both of them now knitting their hands around their skulls and howling—from the room.

"I have a saying about democracy," Wilhelm goes on. "Democracy is a party where everyone is invited. That's my saying: democracy is a party where everyone is invited. And our job is to see that as many people get to that party as possibly can. We hope to hold right here the biggest party in Freeland's history." Snowy sleet lashes the windowpanes. "Now you might well ask us how we hope to make sure that as many people get to our party as possible."

Wilhelm pauses with the surely justified assumption that his interviewer *will* ask. But the interviewer/photographer, showing admirable powers of abstraction, doggedly says nothing.

Fortunately for Wilhelm, his colleague Paradiso is suddenly bitten by curiosity. He says, "The biggest party in Freeland's history—how *do* you plan to do it, Kevin?"

"Well, Tony, our plan is to hit the ground running. We're planning to spend the first couple of days rubbing shoulders with the electorate down at the grass roots, not talking but *listening*. Our immediate goal will be to locate and quantify the focus groups. This will allow us to set up provisional data tables, with the help of Ken here, our numbers man, from which we can prioritize the leading issues." Sleepy Ken Kanekyu has a perfect oval of a face; the numbers man has a zero for a head. "By this means we will be able to quantify, scientifically, the sectors in which the present system is failing to address the—"

But what in hell is he talking about? Eggert prides himself on his command of idiomatic English, and on his long familiarity with political tactics, but he doesn't begin to grasp how the words issuing from Wilhelm's overtoothed mouth conform to any mappable reality. *What is this?*

"Is this a simple process, Kevin?" Paradiso asks his colleague.

"Oh it's never a *simple* process, Tony, because each political system has its own constellation of need-structures. That's where the importance of *listening* and *targeting* comes in. We're here to see that all conclusions are strictly subject to constant inputting. I have an expression for what we plan to do: we're going to *fix on the flux*. You know, it just now strikes me that the whole process is a lot like being a doctor, Tony."

"A doctor, Kevin?"

"On the one hand, you need a good bedside manner. You need to *listen* to what the patient is trying to tell you."

The patient? Is Freeland the patient?

"On the other hand, you need the very latest in research and equipment. That's why I say a *doctor*, Tony. We need to be one part old-fashioned general practitioner and one part technocrat."

"Yes," Tony cries. "I see what you're saying, Kevin."

And an exchange of looks between them. Both glance impatiently at the interviewer. He's apparently in the midst of quantifying the patterns the sleet makes against the window. Tony goes on, "You know I find myself wondering, Kevin. I know you've just arrived. But I find myself very curious to hear your first impressions of Freeland."

"Well, Tony, that's a very good question. It's immediately clear it's nothing like all the stereotypes, is it, Tony. Good God no. Forget the myths. Forget the myths. It's a much more complicated and interesting place than *that*. . . ."

The three Americans have come down from Heaven, surely. Supplied by Providence. Earlier in the day, not having the heart to banish Baldur, I'd stopped my game of Twenty Downed at seventeen. But these three are an inspiration. The propeller plane that carried them here? The one now shivering on the runway under a gray veil of sleety rain? Hurry. Restart the engines. It's time for a departure. Don't worry about topping up the gas tank. This will be a one-way flight. Eighteen, nineteen, twenty . . . I have filled up my Isle of Exile.

44

Dotty

He is being nagged at or lectured to, insistently and tediously, and even in his present condition he feels confident he can charm his way into some sort of reprieve. His gifts travel with him. This bright belief in himself penetrates even here, into the warm, shadowy, occasionally treacherous, natal land of dreams.

In his sleep he flutters one hand, disarmingly, a motion one part contrition and one part deft insouciance, and he smiles, shyly and winningly, at his persecutor.

But the nagging lecture goes on.

Again he flutters his hand, again he smiles, but still the haranguing continues, until his face undergoes a troubled dissolving alteration and his eyes flutter open.

He does not recognize the room he is in. His head is pounding, slightly. Bells are pounding. Bells—it is the *bells* nagging at him, they've been ringing and ringing, the bells of Mariners' Church, announcing news of another tragedy, but who or what could it be this time? Honestly, why are people forever making such messes of their lives?

He swings out from under the blanket and discovers he's naked from the waist down. He has an erection, a full one, risen so high it nearly touches his navel, though at the moment what it demands most pressingly is only a place to urinate. . . . Where is he? It doesn't matter, really, provided there's a toilet nearby. *Then* he can get around to figuring out where he has awakened this morning.

Or *is* it morning? Is it afternoon? What time is it?

Meanwhile, the erection poses a potential embarrassment, for there's no saying who might be encountered on the way to the toilet, but it's not enough of a problem, finally, to induce him to struggle with the wadded underwear on the floor. Hell, his head is hurting, a little.

And his throat's dry. In addition to a toilet, he needs a Coca-Cola, and maybe some french fries or pancakes to settle his rumbling stomach, and also he needs to figure out where he is. Lifting his T-shirt to scratch at the center of his hairless chest, he wanders down the dark hall, into a bathroom where he has to thrust his shoulders well forward in order to cant his stubbornly upright penis at a serviceable angle. Youth's swollen, heavy burdens compel him into an elderly stoop.

The very moment his hot urine finds the cold upper reaches of the bowl a variety of useful information revisits him. He recollects the outlines of the night before, if not every detail, and he has a pretty good guess whose house this must be. Eyjolfur's. He remembers swigging vodka with Eyjolfur in the parking lot behind the Cinemaharbor.

He examines himself in the mirror over the sink. The thick dark hair is tousled. Though the whiskers on his chin daily disappoint him—too sparse—he likes this stage of unshavenness: he has this morning an appealing careless stubble. Overindulgence in drink has brought a fair flush to his cheeks, and the effect of the ravages of the night before is, if anything, to render the most beautiful boy in Freeland yet more beautiful.

Still naked but for his T-shirt, Vikram pads back down the hall. He slides into the underwear on the floor, and into his pants—a pair of black jeans. But where's his shirt? He opens a door that turns out to be a closet. Whose clothes are these? He helps himself to some black socks. On the upper shelf a yellow sweater—almost the color of his car—catches his eye and he brings it down and holds it out, unfolded. A little large, but quite promising. Yellow suits him. It's one of his colors. He lifts his arms and throws the sweater over his head.

It turns out to be a little long in the sleeves, but these are all right once he rolls them up a couple of times. It's also large in the shoulders, but that's just fine: he likes this combination of tight jeans and baggy sweater. Perhaps he ought to leave some sort of note? Explain he'd borrowed an item or two? He locates his loafers—one by the door and one under the bed—and slips into them. His bottle-green suede coat is in the corner.

Gloves? Didn't he have some gloves? No matter—if he did he can come back for them. The bells of Mariners' Church are still jangling portentously, resonant with tragedy and woe, and as he throws the coat over his shoulders a woeful, a tragic suspicion stabs him straight on, in the forehead: Where is his car?

Where is his car? He taps—quickly, frantically—the pockets to his pants and his suede coat. A dim memory arises of—but could he really have lent out his *car?*

Suddenly a sense of emergency's upon him and on a born dancer's skimming feet he breezes downstairs. "Hullo, hullo, *hullo,*" he calls. The place is in long-standing disarray: newspapers, clothes, record albums, chess pieces, beer bottles. He bursts into a bedroom and calls, "Eyjolfur! Eyjolfur!"

But the body sleeping in the bed isn't Eyjolfur—Eyjolfur doesn't have blond hair, doesn't wear an earring. It's Jon Pall.

"Jon!" he calls. "Jon!"

"Mmm." Jon is lying on his back, with an army blanket thrown over him. His knees are up and an elbow is folded over his face. He does not remove the elbow.

Vikram gives his friend an urgent shake. "Jon Pall."

"Mmm?"

"Where's my *car?*" He gives his friend a more vigorous shake.

"Don't blame me."

"I'm not blaming you. Just tell me where it is."

"You lent it out."

"Lent it out? Who lent it out?"

"We did. You did. To Thorsteinn Thorsteinnsson. Remember? Exchange for a pint of vodka. Desperate—we were desperate."

"To *Thorsteinn Thorsteinnsson?*"

"Exchange for a pint of vodka. We were absolutely desperate."

"And where's the car now?"

"Out front, probably. He promised to drive it back. It's out front?"

"Are you sure? Where are the keys?"

Jon Pall still has not removed the elbow from his eyes. "In the car probably. Probably down the street. Thorsteinn's probably upstairs. Sleeping."

In an instant Vikram has flown back upstairs. He peers once more into the room where he'd slept—though surely Thorsteinn can't be in it—then throws open the door of the only place up here he hasn't already explored this morning: it's a storage room, piled high with cans of motor oil, magazines, kerosene lamps, fisherman's waders. But no Thorsteinn.

Vikram races back downstairs, into the room where Jon Pall's dozing, then into the living room, the kitchen, the bathroom: no Thorsteinn anywhere.

"Jon Pall!" he calls from the doorway. "He isn't here."

"Who?"

"*Thorsteinn.*"

"Thorsteinn?"

Vikram pauses. What is he to do? "Are you getting up today?"

"Today? Maybe not today," Jon Pall says.

"I'm going out to find my car."

"Right."

"Oh," Vikram calls from the doorway. "I borrowed your yellow sweater."

"Mm? Don't have a yellow sweater."

Vikram shrugs, zips his green suede jacket halfway up his chest, and steps outdoors. The church bells are still ringing.

It's the oddest feeling in the world: not knowing where his car is. Never in his life has he had no idea where his car is. It's almost as though part of him lies elsewhere, as though he were detached and distanced from his own body. He floats unreally down Grettisgata. He might almost be a ghost.

One after another, the afternoon streets are strangely deserted. It has been raining—the sidewalk is wet—but now a wavering mothlike sun flutters here and there across a mottled metallic sky. Its patchy light reveals no yellow Mustang convertible—no yellow car at all. He's feeling desperate. And hungry. Nervousness is one of those sensations—like fatigue or restlessness, or joy or sorrow, or boredom or excitement—that whet his appetite, and surely the search would better be carried out with a cinnamon roll in hand. He steps round the corner to Ursula's Bakery, whose door rings as he steps inside.

Behind the counter Ursula is leaning over a hot tray of fresh doughnuts. She has always had a soft spot for him. Yes, she can be something of a dotty old lady—she talks too much—but he's genuinely fond of her, and grateful for the little something extra she regularly nudges his way: three cinnamon buns when he's paid for two, or a bar of Dutch chocolate beside his sesame roll, or a doubled wad of ham on his sandwich. It's been a couple of days since he last saw the old woman and he has every reason to expect a warm welcome. But he's almost overwhelmed when her jaw quivers and plunges at the sight of him, her hand floats up and points, her wide body scampers around the counter with girlish quickness and, throwing her fatty arms over his shoulders, she kisses him—smack!—on the center of the forehead, on the cheek, on the nose. "You're alive, you're alive, you're *alive!*" she cries.

Vikram laughs, a little uneasily. "Of course I am . . ." Dotty. Truly she *is* getting dotty.

The bell on the door jangles behind his back, and another voice—another woman's voice—cries, "He's *here*, oh precious Heaven he's alive. He's alive he's alive he's *alive.*" Vikram swings around. It's old Solveig, who once tried to teach him English at the Superior School. Fat tears spring into her eyes. Indeed, both women are crying.

He finds it isn't unpleasant, exactly, to be standing in Ursula's Bakery with two old women embracing and petting and pinching him—he's used to the oddly urgent embraces of elderly women—but on the other hand this talk of theirs *is* a little disconcerting. When they calm down, when they give him a chance, he asks the obvious question: "But why wouldn't I be alive?"

And the room falls silent.

Once again the bell on the door tolls behind him. This time it's Tryggvi Gunnarsson, whom Vikram knows from television: he's the man with the eyebrows, the one who took part in the recent debates. Tryggvi has a pipe in his mouth, and it actually drops—falls with a clatter to the floor—in that moment when he lays eyes upon Vikram. "Good God, my boy, you're alive. . . ."

Vikram is rarely petulant toward anybody—and *never* toward adults—but his voice has a honed edge as he protests, "Why on earth wouldn't I be? What else could I possibly be?"

Again the room hushes.

Wide-eyed, the two old women, each squeezing one of Vikram's forearms, stare at each other. Glances flying back and forth, they turn to Tryggvi, who as an editor at *The Torch* might logically be expected to deliver up any sort of momentous news.

But Tryggvi, too, says nothing. He peers at Vikram from underneath the thickets of his eyebrows and then stoops to the floor to retrieve his pipe. While in his crouch he says, "Tell me, were you with Thorsteinn Thorsteinnsson last night?"

"Yes—yes I was. He *has my car.*" A terrible fear wrenches awry Vikram's beautiful features.

Tryggvi rises to his full height. "Well, Thorsteinn's dead, my boy. He drowned in the Two Day River."

Now Vikram's precise response—the question he posed in answer to this announcement—is indisputable. But as old Ursula and old Solveig were quick to point out, nobody makes much sense when confronted with a shocking, brutal loss. What Vikram said was: "But what about my car?"

"The car is fine," Tryggvi reassured him. "It's at your parents', where your mother's absolutely desperate for news of you. Your father's out by the Two Day, along with hundreds of others. They're looking for your body."

For a moment, no one said anything. Then old Ursula, recognizing that the boy was suffering from the shock of his life, commanded him to sit down in a chair by the counter and eat a warm doughnut and drink a calming glass of milk. And while she was ministering to him, Old Solveig got busy. Weeping with joy, she telephoned Vikram's mother, and the police, and the radio station, and various friends. She made one call after another.

Vikram, famished by shock, finished off a couple of doughnuts and ate a ham sandwich. A crowd began to assemble in Ursula's—one that was soon too big for the store, and everyone shifted over to the Hotel Snorri. A newspaperman showed up and flashbulbs began to pop like fireworks. Bottles, as well as flasks in paper sacks, began to circulate through the crowd and the boy's heroism was repeatedly toasted.

Then Vikram's mother, our dear Perla, came quivering forward, and there were new explosions of flashbulbs as she wrapped the beaming boy in her arms. Scattered calls for a speech went up, but Vikram, with a toss of his curly-haired head, modestly demurred. Soon Jakob appeared, triumphantly holding aloft the keys to the Mustang, and father and son fell into another tearful, lustily applauded embrace. Amid hoots and laughter, with a crowd following at a respectful distance, Vikram marched outdoors behind his father to inspect the car. The Mustang glowed ravishingly in the gathering dusk.

The bells in Mariners' Church had stopped ringing.

45

The Triple Man

I receive a telephone call from my son. We haven't spoken in quite some time. How long? Anyway not since before the night when a Lilja in hospital pajamas broke the news about Sindri's "private life." I suppose I'm expecting to hear in his delivery something flustered, a few notes of stammering embarrassment, but I detect nothing of the sort and I'm left wondering: can it be he doesn't know I know? But surely Lilja has told him about telling me. They don't long keep secrets between them, those two.

Is there something aggrieved in his tone? Doesn't he maybe feel I've been avoiding him? Not that I have. It's simply been a matter of my not going out of my way, in a time of extraordinary busyness, to seek out a conversation.

In truth, once we've waded through our initial pleasantries, Sindri handles the matter impressively, with atypical forthrightness.

"I haven't seen you for quite some time," he begins.

"You know what the end of a campaign is like."

"I thought if you had the time I might treat you to coffee and cake downtown."

Treat me to coffee and cake? Downtown? This isn't the sort of activity, or the sort of language, we customarily share. To hear him talk, we might almost be business associates, author and editor, say, meeting to discuss revisions and publication dates. Still, even while scrambling for cover in this new conversational terrain, I have to admire this gambit. Any strategy which might foster between us an adult-to-adult professionalism is surely to be welcomed.

We agree to meet that very day, in a couple of hours' time. In closing, Sindri says something very peculiar: "I look forward to seeing you."

Has he convinced himself this is some sort of business meeting? A job interview? *I look forward to seeing you*—honestly, is that any way for a son to address his father? Gloom settles over me as the appointment approaches. With half an hour to go, I pour myself a generous Scotch.

I arrive at the Hotel Snorri a couple of minutes early and Sindri is already seated, a thermos before him. As I'd feared, he's wearing a black shirt, with the top button buttoned. His coffee is black. He looks vampirically pale. We shake hands. His is clammy. It occurs to me—as it so often does—that it was in this very restaurant I first laid eyes on Constance Q. Simple, and further occurs to me, as I drop heavily into my seat, that Sindri presumably will never meet a woman for an assignation here, or anywhere else.

"How's the fish business?" I begin.

"Cold and wet."

"It's a job."

He tests me in English: "Is that a commendation or a condemnation?"

There's a sort of—what?—defiance in his gaze. What is this toughness in the boy? Where in his eyes am I to locate that familiar look—that character-defining expression—which says, *I implore you. . .* ? I can't find it. I've long accustomed myself to the notion that the boy isn't my biological son, and yet I'm finding it vexing, all the same, to assimilate the complementary notion that he might be somebody I don't thoroughly know.

"Forgive me if I seem a little abstracted," I say. "This is the most brutal campaign I've ever been involved in."

"The election?" He is, in his way, as clumsy as I am.

"Nothing else." And I talk for some minutes about the various speeches I've written, and when and how they were received. He pours me a coffee. I go on talking. After a while Sindri interrupts me:

"Lilja tells me she spoke to you."

"Spoke to me?"

"About me . . ." His gaze bobbles in its old way, which reassures me, but then it comes up chilling and steady: "About my sexual orientation."

My glance darts round the room. His voice, though not loud, could certainly be a bit more subdued.

"Yes . . ." I whisper at him.

"I just wondered if that's going to cause problems," the boy goes on.

"Problems?"

"For you."

"Ah, but I should have thought it would cause problems for *you*," I answer him.

I've long accepted the proposition that there are three and only three great preoccupations in my life: writing books, pursuing the love of women, and furthering, by all necessary means, the great cause of Freeland. It is perhaps a failing of mine—though I would naturally prefer to think it a wise, instinctual budgeting of internal resources—that life, outside my three preoccupations, by and large bores and wearies me. I admire—but oh, at such a distance!—the home handyman, the gardener, the woodworker, the amateur musician, the watercolorist, the ceramicist, the meditater, the religious pilgrim, the black-belt karate instructor. As I sip from the coffee my son has poured for me, what I realize, and haven't the heart to tell him, is that at the tripartite core of my life he and I have nothing in common. My own narrowness may be at fault. I certainly don't hold it up as a virtue. Yet I wouldn't call it a vice either. It's just a fact. There it is.

So, though he pitches eagerly forward on the table, training upon me a look of almost invincible winsomeness, there's an unbridgeable chasm between us. That's a word—*chasm*—bound to have for any Freelander a more than metaphorical potency. It sometimes seems as though our land itself, so riven by volcanic fissures, was outspread before us as a constant reminder that the physically proximate may turn out to be unreachable.

"It *has* been," Sindri says. "A problem. For me."

Delicately, I hold out the prospect of freedom to the boy: "You may want to go away. Surely there are places that might be more—" how to put this sympathetically?—"more congenial to someone of your type."

Outside the window, bouncing along in absurd orange sweatpants and lime green tennis shoes, ragged old Odin, head of the Psychics Guild, crosses Independence Square. People say he can see a person's "aura." Do homosexuals, as a class, have a signature aura? Had Odin, too, figured out the truth about my son long before I did?

"I may go away. Is that what you want?"

"Me? Surely my wishes are secondary in the matter. But I suppose it's what I want only if that's how you'd be happiest. Your sister and I would miss you, naturally."

"Does it make you uncomfortable?"

"Uncomfortable?"

"My orientation. My—sexual tendencies."

He looks nervous. And there's a faint stutter, curiously not over "sexual" but over the euphemistic "tendencies." Yet isn't there on his face, in addition, the hint of a gloating, pleasurable anticipation? At this particular moment, isn't his prime "tendency" a desire to make me uneasy? If so, he won't be offered *that* satisfaction, anyway. I tell him what also happens to be true: "Sindri, your father's a very worldly man—at least by Freelandic standards. I've seen all sorts of things."

"Well I may go away. But not yet. I'm in the middle of things."

And what does he mean by this? I would almost swear he's preparing to spring another announcement on me. "Well these are busy days," I remind him.

"I can't *tell* you how glad I am that Lilja broke the news to you. About me. Of course I should have told you myself. But I was worried that you'd feel—disappointed. Or even disgusted."

And with this last word, for the first time in this encounter, Sindri's face is truly and utterly Sindri's face: not just the bobbing, imploring gaze, but the outthrust and yet vulnerable please-don't-hit-me chin, and the lower lip clamped by his upper front teeth, as if to arrest its trembling. Disappointed? Disgusted? Neither begins to describe what I'm feeling. I'm struck most forcibly, I suppose, by a sense of weary inevitability: it seems everything the boy does underscores the same habits of debility. On the evening when Lilja first informed me about the boy's "tendencies," my immediate response had been to exclaim *But that's impossible*. But now I say, Of *course* the boy had taken up with a scrawny-mustached Norwegian linguist. One says this just as one says, Of *course* the boy catches fish for a computer, or, Of *course* he dresses like an undertaker, or, Of *course* he lingers on in Freeland when other young men his age are exploring the Australian outback or the Tanzanian highlands.

"Already I feel better," the boy tells me.

"Well there are strains to living a double life," I answer him. "There's a pressure not for the weak-hearted."

"It's like taking off a heavy backpack you've been carrying so long you almost forget you have it on. It's hard to believe: I don't have to lead a double life anymore. Or less of one. I mean—there are other things. All sorts of private preoccupations."

Other things? Private preoccupations? I wasn't at all sure I was catching the boy's drift. Was he hinting at further revelations? What in the world *further* could he possibly confess to? Has he become (a) a satanist, (b) a necrophiliac, (c) a speaker-in-tongues? In any event, for our mutual benefit, I cut him off stoutly: "A moment ago, I was thinking that I have only three great preoccupations in my life. I say 'only' but perhaps that's too many—I sometimes feel I'm spread too thin. Still, I don't know what I might eliminate. A life without any of these three is all but unimaginable to me."

Sindri's face showed some puzzlement—as well it might. It was time to collect my wits and lay it out more cogently: "I have three great preoccupations in my life," I declared. "The first is writing books, which I seem to do as compulsively as a rabbit breeds rabbits. I've published forty-nine. Did you know I once finished a novel in the morning and started a new one after dinner? The second preoccupation is the love of women."

He interrupted me: "But we both love women. We both love Lilja, anyway." And looked at me slyly. I don't always care for his taste in paradox. . . .

"Let's call it romance, then, which in my case, perhaps rather unimaginatively, means full-grown women exclusively. I've been a good deal less successful with them than I'd like, frankly, both in getting the ones I wanted and in keeping the ones I got. But there it is—it's been an obsession from the outset. And third, I've fought for Freeland. For the language, of course, but ultimately for the spirit of the place."

"It's as if you feel you have a monopoly on patriotic—"

I silenced him with an uplifted hand. "Let me finish, boy. As I said at the outset, I'm a narrow person. Doubtless you have your own preoccupations. Who knows, perhaps they're as rich as mine. Or richer. But whatever they are, they're *not* mine. Your Freeland's not my Freeland, and my ruthlessness in defending it may make me a fascist or a madman in your eyes. My romantic pursuits, God knows, aren't yours. And my shelf of books is a long way from your computer at Freefiskur."

And at this, the eyes in the boy's wan face sparked: they flared, they took fire. Was this a homicidal—patricidal—flame? Was he feeling desperate? Heartbroken? Illuminated? Liberated? I don't know. . . . In any case, I went on hastily: "All I am asking for, son, is a certain measure of patience. If I fail to understand you, you must keep in mind that inevitably there is a great chasm between us."

"A chasm?"

It was heartbreaking—Sindri's uncomprehending delivery of this question. In that moment he might well have been the merest tyke of a child, perplexedly asking *why? why? why?* Could there possibly be any more telling demonstration of the distance between us than this pinched-voiced crestfallen inquiry?—this utter inability to surmise just how impassably deep was the chasm we called across in speaking to each other?

46

The Flag of Night

Freud in his *New Introductory Lectures on Psycho-analysis* tells us that there are "two essentially different classes of instincts," the sexual and the aggressive. It's our old friends Eros and Thanatos, aka Love and Hate—that pair of bumbling colossi, locked in an uneasy waltz across the millennia.

Freud is hardly to be faulted for failing to intuit the existence of a drive more primal and powerful still. That it fell to Eggert Oddason, one afternoon in Wilmington, Delaware, to plumb finally to the sunless core of the human personality, to glimpse the soul unshelled at last, was a result of timing and chance as much as psychological penetration. You see, I make no extravagant claims for myself. The technology simply wasn't in place that would have permitted Freud to get there first.

I'd had no intention of visiting Wilmington. My goal was Washington. This was on my last trip to America, in 1991. I was between books. I was recuperating, I was revitalizing. I was flirting with the devil. This would be my first visit to Washington since I'd guiltily fled the Simples eighteen years before. What had happened to them? Not surprisingly, we'd lost all contact. Had Geoffrey recovered his vision? Had little Bella, now a grown woman, ever located the intellect that had somehow gotten misplaced, like a little dolly tumbled behind a radiator? And Connie—what of Connie? I rarely thought long about the Simples, having relegated them to that dark corner of the mind where is stored the file called People Who Probably Came to a Depressing End. Of course, given my dealings with them, they were cross-referenced under Behavior Even a Prideless Man Must Be Ashamed Of. Well, I was returning to the scene of a crime, I suppose, and a delayed but terrible system of Criminal Justice came down, literally, upon my head.

I never got near enough to the Simples even to contact them by a local telephone call. I left New York's Penn Station in the early morning, suffering from toothache and hoping the motions of the train would lull it to sleep. But by the time we reached Newark I was already limp and miserable and half-deaf with pain. A situation that seemingly couldn't get worse got worse. My only ambition—I suppose I wasn't thinking clearly—was to reach Washington: it was as though I would be mystically restored if only I could attain my original goal.

And still the pain sharpened. The train halted for a long infernal interval in Philadelphia, but I held on.

I finally stumbled off in Wilmington, located a phone, spoke with someone in a dentist's office, and found myself to a cab, to a dentist's chair, to the most delicious object in the universe: a hypodermic needle steeped in novocaine. Even so, pain continued hammering my skull. The source was an upper wisdom tooth, firmly rooted, and the dentist was an ancient snowy-haired man who years ago had lost—if he'd ever had it—that brute forearm strength which even now remains an essential of the trade. He pulled and pulled and pulled. It was the first time I'd suffered an extraction. The tooth, it turned out, was a little pillar, on which was erected the temple of my brain. When it budged, at last, I felt my intellect shiver and slide.

Later, my damaged head and I found our way to a hotel. I was good for nothing. Although the pain had changed shape, it was still with me and to distract myself I turned on the television. I watched the little screen all day, one talk show after another, in a gathering horror that finally crystallized in that bleak realization of mine which extended Freud's insights to the endmost step. . . .

The most powerful, primal impulse in the human psyche? It's the *desire to appear on television*. No body of creeds or convictions, no work of hand or heart, can stand up to it. It razes every scruple, every aspiration, every value. For the chance to appear on television, a wonderfully dutiful veteran bookkeeper, in a gray bun and Peter Pan collar, a woman so punctilious she frets all weekend over having inadvertently left the office on Friday afternoon with a company pencil in her purse, will confess, falsely, to years of embezzlement. A middle-aged gentleman so prim that his cheek pinkens at having been glimpsed early on Sunday morning wearing bathrobe and slippers as he gathers his newspaper from his front porch will, for the chance to appear on television, don an enormous diaper and jam a pacifier into his mouth. A nun so impeccable that for two decades her greatest succumbing to fleshly temptation has been the gooseberry jam she allows herself at Christmas will, for the chance to appear on television, confess to heaving fornications with the gardener's idiot son. It is our new, true god, and oh there is nothing we will not do for the chance to undergo that mystical, fundamental transubstantiation by which flesh and blood are momentarily converted into a matrix of glittery pixels.

In the Freelandic folktale to which I've already alluded—that of Annasigga and the Trolls—one finds a lovely phrase. When the little girl stumbled into the trolls' cavern and beheld its illimitable riches, her "gaze turned to butter." She lost track of who she was and where she was and the danger she was in—the glow of the treasure had melted her common sense away.

Doubtless, future scientists will be able to explain to us the complex interweavings—the microaffiliations of neurons and cathode rays—that fully account for the way in which, in the glow of the television lights, we forget who we are and where we are; our gaze turns to butter. But until they do, what's to be done by those who perceive the danger? We can only resist it as best we can. Which is the job I've undertaken, and if most of the time it's a highly abstract task, every now and then, rather hearteningly, the enemy takes a highly visible form. . . .

Which is to say, the American Visitors make their presence felt with remarkable swiftness. Tuesday evening, two days after their arrival, I turn on my television and, in the guarded, squinting fashion I employ at such times, begin watching "Youth Hour." Nonni Karlsson is seen delivering a speech to the Giant Island Women's Club. My first thought is that he has injured his arm, which flails around in a jerky, disconnected way. Slowly I come round to recognizing that the motions are deliberate—they are one aspect of what aspires to be a new mode of oratory. He has been coached.

What have the "election consultants" taught him so far? He has learned to pound with his right arm as a means of emphatically agreeing with himself and to introduce his observations with a *That's an issue I've been hoping to address.* He has learned to grin while being asked a question and to say *I have a three-part answer to that* even if he subsequently demonstrates he cannot count up to three. You might expect I'd be overjoyed to see our opponent make an excruciating ass of himself, but the truth is it's *so* excruciating I find no pleasure in it. No, he stirs in me a sense of piercing shame. This buffoonish figure, this malfunctioning automaton got up as a grand statesman—*he's* being earnestly advanced as a candidate for President of my nation? Statistically, most people in the world have never heard of my homeland, and among those who have we're seen, sketchily, as a risible nation—comically small, comically northern, comically bibulous. But while we have, admittedly, countenanced as President someone who has taken a barmaid for his woman and who scavenges wood scraps out of vacant lots, we will not accept, surely, a President who in response to a question offers the glazed spasmic grin of a ventriloquist's dummy and who says things like *I'm glad you asked me that.* We have our own internal codes of respectability.

Nonni's charm and dignity—such as they are—have always lain in his genial incompetence. He has good intentions; he has always stood for the earnest desire to stand for something. And now, wretchedly misled, he was trying to talk as others told him to talk, gesture as others told him to gesture, even grin as others told him to grin. Through sheer agreeableness, he'd rendered himself painfully disagreeable. I scooted over to the phone to call Hannibal. "Are you watching?" I said.

"Mm?"

" 'Youth Hour.' "

" 'Youth Hour'?"

And Hannibal? He sounded vacant—had I awakened him from a nap? "Turn it on, Hanni. I'll call you when it's over."

I returned to "Youth Hour," where a "music video" had succeeded Nonni. Silencing the set, but allowing the pictures to run lest I miss any further political item, I dipped into an old Danish newspaper. After a few minutes I glanced up and there in the background loomed Great Blue Mountain. In the foreground, shirtless, his hairless chest blue with cold, a young man was lying on a moss-covered hummock, fondling a guitar. He was surrounded by tapers, hundreds of them, most but not all of them lit. Evidently the breeze had snuffed the rest. I scrutinized the television screen. It took me far longer than you might suppose to ascertain that this was a bit of domestic programming. I restored the sound. Some clatter was just then diminishing and a voice announced, "That was Elmar 'Elton' Jonsson singing 'Candle in the Wind.' " Local programming. The local music industry. This was everything I'd fought for, oddly enough. I'd helped give birth to the Freelandic music video industry.

Next appeared a woman in army fatigues and a boy in a double-breasted lavender suit. There was some back-and-forth banter—comic in intention, evidently—and then another music video, this one imported, and then the Wolf's Puppettheater, in which Charlemagne/Hannibal kept pinching a blond girl on the bottom while being lectured to about "proper decorum" by his arachnoid SS-uniformed adviser, and then a return to Nonni Karlsson. This was out on Diamond; I recognized the school auditorium. A young man with shoulder-length hair—interchangeable, so far as I could tell, with Elmar "Elton" Jonsson—asked, "Under your presidency, what will be the policy toward foreign rock music?"

"I'm very glad you asked me that," Nonni began and grinned his rictal grin. "Now I have a three-part answer to that. First, one of my teachers at the Middle School once told me that music is the *universal language*. The *universal language*—I've always been grateful for that amazing concept. Now what some people in this current administration don't seem to realize is this: they don't see that by promoting a universal language we are promoting international understanding."

—and the music video's shirtless boy in the lava fields is a cultural ambassador.

"In my administration I want to see the promotion of all"— thump the table—"forms"—thump—"of music"—thump. "Because—because, third, I have a theory that each and every one of us has a song in—"

I moved quickly and extinguished the set.

I dialed Hannibal. "Well?" I said.

"Well?"

"Have you ever in your life seen anything like it?"

"Like what?"

"Like Nonni."

"Oh, Nonni," he said, and snorted.

"You haven't been watching?"

"Oh I've been watching."

"And you don't think it was the most appalling spectacle you've ever seen in your life?"

"Was it more appalling than usual?"

"How can you say that? How can you *say* that?" What was wrong with him? "Hanni, take it from your speechwriter: a nation is best judged by what it fails to laugh at. If people honestly don't think Nonni has now become *laughably* ludicrous, we're far more debased than I'd thought. Listen, I'm going to come visit. Is that all right?"

"Suit yourself."

I hung up the phone. Clearly, he needed peering at. Why did he sound so vacant? Could anyone fail to see that a new nadir had been arrived at in our politics?

Or was I losing my mind? Was it possible that tonight was no more appalling than usual? I dialed Lilja's number.

"Did you watch 'Youth Hour'?"

"I'm *watching* it. It isn't over yet."

"And you're not horrified?"

"Horrified?"

"At Nonni."

"Mm?"

"At what they've *done* to him. Surely you see they've been trying to teach him how to speak?"

"That's not a bad idea. As you yourself are forever—"

"But surely you see how horrifying it is?"

"Horrifying?"

I got her quickly off the phone and drove out to Founders' Point. I opened the front door and called a greeting—there was no answer, no one there. Where was Hannibal?

But perhaps I ought to pause a moment here. Is the significance clear? Freeland is a country where the President does not bother to lock his house. . . .

I poked around downstairs, calling out an occasional halloo. The rooms were in a state of multilayered disorder—papers, books, clothes, dishes, empty bottles. That greatest of luxuries in our treeless land—a crackling blaze—danced in the fireplace. *The Saga of the Volsungs*, one of the most magical of the old tales and the source of Wagner's *Ring*, lay on the seat of the armchair opposite the blaze. Perhaps it was open to the page where the old King declares: "Maidens will not taunt my sons during games by saying that they feared their deaths, for each man must at one time die. No one may escape dying that once, and it is my counsel that we not flee, but for our own part act the bravest."

I went back out on the front porch and loudly boomed Hannibal's name into the darkness. I scared up no answer. The northern lights were loose in the sky. I called again and this time I summoned, from well down the shore, a distant "Eggi!" I waited. The sea was calm.

After a while a figure materialized—a dark hunched grunting shadowy shape. Hannibal was dragging something. It was a big log. No, it was the many-armed branch of a tree. Driftwood. He'd scavenged some more fuel for the hearth.

I went across the slick rocks to assist him. The branch was both slippery and abrasive on the fingers, and heavy against the arm, but we managed to drag it around to the front of the house. Limping, Hannibal went inside to turn on the porch light. He came back with an ax.

I stood there shivering. He was, needless to say, a master with an ax. The blade swung—a dull glint in the darkness—and the wet wood splintered and gave way.

"What did you think?" I said.

"Think?"

"Of Nonni Karlsson."

"What in the world"—crunch—"is there to think about"—crunch—"Nonni Karlsson?" These were northern lights of that sort which continually roll and flicker while seemingly maintaining some pliant but ultimately fixed shape—like a flag or banner in a stiff breeze. It was as though, far off, out between the stars, a storm were coming in. As though we inhabitants of the earth—that becalmed blue isle in the black sea—inhabited the eye of a storm. The real weather was elsewhere. Down here, we didn't feel a thing. Up there, out in the elements—the elements we didn't begin to apprehend—the Flag of Night was being tugged and tugged at.

"They're teaching him. How to talk."

"They have a long way to go."

"That's not the point," I say.

Hannibal then volunteers something unexpected: "I let her go. Elva. I let her go."

The phrase might be interpreted in any number of ways, but oddly what I think of first is the commuting of a prisoner's sentence: Hannibal might be some governor, explaining why a criminal has been released.

I weigh my response. "I'm sorry," I say.

"So am I," my friend replies.

The blade arcs upward, seems for an instant to catch a flicker of the aurora borealis on its metal flank, plummets down through darkness.

"Should we go inside?" I suggest.

"Why don't you come by tomorrow?"

"A drink?"

"A drink tomorrow."

I pause another moment, nod at him, turn to go, turn back: "Surely no one's going to vote for him now. He has declared himself a zero to all the world."

"Maybe that's a number most people can live with. . . ."

And I offer what I suppose might have sounded like an odd form of solace: "As for me, I've never in my life been with such a beautiful young woman as that. Nothing like."

Hannibal understood me. He countered with an equally odd assuagement: "She's prettier even than you know."

Prettier even than you know: the phrase followed me home. As I drove past the Customs House I thought of Elva, for it was here, on a night too windy and icy for vertical movement, I first laid eyes upon her. White legs flashing, she'd been down on all fours like an infant, or like some strange mythological marine creature crawled up from shore. Was her generation truly going to elect Nonni Karlsson to steer them into the future? Surely I wasn't wrong in thinking Nonni had dealt himself a blow? The next morning I scan *The Torch* with incredulity. Although this is "our" newspaper, all they see fit to observe is that "Nonni Karlsson seems to be making some effort to speak more forcefully and cogently. While this is a sorely needed effort, we must report that he still has some work to do. . . ."

It seems I'm out of joint, out of synch, out of touch. I'd expected Nonni's "makeover" to be the topic of the day, but as I go about my business—buy a loaf of mountain-bread at Ursula's, have a morning coffee at my "annex office" at the Snorri—it soon becomes clear that the pressing political topic is something else entirely. It relates to a little story at the bottom of the first page of *The Torch*: "'Poll' Predicts Nonni Victory." Freeland's first political poll. Nearly two hundred Freelanders, selected randomly through the telephone book, had been asked whom they plan to vote for. Fifty-one percent of respondents had endorsed Nonni, thirty-two percent Hannibal Hannibalsson, and seventeen percent were undecided. Kevin Wilhelm—for of course it was our three Visitors who lay behind the whole business—was quoted as follows: "It seems greatly significant that even if every Undecided were to vote for the incumbent, Candidate Karlsson would still give him a drubbing." This is, I discover, what everyone wants to talk about: not Nonni Karlsson's transformation, but this 51–32 "drubbing." What do I think? Will it be as bad as that?

I remonstrate, I complain, I cast aspersions, I pooh-pooh and throw doubts, but the more I talk to people the clearer it becomes how incisively these figures penetrate the national psyche. Haven't these computations been brought to us from America? Aren't these visitors genuine Experts who have served overseas in various political campaigns that dwarf our own? Who do *we* think we are to dispute them?

Such is our reverence for Outside Experts—think of those Copenhagen scientists who have formulated Danish Blue, a soap designed exclusively for polar regions!—that we instinctively respond to the poll not as an intrusion but as an illumination. The wonders of modern science have contrived to explain our electorate to our electorate. And for those among us who continue to support our flailing President—aren't we now obscurely tainted? Aren't we all just a little ashamed to learn beforehand—in cold, naked numbers—just what losers we really are? The American Visitors have so arranged it that we've suffered a defeat before a single vote has been cast. At the moment, there *is* no other issue.

By the time *The Daily Liar* comes out, later that day, it can run as its headline, *Experts Call It: LANDSLIDE.*

That's explanation enough. We're now old hands at reading polls. No one's confused for a minute. . . .

47

A Sensation of Nondishonesty

The next day, a sunless day, all the darkness in the world is encapsulated in the phrase *dropping fast*. It begins on Skeggjagata, when I run into Tryggvi, he of the shaggy eyebrows and the maundering questions at the debate.

He's an old friend, whose newspaper's support of Hannibal has been unwavering, but as he buttonholes me on the street, in a slight drizzle, I find I'm in no mood for someone who, if he came home one night to discover a blaze in his living room window, couldn't yell "Fire!" in less than twenty words. His topic today, so far as I can discern it, is "restlessness" at the newspaper, particularly among the younger journalists. Evidently, they're growing "impatient" with Hannibal. *Well, who isn't?* I want to say. *But our goal is clear, isn't it? We simply must keep such restlessness in check.* Of course I'm not quite as direct as that. He pours vaguely worded discontent my way; I waft vague assurances back at him.

We seem to reach, finally, a satisfactory halting place and I turn to leave. "Oh, by the way, do you remember Gudrun Haraldsdottir?" he asks me.

I swing around on my heels. "Of course."

"Old Harald Haraldsson's daughter? She went to school with us. She used to live on Lidgata?"

"Of course of course."

"She married Baldur Hermannsson, you remember. And by the way I hear he'll be declaring bankruptcy again. If ever there was a man who had what you might call a non-Midas—"

"But what about her? What about *Gudrun*?"

Under the ledges of his eyebrows Tryggvi's eyes pop with pain. "Well, you know she has cancer. She has a very rare—"

"Yes I know," I interrupt again, and his eyes pop once more.

Tryggvi says, almost apologetically, "Well, I just hear she's going down now. She's back in the hospital. Dropping fast."

Encapsulated in that phrase is not merely the dark of that dark day, but all the pooled, intensified blackness of the upcoming arctic winter, when Hannibal will have been bounced from office and the quarters of my Freelandic Language Committee will doubtless have been requisitioned for a Rock and Roll Museum. *Dropping fast.* I go home and contemplate a blank paper—am I seeking to pen a speech? a poem? my fiftieth book? a funerary elegy?—and nurse a Scotch and nurse a second Scotch, as the rain intermittently fingerpaints my study window.

At six o'clock I head over to the hospital. I rarely come here on my own. Usually I'm with Hannibal and we're bound for the Eldershelter. This time, I head to the building's other wing. Both sides in this, Freeland's costliest structure, offer views of Great Blue. *Is Gudrun Haraldsdottir a patient here?* Yes, she's on the fifth floor.

Well, she's at a good height—a good vantage for "mountain viewing."

Should I have tried to telephone some sort of message first? Perhaps, but somehow I can't bear to. She will have other visitors, no doubt. And I will simply have to put up with them.

I find her room and pause at its threshold. I'm a man imperiled, a creature with a snagged thorn ripping at its heart. She doesn't see me. Her eyes are closed. Behold my virgin muse, my schoolgirl Beatrice and Laura and Venus all wrapped into one: she's a frail, a shop-soiled doll. Death, in stepping close to my Gudrun, has come between her and the light. Her face is smudged with shadows—under her eyes, at the side of her nose. "Gud-run," I call but my voice cracks on the first syllable—that *gud* which means God, which means to me all goodness—and she does not hear. "Gudrun," I call again, vowing to be on my way if this summons fails to rouse her. It would be wrong, surely it would be wrong to awaken this woman.

Her eyelids flutter open. She peers at me in the doorway and for just a moment alarm distorts her features. To judge from her expression, it might almost be I and not she who has been cruelly transformed.

But the next moment she smiles once more, warmth spilling into her eyes, and she is as much Gudrun as any wasted creature in a hospital bed could possibly be.

"Eggert Oddason! What a"—she pauses, as though seeking some nimble turn of phrase, the very mot juste, and concludes—"lovely surprise." It was that old conversational trick of hers. Never, I've never known anybody else who could deliver the expected response with quite such winning panache—who could utter a cliché with the same infectious felicity.

"I heard you were here and I thought I might stop by for a moment."

"How *kind* of you. How very considerate. I'm afraid I must have been dozing just now."

"That's good. You need your rest. That's what you need to get better."

"Better . . ." Gudrun echoes, with what might be called a cheery wistfulness, and what is it about this woman that so captivates me? Why does merely hearing her utter my name burn my eyes as though ever-tearless Eggert Oddason might begin to cry? Maybe it's the way she says it—*Egg*ert *Odd*ason!—as though somehow it were some particularly clever, splendid feat, this daily business of being me. . . . No one else has ever uttered my name so as to suggest I'm some sort of marvel—and isn't this the reason why these little solicitous remarks I tender in return feel so natural? When I'm with Gudrun, I have an odd, disorienting sensation of full honesty—of, at least, nondishonesty. I say "It's nice to see you" and discover, studying my response, that *it's nice to see her.* I say "That's thoughtful of you" and find, indeed, that she has been thoughtful. . . . It's as though she takes my words in her hands like so many muddy pebbles, lays them under the cold plunge of a miniature waterfall, scrubs them clean. . . . Dear creature, dying but enduring creature, you are my muse even yet. For you have brought me to this lovely phrase I would never have found without you: a *compact cataract*.

"I suppose it's all the visitors, tiring me out."

"Perhaps I should come again another time."

"Oh I have enough energy to see *you*—one of my oldest friends in the world. Come sit beside me."

Hesitantly I take a seat, on the mattress, beside my friend. It's the first time, I'm keenly aware, we've in any sense shared a bed.

"You've had many visitors," I begin.

"Well Baldur has been here. You know Baldur."

"Of course. And how is Baldur?"

"Very well, thank you, Eggert, very well. He's in electronic equipment now, those I guess you call them youth-oriented games."

"Yes—"

"And doing very well at it, I'm happy to say."

She hasn't been told the truth, obviously, and I squelch the cruel desire to correct her. But since I'm not used to being so noble, I'm left feeling angry with *him*—for failing in business once more. Or maybe for receiving undeserved credit for success.

"And my boys were here."

"Your three boys."

"Three boys. Such fine boys. I've been so lucky, Eggert," the dying woman marvels. "Sometimes I don't know what I did to deserve such good luck."

"You deserve everything you've had and more, Gudrun," I tell her. And now my anger has moved outward: it's life, or God Himself, I'm outraged at.

"Oh but I don't really. Who does?" She laughs. "It's just good luck. You've been lucky, too, haven't you, Eggert? You've had so much good fortune."

She lifts her arm from the bed and takes one of my hands and although it's a revelation that certainly ought to have hit home long before this, only when the papery flesh of her hand contacts mine do I fully accept that we will never be lovers. Gudrun will never recover, and I will never confess quite what she has, all along, symbolized for me. I suppose that, in some stubbornly irrational corner of the mind, I'd been harboring the piquant notion that Gudrun Haraldsdottir would eventually cast off her dim and feckless husband—just as, with the help of Outside Experts, she would cast off her rare carcinoma—and that the passion of mine which originated more than a third of a century ago, in a flurry of poems and unspoken avowals and night-pilgrimages past her home, must find its just consummation.

That smooth oval face of hers, which in youth had lent her a precocious stateliness, and which in early middle age had gone perhaps slightly too soft, enhancing her sweetness as it undermined her painful attractiveness, in the onset of mortal illness had given way to dents and bruises. Was she still beautiful? If not, it was a testament to something rarer than beauty that she held me wholly with her hushed, contented voice, her benign gaze.

And me—what does she observe when, her hand in mine, she looks up at me? Does she see me at all? Over the years there have been many appealing women—too many to count—who have somehow conveyed that my hedgehog's features repulsed them. And there have been some fair women—too few to mollify me, finally—who have somehow signaled that that hint of something furtive and four-legged about me was exciting. But Gudrun was the only beautiful woman in my life—or so I would be prepared to swear as I perch on her bed in an unmercifully bright hospital room, her hand in mine—for whom my appearance had been largely irrelevant.

"Look!" she exclaims now, "look what somebody gave me."

On the bedside table to my right lies one of my books. Though it lies backside up, I know it is mine. I recognize the colors.

One of my books. Its presence makes me nervous, and my hand advancing toward it goes all quivery and tickly. I turn it over with a sense of squeamishness, as you might turn over a flagstone to see what wriggles beneath, and also with a sense of bashful pride, like a pint-size schoolboy who, yielding to entreaties from his pint-size beloved, hands over the taped and pasted valentine so painstakingly constructed the night before.

It's an old novel. *The Runner on the Hillside.* Book fifteen or so.

"You've written so many books," she marvels.

"Forty-nine."

"Forty-nine! Imagine. Forty-nine offspring! What a patriarch you are."

"Some would say I've produced more than my share of bastards."

"You must never listen to nasty people, Eggert."

"If I didn't, my world would be a *very* quiet place, Gudrun."

"That's that *wit* of yours, isn't it. What your critics call your mordant wit."

"There isn't a critic under the age of forty in this country who doesn't disparage me and my work. Not one. It seems we have nothing to say to each other—the young and I."

"I know you don't believe that, Eggert."

"They're creating a world I don't recognize—one that no friend of Freeland would recognize."

"They're creating their *own* world, their own future. And that's how it should be."

"I envy you your faith, Gudrun."

"And perhaps I should say I envy you your doubt. Is that what gives you your energy, Eggert? Truly there's no one like you in the whole country, is there—forty-nine books! Just look at you." And Gudrun Haraldsdottir—let it be recorded here, memorialized here—shakes her beautiful head in admiring wonder at the sight of her grizzled old ugly friend. "Forty-nine books," she says once more, "and I bet you have the fiftieth well under way."

"At this point it's no more than a germ, actually."

"Oh but it must be something very special, don't you think? For your *fiftieth* book . . . Promise me you will do something special."

"I try to make them all special," I tell her. "It's hard to say if I achieve it."

"Of course you do." Gudrun muses a moment. "Well then, promise me at least that you will fill it with special people."

"That I will do," I pledge to her. "At least one. However nasty my story is, there will be at least one wholly kind and special person."

She releases her hand from mine to glide a forefinger along the spine of my book. It might just as well be my own bumpy spine she strokes. Her hand goes through me. "*The Runner on the Hillside*. It's a lovely title."

"Thank you." Of course I'm having to wrestle with all of my disappointment in perceiving that she hasn't yet read it. "It seems so long ago now, writing that book. Almost as long ago as the days when I fancied myself a runner."

"Ah but you *were*. You used to be quite fleet."

"It was a secret I kept from the world for a long time. I planned to spring it on them at that Olympics. You remember. It was the first, Freeland's First Olympics. June 21, 1958."

"Oh of course I remember. I was right there. Cheering you on."

"Yes. I saw you. I'll never forget. You did cheer me on."

"What a day that was!" Gudrun exclaims, and then adds a remark, in the same pleased exclamatory tone, which is one of the oddest things I've ever heard in my life. Truly, for just a moment I can scarcely believe my ears:

"That's when you won the gold medal in the Long Run."

For a moment my gaze burrows frantically into hers. Is she teasing, mocking me?

No, Gudrun does not mock. Her sincerity is unimpeachable. She honestly believes that the man sitting before her won the race.

I speak slowly: "But I didn't win, Gudrun. No. No, no, no," I protest and I'm so flustered I snatch at her hand once more. "It was Hannibal who won. He won everything. Everything!"

"Now isn't that peculiar . . ." Gudrun ponders, and once more her voice has gone wistful. "I *clearly* remember you winning that race. Of course it was very long ago . . ."

Yes, it was more than thirty years, Gudrun, it was many lifetimes ago: a blue sun-polished day when it seems half the men of Freeland broke into a run at the crack of an antique pistol. And yet why does this little misunderstanding in the hospital room, on a night when graver matters are so painfully before us, absolutely devastate me? Have I never fully abandoned the suspicion that it was by losing the race that I lost you? Yes, I'd thought so at the time—or at least had wanted to think so. What did I have to offer you, back then, except my scooting drive, my covert ambition, my will to outstrip my fellows—and weren't these the very traits you'd seen defeated?

What upended me in the hospital room, I suppose, was the question Gudrun's question compelled me to face: If it wasn't the race that cost me her love, what was it?

Where and how had I lost her—and lost nearly everything she represents? I look back, dazedly, over all my messy and vindictive romances, whose sum has been to leave me, at fifty-five, with nothing—solitary and loveless and soured and confused—and surely it's clear *some* other race has been run from the outset, one in which I've been trounced . . . but what was the race? Where did I stumble?

"I'm feeling tired suddenly, Eggert," Gudrun apologized. "I'd better close my eyes a moment."

She did so.

My own eyes drifted to the window. Stare hard as I might, though, the night's blackness would not reveal Great Blue, upholding its crown of snow in a veil of rain. All the glass would do was cast back at me ourselves. Two longtime, middle-aged friends.

All it would reveal was a white hospital room where a woman was impeccably dying

—and where a fierce little gray-haired man stared fixedly out, his features in that moment less feral than frightened.

48

The Real Rain

I was a man pursued by a phrase, *dropping fast*, which threatened, if I were overtaken by it, to undo me utterly; everything I valued was about to be hurled down some lightless abyss. . . .

As scheduled, the world was slated to end in less than two weeks. September was coming to a close, the election was arriving on October fourth, and the campaign was still faltering. Hannibal was looking stooped and his speeches, for all my efforts, had turned into limp and rambling affairs. It was difficult to counter the charge, increasingly more pervasive, that he was hoping to lose. He was looking forward—so the theory went—to setting down his two-decades-long burden.

Infuriatingly, the opposition—Nonni, Nonni's advisers, "Youth Hour," *The Daily Liar*—kept playing up Hannibal's age. Yes, true, he might fairly be described as an elder statesman—after all, how many elected leaders the world over have lasted twenty years?—but he was still a man in his mere fifties. Even if his knees had given out, he remained a powerful swimmer and a tireless rider, and we'd always taken heart in the knowledge that, in a crisis, his energy would outstrip everyone's.

Now, though, and overnight, my friend began to look aged to me. He was *dropping fast*. He was about to be defeated, and how in the world was he going to live out the rest of his days? Perhaps I come closest to encapsulating Hannibal's singular character in a sentence when I say that at this juncture the only job I could possibly imagine for him was the presidency of Freeland.

The third and last debate broke my spirits; most of my remaining hopes went down with it. I arrived at the television station to discover that behind what would be Nonni's lectern a pair of banners had been mounted. The first said "Innovation Through Tradition," which enraged me on a number of levels—not least being its utter nonsensicality. The second was in English. It said "Freeland, Free as Our Name." The English-language election slogan, too, had come to my country.

Naturally, I protested—raised a spiteful fuss, cursed and hollered, demanded their immediate removal. A couple of Nonni's handlers countered by brandishing in my face the "official terms" of the debate agreement, a one-page, scattershot document that vaguely endorsed maps, charts, visual diagrams. These banners? Nothing more than "visual diagrams"—an assertion posed with such shameless smirking grins I knew they themselves didn't see any likelihood of the things remaining aloft. Just at that moment, though, Hannibal showed up, some twenty minutes early, and he grandly declared the banners "perfectly unobjectionable." He appeared to find them amusing. From his point of view, indeed, the entire subsequent debate seemed, when he could rouse himself out of an indrawn lassitude, an amusing business. *Isn't this remarkable?* his crooked half-smile seemed to be asking. *I'm being attacked by my ex-wife's cousin.* And, *Isn't this priceless? They've all turned on me.* Having played, handsomely, so many glamorous roles upon our public stage, it was as though he'd vowed to render this one, too—that of the martyred statesman—with full-bodied piquancy. There were no attempts this time at a soaring rhetoric. No summonings to a brighter future, no invocations of our sacred suffering past. His answers were rueful and supine. *Where was the price of cod heading?* God knows that depends on a great many things, doesn't it? *Will our growing involvement with the Japanese pull us out of our economic slump?* I'd hate to count on that, wouldn't you? *What was being done to increase tourism during the winter "slow season"?* Well, studies continued over in our Department of Tourism, but the stubborn fact was that, among the comfort-addicted folk Down Below, resistance remained strong to the prospect of wintering in a blizzard-prone country where, on the shortest days, sunrise didn't arrive until noon.

Meanwhile, Nonni Karlsson, irredeemable as ever, demonstrated that in the realm of public debate, as elsewhere, the phrase *quick study* wasn't to be applied to him. The right hand continued to chop spasmodically, and the grin to light in disconnected moments, like a lamp with faulty wiring. He had added a new phrase, *no tariff on ideas*, which he repeated a number of times. I suppose he meant to suggest, or his handlers meant him to suggest, that the various limitations we'd imposed on radio and television programming, as well as the cinema tax and the video tax—policies designed, it need hardly be said, to safeguard the unique cultural quiddity of our island nation—were somehow comparable to the duties we'd imposed on the importation of cheese, meat, chocolate.

I was sitting in my isolated corner of the studio, my dismay alternately veering from one debater to the other, when the slogans over Nonni's head at last caught my full attention. "Innovation Through Tradition" was meant to draw the older vote. "Free as Our Name" was designed for the kids. Nonni was speaking Freelandic to the one group, English to the other—encouraging either to tune out what they didn't want to hear. There was, I grudgingly conceded, a subtle cleverness to it. . . .

Rumor had it that another damned poll was forthcoming. Whether our Visitors' polling techniques were straight or crooked, sound or shaky, was—I'd come to see—irrelevant; I knew in my bones the numbers would hurt us. Actually, it took no pollster to see where things were going: Hannibal was *dropping fast*.

The words echoed in my ears. . . .

Later that night I was awakened by the telephone. It was only 11:30, but I'd gone to bed early, hoping to make up for too many sleepless nights.

I was groggy when I answered, which may explain, but only partly, why I found the call so befuddling. I'd never experienced anything quite like it. This was—*this was no hoax!* No, this was an honest-to-goodness poll-taker. Somehow, I had been selected—randomly selected—to express my views in regard to the upcoming election.

Now, was it possible that the Visitors, or at least some of the local help they'd hired as assistants, were truly so inept as to include in their random sampling the campaign manager of one of the candidates? Apparently. Could they *be* so dumb? Evidently. During his rote enumeration of what this poll-taking process consisted of and what its huge benefits to our nation would be, the male voice at the other end sounded young, sleepy, sloppy, and—perhaps—tipsy. I waited patiently. In the upcoming election, now a mere nine days off, had I made up my mind about which of the two candidates I planned to vote for?

"Erik the Other!" I bellowed, and slammed down the receiver.

My joy was intense but short-lived. As I sank back into my mattress, it dawned on me that the sampling might be sufficiently small that I'd actually cost Hannibal a percentage point. Had I, significantly, contributed to his decline? Was I one of the reasons he, too, was *dropping fast*?

I lay there in the darkness, like a turtle on its back, the promise of sleep all but obliterated. *Dropping fast* . . . In a hospital nearby, in a fifth-floor room, Gudrun Haraldsdottir was quietly dropping fast. As was, out on Founders' Point, Hannibal Hannibalsson, contemplating the waning embers in his fireplace. And to entertain myself, in lieu of counting sheep, I let this *dropping fast* summon up an interlocking cataract of images. . . . Everything in this world was and always had been sinking: think of a saber-toothed tiger oozily embraced by a tar pit, braying as the tenacious gum clutched at its haunch; think of wooden ships, of ships going down with a splintery hole in their belly, and a lamb slipping off a foggy cliffside, virgin wool dropping into mist; of a cow elephant crumpling to its wrinkled washerwoman's knees when the steel slug tears into the lofty dome of its cranium. . . . Think of the wet brown paper bag jaggedly bursting in the arms of an old Dutch *huisvrouw* winding home on drizzly Prinsengracht and ruptured eggs wandering the mazy cobblestones, of the old rope in the well snapping and the bucket that had climbed near enough to the sky to catch a glint of sun on its tilting surface now plummeting toward its dark swallowing crash, of the drooping chinless throat of Perla, of the young mother's milk-heavy breasts; think of the eyelids collapsing on the ancient, slit-gazed Inuit, all but blinding him, of the newborn puppies back in a sort of womb—although this womb is dry and made of burlap—tumbling over each other in a weighted sack that has just now been tossed over the rail of a bridge.

Think of the sea, and it is into the sea all images of subsidence eventually drift and dissolve . . . of the illimitable metric tons of dead creatures that daily, steadily inch their way further into the benthic blackness. From the lit upper galleries, glinting like raindrops, the fish descend. In the sea's cellars, it rains black corpses perpetually. The dead are always coming down.

49

Hell's Belle

At wits' end, at hope's end, I telephone my Lilja. It's getting on toward midnight. I don't usually call so late and she wonders what I want of her. *I* wonder what I want of her. "Pabbi," she says, "can I do something for you?"

"Not really," I tell her, and add, "Are you looking for company tonight?"

"To tell you the truth, Helmut and I were going out. But if you're looking for company, I'm pretty sure Sindri's free."

"Actually, I've got plenty to do. Actually, I *always* have plenty to do. It's a bottomless task, so far as I can see—trying to figure out just *why* we're losing so badly."

She came back at me hesitantly, after a pause: "This might sound crazy, but maybe you'd want to join Helmut and me? We're going off to a club, a disco, and don't say *no* until you've heard me out. Nonni Karlsson's going to be there—I think he's going to give some sort of speech. A toast, anyway. The band's Danish but their name is English—Let's Call It a Day—and you'd despise them utterly. You remember, some weeks ago, I gave you a little tour of the town? We went to a couple coffee shops, I was giving you a youth's-eye view of the city? Well, you claim to be looking to understand why Hannibal's losing so badly, you could consider tonight a continuation of that tour. I'm dead serious. You'll learn something, Pappalingur. You owe it to yourself to go. You owe it to the campaign to go."

It was the world's least appealing proposal—which was why I agreed to it. I owed it to the campaign? I was going to learn something useful? No, no—I wasn't looking for something helpful, but something hellish.

My goal was that personal abyss from which, the depths having been sounded, I might begin to reascend.

And it was fun to flabbergast the girl. When I said, "I'll come," she said, "You'll come? You mean you'll come? You'll honestly come? Good, wonderful, that's great. That's just—great. Now we weren't actually going to head over there until about one. I hope that's not too late . . ."

"That's fine. Proceed as though I were not along."

"The place is a little pricey. It's a thousand kronur."

A thousand kronur! Did Lilja have on hand a thousand kronur to throw away on a Danish rock band called "Call It a Day"? Clearly, I'd been much too generous with the girl for years. But I said, "Whatever it takes."

I went along with everything she proposed, although some saving instinct for flight induced me to refuse the offer of a ride in Helmut's car. We would go in mine. I'd be at their place a little after midnight.

The absurdity of the whole undertaking left everyone feeling clumsy and miscast. We had no protocol. When I arrived Helmut—whom, it seemed, I soon must begin thinking of as my son-in-law—offered me a drink. I accepted. To my surprise, and relief, the bottle of whiskey he unearthed bore the official stamp of the state liquor store. Our smuggling problem worsens by the day.

Lilja, conscientiously demonstrating that she'd profited from her recent visit to the hospital, made a show of producing grapefruit juice for herself. She was watching after her baby. Which I appreciated. My little granddaughter—I continued to trust my poet's intuition about the child's sex—was not yet a visible presence. But there was a flush to Lilja's face, and perhaps the first faint traces of a swelling amplitude—oh, the girl looked splendid! I've always had a special softness in my heart for pregnant women. . . .

What did the three of us talk about? I don't recall—though I do remember being grateful that the subject of the campaign wasn't broached. I suppose they were trying to cheer me up. Hapless Helmut even attempted to tell a joke—something about a family of Sicilians visiting Germany for the first time. . . . I must have drifted away for a moment. . . . I recall Lilja's ringing accelerated laughter and a sudden common recognition, accompanied by much zipping and buttoning, that it was time to leave.

The "club"—Lilja's word for the place, one more borrowing from English which the Freelandic Language Committee was not about to legitimate—was called "The Camel's Hump." It was owned by one of my former Superior School classmates, *not* a friend, who was reputed to be a primary contributor to Nonni's campaign. One, two, three, we each stepped up meek as lambs and were shorn of a thousand kronur. And we entered a place that managed, with wrenching simultaneity, to offend the ear, the eye, the nose.

I would begin with a description of the music, but a stern internal voice calls, Halt. It asks, Is there anything in the world more tedious than complaints about rock music uttered by a late-middle-aged man? So I stop dead, my pen arrested in my hand, until another voice replies, Yes, there *is* something still more tedious, and that's the din of the Danish band Let's Call It a Day as they entertain a seething crowd of Freelandic youth. . . .

Thudding, thundering, the music was colossal and cruel—like the thousand-times-amplified scrapings of cars skating into each other on an icy highway. Like the sound of a bountiful chandelier splintering price-lessly on a marble floor. Like the high roar of a dentist's drill, assaulting the ear in two directions, from inside the head as well as outside, sharpening its pitch as it prises out the quivering raw nerve it seeks. Spotlights slithered over the walls, momentarily turning cobweb-gray faces a cadaverous white-green. Meanwhile, faint but unmistakable, a low stink of vomit lurked at the bottom of each breath.

The three of us stood in a corner and yelled at each other for a while—our speech, punctuated with frequent hand and facial gestures, suggesting the first fumbling ums and ers, the Ur-ers, of some Neanderthal proto-language. Helmut disappeared and eventually returned with two red paper cups and a little can of pineapple juice. He handed me one of the cups and I obligingly drank. It seemed to be Coca-Cola, laced heavily with something like vodka.

We made our way—with painful slowness, past various lurching young people—toward what turned out to be a stage. Let's Call It a Day were writhing and leaping. On the wall behind them blazed a number of spotlit banners, all in English: "Liberate the Music," and "Free Music for a Free Land," and "It's *Our* Rock 'n' Roll." That was only a start. Lilja pointed. Right there before the stage was Nonni Karlsson himself. He was dancing, I guess—turning round and round like a rotisserie chicken.

I felt ashamed, for him and me both, as though I'd caught him— what?—got up in woman's clothes. He was in his "youth mode" clearly: lavender suit and tennis shoes and open-necked mustard-yellow shirt, his hair mussed roguishly.

Lilja wanted to dance with Helmut and would I hold her drink? I would. I stood there fifteen minutes? Twenty? I'd crossed into a new domain, where time itself fractured. . . . I watched Nonni dance with a blond girl, and then a bookish-looking brunette in severe black glasses, and then—here was a politician with catholic tastes—a redhead. In my distraction I sipped not from my own drink but Lilja's. Her lily-pure pregnant-girl's pineapple juice floated in a sea of vodka.

Like a train derailing on a bridge and tumbling, car by car, into a bouldered gorge, the music came to a close. A microphone squawked. One of the members of Let's Call It a Day announced, in lightly Danish-accented English, "And now I'd like to introduce the bright hope of the nation. Ladies, gentlemen, the next President of Freeland . . ." Applause. Whistles. Nonni stepped up onto the minimal stage. An errant spotlight found his red, jubilant face, licked with sweat. "Good evening," he bayed, and laughed, too close to the microphone. A wrenching squeal boomeranged through the cavern. He started again: "Fellow music lovers." Laughter, whistling, applause.

"I want to thank various people. I want to thank first Hannes Kristofersson, owner of the Camel's Hump, who proposed this rally tonight." Applause, applause. "And I want to thank the people who put up the banners." Applause. "And of course the members of Let's Call It a Day, for bringing us their fantastic musical talents." Applause, laughter, whistles—and the rumble of a bass guitar, a stomping thump-thump-*thump* of a bass drum.

"Now I'm hoping many of you won't recognize me as a politician." Laughter, applause. "But we do have an election coming up next week. And I need each and every one of you. This election is about something significant. It's about your fundamental rights—including your right to the music you love. Now I'm hoping you're all having a wonderful time tonight, but this evening is about more than just good times. It's a rally, isn't it? A demonstration. By being here, each and every one of you is making a powerful personal statement about your *most* basic human rights, aren't you?"

I'm hoping it's clear by now that Nonni's impromptu remarks came to me as a revelation. This was the first time I'd ever heard him speak in public with any facility, directness, or confidence. He had found his subject and his venue and his audience, hadn't he?

"By being here, each and every one of you is making a potent self-assertion. You are speaking up for a new Freeland. . . . The future begins *right here,"* Nonni declared and lifted his arms, symbolically embracing, through the smoky air, *each and every one of us.* I downed, at one go, my daughter's drink. Evidently, someone nearby had made a more powerful self-assertion. A fresh smell of vomit pressed itself upon me.

"I look at the crowd assembled before me and I ask myself, Who are these people? Do you know who you are? Friends, you are *freedom fighters.* Tonight you are battling for your *most basic civil rights.* . . ."

It was time to leave. I'd seen what I'd come for. I pushed through the audience, in search of Lilja. Nonni continued to applaud the crowd, and the crowd Nonni. Everyone in this place seemed at least half a head taller than I. Pushing, squeezing, elbowing, kneeing, hipping, I made my way from the stage to the far wall and back to the stage once more. I decided to—to call it a day. Lilja was a quick girl; she would guess what had become of me. At the end of the night someone would drive her, and the baby inside her, home where they belonged. Both would be tipsy, I supposed.

A sense of hopelessness, of physical impotence, swept over me as I jostled and jolted toward the exit. I'm a bit of a claustrophobe and it was like having Michael McKaig straddled atop me, panting in my ear, my face wedged into the crotch of his arm. Panic squirmed, screwed its way through my chest, and I pushed harder, ducked and shoved my way toward the door. I was sweating. The music cranked up once more, huger than ever. I was cursing loudly, though I don't suppose anyone heard me. I caught a pointed elbow in the ribs and a queasy light-headedness ricocheted through me and I thought I too might vomit. But here was the door.

And now, just as I was about to squeeze through the clogged exit, someone fiercely grabbed hold of my forearm. I swung around desperately, venomously. In my rattled state I didn't for a moment recognize my captor.

But I did understand, at once, that she was young, and fair-haired, and overtakingly beautiful.

50

Karmically Entwined

"**E**ggert!" she shouted over the din. "*Good Lord!*"

"*Elva!*" I shouted back. "*What are you doing here?*"—a question she might better have asked of me.

She weighed it seriously, though, a look of deep furrowed cogitation ruffling her normally smooth features. "*Drinking too much!*" she eventually concluded. "*What about you?*"

"*Not enough.*"

"*What?*"

"*Drinking not enough.*"

She had hold of both my arms; our shrieking faces were in each other's faces. Really, the racket was beyond belief.

"*But what are you doing here, Eggert?*"

"*Leaving.*"

"*What?*"

"*What I'm doing is LEAVING.*" I pointed to the doorway.

Elva followed me outside. The rain had stopped but the wind had a predatory edge. She too must have been preparing to leave. She had a coat under one arm and a black sweater under the other. In the heat of the Camel's Hump she'd been wearing a short red skirt and a turquoise leotard. The night was much too cold to be dressed as she was, but I said nothing. We walked down Sudurgata. My car was some ways off.

"What were you doing there?" Elva shouted—not yet having adjusted to the quiet of the street.

"I came with Lilja—my daughter, Lilja," I answered, softly. "She said it would educate me. I suppose she wanted me to see and hear Nonni Karlsson."

"He's disgusting." Elva spoke with real bitterness.

"A shame more people your age don't think so. It's the youth vote that's going to kill us."

"They say you're a fascist—some of the kids do."

"I know they do."

She brought her voice down. "They say you're dangerous."

"Dangerous?"

"That's right."

"I wish I were, Elva. It's one of the great regrets of my life that I don't hold enough real power to be dangerous to them—to anyone."

"I tell them, he's not dangerous. He's just very peculiar."

"That's good of you."

Her shoulder jounced mine, solidly. It seemed she was a good deal drunker than I'd first estimated and this knowledge invested me with *one* form of authority, anyway. I said to her sternly, parentally, "I want you to put on your coat."

Elva eyed me in the darkness, the beautiful disc of her face tilted to one side, skeptically, and then she shrugged. She put on her cardigan, not her coat, but I wasn't about to argue the point.

"Button it. I don't want you to catch cold," I told her. "You're sweating."

She buttoned up the sweater.

"Where are you headed now, Elva?"

"I'm walking with you. I thought *you* knew where you were going. Christ, it's ugly, isn't it?"

"What is?"

"Goddamned Thorskrist."

"Ugly compared to what?"

She answered me indignantly: "Ugly compared to Thorskrist."

"I was heading home," I said. "I could make you some coffee at my place."

"Coffee?"

"At my place."

"Your place?"

"Here's your chance to see ugly Thorskrist from the penthouse of Skyscraper Tower."

"Coffee out somewhere else maybe? Would you take me for coffee out somewhere else maybe?"

"Gladly," I said.

I was feeling less carefree than I perhaps managed to sound. It excited me, yes, to envision myself escorting a beautiful young woman into a coffee shop, but under the circumstances—the hour, her visible drunkenness, her recent affair with Hannibal—it disquieted me, too. Still, I led her to my car, held the passenger-side door open, came around and settled myself behind the steering wheel.

There was a hole-in-the-wall down by the waterfront, Hansen's, which stayed open until all hours. I drove there in roundabout fashion, letting Elva sober up a bit, letting the din clear from my ears. I turned on the heater. Elva slumped against the door of the car. I thought for a moment she might have fallen asleep. But when she spoke, without stirring from her slumped position, hers was a wide-awake voice: "Do you believe in Hell?"

"Believe in what?"

"In Hell. Satan's Hell. Eggert, do you believe in Hell?"

"Heavens no. Maybe that's one of the benefits of not believing in God."

"I hope so."

"You hope what?" I said.

"Hope there's a Hell . . ."

The heater ticked and purred. "I take it you know some person or persons whom you would wish to see burn?"

Elva didn't answer. I pulled into a parking lot around the corner from Hansen's. "Here's coffee," I announced. I got out of the car. Elva didn't move. Again I thought she might have fallen asleep.

I came around the front of the car and, tenderly, undid the passenger-side door. She sprung to attention—unpacked herself from the front seat, eyed me with owlish suspicion, then strode off in her heels and red miniskirt. I followed her inside.

Hansen's had five or six tables but only one booth, which surprisingly was empty. Elva crawled into it. She'd left her coat in the car. She removed her black sweater, stripping down to her turquoise leotard once again. I took a seat across from her and ordered coffee and a couple of salami rolls, although at this hour these were likely to be hard as bricks. The fluorescent lights of the place always made everyone but the youngest of children look as though they had one foot in the grave. It was alarming to discover just how beautiful Elva—hair in disarray, eye makeup smeared—still managed to appear.

"I have a friend who believes in reincarnation." Her voice was again too loud. "She says you go on meeting the same people, one life after the next. If two people are really *close*, what she calls karmically entwined, they're going to keep on meeting, one life after the next. They're always together."

"It's an attractive theory in many ways."

"It's probably not worth a sheep's turd. I'm no fool, I'm leaving here."

"Leaving?"

"Leaving Thorskrist and Freeland and politics and the Camel's Hump."

"Where are you going?"

"To Paris," Elva declared. "I'm going to go to Paris and become a waitress. I have a girlfriend who's a waitress at one of the fanciest restaurants in Paris and do you know what two people spent for dinner?"

"I don't think I do."

"It came to forty-five thousand kronur!" Roughly five thousand francs, or about nine hundred dollars. "Imagine trying to spend forty-five thousand kronur at—at you name the restaurant in Thorskrist!"

I suppose it runs in the very fiber of my character to feel a potent physical attraction whenever a woman—almost *any* woman—imparts a secret aspiration. And all the more so if the wish in question seems narrow, callow, unimaginative, mundane. That a job as a *waitress* would be the luminous sanctuary Elva divined for herself—some Parisian eatery where the besotted rich consumed oiled snails and larvae—broke my heart, and in breaking my heart Elva had never seemed quite so desirable. Her ambitions stirred in me a contending host of feelings—pity, superiority, solicitude, and a born pedagogue's hope that I might instruct her to her betterment. Illusory it may be, but it is—along with the phrase *Christ, she must be six feet tall*—one of the most dynamic aphrodisiacs I know: the soft voice in my head which now and again announces, *She needs my advice.*

"Have you been to Paris before, Elva?"

"Have I been to *Paris*?"

This emerged bitterly, and stridently. No, hell no of course not, for she'd never been *any*where don't you see, except once to damned Iceland, where it rained for four days straight, and once to damned England, where it rained for eight days straight, and how was she supposed to go *anywhere* given the sort of life she'd had?

Back and forth, piecemeal, in leaps and loops and pauses, a young Freelandic woman's life story emerged. I knew this sort of tale. She was the eldest of seven children and her father, who died when she was nine, had been shiftless anyway. Her mother drank and, shiftless herself, had relied on Elva to oversee the younger siblings, and it was only *now*, having attained the advanced age of twenty-four, that Elva's brothers and sisters were getting old enough to fend for themselves, damn it, and she was off to Paris where her friend was a waitress in a chandeliered restaurant where one couple had run up a bill of forty-five thousand kronur. . . . "Let's get out of here," she said.

I picked up the check. "The bill is hardly forty-five thousand kronur, but I can handle this," I told her. It was an extraneous protestation; she was making no motion to cover her share.

We climbed back into the car. "Will you do me a favor, Eggert?" she asked me.

"Anything, Elva."

"Will you take me somewhere?"

There was something new and urgent to her voice, a scraped-raw, intimate strain. It was precisely the voice I'd wish to hear on my deathbed. It was a voice to wake the dead.

"Anywhere you ask, Elva . . ."

"Okay. All right then. Thank you. Then all right drive me out to Founders' Point."

I didn't answer.

I nodded in the darkness.

I took an indirect route, in order to circle by the Customs House. What more tantalizing memory could a man have than that of rescuing a beautiful woman, crawling like a beast on all fours, from a deadly storm? As we drove past, did Elva recall that night? Did she remember plucking her black stockings from her pocket and casually slipping into them in the very seat where she now sat?

"Do you believe in Fate, Eggert?"

"In Fate? I don't know. Having thrown off God, it seems a little silly to let Him in by the back door by believing in Fate. But tell me what you mean."

"Do you think two people can be fated to be together?"

"I believe it can certainly feel that way. And maybe if it doesn't feel that way, it's not the real thing. But what would I know of such things? Who am I to use the phrase *the real thing*?"

I cut the headlights as we swung into Hannibal's long driveway. We sat in silence.

Somehow it didn't surprise me that, although the house was dark, smoke was wisping from Hannibal's chimney. Was he living round the clock in his study? The dimmest of red glows issued from within. I pictured my friend seated in there, slumped and brooding before a vanishing constellation of embers. How long, how many hours could he spend staring into his meager fireplace?

I realized that I'd realized a minute or so before that Elva was shaking, and not with the cold. In the darkness, right beside me, a beautiful young lady was weeping.

Neither of us said anything for a minute or two. Of course I wanted to take her in my arms, to take her home, take her to a church and marry her. Why couldn't she understand that I was nothing like everything that I was? I wanted to tell her we were karmically entwined, she and I, that life at bottom is a sort of desert island, and any single lifetime is but a day, and yet to those actually living on the island, those who have reached the final round of Twenty Down, there are to be years and years and years together. I listened to her weep.

"You're truly in love with him, aren't you?" I said.

Her reply shot back with crisp defiance: "In *love*? Damn it to hell, you think I'm stupid? Well, I'm not so stupid as to be in love with somebody who no longer loves me."

"But think of Hannibal," I pointed out. "Think how stupid *he* must be. To be in love with an entire nation that no longer loves him."

51

What "Isn't Done" Is Done

I was working on a speech the following afternoon when Lilja telephoned. I assumed she was calling to reproach me for abandoning her and Helmut at—or upon—the Camel's Hump. Or perhaps calling to apologize for having led me there in the first place. But none of it. She asked me, with an unnerving quickness, whether I'd seen *The Daily Liar*—actually, *she* called it *The Daily Ledger*. When I told her I hadn't yet, her response was, "Maybe you'd better."

It was ominous—her clipped urgency.

"Are they calling me names again?"

"They have some photographs?"

"Photographs? What photographs?"

What in the world had I done? Or what had they caught me at?

"Of Hannibal."

"Of Hannibal? Photographs of Hannibal? What's he doing in them?"

Oh, to judge from her voice, he might be got up in a schoolgirl's uniform, or feeding drugs into his arm with a hypodermic needle.

"He's—well he's just being Hannibal. But the effect is—painful."

"I'll go see for myself," I said. "I'll call you later, thanks, good-bye."

I made my way over to the nearest newsagent/tobacconist. Was I kidding myself, or did old Helga behind the counter give me a shamefaced and sympathetic look? She folded my paper in half before handing it over. And, after calling a jaunty good-bye, I left it that way until I'd stepped back into the Skyscraper Tower elevator.

Is This the Man to Represent Us to the World? the headline demanded. There was almost no other text. The whole front page and the whole back page were devoted to photographs—eight of them.

As Lilja had said, what they illustrated was just Hannibal being Hannibal. But they were also, as she'd said, *painful*. The first photograph caught Hannibal standing among a crowd of men in suits—some of the country's top businessmen. He was scratching ruminatively, scoopingly at his testicles. In the second he was seated at a banquet. He must have spilled a morsel of food, for why else would he be sucking on his necktie? In the third, clutching a bottle in one hand, he was rising from the floor—apparently having fallen. In the fourth, he was yawning—hugely, cavernously—straight into the face of a man identified as the Danish Ambassador. In the fifth, he was reaching toward a young woman—I thought I recognized Elva, although her face was clipped at the side of the picture. My guess was that he'd been reaching toward her shoulder and had missed by a little, but another viewer might regard him as groping a girl's breast. In the sixth, a man identified as "Kobo Kumano, Leading Japanese Fish Importer" was standing at a dais, delivering some sort of oration. Seated beside him was Hannibal, head thrown back and mouth agape, evidently snoring soundly. In the seventh photograph, Hannibal was again on the floor—those knees of his were forever deserting him. This time he was brandishing a beer bottle, and Reverend Gudmundur, perhaps the country's leading religious figure, was glimpsed standing behind him. The final photograph had been taken at the public pool. It caught Hannibal from behind. He was climbing out of one of the hot tubs. His swimming trunks had slipped, and an inch or so of the cleft of his buttocks was bared for the world to see.

I should perhaps begin by saying that in Freeland this sort of exposé—or whatever it could politely be termed—"isn't done." Our politics might plausibly degenerate into name-calling or even fisticuffs, but we don't publicly distribute photographs of each other's buttocks. It isn't chiefly modesty or prudishness that restrains us—although there may be a fair measure of such things at work. No, I suspect it's a feeling, all the more powerful for being inchoate and instinctual, that ours is a country so vulnerably small, so negligible in the eyes of the world, that we can scarcely afford any public exhibition that would make our statesmanship look ludicrous. Hannibal had been our President for twenty years. And here he was, the soi-disant father of the country, on display openly scratching his balls and groping young women and falling down drunk and mooning the world at large. Far more than I would have thought possible, the photographs unnerved me—*dislodged* me, *uprooted* me. Could it be that I, so proudly cynical and jaded a public man, had just had the last of my illusions shattered?

And hadn't Lilja suffered much the same blow? Wasn't that what I'd heard in her urgent terseness? Charter member that she was of the Chuck-out-the-old-bastards-and-their-old-bastard-ways Party, she might be expected to relish this sort of attack, but her voice said otherwise.

Dismay, shock, and a sensation of shamed impotence . . . No one among us knew what to do about this collapse in community standards. That's the lesson, anyway, I took away from my afternoon at the Hotel Snorri. As soon as I saw the photographs I telephoned out to Founders' Point. No answer. I then donned a suit and tie—this seemed a day for especial finery—and drove over to the hotel. The circumstances called for a display of unflappability. I found my seat, ordered a thermos of coffee, made a show of flourishing pen and paper. I was writing, or was making a show of writing, a new speech.

With low, uncertain voices, with the timidity of wrens hopeful for a handout, they kept coming forward, usually one at a time, sometimes in quiet groups of two or three—troubled souls, awaiting from me some signal as to how they ought to be responding to this outrage. *Had I seen today's* Daily Ledger? Oh yes, I'd seen it. *And the—the photographs? I'd seen those?* Oh yes, I'd seen them. *Weren't they outrageous?* Oh yes, definitely outrageous—as well as libelous. No doubt the matter would end up in court. We were confident of a happy result in the long run. They had really dug their own grave this time, hadn't they? *But in the meantime, what were we going to do?* And this was the question that repeatedly stumped me. Did they sense that I had no real answer?

What to do? What I did next was to drive out to Founders' Point. Hannibal's Land Rover was in the driveway but he didn't seem to be at home. I went out back, to the barn. The horse, Blesi, was missing. Hannibal had gone riding.

I drove back into town and wandered up and down Skeggjagata. *Had I seen* The Daily Ledger? Yes, I had. *And wasn't it outrageous?* Yes, and libelous, too. *And what were we going to do about it?*

What were we going to do about it?

And everywhere I went: the same stammering combination of ire and shame. The air was charged with it—as must have been apparent even to Kevin Wilhelm, who appeared that night on the television news. He hastened to assure the people of Freeland, with a blend of large-eyed sincerity and fluorescent grins, that the "photo spread" had been solely his own idea. Nonni had had nothing to do with it. He hoped the good people of Freeland would take it in the "spirit of fun" in which it was conceived. He was certain that Hannibal Hannibalsson did. It was also a supreme testament to the decency and maturity of this great nation—a place which, frankly, impressed him more and more with each day of his stay—that it would allow this type of political freedom of expression. In fact, looking at the photo spread, we ought to feel *proud*—proud of the enlightened liberty and the vigorous exchange of ideas it represented.

Hannibal's buttocks as a *vigorous exchange of ideas*?

But Wilhelm also sincerely hoped that, amid all this fun and amusement, the people of Freeland did not lose sight of the fact that each and every photograph was taken in a public venue. This was no invasion of privacy. There was nothing on exhibition here that hadn't been, already, presented to all. The question now put to the people of Freeland was whether such behavior from our nation's leader, on display to every foreign tourist and businessperson who comes to this wonderful country, is not perhaps a little—unsuitable? Did Hannibal's deportment fit with our notions of a modern, civilized nation?

I flicked off the set. I was alone in my apartment. I got down a bottle of Scotch and did what I rarely do on my own: I took a deep dive into it.

I hunched over my desk. The wind had started howling. The eight pictures were before me. I went over them time and again. . . .

Some years ago, as he hit middle age, Hannibal had had to confront the question faced by everyone possessed in youth of an effortless beauty. Would he remain true to his looks, maintaining them at whatever cost, or remain true to their effortlessness, let the looks go where they may.

One often reads how American politicians, their fates increasingly wired to the television screen, divide their time between their plastic surgeons and their makeup specialists. But while it sometimes grieved me to see what a wreck Hannibal had become, with his sprawling gut and his thinning hair, his drink-ruddied face and his gimpy knees, wouldn't the loss have been greater still—wouldn't Hannibal have ceased utterly to be Hannibal—had he chosen the other path? To envision a cautious, abstemious, hair-transplanted, liposuctioned Hannibal was to conceive of a denatured—a monstrous—thing. Wasn't there, once one struggled past the photographs' buffoonery and tawdriness, an element of nobility in the generous-hearted decline they documented?

Admittedly, there might be those in the population who would fail to see anything noble in a President whose photograph effectively declared, My name is Hannibal Hannibalsson and here is a view of my big and sagging bottom and I hope a week from now you will vote for me.

52

Ashed In: Waiting for
Our Miracle

We have an expression in Freeland, *up to our ears in ash*, roughly equivalent to *in hot water* or *up the creek* or to various scurrilous or scatological alternatives, but our phrase has a quality of tactile desperation the others lack. Peer deep into our souls and it's clear most Freelanders envision the end of the world as a brilliant fountaining of lava and ash. In just such a fashion were we once almost annihilated in the past, in the eruption of Great Blue in 1810. Some few were killed by the fire, but most died from the ash.

It must have been a sort of lithic snow, gray and dainty, all but weightlessly coming down—and coming down and coming down. The sun, glimpsed through a heavy curtain, was nothing but a candle flame. The pastures were choked, the garden plots buried, the rivers clogged. Ours was a newly lunar land where terrestrial creatures had no place. With nothing to graze on, our livestock began to starve. And the people after them. Frantic appeals were sent to Denmark, but these went unheard, or unheeded. . . .

On the morning of September 29, the Wednesday after the Sunday when *The Daily Liar* offered its photographic gallery, I drove out to Founders' Point. Up to his ears in ash was the fitting phrase for Hannibal Hannibalsson. There were exactly five days remaining to the campaign. I had a copy of *The Torch* with me—the so-called friendly paper. My hope had been for a savage riposte. I'd looked forward to extravagant fulminations—outrage, fury, indignation, censure. Nothing like. Though their editorial did inveigh against "journalistic excesses" and the "lures of the gutter press," protests in that direction were tempered. Reading between the lines, one might fairly say that the harsher criticisms lay elsewhere. There were scattered hints that Hannibal himself was culpable. While breaches of journalistic etiquette may have been perpetrated, the photographs did bespeak a certain lack of "desired dignity and comportment" in our highest elected official, and so forth.

How in the world could *The Torch* do this to us? In addition to their tepid, "balanced" rendition of *The Daily Liar* fiasco, they'd accorded prominent coverage—front page—to the latest poll. We were now down 61–29, with ten percent undecided. We were losing ground. Ken Kanekyu, the "numbers man" of the American consultant trio, explained that the election seemed to be moving from a landslide "to whatever the word might be that describes a contest even more one-sided than a landslide." And the editorial page contained a murky analysis of the problems of the stumbling incumbent's campaign, noting that he "appeared to have unwisely heeded the counsel of a number of advisers who have too often held fanatical views that are no longer in harmony with the nation at large. This has been particularly the case in regard to the issue of 'protection of the language,' where a certain overzealousness has led to unnecessarily severe restrictions on foreign music and foreign—" And so it went, with a prolixity suggesting that our friend Tryggvi himself might have been its source. Hadn't he warned me of his desertion when I'd run into him on Skeggjagata recently, the day he'd complained about "restlessness" at the paper and added, as an afterthought, that Gudrun Haraldsdottir was "dropping fast"? *The Torch* was of course calling for my resignation. It was some consolation—though not enough—that its editorial, while decrying "overzealousness" in matters of language, fell guilty of one hopelessly mixed metaphor and two solecisms. . . .

I hollered a greeting and let myself in and found Hannibal—where else?—slumped in his study. Had he slept in his leather chair? He was wearing what might charitably be called his pajamas: a baggy pair of elastic-waist cotton bottoms of indeterminate color and origin. They were four or five inches too short and looked like something that might once have been worn in a hospital, for an extended period, by a terminal patient; they looked not so much lived-in as died-in. His feet were bare. His shoulders and chest but not quite all of his stomach were covered by a yellowed, rust-spotted T-shirt that was frayed at one shoulder. I'd seen him many times, Lord knows, looking not his best in the morning after an ill-judged night, but the sight of him today was something of a shock. I guess

I hadn't quite grasped just how far his appearance had degenerated over the last few weeks. His face was pouched with fatigue and looked flabby and sallow. His nose had the ruddy, open-grained look of the perpetual boozer. His mustache was ragged and it held, besides, what might have been scraps of food or newspaper. His shoulders wore the slump of defeat. He desperately needed a haircut. He was, unmistakably, *up to his ears in ash.*

In addition, an acrid, unnatural odor pierced the room. This wasn't the familiar, gray, depleted smell of a cold clogged hearth. Whatever it was, it was bright and *evil.*

"What stinks in here?" I offered by way of greeting.

The voice had something of the lightness and dryness of ash: "I made a fire. One of the pieces of wood had paint on it. Or maybe there was a bit of plastic attached."

"I don't know how you can sit in here. . . ."

"I've had quite a bit of practice. You get used to it."

I perched myself lightly on the broken-backed couch. "You've seen *The Torch* this morning?"

"I don't suppose I have. And please don't tell me I need to."

Sorry as I felt for him, the truth is I felt angry, too. Or perhaps the word is betrayed: tricked and misled by that big partially dismantled body in its elastic-waist pants and frayed T-shirt. Somewhere in this vast warehouse of a book I've referred to myself as the brains of the body politic—the head of the Language Committee, the preserver of Culture—but I now understood it was far more truthful to say that here before me slumped the heart, the faithful but enfeebled heart, of Freeland. Were we really beaten? Beaten not in terms of votes but in the blood-pumping core of our beings? No doubt there was something spiteful in my voice as I announced, "There's a new poll. We're losing worse than ever."

"Does that surprise you, Eggert?"

"A little. I thought we'd already hit bottom, Hannibal." Two could play at this game of cold Christian names rather than nicknames.

"Evidently it's a long, long way down."

"And while they do criticize *The Daily Liar* for 'journalistic excesses,' they also question the 'dignity and comportment' of our 'highest elected official.'"

"Does that surprise you?"

"It *does*, frankly. They've been good, long allies of ours."

"Yes, and they're the last people in town who have accepted the notion that I'm going down to a big defeat at the end of the week. They're belatedly making peace with what will be the new administration. These are rats that aren't going to go down with the ship."

"There was also an editorial suggesting that your 'advisers' are fanatics—particularly in the matter of language preservation, regulation of radio and music and the like."

"Now *who* in heaven could they be talking about. . . ."

"They were suggesting you might get rid of me."

At this, Hannibal looked up, sharply. His head was tilted and from this angle there was something queerly asymmetrical about his features, reminding me of—of all people!—Michael McKaig, whose lopsided face, so many years ago, used to study me with such simian cunning as we warily circled each other, the first step in that rite which concluded with his knuckling raw the back of my head. For just a moment, with this odd ghost of a linkage in my brain, I wondered whether Hannibal might truly be going mad.

He spoke in a cracked voice: "*You aren't abandoning me too?*"

"Christ, of course not. I'm only suggesting that if you think it would do the campaign any good, I'd be glad—"

"Not you too! You're not jumping ship too?"

"Good heavens no: this rat plans to go down with the ship."

It says something about the pitiful state we were in that I would offer such words in solace, and that Hannibal would welcome them as such. "I knew I could count on you, Eggi," he murmured, and stared once more into the nonexistent blaze in his hearth. He'd promised that I'd get used to the smell in here, but I was beginning to feel sick to my stomach.

Hannibal's generally not a man given to nostalgia, but there was a tender wistfulness in his tone as he asked, "Remember you once wrote a Charter for the New Republic of Freeland?"

"Do I remember? I can tell you exactly where I wrote it: I wrote it on a plane from Reykjavik to Thorskrist, on my way back from Washington, the summer of 1973. And I can recall pretty much word for word the letter that inspired it: 'Come back, come back. I'm running for office and I need your help.' There was a footnote attached, in which you explained that the office you were running for was President."

"Yessss." I'd amused him, a little. He said, "And the first part of your Charter was something about limiting tourists."

"It was the third part. Right after the prohibitions on pastel sweat suits and frozen waffles. It was the Fair Weather Friend Provision. It stipulated that no tourist would be allowed to visit Freeland only in the summer. Your passport would be stamped, and if you came once in the summer, next time you'd have to come in the winter. None of this attempting to cheat Mother Nature. If you came for the white nights of summer, you had to come for the black days of winter. You had to take the dark with the light."

"Dark days will be here soon," Hannibal said. "Winter's coming, and this year we never had much of a summer. . . ."

"Dark days are good for the soul."

"I've been thinking about the Visitors, the what Nonni calls electoral consultants. You know what, Eggi? They're evil."

And his words, instantly, cheered me to the marrow of my bones. "But that's just *it*," I cried. "Don't you see? That's just exactly what I've been saying all along."

"When they first appeared, I thought they were amusing," Hannibal went on, in the same tone of earnest and mournful expostulation, as though he hadn't heard me. It appeared that, just as he'd had to reach this conclusion himself, he likewise needed to express it unassisted. "But what they represent is hardly amusing. There should be a Charter against them. It's the death of everything you and I mean when we speak the word *politics*."

Did he know what he was saying? Just how deeply—in his mulling way—had Hannibal grasped the significance of our Visitors? He understood a great deal, I suddenly felt prepared to say. Yes, the three Visitors were buffoons—a team that, in their native land, might be brought in to supervise a mayoral election in a middling-size city in a middling-size state. They were mediocrities. Even so, we needed to look further. . . .

Had Hannibal come to understand, in these past few weeks, that the profession of poll-taker—ostensibly so technical, so dry, so neutral—was inherently corrupting? Did he see that much? And did he see more? Did he see that mendacity was to the poll-taker what black lungs were to the coal-miner—a malady absorbed with the very air they breathed? Had he envisioned yet a commonwealth where a politician might plausibly say, *I will tell you what my heartfelt convictions are just as soon as the latest polls arrive*? A world where statesmen are coached in spontaneity?

And did he see even beyond such things, venturing still farther out to the world we're all rapidly approaching: the one where the demographer marries the marketer, and effectively only two groups of people matter any more—those who make television pitches for whoever will pay them to make pitches, and those who, ensconced in their easy chairs, let the pitches roll over them? Everyone else will be—as a statistical portion of the market, or the electorate—an irrelevance. . . . Did Hannibal see all that?

I said to him, "I read not long ago about a new practice in American campaigns. Candidates will fly into local airports but they won't really land, at least in any meaningful sense. They will be filmed stepping down from the plane. Then they get back in and fly to another small airport, in order to repeat the process. They've learned, you see, that if they arrive at a local airport, they'll get their faces on local television."

Hannibal took a little time to digest this practice. "Up until recently, I'd always assumed they were simply sillier than we are—the Americans."

"What the Visitors have come to teach us is that everyone's as silly as the Americans. Potentially."

Hannibal finished my thought quite neatly: "And that's why the Visitors have come. To fulfill our potential."

"It's like dealing with a kid you have to humor because it's *his* birthday, and *his* birthday party. The only trouble is, it's always, every day, the Americans' birthday—and their birthday party."

Again Hannibal added just the right embellishment: "Wouldn't you think, with all those birthdays, they would eventually grow up?"

"Hanni, to the *contrary*. We're talking about a country that will not rest easy so long as there remains one grown-up nation on the planet."

"But Eggi: *why are they like that?*"

Probably no more than once a year, certainly no more than twice, Hannibal turned on me the expression I read on his features now. It was a look of burning inquiry. It was a face that effectively said: *I have only this instant recognized that some vital piece is missing in my world-view.* Oh, of course Hannibal was forever pretending to solicit my advice—which I dutifully and at some length provided, even while knowing he generally inhabited a realm all but inaccessible to my words. Yet a moment like this was different: with his whole heart and soul, he was prepared to listen.

I proceeded cautiously. "I can't give you a full answer," I said, "but I can give a partial explanation. They don't feel they have to clean up after themselves. Most rich countries are like that. The Germans have brought in the Turks to sweep their alleyways and peel their potatoes. The French have allowed in the Algerians to scoop up after their dogs. The

Arabs fly in their maids from the Philippines. When I was in Texas, it was all Mexicans who made the hotel beds, washed the dishes, shoveled up the muck. But in Freeland, who takes out the trash? Freelanders. Who cleans the septic tank? Freelanders. We've had the historical advantage of our powerlessness."

Hannibal looked skeptical. "There was a time—" he began, and was he about to launch into our great Viking heyday?

I interrupted him: "The Americans? They're infantilizing the planet. That's why they sent the Visitors, who are contract killers. They're hit men, whose intended victim is named Freelandic Culture. You do understand that, don't you, Hanni?"

"It's just four more days. Then it will be over. They will go away."

"It will *never* be over. They won't be done till we're done in. But we've got to fight it out to the end anyway, Hanni."

"Fight it? Fight it out? And just how, may I ask, am I supposed to fight it out? Let me guess. I'm to give one more talk to the Chamber of Commerce? Promise them all higher profits and lower taxes? Or give a speech in a discotheque? Or I'll announce a condom giveaway on 'Youth Hour'?"

Sarcasm has never been very becoming in my friend. It's always been more in my line, actually. He lacked the necessary wit, as well as that hint of something pinched in the spirit; his outsize temperament got in the way whenever he turned mincing or carping. Nonetheless, I saw what he meant. He was feeling no reluctance to fight. No, he was feeling instead a befuddled sense that the only fighting now permitted wasn't anything he quite recognized.

Oh, his whole life he'd been waiting to fight! He was waiting—even now, I suppose—to hear that an expeditionary force of colonialist Danes, wearing lava-gray camouflage gear, was climbing Great Blue with flag in hand, intent on wresting sovereignty from us once more. He was waiting to hear that an army of Greenlandic Eskimos in polar-bear parkas, riding an armada of kayaks, had sneaked ashore during a blizzard and was ambushing one sheep farm after another. Oh, the poignancy of a life that waits always for an invasion that never comes! Where does it naturally lead, except to a man in a brown study in a brown study?—to a room stinking of burnt plastic and to a slumped torso in a ripped T-shirt canted toward a dead fireplace?

"We're awaiting the end," Hannibal said.

I meant to cheer him, though the correction issuing automatically from my lips wasn't very encouraging: "No we're not, we're waiting for a miracle."

"All right. That's what we're doing. We're waiting for our miracle."

"If that's the case," I said, "we might as well do so without freezing. I'll make a fire."

"There isn't much wood."

"I'll make a small fire."

"There may be a couple of scraps at the side of the house."

I left Hannibal in his chair and stepped outside.

The sky was overcast but glazed: a silver, timeless expanse whose illumination seemed to have less to do with the sun—with generous, gold, solar illumination—than with some sort of celestial fluorescent strip-lighting. The cosmos was economizing. Firmamental cutbacks. The scraps of wood—more of Hannibal's scavenging—were a sorry lot: a triangle of plywood, the leg of a chair, a silted piece of driftwood, the ribs of an old fish crate. I could carry in most of it in a single load.

Inside, tinder, too, was scarce. There were a couple of cardboard boxes and some paper plates. With hands and feet, tearing and stamping, I readied the various ingredients. The fireplace, too, like its owner, was "deep in ash." I laid in the paper plates and propped the wood in a tentlike wedge over them. For someone who doesn't own a fireplace, I've maintained a good touch for a blaze.

Still, this wet and muddy collection was slow to catch. The fireplace coughed smoke into the room. "I know what this fire lacks," I said.

I rose from my crouch and retrieved the offending newspaper. What better way to start a fire than with a *Torch*? Hannibal didn't need to read it. I balled it up, page by page. Then I struck another match. This time everything caught. Still stooping before the fireplace, I spoke to the newspaper balls, as they, too, gave way to ash: "I may be among the damned," I began, in a show of vacant histrionics, "but I consign all of you to the fires of Hell."

53

Our Miracle:
Rut Lifts a Finger

That night I went to bed at three in the morning and I dreamed that Sindri and I were sitting at a sunlit kitchen table, we were chatting in an amiable and comfortable way. And he made me an offer, he said, "Would you like to see my children?" and I answered, "Wholeheartedly, my boy," and so Sindri led me upstairs to his bedroom and I knew this place, I'd been in here before. For this room was my old room, the one I'd rented from the McKaigs in Detroit. These were the walls of the dead boy's room—the shrine in which I'd cohabited with a dead son's ghost.

"Here are my children!" Sindri announced jubilantly and pointed to the floor.

And I saw that the boy all along had been pulling my leg, for there upon the rug was a menagerie of creatures each no larger than my thumb. All were ambulatory. I looked closer and I spotted a giraffe and a bear on its hind legs and a waddling duck and a plump donkey and a little furry mouse, and I said to him, "Quite ingenious. But they're not alive, Sindri my boy."

Each one, on nearer inspection, bore a silver key on its back. Sindri's *children* were windup toys.

But "Oh yes, they're alive," the boy persisted, in that maddeningly sincere way of his. "They're alive but they are *ever* so delicate. You must be careful with them, Father."

But they're windup toys, I told him again, and he stubbornly maintained his position—*alive . . . alive . . .* And he beseeched me again to treat them with greatest delicacy.

And in my impatience I snatched up the mouse—a sharp-nosed ugly little dustball—and said, "Here, *look*, son, *look*, it's dead, son, dead, my boy, *look* . . ." And something stirred—gently, horribly—in my closed hand. A vibrant little face angled its way out, out through the gap between my thumb and index finger, and for one electrified instant our gazes met—its bright little eyes were like the pointed ends of a pair of scissors—and then the creature opened up its face and savagely bit me, a ripping gaping razor-toothed bite, and leapt like a rocket from my hand. . . .

I woke, and sunk my hand, which stung as though it *had* been bitten, tight between my legs. It was four in the morning. The wind was blowing. A titanic wash of despair slid over me. I saw that all sorts of jagged pieces of my life informed the dream—I'd blended together, among other things, the live child Sindri and the McKaigs' dead child Steven, as well as my life-long identification with rodents, and the recent revelation that Sindri would probably never give me a grandchild. All had agglomerated to create a multistranded narrative, but under the circumstances I hadn't either the strength or the desire to piece it out. What possible benefit was going to come of psychoanalyzing myself once more—what insight could I, at this point, possibly grasp that would go any distance toward amending myself? No, the patterns of my life—as I woke at four in the morning, Thursday the thirtieth of September, four days before the election, and the tiny, embattled culture I'd stood for and fought for about to go smash—constituted an intricate, tightening web of reproaches. For all my rounds of Twenty Down, all my frantic romantic pursuits, I'd wound up alone on my deserted island, whose name was Bare Subsistence. I lay in my bedroom in the dark, half-dozing, and the whole bitter business of the years was all jumbled together: Gudrun in her hospital bed convinced that I'd won the Long Run at the First Freelandic Olympics, and Geoffrey Simple going blind, and Meg's dirty pink Bermuda shorts and her dead son's dusty airplanes, and the children calling me Wharf-rat when I was a schoolboy, and Lilja saying *He's gay, Pabbi*, and that sweet-faced girl Bella Simple peering thoughtfully at my leaky erection, and my father-in-law's rotting swamp-colored mouth, and the crack of Hannibal's buttocks on the front page of the newspaper, and my skin turned to pus and fungus in the Washington heat and old blind Thorgunnur seeming to smell me out rather than see me, saying in that stern unquestionable way, *It's Eggert, isn't it?* . . . Everything was jumbled, everything was jagged and accusatory, and I lay helpless there, not quite dozing, hating my face, hoping sleep might return before the dawn.

When I woke next it was a little after one—it was afternoon! I felt rattled and upended—I never sleep to such an hour—and for a moment didn't realize it was the phone that had roused me.

"Eggert—Eggert, I've got the pictures!"

"The pictures?" What in the world was this? *Who* was this?

"Of Rut. I was there. I've got them. They're beautiful."

"Of Rut?" Beautiful pictures of *Rut*? Another one—another Freelandic madman. It's the Arctic darkness, or it's the cold and the drink, or it's our inbreeding: our land abounds in lunatics.

Then I realized who my caller was and despair laid its cold hand upon my chest. It was untrusty Trausti, the world's worst photographer— *our* photographer. Doubtless he was drunk again, for he somehow managed to be perpetually drunk, and even so Hannibal wouldn't hear of my firing him.

"You remember I've been tailing them?"

"Tailing them?"

"Nonni and his gang. Remember? Waiting—I've been waiting. Well, I didn't get her actually delivering the first blow, front on and all that, more's the pity, but I do have a shot, pretty as you please, of her giving him a swift kick to the hindquarters."

"Trausti, what are you talking about?"

"You mean you haven't heard?"

"Haven't heard what? I've been asleep. What in the world are you on about now?"

"I thought *every*body'd heard. Well this is something. This is really something. You might say he took a sampling from a section of the electorate he hadn't met yet. Or he tapped into deep-rooted feelings that hadn't been expressed. She decked him, she did, right flat out. Knocked out two of his front teeth."

"His two front teeth . . . Hannibal's two front teeth?"

"*Hannibal's?*" Trausti cried, and laughed so explosively I felt as if, through the phone, he'd sprayed saliva in my ear. "No no *no*. *Hannibal?* No, the *American*. The one with all the teeth. Or the one who used to have all the teeth, for however many he still has, he had two more of the things when he woke up this morning. He's unmistakable, Eggert, I don't see how you could get the two of them confused. Wilhelm, Kevin Wilhelm. Decked him is what she did. Right flat out."

Inside my chest a pair of great wings, though heavily weighted, extended themselves and flapped, once. Up to its ears in ash. Up to its ears in ash, a scrawny but colossal bird shrugged and twisted and yanked and yanked its wings free and flapped them, once, and flapped them once more.

"Now let me get this straight," I said. "Slow down, slow down. Damn it, speak straight. Are you actually telling me you have a photograph of Rut Bjartardottir delivering some sort of blow to Kevin Wilhelm?"

"Some sort of blow? I say, Speak straight, Eggert. I say, Let's call it one hell of a mighty kick in the ass. Square in the backside. Right flat out."

"And you're at home? You're calling from your house?"

"Sure I am. I've been in the darkroom."

"Don't move, Trausti. Don't go anywhere. Don't talk to anyone. I'll be there in two minutes."

I think I made it over there in one. He sat me down at his kitchen table. Somewhere far away a voice buzzed and droned beside my head. It was that endearingly tipsy fellow, Trausti Hauksson, explaining to me what I was looking at. I scarcely heard a word. I had no need of explanations.

For these were, without question, the most dizzyingly beautiful photographs I'd ever seen.

Here was Rut Bjartardottir tossing Kevin Wilhelm, his jaw spilling blood, out of the Cod's Head. Here she was—yes—gorgeously landing a big booted foot square to his backside. And here was Kevin Wilhelm at last getting a close firsthand look at Freeland's "grass roots": he was prone in the mud and gravel.

When at last I'd calmed down, I had Trausti repeat his entire account. Needless to say, some details were blurry, but what did this matter when the photographs were so crisp and clear? Eventually, as this most delicious of days wore on, I assembled a full narrative. . . .

It seems that on this Thursday morning Kevin Wilhelm, having heard about our quaint custom of serving "strong coffee" in a "fishermen's bar," had gone off in search of a cup. Two days before, on Tuesday evening, he'd appeared on television claiming that the "photographic essay" in *The Daily Liar*, including that shot of Hannibal's bare backside, had been purely his own idea. Evidently Rut, having had some thirty-six hours to brood over the matter, still didn't find it amusing. . . .

Meanwhile, equally outraged at the "photographic essay"—as well as feeling personally miffed, no doubt, at seeing a competitor's work become central to the campaign—our endlessly resourceful official photographer, Trausti Hauksson, the Lord God bless him and keep him, had spent the last couple of days following Kevin Wilhelm. Trausti had "just had a feeling" that some sort of indiscretion or embarrassment would manifest itself.

Trausti hadn't actually followed Mr. Wilhelm inside the Cod's Head, and so he'd missed the bewitching moment when Rut came forward and asked Kevin to stand up. The American had readily complied, no doubt curious to see what colorful native custom was about to be enacted. Reaching deep into the thick muscles of her shoulder—summoning them in a way she hadn't, presumably, in a third of a century, not since that mid-summer night when a young Hannibal Hannibalsson, flush with Olympic glory, had stolen a kiss from her and she had responded by breaking his nose—Rut this time drove a square, uncompromising fist square into Mr. Wilhelm's mouth, dislodging his upper two front teeth. As Kevin, in a stunned horror of pain and stupefaction, was scrambling about on the floor, searching frantically for those mainstays of his winning smile, Rut had picked him up by the scruff of the neck and tossed him, Photograph #1, out the doorway of the Cod's Head. Still not quite satisfied with her handiwork, she had planted a booted foot in his backside, Photograph #2, and left him prone, Photograph #3, in the mud.

"Maybe this calls, perhaps this calls for a little celebration?" Trausti tentatively suggested.

"Trausti, my friend, this calls for a celebration involving the finest spirits you have available."

He brought out a couple of coffee mugs and a bottle of *brugga*—his own brew. Freelanders have long speculated that it's only a matter of time before Trausti confuses his photographer's and his moonshiner's chemicals and poisons himself. Trusting that *this* wouldn't be the day, I emptied my mug at a single go. I was too rapturous to sit still. I could have kissed him. "Make me as many more prints as you can," I called from the door. "I'll be back. We'll distribute them everywhere. . . ."

I scurried along. Oh, I was a busy mouse. . . . I was over at the television station: I have a few photographs that might be of interest to— *Yes, oh good God, yes, these could go on the air tonight.* I was over at *The Torch*: I thought you might be interested in these— *This is front-page material!* I was over at the printer's: Was it possible that we might place an express order on some posters or handbills or whatever— *Right away, but what about a caption?* Yes, let me see. A caption. How about "Freeland Fights Back"? I think I like the sound of that. . . .

And where, meanwhile, as I race from place to place, as the capital buzzes and swirls and guffaws and shouts, is Hannibal? The man of the hour? The fond subject of every conversation? He's nowhere to be found. Rumor has it that he took the ferry to Giant Island. I envision him seated beside the Waters of Truth, contemplating the bubbling end of the world, but the end may not be so imminent as he supposes. . . .

Rumor also has it that Kevin Wilhelm has already departed our shores—that, not finding a scheduled airline to his liking, he'd chartered a private plane to Reykjavik, whence he hoped to get a quick flight home. It seems that, for all his marveling over Freelandic competency and sophistication, he'd not wanted to trust the repair of his mouth to any but an American specialist.

Later in the afternoon I place a phone call to Rut at the Cod's Head. Wary allies at the best of times, we've exchanged no more than a handful of words since Hannibal declared his candidacy. Even now, I suppose, I'm a little leery of confronting her in person. The phone seems safer.

An unfamiliar voice answers—a young woman's—and I identify myself and ask for Rut. Such a long pause ensues that I fear I've been placed in telephonic purgatory, but finally Rut's voice breaks in: "What do you want?"

"To say hello, among other things. It's been a long time."

"I've been getting calls all day. I've got work to do, Eggert, so what do you want from me?"

"I've been worried that you're angry with me, Rut."

"Stay worried. I am."

"Did you really knock out two of his teeth, Rut?"

"One, as far as I know. I found only one on the floor. You see how this goes? Everybody wants to make the incident into something much bigger than it was. *Two* teeth. Well I only found one."

"And then you tossed him out on his ear."

"Listen, Eggert, I think you better get one thing *clear*. All sorts of people around here seem to believe that what I did represents some change of heart. Well, I've had no change of heart. Or they see what I did as *soft*-hearted"—she expelled a scornful sound, half laugh and half grunt—"but what's so soft-hearted about knocking out somebody's front teeth, I ask you? A lot of people around here seem to believe that what I did represents some sort of new endorsement. Well, I'm not endorsing anyone, Eggert. You understand me? I don't have time for politics. I have coffee to serve."

"So that's what many people are thinking, is it?"

"Listen, Eggert. If you're calling me in the hope I'm going to declare my support for that broken-down fool of a friend of yours, you're wasting your time. You're wasting *my* time. If you're looking for an endorsement, you're looking in the wrong place. Listen, I have always reserved the right to sock in the jaw anybody who interferes with the proper atmosphere of my establishment. I'm a businesswoman. That's all it is, Eggert. You're wasting your time."

"But I didn't call for any sort of endorsement," I replied. This wasn't strictly true. But my words had that special aptness which imparts what might be called a retrospective veracity: they *became* true by being heartfelt. "I'm calling for another reason entirely. I'm calling just to say one thing."

"Mm?"

"You've served our boy handsomely. In fact, there's nothing you could have done that would have benefited him more, and I'm calling just to say thank you, my dear."

For thirty-plus years I've been contending with this woman, but this was perhaps the first time I'd so outmaneuvered her as to leave her speechless. Gently as you'd arrange a quilt around a newborn baby, I settled the telephone back in its cradle.

54

When Any Two Stones Speak

Anoint his feet and his hands and his head with oil, clean and clarify
the whites of his eyes, widen his shoulders and tauten his middle, O
Genius/Goddess who for a vexed millennium so capriciously has overseen our troubled archipelago. Bring on lusher lights, nimbler phrases—yes, enwrap
his limbs once more with that numinous nimbus, glory's high-flown glow. . . .

Or, hell, at the very least present him to us in his very best suit of
clothes—a double-breasted royal-blue serge from Denmark—and a silk
Italian necktie of alternating vermilion and lemon stripes, and newly pol-
ished shoes of a black so lustrous it's constantly throwing off diamond
highlights, and let us see his hair unknotted and neatly parted and his
ragged mustache trimmed to a virile arc and the gray shadows chased from
his features and a good biting acquisitive gleam in his eye. Let the cry go
up on every street corner: Hannibal's back. . . .

Hannibal's back and moving jubilantly through the little crowd that
moves along with him, unwilling to let him go. They yearn once more to
shake his hand and to share with him an anecdote—or merely to watch
him shake another's hand, nod appreciatively at another's anecdote. Just to
be in his proximity is sufficient. He has something to give: himself, his
mere presence. That's who he is: someone whose mere presence is a gift.

Has he heard that Kevin Wilhelm, hand clamped over his vacant
mouth, has fled the country? *Yes, yes*—Hannibal roars with laughter—he's
heard a rumor or two to that effect. And has he heard that Nonni Karlsson is now admitting to "lapses in taste" in his campaign? Well, is that so?
And is Nonni perhaps referring to his own decision to run for President? Again
Hannibal erupts with laughter and the grateful crowd erupts with him.

The whole business has suddenly become utterly *simple*, with so much accumulated anger and puzzlement dissipated in a twinkling. . . . For such a long stretch of days we've been worrying ourselves: What can we do, now that the Visitors have come? What's to be done in the face of the heartless progress they bring? And the answer is: in the face of it, you punch it right *in* the face. A solution was present all along: you plant your feet, you rear back your arm, with one beautiful throw of your fist you cast a pair of teeth like a set of dice to the ground. . . .

It required a woman to show us this dazzling insight, but that's all well and good, for haven't we Freelanders, ever since Saga days, reveled in and relied on strong women? Think of Ingigerd in *Halfdan Eysteinsson's Saga*, disguising herself as a man and taking up arms to avenge her father. Think of the princess Thorbjorg, who dressed in armor and insisted on being called "sir." When we've let our shoulders slump, when our hearth fires have cooled and lassitude overtaken us, we have always counted upon a strong woman to reawaken our best selves, to rouse us to a sense of duty.

When the crowd reaches Independence Square, it is decided that a brief impromptu speech ought to be delivered. Yes, *it is decided*—for this isn't a case of Hannibal himself making the decision. Nor is he responding to any individual outcry. Rather, the speech shall manifest the collective desire of the crowd, which rings round him eagerly. Hannibal mounts a cement bench that will serve him handsomely for a stage and pulpit. It is a small band before him—thirty or forty souls—but as he speaks, the audience rapidly multiplies.

He has—what?—a hundred people before him. They are tumbling out of doorways and jeeps and alleyways, and as he stands contemplating Great Blue Mountain he entertains a sense that the people are coming down from the very hills to hear him. He has—what?—two hundred people around him and at the present rate of expansion just how long must he go on speaking before he has assembled at his feet every living Freelander?

What does Hannibal say to his people? He begins lightly: "Some of you may have heard that we have an election in three days." Warm, appreciative laughter. The crowd is growing. He says, "And to tell you the truth, I'm one of the candidates," and the laughter amplifies. Along with everything else, he possesses, this leader of ours, a bright and biting wit.

"I'm a candidate once again, as I have been in the last four elections," Hannibal tells us. "I'm looking for your vote. Now you may well ask yourself, What sort of man is this who would come before us time and again in the role of beggar? You may well ask yourself, What in the world is this strange phenomenon? What is an old politician?

"It's the question I asked myself this very morning, as I pondered my reflection in the mirror. I asked myself, What is an old politician? And do you know what a voice inside me answered? It said, He's a pitiful old clown. It said, He's a creature that has necessarily sacrificed principle for self-advancement. Yes, he's a broken-winged seagull reduced to begging fish heads from the fishermen on the docks. He's an old dog too fretful and feeble to chase the cats away from the garbage cans behind the cafe so he can have a go at them himself. . . ."

The growing crowd waits patiently, contentedly. We're charmed by this broken-winged gull, this pitiful old hound—we dote upon all the members of Hannibal's lame and wayworn menagerie. There isn't a soul in the crowd who does not appreciate the design and the cadences of this brand of oratory. Politics? This is what we mean by politics. Over the years, this has become the very essence of our political rhetoric: we depend upon this particular ritual of despair, this passage through self-negation, before pride in ourselves can justly be advanced and hope replenished. The stronger and more virulent these expressions of bleakness are, the better we like them, and no one among us has ever excelled Hannibal in evoking grimness, futility, inanition. We are the denizens of a scarred, wind-ripped landscape whose grandest mountain bears upon its neck a perpetual, a staggeringly heavy crown of murderous ice, and to attend to Hannibal is to absorb our stony birthright.

"He's an old sheep who, even on the balmiest days of midsummer, lacking the gumption to climb the slopes where the lushest grasses are growing, thinks to himself, Tomorrow may be warmer. He's an old whore so gone in the teeth that virtue may at last be achieved through the falling off of customer interest. He's a lone sailor who has lost his compass and declares in resignation, I will let the wind steer me.

"That's what he is unless—"

Unless, yes: we have waited with forbearance and now the turn has come.

"—unless he wakes one morning and the landscape of his nation, wherever it happens to be, begins to speak to him. I say 'wherever it happens to be.' . . . For let us say this politician is an African chieftain. He wakes within the tropical rainforest of his kingdom and the magnificent trees in their exhilarating height and breadth say to him, You must go forth and create a commonwealth suitable for us.

"And a sheik wakes in his desert domain and the stupendous patternings of the sand-ridges, the dunes that out-roll themselves for miles before him, summon him to his labors. And a fifty-six-year-old Freelandic politician rises this morning and he looks out at Great Blue and the mountain says to him, You must help build the polity anew.

"The people who founded our nation were people to whom the land regularly spoke. These were independent folk who could not see one flat stone beside another flat stone without hearing the two stones asking to be piled one on the other, as the start of a sheep pen or a stone wall."

Steadily, splendidly, the crowd grows, goes on growing. Independence Square is filling. Yes, if only he could continue orating fervently enough, Hannibal would have the entire nation ranged before him. He feels in these instants that his voice is, on its own power, capacious enough to enclose them all. The whole assembled nation. It would be an exact overlap. Onto the broad circle of the crowd the broad circle of his voice could be superimposed precisely.

"I woke this morning and it was as though I heard a speaker I hadn't heard in weeks. I walked out along Founders' Point, there where Erik the Other first beached, and the land was addressing me once more, it was saying that the great quest I've undertaken is a necessity. I am asking for your vote. The reason I can do anything so shameless, and the reason you ought to give me your vote, is a simple one: the stones of Freeland speak to me.

"The question *anyone anywhere* ought to ask before casting a vote is, Do the stones of our nation speak to the person I'm planning to vote for? Lithuanians ought to ask it, Americans ought to ask it, Zaireans ought to ask it. These are the very words that ought to be inscribed above every voting booth in every nation in the world. How *could* you, in good conscience, vote for someone who was deaf to the stones at his feet? Well, the stones speak to me. They say to me, Pile one of us on another. They say, Let us construct a home together."

In all of his life, it's the richest vision the world has ever granted him: a populace co-extensive with his voice, the crowd and his oration a tailored fit, like sun and moon in that moment of eclipse when together their material bodies are subsumed within a ring of holy fire. It is richer than the sight of a net being hauled from the sea, straining with its opulent load of twitching, living silver. Richer than a first walk down Copenhagen's Vesterbrogade, on a golden day in June 1960; and richer than the sight of sleeping Elva Gizursdottir's breasts in the low light when a middle-aged man returns to the bedroom after a painful piss; and richer than the vision of the finish line of the Long Run when you've just surpassed the final runner and nothing human stands between you and undivided glory; and richer, even, yes, than a walk around Great Blue with a pigtailed Rut Bjartardottir, a lifetime ago, when you first conceived the pattern of alternating blandishments and affronts, oh my angel, my pail of reeking fish guts, my fair one, my sow's belly, and thereby managed to so fluster the girl that, miraculously, her opposition dissolved and she was as much yours as you were hers, two young bodies bare in the long-slanting shadows of an Arctic midnight sun.

Richer still is that vision of a world shepherded, soul by soul, into a unified mass. It's the vision of a nation where, by unflagging oratory alone, he can convince all the doubters and convert all the opposition. Where every placard and poster in the town bears his face. Where his name alone adorns the ballot. Where he can bring his country to its foretasted singleness: induce them, by power of his voice alone, to celebrate their authentic unanimity.

55

Dedication

On Election Day, quite early in the morning, someone thumps commandingly on my front door. Rat: rat-ta-tat-*tat*. Rat: rat-ta-tat-*tat*. I'm in the middle of shaving, but it isn't this so much as simple heaviness of heart that leads me to ignore my visitor. I'd recognize Hannibal's knock, and there's nobody else on earth I care to see right now.

Another peremptory thumping, and a long wait, and then another. All right. But as a way of illustrating the intrusiveness of so early a visit, I leave the lather on my cheeks and carry my razor with me. Hence I must be looking both vulnerable and adversarial when I throw open the door. It's an appropriate blend of impressions, it turns out, for my visitor is Sindri. I'm surprised: those knockings had been uncharacteristically forceful.

"Father!" he calls joyfully—I wish he wouldn't do that—and adds, "I'm so glad to see you."

"Sindri?"

"You busy?" he asks nonsensically.

"No, no. I was thinking I'd leave the remainder of my shaving until tonight."

If he hears my reply at all, he utterly misses its caustic edge. Eagerly he strides in. His normally pallid face is flushed. Odder still, he's wearing a tomato-red V-neck sweater. Where is his mortician's black? He has a paper bag under one arm and there's something disquieting about his solicitous, tender style of carrying it. From the first, that bag unsettles me.

"It's quite a day, isn't it!"

"I don't know. I haven't yet been out."

"I mean the election! Hannibal seems to be making quite a comeback."

"If Rut had only decided to take a swing at Nonni Karlsson, instead of Mr. Wilhelm, I suppose we'd have a fighting chance. As it is, I'm not very hopeful."

"But Father, when have you ever said, I'm feeling hopeful? I don't know in my whole life if I've ever heard you describe yourself as hopeful." Sindri laughs brightly. "Always seeking out the dark side of things. Always claiming, for instance, that there isn't a young writer in this country who admits to admiring you."

"They're fading fast—the literary values I stand for. Hell, that sentence is overqualified. Forget 'literary.' "

"Admiration takes all sorts of unexpected guises. . . ."

And what is the feather tickling at the boy this morning? *Something* is getting at him. He's treating me with a sort of broad-gesturing chumminess I've never seen before. He's *joshing*—seems but one step away from giving me a wink, a clap on the back, a nudge in the ribs.

"You might want to finish your shaving," he says and, miming, takes a few swipes at his own chin with an imaginary razor.

I peer quizzically at the boy, then nod and pad back into the bathroom. Sindri follows. I apply the razor to my face.

"This is a big day for me, too," the boy says. "I have an announcement to make."

Once more I turn and peer at him. His proud, sly, shy, foot-shuffling manner suggests the inconceivable: he looks exactly like a young swain come to declare his intention to be married.

"An announcement?" I echo. And why in the world the tomato-red sweater? Why this dramatic shift? What's the matter with *black*, for heaven's sake?

And Sindri says: "Great Blue Press has accepted my first novel!"

My answer ejects itself from my mouth instantly, reflexively: "But that's not possible," I tell him.

Not long ago, I'd made a similar proclamation in regard to the boy. *But that's impossible* I'd declared to a wan-faced Lilja, looking fragile and small in her hospital bed the night she'd had her fall and almost lost her baby. Those had been my words when she'd reported, *But Pabbi, Sindri is gay.* Was there, even so, *anything* impossible so far as this unshakable young man was concerned?

"What I mean is—" But what do I mean? I feel a paternal need to protect the boy. I sense he's talking nonsense, airing grand but groundless dreams. Clearly he's ripe for some bruising disillusionment; he's going to get hurt. "This isn't America, son. Great Blue would never agree to publish a first novel until it's finished," I explain to the boy.

"But it *is*, it *is* finished." He laughs and jiggles the babylike bundle cradled in his arm. "All six hundred pages of it!"

Six hundred pages?

"Well if they—if they—Sindri, you'd best be careful. I've made a name for myself at Great Blue, needless to say, and if on the basis of that name they were willing to bend certain—"

"But I submitted the book under a pseudonym!"

"Under a pseudonym?" One marvel on the heels of another. I felt dizzy, suddenly. I gazed—gaped—into the bathroom mirror and beheld the face of a man who needed to sit down.

"Yes, a pseudonym. I didn't want special treatment, you see."

"So what pseudonym did you select?"

"Oh, Father, you're going to love this! Georg Samuelsson." Sindri eyed me expectantly. His gaze positively effervesced.

"Georg Samuelsson . . ." The syllables of the name were like the wind-borne tolling of a church bell in another valley. Just as dim and fateful as that. Why did they sound so faintly but so profoundly familiar?

"Yes, that's right! From *your* first novel . . ."

"*My* first novel?" For just a moment I still couldn't fix the connection. Then it came to me. Sindri had dug hard. Georg Samuelsson. A minor, a tertiary character: a village orphan who, swept overboard in a storm, is naturally presumed drowned. But he's discovered some weeks later on a skerry, having managed to survive on seaweed, birds' eggs, beached fish. . . . My eyes focus on the blade of my razor: a killing sliver of steel in a cloud of foam. I didn't know what to say to the boy.

I begin again: "But a six-hundred-page novel . . . There simply hasn't been time." A painful possibility strikes me. "You haven't quit your job?"

"No, no. Though I plan to, soon."

"But when would you have—"

"Let me show you something, Father," Sindri says, and his eyes brim so full of proud boyish ingenuity that he truly can't be more than twelve years old. He unfastens his black wristwatch—what in the world is he doing?—and presses a button on one side. He hands it to me. "Do you see this? Can you read that?"

The watch weighs nothing—nothing at all. It must be made of

plastic. I peer into the square, narrow window of its face—peer, like a Peeping Tom, into the House of Time. Ugly, black block numerals. They read 4:59.

"Yes?" I'm not at all sure what he's getting at.

"The watch has an alarm. Four fifty-nine, a.m. That's when it's been going off, day after day, seven days a week. I've been writing in the mornings. Three hours each day before heading off to work. It goes off at four fifty-nine so I can regard as a wastrel and a slugabed anyone who gets up at five." In his tomato-red sweater Sindri looks, I'd have to say, remarkably well rested. His face is thin but bright, as is his laughter.

"And after work I'd go home and write. It was the same when I moved in with Dag. That's what broke us up in the end. One day he declares, I could put up with rivalry from some other man, but I won't compete any longer with that damned manuscript of yours."

I go right on staring at the boy. I suppose my mouth is agape.

"Nineteen months ago," Sindri says, "you gave me some wise and wonderful advice. I came and told you I wanted to be a writer."

"And I told you to give it up. . . ."

"Not exactly." Again more laughter. I don't know if in his entire life I've ever seen him quite so jolly. "You told me the writer's life wasn't for anyone so lackadaisical as me. And naturally I went away in a blue funk. Oh, woe is me, I said, my father doesn't understand me. But of course you were absolutely right. You sent me packing. And for thirty-seven days I didn't do *anything*. I sat in my room and contemplated the wall. I contemplated my life and I didn't like what I saw. Then one night I go out for a walk, and it's three-thirty in the morning and I wander over this way and I look up at Thorskrist's sole skyscraper and every light is off—except one. Can you guess which one?"

"It doesn't necessarily follow that I—"

"It was *your* study light. And I knew right then that *you* couldn't sleep any better than *I* could, and that's when that phrase came to me, *The fruit doesn't fall far from the tree*, which is I guess a proverb in all sorts of languages but which has always seemed pretty absurd in Freelandic, hasn't it, given that we don't really *have* trees, let alone fruit. . . . Nonetheless, that night the phrase popped into my head. Don't you see? I saw right then how *similar* we are—"

"*Similar?*" My eyes pored over the boy's face, and wasn't there something almost preternaturally bright about that gaze of his? Why were his cheeks so deliriously flushed? Was it possible that he, like many a sexual deviant before him, had taken refuge in drugs?

"And I said to myself, I'm going to go home and begin writing a book called *Not Far from the Tree*, and six hundred pages later that's just exactly what I've done."

He paused, perhaps for breath. *I* certainly was breathless, even though I hadn't been doing most of the talking.

"A novel isn't something you just go and write on a whim," I pointed out. "It takes planning. You have to be willing to go over and over and *over* the same pages time and—"

"I wrote two hundred and twenty-seven pages the first month, and then I looked at them one morning and I said to myself, *They're not right*, and I burned them and started over. I've been writing something like ten pages a day. The book"—and here he patted that suspicious-looking sack under his arm—"has gone through six drafts."

"The point with revisions is that you can refine the life out of something," I told him. "It's a dangerous business, this going over and over the same—"

"And I sent them off to Great Blue Press under the name Georg Samuelsson, and last week I hear that they're willing to offer me an advance of five hundred thousand kronur—"

"Five hundred thousand kronur!"

Five hundred thousand kronur! Something like ten thousand dollars! This, in a country whose total book market is restricted to some fifty thousand souls. . . . "Why for my last book, I hardly—"

"They said I'd captured the Youth Experience. That *every*one is going to read it, the young and the old. That I'd captured what it is like right now to be growing up in a little Nordic island nation at a time when the outside world is impinging as never—"

"Oh *well*," I said. "The Youth Experience. You've got to watch out, lad, regarding the perils of a career built on the fads and trends—"

"And what I wanted to say to you, this morning, is that I really owe my success to you."

"To *me*? To *me*? Oh I don't think, whether it's blame or—or the contrary, whatever, you want to be attributing to me any—"

"You've been extremely tough on me—just as you should have been. You've been a true exemplar. I know that today is a big day for you. You have a great deal riding on the election. So I saved this announcement of mine until today. I've brought this manuscript as a gift, you see. My thought was that this way you couldn't really lose. Even if the election went against you—well, you'd still have my book. *Not Far from the Tree.* It's dedicated to you, incidentally."

"To me?" My voice came out as a chipped whisper. These might almost have been the last words I would ever utter on this earth.

"You do realize that you're bleeding?" And Sindri laughed once more.

I returned my gaze to the bleached rat's face in the mirror. I'd nicked myself with the razor. A single droplet, redder than any rose, slipped from my chin into the white enamel basin.

56

The Old Newlyweds

Shortly after noon the storm came swooping down. A besieging circle of gray mist massed around the base of Great Blue Mountain and quickly its icy crest went under. There followed a minute or two of fluid, floating suspense—while the heavens hung in the balance—and then the wind began to howl, the snow to fly.

Logic told me the storm might work to our advantage. Presumably, Hannibal's supporters were hardier folk than Nonni's, and far less likely to be discouraged from voting by the mere sundering of the firmament. All the same, there was something ominous, and spiteful, about this turn in the weather. When I stepped outside, it certainly *felt* like a slap in the face. The wind ripped and the snow exploded. Three months ago, this mad electoral quest of ours had commenced with one vision from the heavens—a rainbow over Great Blue Mountain—and it was closing with another: a holocaust, though of flakes rather than flames. The world was frigidly burning.

Hannibal and I were actually on Diamond Island when the storm broke. We'd taken the ferry out early that morning. Hannibal delivered a speech in the Hollhovn town square, where he clapped the men on the back and hugged the ladies and kissed the babies—and all the while the storm was brewing. We'd been planning on taking the two o'clock ferry back to Thorskrist—we'd scheduled a final speech in Independence Square—but the weather rewrote our plans. The snow was so thick the ferries stopped running. To venture out on seas like this was to be sailing blind.

We took temporary shelter in Hollhovn's one restaurant, the Mended Net, where we ate fried haddock and drank buckets of coffee and watched the warehouse across the street drift in and out of visibility. We were marooned.

There was nothing for it but to sit and wait. We had to confront the possibility of an extended—an overnight—stay.

But Hannibal didn't share my resignation. He kept rising from the table, pacing the Net like a caged bear. He telephoned the ferry office, repeatedly. Was the weather clearing? Did they expect to be going off soon? It wasn't and they weren't. . . . The Net's owner eventually took pity on the President—pacing back and forth, back and forth—and a mostly full bottle of *brugga* materialized, from which Hannibal sucked greedily. While there was still something to siphon off, I splashed a good amount into my coffee cup and swigged away, eager to ease my nervousness at *his* nervousness. Three o'clock. Four. We drank, and the wind howled, the snow came thronging down.

"It's not as though we'd be any better off in Thorskrist," I reminded him. "It's not as though you could actually make your final speech in Independence Square. I don't think we could *find* Independence Square in this weather. . . ."

"We've *got* to get over there, Eggi."

"But we'd be doing just what we're doing now. Sitting out the storm somewhere. We can vote over here."

"There's got to be a way over. . . ."

"But there isn't any *point*, Hanni. Why in the world would we try to get across under these conditions?"

He looked at me reproachfully. "Why, for Thorgunnur," he announced, with the indignant, lifting pitch of someone asked to explain the painfully obvious.

"Thorgunnur?" What in the world was he talking about?

"I promised I would escort her to the polls. It's a tradition. I have done so every election for twenty years."

"But surely she'll understand. This is hardly the first time a storm has—"

"We've *got* to, Eggi. We've got to get across." We both glanced out the window. The wind was shrieking. The snow was as thick as ever.

Hannibal resumed his pacing, now and then upending the bottle of *brugga*. He spoke animatedly, about the weather, with an old fisherman named Lars Olgeirsson. The two of them alternated pulls on the bottle. I remained at my seat, sipping from my mug, letting my thoughts drift.

Five hundred thousand kronur. For a novel entitled *Not Far from the Tree*. Written by Sindri Eggertsson. Under the pseudonym Georg Samuelsson. A name lifted from *The Annals of Nils*. I took another sip. If the world indeed was—as all appearances suggested—coming to an end, I was determined to see it through in the proper state of numbness. The clock chimed. Four-thirty.

Hannibal rejoined me at the table. His face was red and jubilant. Trouble was afoot—I knew, all too well, the import of that bright, stupid look in Hannibal's eyes. "Lars has agreed to take us!"

"Come again?"

"Lars Olgeirsson has agreed to take us."

"To take us? What do you mean?"

"In his boat."

"In his boat? When?"

"Now. . . ."

"*Now?* He's going to take us *now*? In *this* weather? Are you crazy, Hanni?"

"We've seen worse."

"You're going to drown," I said. "Which perhaps wouldn't be so bad except by drowning you're going to confirm everything they've been saying about you. They're all saying your whole campaign reveals a self-destructive—"

"Lars knows what he's doing, Eggi."

"The man is drunk." And suddenly the whole thing came clear.

"In fact, you're the one who got him that way. You got him drunk so he'd be willing to go across in a storm like this."

"You don't have to come. You can stay right here."

My voice lifted: "All I want is to get this absolutely straight. *That's* my goal. Let's spell this out, shall we? You're planning to go across White Seal Bay in heavy seas and blinding snow, in a little motorboat operated by a drunk, all so that you can keep the promise you made to your retired schoolteacher—who happens to be a blind nonagenarian—that you would escort her to the voting booth. Do I have the gist of it?"

For one moment, Hannibal looked offended, defensive. The next, a buoyant, merry acceptance swam into his gaze. He grinned at me. "I'd say that's pretty accurate. Boy, there's no sense trying to pull the wool over *your* eyes. I've always said that for sheer psychological penetration, you—"

"Do shut up, Hanni."

Our positions—our physical positions—only accentuated the root inequality of our debate. Hannibal was standing. I was sitting—being looked down on, being boozily breathed on.

I suppose I'd come to a branching in the road. On this Election Day, did I prefer to loiter in the Mended Net, which was a snug and by and large extremely comfortable place, sipping warming spirits and eating delicious fried haddock, or would I prefer to be pounded by the wind and the sea, to feel my stomach lurch as the little boat churned blindly along, and in the end to drown in White Seal Bay?

"Leaving now?" I asked.

"Right now. Come on."

We stumbled, the three of us—drunk Lars in the lead, Hannibal behind him, me in the rear—out into the storm. I wasn't wearing proper all-weather gear. I had on my "good" wool topcoat, which didn't button tight at the neck, and a pair of black leather dress shoes that slipped and slid hopelessly in the snow. I reached into my coat pockets and they came up empty; evidently I'd left my gloves in the Mended Net. I shouted Hannibal's name, cried out my need to go back, but he continued trudging along. Apparently he hadn't heard me. The wind stole my voice away. This was Nature's answer to the Danish rock band Let's Call It a Day.

Eventually we made our way down to the dock. My hands went numb in my pockets. My face was burning. The sea was jumping. The air was full of salt spray, as well as snow. When it was my turn to climb down the dock ladder into the boat, my shoe slipped, and for just a moment I dangled—dangled just above drowning. A hand reached out for me and my body ended up in the back of Lars's little motorboat. The engine coughed weakly. We began to move.

Time and again and time and again the sea picked us up, dropped us down, heavily, *thump*, heavily, *thump*, heavily, *thump*, icy spray went over us, through us, and we dropped down heavily, *thump*. I'm no more a sailor than I am a horseman and I vomited up the haddock and the coffee and the *brugga*, all over my overcoat. I hunched down and wrapped my head in my hands and looked backward. In all the snow, Hollhovn had disappeared. Thorskrist was invisible before us—assuming it *was* before us and drunk Lars hadn't gotten turned around and veered off toward Labrador. Snow was falling into the sea, chilling its iciness. I sunk my head back between my knees and closed my eyes. Could Lars, our pilot, see any better than I could? The boat—the *Little Titanic*—slipped and tumbled and slapped down hard and the sea broke over us and the snow came down

and this would be something for the annals of our nation, wouldn't it?—
the Election Day when the President and his campaign manager drowned
in White Seal Bay. . . .

We pitched and fell, pitched and fell, and far off, way in the back of
my head, a snatch of "The Ancient Mariner" unfolded:

> And now there came both mist and snow,
> And it grew wondrous cold:
> And ice, mast high, came floating by,
> As green as emerald.

I'd translated that one, hadn't I? Into Freelandic, a vanished lifetime and a
vanished world ago: at the age of twenty-one, at the Ansons' farm in Nova
Scotia, during my first voyage to the New World. When *The Annals of Nils*
was brewing. Vomit welled in my throat and flung itself once more over
my overcoat. I huddled tighter, made myself still smaller—aware that my
only hope of preservation lay in shrinking myself to the point where the
hawklike Gods of Heaven might overlook me.

We made it across the Bay. Mercifully the wind eased, just a little, and
the snow let up, just a little, and we found the dock. I lost my footing getting out, but a strong arm—Hannibal's or Lars's, again I'm not sure—
hoisted me upward, forward. We made our way around the edge of a
warehouse, into the lee of the wind; we were alive, we were in the capital
city once more.

I was wet and sick and maybe still drunk and absolutely wretched
with the cold. Hannibal and Lars bade each other farewell. Hands were
shaken, cries of comradeship exchanged. Hannibal took me by the elbow.
"Come on," he shouted over the wind. "We're heading to your place."

The wind was still vicious and the snow already deep—and I fell a
couple more times. I was more dead than alive by the time we straggled
into the elevator of Skyscraper Tower. "Jesus," was all I said, and Hannibal
laughed and I tried to laugh with him. How did he look? Ruddy—ruddy
with that high color which triumph alone instills. Perhaps he'd had *fun*?

Even so, he was limping, badly, as we made our way down the corridor to my apartment. He'd twisted his knee, evidently. I unlocked the door
and the first thing each of us did was throw down a tumblerful of whiskey.
Then we stripped off all our clothes, most of which were dripping wet,
and laid them out on the radiators. I wrapped myself in a bathrobe while
Hannibal took a short shower.

I took a long shower and by the time I emerged Hannibal had dressed once more. Redonning those soaked clothes couldn't have been *much* fun. But he was a man in a hurry.

"We've got to be on our way," he told me. "I promised Thorgunnur we'd be there at five-thirty." It was nearly six.

While I put on dry clothes and waterproof rainpants and jacket, Hannibal resumed his pacing. We took the elevator down to the parking garage. Driving conditions were awful—slippery roads, tugging winds, blinding snow—but after our passage across the bay I wasn't about to complain. I was safe and dry and what else mattered? The car crawled along. The day had been dark for so long that I only now realized night was falling. We made our way in silence. We were both exhausted.

The ride in the car did nothing for Hannibal's knees. By the time we reached the seventh floor of the Eldershelter, he was grimacing with every step. Still, it was with a light and chipper voice that he called from the threshold of her doorway, "Hello, auntie."

"You're late, Hannibal." Delivered with an imperious lifting of her schoolmarm's chin.

"Yes, I'm sorry. Bit of a blow out there."

"Ours is a country where you have to make allowances for the weather," she pointed out. "That's what I always told my classes. In more than half a century of classrooms, I never once accepted excuses on account of the weather."

"I remember. And you're absolutely right, auntie. Where would Freeland be if we'd let the weather get the best of us?"

"If *I* could get to class, I expected others to do the same."

"I was out on Diamond, you see, and the ferries quit running."

"That's what Iris Birgisdottir told me. She's down the hall. She'd heard it on the radio. She said you were over on Diamond and the ferries weren't running and you weren't going to be here. And I told her you always come on Election Day to escort me to the polling booth. He'll be here, I told her. I would have felt quite the ninny if you'd made a liar of me."

"Well here I am," Hannibal announced, with a schoolboy's pride.

"*Late . . .*" pointed out Thorgunnur, whose role it still was, naturally, to keep any schoolboy's soaring boastfulness in check.

Duly chastened, Hannibal murmured, "Auntie, it won't happen again."

"You have to allow for such things," Thorgunnur continued. "The occasional bit of a blow . . ."

"You're absolutely right. You set the example for us, didn't you? If *you* could make it to class, the rest of us could too, isn't that right?"

"That is correct." But delivered tentatively. Thorgunnur prefers, I suppose, to make her own self-assertions. And balks at having the roles of teacher and student reversed.

"It was of course in your classroom that I gained an appreciation of our literature," Hannibal observes. And what is he steering at? Why does he wear such an absurd smirking expression? "*You* told us that if we were searching for the soul of our country, it was to the great Sagas we must look—more of Freeland being located in them than in Great Blue Mountain even. *That's* what you taught us, wasn't it, auntie?"

"*Tried* to teach is more like it. . . ." Thorgunnur keeps her voice tentative. Her nose has lifted, as though to sniff out the scent. She doesn't need to be able to make out Hannibal's smirk to know some sort of schoolboy mischief's afoot.

"But auntie," Hannibal goes on, "I have an important announcement to make."

"Yes."

An announcement?

"It's something you've long wanted to hear, auntie."

"Yes . . ."

Hannibal, too, has an announcement? What *sort* of announcement? Good God, haven't we had enough announcements today? Five hundred thousand kronur—that's what Sindri was offered for a novel about the Youth Experience. . . .

"It's actually something the two of us have long looked forward to, auntie."

"*Yes* . . ."

What in the world is Hannibal up to? Why is he stringing her along like this, deliberately trying to exasperate her? What conceivable news could he be holding in reserve? Hannibal looks hugely, horrifyingly pleased with himself.

And he teases out the moment a little farther.

"I believe you have charged me with a very important duty. . . ."

"Good heavens, what *is* it, Hannibal?"

But still he isn't about to satisfy her. No, not quite yet.

"And there may even have been times when you thought me some-what late in regard to *this* matter, too. But one does what one can. We mustn't be hasty, isn't that right?"

Thorgunnur sniffs the air by way of reply.

"And it's very tricky, of course, negotiating with those people, as you yourself know better than anyone."

"Speak *plainly*, Hannibal."

But he doesn't: "Needless to say, in *this* matter you have to make allowances for me, given the long-standing difficulties, and the issue of competing national pride—"

And now the break. Thorgunnur cries, "What damned thing are you on about now?" He has won: schoolboy had gotten a "rise" out of school-teacher.

Yes, he has broken her and have I ever in my life seen him looking more exultant? "Why, about *The Freeland Saga*, of course," he replies. With a look of invincible sham innocence on his face. "I've arranged it. With the proper authorities in Iceland. It's going to be ours again, auntie. To keep. The original sheepskin manuscript of *The Freeland Saga*. The best-illustrated Saga manuscript in all the world. It's coming here. To Thorskrist."

It was a day on which I'd already heard one electrifying announce-ment—five hundred thousand kronur!—and a day in which I'd only very narrowly escaped drowning, and I wouldn't have thought I had remaining in me much capacity for wonder. But my jaw dropped. Could he—had he really done it? Had Hannibal arranged to fulfill Thorgunnur's eternal quest?

Or could he be lying? Was it possible that, yearning to comfort her, he'd offered her the prize she'd coveted for a lifetime?

But I studied his face, rapt with triumph and devotion, and I knew he was speaking God's own truth. What in the world had he bartered away in exchange for a priceless one-of-a-kind medieval manuscript of this sort? Had he forfeited our best fishing rights for the next twenty years? Had he signed away Great Blue Mountain?

A stunned silence ensued. Without question it was one of the apical moments, perhaps *the* moment, of Thorgunnur's life. Her face began—well, her faced seemed to be *dismantling* itself: a nerve throbbed in her cheek, her jaw drifted out of line, her lips moved soundlessly.

And I? I felt tremendously fearful, all of a sudden. What if the old impossible bitch wasn't up to the occasion? Notwithstanding the decades of dismissal she'd shown me—me, who by rights should have been her spirit's natural son—it turned out I wanted to see her come up equal to the moment.

Is it all clear? I was *surprised*—I never would have thought I could have worried so much on her behalf. . . . But she was, after all these years, a fragile vessel, and truly I feared that this consummation of her wishes would dismast her, scuttle her. I'd only recently, an hour or so before, escaped drowning myself, and I knew what it was to feel yourself going down.

But a marvelous thing unfolded: the woman collected herself. She sat bolt upright in her bed and her sightless face went radiant with victory. Her face sought out neither one of us, she stared off searchingly in the direction of Great Blue Mountain, and her voice, rapt as that of a prophetess, was one I'd never heard: "I *knew* it, I *knew* it, dear sweet Jesus, all the time I *knew* it."

The wind tore hungrily at the pane and you had to shudder to think what the seas out there were like. But Thorgunnur, evidently, had found at last her holy harbor: "It was forty-two years ago, Hannibal Hannibalsson, you first stepped into my classroom, and it wasn't long at all before I *knew* you were the one. Oh, I'd had cleverer boys, probably, and harder-working boys, surely, and maybe even one or two better-looking boys, but it was you and you alone that had the glow about you. You see, no other boy, ever, had quite that same old-time glow. It's a light long dimming from these islands. And perhaps it's only the once, you see, the one time only, that the inkling comes to a teacher, the feeling that *this* is the student who will make the difference, *this* is the one to whom the future properly belongs."

Glow—the old blind teacher had spoken of *glow*—and her fissured features shone with the vindications of a lifetime. Aglow, too, was the object of her praises, the President who was, even now, more Student than President perhaps—as eager as ever for Teacher's acclaim. Meanwhile, the all-but-forgotten, gray-haired, gray-faced, ever-glowless Eggert Oddason looked on transfixedly, scrupulously, ravenously, missing not a single detail.

Into the silence rushed the sound of the wind, blowing and blowing, miles-long wails of spite and discontent.

"It's a bit rough out there, auntie," Hannibal said.

"I can hear it for myself, young man," Thorgunnur countered. She drew a handkerchief from her lap and honked her nose. If, in my entire life, I've ever seen Thorgunnur embarrassed, this moment of recovery was the occasion. Her cheeks had pinkened. Never before, surely, had she opened her soul to a student as she had just now.

"You know, auntie," Hannibal said, "given this weather, you might prefer not to go out tonight."

Thorgunnur was a great one for feigning incredulous confusion on meeting something she didn't approve of, but this time she seemed authentically perplexed. "Not want—"

"Maybe you want to stay here? Stay in tonight?"

"Stay *in*? But tonight's election night." Her tone was forthright, as though Hannibal himself might somehow have overlooked this fact.

"I know I have your support," Hannibal said. "That's the important thing."

"My *support*," Thorgunnur cried. Oh, it had taken her a moment to interpret his proposal, but now its full import had come clear: he was suggesting that *she fail to cast her vote!* "Are they going to count the *support* of those who sit in their rooms all day? Is that what they're tallying? Is that what an Election Day is all about?"

"Since it's only one vote . . ."

"It's *only one vote*. . . ." Yes, he'd cut her deep this time, the careless blade had riven tendon and bone, but she was more than equal to him. Christ, she was more than equal to anyone! Her bony jaw broadened and stiffened, and in a voice that brooked no back talk—the voice of the veteran schoolmistress who has met some japery that simply *will not be tolerated*—she declared: "If you and that friend of yours are daunted by a little blow, why that's your business. You boys are free to remain here in my room. You may even help yourself, one each, to a butter biscuit. On the other hand, I have a vote to cast and it's getting late. Now if you will hand me my cane, Hannibal Hannibalsson, I have better things to do than to sit and listen to such balderdash."

A chastened Hannibal retrieved her cane. Her gnarled hands seized upon it with a blind person's clutching avidity.

"My coat," she said. "Eggert Oddason, you bring out my black coat from the closet."

I fetched her black coat. The old woman rose unsteadily to her feet. She lifted one arm, and I slipped the sleeve onto it. She switched hands on the cane and I fitted the coat over her other arm.

Thorgunnur lowered herself once more to the side of the bed, placing her cane beside her, which freed both hands for the buttoning of her coat. She was out of breath.

"My gray hat," she murmured, and indicated the closet. Hannibal brought her her gray hat.

"My brown gloves," she said, and I presented her with her brown gloves.

She performed the donning of each of these articles with a lentor that only a majestic stateliness could have rescued from absurdity. Everything had to be done by touch and yet appear as though it were not being done by touch.

When Thorgunnur stood, eventually, she declared, just as though we and not she were responsible for any delay, "*Really*, I think we had best be going."

Slowly, slowly we made our way down the Eldershelter hall. Hannibal took her arm. Could she, even in the dazzling light of the corridor, make out the elevator doors at its end? Did she notice how the "boy" who had taken her arm, to whom she'd offered a butter biscuit, was walking with as much difficulty as she herself? Something dreadful had happened to Hannibal's knees. Upper lip clamped grimly over lower, his face was contorting with each step.

When, finally, we entered the elevator, Thorgunnur announced confidently, "It sounds as though the storm is dying down." Did she realize where she was? Did she even know an elevator's muffling walls surrounded her?

Slowly, painfully, we made our way to the Eldershelter exit. The storm was *not* dying down. The wind was blasting. Snow whipped against the glass.

"It's a little rough out there," Hannibal said.

"Oh?" Thorgunnur replied. Warily. She was ready to fend him off, should he once more attempt dissuasion.

"There's heavy snow," he said, "and a very big wind."

"Oh?" Coolly.

"It's hard going, auntie," Hannibal said. "Maybe you'd better be carried."

"Carried?" she said.

"Just out to the car . . ."

"Carried?" she said.

I stepped forward. "I could do it, auntie. I could carry you."

"*You?*" Decades of skepticism reverberated in her voice. Thorgunnur swung her face toward mine and in the bright whiteness of the entryway she blindly regarded me. She didn't like what she saw, evidently. "Now I hardly think . . ."

"I suppose I could carry you," Hannibal suggested, softly. "Just out to the car."

She pondered her student's proposal. "Yes," she relented. "Perhaps out to the car . . ."

Hannibal placed one hand on the small of her back and, stooping, one hand behind her knees, and, with a grunt, he took his big-boned old teacher up into his arms. A yanking pain registered on his features and I thought sure his knees must buckle under him and his precious living load tumble to the floor. But he held steady.

And I?—I opened the door for the pair of them. There was a touch of parody to the scene, perhaps, in which Man crosses threshold with Woman in his arms. They might almost have been newlyweds—only, the limping husband was middle-aged and the wife was ancient and the "home" whose threshold he carried her across was the ravaged wastes of Freeland itself.

There was a touch of parody, certainly, in the hyperbolic way I played the jilted lover: the truth is I'd begun to weep. I, who never cry, was blinded by tears as the two of them ventured out on this Election Night, arms wrapped round each other, straight into the all-swallowing storm.

57

A Little Squiggly Shadow

I was heading toward the door, about to make my long-delayed escape, when the doorbell rasped. Had it been the phone, I would have let it go unanswered. But whoever was outside my door would have to be dealt with—dispatched—before I could be on my way. My little suitcase was packed. There was nothing but this one last visitor to keep me a moment longer in the city.

I opened the door and found my daughter waiting, a satchel under one arm. "You just caught me," I told her. "I'm heading out."

"Out?"

"To the summerhouse."

"Right. Just what you've been promising yourself. Win or lose, you were going to give yourself a few days alone."

"I have a book to write," I told her. "My fiftieth . . ."

"Well now, that's a task that can be put off a moment longer, isn't it?" And Lilja breezed on past me into the living room.

Her stomach grazed my ribs and I was made aware, belly to belly, of the child within her. To a stranger's eye, the girl wouldn't yet be unmistakably pregnant. Her figure had taken on that equivocal feminine fullness which may be the loveliest sight in the world.

"Actually," she called, over her shoulder, disappearing into the kitchen, "I was hoping you'd come to dinner at my place tonight. I've invited Sindri already. It's to be a sort of celebration. For him and his book. And for you and your soon-to-be-written fiftieth book. A little family affair—the first one in months, I'd add. Just the four of us."

"Four?"

"I thought I might invite my husband. I thought we should all get together again now that the election's over."

"I'm away to the summerhouse."

"Well, can't you reaway? Back to town tonight? Just this once? Say seven o'clock?" She has opened the cupboard and begins to make herself—to make both of us, I suppose—some coffee. "Do say you will, Pappalingur. I'm counting on you."

"Lilja," I protest, "I need to concentrate. No distractions. I've had nothing but distractions for months on end."

"We've all had distractions. We also need to treat ourselves to a little family celebration."

"This is a serious business: starting a book."

"Have you been outside today?"

"Hm?" Was she listening to a word I said? Blithely, busily she was setting up our little kaffeeklatsch: milk, sugar, crackers, oatmeal cookies.

"It's just so amazingly *warm*, Pabbi. For this time of year. For *any* time of year. You see I've worn no sweater or jacket. Here it is October and *I've got no sweater or jacket.*" She was wearing an olive green work shirt and a pair of jeans. Her blue hair band matched her eyes, as did her dangling turquoise earrings. How in the world did *I* ever conceive such a beautiful daughter? "And to think just a couple days ago, Election Day, we had all that snow. There's no rhyme or reason to it, is there?"

For my taste, the girl's always a little too quick to ascribe inexplicable—mystical—causes to the everyday. "There's a reason to it," I told her. "I heard last night on the radio that we're entering some sort of unusual high pressure zone. Or low pressure zone. Up from the Gulf Stream. The result of the storm down there. It's a rare but not-unheard-of phenomenon. A bit of Caribbean weather heading toward the Arctic."

"That's not what Odin at the Psychics Guild is saying. . . ."

"No?"

"He's saying the weather's shifting. Long term. Who knows? We may yet see trees in Freeland."

"Not in my lifetime, let's hope." I drop into a chair at the kitchen table. "I think I've finally grown used to the place as it is. Barrenness suits me."

"But that's exactly what Odin says he saw in a vision. A lush, forested Freeland . . ."

"One more way in which my own country becomes unrecognizable to me," I point out.

"Oh now *honestly*," Lilja says, in what I think of as her curmudgeon-shushing way, "why all the grumbling?" She sets a steaming coffee cup before me. "Seven, seven-fifteen would be fine," she goes on, settling in across the table with a cup of her own.

"Hm?"

"Tonight. Seven, seven-fifteen . . ."

"I don't remember having agreed to come," I remind her.

"That's all right. I know you meant to. So I'm not feeling hurt." And she sips from her coffee.

I suppose I like being outmaneuvered by her—how else to explain why I let her manipulate me as she does? I sip again from my coffee. Pregnancy so strikingly becomes her. If her beauty has any significant flaw, it's the touch of something cold or remote about her—something to do with the breadth of her eyes, no doubt, what I like to think of as her steppe-surveying queen-of-the-horde gaze. In addition to lending her some color and plumpness, pregnancy gives her a nearness, a permeability, a veined connectedness—oh hell, my description is awkward and approximate, but the object under scrutiny is all the more appealing for its resistance to phrasing. . . .

She said: "I was reading in the paper today an interview with that man Kanekyu. Did you see it?"

"Who?"

"Oh come on. Do stop it. The pollster. He was trying to explain why their polls were so wildly inaccurate."

"I've given up on the newspaper. *All* newspapers. It's a postelection luxury I allow myself."

"It's really quite beautifully hilarious, Pappalingur—you're missing the best entertainment in town. Here they were predicting Nonni Karlsson to win with seventy, seventy-five percent of the vote, and now they've got to explain why they were so *laughably* wrong, and of course they can't begin to admit that the largest consideration was the fact that one of their own pollsters got a sock in the jaw." Lilja laughs—that giddy girlish easy-flowing laugh of hers.

"So?"

"So they're stuck having to announce that it was the blizzard, or it was better fish catches in the days right before the election—though from what I've heard those were anything but good. And also—now this is the one you're going to love—they blame it on an 'unsophisticated electorate unacquainted with modern polling techniques.' Don't you just *adore* it? As though it's our *fault* or something? We're too unso*phis*ticated for those super-sophisticates to read our minds. . . ."

"Presumably, when we're less primitive, they will be able to predict our every move."

"*Exactly*. Here they were, predicting Hannibal's going to get twenty-four percent of the vote, and he gets nearly *twice* that!"

"More than twice," I correct her. I sip from my coffee cup. "Forty-nine point two percent."

"Forty-nine point two percent," she marvels. "That's something."

Yes, it is—but something less than Nonni Karlsson's fifty point one. I drain my cup. "I've got to go, child," I tell her.

"Not quite yet, Father," she answers me, playing on my calling her *child*. "I have something to give you first."

Am I to be blamed if at that moment my heart quailed? Dear God, not another present from one of my children!

A gift from Lilja? Has she commenced the study of incendiary devices and assembled a monogrammed hand grenade? Taken up home pharmacy and decocted a toxin-laden vitamin tonic?

"To give me?"

"To give you."

From her satchel she draws a paper tube encircled by a rubber band.

Gingerly, I remove the rubber band, unfold the paper. It's a picture. A photograph. It's something dark and spectral—there's an overlay of horror to it. . . .

"I'm not sure—"

"It's your grandchild," Lilja announces.

"My what?"

Lunatics—I'm forever surrounded by lunatics.

"It's the baby, Pabbi. The one in my tummy. Don't you see? It's a sonogram."

"Hm?"

"Something like an X-ray. . . ."

Well, it makes me feel quite queer, taking my unborn grandchild into my arms. I've never been quite comfortable with very small children, and this is, needless to say, the smallest child I've ever held. My eye wanders warily across the dark shiny surface—Lilja's womb—in whose menacing murk I begin to discern a vaguely humanoid shape.

"The baby?"

"Your grandchild."

"Forgive me if I don't spot an immediate resemblance."

"*No resemblance?* Why just look at these feet!" She points to a pair of splayed dots, as far from anything human as are the scratchings in the mud that a scampering archaeopteryx might have deposited on the floor of an antediluvian swamp. "Those are *your feet.* I'd know them anywhere as yours."

You do have to love the girl. . . .

"And look at these arms!" A pair of sodden-swollen twigs. "Why, you must feel you're looking at yourself in the mirror. And the *head . . .*" A little oval the shape and size of the stone of a peach, and fuzzy the way some peach pits are when you eat them—the flesh of the fruit, instead of breaking cleanly from the stone, clinging in wispy, slimy strands. "Look what an intense, knotted, *brooding* head we've got here, just *packed* with gray matter." A brain that must be about the size of the inner stone inside a peach stone. "Why, you're as like as brothers. *Twins!* people will cry. *Twins!*

"And look at it—look at it here," she crows, and comes down crisply, with a gleaming red fingernail, on a spot between the creature's legs. It's the crotch—that's what her blood-red fingernail rests upon. "What do you see?"

"I'm afraid I—"

"You see this shadow here? This little squiggly shadow? Now the doctor's being very coy, refusing to commit himself, but isn't it clear even to the untrained eye that what we've got here is a penis?"

"A penis?" I search for it in vain. . . .

"*Here,*" she says, fixing it under her nail, "doesn't it look like a penis to you?"

"Not *exactly . . .*"

"You see?" She laughs triumphantly. "Remember our battle? My feminine intuition telling me *boy* and your poet's intuition telling you *girl?* Well, *I* see a penis!"

"Do you? Is that what you see?" I nudge the paper toward her. "We'll know in time. . . ." The photograph immediately curls up into what I suppose you could call a fetal position.

"Pappalingur, that's *yours,*" the girl cries. "It's your gift. Your very first photograph of your very first grandson. And to judge from his virile equipment, he's going to be quite a ladykiller." More laughter.

Honestly, where does she come by humor of this sort? Certainly not from me. I rise from the table. "Well," I say. "Thank you," I say. "And now I'd better be off."

Lilja follows me into the living room, watches me open my travel bag. I need to shelter the photograph against something, so it won't get crumpled.

It occurs to me that it might just be placed against Sindri's manuscript, which I must soon investigate. Perhaps today. I've been putting it off until some leisure time stretched before me. The two gifts belong together, I suppose: the photograph of my first granddaughter with her shady penis and the first literary offspring of my homosexual son. I zip the bag shut.

"Well, it's been a long season, with more than enough nonsense," I announce. "And now it's time to turn the calendar page. It's time for the serious work to begin."

58

Double Inversion

H annibal's big right hand gathers itself into a fist and for a poised, impossible moment—like a diver doing a handstand on the edge of a tensely quivering board—hangs suspended in the air. Then it comes down decisively upon the wood of the door, once, twice, thrice. Somewhere above, from a rooftop nearby, a seagull looses a noncommittal cry. The morning sun evenly, cheerfully exposes every bubble and broken blister on the white paint of this door he has not stepped through for months. Really, it is an astonishingly warm day for October. The weatherman had explained how a "rare double inversion," or some such thing, had carried a colossal bubble of balmy Caribbean air up the Gulf Stream. But on television last night he'd also seen old Odin Palsson of the Psychics Guild—as trustworthy a source, taking all with all, as any television meteorologist. And *he* had divined that a "new warm age" was coming to Freeland. It made sense. Dirt, smoke, poisonous effluents—all those atmospheric cast-offs which were already rendering the countries Down Below unlivable—soon would combine to raise temperatures across the planet. In their shameless, choking squalor, those people Down Below would usher in a sweet ample new age for our Arctic island nation.

He hears a stirring within the house, which reassures and unnerves him in equal measure. Fear and hope contend in his heart this morning. When the door eases open he says the one thing he has prepared to say: "I've come to let you laugh at me."

He's grateful for the witty bite of this opening remark, and yet relishes as well the sense of sailing henceforward without a compass. As the nation's first settlers did, he will steer by the sky and the currents and the wind—he's on his own.

With her good eye, tilting her head slightly, Rut inspects him, up and down. She does not utter a word—indeed maintains so prolonged a silence that, discomfited, he repeats himself: "I've come to let you laugh at me."

Then he says: "You may recall the last time we spoke. I declared *There will be laughter in any case*, since you were intending to laugh at me when I *lost* the election and I at you when I *won* it. All right, Rut: you may now feel free to laugh at me. . . ."

And still the woman said nothing. She canted her head to the other side, as though now filtering him through her bad eye—the timeless, intuitive eye. She said, "You? You're too sorry a spectacle for laughter."

What to make of this? Hannibal scratched vigorously at the ball of his nose, threw skyward one bright abrupt gout of laughter, then immediately fell silent. The gull voiced another ambiguity. The sun was blinding.

Was Rut going to invite him in? And was this invitation what he was aiming for? Should he have drawn up plans? Was it foolishness to suppose that tactics would simply come to him as needed?

"It's amazingly warm," Hannibal volunteered. "The meteorologist said that we're in the midst of a rare double inversion, which is sending—"

"*Meteorologist?* If by that term you mean that boy on the television, Ingolfur Jonsson, I can tell you what my father used to say about *his* father, old Jon Jonsson. My father said he didn't have the common sense to move aside when a horse started pissing on his boots."

"And Odin Palsson, too, he says we're beginning a whole new age of warmer weather. It's going to be hell for the countries Down Below. They're going to boil and fry and we're going to have a sweet and easy time of it."

"Odin Palsson," Rut repeats. In truth, she isn't about to say anything derogatory about the head of the Psychics Guild. "It is unusually warm," she concedes.

"I thought you might want to come out in it," Hannibal tells her.

"Out? Well that's exactly where I'm headed. I must be off to work soon."

"I thought you just might wish to take the day off from work perhaps," Hannibal continues.

"Oh you did, did you?" Her hands are folded across her broad chest.

No doubt about it: every step. Yes, he's going to have to battle her every step of the way.

She says: "And I suppose I should just let the man go thirsty who comes to my establishment looking for a coffee?"

"I thought you might get someone to run the place in your stead today perhaps," Hannibal continues.

"Oh you *did*, did you?"

The second time around, her question loses a good deal of its arch forcefulness—a fact Rut herself tacitly acknowledges by repeating it again, this time with an altered emphasis: "Oh *you* did, *did* you?"

"We won't see another day like this this year, that's certain. It will be next summer, if then, before we have so fine a day, and I've been thinking," Hannibal says, just as though this idea hadn't come to him seconds before, "you might want to head out to Blue with me." Blue: Rut's home island.

"Blue? And what's going to take you out there?"

"The weather, my dear," Hannibal declares and gestures grandly, openhandedly at the skies.

"I'm nobody's 'dear,'" Rut counters.

"A slip of the tongue, my pet. Force of habit."

"I'm nobody's 'pet.' You're slipping more and more these days, Hannibal."

"You may feel free at any time to laugh at me. . . ."

But she does not laugh. Instead Rut says, thoughtfully, "Blue Island."

"I thought we might head out there together."

"Blue," Rut murmurs yet again. "I do have a few errands out that way. . . ."

"I thought we might go together. The two of us. Will you perhaps come with me?"

"Certainly I will not. I'm not about to go out there with you. Yes, I do have some business out that way, and I don't suppose if you're also heading in that direction I could do anything to stop you. But let's have one thing absolutely clear: I'm not about to go to Blue with *you*, Hannibal."

"There's a ferry leaving in twenty minutes," Hannibal points out.

"And you're free to be on it. But I have some telephone calls to make and it isn't at all clear that I will be on that particular ferry. I have various responsibilities. I have a business to run."

"There are those who might perhaps suppose I, too, have various responsibilities. I'm still the President of the country."

"Not for long," Rut points out, and another sunlit silence falls.

"I'm going to make my calls," she then announces.

She does not invite him in. That's all right with Hannibal. The un-
seen gull, having moved to a new lookout, signals again, and this time he
hears in its narrow-throated observation the craftiness of a co-conspirator.
Bless them, the birds are still loyal, still behind him—as are the sheep. If
suffrage ever becomes *truly* universal, he won't have a thing to worry
about. . . .

Hannibal shuffles in the doorway, runs his hand through his thinning
hair. He's wearing gray cotton trousers and hiking boots and a big brown-
and-gray wool sweater. He needs no more clothes than this. When, in the
millennium-long history of Freeland's habitation, has there ever been so
fair an October day?

When Rut returns, he notes with satisfaction that she has brushed
and pinned her hair. She, too, is wearing hiking boots and cotton
trousers—hers are olive green—and a baggy brown wool sweater.

They walk in silence from the house. The gull calls a terse all-clear.
Hannibal turns left, toward the harbor.

"It's Eggert's car," he tells her.

"I think I recognize it."

"Were you surprised to see me just now?"

"I thought I recognized the knock."

"I didn't know I was going to come see you today," Hannibal con-
fesses. "Oh, I knew I would come sometime, and before too long, but I
was waiting for some sign, you see."

"And then it came to you? Your *sign*?" There is no mistaking her
skepticism.

Nonetheless, he pretends not to notice it: "Yes, today it was, and I
suppose it was a sort of vision. I went out riding, early this morning, way
out near Drangurfell. I was heading along the Two Day River, in fact, and
I had a vision of myself standing at your doorstep."

It is, by chance, the river her father drowned in.

"You've been riding too much. Jumbled your brain," she says. "You
and your *visions* . . ."

Only now does he recall that what got him into trouble with her in
the first place was a vision—of himself running for a fifth term, which had

come to him also on horseback, while contemplating Great Blue in the distance. He'd somehow forgotten.

He brazens it out: "Yes, a vision. Of me on your doorstep. Of my fist coming down upon your door. Of myself announcing, *I've come to let you laugh at me.*"

"You deserve to be laughed at. . . ."

"Do feel free, my dear. Everyone else has. But be that as may be, I had my vision this morning on horseback, out by the Two Day, and I knew instantly I must stand before you as soon as possible. Well, by then I was in Birch Valley, near Eggert's summerhouse, and what do I see by the side of the house but Eggert's car? And no Eggert. I stop to borrow his car and he's not there. Must have been out on one of his walks. So I look around and find his keys and steal his car and here I am."

"You left him your horse?"

"Yes. Old Blesi."

And now, at last, as she has been invited so many times to do, Rut laughs. The thought of her old adversary being stranded in this way, that pinched little man who rides like a city schoolgirl, tickles her. "So here you are," she says.

"Here we both are."

Yes, it's true. They are sitting companionably in Eggert's Volvo, after weeks without a word exchanged. They're riding out to the harbor together.

The ferry's going to be crowded—the brilliant weather has attracted quite a throng. Hannibal pulls into a line of cars that will be stowed in the boat's belly. He and Rut sit in silence, in a bath of Caribbean sunlight. Quite a peaceful sensation.

After they have secured the car in the lower deck and climbed to the passenger cabin, however, Rut experiences an unusual uneasiness. It isn't often she worries what people will think of her—that's a vulnerability she overcame decades ago—but she can't help fretting at the thought of how the other passengers may stare at her and whisper. It would be a shame if anybody were to conclude, just because she and Hannibal happen to be traveling out to Blue on the same ferry, that they've reconciled. She sits, pointedly, with an empty seat between her and him, and sets an explanatory scowl on her face.

Yet no one seems to notice. It is as though they've all succumbed to some sort of spell—bewitched by the weather. Really, it is quite something: what in the world has happened to the *weather*? Everything feels giddy and aimless and when exactly did she last experience this sort of heady open-endedness? She's reminded, as the boat chugs over a blue sea overlain by a shifting net of solar knots and cordage, of her childhood on Blue Island. She recalls her gruff father, who one Christmas Eve said of her—of her! who today must weigh at least a hundred and sixty pounds—"Each man must have a flower in his life, and you are my flower. . . ."

When Hannibal scoots over a seat, to murmur in a low voice, "Are you hungry? I'm feeling hungry . . ." there seems no point in challenging this minor physical advance. No one is noticing and if they are, what of it? When was she ever someone to worry about the idle misapprehensions of her neighbors? She shakes her head at him—*no*—and lets the matter drop.

Hannibal nods in return, then rises gingerly to his feet and makes his way over to the little refreshment counter. He's limping heavily these days, which distresses her—which doubly distresses her. She worries not only about his knees but also about how the sight of him limping tugs and tears at her chest. Is she turning sentimental in her old age? It's always a mistake, pitying Hannibal.

He returns with a Snickers and a bag of Tropical Fruit Jellies. He unwraps the candy bar and offers her the first bite. She refuses with a toss of her head. He nods again at her—he has such a thoughtful, abstracted look on his face this morning—and in three large absentminded bites consumes the bar. Actually, she *is* feeling hungry.

When the ferry docks in Hollhovn, most of the crowd disembarks. She's hardly surprised at this. Diamond has always been a "fun" island. She distrusts it—as her father always did. The grass was richer, greener over on Diamond, and the people correspondingly weaker and more shiftless. They lacked complete depth, those Diamonders.

But when, twenty minutes later, the ferry pulled into her own Blue, she felt the full *rightness* of their destination. Didn't the air suddenly smell better? The two of them went below, climbed into Eggert's car, drove off into Halldorshovn. It wasn't many minutes before they'd left the town far behind them.

They were circling around Great Blue. Its bulk was too near to get any sort of perspective on it. She merely felt an ascending presence on her left, a gray slope dotted with stubborn mossy patches of green. She'd lived her life—her early life, her irreplaceable girlhood—in the mountain's shadow.

Indeed, Hannibal is driving her not so far from the old farmstead. It's deserted now, of course, like so many of the old crofts. The whole valley's deserted—except for the ghosts—and the gravel road worsens every year. But this is still a place where you can trace the paths cut by generations of sheep and horses two, four, six, eight hundred, a thousand years ago. The centuries lie exposed, side by side, in these paths scored into the flank of the mountain. Hannibal pulls the car to the edge of the road. "I thought we might take a walk," he tells her.

"Might as well. Since we're here anyway."

They start down one of the sheep paths. The vast resplendent mazes of Thorskrist—a megalopolis of some nineteen thousand souls—glitter across the Bay. They walk side by side. Hannibal is limping.

"You haven't yet laughed at me," he reminds her.

"Do you honestly need someone else to laugh at you? Good Christ, I would have thought you'd been laughed at enough."

"But I lost the election, Rut," Hannibal says.

"You lost the election, Hannibal," she tells him.

"Just as you told me I would."

"Just as I told you you would."

"I did come close to winning," he points out.

"Closer than I would ever have thought possible," she admits.

The sea lies on one side, the mountain and its glacier on the other. The breeze is balmier than it has any reason to be.

She adds: "And you did get *The Freeland Saga* back."

"That's when I knew I must be doomed—when the Icelanders agreed to relinquish the damn thing. If they'd thought I had a chance in the world, they would have held on to it another five years, anyway. They do love an argument, those people."

"Yes . . ." she says, and looks pleased, almost as though she has received a compliment.

"They were having fun goading me with it. Making sport with me. They'd goaded me for twenty years."

"You got it back," she repeats.

There's a crinkling sound and Hannibal absentmindedly places something in his mouth. It's one of those Tropical Fruit Jellies.

After only a moment, his hand fishes into his pants pocket once again and there's another crinkling, ripping sound—which rips at *her*. He's going to eat them all, isn't he, every single last one, the appalling glutton. . . . If she doesn't watch out, he's going to toss the lot of them rapidly, thoughtlessly into his gullet, swallowing them down without even chewing.

On the other hand, she absolutely will not offer this man, who too often gets his way, who too often for his own good is approached by supplicants, the satisfaction of seeing her beg for anything. So when he next dips into his pocket she halts her walking and peers hard at the private region where the crinkling emerges. His wrist jerks guiltily. A sheepish, awakened look realigns his features. He brings the cellophane bag forth in his palm and extends it to her. "Want some?"

"I don't think so," she says and accepts four of them. Two yellow, a red, and a green.

"I've been thinking about elections," Hannibal begins again.

"Oh?"

"About the voting process. Now on Election Day, each one of us casts our ballots in private. Which means, there's no saying who any of us actually voted for. . . ."

"That's right." She lays a yellow Tropical Jelly on her tongue. It's covered by a lovely, delicate, thick crust of sugar.

"Now it seems to me I recall your swearing to me, on that day when I first announced my plans to run one last time for President, that you planned to cast your vote for Nonni Karlsson. But in truth, I don't have any way of *knowing* you actually did so, do I? You see? Even if you *told* me you did, I wouldn't really have any way of *knowing* you did, now would I? Which isn't to say, of course, that I'm one to doubt your veracity. . . ."

Across White Seal Bay, the capital basks in the sun. He is a sly one, Hannibal Hannibalsson is. Always such a sly one . . .

"I am a woman of my word," Rut points out. "Just ask anyone."

"Oh agreed, agreed, there's no disputing your stubbornness about sticking to a resolution, now is there? I've never known a Freelander yet who wouldn't concede your stubbornness."

He is bending her words, slightly, playing with their meanings. Hastily she swallows her Tropical Fruit Jelly and cries, "Has it occurred to you that on Election Day I may have had things to do! I have a business to run. Maybe I have better ways to spend my time than to head out into a blizzard to cast some vote for some silly election?"

"Oh you're a busy woman—no one would disagree with you there." His tone is peaceful, appeasing. "But I've never yet seen the storm could keep you indoors on Election Day. No, no," Hannibal announces sagely, "that sort of storm hasn't been invented yet."

He's flattering her, she realizes; she must be on her guard. "Now it may be," she concedes, "that I did get out to vote. I hardly remember. I'm a busy woman."

"Indeed, indeed," he concurs, in that same soft and insinuative manner. "But you know what the odd truth of the matter is? Admittedly, I will never know. It's a completely private affair, as I say. But would you like to hear something quite odd? In my heart of hearts, I can't see you *voting* for Nonni Karlsson. Despite your vow. Yes, despite your vow. Of course, you were publicly obligated to do so. . . ."

Well: her chest throbs. He's getting close—he's hot upon her shameful secret. . . . Savagely she cries, "There isn't *anybody*, not a soul in all of Freeland, who can claim that I supported you."

"Oh agreed, agreed," Hannibal murmurs, in that maddeningly measured, that sham-humble voice of his. "No one can taint you with that, Rut-my-dear. No one's going to say of you that you supported your man."

"Goddamnit, Hannibal, whatever I did in the privacy of that voting booth"—and who in the hell is *he* to have guessed the truth about her?—"there isn't a single soul who can accuse me of going back on my word."

"Indeed, indeed," he intones, sucking another of his Tropical Fruit Jellies. Oh and what a scheming bastard he is! "It's no one else knows the truth. No one but you and me, my dear."

"You do realize you're the most insufferably arrogant man I've ever known?"

"Arrogant? Oh well, yes, yes perhaps," he muses. He runs a hand through his sparse, once red-gold hair. "But I suppose I've had my comeuppance now and then. Life has a way of bringing the arrogant back to earth with a painful thump, now doesn't it? If memory serves me aright, it was along this very path a young farmgirl broke my nose, thirty-some years ago."

And now she cannot help it: she must grin at him.

It has remained their secret, that blow she landed when he dared to presume he might kiss her—so tightly, breathlessly, hungrily—without first obtaining her permission. . . .

It has all along remained their secret, and when Hannibal turns and catches Rut's grin, the look in her eye thrills him. Oh, the *spirit* of this woman, her gloating pride in having shattered the face of a lover who dared take advantage of her. These days she's missing a tooth, an upper canine, and the glimpse of a slick seal-like gray tongue prompts him to remark, "I feel now what I felt then: you're still a very attractive girl, Rut."

The words, once loosed upon the air, doubly astound him. For one thing, he hadn't planned on making any such declaration. For another, they prove, unexpectedly, to be true: he desires her. His body is craving hers. . . .

"And you're an old has-been," Rut swiftly responds. "You're a failed politician bounced out of office."

"Oh no one's likely to dispute you there," he croons. "I don't suppose there is anyone around here likely to say that the man before you, though he served as President of his country for twenty years, is still someone to reckon with. You're quite right. No, no, I am nothing but a gimpy old has-been. Agreed, agreed. Ah, but you, on the other hand, are a fair princess. You are the queen of the fairies. You are a celestial apparition. You are earth's fairest flower."

Damn it to *hell*, she's not about to put up with any such talk as this! There was another man, many lifetimes ago, who used to call her his flower, but he died—that man, Bjartur Jonsson, drowned nearly thirty years ago in the bitterly, unthinkably cold Two Day River—and she isn't now going to listen to any lying fake sham of an impostor wafting such high-blown language her way.

"Failure!" she calls him. "Gimpy, broken-kneed stumblebum."

But he is close upon her, Hannibal Hannibalsson is close at her side with all of his venerable but still formidable tricks. "You're my bristly old sow's belly," he exhales in her ear. "My very own fly-dotted sheep's dropping. Fish stink and rat's plunder."

That's more like it and she answers, "Mud spawn, slime bucket. You old goat-breath."

In truth his breath smells of his magical imported candies: his lungs are dark cargo-vats full of pineapple and coconut, of papaya, mango, passion fruit. . . .

"Oh but my dearest angel," he counters. "My tenderest papery butterfly. My nightingale. My mimosa flower." He has taken her hands. Actually, he has taken both of her hands in one of his big hands and his other hand has slipped beneath her sweater. It is climbing, up and down, up and down the rungs of her spine. Briefly he lays his mouth upon hers, once, firmly, fiercely. Kisses her. Kisses her on this path, on the western shore of Blue, where, one glorious midsummer's eve, in response to a similar kiss, she broke his nose. Does he think he can get away with this? When will the man learn?

"Swamp-muck," she whispers in his ear. "Lice brain."

"Pig's hoof," he calls her. "Cat piss. Cat piss."

There's a bed of moss, some ten yards over on the left, which he may not yet have seen, and it is almost as if, although she is fending off his every advance as best she can, her step-by-step retreat is leading them there.

"My dearest, my fair one, my ugly, my brute, my soul's star," he is gibbering into her ear, mixing everything up, he hasn't a clue what he's doing, the fool. But she hasn't a clue either, and when, moments later, she's supine upon the bed of moss and feels, against her bare backside, the earth's sweet wet roused vegetal embracingness, seeping upward, through the sweater deposited there in haste, she's no longer herself at all, damn him, and what is the name of this infernal emotion that would lead her to behave so ridiculously? Will someone tell her its name? Her powers of vituperation are dissolving away, though she manages even yet to hurl at him a final anathema. She summons up one more unutterably nasty insult: "You *Hannibal*," she whispers in his ear. "You *Hannibal*," she accuses. "You *Hannibal*."

He retaliates powerfully: "My bloom, my blood," he says to her. "My flower. My fairest flower."

59

The Poet of the Glacier's Edge

I suspect you'd have to live at least a year or two at or above the Arctic Circle to understand the essence of winter light in the Far North. There's little of it, of course. But the crucial aspect isn't amount or duration so much as direction. At the start of one of winter's abbreviated days the sun doesn't come up, and at the close it doesn't go down; it moves sideways, mostly. Hours before it actually nudges into view you sense it there, just below the horizon, intensely weighing the prospects of that momentous thing, the breaking of a new day. And for hours after its setting it wanly tints the heavens, still mulling over its passage. This is a contemplative's domain. You're constantly mindful, in Freeland in winter, as you're rarely mindful in southern climates, of what's beyond the horizon. Even those of us who have never left these islands speak naturally of the world Down Below.

By contrast, anyone who has ever visited a tropical island knows how at nightfall the sun, having put in another workday, is all but tossed out on its ear. Gone—with startling rapidity. Bring on the stars. There are to be no second thoughts.

Ours is, paradoxically, a gentler place than any tropical paradise. There's a tenderness to our winter light, a distant but voluptuous elongation of its pleasures which hints, perhaps, of sentimentality, killing though our climate may be. . . .

October had come and another killing season was approaching. But my summerhouse looked set to weather another winter. It was provisioned against all seasons, a repository of everything a man might reasonably ask for: a ream of good English paper, two German fountain pens, half a dozen ink cartridges, half a dozen wool blankets, a crate of Polish coal, and a pantry stocked with potatoes, dried fish, onions, beans, rye bread, carrots, lamb steaks, coffee, gin. I had everything, indeed, but some germ of inspiration—everything but the vital quick of my fiftieth book. So I took myself out on a long walk.

My nation's islands, in their asteroidal smallness and grayness and bleakness, may not be what I would like to think them: infinite in their inspiration. But I had no doubt the terrain was bountiful enough to launch me one more time. In my quest for the opening to another tale, I turned instinctively and hopefully to Freeland's fissured slopes and spindly, cold, haphazard streams. I felt—does this sound absurd?—the land owed me nothing less. Over and over hadn't I stayed inexplicably loyal to this place which everyone might have expected me to abandon for some larger and milder Elsewhere?

I was seeking repayment. I would take what I could get, but I suppose my tender hope was that these past weeks had added up to something other than themselves. All our pandering attempts to satisfy some nebulous collective entity called the Electorate were now to be transmuted. Our rhetoric—full of words like nobility and fidelity and strength—would be revealed as noble, faithful, and strong after all. I let my mind sally back and forth over the campaign: the fateful day when Hannibal announced his "vision" of another run; the televised declaration of his candidacy out on Giant Island, while the rain came scissoring down and a sheep dropped a load of turds behind him; the arrival of the three Visitors—Wilhelm, Paradiso, Kanekyu—looking for all the world like some parodic embodiment of the Axis Powers; Nonni's pitiful attempts to remake himself into a dynamic speaker; the arrival of Elva, first glimpsed on all fours in a blizzard, her black stockings safeguarded in her pocket; Nonni's wonderfully lamebrained suggestion that we stop importing Danish Blue; Hannibal's increasing lethargy, slumping deeper and deeper into his armchair, as the hearth before him cooled; Elva in her turquoise leotard, crying in my car *I'm not so stupid as to be in love with someone who no longer loves me*; Rut's saving blow to Wilhelm's face. . . . For months now I'd had no time for true work, I'd sacrificed my best self to the toilsome imbecilities of the campaign—to reassuring words designed for the hard-of-hearing elderly, to eloquent turns of phrase destined for crowds of boors and hooligans—but all along, or so I'd been reassuring myself, a new book had been amassing. Surely I hadn't been wasting my time completely? Wasn't something worthwhile about to crystallize?

With my netherworldly photograph of my grandchild tucked into my bag, I'd left my apartment this morning by a little after nine. It wasn't quite ten when I'd settled myself into the summerhouse and seated myself at my desk with a virgin sheet of rag paper before me. For long minutes I'd stared at it, then I'd written "Page One" sturdily and handsomely with my German fountain pen, and again I'd contemplated the page. It was like staring down at an unbroken bed of clouds from a jet's round window, mile after mile, then having the clouds thin and break to reveal—to reveal another, lower bed of clouds. Where was my land? Who were its people? When was I going to spy the contours of my fiftieth book? At eleven, I set out on my walk.

The weather was extraordinary: blue, limpid, and balmier than any October day in Freeland I could remember. Just a few days before, on Election Day, we'd had snow, a big fuzzy blizzard, and the earth was wet and soft, oozy with snowmelt. Miniature impromptu waterfalls, delicate as the strings of any lute or lyre, threaded down cliff sides and over boulders. Freshets braided across ancient sheep trails, rockfaces dripped and shone. The ground was awash, a-rush. We'd had a cold summer—even by Freelandic standards—and I suppose these pages are full of an unseasonable share of icy drizzle and numbing winds, gray skies forever giving way to shrapneled explosions of snow and hail. But this was a day to induce a stunned, beatific amnesia: hadn't it always been like this? Wasn't ours a land of cerulean skies, of clouds of the softest carded virgin wool, of hills into whose slopes hundreds and hundreds of rainbows had been ground?

The earth was stirring, quickening in the unforeseen warmth and light, and everywhere you felt the same overrunning wish: in the beds of moss, in the nervous tipped reed beds along the Two Day River, in the little incandescent pools on either side of the sheep paths, even in the massed, ungiving hills themselves. Here was the hope that the warmth might somehow persist, that a cruel season might be circumvented. For the first time in the thousand-year history of these islands' habitation, might we not be spared the killing brutalities of winter? Why must we always pay so dearly for our annual birthright? Why must we suffer so horrifically just to glimpse the spring?

Somewhere far back in my mind I recognized this day as an illusion, a dazzling false promise. . . . Its warmth couldn't possibly hold, winter never be averted. The terrible ransom must be paid; the trolls living within Great Blue Glacier must all be fed their pots of snow and ice, one after another after another, before a single vernal blossom could be granted us. The presiding genius of our land abided.

I've visited some locales where the spirit of the land has been successfully overthrown. Swamps were drained or deserts irrigated, truckloads of air-conditioning units were shipped in, refrigerated shopping emporia were constructed. Think of Miami, of Phoenix. But in Freeland we hadn't yet found the means of carting away Great Blue Glacier, of sending the North Wind packing. . . .

Even so, hiking among the hills—for an hour, for two, for three—I was grateful for the day's deceptions. When I was in Copenhagen once, years ago, I remember a January that ushered in a sunny interlude so mild it unfurled the forsythia. I'd never seen this happen before, which perhaps explains why I was so touched by the heraldic boldness of their dumb, doomed yellow. The bushes didn't know any better. The forsythia's sophisticated network of roots and branches was, in the end, easily hoodwinked. Millions upon millions of years of evolutionary refinement, the epochal triumph of the angiosperms, and yet they remained a soft touch. Merely treat them gently and they will unfold. Suckers for a spot of sun . . .

But now it was October not January, and Freeland not Denmark, and the Arctic winter dark was bearing down. Only a few days ago we'd suffered a blizzard. Who could deny what lay before us? Yet everywhere I walked, the hills and valleys, cirques and basins declared in sun-glazed stupefaction, *It's come, it's come.* Declared: *Spring is on the way.* I wandered without aim, but with purpose, over hilltops and down into narrow canyons, listening to the endlessly modulating music of running water—babblings, bubblings, burblings, gurglings, whispers, whimpers, splashings, shushings, frothings. The music was soothing, it was cleansing. I'd been sullied. For weeks and weeks. The hectic hurry of the campaign had left me dirtied and diminished. It had turned me into an urban rat, whereas it surely lay within my nature to be, at least, that diminutive but admirable being, a Freelandic field mouse—a creature flush with grace and hope even as, eyeing the heavens for a hawk, it darts from one moss-tuft to another. I had betrayed my better self.

I was crossing a sandbar of volcanic ash, a blue, still pond to my left and a gold, rushing river to my right, when it came to me that my fiftieth book would have nothing to do with the campaign. Its pages would shun altogether the burly allure of politics. I would dismiss them all—Hannibal, Nonni, Rut, the Visitors. Like a river myself, I would flush them away. My book would aspire instead to the hues and harmonies of this peerless afternoon. Its prose would have the good slight give of this sandbar under my feet. I would seek to re-create nothing less than the erosive, rock-ribbed beauty of Freeland. Oh, I'd steered at this before, sought many times to be the poet of the glacier's edge, but this time around I would bring to it the savor and the dolor of the aging man who realizes, almost too late, how he has squandered his energies on phantoms and ephemera. I would emulate lightness, brightness, clean stones and low, earth-hugging flowers. I would begin to write on the morrow. Today I would do nothing but walk—soaking it up, taking it in, letting the landscape work its recu- perations on my soul. And at dusk I would go, as pledged, to my daughter's for dinner, where, cordially installed at the head of the table, I would ease whatever familial tensions had burgeoned over the last few weeks, making amends with both my androidal son-in-law and my biologically inexplic- able son. And after dinner I would telephone Hannibal, and perhaps head briefly over to Founders' Point, where the two of us might clink glasses in a toast to a battle well and bravely waged. Finally, I would shake Hannibal's hand, bid a fond adieu to my old comrade-in-arms, and drive out once more, under pitch-black skies, to the summerhouse. And in the morning I would unlock and open—my pen serving as a key—a first chapter, a new book, its pages perfused by lightness, brightness, clean stones and low, earth-hugging flowers.

I kept stooping to the earth. I came upon lichens of a mazed ornate- ness not even the most painstaking eye could negotiate. They were cen- turies old, some of them—they had first felt the sun in a year and a season when the men of these hills wore armor. . . . And here were the remains of pinks, bedded among volcanic cinders, like little hefty galactic clusters scattered over a night-universe of ebony. Here was a wall of obsidian— Nature's original "glass darkly." Here were heaps of red pumice, stones that had lost the heat but held the hue of their infernal birth, and here were collapsed lava tubes, looking like desiccated riverbeds, like moles' tunnel- ings, and here were black stone beaches strewn with orange and white kelp in tangled heaps, like torn, discarded party favors. Here was a white tern by a green tarn.

When had I last experienced such a happy sense of resolve? I re- member I was humming a song as, after five hours of walking, I mounted the final sheep path toward a ridge from whose crest Birch Valley and my little summerhouse would spring into view.

But at the crest I halted, troubled. Something was gravely amiss in the valley outstretched below me. What was it? Why did it feel like a vandal- ized painting?

There, just where it belonged, was the summerhouse, its walls an inviting red, its corrugated roof a cheery sky-blue. There was the stream that ran beside it, and there was the ruined stone wall that spoke of the farmstead that once, lichenlike, had affixed itself to these rocky slopes, only a few generations ago, and there were the scrubby bushes in the lea of the hill, and there was the winding gravel road that meandered over to the next valley.

And there—so to speak—wasn't my car. My car was missing.

Missing? My car?

Had it been carried off by a giant eagle? By a colossal troll who had strapped it on his back and humped on over the hills? These seemed explanations as plausible as any, for cars in Freeland are not stolen. There's nowhere to hide them, nowhere to take them to.

I should have guessed immediately at the cause, of course, but somehow I didn't. A muddy wave of nervousness went slopping over my head; my brain ceased to process information. Hurriedly, incredulously, I pitched down the hillside. I stepped into a sinkhole, sending icy water plunging over the top of my boot, and a few steps farther on I came down heavily on a loose rock and gave my ankle a wrenching—ours isn't a landscape meant for hurtling motion. Still, I raced on.

The car was gone. I looked around, up and down the valley. My Volvo had disappeared. And yet, somehow expecting it to reemerge on its own, I stared hard at the spot where I'd left it, as though by dint of forceful inspection I could compel it to materialize. I then began combing the ground for tire tracks, as though to prove to myself—what? That for the last four years I hadn't simply *imagined* owning a 1985 white Volvo?

How could anyone have stolen my car, given that I held the keys in my pocket? But they weren't in my pocket—they were inside the house. The house? I glanced toward it and saw a scrap of paper wedged between door and frame, ten or so feet away, and even at this distance I recognized the big sprawling scrawl. Oh, I knew that heedless, headlong, space-arrogating penmanship.

The note was brief:

Emergency. Have traded modes of transport.
Look behind house.

H

I circled the house. There stood Blesi, Hannibal's horse. Strapped to a fence paling.

Inside my head, worry and confusion hadn't yet given way to fury.

They did so now. It was the shamefaced look that Blesi bestowed upon me—that's what hurled my emotions over whatever boundary heretofore had contained them. I swear that that creature regarded me as an equal: he shot me the look that one dupe or pawn or patsy or gull or fool exchanges with another. He saw me—I swear!—as a fellow victim. Exasperation, resentment, wrath welled up within. *He rides roughshod over me, too*, was what old Blesi's sunken-headed glance confided in me.

A voluminous vat, a troll's cauldron, began to steam and bubble and pop inside my chest. I felt a pronouncement—an anathema—inspissating within it. And since there are few pastimes more delectable to the Freelandic soul than the ceremonious recital of a malediction, I also felt a happy expectancy. I lifted my chin, I threw back my narrow shoulders, and I addressed the surrounding hills:

"I bid farewell to lightness and brightness and the coming of spring. Farewell to clean stones and low earth-hugging flowers. For my fiftieth book shall be a harsh and uncharitable exposé, a chronicle of all the indignities and imbecilities you've put me through, Hannibal Hannibalsson, decades and decades of your overweening foolishness, your fatuous bloated self-important mystical blathering, and I shall protect you from nothing. I will not even spare you your drunken stumblings, or the sight of you at some grand political occasion sucking your necktie clean of the food you've spilled upon it. No, I will not even spare you the sight of your bare buttocks on the front page of *The Daily Liar*."

My words reverberated throughout the valley. Blesi eyed me dolefully. *Why don't you take it easy?* Blesi was asking me. But hell no I would not take it easy. I would construct a novel thick with hail and wind and monumental, doomed foolishness—this book—and in my unstinting pursuit of bitter truths, my cold dissection of my nation's follies, I would prove myself willing to betray everyone, my friend Hannibal most of all. (I boast of my eagerness to expose and betray, and yet my dearest wish, as perhaps at last shows plain, is that in my fashion I've proven to be a scrupulously faithful man. I mean to be true to you alone, Reader, although at this *very* moment I'm hoping you're feeling a little puzzled and more than a little betrayed. The last time I spoke to you directly and at length, some fifty-three chapters ago, I vowed that there would appear in my book no more parentheses, and yet here we find ourselves closeted within one, and now I'd better confess that even as I was making that pledge I intended to violate it. Even then I was hoping for a Reader who eventually would recollect that faraway promise and wind up feeling double-crossed, and even then I was looking forward to offering him or her an apology. Within that previous parenthesis I spoke of my endless, solacing musings upon my ideal reader. . . . I spoke of you as a retired American schoolteacher, vacationing alone in the Yucatán; as a young Irishman in Brooklyn; as a mother of twins; as a shipping clerk in Rotterdam. Is it not apparent that *you* are my reality and none of the others signify, that everything contained herein—except this pair of far-flung, sibling parentheses—is a complex of lies? Think of their shape—a pair of parentheses—the only punctuation marks of any grace and comeliness, cupped as gently as a pair of hands in prayer. This is a large enough book that two parenthetical glosses might plausibly get lost within it; if you were to conceive of my novel's sixty chapters as the minutes of one hour, our two pairs of parentheses, our two little prayers, would occupy no more than a few seconds. And yet only in those seconds do I feel I can speak with any candor. Oh I've done my full conscientious best to render my portraits with the most minute verisimilitude. Think for a moment of all the intricate fussing that has gone into the delineation of dear Lilja's eyes. Have I conveyed a sense of their chill and breadth and preternatural clarity? With my whole heart I hope so. Certainly I've offered you some lovely touches. Recall Kornelia's Freelandic cream ships, those pathetic native pastries on which "the light of all the world had been spun, miraculously, into a nourishing froth." Or recall that reconstructed moment in Buck's Eat Shop when eggs hit the skillet with a "searing, cohering kiss." Recall, just a few pages back, "a white tern by a green tarn." But of course yes they're all lies. I have given you, by way of a series of painful poignant couplings, a self-portrait of a man doomed to drift unhappily in love: think of Meg, more intimately attached to her dead son's model airplane, hanging from the ceiling by a string, than to the living organ that probed her; think of gluttonous Kornelia and her ever-dwindling series of lovers, whose sexual life if extrapolated to its logical termination leads to a woman the size of a pickup truck who carries a man the size of a screwdriver in the pocket of her overalls; think of Connie taking into her pristine, generous-hipped body a rash-ridden, scrofulous Eggert while downstairs her idiot daughter beams beatifically at the bare walls of her room. But the real affair, the sweet and genuine and chaste intimacy that has concealed itself behind all those distasteful exhibitions—the real affair has been my soul's concern. It is—dare I say it?—something the two of us have shared, for I've sought from you the rarest and purest gift in all the universe: true friendship from a stranger. And as a challenge to you, as a way of making yours a task worth the undertaking,

I've systematically imbruted myself: sharpened my ratlike features, high-lighted my narrowness and selfishness and cruelty. Still, you were not taken in? Not fooled, for example, by the mock-viciousness heaped on our Sindri-Cinderella? Well, possibly I've already said too much, but if you're an authentic friend my garrulity will be excused, and if you are no friend no excuses matter, and having waited so long to open myself to you I must babble a final few words. I must say something more than fare-well. I would say also, *Bless you, reader.* Would say, *Bless you, friend.*)

Blesi shits, copiously, with a grunt of satisfaction, onto my woodpile. He blinks, once. *What else did you expect?* his gaze says to Eggert. "Not a damn thing," embittered Eggert answers, aloud.

Eggert stamps into his summerhouse. Damn, damn, and double damn. It's time he was off to Lilja's. He must be on his way.

Presumably, if he rides Blesi over to Founders' Point and deposits him there, he could then catch a bus over to his daughter's, with luck arriving no more than half an hour late. The working assumption is that Hannibal, one way or another, will return the car tonight. If Eggert spends the night in Skyscraper Tower, he can head out to the summerhouse tomorrow morning. He has a new book to write.

And what does he need to take with him if he's heading back to town? Surely, soon, he must begin his son's manuscript, *Not Far from the Tree*, which is sitting on the desk. Eggert lifts it up—the Youth Experience! how presumptuously heavy it is!—and carries it outside and stuffs it into Blesi's saddlebags. What else? As a sort of counterweight to the boy's bulging manuscript Eggert packs as well one spectral photograph. His "brooding" and sexually ambiguous grandchild.

Eggert has never liked to ride. He mistrusts horses. So it's with feel-ings of distaste and uneasiness that he mounts another, a final, creature. His feet find the stirrups.

Eggert sets forth, claimed by a land he has sought to claim as his own. He rides and, simultaneously, he observes himself riding. He feels his being being absorbed. It's happening. Yes, the quale of this magical land of Free-land is beginning to assert itself: a process of transfiguration whereby the living are woven into a rag-paper tapestry—a tapestry in which feelings are the needles and words are the thread. He is becoming a *character*.

And as he and Blesi make their plodding progress up the rubbly side of the hill, it dawns on him just what an appropriate, what a fittingly ab-surd, conclusion this journey on horseback provides for his portion of the tale. Eggert is riding off to visit his pregnant daughter and his inverted son.

The most amazing thing in the world has transpired. That son of his has actually written a novel—now banked in a pair of saddlebags—entitled *Not Far from the Tree*, which has drawn a five-hundred-thousand-kronur advance, and at the thought of such a wild monstrous improbability Eggert tosses back his head and projects a jagged and defiant peal of laughter at the broken hills. Let *that* be his final judgment on the world!

Yet Eggert shall not have the last word. With vexatious aplomb, with maddening magnanimity, the dream-laden hills of Freeland echo the sound. In myriads of little liquid rustlings, the land itself speaks: purlings, gurglings, all the bright, light, ministering whispers of water dancing over stones.

60

The Art of Bold Design, or,
A State of Mind

Buttocks oddly warmed by sunlight, Hannibal awakens from his doze. He realizes, with a panicky jerking thrash of his limbs, that there's a woman underneath him. But then it turns out to be all right after all: it's Rut. She's dozing too.

He mounts slowly to his feet—his knees are giving him trouble—and draws up his underwear and trousers, smooths his upraised sweater over his broad belly. Rut whimpers in her sleep but does not wake. Her broad pale legs are lying open and he glances, fleetingly, at her crotch and a broad, tidal melancholy floods through him. This is something he has never been able to confess to anyone, not even to Eggert, who probably couldn't begin to comprehend it.

How could the truth ever reach Eggert, who in his harried, hurrying, lurching, clutching way has shown himself time and again willing, irrespective of her looks or temperament, to lie down with any female whatsoever who does not positively shove him from her side? Eggert has never had the time to see what this business of the body is really like. Perpetually driven by a sense of deprivation, of being thwarted at every turn, Eggert has never had the disinterest and the leisure needed to detect the pervading sadness under it all. How could anyone like Eggert, so bent on proving himself the equal to other men, ever grasp just how painfully deficient we *all* are, the men of the species, in this business. . . .

Eggert doubtless cannot feel the pain a man by all means ought to feel while contemplating the naked body of a woman. In due time,

Mother Nature will probably set things right. She will devise a race of men fully equipped to handle the rich inward intricacy of the female form. They—these superior men of the distant future—will be different. They will no longer have to depend upon a blunt dumb instrument, as sensitive as a crowbar, as adaptable as a birch log. Always so intent on his manhood-vindicating triumphs, Eggert simply cannot afford to see that such triumphs are, even for the best of us, a hopelessly compromised and approximated matter. Surely, he cannot bear to contemplate how much more we might accomplish, even in our most successful couplings, how painfully each is a falling short. . . .

Hannibal feels himself in need of solace, and is there any comfort in this world greater than a walk beside the sea? At his feet, as bright as coins still warm from the stamp of the mint, a few shells spark among the heaps of dark wet pebbles. Eggert sometimes speaks knowingly of "postcoitum tristesse," but what honestly could he know of its riddles—of the full emptied abyss of the thing? For he's a romantic, and therefore constitutionally unable to appraise the true cold expansive eddying wastes of love, of art. He writes poems about the sea but the sea itself doesn't deeply involve him. He is always careening elsewhere, carrying the "sea" elsewhere with him. Even on the beach, there are no stones for him but steppingstones.

Hannibal comes upon some kelp, brown ribbons of such sharp edges and uniform widths as to look artificial—as though they'd been run through a vast marine paper shredder—and a couple of modest lovely fist-hunks of driftwood. And here too, of course, are all sorts of cast-off garbage, transported from Down Below: bottles, cans, a pair of white plastic sunglasses, a key chain that has lost its keys, lids without jars, jars without lids. They produce so much refuse there, Down Below, that not even the most monumental of their computers could begin to keep an accounting of it all. Waste is forever leaking and spilling forth from their shores; they amass and expel their mountains of trash as automatically as a glacier calves another iceberg. They've never heard of Freeland, most of the people Down Below, and yet in their colossal spewings they are forever sending forth offerings to us all the same. Poisons. They are killing species that haven't yet been christened. Trashing the bottom of the sea. Contaminating hills and valleys whose existence hasn't yet reached them.

This thought, too, brushes him with melancholy, and Hannibal strolls for a while down the shore with his chin uplifted, eyes hard at the sun, lest he glimpse at his feet one more thoughtless throwaway. Really, the day is amazingly warm. *Straight from the Caribbean*, that's what the meteorologist on television had said. This weather has been sent, intact, right up the long aerial chute of the Gulf Stream, from a region where pineapples and mangoes and oranges fatten on the branches.

There once was a time, long ago, when it seemed as though all of those countries Down Below might too be his. This goes back quite a ways, when he'd first voyaged to Copenhagen, for the Great Danish Steamship Company. He'd been a very young man and everything had seemed possible.

But a confusion had descended on him—the largest confusion of his life, perhaps, a mist that maybe he hasn't yet steered himself free of. The world was, he'd had no doubt, calling upon him to undertake some stupendous project, but what precisely was being requested? Oh he'd been ready—he'd always been ready—to attempt to square its demands, but wasn't it only fair and just, given his willingness to hurl himself into any enterprise, howsoever outlandish or foolish or hazardous it might be, that the world at least specify what it required of him? In time he'd left Copenhagen—maybe the confusion had mastered him in the end—and returned to Freeland, and eventually he'd located what he was manifestly intended to do, for wasn't it his true task in life to serve as his nation's leader? But if this is indeed meant to be his life's work, why was he feeling such terrible uncertainty now? Life couldn't possibly be saying to him, *Your lifework is over*, could it? But then why had his own people repudiated him?

He keeps expecting the next breeze to be colder, and yet each seems, if possible, warmer than the last. *We're entering a new warm age* Odin Palsson of the Psychics Guild had announced, and only now does Hannibal perceive that crazy old Odin has it exactly right. *A new warm age*. All this garbage at his feet, all the junk and filth and crap and trash that the world Down Below sends as its only bulletins this way, don't they, too, affirm the new, warm age? Isn't that the message decipherable in the runic strew of rubbish lining the shore? They're overheating, those countries Down Below. Racing too fast, like turbines idling at a furious speed. They're producing much too much, and it's only natural, it is indeed inevitable, that they must finally so congest their skies with smoke and soot and gas that temperatures will climb and they'll begin to cook themselves. The greenhouse effect. Odin has probably never heard the term but he doesn't need to. Odin has second sight.

Hannibal sees that, beautifully, the whole elaborate process makes perfect sense: hasn't he understood from the outset that the rest of the world must go, literally, to Hell? Hasn't he always known that in Freeland alone lies the world's salvation?

For Freeland is about to enter a *new warm age.* While the peoples Down Below are beginning to hiss and sizzle like fish in a pan, Freeland will be basking under a clement, a fertile, a sweetly fulfilling sun. He holds it in a sort of vision: oh, it's to be a kind of love affair, with a doting sun beaming down upon Freeland and Freeland, yes, its every hillside blushing brightly, shining back at the sun. Our weather will be both passionate and exquisite. . . .

How it all must turn out—the denouement, that is, of *The Freeland Saga,* whose first pages were inscribed on sheepskin seven hundred years ago—comes clear to Hannibal and his chest hums and aches with the inclusive global splendor of his vision. His melancholy slips distantly away, like a cloaked man glimpsed on the far rise of a valley, arm uplifted in farewell. Oh, he hasn't time for it now! He is beginning to discern the future dead square on at last! Of course they will want to emigrate to Freeland. All those people Down Below, they will want to pack up and move right here. . . .

And now his brain is whirring, quick and clear and powerful. . . . The ramified richness of this future necessitates the wisest planning, of course, the finest possible calibrating of consequences and of the consequences of consequences. The task demands a leader of strength, of audacity, of valor. . . . Things must be mulled over, seen through. . . . Oh, he's had a bit of valuable experience in such matters—hadn't he planned a Little Saigon in Thorskrist back when the country welcomed its first Vietnamese refugees? But the present situation requires far more discernment, and far, far greater concentration. It calls for vigor and experience— it calls for a youthful veteran. It's even possible, yes, that an entire new city must be erected, *yes,* perhaps here on Blue. It might be a kind of cosmopolitan counterpart to Thorskrist, one perhaps named for Rut's own father: Bjartsvik. And this new metropolis would be a haven for emigrants, a warren of foreign enclaves, with a Little New York, a Little London, a Little Paris, a Little Berlin. . . . And they must display kindness and generosity, his countrymen. They must admit the desperate defeated foreigners without gloating or recrimination.

He turns and stumps back down the beach. Rut! He must wake Rut! She must be made a party to his vision. . . .

And yet Hannibal, even before he reaches her, feels inside himself a still more forcible need. Yes: he feels within the vault of his chest a proclamation burgeoning.

He lets it build, nursing it along by actively avoiding any attempt to articulate fixed phrases. He isn't at all sure, yet, what he wishes to say and knows he must carefully husband the impulses within. When he has nearly reached Rut he swings left, toward the sea, instead of right, toward her dozing body. Out there there's a flat boulder that wants standing upon.

The water is cold, he supposes, though this isn't something to concern him as he pushes out into it. The sea has climbed to his knees, which are not hurting him at all, before he hoists himself from the water onto his flat ledge of basalt.

He turns and looks south, over the ocean. Great Blue is on his right; Thorskrist, across the bay, is on his left; but he looks toward neither one, he looks toward the invisible warmth, toward the continents Down Below. His audience is the sea, out to the blue horizon itself, and he speaks in a lofty voice whose grand arc is that of the curvature of the globe. "I have always believed in the art of bold design," he begins. "I think of my namesake, who brought African elephants over the Pyrenees and the Alps, who fought at Cannae and on the plains of Zama and who was hounded all the way across the Mediterranean and still would not surrender. And I think of Leif Eriksson, who, sailing without a compass, found a new world. I think of Grettir the Strong, who was avenged in Miklagard after his nineteen years of outlawry." He pauses. How is he doing so far? Beneath his feet, his audience shifts uneasily, restlessly, rolling back and forth between the horizon and the shore. He hasn't fully reached them yet. Hasn't yet *gripped* them.

"And I think of Sir Ernest Shackleton, whose ship was crushed after drifting in pack ice for nine months and who led his crew across hundreds of miles of antarctic wastes without losing a man. And of the black slave Enrique, who had already traveled many miles before meeting up with Magellan, and who therefore seems in fact the first man ever to circle the globe."

Still the sea goes back and forth. Still it is not fully his. Not satisfied? Not satisfied. Not satisfied? Not satisfied. It wants *more*, it requires that he hold nothing back, and who is he to deny the sea's wishes? After another pausing, after a moment's resistance, he softens and accedes to its demand: "And, yes, I think also of Fred Astaire, who in *Top Hat* danced as no one has ever danced."

"You're a damned fool, Hannibal Hannibalsson," a voice from else-where—from behind him—calls. "You may be the biggest damned fool I've ever met in my life."

The words are thrilling, naturally—they're quite a concession!—and he turns toward them jubilantly. It is his Rut speaking, his own dear time-less Rut. On ageless knees he splashes his way to shore and climbs the gen-tle slope, feet sloshing in his boots. He mounts to the bed of moss where she, loins still bare, awaits him.

"Rut, Rut," he calls, "I made a mistake."

"Not your first, I daresay."

He drops beside her on the bed of moss. "Do you remember, Rut, the first debate, when I made that remark about Freeland's being a mental condition?"

"Perhaps you think I've got nothing better to do with my time than to watch some asinine political debate?"

"I was talking about Freeland and I said, We are not a place but a mental condition."

"You did not," she corrects him. "You called Freeland a *state of mind.*"

"That's right." Good, wonderful Rut, with those crossed eyes of hers. Peering two ways at once, always has been more precise than he has. "But you know what? I had things exactly wrong. And *that's* why I lost the election." It is all clear to him now. "I deserved to lose, you see. I had things exactly wrong."

He takes her upper arm in his hand. He'd needed the strength of this arm. With this arm, when he'd lost his way recently, she'd delivered the clarifying blow that had put the grinning invaders in their place. By knocking out the front teeth of a man whose teeth cried out for removal, Rut had brought the nation to its senses, and recalled her man to his sta-tion. She was the closest thing he'd ever known to a true hero—how could he do anything but love her?

Hannibal gazes out over the sea. He has a message for them, for those countries Down Below. He speaks quietly. It doesn't matter if they do not hear—indeed, they *cannot* hear and that is precisely the point.

Hannibal says, "It's those other lands, my dear. They're the ones that are not genuine." Of *course* they cannot hear him. "They don't exist, really, those countries Down Below."

This may be, he senses, the largest utterance as yet to escape him. To proclaim these words is to line his lung-tissue with air that glitters—he is lit from within. And it is to acknowledge simultaneously the need to reconceive himself and the possibility that his service to his homeland perhaps only now is about to commence. He squeezes that arm which has proved to be even more dependable than his own. "Those countries Down Below are a passing affair," he tells her. "Don't you see? In the end, only Freeland is real."

Brad Leithauser was born in Detroit and graduated from Harvard College and Harvard Law School. He is the author of three other novels (*Seaward, Hence, Equal Distance*), three volumes of poetry (*The Mail from Anywhere, Cats of the Temple, Hundreds of Fireflies*), and a book of essays (*Penchants and Places*). He also edited *The Norton Book of Ghost Stories.* He is the recipient of many awards for his writing, including a Guggenheim Fellowship, an Ingram Merrill Grant, and a MacArthur Fellowship. Emily Dickinson Lecturer in the Humanities at Mount Holyoke College, he lives in South Hadley, Massachusetts, with his wife, the poet Mary Jo Salter, and their two daughters, Emily and Hilary.

A NOTE ON THE TYPE

The text of this book was set in a film version of
a typeface named Bembo. The roman is a copy of a
letter cut for the celebrated Venetian printer Aldus
Manutius by Francesco Griffo. It was first used in
Cardinal Bembo's *De Aetna* of 1495—hence the name
of the revival. Griffo's type is now generally recognized, thanks to the research of Stanley Morison, to
be the first of the old-face group of types. The companion italic is an adaptation of the chancery script
type designed by the Roman calligrapher and printer
Lodovico degli Arrighi, called Vincentino, and used
by him during the 1520s.

Composed by Crane Typesetting Service, Inc.
Charlotte Harbor, Florida

Printed and bound by
Quebecor Martinsburg,
Martinsburg, West Virginia

Typography and binding design by
Dorothy Schmiderer Baker